ADAM HAMDY

was born in London in 1974 and read Law at Oxford, and Philosophy at London. He spent a number of years working as a management consultant before embarking on his career as a writer. His debut feature film, *Pulp* will be released in 2013 and he is currently working on his second feature. His critically acclaimed debut graphic novel, *The Hunter* (2007), has become one of the most widely read independent titles in recent years. His second graphic novel series, *Starmaker: Leviathan* (2010) was described by IndieComicReview as 'lightning in a bottle'.

Adam currently lives in the UK with his wife and three children.

Also by Adam Hamdy

GRAPHIC NOVELS
The Hunter
Starmaker: Leviathan

FILMS
Pulp

BATTALION

Adam Hamdy

BATTALION

A Dare Book

Second edition published by Dare Books,
a division of Dare Productions Limited 2012

Copyright © 2012 Dare Productions Limited

The moral right of the author has been asserted.

A CIP catalogue record for this book is available from the British Library

ISBN 978 0 9565020 3 2

Never, never, never believe any war will be smooth and easy, or that anyone who embarks on the strange voyage can measure the tides and hurricanes he will encounter.

- SIR WINSTON CHURCHILL

PROLOGUE

The man in the shower was supposed to die today. The Agency had put a fifty thousand dollar bounty on his head, and the Nazi Lowriders were coming to collect.

Scott Pierce hid in the alcove that housed the boiler unit and watched the corrupt prison guard exit through the door at the other end of the shower block. Rahim's two personal bodyguards did not even notice the uniformed man's departure. They stood either side of the tiled entrance to the communal shower and stared vacantly into space. Men hired for their muscle, not their competence.

As he waited Pierce thought about the man he had come to jail for: Idris Rahim, a drug dealer whose two-year sentence for tax evasion masked far more heinous crimes. Good behavior would see him out in one. And even that one year would be passed in relative comfort; privileges such as showering alone were expensive but Rahim could afford them.

The shower block door opened and five huge, menacing figures entered. The sleek domes of their shaven heads reflected the low-level lights as they moved silently and purposefully towards the two dozy bodyguards. The Lowriders efficiently overpowered the bodyguards and opened their guts with a couple of shivs. Both men crumpled to the floor, bleeding and screaming.

Their howls alerted Rahim to the presence of danger and the naked Somalian stepped tentatively out of the shower. Dillon Williams, the leader of the Lowriders, gave Rahim a macabre smile, unveiling two rows of filed teeth with which it was rumored he liked to rip out his victim's jugulars.

Pierce stepped out of his hiding place, catching Dillon off guard.

"This doesn't concern you," Dillon snarled.

Pierce saw the Nazi hesitate, as he tried to work out how to deal with this unknown quantity. Since his arrival a year ago, Pierce had failed to slot into the neat social hierarchy of the jail yard. He had a reputation as a loner who knew how to handle himself.

Pierce stepped forward and placed himself between Rahim and the five skinheads.

"We can kill two as easily as one," said Dillon, shrugging at his comrades.

Take out the leader, Pierce thought as he came in low and hard, and the rest will fall. His knuckles connected with Dillon's solar plexus, and there was a satisfying crack. The big man tried to bring the shiv up, but Pierce blocked the blow, fracturing Dillon's wrist in the process. He disarmed the Lowrider, then stabbed him in the gut, and turned to face the other four men, who came at him as one.

Pierce sidestepped a second shiv, and planted his own blade in the swiper's neck. The man's curdled screams unnerved his fellow Nazis and gave Pierce a moment's edge. He stepped inside the reach of the third Lowrider and quickly speared the man in the thigh and under his arm; both non-fatal blows designed to cause maximum pain.

The fourth man had heavy fists, one of which connected with the back of Pierce's head. He span round and tried to keep his vision focused, as the heavy fists came at him again. Pierce dropped to the floor and caught the man in a scissor kick. As the fourth Nazi fell, Pierce plunged the bloody shiv into the man's abdomen, just above the groin.

The talentless do not recognize the talented at work and ascribe any success to luck, which is why the fifth Lowrider did not have the sense to run. When the man kicked him in the face, Pierce simply stepped back for a moment to spit blood on the floor and then turned his attention to this final piece of business. Number five came in high, flinging his fists wildly. Pierce punished the man's inefficiency, ducked and moved inside to plant three holes in the man's chest. It took a split-second for the man's disbelief to turn to agony, but Pierce saved him from prolonged pain by punching him in the face and knocking him unconscious.

Pierce grabbed the only towel and hurled it at the stunned Somalian.

"We can't be caught here," he cautioned.

Rahim stared at his injured bodyguards and the five fallen Lowriders. He was struggling to come to terms with his close call, but Pierce did not have time to indulge him.

"Let's go!"

Pierce grabbed Rahim and hustled him out of the shower block. As they stepped through the door, Pierce dropped the wet shiv. Every fiber of his being had wanted to thrust it into Rahim's heart. But the satisfaction of seeing an evil man die would have to wait for another day. Saving Rahim was business and whatever else had gone wrong in his life, when it came to business, Pierce still considered himself to be a professional.

"You have done me a great service," Rahim said, as they hurried towards the safety of the main prison complex. "God sent you."

How wrong the Somalian was. Pierce was not the righteous hand of some divine force. He had discarded what was left of his morality the moment he had pushed for this mission. Whatever drove him forward had nothing to do with God. The bleak vacancy where he had previously felt a soul suggested whatever initial rage had compelled him to take this vile assignment had long since withered. He no longer felt the furious heat of someone out for revenge.

In his more honest moments of reflection, Pierce knew what kept him going, but fear that he had a problem - that he might be sick - prevented him from ever holding onto the truth for more than moments. If he could not trust his mind, if he was not in control, Pierce feared losing his grip on reality altogether. Somewhere deep inside he knew what kept him going was a compulsion, a sickness, an addiction. Like a junkie with a thousand-dollar-a-day habit, Pierce took no joy in what he did. Each step nearer his target was a fix, a momentary flash of euphoric understanding that he was a day closer to completing his grim task. His mind, reality, his emotions were all slaves to his mission. Once he had killed the man known as the Spider, Pierce would be free. And once he was free, Pierce could consider how best to join the woman he loved.

CHAPTER 1

Nature had reasserted its supremacy. The only things reflecting off the surface of Lake Michigan were the moon and stars. The silhouettes of the skyscrapers lined the shore like dark sentinels watching over a shimmering beauty.

Pierce stood at his hotel window watching the moonlight dance across the surface of the lake with the absentmindedness of someone who considers life a distraction. He was hungry for his next fix, but it would not do to arrive early. Keep treading water. Keep passing time. Behind him the OLED screens on the wall were tuned to a panel discussion program. The panelists were talking about the energy shortages and civil unrest for the hundredth time. None of them had anything original to say, but the network had air to fill and advertising to sell so it didn't hurt to exploit the nation's fears just one more time.

"We've got energy shortages, the economy is contracting, we're fighting multiple wars and we're facing a terror threat greater than at any time in our history," spat the bald man with hate in his eyes, "I'd like to know when the administration is going to act."

"Until we get the nuclear program back on track there isn't a heck of a lot they can do," said the blonde woman with the angular face. "We're paying for the excesses of past generations and their inability to make tough decisions."

Pierce switched off the vitriol and turned back to the darkness of Chicago. Movement in a window in the building opposite him caught his eye. Set against the eerie blue light emitted from a low energy bulb, a naked woman toweled herself dry in her bedroom. There was an easy beauty in the unselfconscious way she moved, but even she failed to hold Pierce's interest. He glanced at his watch: time.

He had checked his pistol earlier, but habit is the savior of those who live on the edge. Pierce reached a gloved hand inside his suit jacket and pulled out his SIG Sauer P267 machine pistol. He checked the clip and then replaced the weapon in its concealed holster.

As he crossed the identikit hotel room towards the door, Pierce performed a final visual check. The bed had been unused, he'd left no physical traces, and the black satin gloves he wore ensured there would be no prints. As the door swung shut behind him, Pierce was satisfied the anonymous room would give up no evidence of his existence.

The ninety-fifth floor of the John Hancock tower offered a tremendous view of the Illinois plain. The city and suburbs that once twinkled like a manmade sea of stars were now dark, the buildings cutting the horizon like black teeth.

Richard Sullivan checked his watch and rolled his eyes, irritated that his connection was late. He signaled the waiter with casual confidence, and raised his glass to indicate he wanted a refill of wine. With only nine diners in the restaurant, service was attentive, and the waiter instantly set about fulfilling Sullivan's request. One of the many advantages of having money in these impoverished times, Sullivan reflected, was the eagerness with which people tried to please you. Ever since the second wave of oil price shocks in 2015, few could afford to properly light and heat their homes, let alone stretch to the luxury of a meal out. And dinner in a place like this was the preserve of the rarefied few who were not afraid to continue to flaunt their good fortune. Sure, the ever encroaching tendrils of the Energy Acts had even robbed fine dining of its luster. Table coverings could only be laundered on every fourth sitting, and diners had to reuse their cutlery for each course. Sullivan could live with having to lick his knife clean, and did not mind the residue of other meals on his table cloth. This was his regular table, and with business as slow as it was, the chances were, it was his own detritus keeping him company.

The waiter brought Sullivan his fresh glass of Chablis. If he took offence when Sullivan totally ignored him, he could not afford to show it; tips were few and far between. As the young man backed away, Sullivan lifted a pair of night vision field glasses to his eyes and leaned towards the window to get a good view of the street.

Hundreds of feet below, standing in the small park that bisects East and North Shore Drives, was an impatient man. He held a pair of black flight cases and carried out a continuous sweep of his surroundings, alert for the danger of a fool stupid enough to try to rob him.

"See anything you like?" Pierce asked impassively.

Sullivan knew Pierce was not slightly interested in the answer; he just wanted to show how easily he had been able to approach undetected. He was annoyed that Pierce had been able to sneak up on him. As he lowered the field glasses Sullivan tried to mask his irritation.

"You're late."

Pierce was always late for their meetings and never once felt the need to explain himself. Sullivan was not used to such confidence. Most of his associates lived in terror of him and his reputation. Pierce seemed smart enough to have done his homework, and yet he treated Sullivan with no more deference than one might give to a checkout operator.

As per their routine, Pierce handed Sullivan a brand new I-Phone. The transfer window for the Swiss bank account was already open. All Sullivan had to do was enter the currency, amount and his pass code. Their business was concluded in a matter of seconds.

"Where oh where does all this money go?" Sullivan asked as he handed back the phone.

"Alimony."

Pierce cracked an emotionless smile, removed a second cell-phone from his pocket and dialed a number.

"You're good to go," he said into the phone.

Sullivan used the field glasses to check the scene below. His bagman in the park approached the sidewalk, as a silver composite alloy electric car pulled up. Doing business with the unseen occupants of the car, the bagman traded the black flight cases for a pair of silver ones. As the car pulled away, he retraced his steps into the park.

"Are we done?" Pierce asked.

Sullivan lowered the field glasses.

"We're done."

Another rat feasting on the bloated corpse of a once decent society, Pierce thought as he watched the numbers on the elevator display cycle through the descent. Sullivan made his skin crawl, but this was yet another instance where he forced himself to conceal his true feelings. Looking the other way had become an unpleasant habit. If Pierce thought about the number of evil men he had passed on his journey, men who in a previous life he would have been compelled to bring to justice, he felt a vague stirring that might once have been shame. He kept telling himself that people like Sullivan were not his concern; they would be dealt with by others. Pierce's target was a different kind of evil altogether.

One of the apes behind him shuffled on the spot. Sullivan was not subtle; when he employed muscle he wanted people to know what it was there for. The shorter of the two men behind Pierce was six feet six and must have weighed three hundred pounds. They concealed their weapons well, but Pierce had no doubt they were armed. He wondered what regular patrons felt when they rode the elevator with two killers paid to neutralize any potential threat. It was a meaningless display. If someone truly wanted Sullivan dead, an apartment on the seventieth floor of the building opposite offered the perfect nest. Sullivan always sat at the same table and a sniper would have no difficulty picking him out, silhouetted against the low level lights of the Signature restaurant.

The short ape handed Pierce his Sig as the elevator slowed. It was in its holster by the time the doors open with a ping, which was fortuitous, because the Feds swarming all over the lobby might not have reacted well to the sight of an automatic machine pistol. Six FSA agents in lightweight body armor and full face helmets dragged Pierce and the two simians from the elevator. Pinned up against the wall, Pierce knew the routine; a sweep with a handheld detector would find his ceramic gun and a physical search would uncover his phones and wallet.

"You're wasting your time!"

Sullivan got the words out, but from his position, pinned cheek down to the stained tablecloth, he was not sure whether any of the federal goons heard him.

If this was their best move, Sullivan almost felt sorry for them. A private citizen out for a quiet meal, they had absolutely nothing on him. Let them inflate their arrest statistics with a pointless collar. Even as his confidence almost got the better of him, Sullivan felt a nagging concern; maybe there was more to this than an empty gesture. As he was led toward the elevator by the faceless FBI agents, Sullivan started to wonder what they knew that he didn't. He felt the bitter sensation of acid coursing over his stomach lining and realized he was afraid.

The military grade hardware the FSA agents had set up on East Shore Drive had been superfluous. The moment the occupants of the silver car had seen the barricade, the vehicle had come to a controlled halt and the two men had surrendered. They had not even bothered to try to hide the pair of black flight cases, which were now on the hood of a Federal sedan. The agent in charge had one of the cases open and was satisfied to be staring at over ten million dollars in unmarked hundreds.

The bagman had been ignoring the bad feeling for weeks. August seventeenth was two weeks away; his fiftieth birthday. He had not been busted since the start of the trade crisis in 2021 and felt that he'd been riding the crest of his luck for the past ten years. He knew that wave had crashed the moment he saw the four suits exit the unmarked sedan. The forty keys of heroin in the two cases were probably sufficient to put him away for twenty years. His greatest fear had always been that he would breathe his final breath in jail; a piss soaked old man dying in a rotting bed shadowed by jailhouse gangsters, perverts and murderers. The bagman was not about to let that happen. Thinking of glory was easy when he dropped the cases and drew his Heckler & Koch MP12. When the Federal bullets shredded his abdomen, glory was the last thing on his mind. As he dropped to the ground, the hot metal that tore his vital organs chastened him with excruciating pain. The bagman took his last breath, conscious of his embarrassment that tears were running freely down his face.

Pierce knew they would be in there talking about him. He stared through his reflection, trying to penetrate the optical illusion of the one way mirror. It was a trick he had not yet mastered, although he had heard it was possible. To the police officers either side of him, Pierce was aware that he probably looked like a smug suspect, confident that they had nothing on him. They would never know the truth. As far as Pierce was concerned, two people in on a secret was one person too many. He risked too much every day to ever see it compromised. Pierce considered what words were being spoken in the adjacent room. He had been held for longer than usual. They usually tossed him the moment the paperwork was complete on all the real targets. Perhaps someone had finally woken up to the danger Pierce presented.

Elizabeth Catlin wondered what the years had done to the man on the other side of the mirror. He had changed physically, of that there was no doubt. He did not carry a single ounce of excess fat, and his face had the pinched look of a determined athlete. But physicality was not Catlin's prime concern. She wanted to know what lay behind Pierce's cold eyes. If the journeys we take are etched on our souls, she could only imagine the imprint left on Pierce.

"Who'd we bag this time?" Van Zyl asked.

Catlin doubted that the man standing next to her would have the time or appetite for a metaphysical contemplation of Pierce's soul. Carl Van Zyl was career. Emerging from a restricted past ten years ago, Van Zyl had risen rapidly to become section chief and deputy director. When making such rapid ascents, people like Van Zyl rarely look down to consider the welfare of the porters upon whose backs they have been carried to the summit.

"David Sullivan. Runs a courier company in Manhattan, which fronts for an East coast heroin distribution network. His bagman committed suicide by cop, but we've got enough background surveillance on him to bring a case."

Van Zyl nodded towards Pierce.

"You think we should bring him in? His luck must be running out."

In spite of her worst fears about Pierce, Catlin had to remain loyal.

"He'll deliver. He's got more at stake than any of us."

Van Zyl considered her words for a moment. Catlin knew he was not considering strategy or tactics, and least of all Pierce's welfare. Van Zyl was weighing up his exposure and the risk the man posed to his career.

The date shocked Pierce; August 3rd, 2031. Three years since he'd got out of jail. Six since London. This would happen every so often. A newspaper, a ticket, or, in this case, the digital tablet he had to sign to recover his possessions, would remind him just how long he'd been looking for the Spider. And with each reminder came a renewed sense of failure. A better man than he would have accomplished his objective by now. He was weak, unworthy and talentless. The sudden realization that his life was a staggering abortion sapped the strength from every cell in Pierce's body. He was sure his psychological decay was transparent, but the overweight desk sergeant did not skip a beat. All he probably saw, as he handed over Pierce's phones, gun and wallet, was a cold-faced perp whose rightful place was in a cell.

As Pierce stepped into the balmy Chicago night, his nerve returned. The panic of failure was replaced with the familiar calculation that now defined his life. He may not have completed his mission, but in his business, each day he survived had to be considered a success. More than that, each passing day brought him a painstaking breath closer to his target. Barring any serious fuck ups, at thirty-two, Pierce had plenty of years left to accomplish his objective. The prime time of his life lay before him and he stepped to meet it with grim determination.

CHAPTER 2

The Lady was draped in the red lights of a whore, Melvin thought as he looked out of his open window. Fucking energy efficiency. America is supposed to be a beacon for the world and here we are living like trolls in the fucking dark. We're savages squatting in the ruins of a dead civilization. As a child, Melvin remembered crossing the Brooklyn Bridge at night, marveling at the Statue of Liberty lit up like she was standing in sunlight. And here he was; same fucking bridge, same fucking statute, different fucking times. Who gave a shit about infra-red? Better leave the Lady in the dark, than give her half-light by which she could see the shadows of the world she once knew.

Damn, he was mad. God help the first asshole crazy enough to cross him tonight. The fucking traffic never helped. Melvin was convinced the checkpoints were just part of the wider government conspiracy to persuade people to give up cars. He could see the mercenaries of the Fortress Corporation at the Manhattan end of the bridge. Their night vision goggles and gamma scanners gave off a ghostly glow. They checked every single vehicle passing in and out of the city. That's why Melvin only drove his cab at night. During the day, it could take up to three hours just to get onto the fucking island.

Melvin threw his cigarette out of the window and turned on the air conditioning. Humans are ingenious monkeys, he thought as he closed the window. The rising glass gave the city a new lease of life. Like the windows on most vehicles, those on Melvin's cab were chemically treated to react to low frequency light. This meant that headlamps that looked dark to the naked eye, gave off a red tinted glow through the glass. It also meant that the advertising pimps could do their bit to keep the economy going. The hoardings on the sides of buildings all over the city, which had looked dark moments earlier, were now alive with animated low light advertisements.

Sitting in his cab staring at the tailgate of the truck in front of him, Melvin considered that he was Satan's bastard son if this miserable fucking life was all he could ever hope to aspire to.

The G-20 swooped low over the bay, its graviton engines humming as they resisted the pull of Earth's natural gravity. The landing pad on Governor's Island was illuminated by a circle of infra-red approach lights. Eighty feet long, looking a little like a semi-circular sea-shell, the G-20's rotund design belied its speed. The prohibitive cost of graviton technology limited its availability to the usual early adopters; the military, multi-national corporations, and the extremely wealthy. The G-20 that touched down on Governor's island carried the Fortress Corporation livery; a chess castle inside a golden triangle.

The darkened buildings of the Fortress Corporation's command base could not be seen from the sky, and if it were not for the landing lights, the island would have looked uninhabited. Once on the ground, Commander Neil Alder, the officer in charge of the Manhattan battalion, could see some of the men and women who staffed the nerve center of the New York operation, as they criss-crossed the base on company business.

As he descended the G-20's passenger ramp, Alder was met by his adjutant, Hector Cyrus. Both men wore the quasi-military uniform of the Fortress Corporation, the only difference being the number of stripes on Alder's shoulder. His four to Hector's three denoted his superior rank.

"Anything to report?" Alder asked.

Hector shook his head as he handed Alder the evening's status report.

"Nothing. The city's quiet."

Hayley Jackson adjusted the filter on his night vision glasses. Permanent marker on the side of his helmet identified Jackson's preferred moniker; Rooster.

"Quit playing with yourself, Rooster," one of the guys behind him shouted.

The face masks made it difficult for anyone to recognize voices. It was probably Alvarez, whose fat head was poking out of the turret of the T1 Abrams tank. Mask or no mask, there was no mistaking that fat bastard's bulbous dome.

"Just getting warmed up for your mom," Rooster shouted back.

Alvarez dropped the massive barrel of the Abram's gun so that it was level with Rooster's head.

"Just try saying that again, Cockerel!"

Rooster ignored the empty threat and waved the next vehicle forward; a light alloy sports car. Whatever words might pass between them, Rooster felt warm every time he thought of Alvarez sitting inside that smiting piece of hardware. Powered by a mini-nuke reactor that Alvarez rested his coffee cup on to keep it warm, the tank was capable of over one hundred miles per hour, and that big gun could fire a tungsten rain of death to a range of forty miles.

Whatever Rooster might face on that bridge night after night, he felt better facing it with some of the best military hardware in the world behind him. The two Cougar APX armored personnel vehicles that completed the Brooklyn bridge checkpoint seemed hardly worth thinking about when stacked against the monster Abrams. Rooster would never share that thought with the guys who operated the guns on the APXs, but it was true nonetheless.

The handheld gamma scanner offered a real time x-ray scan of whatever it was pointed at. Rooster had it pointed directly at the hot brunette who drove the sports car, but instead of anything interesting, it just revealed her skeleton. After using the scanner to check the rest of the car, Rooster waved her through the checkpoint and signaled his colleagues to let her pass.

Rooster watched the brunette until she was out of sight, then turned his attention to the next vehicle; a truck. He waved the driver forward.

"You think you had a chance with her, Cockerel?"

Rooster knew it was Alvarez that time.

"Better chance than you, fatboy!"

"Hey fuckface! Move your fucking ass!"

Rooster turned to see a cab driver leaning out of his window shouting in the general direction of the truck in front, which had failed to move forward in accordance with his signal. Something about the cab driver made Rooster smell trouble. He looked like one of those guys who was always in the market for a fight.

"Stay inside your vehicle, sir!" Rooster barked at the cab driver as he stepped forward to take a closer look at the truck.

"Driver, you may proceed."

Still no movement. Rooster pointed the scanner at the truck to reveal a lone driver seated at the wheel. Now level with the driver's door, Rooster used the tip of his MX18 assault rifle to tap on the window.

Rooster kept his gun trained on the driver, as the window lowered to reveal a man wearing a pair of opaque shades. The hairs on the back of Rooster's neck stood on end, and years of experience and military training kicked in.

"Step out of the vehicle, sir!"

Rooster activated his collar radio, "I gonna need a jump team."

Shades watched, as a squad of armored mercenaries leapt out of the troop compartment of one of the APXs.

"Get out of the fucking truck!" Rooster shouted.

Shades turned, acknowledging Rooster for the first time.

"Your days are numbered, American."

It was at that point that Rooster noticed Shades' raised right arm, and the remote detonator held in his clenched fist.

Rooster got one bullet off before Shades pressed the detonator, but by the time it shattered the left lens of the sunglasses, the back of the truck had exploded in a huge fireball. Rooster was incinerated on the spot. Melvin didn't even have the time to curse his murderer before the fireball vaporized his vehicle and thirty more behind it.

The mercenaries manning the checkpoint, and their comrades in the APXs were blown to pieces in an instant. Only Alvarez's quick reactions in sealing the main hatch kept him and the other three members of the T1 tank crew alive. Unfortunately for them, the massive explosion had weakened the structural integrity of the bridge. Huge sections of masonry fell into the river. Moments later, the mass of the T1 caused the weakened structure to collapse underneath it, and the tank fell through the bridge and plummeted towards the East River.

Alvarez knew they were falling, but he could not believe it. Nothing prepares a person for the sensation of falling in a hundred and fifty ton vehicle. It felt like he was weightless. The crew stared at him in misty eyed shock, until they heard the crashing splash, and were flung against the walls of the cabin by the force of the impact. Then Alvarez saw the first water streaming through various cracks in the chassis. That's when panic set in; they all knew the tank would sink fast.

As the tank tumbled through the water, Alvarez lost all sense of direction. He reached out for the lever on the main hatch, as the electrical circuits shorted and plunged the tank into darkness. Someone started screaming. Alvarez flipped the lever and the main hatch popped open, flooding the cabin with ice cold blackness. Alvarez held his breath and tried to keep a lid on his rising fear. By now he was being bucked and tossed as though on some macabre rollercoaster. He'd lost all sense of where the hatch was, and found himself praying he'd smash his head and blackout rather than have to face the prospect of taking that first lungful of water. He wondered what it would felt like to ingest something that he knew was death. His chest was starting to burn and he felt his ears pop as the tank fell ever deeper. Something touched his leg, and he reached out a hand. It was a body, and, whoever it was, he wasn't moving. Alvarez clutched onto what felt like a shirt collar unwilling to let go of what would be his last human contact.

Alvarez thought of his wife and three-year-old girl, and the tragedy of never seeing again struck him like a blow. His lungs were burning, but he was determined he would not breathe the water. It was so difficult to resist. Every fiber of his being wanted to breathe, to inhale whatever was on offer, but he would not. It was then that he saw the light. In later years, Alvarez convinced himself it was a flashlight, or the lights of another vehicle tumbling through the water. The only problem with such rational thought was that in this energy deprived world, such bright lights did not exist. In the rapture of the moment, Alvarez knew the light had a divine source, and holding onto the fistful of fabric, he kicked towards it. Alvarez and the man whose life he had saved, gunner Ernie Wallace, popped out of the Abram's main hatch, as the tank spiraled towards the river bed.

The lungful of air Alvarez took when he reached the surface would always stay with him. Above him, the Brooklyn Bridge was burning.

CHAPTER 3

The jolt of the Boeing 877 dropping into its approach pattern woke Pierce. He lifted the window shade and sunlight flooded his private cabin. Below the large commercial graviton jet liner, Pierce could see Cairo airport set against the desert sand. A couple of Boeing 877s and an Airbus 510 stood at the new terminal. At two hundred feet long, the curvelinear 877 was a small, sleek aircraft. The Airbus 510 looked like a giant boomerang, its four hundred feet airframe dog-legged around the cockpit. Neither aircraft had wings – graviton technology had dispensed with the need for them.

Since the demise of cheap oil, air travel had become so expensive that the remaining carriers had dispensed with economy and business classes. Flying had once again become the preserve of the privileged. Commercial airlines, using expensive graviton technology, now only offered first class private cabins at exorbitant prices – his ticket to Cairo had cost fifty thousand dollars.

Beyond the airport Pierce could see the giant airliner parking lot where mothballed jets from the Oil Age were preserved in the dry desert heat, waiting for the unlikely day when they would fly again. Boeing 747s, Airbus 380s and countless other jets baked in the desert heat, preserved like relics of a bygone age.

Pierce had been summoned. The coded message he had received through a series of cutouts left no room for misinterpretation. He had met the Engineer only once before, so either he had done something very right, or very wrong. Pierce suspected the latter, but would never deny himself the opportunity to stand at the epicenter of the organization. All he needed was one misspoken word, one unremarkable slip in their rigid security protocols, and he would find the Spider.

Edfu Yaseen watched the holographic display with an expression of deep boredom. He could feel the sweat pooling at the base of his spine and offered a silent prayer for the government to complete their rollout of nuclear power stations, so that the country might have access to air conditioning once again.

The gaunt, nervous privates, who stood at either shoulder, looked ever fearful of a command they could not meet with immediate satisfaction. Yaseen's insouciance befitted a ranking colonel in the Egyptian army. Outwardly everything appeared exactly as it should. Inside, Yaseen felt the comforting satisfaction of another successful mission, as the hologram showed American news footage of the Brooklyn Bridge burning.

The first passengers from flight UA 832 shuffled into the arrivals hall. Graviton travel did strange things to a person's legs. If he experienced such lumbering ill effects, Pierce did not allow them to show as he passed through the opaque automatic doors that separated the customs and arrivals halls; he walked with a confident and easy stride.

Yaseen had disliked the American from the beginning. Pierce had saved the life of a mid-level functionary while in prison and came with a strong recommendation from their associates in the United States. The Engineer had seen something in the man and had given Pierce the opportunity to prove himself. Whatever his personal feelings towards the man, Yaseen had to admit that Pierce had been effective. Within three years Pierce had risen from running distribution in Arizona to handling their entire American operation.

"Salam alekum," Yaseen said as he offered his hand.

Pierce shook it, but there was no warmth in the greeting.

"Wa alekum salam."

Yaseen turned to the private on his left and commanded, "khod shunta, ya."

The private grabbed Pierce's suitcase, and Yaseen ushered the American out of the airport.

Mido looked over the plastic carousel of sunglasses that had held his attention for ten minutes and watched the colonel exit the airport with the American. Mido walked out of the gift shop, and followed the colonel, drivers license at the ready. Egyptians were required to show identification when entering and exiting all hotels and public buildings. The police officer gave Mido a cursory glance and waved him through.

Mido made a mental note of the number plate of Yaseen's car as he descended the steps to the parking lot. He considered the prospects of a country where corruption was so blatant. Yassen's brand new Japanese electric sedan would have cost a small fortune. The import duty alone would have been more than the annual salary of ten Egyptian colonels. Such opulence sent a message that it was better to be corrupt than diligent and skewed the minds of the nation's youth against honesty. Mido could see one of Yaseen's men loading the American's case into the trunk, while the other slid behind the wheel. Yaseen and the American took a back seat in air conditioned comfort.

Mido jumped in the driver's seat of his old Egyptian taxi, which had been converted to run on some kind of corn oil. Henry Morgan, his American passenger, sat on the flea ridden blankets that covered the back seat. Morgan's pink skin glistened in the heat.

"Yaseen has him," Mido reported.

Mido turned the ignition key, and the noisy engine sputtered into life. Keeping three cars between him and the slick electric, Mido followed Yaseen's car towards the exit.

Morgan activated a microphone concealed in his lapel.

"We're on the move."

16

Catlin never ceased to be amazed at the clarity of the image. Three hundred miles from Earth and the satellite could read the letters on Yaseen's license plate. The OLED screens that made up one wall of the operations room broadcast a crystal clear image of Yaseen's car as it passed through the Egyptian army checkpoint at the airport exit. Three cars behind, she could see the outline of Mido's face at the wheel of the old cab.

Catlin had a dozen Federal agents under her command, half of whom were in the operations room monitoring their computers. Catlin eased over to Belle Pearlman and watched her practice her voodoo at the holographic controls of a computer terminal. Most agents in charge would never have given the studs and chains that adorned Belle's face a chance, but Catlin was experienced enough to know that extraordinary talent can be found in the most unlikely places. Her reward for taking a chance on this reformed Goth – the studs were gone but the death black hair and nails remained - was a technical officer who was the envy of the entire division. Catlin watched, as Belle tasked the satellite to track Yaseen through the suburbs of Cairo.

The journey had passed in silence. Pierce was puzzled at the lack of tradecraft shown by Yaseen's men. No random stops or U-turns to check for tails, no tunnels to avoid satellite imaging, and so far no scans to check him for surveillance devices. It was the kind of carelessness Yaseen had never shown before. Or perhaps it was over confidence. Either way, it was unusual and, like all changes, it made Pierce feel uneasy.

The minarets of the Citadel split the blue sky ahead of them. The streets were full of Egyptian families thronging towards the ancient fortification. As the car neared the outer walls, Pierce saw that small patches of grass, sidewalks and tops of wide walls had become makeshift picnic areas for hundreds of families.

"The tourist authority closes all monuments on national holidays, so that we Egyptians don't ruin everything for important foreigners such as yourself," Yaseen said.

The car turned into a narrow street that led to the side entrance of the Citadel.

"Luckily, we have friends everywhere," Yaseen continued.

The car did not slow as it approached the tourist police checkpoint. The metal barrier that blocked the entrance dropped so that it was flush with the road surface, and a police officer emerged from the adjacent hut to salute.

As Pierce was driven into the Citadel compound, Yaseen drew his attention to the rear window.

"It seems that not everyone has such good fortune."

Behind them, Pierce saw a battered old taxi that had been stopped at the barrier. The Egyptian driver was arguing with the police officer, the unfriendly face of a bureaucratic nightmare.

Even when transmitted through the vacuum of space, Mido's frustration was palpable. Catlin watched the satellite image, which showed the young Egyptian get back in the cab and reverse it down the street.

"We're falling back," Morgan's disembodied voice reported over the satellite radio.

"We've lost our tail. Keep that satellite on them," Catlin instructed Belle, who responded with a casual nod.

Pierce stepped out of the car and was greeted by an unnamed Egyptian who held a gamma scanner. He looked at Yaseen over the roof of the vehicle.

"You know the rules."

They were being as cautious as ever. Pierce masked his relief and gave Yaseen a look of pure frustration.

"When are you going to learn you can trust me?"

The colonel smiled, "When one of us is dead."

The scanner showed nothing, and Yaseen waved Pierce forward, towards a narrow passageway.

"Through there."

The significance of the location did not escape Pierce. The Citadel had been fortified by Salah El-Din to offer protection to Cairo's citizens during the third crusade. Pierce followed Yaseen's instruction and walked along the narrow passageway, which ran behind a low brick building. It led him to a service road opposite the mosque of Mohamed Ali. The building was designed to inspire faith. The silver domes that crowned the mosque glinted in the harsh sunlight. The omnipresent glow reflected by the alabaster that clad the lower levels of the building added to the sense that Pierce was somewhere ethereal.

Pierce passed the southern corner of the mosque, crossing a small courtyard that was peppered with motionless palms. He headed for the only other person he could see. This was a magnificently simple yet impressive display of power on the Engineer's part; he had turned a large section of one of Cairo's foremost public locations into a private meeting place.

The Engineer was silhouetted against the Cairo skyline. Pierce had only met him once before, and as on that occasion, the man wore the simple robes of a preacher. Everybody called him the Engineer as a mark of respect, but he had introduced himself as Azzam. As he drew closer, Pierce considered how easy it would be for him to kill this man. Azzam stood at the very edge of the high plateau that ensured the defenders of the Citadel could see would-be conquerors from whatever direction they approached Cairo. A short wall separated him from a plummet to a painful death on the rocks below. This man, who was responsible for so much evil, could be dispatched so simply.

"Beautiful, is it not?" Azzam asked without turning.

18

Pierce stowed his murderous thoughts and focused on the desert to the south west of the city, a few miles beyond the Great Pyramids of Giza. The telltale flashes of an artillery exchange illuminated the cobalt blue sky.

"It is the beauty of belief," Azzam continued. "Every day from villages along the Nile, we bombard Egyptian army positions."

Four G20 Egyptian air force graviton jets flew low over the Citadel, heading straight for the battle zone. Azzam glanced skyward at their sleek, wingless fuselages.

"And every day the government sends jets to bomb its own people. Many of our followers shall die, but in the end we will win. Bombs cost money. Belief costs nothing. It is simple economics."

Pierce had heard enough of the sermon.

"Why was I sent for?"

Azzam turned to face him for the first time, his face fixed by a smile that would have frozen the scales off a snake.

"I know that you long to fight for our cause."

Pierce remained impassive.

"You view your position as our chief importer in the United States as an insult, when you are clearly capable of so much more."

Pierce tried not to let his skin crawl as Azzam touched his shoulder.

"We have a new contact at the American embassy who claims to have use of the diplomatic pouch. Prove yourself on a field mission for me, and I shall send you to join the Spider. He has something spectacular planned that I know you will approve of."

It took great effort of will for Pierce to remain impassive. After all these years, he was being offered the opportunity to join his quarry. He calmed himself with the thought that this was only the beginning of the end. The time for celebration lay ahead.

In the cool operations room at Langley, Catlin wondered what the old man was saying to Pierce as they stood on the edge of the Citadel. For all its magic, the satellite was still unable to provide them with a way to read lips.

"We believe he's with the Engineer, but we lost direct contact," Catlin said into the phone. "I have another team working on re-establishing visual."

It was a humid day in Washington and Van Zyl was keen to get inside as quickly as possible. He climbed the steps to the Capitol Building, cell to his ear. He spoke rapidly, habituated as he was to having his commands followed.

"Keep me posted."

Van Zyl handed his identification to the Resolute Corporation mercenary stationed at the building checkpoint, near the main entrance. A dozen mercenaries performed provisional security checks on everybody entering the building.

Fingerprint and retinal scans would be carried out by the Federal agents inside. The mercenary returned Van Zyl's identification.

"You're clear, sir," he said crisply.

Abdul Nour, a stout Egyptian, sat in his favorite armchair and watched television. His wife nursed their infant son with a bottle and his eight-year-old daughter did her homework at the family's small dining table. It was not a lavish existence but, as the son of a peasant, Abdul Nour had come from nothing to a three room apartment in Cairo and he took pride in his achievement. He was basking in the perfection of the simple family scene when the doorbell rang.

Abdel Nour glanced at his wife, but it was clear from her expression that she was not expecting visitors. He slipped his feet into his house shoes and shuffled to the door, gathering his galabaya in front of him. He opened the door to reveal two dark, fit young men on his doorstep.

"We need to use your apartment," one of them stated in fluent Arabic.

"Who are you?" Abdel Nour asked in genuine bemusement.

The other pulled a bundle of cash from a leather satchel he carried over his shoulder, and thrust it into Abdel Nour's hands.

"One thousand pounds."

Without waiting for an answer, the first man pushed past the fat Egyptian and entered the living room.

"Everybody out!"

Abdel Nour looked first at the confident young man who had issued the command, then at the cash in his hand.

"You heard the man; out!"

As the fat Egyptian hustled his bewildered family out of their home, Saul removed a digital tablet, known as a Surveyor, from his satchel. Saul shut the door on the departing family, as his partner, Wycliff, approached the nearest window, which had a clear view of the Citadel. The Surveyor sparked into life; the seven by four inch flat screen displaying a crystal clear image of the scene outside the window. Wycliff operated controls on the side of the device and the image on the screen zoomed in on Pierce and Azzam at the edge of the Citadel.

"We have visual. Are you getting this?" Wycliff spoke into a concealed microphone in perfect English.

Catlin looked at the image on the OLED screens in the operations room, which was an exact replica of what Wycliff had on his Surveyor.

"Loud and clear."

Belle matched the Surveyor's image of the old man who stood next to Pierce to a grainy file photo they had of the Engineer.

"It's him," Belle confirmed with a smile.

The image on the Surveyor showed Pierce and Azzam shaking hands. Pierce returned the way he had come, while Azzam walked towards a low building on the south side of the courtyard.

"Both targets are moving," Wycliff said. "Target one is headed for the palace, service entrance."

Catlin's voice crackled over the airwaves into a tiny speaker hidden in Wycliff's ear.

"Exits?"

Saul checked the building schematics on a tablet PC he had produced from his breast pocket, before he responded.

"Two. One on Al-Armidan and the second on Al-Mahgar."

They did not have to wait long for Catlin's command.

"This is the first time the bastard's broken cover in three years. Bring him in."

Abdel Nour was trying to explain to his wife why he had been complicit in their eviction when the two young men burst from their apartment at full sprint and leapt down the stairs three at a time.

Avoiding the usual mix of donkeys and horses and carts, Mido pulled the cab to a halt near the Al-Armidan exit. He and Morgan stationed themselves against the baking hot high walls of the Citadel and watched the gate to the ancient complex.

In the operations room, Catlin watched the satellite feed, which showed Azzam step into a low building.

"Can we get infrared?" Catlin asked.

"Not with the latent temperature; it's too hot. But we should be able to get a gamma image."

Belle manipulated the holographic controls of the satellite. The onscreen image shifted to a continuous x-ray, but while the occupant of an adjacent building was laid bare beneath the roof of his building, the building Azzam had entered showed up as a dark shadow.

"Shit! I think it's got a lead roof."

Azzam entered the Gawhara Palace through a heavy wooden door marked private. The curator was waiting for him, as instructed. The once grand palace was now a national museum, and apart from himself and the curator, the expansive great hall was empty. When the gaunt man bowed with marked reverence, Azzam felt satisfied with the reach and reputation of his organization.

"Please follow me, my lord," the curator said. One of the most powerful men in Egypt stood before him and he was terrified of doing anything wrong.

"You are a loyal servant," Azzam responded, touching the man on the shoulder.

This simple human gesture put the curator at his ease, and he led Azzam towards the impressive gilt throne of Mohamed Ali Pasha. The curator touched a hidden button underneath the right arm of the throne and part of the wall behind the seat of kings clicked open. The curator pulled the panel open and gestured for Azzam to enter.

"There is no God but God," Azzam said as he entered the secret passageway.

The tunnel was lit using tiny mirrors strategically placed to reflect the rays of a single, unknown light source. The curator watched Azzam until he disappeared from view, then pushed the panel shut. For a few brief moments he had been in the presence of greatness; it was a day the curator would remember for the rest of his life.

Wycliff had a few yards on him, but Saul consoled himself with the thought that the race was not always to the swift. The two men rounded the corner of the Citadel wall and burst onto Al Mahgar street at a sprint. Both were sweating, but nowhere near as badly as the time Saul had chased down a suspect in Singapore. Cairo's arid heat did not have anything on that oppressive humidity.

Wycliff slowed to a walk and Saul drew alongside him.

"We've lost the satellite," Catlin disembodied voice spoke into Saul's ear. "I'm counting on you."

Without a word, Saul and Wycliff took up positions either side of a wide timber door cut into the Citadel wall.

Pierce was working the angles as he walked towards Yaseen. The Egyptian Colonel stood beside his car and smoked a cigarette. Pierce had been committed to this for over five years, two of which were spent in jail, but still it felt too easy. So much time, emotion and energy had been invested in getting to this point that the event had taken on a significance that warped Pierce's natural responses. He struggled to differentiate between ingrained paranoia and good instincts. Gaining access to the Spider had been the objective from the outset, and here it was being offered to him. If the introduction was ever going to come, it would be the Engineer who made it. What was happening was exactly as Pierce had dreamt it a thousand times. Perhaps it was his proximity to a dream that made Pierce feel uncomfortable. Or perhaps it was instinct telling him that the evil men he worked for were setting him up. One thing was for sure; whatever they wanted him to do next would be unpleasant. Pierce wondered just how much morality he had left. As he got in the car and was greeted by Yaseen's smiling face, Pierce realized he had no choice but to play on.

Azzam descended the last of the ancient steps and approached a man who stood beside the tunnel door. The doorkeeper gave Azzam a deferential nod and drew back the heavy bolts at the top and bottom of the door.

Saul had learned to control his impatience years ago, but something about the situation made him uneasy.

"Anything?" he spoke into his concealed microphone discreetly.

"Nothing," came Mido's response over the radio.

Saul looked at Wycliff who shared his thoughts; the most wanted man in the world was not about to step through this door into their arms.

If Saul had looked six hundred yards down the street he would have known his assumption had been correct. A section of a large advertising hoarding set against the Citadel walls opened. The bleached and peeling sheets of the old advertisement extolled the virtues of a popular brand of detergent. Azzam did not give it a second look as he stepped through the secret door, crossed the sidewalk and climbed into the ancient black Mercedes that waited for him.

The car passed Saul and Wycliff seconds later, but all they saw in the black windows were their own reflections.

CHAPTER 4

The instant message from Elizabeth Catlin read, "we lost him."

Van Zyl masked his frustration, and put his PDA into his jacket pocket. He had spent little time overseeing field operations but was convinced he could have performed better than his subordinates if he had been so inclined. He had an unerring attention to detail, which he would employ when examining Catlin's report. She would take some heat for letting the Engineer slip through her fingers.

Van Zyl turned his attention back to the Senate hearing. Patricia Nelson, the ranking senator from New York and chair of the committee, was just getting started. The other members of the Homeland Security Appropriations Committee were trying their best to look somber - the modified behavior of men and women who knew their every move was being captured for the masses. Van Zyl had little time for Nelson, who was widely regarded as a liberal. Senator Robert Stovall, a gruff, heavy man from Wisconsin, was tipped for the committee chair as soon as a reason could be found to ease the New York senator out of her position. Van Zyl had a lot of time for Stovall, a man who shared many of his own stringent views on law and order.

The committee room was packed with journalists, lobbyists and political tourists; members of the public who felt they had some kind of legitimate interest in proceedings. Van Zyl would have felt more comfortable if the committee had held its sessions in camera, but the trade-off for the CIA/FBI merger ten years ago had been greater oversight and public scrutiny. The activities of the Federal Security Agency filled otherwise dead air on dozens of twenty-four hour news channels.

Seated at the witness bench was Van Zyl's old comrade, John Creed. Creed had let himself go since their days in Iraq, and was carrying an extra twenty pounds. The weight showed around his face, softening his features. Van Zyl did not approve; physical excess was a sign of emotional weakness.

Van Zyl only knew Sam Solomon, the young man seated next to Creed, by reputation. He was said to be the real force behind the Resolute Corporation's success, and the younger man looked sharp in every sense of the word.

"Before proceeding with committee business," Nelson began, "we would like to express our condolences to all those who lost loved ones in the Brooklyn Bridge attack. Our thoughts also go out to the injured survivors."

Quiet swept the room, as people bowed their heads in silent contemplation. With an average of three terror attacks per month, the Agency was fighting a never-ending battle against a disciplined, efficient, but invisible enemy. Van Zyl wished he could say that the capture of the Engineer would have been the panacea everybody was looking for, but the truth was that the cell structure operated by these terror groups meant the Engineer would have been replaced within hours, without the organization skipping a single step.

At a nod from Nelson, the committee clerk broke the silence.

"The Senate Homeland Security Appropriations Committee is now in session. Continuing their evidence before the committee are John Creed and Samuel Solomon, senior executives with the Resolute Corporation."

Senator Stovall smiled at Creed and began.

"Thank you for returning, mister Creed. The events of last night put this hearing in a very different context."

"We've offered Fortress any support we can give," Creed interjected.

"Since the Sentry Bill became law four years ago, your company has been responsible for physical security in five cities; Detroit, Seattle, San Francisco, Chicago, and of course here in Washington. Under changes proposed by the administration, you would also assume responsibility for Boston, New York and Los Angeles. That's quite a burden you'd be carrying."

"We feel confident we can continue to offer exceptional levels of security," Creed replied.

"Do you share your chief executive's confidence, mister Solomon?" Stovall asked, as he turned his attention to Solomon, whose mind was elsewhere.

"Mister Solomon?"

Creed coughed discretely, drawing Solomon's attention.

"I'm sorry," Solomon offered.

"I wondered if you shared your CEO's confidence."

Solomon took Stovall's gaze and held it.

"We can sit in this room all day and talk about how to make this country safe, but it seems to me that if you have a genuine interest in the security of those cities, you'll recommend the security contract is transferred to us. We're the only company authorized under the Sentry Act that has maintained a clean sheet. Not one single attack in any of our control zones since the Sentry program started."

"An admirable achievement," Stovall acknowledged.

Van Zyl could see by the expression on Senator Nelson's face that she was less than impressed with Solomon's response. He wondered how much of that feeling was genuine and how much was a reaction against the obvious soft questioning Resolute were being given by her political opponent, Stovall.

"Mister Solomon, you served in Iraq with mister Creed for two years. Special forces if I'm not mistaken."

"You're not."

"Four years ago, you helped mister Creed found Resolute Corporation. Why?" Nelson asked.

Solomon hesitated, so Nelson, who had taken lessons in political theatrics from the best, picked up a dossier and continued.

"According to your file, you're an unassuming Jewish boy from the Catskills. Unremarkable childhood, mediocre school record and until your appearance in Colonel Creed's unit, an undistinguished military career. I wondered why the sudden grand ambition?"

Van Zyl could see that Solomon was irritated by Nelson's personal attack.

"I want to serve my country."

"You were doing that in the army." Nelson heaved a sigh, "Mister Solomon, I get very nervous when I see mercenaries on American soil. Soldiers would be bad enough, but at least their commander in chief is the President – yours is the dollar."

"We're not here to debate the merits of the Sentry programmed," Stovall interjected.

"I'd like to," Solomon said, throwing down a clear challenge to Nelson. "Perhaps the senator can explain how else to secure our cities whilst fighting three wars overseas."

"Maybe the military wouldn't be stretched so thin if the private sector wasn't offering such high salaries."

Nelson had taken the predictable path in an attempt to play to the gallery, but her argument was well-rehearsed, and as such, Solomon was clearly prepared for it. He held his own dossier aloft.

"This is an advanced copy of the Federal audit of the Sentry program. It states what those of us working in the industry have known for a long time. As a private company we are able to hire the best and brightest military and law enforcement personnel from around the world. Forty percent of our people are hired from friendly nations. The Sentry programmed has had the net effect of increasing our military capacity by ten percent."

Unaccustomed to having the ground blown from under her feet, Nelson went on the offensive.

"This committee is not fortunate enough to have received copies of the audit yet, mister Solomon, so perhaps you and I can continue this conversation at a later date. You still have not answered my question. What are your ambitions, mister Solomon? Do you dream of taking control of every city in America?

The veneer of respectability was slipping away. Van Zyl believed Nelson had made an error by reacting to Solomon's bait exactly as he had expected her to, and now everyone in the room could feel the tension between them. Solomon was used to the pressure of a battlefield and kept his cool.

"You know our record, senator. No attacks in any of our control zones. Our tactics work and they keep people safe. If we have to take command of every city in the United States in order to protect our citizens, then so be it."

They had stopped outside a flea-infested hotel in central Cairo, and Pierce had waited with the driver while Yaseen went inside to change into civilian clothes;

a black shirt and jeans. The Egyptian colonel looked trim, his muscles rippling under the silk. The Sons of September was a brutally efficient organization; it had no room for the frail, indolent or sluggish. Pierce surmised that Yaseen's physical condition would be an accurate echo of the state of his mind.

The car had dropped them outside a warehouse in Mohandesin, one of the more fashionable parts of Cairo. The lightly spiced night air evoked a childhood memory; a summer vacation in Spain, dining on tapas every evening outside rustic beachside restaurants. Pierce extinguished the thought of happier times and followed Yaseen into the warehouse.

Pierce contemplated killing Yaseen the moment he saw the truck. A late-model electric Volvo. The cab was secured to a bare flatbed that rested on ten wheels. Something about it, standing alone in a vast warehouse, made Pierce's sixth sense tingle. He had little time to indulge in reflection if his instinct was to be acted upon. They were alone in the warehouse and Yaseen was three paces ahead; this would be an ideal place to kill the colonel. But kill Yaseen and he would never get to the Spider. It was a trade he was not prepared to make on the basis of an irritating doubt. As he joined Yaseen in the cab, Pierce took comfort in the knowledge that he could kill the man as easily in the truck as he could in the warehouse.

Van Zyl kept an eye out for Creed, while his deputy, Porter, showed him some last-minute reports. The corridor outside the committee room was thronging with people keen to beat the traffic. His scheduled testimony meant Van Zyl did not have the luxury of that concern; he would be stuck in Washington until much later. Van Zyl saw Creed some way down the corridor and caught his old friend's eye. Creed and Solomon approached.

"You up next?" Creed asked.

"Strategic briefing. I'm supposed to put the Sentry program into a global perspective."

Van Zyl's response was more skeptical than he'd intended.

"Good luck with that."

Solomon clearly had a low opinion of the committee members.

"Have you two met?" Creed asked of Van Zyl, who shook his head in response.

"I don't think so."

Solomon offered his hand and Van Zyl took it.

"Sam Solomon."

"Carl Van Zyl."

"Carl and I served together in Iraq, long before he became classified. Sam's my number two."

"Nice to meet you, mister Solomon."

Van Zyl tried to turn on the charm. There was no harm sweetening

28

high-flyers who might be of service to him one day.

The committee clerk appeared at the door.

"They're ready for you, deputy director."

With the public gallery empty, the atmosphere in the committee room was very different. The senators were hearing privileged testimony from a high ranking intelligence official. Van Zyl noted that they were no longer playing to the crowd, the bluster and posturing replaced by attentiveness and a genuine willingness to listen. Only the senators, the clerk, the stenographer and three administrative assistants who had been cleared top secret were exalted enough to hear what he had to say. Van Zyl relished being at the center of such rarefied attention.

"What you seem to be telling us is that we can do nothing to reduce the frequency and severity of attacks," Stovall postulated.

Van Zyl signaled Porter, who sat next him at the witness bench.

"Bring up the Mid-East."

Porter operated a computer remote control and activated a holographic display unit that stood below the senators' bench. A hologram image of a satellite map of the Mid-East was projected into the air directly in front of the senators. The map was marked with territorial boundaries, US military installations and key oil and gas reserves.

As Van Zyl spoke, the relevant sections of the map highlighted in red.

"Our military is stretched as never before. We're peacekeeping in Iraq, Iran, Afghanistan and Indonesia. We have army, marine and national guard divisions protecting the Rosetta gas deposits in Egypt, the Garwar oil field in Saudi, North Pars in Iran and the In-Salah and In-Amenas gas fields in Algeria. Until our nuclear power program ramps up, these reserves are crucial to our economic and social well being. Without the mercenary forces provided under the Sentry program, the homeland would be completely open and vulnerable to attack. Our law enforcement agencies are simply not up to the task of providing ringfence protection of all our major cities."

Patricia Nelson leant over the bench and stared at Van Zyl.

"Deputy director, you insisted your testimony be heard in camera. Well, here we are, no press, no members of the public. In return for this, we expect a proper briefing. Everything you just told us is on public record."

Van Zyl signaled Porter, who killed the hologram.

"If you're looking for names and addresses, senator, you can forget it. The early wins we scored just after September eleventh proved the truth of Darwinism; survival of the fittest. The enemy we face now is smarter, more professional and better equipped than ever. We're dealing with levels of tradecraft that rival the Soviets during the Cold War. Without knowing the intimate details of each and every member of this committee; who you work with, who you eat with and who you sleep with, I'm afraid certain things are going to remain secret."

"Deputy director," Nelson tried to interrupt.

"I'm not prepared to reveal live intelligence and risk the lives of field agents who have spent years working to give us an edge."

Nelson admitted defeat.

"What are you able to share with us?"

"We believe the man responsible for the London and Rome atrocities, known as the Spider, has infiltrated the United States. If he is here, he will have established a deep cover terror network and will be planning a major attack. We believe that if we can't find and stop him, the Sentry program represents the best hope we have of protecting America from whatever devastation he has planned."

CHAPTER 5

Pierce relaxed into his seat the moment he saw the signs, which advised drivers to proceed with caution as they were nearing the American green zone. A ring of steel and concrete around a ten block upscale Cairo neighborhood protected the embassy and the homes of all the resident US workers. If Yaseen planned murder, it would not be tonight. The scanners at the green zone checkpoints would red flag so much as a paperclip.

As if reading his thoughts, Yaseen revealed, "we're testing the effectiveness of our new contact at the embassy. We shipped a consignment of office equipment from Thailand, using the diplomatic pouch. Hidden inside the shipment are forty kilos of raw opium. If this man can get it into the country undetected, it will halve our processing costs."

Pierce responded with a contemplative nod. He was considering ways to expose a traitor within the American embassy without revealing himself as the informant.

What had once been a green and pleasant neighborhood was now a fortified compound within a predominantly hostile city. The ruling elite still supported the United States, but the majority of the population had long since turned against Uncle Sam. The wide tree lined avenues were encircled by twelve feet high, razor-wire topped walls. The neighborhood's large villas, which housed the embassy workers, had steel mesh over the windows and tempered steel shutters over every door. Marine checkpoints guarded the four routes in and out of the Green Zone and restricted entry to authorized personnel.

The marine checkpoint they now approached was a very effective deterrent. Concrete doglegs positioned along the road from a distance of half a mile forced vehicles to a crawl. A reinforced pill box manned by two marines stood a quarter-of-a-mile from the main checkpoint. It allowed the two stoic marine observers inside the opportunity to perform a quick visual on approaching vehicles. Anything immediately suspicious could be stopped or cut to pieces with the 50-calibre machine gun mounted in the center of the fortification.

The main checkpoint was staffed by a platoon of marines in full body armor. In addition to extensive protection, the armor gave the men a preternatural presence; faceless, invulnerable sentinels guarding a seat of great power. The platoon was split; two marines used handheld gamma scanners to check vehicles, occupants and cargo; two operated communications equipment in a concrete bunker that stood beside the five foot cheese wedge barrier. The remaining ten marines were on weapons duty. Eight carried a mixture of light machine guns, while two manned the XM309, a turret mounted grenade machine gun capable

31

of strafing anything within a five mile radius with ten grenades per second.

The truck cleared the concrete doglegs, and Yaseen brought it to a halt at the main checkpoint. A masked marine approached.

"Identification."

Of all the possible responses, Pierce had not expected Yaseen to ignore the request.

"I need to see some identification," the marine said.

When Yaseen raised his eyebrows and shrugged his shoulders, Pierce was not sure whether the gesture was meant for him or the marine.

"Both of you out of the vehicle now!" The marine called to his comrades, "We've got a situation!"

Three armed marines approached the truck and the barrel of the XM309 was swung in the direction of the cab. Pierce knew they would never use the weapon in such close proximity to their own men, but the move had the desired effect of making him nervous. If the marines ran Yaseen's prints there was a good chance he would be flagged as a hostile operative. If they ran Pierce's, he risked exposure. Pierce looked at Yaseen again, wondering what the man hoped to accomplish from such inanity. Yaseen simply smiled back as he reached for the door handle. Pierce decided he could not risk letting events unfold without intervention.

"I have my identification," Pierce said as he reached into an inner pocket for a small plastic card. The hologram imprinted on the chip next to his photograph bore the legend; Federal Security Agency.

The marine accepted the card.

"And him?"

"My driver," Pierce covered for Yaseen.

Pierce watched the marine signal his colleagues to stand down. He waited until the marine was busy running his identification before he turned to Yaseen.

"Fake FSA identification. Accepted more places than American Express."

"You are a resourceful man," Yaseen said finally. "That is why we like you."

Buck, the young marine inside the body armor, did not like the smell of the two guys in the truck. The silent one had terrorist written all over him, and the American was as corrupt a man as Buck had ever had the misfortune to cross paths with. Buck ran Captain Corrupt's card through the handheld digital scanner and the machine came back with a flag. The scanner automatically dialed a secure connection and patched it through to Buck's in-helmet radio.

"This is Belle Pearlman, agency operations," said the honeyed voice. It made Buck think about just how much he missed his girlfriend.

Belle waved at Catlin, who sat in a large office that was separated from the rest of the operations room by floor to ceiling glass panels.

"Tell me what you've got," Belle spoke into her headset, as Catlin rushed to join her.

"Two guys in a truck giving me a bad vibe. Ran the I.D. on one of them and the machine patched me through to you."

Belle brought Catlin up to speed.

"Pierce is at a Green Zone checkpoint in Cairo. He's got a travelling companion."

"Any visual?" Catlin asked.

"You got a camera?" Belle tried.

"Tag number six-niner-zero-four-seven-one," came Buck's response.

Belle typed the numbers into a surveillance system on her computer. The system sequenced through a series of networks to link with the specified node, and within seconds an image from the surveillance camera at the Green Zone checkpoint was displayed in front of Belle and Catlin.

"It's Yaseen," Catlin observed.

"Should I pull them?" Buck asked over the radio.

Belle looked at Catlin for a response.

Catlin shook her head. Then added as an afterthought, "and don't scan them either. One of them might be carrying a weapon, and it will look odd if they didn't get pulled after being scanned."

Belle relayed Catlin's orders.

"You're clear, sir."

Pierce was unsure what to think when the marine handed back his identification. He had been counting on the security apparatus of the Green Zone to provide him with a safety net, but here they were being waved through without so much as a cursory scan.

"You're not going to scan us?" Pierce asked, avoiding eye contact with Yaseen.

"No need, sir," came the marine's friendly response. He signaled for the giant barrier to be lowered.

Pierce considered his options, as Yaseen rolled the truck forward into the Green Zone. He realized that he could do nothing without exposing himself. He was cornered.

The reinforced embassy wall loomed to the left of the truck. Yaseen parked in a restricted zone. Pierce was very uncomfortable with the situation.

"What now?"

Yaseen cut the motor, and opened his door.

"We go."

Pierce followed, exiting the cab onto the quiet street.

"We're right behind the embassy. It's a no parking zone. It will be towed."

"This is where the contact wants it. He will load the shipment and we shall return to collect the truck tomorrow."

Pierce looked at the vehicle, as Yaseen started walking away from it. There were dozens of places to conceal an explosive in the cab, but a device that small would not penetrate the embassy defenses. Pierce crouched to tie his shoelace and checked under the flatbed; nothing there. If there was a device in the truck, the only risk was to the chance passerby. Pierce could only trust that his handlers would do the right thing and get the truck moved. He turned and followed Yaseen down the dark street.

Van Zyl answered his ringing cell-phone and motioned for Porter to continue walking along the corridor towards the Capitol building's grand exit.

"Go ahead, Liz."

Elizabeth Catlin sat in her spartan office. The walls were bare and her desk was unburdened by photographs. Watching her team through the glass panels was sufficient to keep her amused during the few moments of inactivity she might be lucky enough to get each day. Not only were personal touches redundant, their absence also made her office more secure; fewer places to hide a bug.

Catlin had one eye on her team as she spoke into her phone, "Pierce just delivered a truck into the Green Zone in Cairo."

Van Zyl's response was immediate.

"You know about this?"

Catlin could only cover her people so far.

"No."

"We're giving him too much latitude. Bring him in at the next opportunity. Find out what's going on."

Buck did not question the logic of his orders. The same person that had cleared Pierce for entry into the Green Zone, now wanted him and his sidekick captured. The instructions were to do it quickly and quietly, no uniforms. Buck had relayed the order to two of the many plain-clothed marines that patrolled the Green Zone perimeter. Armed with concealed machine-pistols, they were a line of defense few people knew about. His two colleagues stood near their car a short distance away from the checkpoint. They were waiting for Buck to identify the target. Similar teams were standing by at the other three checkpoints, and Pierce's photograph had been circulated.

These guys were creatures of habit, Buck wagered, just like every other human being on the face of the Earth. People sleep on the same side of the bed, sit in the same chairs, and leave a place by the same door they came in. It was one of many bets with himself that Buck won. He watched Pierce and his silent companion, as they walked out of the Green Zone and passed through the pedestrian exit gate, which was no more than thirty feet away. He gave his two plain-clothed associates a nod, and they set off behind the targets. As Buck watched them, he deactivated the safety switch on his machine gun. He and his team stood ready to provide support in the unlikely event that things got heated.

Pierce was aware of the tail the moment he and Yaseen turned onto the wide street that was lined with colonial villas. The two men were about forty yards behind them, and closing at a pace that was designed to look casual. If he noticed, Yaseen gave no clue. He walked at the same brisk, military pace as usual. Foot pursuit this obvious could mean only one thing; he was about to be brought in. Someone else must have felt uncomfortable about a potentially hazardous vehicle taking up residence next to the embassy. Pierce just hoped the men behind him were professional enough to make the pull look convincing.

As he and Yaseen rounded the corner into Ismail Abaza street, Pierce saw an unmarked van approaching them at speed. He tensed, ready to put up convincing resistance to the arrest. When the van jerked to a halt and the side door slid open, it was not an American face Pierce saw. Instead, it was one of Yaseen's army privates, now dressed in civilian clothes.

"Get in, colonel," the man said in Arabic.

Yaseen entered and Pierce hesitated, but only for a moment. This van led to the Spider. Pierce clambered aboard and did not look back as the side door was shut. A man Pierce did not recognize was at the steering wheel. He slipped the van into gear and sped away.

The two marines tailing Pierce had been startled to see their targets jump into the van, but they were too professional to be phased for more than a moment.

"Command, this is unit two-niner, targets have moved to a vehicle. White Volkswagen Transporter, license eight-one-five-three-two."

Two streets along, an electric Fiat pulled out in pursuit of the white van that had passed it moments earlier.

Zane, the driver, was careful to keep some distance between him and the target. Beside him, his partner, Roth, activated his radio.

"We're turning onto the Corniche. Request satellite tasking to this transponder location."

Zane followed the van onto Cairo's grand riverside boulevard, the Corniche. The dark city reflected in the murky, moonlit waters of the Nile. With more traffic on this arterial road, Zane was able to keep a four or five car buffer to make the pursuit less obvious.

"Embassy control has tasked a satellite in response to a request from the marine team in pursuit," Belle said as she operated the holographic controls of her computer. "I'm patching into their feed now."

As she finished speaking, the OLED screens on the far wall flickered into life and filled with the real time image of Zane's car. Five vehicles in front was a white van.

"Can we get more units on this?" Catlin asked.

"Embassy control won't assign us any more," Belle's responded. "They have strict protocols about sending units out of area. We want more support, we'll need to get our own people there or use Lansing."

When the private handed Yaseen the pistol, Pierce started to feel less like an accomplice. Accomplices get weapons of their own, and the move was a clear slight. At the very least, it was a way of Yaseen demonstrating his superiority. At worst it was a sinister indication of what was to come. Pierce suspected he was the only unarmed man in the vehicle and could not escape the uneasy feeling that he had made the transition from accomplice to prisoner.

The riverside apartment buildings started to show signs of wear and tear as they headed further north. Within fifteen minutes, the surrounding architecture had changed from late twentieth century to late nineteen century colonial. Many of the ancient apartment buildings looked like they were on the verge of collapse, held together by the hopes and prayers of the impoverished inhabitants. They were headed for Imbaba; Cairo's poorest neighborhood. A hotbed of social, religious and political unrest that was so volatile that even Egypt's brutal security services declared it a no-go area.

The driver turned off the main road after twenty minutes, and steered a course through the labyrinthine streets and alleys that cut through Imbaba. Two-hundred-year-old apartment buildings intermingled with modern constructions of concrete and bare mud brick. Dozens of makeshift huts on every vacant lot created isolated shanty towns in the shadows of the tall buildings. They drove along roads that had not been resurfaced in decades, some cobbled, others no more than mud tracks. The van finally came to a halt outside a decrepit four storey colonial apartment block. There were two similar buildings on either side, and together they formed a terrace, which in tender hands could have become an architectural monument to a bygone age of genius. Instead, the dank, dark, damaged blocks looked to Pierce like the type of place animals go to die.

CHAPTER 6

Roth used a pair of night vision glasses to watch the four men enter the rundown building. He glanced at his PDA to check the digital photo that embassy control had transmitted, and saw that their primary target was the second man to walk into the building. One ahead, two behind – jailhouse rules. Before he joined the marines, Roth had done time as a guard at the Supermax in Beaumont, and he recognized a convict transfer when he saw one. It was subtle enough for him to wonder whether the primary target even knew.

"What do you want us to do?" Roth spoke into his radio.

"Sit tight. We're patching you into the satellite," came Belle's reply.

Roth grabbed his scanner from its holster behind Zane's seat, and switched it on. The thin digital tablet displayed an infra-red satellite image of the interior of the building. Roth adjusted the resolution to zoom in on four heat signatures climbing the stairs. On the floor above them was a cluster of over a dozen human heat sources. Roth doubted it was an AA meeting.

"We have your feed, Langley," Roth confirmed over the airwaves.

Belle, Catlin and the rest of the team watched an exact copy of the infra-red image broadcast to Roth's scanner. The four man-shaped red signals were almost at the top of the first flight of stairs.

"You want the surveillance team to get him out?" Belle asked.

"It's too dangerous. Scramble an evac team from Lansing." Catlin hoped that Pierce would not need their help.

Water dripped into the central stairwell from the rotten ceiling three storeys above. With the driver ahead of him and Yaseen and his private behind, Pierce felt like a condemned man. The apartment they passed on the first floor was missing its front door, which allowed Pierce a clear view of the twenty or so armed men inside. Two of their number were playing backgammon, and the rest were busy arguing about whose tactics were best and their own legendary victories. Most of the men carried AK109 machine guns, the AK47 replacement. Two of the men held M240 mid-calibers. The sight of this well-equipped unit did little to allay Pierce's discomfort.

"Everybody up," Major Byrd yelled as he turned on the lights. "This is not a drill!"

His squad were well trained, and were out of their bunks and on their feet in an instant, grabbing their gear and hustling out of the barracks moments later. Byrd followed them into the night.

Outside, a marine corps G-20 graviton jet hummed on the landing pad. Byrd joined his men in the troop compartment, signaled to the pilot and sat back in his jump seat. The jet climbed into the sky, and the huge expanse of US Combined Forces Forward Base Lansing, which sprawled over the desert sands, shrank into the distance, as the jet raced north.

Pierce spent the next flight of stairs studying what he could see of the building. In keeping with most colonial buildings, the architect had opted for few apartments with big, high-ceilinged rooms. If the layout of the first floor was replicated, there would be three apartments on each floor; one central, one east and one west. Pierce reconstructed the external street scene to give himself a better idea of dimensions, routes into other buildings, possible methods of escape. If the time came to peel, he would not have much breathing room.

The driver knocked on the door of the central apartment on the second floor, and an armed man opened it. As Pierce was ushered inside, he saw Azzam rise from an ornate gilt chair and approach. Two more armed men stood behind the Engineer. Pierce scanned the room; two small windows on the east wall, a corridor to the west that led further into the apartment, and large French doors directly opposite that opened on to a small balcony. The whole place was in a state of terrible disrepair.

Azzam approached Pierce with his arms outstretched, "God favors those he loves."

At the prearranged signal, the armed man who had opened the door cracked Pierce on the back of the head with the butt of his machine gun. Pierce fell to his knees, all thought of escape temporarily shattered. His immediate concern was staying conscious.

In the operations room, Catlin saw Pierce's heat signature buckle under the force of the blow from the other man.

"Evac one, what's your ETA?" Belle asked.

"Ten minutes to target," Byrd responded, the low hum of the graviton drive audible in the background.

Catlin knew they could not wait.

"Tell them to get him out."

Roth and Zane were already at the trunk of their car, when the call came through ordering them to extract the target. The odds weren't in their favor, but they carried something that would help level the field. The two men lifted a large flight case from the trunk and placed it on the ground. Zane punched a code into a secure keypad and the flight case lid popped open. Inside, resting on custom shaped foam, were two machine guns, protective vests, and at the center of the case, an MS9. The Metal Storm series nine was a formidable weapon.

Built around a miniature graviton drive, the MS9 was a remote drone that carried a Firestorm M2 machine gun capable of delivering four thousand fifty millimeter rounds per minute.

Zane removed the MS9 from the flight case, while Roth put on the operator's system; digital goggles and a pair of touch sensitive gloves. Roth activated the system and brought the MS9 to life. The graviton drive powered up and the weapon rose gracefully into the sky.

Azzam crouched and touched Pierce gently on the chin.

"Please stay with us, mister Pierce. I feel that I am meeting you properly for the first time – as an employee of the Federal Security Agency."

Pierce forced back the clouds of darkness that crowded his mind. Pass out and die, he kept telling himself.

"You're not talking sense," Pierce struggled to get the words out in Arabic. "I am a soldier of God."

"I will ignore your insult to my intelligence, agent Pierce, as the desperate efforts of a frightened man," Azzam said as he raised himself to his full height. "Some time ago, a source within your organization informed us that there was a traitor among us. Your cover is so good that we initially looked elsewhere - one of our other associates in the United States who is now dead."

Azzam nodded at Yaseen, who hauled Pierce to his feet.

"It took us a long time to work out that you were feeding information to your masters. Just enough to make life difficult for us, but never enough to compromise your mission to infiltrate the Spider's network in North America."

Pierce composed himself, and stared at Azzam with indignation.

"The trouble is your masters got greedy. There were too many coincidental busts of our heroin shipments, too many arrests of distributors and dealers associated with our cause."

"You've got the wrong guy," Pierce said with conviction.

"I don't think so." Azzam stared him in the eye. "We set a final test tonight. The chassis of the truck you delivered was specially fabricated from an explosive resin."

Azzam checked his watch.

"In exactly twenty minutes, the American embassy will be wiped from the face of the Earth."

"You're lying." Pierce regretted his decision not to finish Yaseen in the warehouse.

"I knew only a real agent could get it into the Green Zone. Your handlers would not want to blow your cover by running a scan. Had you not been CIA, Yaseen was given instructions to make martyrs of you both and detonate the explosive at the checkpoint. One way or another, you were destined to die tonight."

The view from the MS9 was broadcast via a short-range digital relay to the goggles Roth wore. He could see a night vision image of the apartment through a set of French doors. The primary target was directly in the line of fire. He stood opposite an older, gaunt man who appeared to be the leader of the other six men in the room. As long as the primary target remained where he was, he acted as a human shield, and Roth could not risk opening fire.

"What dedication! Your commitment rivals our own. You willingly spent two years in jail, enduring all kinds of torments, just to get a credible introduction to our organization." Azzam was genuinely impressed. "What drives a man to such extremes?"

Pierce could only hope that his tail at the embassy had not given up, and that someone from the Agency had eyes on him. A prayer for the cavalry was palliative, but stalling for time was practical, so Pierce unburdened the evil secret that set him on this dark road.

"On the tenth of August two-thousand-and-twenty-five, my wife was boarding the Eurostar at St. Pancras station in London."

The date resonated with Azzam.

"You want Karim?"

"Karim Al Kamal, also known as the Spider. Mastermind of more than eight major terror attacks. Responsible for the deaths of more than twenty-thousand people. The man who murdered my wife."

Roth knew it was a risk, but it was the only alternative to entrusting the future to fate. As he activated the laser sight, Roth prayed the primary target was alert.

Pierce was about to try to buy more time when he noticed the split-second flash of a pin-prick laser sight. Instinctively, he threw himself to the ground, and as he hit the wood-wormed floorboards, he heard the rapid fire of a high caliber automatic weapon; an MS9.

The room shattered and fragmented into thousands of pieces as it was strafed with more than sixty bullets per second. Two of the armed men, and Yaseen's driver and private were shredded in an instant. Yaseen, Azzam and the other armed man followed Pierce to the floor, and tried to shield their heads from falling masonry and shards of flying glass.

Roth knew he had scored multiple hits, but there was so much debris and dust in the air that it obscured his view. He needed to take a closer look.

As the MS9 flew through the splintered French doors, the surviving armed man opened fire with his AK109. The bullets ricocheted harmlessly off the remote craft's armor plating, but the attack provided Azzam and Yaseen with enough cover to escape the apartment. Pierce was nowhere to be seen, having fled in the midst of the initial assault. As they made it to the safety of the second floor landing, they heard the sound of the MS9 executing their brave comrade.

Yaseen caught sight of Pierce racing up the stairs between the third and fourth floors, and managed to fire a couple of rounds from his pistol before the American disappeared from view. Azzam's guards spilled up the stairs from the apartment below. Yaseen grabbed two of them.

"You two with me. The rest of you; after the American. I want his head!"

The three apartments on the fourth floor were all locked. Pierce thought about kicking one of them open, but his options once inside would have been limited. The interior beyond the first room was a mystery and if there was no obvious exit, he'd be trapped at the mercy of the men he could hear rapidly climbing the stairs. Pierce cast about him, looking for an exit route. He noticed tiny shafts of moonlight on the cratered plaster wall, and followed their source to the gaps in the rotted ceiling.

The approaching men sounded close, and Pierce knew he had no time to consider the lunacy of his plan. He sprinted towards the stairwell railing, jumped and used the railing as a springboard to propel himself up so that he could grab an exposed structural beam. Pierce hoisted himself up and forced his way through the derelict ceiling. He had his shoulders through when the men on the stairs beneath him opened fire. Pierce felt something burn his leg as he pulled himself through the rotten wood and plaster. Trapped in the space between the ceiling and the roof, Pierce crawled forward on the structural support, as bullets peppered the ceiling around him.

Yaseen and the two guards exited the building and scanned the street. Yaseen caught sight of the Fiat and the two men beside it. One of them was wearing a headset and strange gloves. Yaseen opened fire with his pistol and his two associates followed his lead, bombarding the men and their car with bullets.

Roth ducked behind the car, while Zane used his machine gun to return fire. Roth removed the MS9 goggles and saw three hostiles back into the doorway of the apartment building, pinned down by Zane's weapon.

"We could use a little more firepower," Zane called out.

"I'm on it," Roth responded, as he replaced the goggles.

The flaked concrete gave at the second punch. Pierce's hand pushed through the hole and felt for purchase on the rooftop. Using the surface as leverage, Pierce forced his head, then his shoulders through the crumbling masonry; as aberrant a birth as the world had ever seen. Exhausted by the effort, Pierce staggered to his feet and took stock. The roof was home to dozens of families who had erected single room shanties out of wood, corrugated steel or mud. The adjacent rooftops were similarly covered; a small city of paupers living in the clouds.

Pierce heard the crackle of gunfire before he saw the armed men who had burst from the stairwell. He set off at a sprint, and headed for the adjacent building. Pierce did not have time to gauge distance, so he simply hurdled the low parapet and hoped. He soared, as bullets seared the air around him, and landed with a crunch on the roof of the next building. Pierce rolled to his feet in a single, fluid movement, and sprinted into the maze of shacks.

Yaseen had dropped to his knees to provide covering fire to enable Azzam's guards to run to the other side of the street. His squat position saved his life. As he squeezed the trigger, he heard a terrifying noise, which sounded like a thousand clashes of thunder. He felt something wet on his face and looked up to see the two guards robbed of their heads. A flying nightmare was raining death from the sky. Yaseen dived into the apartment building, as the two mangled corpses fell to the ground.

Roth ceased firing once the third man dived inside the building. The MS9's targeting display showed two kills.

"The primary could use some help," Zane yelled, indicating his scanner, which displayed the satellite image showing Pierce ducking bullets on the rooftop.

Elizabeth Catlin's heart was in her mouth as she watched Pierce cross the rooftop. She grabbed the nearest open microphone with an urgency none of her staff had ever seen.

"Evac, what's your ETA?"

The G20 flew over the city low and fast. Byrd peered at the jet's video display, and watched the unarmed target being assailed by over a dozen heavily armed men. Byrd yelled at the pilot with a growing sense of frustration, "Get this hunk of junk moving!"

He checked the vector reading, and radioed a response to Catlin, "We'll be there in four minutes."

Roth heard the radio call, which was broadcast to him and Zane.

"Surveillance, target is in trouble. He needs assistance."

"We're on..."

Zane never finished his sentence. Roth saw the bullet split Zane's head open and knock him to the ground.

Roth dived for cover behind the Fiat, as a squad of armed men ran up the street firing wildly. He manipulated the motion sensitive gloves, and the MS9 swung low along the street and strafed the thoroughfare from gutter to gutter.

Half-a-dozen men went down under the barrage, and the remaining four took cover in the doorway of one of the derelict buildings.

The bullet hit the local man in the heart. He had emerged from his shack to see what the noise was about, when Pierce had raced past him. The local had taken the shot meant for Pierce, and dropped dead on the spot. Pierce's armed pursuers chased him across the rooftop, firing intermittently. Pierce leapt over another parapet and landed on the roof of the adjacent building.

He heard one of his pursuers cry out in Arabic, "One thousand pounds to the man who kills the American infidel."

The night vision capabilities of the MS9 mini-grav were awesome. Through the operator's goggles, Roth could clearly read the maker's imprint on the AK109 as a desperate man poked it round the disintegrating masonry of the building entrance, and fired wildly. Roth targeted the Metal Storm at the gun and shredded it, and the hand that held it. Shocked and in pain, the instant amputee fell into the street. Roth halted the barrage and heard the man scream into the night. One of his comrades reached out to pull him back to safety, and Roth opened fire, killing them both. He switched to infra-red and saw the shapes of two men cowering in the archway of the entrance. Roth fired a burst of shots into the wall level with their heads. He knew that no fighter could keep their cool with a rain of fifty caliber bullets inches from their skulls.

Roth felt the scalding heat before he sensed anything else. Then came the pain, and the sensation of something running down his neck. He raised his gloved hand to his neck and felt the wound; he'd been shot.

Yaseen had recited a prayer as he covered the ground between the derelict building and the other side of the street. If the American had seen him, the deadly firepower of the hovering machine-gun would have been turned in his direction. Yaseen had drawn level with the far side of the car and had seen the American crouched with his back to it. The man was wearing strange gloves and glasses, which he was using to operate the infernal device. Yaseen had sighted the machine-gun he had taken from one of his dead men and had aimed at the American's head. When the shot went low, grazing the man's neck, Yaseen had taken a moment to readjust to compensate for the deficiencies of the weapon.

The American ripped off his glasses and scanned the dark street for the source of the shot. He held a machine-pistol in one hand. Yaseen let the man see him for a split second, before he released a volley of shots that tore into the American's forehead.

The OLED screens in the operations room showed the satellite image of the prostrate forms of the two dead marines. A lone figure approached them, and

43

began looting weapons and equipment. More men approached from further along the street. Catlin could not express her outrage at the men who had killed them and who were now scavenging amid their remains, so she turned her attention to the sole surviving American agent on the scene.

"Where's Pierce?"

Belle adjusted the computer controls and the satellite image panned to reveal a lone figure running across the terrace's final rooftop. Dozens of men could be seen giving chase, pausing every few moments to fire. Then Catlin saw a new addition; figures emerging from the rooftop shanties.

As Pierce raced towards the stairwell on the far side of the roof, local men with aspirations of securing a rich purse emerged from their shacks, armed with any weapons they could lay hands to. Pierce disarmed a one-legged man who tried to aim a World War Two rifle at him. The man topped backwards, and Pierce, still running, swung the rifle by the barrel and brained a man who wielded a large knife. The would-be bounty hunter caught a cluster of bullets in his chest, as Azzam's men tried to shoot Pierce and missed.

If their intention had been to force him inside, his pursuers had succeeded. Pierce had run out of options. The only alternative to the stairwell was a leap over the final parapet. Pierce had given it serious consideration; there was a reasonable chance of surviving a four storey drop, but the guarantee of broken bones would make further flight impossible. When he burst inside the stairwell and the meat cleaver missed his head by millimeters, Pierce wondered whether he had made the right choice.

He was confronted by a mob of locals, the foremost of whom was slashing at him with a dirty, brutal cleaver. The weapon was not in the hands of an expert, but Pierce changed that situation in an instant. He dropped below the butcher's swing, dodged the weapon and rabbit punched the man in the throat. As the man struggled for air, Pierce grabbed his wrist, cracked it, and relieved him of the cleaver. He kicked the man down the stairs, and sent half-a-dozen amateur bounty hunters flying with him. Pierce could hear more locals and Azzam's men pounding across the roof, and knew he could not waste a moment. He jumped the flight of twenty stairs and landed on the crumpled locals. A hand grabbed at his ankle as he tripped his way over the men, but a swipe with the cleaver was rewarded with freedom and a piercing scream.

Pierce kicked clear of the men and half-fell, half-leaped down the next flight of stairs. Three more to go, he thought, as the first bullets punctured the plaster by his head. Pierce could not risk the stairs, so he opened the third floor stairwell door and ran into the corridor.

A peasant farmer thrust at him with a large machete, but Pierce parried with the cleaver, and kicked the man back through his open apartment door.

"Stop!"

Pierce heard the shout in Arabic. Through the darkness ahead of him, Pierce saw one of the residents step out of his apartment. The man wore a junior ranking policeman's uniform, and had his service pistol raised. Instinctively, Pierce hurled the cleaver, which struck the off-duty police officer square in the chest. He grabbed the pistol as he rushed past the astonished, mortally wounded man and spilled into the emergency stairwell on the other side of the building. Shots rang out behind him and splintered the door as it swung shut.

Pierce raced down the stairs, ignoring the pain from the bullet wound in his leg. Hot metal came from above, but this narrow spiral staircase made a strike very unlikely. Pierce pushed open the ancient emergency exit to be greeted by the sight of Yaseen and a dozen men looting two bodies and a car.

The men were startled by the noise, and turned.

Yaseen yelled, "Get him!"

Pierce fell back into the stairwell and pulled the door closed, and a split-second later the first volley of shots splintered the rotting wood. He rolled across the stairwell floor, avoiding the barrage from above, and burst into the building lobby. The main exit was out; it opened onto the street, and Yaseen's men would already be heading for it in an effort to corner him. More shots came from first floor landing, and Pierce knew he was running out of options. As the ancient marble floor crackled with gunfire, a dark doorway to the rear of the lobby beckoned.

Hisham had been a porter in the building for eight years. Being the custodian of an Imbaba apartment block had not been his ambition when he left the Tanta countryside for Cairo, but the job provided him with a meager wage and gave him and his family a safe home. Their room might be small, but they were not like the beggars that lived on the roof, who spent each waking hour wondering whether a heavy rainfall might finally push their shacks through the rotting roof timbers. As he drew his family close to him, his wife clasped under one arm, and his young son and daughter under another, Hisham prayed for their safety. He looked around the damp chamber that they called home, and for once was grateful for their poverty. They had three woolen mattresses to sleep on, a few discarded broken toys for the children to play with, and a primitive kitchen set that tested his wife's talents. There was nothing here that men with guns would be interested in. The danger would soon pass.

Hisham was alarmed when the gunfire grew louder; they were close. His alarm turned to terror when the door was kicked open, and an injured, wild man ran inside, and slammed it shut behind him.

"I don't mean you any harm." The man spoke fluent Arabic, but was obviously a foreigner.

Hisham found a strange calm in his fear.

45

"Please go. We don't want any part in this."

He was a simple man, but Hisham was prepared to defend his family with his life. As the stranger looked around their room, Hisham reached for a rusty knife he had concealed in his robe. It would be like slaughtering a chicken, he thought, just aim for the neck.

Before Hisham could make his move, the stranger pulled out his wallet and tossed American dollars in his direction.

"For the stove," the stranger said as he grabbed Hisham's portable gas stove.

Hisham let go of the knife and started gathering the hundred dollar bills. There were five of them, each one worth more than he made in three years. He raised his head to give the stranger his thanks, but the man had already gone.

The armed men had converged on the porter's lodgings. Yaseen was proud of the way they had handled themselves and was glad he had insisted that Azzam finance the training camps in Iraq. They had left the American with no option but to retreat like a rat into the tiny room at the bottom of the building. The first floor landing was open to the double height lobby, and a dozen men leant over the railing, guns trained on the archway that led to the porter's room. In the lobby, on the ground floor, fifteen men, including himself, had guns trained on the archway. The American would die in this godforsaken building, thousands of miles from home.

"Agent Pierce," Yaseen began, "surrender now and we shall be kind to you."

Yaseen caught one of his men smiling at him. There would be no kindness here; all the training in the world cannot quell a zealot's enthusiasm once he has laid hands on the enemy. Then he heard the sound; something heavy hitting the floor and rolling towards them. Yaseen looked down and saw the portable stove. He saw the gas canister attached to its base.

"Move!"

Yaseen scrambled to get past his men, as Pierce stepped out of the shadows and fired a single shot from a pistol.

The shot struck the gas canister, which exploded. The four men nearest the stove were dismembered, three more were set on fire, and the remainder of those in the lobby, including Yaseen, were blown back against the walls. The men on the first floor landing were momentarily blinded and knocked to the floor. Stunned, at first Yaseen could neither see nor hear, but gradually his senses returned. He became aware of a striking pain in his left leg and looked down to see a twelve inch piece of metal embedded in his thigh. The first scream he heard was his own.

Despite having been deafened and winded by the blast, Pierce knew he had to move; his advantage would not last long. He rounded the corner and ran through the dust-filled lobby, ignoring the men on fire and pausing only to snatch

46

a machine gun from an unconscious man. As he ran towards the exit, Pierce scanned the room for Yaseen. The colonel's death would be some consolation for the blown mission, but there was no sign of him.

Pierce emerged onto the street and ran for the small Fiat that was parked on the other side. The first shots rang out when he was about halfway to the car. Four men with Kalashnikovs ran at him from the other direction. Their shots were wild, but it was only a matter of time before Pierce's luck stuttered to a halt. Pierce pulled the trigger to lay down covering fire, but nothing happened. The lack of resistance against his fingers told him that the firing mechanism had failed. The weapon had probably been damaged in the explosion.

Pierce reached behind him and drew the pistol he had confiscated from the policeman. The primitive service revolver had only three shots left. Out of the corner of his eye, Pierce saw armed men emerge from the main and emergency exits of the building he had just escaped from. He was caught, essentially unarmed, on open ground. The odds had shifted enough for Pierce to consider that he only needed one bullet to join his wife.

The four men running towards him were cut down by a barrage of shots from a Metal Storm M40 so powerful that it cleaved one of the men in half. Pierce looked up to see a marine corps G20 descending, its black hull silhouetted against the night sky.

Six marines leapt from the G20, which was still two hundred feet above the ground. The marines' personal grav-pacs, allowed them to control the direction and speed of their descent. They landed in a semi-circle around Pierce and opened fire on the armed men emerging from the building. More armed men emerged from the adjacent building, and were slaughtered by the M40.

The G20 dusted down, and Pierce was bundled aboard by two marines who had emerged from the grav-jet to recover him. The six marines on the ground laid down covering fire as they retreated into the craft, which took to the sky the moment the last of them was aboard. With Pierce safely recovered, anyone in the combat zone was assumed to be hostile, so the few men foolish enough to fire at the departing aircraft were automatically targeted by the G20's computer and killed where they stood.

"Major Byrd," the ranking marine shook Pierce's hand, "good to have you aboard."

Pierce was not in a celebratory mood.

"Major, I need a comms link to Langley, and we need to get to the embassy, fast. The whole place is about to be blown to hell."

CHAPTER 7

"There's a bomb concealed within the chassis of the truck. It's going to detonate in five minutes."

Pierce's voice came over the airwaves and filled Catlin with dread. An agent under her command had been complicit in staging a terror attack. If they did not prevent the explosion, American lives could be lost.

"Code red," Catlin alerted her team, who immediately started running through their well-rehearsed alert procedure. The embassy would be informed and evacuated, the resident bomb squad would be dispatched and security would be heightened at all US facilities in the target country.

"We're on our way there," Pierce continued, "E.T.A. five minutes."

"Negative. Return to Lansing. The situation is in hand," Catlin countered.

"This is on my head, Liz, I took that thing in there," Pierce responded.

Catlin knew from the tone of his voice that any argument would be pointless.

Standard operating procedure dictated that a marine sweeper company scramble from Lansing the moment Major Byrd's evac team departed. The one hundred and fifty men and women of the MSC were tasked with tracking down and capturing any hostile combatants in the target zone. They departed forward base Lansing two minutes after Major Byrd, taking to the sky in six G20 graviton jets.

Coming in low over the city, Captain O'Connor, the ranking officer in the lead grav-jet, suspected the enemy would maintain their standard operating procedure. She had been in the corps for six years, posted in Egypt for three, and had yet to see a single hostile captured alive. They nested in neighborhoods like Imbaba; warrens of poverty and desperation, where brutal men could melt away into the shadows, protected by locals who shared their rage at a world defined by injustice. All O'Connor and her people ever found were bodies.

The infra red image on O'Connor's scanner showed no movement in the street. The bodies of two plain-clothed agents lay near a small car. Multiple hostiles lay where they'd fallen, their corpses already showing signs of cooling in the Cairo night. The scanner showed heat signatures in the nearby apartment buildings, but they looked like terrified locals huddled in their homes. None of the signals carried weapons. Evidence of a firefight was everywhere, but the men behind it were either dead or had vanished into the night.

Darcy O'Connor was well aware of the technology she had at her disposal. She knew the Agency would have had tracking satellites on the location. She recognized the volume of manpower that would be put into hunting down those responsible for what had happened here. The investigation would begin with her team and the rest of the MSC conducting door-to-door searches and canvassing witnesses over a three block area. As the G20 touched down in the deserted street and the first members of her platoon exited the aircraft, O'Connor could not help but admire her enemy; despite facing such a well-equipped, well-organized foe, they would disappear to fight again another day.

Lamar Jackson was standing in the lobby of the comedy club listening to his Hollywood agent wax lyrical about his comedic talents, when the alarm sounded. Jackson woke with a start, wondering for a moment, whether this world with its small bunk, claustrophobic walls and piercing siren was real or a nightmare. It took a few beats of his heart for reality to click into place; Jackson was not a world famous comedian, he had a far more somber role in life.

He swung himself off his bunk, avoiding the head of his roommate, Nathan Lake, otherwise known as Doctor Love, a fast-talking, smooth operator from Nashville. Love was already in his FibreGuard suit and was strapping on his body armor. Jackson jumped down, opened his locker and removed the custom-made quarter-of-a-million dollar suit that was designed to protect the wearer from a close proximity category three explosion.

Jackson and Love joined the rest of the disposal team in their barracks ready room, which was located in the south wing of the embassy. All eight men were in full armor, including their commander, Curtis 'Metal Head' Ballard, who'd earned his moniker after having half his face blown off in Tehran. Metal Head began the briefing, as Jackson entered.

"We have a suspect vehicle parked against the south wall of the compound," Metal Head growled.

"In the controlled zone?" Jackson could not stop himself from asking in amazement.

As Metal Head turned to Jackson to express his impatience, the monotone strip lighting glinted against the titanium that had been used to reconstruct his face.

"Welcome to the clusterfuck, Lamar. So glad you could join us."

"Looks like an HMX charge piped along the front of the chassis, bonded to an RDX Composition C that is hidden in the hollowed flatbed," Jackson said as he examined the gamma image displayed on his scanner.

The device employed gamma rays to analyze the chemical compounds used to make up the explosive charges. He stood no more than fifty feet away from the suspect vehicle, a Volvo truck, which was more bomb than vehicle. Based on what the machine was telling him, Jackson knew that even in his protective gear, he would have no better than a fifty percent chance of surviving the explosion.

Jackson looked through his helmet's thick Plexiglass and saw Metal Head in his usual position; close to the action. He leant over the space between the cab and flatbed, where he'd uncovered the detonators. Metal Head's voice came over the radio.

"Motion sensors linked to the trigger. We move this thing, it goes. I've got a multi-strand detonator, with double blinds and booby-traps up the Yazoo. Fuck, I can't even tell if it's on a timer or a remote. What's the story on blast containment?"

Doctor Love led the effort to get blast shields expedited from Lansing. Security at the embassy was so tight that they had never expected to need the enormous reinforced concrete slabs used to contain explosions. Love was on his radio coordinating their dispatch with a senior officer at Lansing.

Behind him, the rest of Jackson's colleagues prepared 'Betty', a robot drone that would be used to try to disable the detonator. A cordon of marines in body armor watched from further down the street, which had been cleared of all residents. On the other side of the wall that separated the truck from the embassy, the staff had been evacuated, and had been taken to the north end of the compound. G20s would soon begin ferrying them to Lansing as a precaution against a secondary attack.

Jackson heard the hum of the graviton drive and thought it was the first of the G20s sent to evacuate the embassy staff. So much for military efficiency, he thought, the marine corps grav-jet was landing on the wrong side of the damned compound. As the G20 touched down one hundred yards away from where he stood, Jackson saw a battered and bedraggled man jump out of the aircraft's personnel hatch and run towards the line of marines.

Jackson couldn't hear what the man was saying, but he had been in enough blast zones to know what the man's animated arm gestures meant: clear the area.

Pierce wondered why the disposal team were still around the truck; he'd told Catlin how much time they had to detonation. In a desperate effort to save them, Pierce leapt from the grav-jet, as it landed, and ran down the street screaming with all the force his lungs could muster. His warning came too late. As he raced towards marine cordon, the truck exploded. The last thing Pierce saw before the world turned white were the silhouettes of men consumed by light.

CHAPTER 8

If his partner was disloyal to the cause, he did a damned good job of hiding it, Smit thought as he watched the kid drive. After twenty-five years with a badge, anyone under the age of thirty was a kid, and Amer Hassan, his Lebanese-American partner, was no different. They had worked together for three years; Hassan's first assignment straight out of the Academy. Nobody had said anything, but Smit felt it was his duty to keep an eye open for anything suspicious. He'd read about the Japanese internment camps during the Second World War, and would never suggest going that far. But in his opinion, it didn't hurt to keep eyes wide on citizens who might have divided loyalties. The kid had never shown anything but grit and determination to trudge the streets, knock down doors, and crack heads to break a case – but that was exactly how a sleeper was supposed to behave.

They had spoken about it once. Smit drunk at the bar, Hassan, teetotal, cradling a cup of coffee. Smit had railed against a faith that produced such enthusiastic murderers. He could not remember exactly what had come out of his mouth, but remembered it had tasted bitter. Smit liked to tell himself that it had been a baiting session, that he had been trying to push the kid to express his true feelings, but the truth was that he had simply given vent to years of pent up anger. His opinions may have even been strong enough to contravene the Equality Acts, but rather than report him, to his surprise, Hassan had simply demurred, stating that these men dishonored his faith. One sentence was scoured into his memory: "To aggrandize them with the label 'terrorist' disguises what they really are; common murderers."

In the weeks that followed, Smit worried that the kid's agreement was too convenient. Surely he would have some sympathy for his own people. Perhaps it was a double-bluff to lull Smit into trusting him. Smit pushed such thoughts to the back of his mind, but they never entirely disappeared; in this covert war, the enemy could always be the man sitting next to you.

Hassan drove their government issue electric sedan, and stopped alongside the gatehouse of a large warehouse complex. The laminated sign next to the gate announced that they were about to enter, 'Red Components, America's leading distributor of electronic and mechanical components.'

Smit shuffled in his seat to extract his identification from his back pocket. His shoulders sagged, as if drawn to the bulbous belly propped against his thighs. He had to lose weight, Smit thought, as he handed his ID to Hassan who passed it, along with his own, to the security guard who had emerged from the gatehouse.

"Agents Lenny Smit and Amer Hassan here to see mister Rossi," the kid said.

Franco Rossi looked through a gap in the blinds that lined the inner windows of his office. He gazed into the sorting warehouse, a football field sized semi-automated facility where eighty-three employees worked to fill orders from huge floor-to-ceiling shelves packed with mechanical and electronic components large and small. It was a business to be proud of, Rossi reflected, even if it lost over two hundred thousand dollars a month. They stocked close to a million product lines and serviced more than two million customers, ranging from large corporations to small, garage-based research labs. Some of the pieces they stocked went into equipment so precise that it had to be constructed by other machines.

Rossi's foreman, David Karo, sat on one of the two leather couches that dominated the office. Karo was tall, dark, and heavy set - but it was all muscle. Rossi had worked with Karo for many years and knew the man would never let himself slip in any way. His sense of discipline was admirable.

"Why now?" Rossi had asked of his foreman when he had learnt of the Agency's interest in his business the previous day. Karo's unflinching stare had told him all he needed to know; there was nothing to worry about.

A knock on the door was swiftly followed by the appearance of Maria, Rossi's beautiful, young assistant. His position merited some perks, but his admiration never went beyond his eyes. She led two men into the office. Both were in suits, but the older one was fat and his suit looked shabby and badly cut. The younger man was handsome and tanned, too much so to be from these shores. His features looked Middle Eastern, Jordanian perhaps. Rossi wondered what it was like for the man to work in an agency whose primary mission was to hunt down and kill Islamic terrorists.

The older man led the introductions.

"Mister Rossi, I'm Agent Smit, and this is my partner, Agent Hassan."

As the men shook hands, Rossi introduced them to his colleague.

"This is David Karo, my foreman. Please take a seat."

Rossi indicated the couch opposite Karo. A mirrored coffee table separated the two.

"Drink?"

"No thanks," the American agent responded.

The one called Hassan simply shook his head.

If this putz was clean, something was very wrong with Hassan's instincts. The big guy on the couch had killer written all over him. The little one called Rossi was hiding his nerves well, but the darting looks, forced nonchalance, and controlled movements gave him away.

When Rossi asked how he could help them, Hassan did not wait for his senior partner to take the lead.

"Rossi, that's an Italian name, right?"

"That's right. I'm originally from Ischia, a small island off the coast of

Naples."

Rossi's answer was too practiced to be true. Hassan examined the man closely. He had the kind of features that could have hailed from anywhere in a six hundred mile radius of Alexandria. He could easily be mistaken for Greek, Italian or Israeli, but Hassan suspected he was from somewhere else entirely. The same went for the big killer on the couch.

"Is this about my immigration status?" Rossi continued. "Because I got my Green Card ten years ago."

The look Smit gave Hassan suggested he did not trust his young partner's line of questioning.

"Agent Hassan and I are following a line of inquiry from the Brooklyn Bridge bombing. Forensics were lucky enough to get a fragment of a component. Usually these things vaporize, but this device had not been assembled correctly."

Hassan cut in, "the component traces back here."

Rossi gave his associate a look of dismay. If it was forced, he was an excellent actor.

"I hate to think anything we've sold has been used to harm people, but we're the third largest component distributor in America. We ship thousands of parts every day."

Hassan hid his skepticism.

"Mind if we check your records?"

Rossi smiled.

"Of course not. I'm a patriot, agent Hassan, I love my adopted country. David will give you everything you need."

Smit watched Rossi's assistant walk ahead of them. His eyes were naturally drawn to her curves, as she sashayed along the corridor towards the reception area. For years he had longed for his dirty dog days, when as a single young agent he played the field far and wide. After twenty years of marriage, Smit had finally gotten his wish when his wife divorced him, citing irreconcilable differences. But the life of a young hound and an old mutt had little in common, and Smit spent his evenings alone with the television. A trophy like the woman in front of him was the stuff of dreams and memories, and even they were fading.

As he tried to imagine exotic love, Smit heard his young partner whisper into his concealed microphone.

"You getting anything?"

The vehicle was designed for prolonged surveillance, but despite the creature comforts the Agency had installed; it was still just a van. Comfortable chairs were surrounded by magazines, books, fast food boxes, cables and assorted items of electronic equipment. The cramped chaos forced intimacy. This was Lahm's third assignment with this particular partner, and as a result, they knew each other's habits well. Lahm checked the monitoring equipment; the signal from the surveillance device checked out.

He spoke softly into his radio microphone.

"Nothing yet."

Rossi looked out of the exterior office window, which offered him a view of the main entrance and the street beyond it. He scanned the row of stationary vehicles until his eyes settled on a van parked one-hundred-and-fifty yards from the main gate. The Agency's methods were reassuring in their predictability.

As he looked out of the window, Rossi said, "I want you to make sure those agents have everything we can give them."

Inside the van, Lahm relayed the message, "The boss is telling the other one to help us out."

As they walked through the reception area, Hassan turned to his partner.

"By the way, I think I've finally got my phone working."

Smit nodded at the prearranged signal.

"Good for you, kid."

Rossi turned away from the window. His lips were still but his hands spoke clearly. They moved quickly, communicating the following message in sign language, "Have the office swept for bugs. I believe there is a surveillance van parked up the street."

Karo responded silently, "And the agents?"

"All in good time, my old friend."

The tiny bug Hassan had attached to the underside of the couch heard nothing but the hum of the air conditioning.

CHAPTER 9

The high windows framed the cloudless azure sky and guaranteed that the occupant of every bed had exactly the same view of the world outside. A dozen beds lined the north and south walls of the medical bay. Many of the injuries suffered by the ward's inmates were easy to discern; the arm in plaster, the bandaged head, or the missing leg. Others were more mysterious; vacant men who stared into space, surrounded by machines that piped a variety of liquids into their bodies via tubes that disappeared under sheets, which concealed a multitude of horrors.

Head Wound occupied the bed closest to the widescreen television that was affixed to the west wall. He watched the screen with disinterest. A three minute news update broadcast the latest from back home. A legend at the bottom of the screen informed the viewer that the suited lady speaking was Senator Patricia Nelson, Chair of the Homeland Security Appropriations Committee.

"The Sentry program," Nelson began, "was started four years ago to give America additional security at a time when our military was severely overstretched."

"You're stretching something, baby!" came the contribution from Legs, so named for his missing right leg, which had been amputated just above the knee.

"How the fuck long have you been overseas?" Head Wound was grossed out. "She's, like, ninety-six."

"Tang is tang," Legs responded, as though that settled the matter.

"Your mama's tang," Head Wound countered. "Does that make her game?"

Legs wisely declined to reply and chose instead to flip the bird.

On screen, Nelson responded to a reporter's question.

"That's exactly why we've endorsed the administration's proposed restructuring of the program. We believe it will give America the security it needs."

"Fuck, someone needs to have the balls to bring back the draft!" Gut Shot yelled out.

"Shit, who's got the remote?" Head Wound asked. "I can see all the news I want to just by looking around at you sorry assholes."

"I'm watching," Broken Leg called out from two beds along, as he held up the remote.

The news report cut back to the studio anchor who tailed the previous item.

"Resolute Corporation were the big winners today after Senator Nelson's committee approved White House plans to reorganize the Sentry program."

"I'll play you for it," Head Wound challenged Broken Leg, who nodded.

The two men shook their fists, and counted to three. Broken Leg revealed the split index and middle fingers of a man counting on scissors, but Head Wound kept his fist clenched and won the gambit. Broken Leg tossed the remote to Head Wound, who flipped the channels and eventually settled on a football game.

The sound of the roaring crowd woke Pierce. Someone was tightening a plastic bag around his brain and his tongue was stuck to the roof of his mouth. If he didn't know better, Pierce would have thought he had a crashing hangover, but the near past came rushing into his mind like a flash flood. The last thing he remembered was the explosion. He moved his limbs to check there were no breaks, and was surprised to feel something heavy on his right forearm. Pierce tried to lift it, but could not. He rolled onto his side and used his left arm to lift the sheet. The cuffs that shackled him to the bed told him everything he needed to know about his superiors' view of his performance.

Pierce looked around the room; a standard issue marine corps medical bay. He guessed he was still in country at Lansing. He leant over to the man in the next bed, who had a head bandage. The bandaged man was watching a football game on the big screen.

"Hey, excuse me, how long have I been here?"

The man looked round briefly.

"No idea, buddy. I only checked in yesterday."

"Five days," the man on Pierce's other side offered. His leg was in an elevated cast.

"Thanks," Pierce said as he allowed his head to fall back onto the pillow. He wondered how the world had changed in that time.

As she leant against the wall of the staff room, Catlin knew Van Zyl's anger was not a reflection of his feelings for the six men who had lost their lives in the explosion. He was enraged at the thought that, despite his best efforts, he was covered in shit. As section chief, he was ultimately responsible for Pierce's mission. Looking at the narrow eyed man who stood opposite her, Catlin wondered how long it would take him to calculate a way for her to carry the heat.

"You blew this one, Liz," Van Zyl said, and Catlin realized that he had already got it all figured out. The anger was just for show.

She looked around the room the medical staff used for short breaks, her eyes darting over official notices about camp security, sexually transmitted diseases and emergency resuscitation procedures. Below the official notices, were a number of personal notes fixed to a corkboard. Telephone messages, announcements of sports fixtures and items for sale. Catlin noticed that one of the doctors was trying to sell an exercise bike – hardly used - and thought that if it was not for good intentions the world would be a real hellhole. She longed for the day when people dropped the petty politics and self-interest that made things so inefficient. If people like Van Zyl spent less time covering their asses as they tried to climb the pole, the Agency might stand a chance against an enemy organization in which the self counted for nothing.

"You're not the only one whose neck is on the line." May as well let him know how transparent he is, Catlin thought.

"You should have had tighter control," Van Zyl replied, barely skipping a beat.

"How?" This would be a neat trick, Catlin observed, as Van Zyl had signed off on operational procedure personally, and now he was going to try to disown it.

"You put a wire on him, and they'll find it. You meet with him and someone will spot it. You call him and they'll have bugged his phone."

Van Zyl knew exactly why they had given Pierce such latitude, but that did not mean he appreciated having it pointed out to him. He rounded on Catlin with a passion that made it clear he intended to bury her and climb over her corpse to bigger and better things.

"Don't lecture me!" he spat. "We don't even know what the Spider looks like. We've blown five years of work. Tens of millions of dollars wasted on surveillance, equipment and manpower. Manpower that might have yielded results if applied somewhere else. And all I've got to show for it is an agent who is directly implicated in the deaths of six people."

Letting her go down for a career fall was one thing, but there was no way Catlin was going to let Van Zyl toss Pierce on a murder charge.

"Scott knew nothing about that bomb. He would never go that far. I've known him for ten years."

"The man you knew died with his wife," Van Zyl countered.

Catlin was relieved when a nurse poked her head round the door and brought the exchange to a close.

"He's awake."

Neil Alder's bones ached with fatigue. Four years in charge of Manhattan's security had aged him more than he cared to admit. He could not remember the last time his eyes had not stung with tiredness the moment he opened them in the morning. Sleep had become a constant, unobtainable ambition, but about a year ago his inability to rest had taken on a more sinister dimension. Alder started to wonder if he would only find stillness in death. As a youth, death had terrified him. So, brash and full of confidence, he had chosen a career in the military where he would have to confront death every day. His years in the field did not diminish his fear, but he grew used to the ever present morbidity and learned to manage it. The last four years had extinguished his terror, until one day he awoke from a brief nightmare and found himself relishing the prospect of eternal slumber. Perhaps this is what life did, he thought as he stood on the dais, perhaps it ground a person down until the alternative finally looked appealing.

There were a few television cameras recording his failure, but nowhere near as many as would be present for the official handover ceremony in two days time. Alder questioned his legacy and wondered what the world would remember of him when he was gone. A distinguished career overshadowed by the past four relentless years of struggle against an unseen, unknowable enemy. The media would not report the two dozen attacks his men had prevented; they would focus instead on the six successful ones that had taken the lives of over eight hundred New Yorkers. Let the reporters say what they wanted; people who understood the fight knew what he had accomplished in the face of impossible odds. And his wife and children loved him.

As the Resolute G20 descended towards Governor's Island through the early morning mist, Alder wondered what he would do with his few remaining years. The suits at Fortress Corporation had made it clear that they expected him to put in his papers. The company had lost out in the recent review of the Sentry program and had no need for an old man so publicly relieved of such a prominent command. Sleep, Alder thought, as the hatch opened and the first Resolute personnel exited the grav-jet, perhaps a few weeks in bed would rekindle his fear of death and reignite his spark for life. After that, maybe a consulting or teaching post, and a handful of quiet years passed with his family before the inevitable curtain.

Alder watched John Creed and Sam Solomon approach the dais, and felt a confusing mixture of jealousy and pity. He knew what the past four years had done to him, and did not envy these men their work. At the same time he felt as though he had been robbed of the opportunity to put things right.

Alder stepped forward and shook Creed's hand.

"Welcome to Governor's Island, Colonel."

"You've done a good job, Neil." Creed clasped Alder's hand warmly.

Alder shook his head. "Not good enough, John."

The press pack recorded the handover of responsibility for the safety and security of Manhattan and its citizens. They would insert colorful words like momentous and pivotal, to heighten the drama of the moment for their news consumers, but, Alder reflected, all the handshake really signified was a tired old warhorse being put out to pasture.

Van Zyl held court by the infirmary door. A quiet conference with four agents, who were active on their PDAs, kept him looking busy and important, and left Catlin with the unworthy task of having actual contact with the contamination. She approached Pierce, who sat up as much as his cuffs would allow. This was the first time they had been able to talk freely in years and Pierce felt the awkwardness keenly.

He nodded towards Van Zyl, who was careful not to meet his eye; any kind of contact might taint him.

"He thinks I've turned."

It was a statement, not a question. Ever the diplomat, Catlin covered for her boss.

"He's taking a lot of heat. I thought it better if I speak to you alone."

Pierce could see that Catlin was sitting on something.

"Fuck him, Liz. You know me. What do you think? Am I a traitor?"

"I know you're not. But what I think isn't important. They're shipping you home to face a board of inquiry."

Pierce stared into the distance.

"They forget why I volunteered for this assignment?"

"Five years is a long time to have been living a lie. They're being careful."

Pierce looked at Liz and wondered if she could be the mole Azzam had spoken of. Someone within the Agency was feeding the Sons of September intel, which made the ground on which Pierce stood very unstable indeed. He and Liz had come up through the Agency together. They had known each other for a decade, and yet here he was unable to trust her, in case she was the one betraying her country. From her lack of ease, Pierce could see she was thinking something similar – and with far more justification; he had just delivered a bomb for the bastards.

Pierce cut the angles up in his mind and resolved that if Liz was the mole, he would have been dead years ago. She could have fingered him from the outset. No, the traitor was someone who did not have direct contact with the operation, or someone within who did not know they were being used as an asset. Pierce knew how paranoid Liz was, which ruled her out of being an inadvertent source. Little steps, Pierce thought exhibiting his own paranoia; just give her something small.

"I need you to do me a favor," Pierce said. "Run a search on all visa applications made through the Cairo embassy in the last twelve years. Check for anything unusual."

Catlin shook her head.

"You're clutching at straws, Scott. The bombing was a set-up to make the Agency question your loyalty, and it's worked. They're not going to trust anything that comes out of your mouth until you've been cleared."

"Bullshit!" Pierce said with such passion that the bandaged guy in the adjacent bed looked away from his football game in surprise. "We both know there's no coming back from something like this. Even if they clear me, I'll be assigned to a basement somewhere to handle the Agency's Christmas card list. I'll never get near anything sensitive ever again."

Catlin clenched her jaw muscles and nodded. She was witnessing the death of a talent that had once shown exceptional promise.

"The only chance I've got is to complete the mission. Get to the Spider," Pierce continued. "The Engineer could have set me up anywhere in the world, but they chose Cairo. They could have chosen another target and killed more people, but they selected the embassy. I believe they were using me to cover something up."

"I don't have the resources," Catlin replied. "We've been shut down."

"Fuck!" Pierce's exasperation was genuine. Azzam had successfully sabotaged the one Agency team that was anywhere near him. The Spider could complete his preparations for whatever nightmare he had planned with complete impunity.

Pierce clasped Catlin's arm.

"They got to me, Liz, just not the way the Agency suspects. They're inside my head. I know how they think. There are no accidents with them. Run the search."

If that money doesn't show, then you owe me, owe me, owe. As he hunched over the terminal, Kevin ran through the opening sequence of Jay and Silent Bob, which always brought a smile to his face. He had a reputation within the Agency for being a number monster, crunching data in ways that would have made other people's eyes bleed. Wells, they'd say, what's your secret? How can you sit at that fucking computer for fourteen hours straight and maintain a semblance of sanity? Nobody knew, because a magician never reveals his secret, but Kevin had been blessed with a photographic memory. As he sat chunking data, he'd replay classic movies in his head. That shit is the mad notes, Kevin thought, and smiled.

"This is a nightmare," the F.O.D. said. Kevin nicknamed anyone over fifty a Friend of Death, and Agent Smit definitely fell into this category.

"If you can't hide something, you swamp it," Agent Hassan responded. The two men were supervising Kevin and his team of junior analysts, as they worked in the computer room of Red Components. They had their machines hooked up to the company's servers and were running pattern searches on every component order for the past eight years. There were tens of millions of files, and Kevin wished the agents would go and pound a beat. They just cluttered up the place and broadcast unnecessary bad vibes because they were dealing with something they didn't understand.

"Why don't you guys grab a beer or something?" Kevin offered. "This may take a few days."

Hassan and the F.O.D. shared a look that suggested they did not appreciate Kevin's intervention, but he was saved from a reprimand by the entrance of the man he had dubbed Frankenstein.

"Closing time," David Karo said, as he leant his big frame against the open door. "You guys need anything; you make sure you call me."

"Sure," Hassan responded.

Frankenstein closed the door on his way out.

"Is it just me?" Kevin asked, "Or does that guy give everyone else the creeps?"

The man calling himself Karo waved at the security guard as he drove his car past the gatehouse. The Federal agents thought there was strength in their badges, in their technology, in their numbers. Only the weak are forced to band together, Karo thought, the strong stand alone. Their reliance on technology leaves them dependant and enfeebled. A true warrior was as comfortable without a weapon as with. Of all their faults, it was their obsession with truth and justice that bemused Karo most. All one needed in life was belief. If he had suspected anyone of committing the crimes these agents clearly believed he and Rossi were implicated in, that person would be dead. His belief that God would guide his sword to the guilty neck was the only truth he needed. That was strength. Truth, justice and due process were the crutches these weak men used to prop up their failing system. As he passed the van parked up the street, Karo consoled himself with the knowledge that these Federals would soon know the true nature of strength.

The rifle range was less than a quarter of a mile away, and the staccato bursts of heavy machine gunfire made it difficult for Catlin to concentrate. Colossal equipment trucks rumbled along the street outside the medical bay and threw up clouds of the fine desert sand that covered everything in the camp. Everywhere she turned she seemed to run into Marines being drilled or striding purposefully from one location to another. She had eventually settled on the small paved area behind the medical bay, and kept a close eye on two Marines who were smoking ten yards away. Catlin needed this conversation to be private.

Leaning up against a wall in a small patch of shade that shielded her from the hot evening sun, Catlin placed the call on her satellite phone. Belle answered the phone quickly and was her normal pleasant self. If the Langley grapevine had told Belle anything untoward about Catlin's future, she was not sharing it. They briefly discussed the winding up of the unit and Catlin felt a pang at background noises that would not have been out of place in a classroom at the end of a semester. Catlin could hear people yelling as they moved equipment, their voices magnified by the distinctive echo of a partially empty room.

"You been reassigned yet?" Catlin asked.

"Why do I get the feeling we're all being punished?" Belle replied. "I got economic intelligence. Talk about a comedown."

"I'm sorry. I should've..."

Belle intercepted her mid-flow. "Don't try to sell me your martyr bullshit, Liz. We all did our best on this one. They just happened to be better."

It was the first time Belle had ever cut Catlin off, and they were both a little unsure how to resume.

Belle found her voice first. "How's Pierce?"

"I think he's still in shock. He's been submerged for years, and now the Agency is fitting him for a fallguy suit."

It was now or never, Catlin thought. She held her stomach, and tried to control the butterflies she felt inside.

"I need you to do me a favor."

"Big favor or little favor?"

"Quiet favor," Catlin replied.

"I'm listening," Belle said without emotion.

The final ride around the battlefield, Alder thought, as he scanned the room. Creed and Solomon were on point for Resolute and stood opposite him on the other side of the Tactical Display Unit. A trio of subordinate Resolute personnel held digital tablets, ready to make a note of everything Alder said. Beyond them, his men disconnected and packed their surveillance and communication equipment. This command centre had been Alder's eyes and ears on the city for the duration, and he felt sad to see it being stripped of its soul. He looked out of the second floor window and saw the tip of Governor's Island; the fleet of twelve G20s on their landing pads, the missile silos, the barracks rooms and the equipment stores. Beyond it he saw the New York Bay, and then the magnificent city he had tried so hard to protect.

Alder touched the TDU and the sophisticated machine flashed into life. The TDU was a twelve foot long rectangular Perspex table that housed a sophisticated holographic system, which was capable of projecting three dimensional images on its surface. This one projected a perfect miniature replica of Manhattan Island.

"New York is unlike any other city on Earth," Alder began. "It's the richest, most densely populated island on the planet. You're responsible for two-and-a-half million souls."

Alder tapped the tablet used to control the TDU, and all the bridges and tunnels connecting the island to other landmasses highlighted in red.

"We deployed platoons at all seventeen bridges and the three tunnels. We scanned and searched every single vehicle coming on to the island."

Another tap on the tablet, and Alder highlighted the tunnels of Manhattan's subway network.

"Twenty-five roving squads covered the subway. Thankfully the energy shortages means it's restricted to only running a rush hour operation."

Alder highlighted a number of spots dotted around the city's streets.

"Checkpoints every ten blocks with random and profile stop and search."

Another touch and a dozen points illuminated on the island's perimeter.

"Missile batteries guard against aerial assault."

Alder gestured out of the window.

"And a squadron of jets on twenty-four hour alert for rapid response."

Alder looked at the hologram wistfully; the beautiful city was not his any more.

"The cops pretty much stay out of our way. They focus on investigating crime and leave the streets to us. You need to take the mayor to dinner once a month to make him feel important, but apart from that, you can use as much of our procedures as you want. I'll have my guys give your people a full briefing."

As Creed spoke, Alder struggled to discern what was genuine, and what was merely intended to humor the departing commander.

"Thanks Neil. I'm sure we'll just add to what you've already put in place. It looks like you ran a tight operation."

Something about Creed's complacent demeanor did not sit well with Alder, who found himself saying, "Even with our best efforts we had thirty attempted attacks in the past four years. Six of which were successful. These guys are sharp. They know our procedures and our running orders. Watch your backs."

A handsaw cutting through a pine log, a guttural pig, and a hydraulic pump were the most distinguishable of the cacophony of snores that echoed around the medical bay. While his neighbors slept, most of them with the assistance of the pills the nurses brought round with the evening meal, Pierce lay on his back and stared out of the high window opposite. The stars shone brightly in the clear desert sky.

Despite the cuff around his wrist, and the fact that he was in the process of being burned by the Agency he had served faithfully for the majority of his adult life, Pierce felt strangely relaxed. This was the first time in five years that he was able to stop living in fear. He did not have to worry about his cover being blown, being followed, having his phone tapped, or being interrogated. He could look around the room and not give a shit whether one of these strangers was a Sons of September plant inserted into his life to catch him out. The lie was over.

Pierce knew Liz would be unable to resist checking the embassy files, but he was worried that she might actually find something. In his current circumstances he would have a hell of a time convincing the suits to follow up any of his leads. And he was damned if he was going to let someone else pick up the trail. Nobody had his knowledge of how these sons-of-bitches operated, and there was not a person in the world that had his unique motivation. Pierce had to convince the Agency of his innocence. He had to make them listen to him. And if that failed...well, he would cross that bridge if it became necessary.

CHAPTER 10

The ghostly glow of her computer's holographic display fought back the darkness of the bare room. The transition had not taken long. Apart from her desk, computer and chair, all evidence that there had once been a diligent team in here was now gone. Belle had explained to the moving guys from facilities services that she had to back up her mission files before her computer could be moved. It was a lie, and they had given her until the morning to get her affairs in order.

The hologram displayed the seal of the Department of Homeland Security. In front of the seal, a window indicated that a database search was being run. Files were coursing through the window at a rate of thousands per second. Belle watched them fly past, half hypnotized by their rhythmic progress. She wondered why Catlin wanted to know about visa applications. Her instincts told her it was something to do with Pierce, which would explain why this had to be done off the books; the official Agency line was that there was a risk he had been turned. Nothing he said or did could be trusted. Belle could not believe it, but if the Sons of September had got to Pierce, it would be a magnificently malignant achievement on their part. They had killed his wife in the London attack. To have turned him against the Agency was one thing, to have turned him against his wife's memory was another. But then, Belle told herself, in the world in which they worked, anything was possible, which is why she had taken care to triple route her search and conceal her tracks. She did not want any of this coming back to her.

Catlin struggled with the morning sun. It blazed with an intensity that made her weak, and she could feel her skin slowly dying under the relentless brutality. The open hatch of the Agency's luxury fitted G20 beckoned her with its promise of comfortable seats and air conditioning. The aircraft's large graviton engines hummed loudly behind her, adding to her sense of oppression. Van Zyl and his sycophantic aide, Porter, stood next to her on the landing pad. Three unnamed agents congregated further away, and the whole entourage was guarded by a squad of armed marines, who spread out in a firing line on the perimeter of the pad. All feeding Van Zyl's already inflated ego, Catlin thought to herself, as the military transport approached.

Two outriders on armored bikes and a Cougar armored truck escort seemed like overkill, but the marines liked to follow procedure, and Pierce was now a high category prisoner. The box shaped prison issue J-Wagon was flanked by the bikes and followed the Cougar to the edge of the launch pad. Two Marines exited the heavily armored cab and walked to the rear of the vehicle, where they punched codes into identical keypads on either side of a reinforced titanium hatch. The titanium door slid open, and Pierce, now in full shackles, was ushered out of the vehicle by the four marines designated to travel with him until he was in Agency custody.

The tallest of the three unnamed agents signed a digital tablet that relieved the Marines of their obligation, and his two colleagues took physical charge of the prisoner.

Catlin mouthed the word, "Sorry," at Pierce, but he did not notice. He was too busy staring at Van Zyl.

"Doing things by the book, hey chief?" Pierce waved his shackled wrists at Van Zyl.

The bastard, Catlin thought, he didn't even have the decency to acknowledge the man. Van Zyl continued his conversation with Porter without even blinking an eye.

As far as Pierce was concerned, the whole thing was bullshit for the benefit of the military. It showed that the Agency was not afraid to get tough with its own. As soon as they were on the jet, Pierce expected the shackles to come off and the tough guy masks to come down. When he was pushed aboard the G20, he was surprised to find the rear access hatch open. It led to the containment cell every Agency G20 had in the rear of the aircraft, which was used to transport high risk prisoners internationally; a process that used to be known as rendition.

Pierce turned to Van Zyl and Catlin, who had followed him aboard.

"You've got to be kidding me?"

There may have been the faintest hint of a smile as Van Zyl responded.

"By the book, Pierce."

The expression on Catlin's face told Pierce all he needed to know; this was a shock to her too. Van Zyl was clearly at pains to be seen to be treating a potential traitor as severely as possible.

"Surely that's not necessary, sir," Catlin objected.

"No special treatment," Van Zyl replied as he waved the two custody agents forward.

The men who had hold of Pierce's forearms dragged him towards the rear access hatch. Beyond it was a brushed aluminum door that opened onto a stark, riveted metal four foot square cell. Inside a smooth metal shelf ran the length of one wall, and fixed to the opposing wall was a small toilet and basin.

The agents pushed Pierce into the cell and locked the door, sealing him in. His only source of contact with the outside world was a tiny glass panel cut into the door, which allowed his jailers to observe him at their convenience. Pierce sat on the metal shelf and put his head back against the wall. He wondered how many suspects had occupied this box before him - and how many of them had been innocent. If this was part of an attempt to wear him down, Pierce thought, they were reading from the wrong playbook. He had grown accustomed to confinement in jail, and was not afraid of it. At that moment, his only fear was that he would not be at liberty to pursue the Spider when they returned to America.

The marines were relieved to see the G20's graviton engines power up. Life was complicated enough without a maximum security Agency prisoner on base. The men watched from the perimeter of the landing pad, as the G20 rose steadily into the sky. The guard detail broke up and the marines returned to their regular duties. About two hundred and fifty feet up, the grav-jet's powerful boosters fired, and the aircraft became a distant speck on the horizon.

Creed was proud of what he had built. True, it was Solomon who had instigated his move to the private sector and provided access to most of the financiers, but Resolute was Creed's baby, and it was now the largest provider of private security in the United States. With over thirty thousand employees, Creed had a military force under his personal control that rivaled that of many small nations.

Through the large command center windows he could see the skyline of New York; the tall buildings pointing like dark fingers towards the moon. Governor's Island was alive with activity, as graviton jets ferried Resolute troops and equipment to their new base of operations. Logistics teams used robot lifters to unload heavy machinery, weapons and supplies, and transport them to the appropriate storage facility.

Inside the command center, Resolute technicians were busy installing their communications and surveillance equipment. Holographic computer terminals were starting to line the walls, ready for the arrival of their operators. Creed expected everything to be fully operational by the next morning.

He picked up a nearby radio.

"Road runner, this is command. How are we doing, Sam?"

"Running like clockwork, sir," Sam Solomon responded, as he turned to survey the massive military convoy that ran the length of the Queensboro bridge. Cougar armored personnel vehicles, T1 Abrams tanks, M8 Bradley infantry fighting vehicles, and MIM89 ground to air missile launchers, all filed slowly across the bridge towards their assigned deployment points on Manhattan Island.

Ahead of him, Solomon saw the last troops of the Fortress battalion who were busy dismantling their checkpoint. They would leave like unwanted visitors in the night, and by morning the city would be under Resolute's control. The Fortress mercenaries had made a valiant attempt at protecting the city, but they had been outmaneuvered by a more sophisticated enemy. He almost felt sorry for these foot soldiers; it was their commanders' tactics that had let them down. The men under his command need have no such concerns; Solomon knew exactly how to keep a city safe.

The soft leather of the wide seat did little to make Catlin feel comfortable. All she could think about was Pierce, who, after six years of the most unimaginable stress, was being treated as badly as Van Zyl could reasonably get away with. She looked across the maple wood table at her superior, who had his attention fixed on his PDA. Porter and the other agents were asleep in chairs further down the aircraft.

"You think this is necessary?" Catlin asked. "You think it's right to lock up an innocent man?"

It took a moment for Van Zyl to turn away from whatever pressing matter he was dealing with, but when he did, Catlin could have punched him. He looked like he was about to patronize a three-year-old child - that perfect mixture of arrogance and disdain for the little kid's naiveté captured on his face.

"And what if he isn't innocent?"

As Van Zyl spoke, Catlin found herself actually clenching her fist under the table.

"What if he knew about the bomb? What if he was involved in planning it?"

Van Zyl paused to let the implications of his remarks sink into the naive innocent's head.

"Just how far do you think he would go to get his hands on his wife's killer?"

It was the one question that Catlin had not wanted to ask in all her years as Pierce's handler. She knew that his fieldwork would require him to do things that were illegal, but she skirted around the issue of his morality. Just how far would he compromise himself to maintain his cover. Catlin had underestimated Van Zyl; he did not suspect Pierce of being a traitor in the normal sense, he suspected that the agent had been overzealous in his hunt for the Spider; that he had participated in a terror attack in order to maintain cover and keep his mission alive.

Catlin sat back in her seat and looked out of the aircraft's window. As she looked at the jagged coastline of North Africa thousands of feet below, she finally allowed herself to wonder whether Van Zyl might be right. Catlin contemplated just how far Pierce had been willing to go in his quest for revenge.

His instincts had told him to kill the Egyptian Colonel the moment he had seen that damned truck and he had not listened. Pierce played back the events of the past week and wondered how much he had been deluding himself. It took great strength to hold on to oneself on an assignment such as this. The Agency shrink had cleared him, despite the concerns of superiors who were worried that he had too close a personal connection to the target. Pierce had been able to turn the flaw into an advantage. Nobody else would go through what was required to infiltrate the Sons of September without that kind of motivation. Now, as he listened to the low frequency hum of the G20's engines, Pierce wondered just how motivated he had been.

Years of Agency training had taught him just how malleable the human mind could be. One moment a man could be cursing America's existence, and the next, with the right leverage, he could be taking the oath of allegiance. Pierce wondered how far he had allowed his personal motivation to interfere with his judgment. He had not known for certain that there was a bomb in the truck, but he had suspected that something was wrong. In ordinary circumstances that gut call would have been sufficient for him to take action. It was very well to blame the opposition's deviousness or the impossible stress of the situation, but that approach not only absolved Pierce of his responsibility, it robbed him of his power. He was a senior field agent who had once been the Agency's youngest ever section chief - he should have seen that bomb coming and acted decisively upon that belief. What concerned Pierce most was his growing suspicion that the personal vendetta against the Spider had clouded his judgment more than he had ever admitted to himself. He wondered what kind of man he had become. Maybe at some level he thought it was okay to let one attack slide past him; that the greater good would be served by him laying hands on the Spider.

Pierce slammed his head against the cold metal wall in frustration. Another six deaths. Another six innocent lives brutally cut short. Their loved ones left to forever lament the tender moments that might have been.

He would have many years to punish himself for his failings, Pierce told himself, now was the time to focus on the man who had set this chain of events in motion. Catching the Spider might not absolve him, but it would be a worthy penance.

CHAPTER 11

The old Central Intelligence Agency headquarters at Langley was now Central Operations, Federal Security Agency. The core of the CIA building remained, but it had far more sophisticated security than its previous incarnation. Fortified barriers blocked the roads leading to the Langley complex. Anyone who attempted to gain access by car had to pass through three separate checkpoints before they even reached the parking lot. Pill boxes equipped with M5 machine guns stood either side of each checkpoint, and squads of marines in full body armor patrolled the inner perimeter of the complex. M290 missile launchers were stationed discreetly at strategic points within the treeline. Five G20X advanced combat grav-jets were positioned on quick-release launch pads near the main building. Their crews were on twenty-four hour coverage, three hour duty rotation, and could be in the air within twenty seconds.

Alongside the White House and the Pentagon, Catlin thought, as the jet came in to land, this was probably the most secure building in the world. Catlin's stomach jumped as the G20's engines powered down and there was a momentary lurch towards the ground. The automated landing system kicked in and instructed the graviton engines to apply just enough upward thrust to counter the effects of the Earth's gravity. Mid-air flight was fairly straightforward but the physics of applying just the right amount of graviton thrust to counteract the Earth's gravity during takeoff and landing were so complex that they were beyond human control. Computers were used to interpret the pilot's desires at those key stages of flight, and there was usually a split-second during the transition from flight to landing where nobody was in charge of the aircraft. Catlin did not like to dwell on what might happen if one day the computer did not kick in on cue.

Today was not that day, and the G20 descended smoothly towards the reassigned landing pad. Marines were already using scanners to conduct multi-level, multi-intensity scans of the jet. Once on the ground those marines would board the aircraft and physically scan every passenger, and check every fingerprint and every retina. Catlin sat back; it would take at least fifteen minutes before they were even cleared to disembark.

William Bailey watched the man patrol the cell in a regimented sequence. He started at the north east corner, then traversed down to the south west, paced up to the north west, down to the south east, and finally returned to his starting point, where he executed a decisive turn and repeated the process. Bailey had watched Pierce do this twenty times and the effect was both hypnotic and slightly disturbing. Pierce had been one of the most promising talents in the agency until the death of his wife. What Bailey saw in the containment cell was evidence of a man who had lived too long on the edge; Pierce was exhibiting clear signs of someone suffering from mental illness.

As director of anti-terrorist operations, Bailey was on the line for this. He expected little of Van Zyl, who was a political animal and had minimal understanding of frontline operations. But Liz Catlin was astute and should never have given Pierce the latitude to do this to himself. He was now compromised beyond rehabilitation, and there was a good chance he would have to face charges for his role in the embassy bombing; criminal negligence at the very least. At least six people were dead as a direct result of Pierce's lack of judgment, and looking at the man now, it was clear to Bailey that he should never have been in the position to exercise that judgment in the first place. Bailey only prayed that when they went back over the operation files that there were not more bodies to be laid at Pierce's feet.

"He looks troubled."

Bailey directed his remark at Catlin, who stood next to him in the observation room. Van Zyl was next to her and watched the image on the surveillance monitor with practiced intensity.

"He's just been through a major trauma," Catlin replied.

"What were his most recent psych assessments?" Bailey asked.

Catlin shifted uncomfortably and then admitted, "He hasn't had one for five years."

As Bailey turned to look at her, Catlin continued, "We couldn't risk pulling him out of the field. They have the same equipment as us, they know our standard procedures. Pierce had to be alone out there."

Bailey looked at the floor and shook his head. On its own, that admission was enough to kill Catlin's career. The only question was whether Van Zyl would go down with her.

As he stood before the raised bench, flanked by two custody officers who held his handcuffed arms, Pierce looked out of the window at the grey sky. The years he had spent in London had been dominated by cloud. Back then, any day the sun had shone was worthy of note. The sun had been shining the day of the attack. Pierce had been scheduled to travel to Paris on the Eurostar, but had been called into the Agency for an emergency. He had planned to catch a train the next day and meet Eleanor for their long-planned romantic weekend away. When news of the attack came, Pierce knew immediately that she was gone. A hole opened in his soul and he felt despair unlike anything he had ever experienced. The hole was still there, patched up with survivor's guilt, frustrated ambitions for revenge and a delusive belief that the world might be a just place.

Pierce did not turn to look at the five members of the board of inquiry as they entered and took their seats at the bench. Instead he turned to look at Catlin, who sat next to Van Zyl and one of his functionaries in the observers' section of the trial board chamber. Catlin met Pierce's gaze, then looked away quickly. Pierce suspected that she knew what was coming, and it was not good.

"Agent Pierce?" director Bailey asked. The old man had been one of Pierce's biggest advocates early in his career, but he could expect no favors in this situation.

Pierce acknowledged the director.

"Sir."

"You are here because the Agency has reason to suspect you may have been involved in planning and executing a terrorist attack."

"I had nothing to do with the bomb, sir," Pierce protested.

"That may be, agent Pierce. However we will need to review your case in detail before deciding whether to proceed to a full trial board."

Bailey was clearly not enjoying this experience. His thumb and index finger pinched the bridge of his nose, as though he were trying to relieve an unseen pressure.

"Pending a full investigation, you will be transferred to the maximum security confinement facility at the marines corps brig, Quantico, where you will be denied all contact with the outside world, other than your Agency assigned counsel who will represent you at any trial board proceedings."

They were coming down hard, but Pierce was not prepared to be disappeared without a fight.

"This is bullshit! Can't you see what's happening here? The Engineer is a genius. He's burned the only agent with any traction on his organization and you're helping him bury the body. The Spider is out there and instead of hunting him down, the Engineer has got you to close down our operation and put me in jail."

Pierce looked at the board and saw that they only heard the desperate words of a guilty man.

"Don't you get it? They're playing the game better than us!"

"The investigation may clear you," Van Zyl's voice came from the side of the room.

Pierce turned to look at the man who was hanging him out to dry, and lost it.

"Fuck you, chief! I put myself on the line and you're letting me burn."

"That's enough, agent Pierce!" Bailey's tone suggested he would brook no further outbursts.

Pierce took a moment to calm himself.

"Sir, I have reason to believe that the Spider is planning a major attack on the homeland. I don't care who gets him, but he must be stopped."

"Any intelligence you have will be assessed as part of the investigation into your operation. If it proves credible, we will of course act upon it."

"It may be too late."

Pierce knew he had failed to convince these bureaucrats of his sincerity.

"We will act in accordance with Agency procedure, Scott. That has always protected the United States in the past. This board of inquiry will reconvene in exactly one month." With that, Bailey brought the hearing to an end.

Catlin could not bring herself to look at Pierce as he was escorted from the room. She did not need to; the force of his emotions was palpable. If he was innocent, the Agency was making a mistake that could possibly endanger the lives of hundreds if not thousands of citizens. They would analyze his intel during the investigation, but Pierce was right; that might be too late.

Catlin and Van Zyl followed Pierce out of the chamber. They stood in the corridor and watched him being led away to the transit custody suite.

"Don't let it get to you," Van Zyl offered.

People said he was a smooth operator but increasingly Catlin found that he just pissed her off. Or perhaps she was no longer worth the effort of charming.

"I've been his case officer for five years. I've known him for ten. I don't care what you or this trial board say, I've seen what he's gone through for us. This is wrong."

"This is procedure. Nothing more," Van Zyl said.

You're a cold bastard, Catlin thought, as she looked at his angular profile.

"Get her away from him!" Van Zyl yelled.

He shocked Catlin by starting down the corridor at a sprint. Catlin hurried to catch up with him and saw that the custody officers had allowed Pierce to stop to talk to someone. As Van Zyl cleared her line of sight, Catlin saw that it was Belle.

Van Zyl pulled her away from Pierce and pushed her bodily to the ground.

"What did you say to him?"

Belle responded with indignant silence.

"I'll bring you up on charges," Van Zyl threatened.

As Catlin helped Belle to her feet she advised her, "You should answer."

Belle looked at Van Zyl with fierce insubordination.

"After all this time watching agent Pierce in action, I said that it was an honor to finally meet him."

Van Zyl turned to the two custody officers for confirmation. Both men nodded.

"Get him out of here," Van Zyl ordered. "Nobody else talks to him. I mean nobody."

"You're doing a great job, chief," Pierce said to Van Zyl as he was led away.

As she watched the officers push Pierce through the door, Catlin wondered if the Agency knew what it was doing. Give a man nothing to lose and he will gamble everything.

Four serious-looking guys in suits stood next to the administration desk in the custody suite. From the scars that decorated two of the faces, Pierce guessed they were black-ops heavies the Agency kept locally to handle any unpleasant assignments. The officer in charge sat behind the desk and completed Pierce's digital transfer documents. He signed his electronic tablet and beamed the documentation to the lead Heavy.

"He's all yours," the officer said, and the two custody officers released their hold on him. The relief of the pressure on Pierce's arms was momentary, as two Heavies stepped forward and grabbed him.

One of the custody officers touched the fingerprint reader in the center of Pierce's handcuffs, and a computerized voice asked, "Release prisoner? Lock? Change custodian?"

The custody officer said, "Change custodian."

The computer chip in the cuffs responded by instructing, "Scan new custodian."

The Heavy on Pierce's left touched the fingerprint reader, and the machine confirmed the new custodian's identity.

Pierce felt the refreshing spit of rain on his face as he left the custody suite. An electric SUV waited for him in the Pit, a transit station that was just large enough for one vehicle. Enclosed by twenty feet high reinforced concrete walls on either side, with a solid steel barrier of equal height as the only exit, the Pit was designed to reinforce the claustrophobic message that escape was impossible.

The Heavies bundled him onto the back seat of the vehicle and pushed him towards the far window. His custodian grabbed Pierce's cuffs and locked them to a chain that was attached to a metal rail above the window. As the Heavies clambered into the vehicle, Pierce looked at the flesh colored band-aid that Belle had placed on his wrist moments earlier and wondered what message lay underneath.

The smile was locked on Creed's face. Had the occasion called for more gravity, Creed would have struggled to maintain his feelings of pride and achievement. He and Solomon had started from nothing four years ago, and here they were standing on Governor's Island at the formal ceremony to mark the handover of control of New York. It was a beautiful summer's day and even the water of the Bay seemed to understand the significance of the occasion, as it was unseasonably still.

Alder stood opposite Creed on the other side of the grav-jet landing pad, and two platoons of immaculately turned out Fortress personnel stood to attention behind him. Creed and Solomon had their own guard of honor comprised of their finest Resolute mercenaries. On the south side of the landing pad, dignitaries from the city, including the mayor, sat on a specially erected grandstand and watched proceedings. The media pack were positioned on the north side of the pad to enable them to get good shots of the personalities on the grandstand.

Creed watched a Fortress officer lower the red, white and blue flag of New York City. With all the ceremonial pageantry of a genuine military procedure, he released the rope at a measured pace hand-over-hand. When the flag had completed its decent, the officer detached and folded it. He handed the fabric parcel to Alder, who started across the landing pad. Creed followed his lead, in order to meet him half way. As Creed set off, a bugler played the 'Guard Mounting' bugle call.

Alder and Creed met over the large white 'G' that indicated that they stood on a grav-jet landing pad.

Alder handed Creed the flag.

"Under Sentry directive three-four-six, I hereby transfer responsibility for the security of Manhattan to the Resolute Corporation."

Alder raised his hand in a crisp salute, which Creed responded to in kind. In a move that had not been part of the rehearsal, Alder placed his arm on Creed's shoulder and said, with genuine emotion, "Good luck, John. I hope you don't need it."

"What a fucking life," Lahm observed as he looked through the van's privacy glass at the swaddled hobo who pushed a cart full of cans up the street. His partner, Dewayne, had his headphones on and was listening to loud rock music.

"You say something?" Dewayne said, as he lifted one speaker and gave Lahm a blast of the dreadful noise.

"Forget about it," Lahm replied.

Dewayne went back to his music, which was so loud that he did not even hear the clattering crash of the upended cart and the clanging of the cans as they rolled into the gutter.

Lahm looked out of the window and thought about drawing Dewayne's attention to the tragic figure who was now rooting around in the gutter picking up the trash that had spilled out of his cart. There was little point, Dewayne would probably crack a joke Lahm would not get and then go back to his music. Lahm preferred to contemplate the tragedy alone.

Outside, the man disguised as a hobo removed a device he had concealed in the folds of his sweltering, fetid clothes and attached it to the underside of the Agency surveillance van. He activated a switch on the device then went back to collecting the cans that littered the gutter.

CHAPTER 12

Pierce looked at the passing trees, as the SUV raced along Suitland Parkway. The energy crisis had made heavy traffic a thing of the past, unless one counted the checkpoint queues. They would be out of D.C. very soon and it would not take them long to reach Quantico. This car ride represented Pierce's best opportunity for escape. Once he was at Quantico, it would take months of planning to figure a way out, by which time the Spider would be long gone, with a trail of destruction left in his wake. Pierce recognized that the time was now and came to a decision. His escape would be quick, but it was certainly not going to be subtle.

Pierce turned to face the scarred Heavy seated next to him. The sneer the man gave in response to Pierce's thin smile was cracked from his face, as Pierce head-butted him with such ferocity that it shattered his nose and knocked him unconscious. The initiative would only be with Pierce for a moment.

The man on the other side of the back seat reached for his gun. Pierce was quicker and punched him in the face with his free hand. The goon in the front passenger seat had his pistol out and aimed it at Pierce, who fell into the footwell and leant towards the shot. This brought him under the shooter's arm, as the gun discharged. The bullet embedded itself in the rear bulletproof window. Pierce grabbed the shooter's arm with his free hand, but the shooter fought back, leaning over the head rest and grabbing Pierce in a headlock.

The man Pierce had punched came to his senses and scrabbled inside his jacket for his gun. Choking, Pierce lashed out wildly with his legs, and felt crunching satisfaction as one of his kicks connected with the man's face. Both backseat heavies were out of action, time to work the front.

The shooter was good, he was using his forearm to apply crushing pressure to Pierce's throat, while the two of them wrestled for control of the pistol. The driver had realized the odds were shortening in Pierce's favor, and started to apply the brakes so that he could get involved. Pierce released his grip on the shooter's arm and surprised the man by elbowing him in the face. The momentary advantage was all Pierce needed; he rotated onto the back seat and kicked at the driver with all his strength. The blow cracked the man's skull, and he slumped over the steering wheel. The dead weight of his foot compressed the accelerator and the out of control vehicle gathered speed.

As the dazed shooter brought his gun round in Pierce's direction, the SUV, which was still gathering speed, turned into a turbulent spin, causing the shots to go wide. Then the Earth gave up its hold, and the high sided vehicle flipped.

Inside the car, Pierce let himself go limp as the airbags burst forth from the panels in which they were concealed. The spiraling disorientation, silicon dust and white bags made it impossible for Pierce to know what was happening, but he felt the jarring impacts of the SUV smashing against the asphalt and colliding with other vehicles. Whatever happened, he had to stay conscious.

Andie Washburn was singing along to a classic rock radio station that was blasting out the MGMT, when she saw the SUV swerve on the road ahead of her. Probably a father turning to chastise a couple of kids, Andie thought to herself, but then the vehicle started to spin out of control. People often spoke about time standing still during moments of disaster, but Andie had never experienced the sensation until now.

Everything played out slowly. The whirling SUV collided with a late model Prius in the adjacent lane, sending the smaller car careening off the highway. The force of the collision destabilized the SUV, and for a moment it rocked from side to side like the pimped up dancing cars she'd seen in old movies. Then it left the ground and started flipping. Through the windows, which started shattering on the first flip, she could see the inflated airbags trying to cushion the bodies of an indistinct number of occupants.

Andie felt herself apply her brakes automatically, as the spiraling vehicle struck three more cars and then spun off the highway onto the wide verge. Ahead of her, drivers stepped on their brakes in an attempt to avoid the wrecked cars and debris. She collided with the vehicle in front of her, and felt the jolt of someone hitting her from behind. Another car sideswiped her, and the force of the last impact sent Andie's head crashing against the driver's window. The final thing she saw before she passed out was the mangled SUV crashing into a tree.

The screaming pain in his torso told Pierce that he had dislocated the shoulder of his restrained arm. The vehicle had come to a sudden and crashing halt on its side, and Pierce felt the shadowy tentacles of unconsciousness reach out for him. He bit down on his tongue, hard, which added to his suffering but kept him alert. The shooter in the front passenger seat was down, but not out. He was bleeding from a head wound and was struggling to come to his senses. Pierce had the weight of two unconscious agents on top of him. He reached out and grabbed his custodian's hand, as the shooter started to reconnect with his surroundings. Pierce pulled the custodian's fingers towards his cuffed hand, and placed the unconscious man's index finger on the reader.

"Release prisoner? Lock? Change custodian?" the computer inside the handcuffs asked.

"Release prisoner." Pierce croaked, as the shooter scrambled to find his pistol.

"I'm sorry, I did not understand. Please repeat your command."

"Release prisoner!" Pierce screamed, and the cuffs opened.

Pierce pulled himself clear of the bodies on top of him, and smashed a fist into the shooter's face. The man tried to fight back, but Pierce was frenzied and battered him into oblivion.

Through the shattered rear window, Pierce could see people emerging from their mangled vehicles on the Parkway. Some of them had started to stagger in the SUV's direction. He could hear emergency sirens in the distance. He had to get out now.

Pierce rooted through the nearest agent's pockets and took the man's wallet and cellphone. Then he saw the pistol hanging inside the man's shoulder holster. He grabbed it and tucked it into his waistband, before turning his attention to getting out of the vehicle. Pierce dragged himself through the rear left passenger window, which was now facing skywards. He pulled himself through the hole, ignoring the lacerating remnants of glass. Pierce hauled himself out of the car and saw a small group of drivers approaching. He could see them yelling but could not hear what they were saying; the crash had killed his hearing. The pain from his shoulder was the worst but it had company from other parts of his body. Pierce ignored it all, and jumped down from the vehicle. He landed on soft ground and immediately started running for the tree line.

Buddy had spent the morning checking GasReport.com for details of local supplies. The kid loved computers and Lyle was happy to let him feel he was doing his part to keep the family hobbling along in their hand-to-mouth existence. Buddy had found out about the resupply of the filling station on Meadowview three minutes after the bulletin was posted but by the time they had arrived, there was already a line of old cars a quarter of a mile long, all waiting to get their five gallon maximum.

Lyle stood beside the old Sebring and smoked a cigarette as he watched Buddy play with his PlayStation in the back seat. The rain had soaked him, but getting a quarter of a tank was worth any drenching. The guy beside the car in front leant into his vehicle, grabbed the steering wheel and started pushing. Lyle pinched his cigarette between his lips and did the same. They could not afford to waste gas by having their engines running while in line, so everybody pushed.

The guy in front unhooked the nozzle and gave his Toyota a drink. Lyle prayed that after an hour's wait, the pump would not screw him by drying up. It had happened before. He had once waited for two hours only to be told that the station was out.

Each of the four pumps at the filling station had an armed guard responsible for enforcing the strict ration, and for collecting payment. Lyle watched the guy in front hand over four twenties for his five gallons, and felt the man's pain. People like them were trapped in a cycle of poverty. Lyle needed his car for work - stationery supplies would not sell themselves - but he did not make enough money to buy an electric vehicle, even with government assistance and dealer cash back. So he kept his old wreck going and was shackled to the nozzle.

Buddy wound down the window, as Lyle pushed the car level with the pump.

"When can we get an electric roadster, dad?"

Without malicious intent, kids always knew where the sorest wounds were hidden. The core of who Lyle was as a man was decaying as a result of his inability to provide for his family. Every day he was emasculated by his impotence in the face of economic adversity. Lyle could have allowed himself to rage against the faceless enemy responsible for all his ills, but that is how people ended up in shopping malls gunning down their neighbors.

Instead he smiled at Buddy and said, "When we win the lottery."

Lyle extracted the fuel nozzle carefully to ensure the last few drops were not lost, then paid the guard and jumped into the driver's seat. Fuel efficiency was a mandatory part of the test when he had learnt to drive so a low consumption start was second nature to him. Lyle pulled out of the service station onto Meadowview and cursed when he saw the red light at the intersection. He slowed to a roll, to try to avoid stopping, but when the lights failed to change, he had to stop behind the Toyota that had been in front of him at the gas station.

Lyle thought of the money being burnt in his fuel tank and inwardly cursed the lights. A moment later they turned green. As Lyle prepared to pull away, the nearside rear passenger door opened, and a man climbed in and waved a pistol in his face.

"Drive," he said.

As he pulled away, Lyle looked in the rear-view mirror at the battered man seated next to his son. The maniacal look in the man's eyes put Lyle's poverty in perspective.

"Don't hurt us," was all he could manage as fear for his son's life coursed through every fiber of his being.

Pierce could see that the civilian was terrified. The boy on the back seat with him looked too shocked to express his fear. Pierce was exhausted. His body was suffering intense pain and did not have the energy for pleasantries.

"Just keep quiet, do what I say and you won't get hurt."

The shoulder-rest of the front passenger seat should provide sufficient leverage, Pierce thought. He lifted his dislocated arm onto the shoulder-rest and slammed his body against the back of the seat. As the shoulder locked back into place, Pierce hollered in pain, which alarmed the civilian driver. The kid started weeping silently.

As he sat back and tried to ride the wave of pain, Pierce thought about the fact that he had kidnapped two completely innocent civilians at gunpoint, and wondered about the role circumstance played in defining good and evil. As far as the outside world was concerned, he was now a bad guy.

The epicenter of the incident was the disfigured SUV, which was wedged up against the trunk of a tree. The emergency lights of a Medi-Vac grav-jet flashed in the driving rain, as paramedics loaded the injured occupants of the SUV into the aircraft. A team of firefighters, their truck parked on the verge, worked to cut the driver free. Police cars, ambulances and an incident support truck completed the roster of vehicles at the scene. Police officers had established a cordon around the SUV, and took statements from members of the public who were well enough to describe the collision and its aftermath. Every single one of them reported seeing an injured man flee the scene.

Beyond the cordon, paramedics tended to those injured in the pile up. Nineteen vehicles had sustained some form of damage, but in most instances the occupants had suffered only minor injuries. Of the thirty-four people involved, two had to be transferred to hospital for treatment.

Lieutenant Freddie Carsen surveyed the scene and felt that he had everything under control. Whoever the fugitive was, they would soon have him in custody. He had already assigned four men to canvas the area on the other side of the treeline into which the suspect had fled.

Carsen was surprised when he saw a military G20 begin its descent towards the Parkway. He signaled a couple of his men to accompany him, and headed towards the aircraft.

A guy in a suit was first out of the jet. He was followed by another suit, an attractive woman in her late thirties, some more suits and a platoon of marines.

"Secure the area and see if any of our people are talking," the first suit said, as he studiously ignored Carsen.

"Just hold on there," Carsen interrupted. "Lieutenant Carsen, D.C.P.D. and this is my crime scene."

The first suit held out his hand and smiled like a crocodile.

"Carl Van Zyl, deputy director, Federal Security Agency. That vehicle was transporting one of our prisoners."

"Shit!" Carsen exclaimed. "Why don't you people ever tell us anything?"

"You can question our procedures some other time, detective," Van Zyl said. "Right now, we need to find this man."

One of the unnamed agents held up a digital tablet that displayed the photograph of a man. Underneath were written the words, "Scott Pierce, Highly Dangerous, Use of Deadly Force Authorized."

The second suit out of the jet, who had been hunched over a scanner, suddenly spoke.

"Satellite uplink is operation and we have a signal."

"Where?" Van Zyl asked.

"Three miles north east."

"Let's go," Van Zyl ordered. "Thanks for your cooperation, detective."

"It's lieutenant."

But Van Zyl was already inside the jet. Carsen shrugged as he watched the entourage hurriedly board the G20. As the aircraft climbed skywards, Carsen turned to his subordinates.

"Call our boys and tell them to come back. Whoever this Pierce guy is, he's already screwed."

CHAPTER 13

The twenty-four hour cable news station replayed the clip for the hundredth time. Rossi pitied the anchors. They were obviously college educated but had to repeat the same sound bites with dramatic passion every fifteen minutes; the journalistic equivalent of being stuck inside a hamster wheel, where every development, no matter how small, was seized upon simply because it represented the most valuable commodity of all in this world of relentless news; change. Soon they would thank him, Rossi thought, because he would give them the kind of headline-making change they could only dream about.

For now the anchors had to be satisfied with the lead story, which was the handover of security in New York. Rossi sat behind his desk and watched the television with Karo, whose immense frame leant against the desk.

The image cut back to the studio where the attractive anchor tried to find some new angle on today's events.

"With Manhattan now in the hands of John Creed's Resolute Corporation, the real question is whether New Yorkers will finally be safe."

Rossi picked up the remote and killed the broadcast. He turned to Karo and said two words.

"It's time."

"Hey, how am I driving, man?"

"I think we're parked."

Wells was ten minutes into mentally replaying Up In Smoke, when Frankenstein walked into the room with a short dude named Rossi, who owned the company.

Wells's team of analysts ignored the intruders and kept chugging data on their machines. The Friend of Death, Smit looked up from the printout Wells had given him five minutes earlier, and a thin smile spread across his face.

"Mister Rossi, good timing. Agent Hassan and I have some questions for you."

Hassan, who had been studying a copy of Wells's print out, could hardly contain his satisfaction.

"We've found stock discrepancies. Components that feature on the Agency's watch list just seem to go missing from your warehouse. The kind of components that could be used to manufacture a bomb."

"Or perhaps a remote," the man called Rossi said, as he produced a small radio device from his pocket.

Before Smit or Hassan could move, Frankenstein pulled machine pistol he had concealed in his waistband. The weapon was fitted with a gas compression silencer.

Rossi curled his lip and shook his head.

"You have no idea where you are," he said, and pressed a button on the remote.

Lahm never knew what killed him. At Rossi's signal, the device underneath the van released a tremendous charge of energy, which coursed through the van and electrocuted Lahm and his partner in a painful and protracted death. The street was deserted but had anyone passed by at that moment, all they would have seen were sparks dancing across the vehicle's metal panels.

When Wells heard the screams coming from Hassan's discarded earpiece, he knew they were all going to die. The agent had ripped the concealed radio from his ear, unable to bear the sounds of his colleagues' agony, which were audible from across the room. Wells was never meant for frontline action, but he was damned if he was going to allow himself to be executed. He launched himself at Karo, who shot him dead mid-stride. The bullet pierced the skull and tore into Well's photographic brain, killing him instantly.

"Welcome to the Spider's web," Rossi said.

Karo sprayed the room with silent automatic gunfire.

Catlin had insisted on going inside with the marines. The G20 had touched down in a community park three blocks from the target location. Van Zyl had decided to deploy a dozen heavily armed marines to capture one man and there was no way Catlin was going to let that kind of firepower anywhere near Pierce without someone on the team who remembered he was once one of their finest. Van Zyl had put up brief resistance to the idea, but then Catlin was convinced he had seen the advantages. She would be the agent on point, which translated into yet more coverage for him in the even that things went to shit.

Catlin had grabbed a bulletproof vest and was fitted with a marine vox radio. The tiny sensors around her neck picked up the lightest whisper. The platoon had covered the distance between the grav-jet and the target location in a couple of minutes, and every step of their journey had been watched by Van Zyl, Porter and a group of agents Catlin did not know, who received feeds from tiny cameras concealed in the helmets of two of the marines.

Their target was a place called Kay's Diner. It was a family run place situated on the ground floor of a red brick building on the corner of Walker Mill Drive and Waterford. Three marines pealed off from the main group and rounded the corner to cover the rear exit. The Platoon Leader was the first to enter, and he immediately signaled for the nine patrons and three staff to remain seated.

The Comms Operator checked a scanner, which displayed the location of a signal. He signaled the restrooms, which were towards the back of the diner, on the opposite side of a corridor from the open plan kitchens. The Platoon Leader moved swiftly and silently, despite carrying more than thirty pounds of body armor. His men followed, and Catlin brought up the rear. With all the firepower ranged ahead of her, Catlin felt naked without a gun in her hand. But to draw her weapon was to admit there was a possibility that Pierce was a danger.

Catlin saw the Comms Operator signal towards the men's room, and the marines gathered around the door in a pre-arranged formation. Much to her dismay, Catlin saw the men flip the safeties on their weapons.

"Weapons cold," Catlin whispered.

The force of the Platoon Leader's emotions radiated through the full facemask he wore. All Catlin needed to see were his eyes, which burnt with indignation at an outsider giving orders to his men.

"Deputy director, instruct your observer not to interfere," came the Platoon Leader's whisper over Catlin's radio.

"Back off, Liz," Van Zyl intervened. "Let them do their job."

Catlin fought off the temptation to shout a warning to Pierce, and watched as one of the marines kicked in the restroom door. These men were trained to prepare for every eventuality, but even they were surprised by the sight that greeted them.

"You've got to be kidding me!" the Platoon Leader exclaimed.

Catlin pushed past the marines and looked into the restroom. Tied to a drainpipe with what looked like shoelaces, were a man in his late thirties and a boy of around six. They both had their own socks stuffed in their mouths, which the Platoon Leader quickly removed. The basin nearest them was covered in blood.

As the Platoon Leader cut the kid free, the man opened his clenched fist.

"He told me to give you this," the man said.

Catlin looked down to see the now bloodied tracking device they had injected into Pierce's arm while he was unconscious in the marine infirmary at Lansing.

Pierce tied the makeshift bandage around his forearm as he drove the stolen Sebring through the suburban streets. He pulled the knot tight with his teeth. He had guessed they would tag him the moment his cover was blown. While he was inside, the Agency could not risk a subcutaneous tracking device because it would have been discovered by the enemy the first time they scanned him. Now that he was out and was a suspect in a major terror attack, they would have taken the additional security precaution of having him tagged the moment they were able.

Warning them what would happen if they tried to say anything, Pierce had led the man and his son into the diner, his gun concealed under a jacket he had found in the trunk of the car. Once in the restroom, he had used their shoelaces to restrain them, and their socks to gag them. He had then turned on the cell phone he had stolen from the agent in the overturned SUV, activated the phone's loudspeaker and turned the volume up to maximum. He had then run the cell over the surface of his body, legs first, torso, and finally his arms. When he had held it over his left forearm, he had heard faint interference on the cell phone's speaker. He had swiped the area three times to make sure it was not a false positive and to zero in on the signal.

Pierce had advised his hostages to look away as he had used the screwdriver found in the Sebring's toolkit. It had taken every ounce of his self control not to scream as he had driven the blunt tip into the soft fleshy meat on the underside of his forearm. He had not wanted to do this more than once, so he had worked the wound deep and wide. When he felt confident he would be sure of getting the device, Pierce had inserted the thumb and forefinger of his right hand into the bloody mess. He had almost passed out with the pain, but after a moment of searching, he had found what he was looking for and had pulled out the tiny chunk of metal.

Pierce had turned away from the bloody basin and tore a strip from the man's shirt, which was to be used as a makeshift bandage. Half in shock at what he had done, Pierce had handed the bug to the man with the mumbled words, "Make sure you give them this."

He had known they would be found quickly, so concealing his wound as best he could, Pierce had exited the restroom, mumbled something to the manager about the kid suffering from stomach flu, staggered out of the front door and climbed into the waiting car.

Alone and in no immediate danger, Pierce finally took the opportunity to peel away the band-aid Belle had surreptitiously stuck to his arm. He could see tiny writing on the underside that was too small to read with the naked eye. He would need a magnifier.

Catlin sat opposite Lyle Kaylor in one of the diner's booths and watched as he sipped a cup of coffee and tried to compose himself. He had his arm around his son, Buddy, who twiddled a straw in a glass of coke. Catlin had debriefed Lyle, and when she heard about the tracking device she forced herself to suppress the seeds of doubt that Van Zyl planted in her mind. Only a man driven by demons of righteous vengeance could endure such self-inflicted torture, she told herself. Van Zyl's assessment had been that the self-mutilation demonstrated the warped zeal of a terrorist and underlined Pierce's desperation to avoid capture. Of course, Catlin thought, Van Zyl's assessment might just be colored by his resentment that Pierce had outsmarted him and his team.

With the diner declared safe, Van Zyl, Porter and the rest of his entourage had joined her. Van Zyl stood a couple of steps away from the booth and was giving orders to Porter, who was using his cell phone to relay them to local and state police authorities. Now that Pierce was in the open, Van Zyl had to swallow the shame of involving local law enforcement. Porter was arranging roadblocks, random stop and search, and increased security at bus depots and train stations.

The rest of Van Zyl's men interviewed the staff and other patrons. Pierce had torn out the tracker and left the diner no more than fifteen minutes earlier, so the trail was still very warm and they had to work fast.

Catlin had to get away from Van Zyl and his men, and saw this as her opportunity. She took her leave of Lyle and his son, and approached Van Zyl, who was preoccupied with Porter.

"Carl, I had the best track and trace team in the business. Let me go back to Langley and pull whoever I can to try to find him."

Van Zyl had half heard her, but was non-committal.

"We ran the guy for the best part of five years. If anyone can anticipate his moves, it's us. Let me give it a shot."

Catlin could see Van Zyl calculating the downside. Once again she was stepping into the firing line. If they failed to find Pierce, Van Zyl would have yet more kindling with which to burn Catlin.

"You find him, you let me know immediately," Van Zyl said at last. "He escapes, and careers are going to end."

Not yours, you slick son-of-a-bitch, Catlin thought as she left the diner.

CHAPTER 14

Woodlawn Boulevard was a very appropriate name for the street. The wide road that cut through the quiet suburban neighborhood was lined with mature trees. Manicured lawns ran up from the sidewalk towards large New England style timber homes. This high-end, purpose built executive estate was likely to have exactly what Pierce needed, and he kept to a steady fifteen miles per hour to give himself plenty of opportunity to scan the houses and driveways.

Pierce saw a promising property and turned Lyle's Sebring into the driveway. He parked next to a silver late-model electric Honda, left the engine running, climbed casually out of the car, and approached the front door. As he peered through the semi-circular glass panel inlayed in the door at head height, Pierce gave a series of loud knocks. He waited, and then knocked again. There was nobody home. As he returned to the Sebring and cut the engine, Pierce thought, this will do fine.

This was the culmination of the past twelve years, the man calling himself Rossi thought as he surveyed the eighty-three men who stood before him clad in black boiler suits. All of them were devout members of the brotherhood of the Sons of September.

He had entered America fraudulently in 2019, using the Rossi alias, and established a clean cover for himself. Rossi had a history in Milan that would stand up to any level of intelligence scrutiny. The brotherhood did not just create aliases; they would select what they liked to call donors. A donor was someone who had no criminal record, little contact with friends or family, and who bore a resemblance to the brother they were donating their identity to. The donor would be killed silently, and their body disposed in a manner that left no trace. The brother would assume their identity in the originating country and immediately begin the process of applying for an American visa. In some cases it took scouting teams up to a year to identify and replace a donor.

When Rossi had arrived in the United States, the brotherhood had no immediate plans for him. They had simply wanted to get as many cleanheads into the country as possible. Rossi had taken work in the hotel business in Los Angeles. He had started in the industrial scale laundry of a five star hotel and over the course of three years worked himself up to front desk. Each day he wondered whether the call to serve would come. He longed to be liberated from the torture of being a functionary in a system he loathed. Rossi lived for the day he would be able to pray without fear of discovery.

Three years and four months after he had come to America, an unknown person left a typed message at the hotel's front desk. It was Rossi's activation code. Rossi gave notice and left the hotel two weeks later. Two weeks after that, Rossi met with a man in a park in San Francisco. The man, who he had never seen since, gave him his orders. He was to use a shell company the Brotherhood had established, funded to the tune of three hundred million dollars, to purchase AmCore Components, an ailing Chicago firm that was up for sale. He would run the firm as a legitimate business until given further instruction.

Rossi purchased the company and renamed it Red Components in homage to his Italian donor's name. He ran the business to the best of his abilities and used Brotherhood cash to prop it up when his abilities were not up to the task. He waited patiently for instructions, and over the years they came. His first was to provide a cover for Brotherhood cleanheads arriving in the country. Over time the old employees were all eased out of the business in favor of the loyal men that presently stood before him.

The next instruction had been to start constructing and shipping explosive devices to various destinations around the country. Fully half of the terrorist attacks in the past six years had originated from his warehouse. Rossi was finally having the kind of impact he had longed for.

When Karo arrived five years ago, Rossi knew that they were about to start work on something spectacular. Karo's real name was not known to Rossi but he had suspicions that this huge man might be the one they called the Spider. He certainly demonstrated all the strength and cunning of this legend. Karo had spent the past five years preparing for tonight, and what a night it was to be.

As he thought about all he had been through to get to this moment, Rossi realized that his story was the reason that the Brotherhood would ultimately taste the fruits of victory. Twelve years ago they had planted the seed; one man had entered America. As a result of patience, planning and ingenuity that went far beyond anything their enemies were capable of, Rossi stood in front of a small army that was ready to strike at the very heart of America.

Behind the men, waiting in the warehouse loading bay, were the ten white electric vans that would carry them to their destination. The men were eager to begin their mission, but Karo took a moment to address them. He spoke openly in Arabic for the first time in years, and the language was like music to Rossi.

"By God's mercy we have been allowed to reach this day. All our years of patience will finally deliver the crushing blow. Praise be to God."

Karo turned towards the east and dropped to his knees. Rossi and the men joined him. For the first time in more than a decade, Rossi was able to perform the Asr afternoon prayer without fear that unwelcome eyes would expose him.

The alarm system was sophisticated for a domestic home but Pierce had managed to disable it within the required thirty seconds of his forcing the back door open. The quantity of food in the automated cat feeder told Pierce that the occupants would not be home for at least a week, and were probably away on their summer vacation.

Pierce was counting on the neighbors to be complacent about security, placing their trust in the invulnerability of their alarm systems and the private security company's two minute armed response. Even so, Pierce worked fast, just in case anyone had seen him.

Sports trophies looked down at him as he sat at the computer terminal. Pierce was in a den that he guessed belonged to the man in the family portrait that hung from the wood paneled wall. The man, who was in his mid-forties, had his arm around the shoulder of a younger woman. Two girls and a boy stood in front of them. The smiles on their faces looked genuine and gave the portrait an authentic feel; this was an insight into familial bliss. He tore his eyes away from the picture, and suppressed thoughts of what might have been. Pierce stroked the cat, who had jumped onto the desk to perform a closer inspection of this stranger, and turned his attention to the heavy oak desk.

In one of the drawers he found a plastic framed magnifying glass complete with built-in reading light; a hidden testament to the father's encroaching age. As the cracking code he had downloaded from an Agency web server went to work on the identification database, Pierce used the magnifying glass to examine the coded message written on the band-aid.

He had just decoded the last word, when the computer screen altered and a window popped up to inform him that he had logged on to the Federal Central Identification Database as an administrator. Pierce typed in the address of the property he had invaded, 2242 Woodlawn Boulevard, and five names appeared on the screen, all with the surname Robins. Pierce selected Timothy Robins, and the identification details of an eight-year-old boy appeared on the screen. The face in the file photograph was a more somber version of the kid in the family portrait. Pierce went back to the list of names and clicked on Martin Robins. The father's face appeared in the file photograph, along with his left and right index fingerprints and all his personal details.

Pierce used the computer's inbuilt camera to take a photograph of himself, which he uploaded to the Central Database. He replaced Martin Robin's photograph with his own, and then used the computer's fingerprint scanner to substitute his fingerprints for the genuine ones. With the changes made, Pierce typed a command into the computer, and a window appeared on screen that told him the updates were being propagated.

The cat followed him, but Pierce used his foot to make sure the animal did not stray outside as he shut the front door behind him. Martin Robins was going to have a tough enough time now that his identity had been stolen and Pierce did not want to add to his woes with a missing pet. He crossed the soft lawn to the driveway and placed his index finger over the reader on the Honda's locking system. The driver's door clicked open and the car greeted Pierce by a friendly female voice.

"Hello, Martin, today's temperature is eighty nine and the forecast is good."

The car's systems started as Pierce climbed into the driver's seat. He typed a zip code into the car's satellite navigation computer, selected manual steering, and reversed down the driveway.

The Car Pool was a fantastic concept that was widely deemed to have been an utter failure. A publicly subsidized corporation designed to encourage people to share motor vehicles. Depots scattered around the major cities mirrored the set up that greeted Catlin. Thirty-two parking spaces spread out from a central computer terminal. Fifteen of those spaces were occupied by small electric cars that were locked to charging stations. The intention had been that people take a car from the Car Pool and return it to any other Car Pool terminal in any city in the country when they had finished using it. They would be charged a very low per minute fee for use of the vehicle. Like all communal facilities, hygiene was the first casualty. Customers complained that the vehicles were foul; people would use them to take trash to the dump rather than foul their own cars. There was one case where a renter had found a corpse in the trunk of one of the cars – that had turned out to be a rather amateurish attempt to dispose of evidence after a mob contract killing.

Then the cars started disappearing. People found a way to beat the billing system by using the identification of someone who was newly dead. The cars vanished and never came back. By the time the loophole was closed, Car Pool had lost over half its fleet.

Catlin placed her index finger over the reader on the central terminal, and the computer brought up her identification details. She confirmed liability for the two thousand dollar deposit, and selected her vehicle from the fifteen available. As she hit the confirm button, the restraining clamps detached from her chosen car.

As she walked over to the vehicle, Catlin called the office. Belle answered.

"How's the analysis?" Catlin asked.

"Nothing so far," Belle responded. "You?"

"Van Zyl thinks I'm there, so I need you to cover."

"Be careful," Belle advised, before Catlin disconnected.

Catlin climbed into her small electric car. She pulled away from the Car Pool terminal, and hoped that Van Zyl was wrong about Pierce.

If there was anything wrong with the identification, he would find out in the next few seconds. The Resolute mercenary checked the scanner as it processed through millions of database entries and came back with Pierce's photograph.

"Thank you, Mister Robins," the mercenary said. "You may proceed."

"Thanks," Pierce said as he pulled away.

Pierce navigated through the concrete doglegs that protected the Resolute checkpoint on Interstate 95, and accelerated towards Philadelphia.

As he looked in the wing mirror, Rossi could see the other nine vans strung out behind him like beads on a beautiful necklace. They proceeded along the interstate, the sun low in the sky behind them, and Rossi felt magnificent as he looked at the incandescent ball of fire. He felt such majesty in the occasion that he could quite easily have believed himself capable of anything, even swallowing that celestial ball from the heavens.

Rossi was in the lead vehicle with Karo next to him in the driver's seat. Six men sat on benches in the rear of the van. They all wore the same black boiler suits and waited with quiet anticipation, willing the van on to its final destination, and praying there was no last minute interference with their objective. The van passed a sign that told them they were headed toward New York. Once they were inside the city, Rossi told himself, they would be unstoppable.

CHAPTER 15

Over the years Pierce had learnt that the wellsprings of the evil that contaminates the marrow of society are often found in the most innocuous locations. As he approached the low rise office complex on Callowhill Street, in the outskirts of Philadelphia, Pierce contemplated what he would find inside. Belle obviously thought that the lawyer whose name had been on the band-aid was a worthy target of Pierce's attentions but other than his name and location there was no indication how he was connected to the Sons of September. In the circumstances, Pierce could not complain; he was used to having to improvise.

A drive through convinced Pierce this was not a trap. As he lapped the block, checking for people or vehicles that looked out of place, Pierce told himself that Van Zyl was not smart enough to have engineered a set up like this. The only other risk was that Belle had talked, but Pierce believed he had been keeping Van Zyl too busy with the escape to even give Belle a second thought.

Pierce checked the area one last time and then pulled into the office complex parking lot. The brown brick horseshoe-shaped office building bordered the parking lot on three sides. Pierce drove into a space on the opposite side of the lot from the target address, exited the vehicle and walked across the parking lot.

As he approached the offices of Helmer, Cohen and Hess: Attorneys at Law, a figure stepped out of an adjacent doorway into the late afternoon sunlight.

"Need any help?" Catlin asked a surprised Pierce.

He checked his surroundings and saw no other movement.

"I'm alone," Catlin continued. "Who do you think asked Belle to give you the band-aid?"

"They've got an informant," Pierce said at last. "Someone inside the Agency. That's how they made me."

"I had a feeling you knew more than you were saying," Catlin was relieved. If Pierce had really turned, she would have been dead by now, neck snapped and body shoved in the trunk of a car.

Pierce was silent.

"You're wondering if it's me," Catlin observed.

"No," Pierce responded. "I'm trying to work out why you helped me."

"You said it yourself; we got outplayed. The Agency just shut down the only operation with enough juice to catch the Spider. And if you're right and there is a mole inside, well then you're the only person I can really trust."

Pierce seemed satisfied with Catlin's answer. She pressed him to trust her.

"You know how they think, Scott. What are they thinking now?"

"They're going to strike. And they'll do it soon. The Agency is demoralized and distracted. The timing is perfect. I've got to stop them."

As Pierce started walking towards the lawyers' offices, Catlin fell in alongside him and said, "We've got to stop them."

Pierce gave her an impassive look, and said nothing. He was not used to having a partner but given his current situation, anything that shortened the odds was fine with him.

David Helmer was looking forward to getting home. His forty-six-inch waist was proof that Jenna was cooking better than ever. He started salivating at the thought of the brisket he'd be having tonight. David admired Jenna's discipline; she could make the most fantastic meals for him and the kids but never touched them herself. She existed on green macrobiotic crap that David could not stand the smell of, never mind eat. Fear, David thought, was a powerful motivator and from the day she had heard the 'C' word, Jenna had changed her life completely. Not even when she had been told she was in remission did she deviate from her new regime. While David had got decidedly drunk on a bottle of champagne, Jenna had replied to his repeated toasts with sips from her glass of water, which had been infused with raw ginger and Manuka honey.

He was just contemplating whether it was too early to leave, when his office door lurched open and a badly beaten man and a woman in smart business suit entered. Carol, David's secretary, was doing her best to prevent the interruption.

"Mister Helmer is extremely busy."

"He'll see us," the woman said as she flashed Federal Security Agency identification in David's face, which identified her as senior agent Elizabeth Catlin.

"It's okay, Carol," David said from behind his desk.

Carol looked at him uncertainly and pulled the door closed behind her. David could see that she was trying to work out what the Agency could possibly want with her boss.

David turned his attention towards the intruders.

"Should I call the police now, or wait until you've made your threats?"

"Smart guy," the man spoke at last. He lunged forward, pulled David out of his seat, and tossed him over the desk onto the floor. David landed on his back and felt a sharp pain run down his legs, as his sciatica objected to the rough treatment.

The man knelt and punched David in the gut. It was a powerful connection that made David yowl and brought tears to his eyes.

"Please," he managed. "What do you want?"

The female agent leant down.

"Four months ago you processed a visa application through our embassy in Egypt. A cross reference of visa records show that the same person applied for a visa which he never used four years prior to that. The only problem is that although the name is the same, the photographs are slightly different. The guy

98

you helped get into the country was a ringer."

David cursed inwardly; those fuckers were supposed to make sure the person contributing their identification had never applied for a visa before. He had found out about the screw up when the INS bounced back the application. It was the first mark on his otherwise pristine record and David had been determined to clean it up. He had made a phone call and within a week the applicant had copies of falsified hospital records that stated he had undergone reconstructive surgery on his face two years earlier. David had spent a day at INS headquarters in Washington convincing the paper-pushing government employees that his client was bona fides.

Even though that particular guy got through, the record of his application was a permanent weakness in their operation. David had expected an INS audit as a result of the irregularity, but none came. He had informed his contact within his client's organization, and when the embassy in Egypt was bombed, he knew they had made a half-assed attempt to cover their tracks. Surely they knew there were master records in Washington. David had worried that the attack would only serve to increase the likelihood of some smart agent double checking files while the embassy's data servers were reconstructed. And here, staring him in the face, was the proof that he was right to be concerned.

The agent had pulled a computer print-out from her pocket. Sure enough, there were two different photographs on the same man's applications.

"I can't help you," David groaned. "Visa applications are handled by my paralegals. I can find out who processed that one."

"Don't give me that bullshit!" the man growled. He pulled a pistol and held it to David's head.

The woman seemed perturbed by the appearance of the gun and gently tugged on the man's arm in an effort to get him to put the weapon away. The man resisted and kept the piece pressed firmly against David's temple. Full of fear, David struggled to keep to the official story.

"I swear I don't know what you're talking about."

"Our people are looking at your records very carefully, Mister Helmer," The woman continued. "If you've got anything to say, now would be the time to say it."

David was tempted the break his silence. The thought of dying at the hands of this psychopath almost prized his mouth open but then he remembered what happened to people who crossed the monsters he worked for, and his lips stayed firmly sealed. This man might kill him, but his clients would kill his family and everyone he knew.

After a tense few moments, the battered man put his gun away and walked towards the door.

"We'll be in touch," the woman said as she followed her accomplice.

David fell back against the floor and tried to bring his breathing under control as his heart pounded against his ribcage. There was no way he would enjoy his brisket after this.

If the motherfucker had any sense of responsibility, Van Zyl thought as he stared at the family portrait in his gloved hand, he would have installed a silent alarm to protect his family properly. The forensics team were in the process of turning the characterless home upside down as they looked for any trace of Pierce. Outside, Van Zyl's G20 blocked the road, and locals gathered to peer into the house from the wrong side of a police cordon.

A local cop had spotted the stolen Sebring in the drive and responded to the APB that was now in force in seven states. From the diner, Van Zyl and his team had made it to the location in under eight minutes. A forensics team dispatched from Langley had arrived six minutes later. They had pieced together Pierce's movements within the house and discovered the majority of his time had been spent at the desk in the den.

Porter analyzed the motherfucker's computer and pulled up logs of Pierce's activity on the machine.

"He downloaded one of our hacking programs from a secure server," Porter said as he read the data on the screen, "and used it to crack the Central Identification Database. He's travelling under the name of Martin Robins, the owner of this house."

Porter typed a series of commands and details of the Robins' vehicles appeared on screen.

"Two cars registered to this location; a Honda Rivera, and a Ford Dayliner."

"Put out APBs on both vehicles," Van Zyl instructed Porter. As his subordinate relayed the command to the state police agencies, Van Zyl used his cell to make a call.

"Pierce is travelling under the alias Martin Robins. I'm texting you the guy's social security number. Have your people run a trace," Van Zyl said before hanging up. Keep her involved, he thought to himself, it never hurts to have a little extra cover.

"They know your alias," Catlin said as she hung up. "Van Zyl just ordered me to run a trace."

Pierce sat low in the passenger seat of her Car Pool rental. He stared out of the window as he contemplated the implications of the discovery.

"I can fix this," Catlin said, and tried to dial Belle's number on her cell, but Pierce stayed her hand.

"You can still back out," he said. "You make that call and you're implicated."

"I know dirt when I see it," Catlin replied. "And that lawyer had it all over him. They're going to make their move, Scott. It's not about my job anymore, we're beyond that."

"Can we trust her?" Pierce asked.

"She knew where you were going and didn't turn you in. That's about as much trust as we're going to get right now."

Pierce released his grip, and Catlin placed the call.

Belle answered after three rings, and Catlin put the call on speakerphone.

"Our friend needs a new identity," Catlin looked at Pierce, her expression acknowledging that she had become his accomplice.

"I'll get right on it," Belle responded. "I've got more on the lawyer."

"Give it to me."

"I'm mailing you the files now."

A tone sounded on Catlin's cell, indicating that she had received new mail.

"We've been running through the INS records of every single visa application made through his office. We've been able to go back to source photographs in the countries of origin in about one hundred and fifty cases. The passport and government photographs match the applicant in all one hundred and fifty cases, but we've been able to pull employer records, medical photographs, student union identification for those people. Out of those cases, twenty of the applicants do not match the secondary source photographs. That means that out of one hundred and fifty applications, twenty were bogus."

"Shit," Catlin said, as she digested the significance of Belle's discovery.

"It gets worse. This guy has processed fifteen thousand visa applications in the past eight years. If that ratio holds true, we could be looking at over two thousand target suspects."

"That's not a cell, that's an army," Pierce observed, shocked by the scale of the revelation.

"Keep doing what you're doing, Belle, but I want you to start bringing in the field offices. Have them track down every single suspect you identify," Catlin said.

"Will do. Any movement from the bastard?"

"None. Are we ready for a trace?" Catlin asked.

"Hard lines, cell and email are all being monitored. If he squeals, we'll know."

"Great," Catlin said before she disconnected.

She turned to Pierce and all she could manage was, "Fuck."

"How did they do this under our noses?" Pierce asked. He did not expect an answer; he knew how. They were patient, they were ruthless and they were efficient. The Brotherhood had spent decades learning proper spycraft and had spent the last few years taking it a stage further, incorporating their own devious ingenuity, which seemed capable of beating the Agency's best.

"There's our man."

Catlin pointed to David Helmer, who had exited his office and was crossing the street. Catlin had parked on Callowhill Street, about a hundred yards from the suspect's offices. The position gave her and Pierce an unobstructed view of the building entrance.

As she watched David make it to the other side of the street and duck inside a bar, Catlin dialed Belle again.

"He's using the bar across the street."

"We've got it covered," Belle replied.

CHAPTER 16

The double whisky would make a full dose of Pepto mandatory before he went to bed. David consoled himself with the thought that it would not be burning pains in his gut that kept him awake this particular night. The moment the agents had left his office, panic had consumed him. Carol had come in to check he was okay, and he had managed to keep it together until he had been able to shepherd her out of the office. The moment he had slammed the door shut, he had started to weep. Not a delicate tear or two, but gushing streams of warm salt.

For years he had been telling himself that he was not doing anything too bad. If his clients didn't use him, they would find someone else. They had first approached him when he was a newly qualified lawyer. The year that Jenna's breast cancer had hit. Neither of them had medical insurance and David just wasn't making enough. A man called Paul, who had pronounced his name "Baul", had come into the office and asked if David could get his cousin into the country. Baul offered to pay David an additional twenty thousand dollars to make sure the INS did not find out about his cousin's Spanish conviction for marijuana possession.

Looking back, David saw the genius of how they worked. If he had refused, Baul would have moved on to the next lawyer on his list, and David would have never thought about him again. But with Jenna's medical bills mounting, David had accepted the money without a moment's hesitation. The cousin had come into the country fifteen years ago, and his entry signaled the start of very profitable, highly illegal relationship. Baul had waited for six months before returning to David's office. The second and third cases were similar; convictions for minor offenses.

After the third cousin made it in, Baul opened up and laid out the deal. Fifty thousand dollars per person, no questions asked. He never said who he worked for, and David tried his best to suppress his suspicions, but it was obvious. David was helping enemies who wanted to destroy his country, and after the second year, when Jenna was given the all clear, he had been helping them for nothing more noble than money. By then, David told himself, he was in too deep. An asset as valuable as him could never be allowed to leave the organization so his continued cooperation was not just about making himself rich, it was about keeping himself alive.

A few years ago David had read an investigative piece in one of the glossy magazines Jenna liked to buy. It outlined how terrorists financed themselves, and David read with horrified interest about the likely sources of the money he had received. The article had estimated that the Sons of September had annual revenue of over three billion dollars, mainly derived from the cultivation, export and distribution of heroin. He was not sure if his masters were part of this particular organization, but the idea that his money had the double misery of coming from the drugs trade gave David pause. Then he thought about his wife and kids and their likely fate if he ever stopped, and the guilt went away. The article had explained how he was able to earn over a hundred million dollars in a decade and a half, for bringing in two-thousand-one-hundred-and-twenty-three guys. The money, which had been converted into multiple currencies, gold and precious stones, was waiting for him in safety deposit boxes dotted around the globe.

David finished the searing whisky and looked around the quiet bar. He would come and grab lunch occasionally. Not because the food was any good, but because he wanted to know who the regular faces were. The bar was his conduit to his employers and he wanted to know if that conduit was ever compromised. Apart from a couple of the regular daytime drunks, and Winona, the barmaid, the place was empty.

David dropped off his stool and walked towards the payphone in the back. If Winona thought it strange that a high-tipping lawyer from across the way would use a payphone when he must have had a perfectly good cell, she had the good sense not to say anything. It was the elemental law of the bar; mind your own fucking business.

Belle watched the holographic display highlight the numbers as they were keyed into the bugged payphone. The lawyer dialed a number in Pakistan. As the trace zeroed in, the destination phone was identified as a cell, which was running off a mast in Lahore.

When the destination phone was answered, Belle heard the lawyer say four words in English.

"The network is compromised."

The recording of that short conversation would be all the evidence they needed to convict the lawyer of criminal conspiracy. Anything else would just be gravy.

Belle shifted her attention to the destination phone number and waited to see how good these guys were.

Three hundred pigeon holes lined the wall of Imran's apartment. There was a cellular phone in each pigeon hole. The thirty-year-old double amputee had one job; to relay messages for the brotherhood. Confined to a wheelchair, Imran had been taken off the streets by his old religious studies teacher, who had happened to catch sight of him one day, unwashed, unkempt, hand extended for whatever scraps people could afford to throw him.

His teacher had introduced him to a man whose name he never knew. The man had provided him with work sewing bags that he later learned were used to transport opium resin. When he had proved his worth, Imran was introduced to yet another nameless man, who set him up in this apartment with the wall of phones.

The phones were paired, one for incoming, one for outgoing, but Imran was watching an old Ismail Yasin film on television, and was keen to get back to it. The phones were replaced every four weeks and Imran was convinced that meant there was no way they could be bugged. Instead of waiting for the paired phone to power up, Imran simply made the outbound call on the phone he had just answered. The telephone at the other end rang four times before it was answered.

"The network is compromised," Imran said in Arabic, before he hung up and returned to the black and white comedy.

Not that good so far, Belle thought as she tracked the outgoing call through the Lahore cellular exchange to a destination cellular exchange in Ismailia, Egypt. Moments after the call was received, Belle's holographic display told her that the local cell mast in Ismailia reported that the cell phone had been turned off.

Okay, Belle thought, this is more like it; a challenge.

Abdul Waleed supplemented his farm income by acting as a relay. He had no idea who he worked for, just that his brother had said that they would pay fifty American dollars a month to a trustworthy dependable man. All he had to do for that money was keep a mobile phone fully charged and with him at all times. When he received a call, he had to convey the message to a memorized phone number using a different outbound telephone from the one he received the call on.

Abdul Waleed placed the inactive mobile on the plywood table in the bare plaster hallway in his house, and picked up his landline phone. The sounds of his wife preparing dinner in the kitchen, and his children playing in the yard with a ball echoed around the hallway. Abdul Waleed thought about telling them to be silent, but they would be suspicious of who he was talking to that was important enough to merit silence. Instead, he covered the mouthpiece with his hand and dialed.

In the operations room, Belle ran a vector triangulation to try to get a fix on the last known signal from the Ismailia cell phone. At the same time, she hacked the Ismailia cellular and hard line exchanges and put a flag on all long distance calls. She would have to work fast to catch it.

The vector search narrowed the cell phone's location down to a couple of neighborhoods, and Belle focused the long distance search on exchanges within that neighborhood. She caught the call just as it was answered, and cut into the line to hear a voice say, in Arabic, "The network is compromised."

The destination number was a cell phone in London.

Bobby Shah stood in the service area and stared at the cell phone. Shit! After all these years of carrying the damned thing around at university and on the dole, they finally called him when he was at work. It was the law of the damned, which had followed Bobby all his life. He'd spent four years studying politics at university, only to be told there were no jobs when he graduated; the economic climate and whatnot. Then a year on the dole looking for work he was not too young, too qualified or too proud for. Finally he had managed to get a job at a restaurant in Soho, but it was run by a harpy who had blocked the landline for all outgoing calls.

His sideline started when he had joined the Islamic society at Hull University. Bobby had wanted to do more to serve his community, but did not have the stomach to engage in some of the more hard-line activities of some of his peers. But he was devout and genuine, so one day a man who had come to speak to the society on the different forms of jihad had pulled him to the side and offered him two hundred pounds a month to look after a phone. The money had kept him afloat when the economy and state aid had failed him, and now he felt guilty that he was about to breach protocol by using the cell phone to make the outbound call to relay the message.

Bobby dialed the number he had memorized. It rang twice before it was answered.

"The network is compromised," Bobby said.

Belle looked at the screen and saw the destination number. It was a Chicago cell phone but the network registered the device as currently in New York. When the system informed her that the phone had just moved from one mast to another, Belle was able to lock onto its location; travelling at sixty miles per hour on I-95.

Belle waited for a few moments before placing the call to Catlin.

"No further activity on that cell. It's moving towards New York. Records show it was purchased in Skokie four weeks ago for cash. No details on the buyer."

"You did good," Catlin said. "Send us the tracking details. We're going to follow it up."

"You want support?" Belle asked.

"Not right now," came Catlin's response. "We can't risk it."

Belle finally realized why they were playing this one off the books; Catlin and Pierce suspected a leak within the Agency.

"I understand," Belle said, before Catlin disconnected.

Pierce watched the fat lawyer exit the bar. The whole trace had taken no more than two minutes, and with it they had ensured the fat fuck would spend the rest of his natural days in jail.

"He goes down," Pierce observed, as Catlin started the car's electric motor.

"Count on it," Catlin said.

She pulled away from the kerb and headed for the Interstate.

Karo thought about the call for a moment. Protocol required him to disband the cell and abort the mission immediately, but to have done such a thing would have been to waste a gift from God. They were within striking distance of the city. He wondered if the warning had been in relation to his own problems in Chicago. Perhaps the bodies of the Federal agents had been discovered. If they had, Karo quickly surmised, any retaliation would have been aimed specifically at him and the other men in the vans. All points bulletins would have been issued and they would have been stopped or shot on sight. No, the network was compromised somewhere else, and it unnerved him slightly to think that it had happened this very night. Karo believed in divine providence, but he did not believe in coincidence, and worried that the mission was at risk.

He chose not to talk about it with Rossi. The short man would only worry, which would increase their exposure at the remaining checkpoints. As he held the steering wheel with one hand, Karo reached into his overalls and pulled a coded digital communicator from his breast pocket. He punched in a number and waited for a response.

"Three, this is two," a voice came over the airwaves in Arabic.

"Two, I just received a message that the network is compromised," Karo responded in the same language.

There was moment's silence, as the man on the other end of the transmission considered the implications.

"It is of no concern. God's judgment cannot be stopped."

The moment the line went dead, Rossi turned to Karo, his face full of concern.

"Are we in danger?"

"You heard the man," Karo said, as he put the communicator back in his pocket. "There is nothing to worry about."

Karo focused on the road ahead and gave a silent prayer that the little man sitting next to him would not start overreacting. He had orders to kill anyone who threatened to compromise the mission, and did not feel like adding anymore deaths to his tally before they even reached the city.

David looked out of his office window at the parking lot, which was now a major crime scene. When the first police car had screeched into the lot, lights blazing and siren screaming, David had been convinced they were coming for him. He had considered running, but knew that it would be pointless; there were too many ways for the government to track a person these days. Instead, he had slumped back in his chair and waited for his arrest. After ten minutes had passed, David had allowed himself to think that he might be okay, and had walked over to his window, where he had stood watching for the past thirty minutes.

The first car had been joined by a dozen others, and two military graviton jets, one of which had landed on eight parked cars, and crushed them flat. The owners of the cars were remonstrating with police officers who maintained a cordon that seemed to center on a silver Honda. Men in white overalls, who David took to be forensics officers, searched the car, and a number of men in suits stood in a small group and examined handheld computers. A dozen marines stood guard, stationed at strategic intervals around the men in suits. The police officers that were not part of the cordon were conducting a door-to-door canvas, and were working their way round the offices towards David's side of the complex.

Carol knocked on the door and showed a couple of police officers in. One of them held a photo of the battered man who had beaten David up. Relief swept through his body; he had nothing to worry about. Those fuckers were on the run. That explained why they had been in such a hurry and had not taken him in for questioning. The surge of confidence almost made him talk but much as he would have liked to have played a part in capturing the fugitive pair, David knew that he could not afford to link himself to them and their allegations. Denial was the safest option, and so when the police officers asked him about a man called Scott Pierce, David denied ever having seen him before.

Van Zyl squinted as the rays of the setting sun filled his vision. A police officer had spotted the car in the parking lot, and called it in. So far forensics and the police canvas had turned up nothing, and Porter had not fared much better with his computer analysis.

Van Zyl was getting impatient.

"Anything?" he asked of Porter.

"The vehicle's computer shows that it has been here for just over an hour," Porter said as he checked his handheld computer. "Nobody in the local area has seen anyone matching Pierce's description and there have been no reports of any vehicle thefts. The Martin Robins alias has not been scanned at any bus or train stations and we have no record of any cabs being paid for on that account. It's like he vanished."

CHAPTER 17

The darkness beckoned him. As he looked in the side mirror, Karo saw the last rays of the setting sun slip beneath the New Jersey skyline. Ahead of him, the giant black yaw of the Holland Tunnel promised him eternal glory. The masked young man in body armor who checked their identification represented the last possible obstacle to victory. The Resolute mercenary stood beside Karo's window and examined the digital work order that Karo had beamed to his scanner.

"What kind of work are you doing?" The mercenary asked.

"Systems integration," Karo replied in a faultless mid-Western accent. "There's a bunch of secondary systems that need to be installed for your deployment."

Ahead of Karo, a Cougar APV and Abrams tank guarded the tunnel mouth and half-a-dozen of the mercenary's comrades watched the line of white vans with interest.

The mercenary was not about to take a chance with something like this, and activated his radio.

"Is there a problem?" Karo interrupted. "You've scanned the vans, right?"

"Yeah, but there's a lot of you guys."

"You guys use a shitload of computers," Karo said.

If anything went wrong, the men had orders to storm the checkpoint. It would be a futile gesture, but there was an outside chance that they might be able to take one or two of the mercenaries with them. Karo was confident he could snap the neck of the one who stood next to his window. He would then use the man's rifle to kill as many of the pretend soldiers as possible.

"Command, this is Holland checkpoint," the mercenary said into his radio. "I have a posse of systems engineers seeking entry to the Island. Eighty-three men, ten vehicles. Work order number three-seven-four-nine-dash-five."

Karo felt Rossi shift in the seat next to him. He dared not look at the man, for fear that a shared glance might trigger a nervous collapse. Instead, Karo leant his elbow against the window frame and tapped impatiently on the side of the van.

After what seemed like an age of silence, the mercenary's radio crackled back.

"Roger Holland one, we log eighty-three, that's eight, three engineers on that work order. I'm sending you identification details now."

"Copy, control, Holland out," the mercenary said, as his scanner signaled that a data file had been received. The young man opened the file sent by the unknown voice, and checked the list.

"You're right here on the list, sir," the mercenary said, looking at Karo. "David Karo. Sorry to have kept you waiting. You guys are cool. You're clear to proceed."

The mercenary stepped back and waved to his comrades to let the convoy of vans pass.

As Karo eased the van forward, the mercenary called out, "Welcome to Manhattan."

After fifteen years in mass production, Catlin still felt uncomfortable with the EverLite treatment that covered the windshields of almost every vehicle in America. The chemical was reactive to certain low frequencies of light, so billboards, street lamps and the lights of other vehicles could be seen from great distances despite the fact that to the naked eye, they appeared totally dark. The only problem with this ubiquitous invention was that the chemical did not offer sharp image resolution. The low level lights of the billboard up ahead blurred, as though seen through a rain-drop covered windshield. Catlin could make out the product being advertised, some kind of candy bar, but the overall effect of the advertisement was to make her feel queasy. She focused on the road ahead, which was illuminated by EverLite reactive paint.

Pierce slept in the seat next to her. She had tried to talk to him about what the Sons of September might have planned, but he was a well trained field operative. Hell, he wasn't well trained, Catlin told herself, he was virtually an automaton. Good field agents knew to sleep when not in danger, and to eat whenever food was available. Catlin had grabbed them both Tofu Macs and Synth Fries from McDonalds, and Pierce had inhaled his. Catlin had been less enthusiastic about hers. Ever since the Livestock Laws of 2023, meat of any kind had become an extremely rare luxury. Catlin understood the logic of the environmentalists – one cow ate as much grain in a year as eighty people – but she was convinced that most of these activists were vegetarian and none of them would understand the misery of going through life without meat.

The moment Pierce had finished his food, he rolled his seat back and shut his eyes. Catlin did not take offence, although she had thought he might want to discuss tactics. You're just along for the ride, she reminded herself; this is his show. And so far he had done a pretty good job of running it. Aside from the help she had given him, Pierce had been able to outmaneuver the Agency single-handed.

A sudden yelp sent her stomach into her throat. Catlin looked at Pierce and saw that he was having a nightmare. His hands were raised, as though fighting off some unseen terror, and he was pleading incoherently with whatever he was afraid of. Catlin reached out to stroke his arm and immediately regretted it. Pierce's right hand reached across his body and grabbed her fingers. His eyes opened and he stared at her with a wild look of dangerous incomprehension.

"Scott, it's me," Catlin said nervously, trying to mask the pain caused by him crushing her fingers. "It's okay."

If Pierce registered her words, he gave no sign. He simply released his grip and slumped back in his seat. Moments later his breathing was deep and rhythmic; he was sound asleep.

Automaton, Catlin thought, as she nursed her bruised hand against the steering wheel. She almost pitied whoever was waiting for them in New York.

The tall buildings of Riverside Drive loomed over the vans as they made their way along the wide thoroughfare. Now safely on the island, Rossi felt he could relax. The call his large colleague in the driver's seat had received earlier had unnerved him. It must have unsettled Karo too, for the big man had breached protocol and made contact with their Manhattan liaison well before they were supposed to. If the network was compromised, the threat of exposure dogged their footsteps. The dead bodies back at the warehouse would guarantee their status as enemies of the state, but Rossi knew Agency procedure well enough to know that the search for the missing Agents Hassan and Smit, and their lackeys in the computer room and van outside, would not commence until tomorrow. By which time those dead agents would be at the bottom of a long list of problems facing the United States.

Rossi smiled as he saw the resupply point. The secure parking lot at the base of the vacant high rise contained everything they would need – including weapons. Rossi disliked travelling through enemy territory with nothing more than his hands and his faith to protect him, but it had been necessary to mislead the mercenary checkpoints they had encountered. As Karo used the remote control to raise the chainlink gate that covered the entrance to the lot, Rossi allowed himself to think about all the people they were going to kill tonight, and the millions more that would surely follow them to hell in the coming months. He was honored to be part of such a holy crusade.

Karo led the convoy down to the second sub-basement level, exited the van and turned on the basement lights. The nine vans that followed maneuvered themselves into a circle, their rear doors pointed towards a large stack of equipment crates that dominated the center of the lot. Karo prized open one of the smaller crates and pulled out an MP9 silenced machine pistol. He tossed it to Rossi, who nodded his thanks.

They should have fed him some false information, Belle thought when she saw Van Zyl enter the operations room. After Catlin had received Van Zyl's authorization to reconstitute the team, Belle had been able to pull a handful of analysts together. It was not a patch on the old team, but it was the best she could do at short notice. The operations room was a scene of chaotic evolution, as people scavenged for furniture and equipment and hurried to get up to speed with the situation. Belle had been careful how much she told the analysts, to protect them as much as to keep Catlin and Pierce safe. But with Van Zyl on site, every move they made would be scrutinized. A false lead or two would have kept him chasing his tail until Catlin and Pierce were ready to bring him in on what they had found.

Van Zyl looked around the room and approached Belle.

"Anything on Pierce?"

"We're chasing down a few leads."

Belle made a decision to keep things as vague as possible. She got the feeling that was fine with Van Zyl. Calculated as he was, he had to be feeling some discomfort talking to the woman he had wrestled to the ground a few hours earlier.

"Where's Liz?" Van Zyl asked.

Belle pretended to scan the room.

"She must have stepped out."

The great thing about the powerful is that although their gaze is intense, Bell thought, they lack the patience to keep it on one thing for very long. Van Zyl turned away from her without another word and whispered something in the ear of his obsequious aide, Porter. The junior agent scurried away on some mysterious errand, while Van Zyl and the rest of his entourage entered Catlin's office and made themselves very much at home.

Catlin looked at Pierce for signs of tension, and saw none. He was performing a very convincing impersonation of a harried agent who was near the end of a rough day. Physically he looked different to the nightmare sufferer who had almost broken her fingers earlier that evening. They had pulled in at a rest stop, and he had cleaned himself up to great effect. But the transformation went beyond his appearance; his essence seemed different. The vengeance driven force of nature had been replaced by something human. Catlin realized she was privileged enough to see a very impressive talent in operation, and the effect it was having on the Resolute mercenary who stood next to the car was quite profound. The man had raised his mask and was joking and bitching with Pierce about paperwork, asshole bosses and the insanity of risking one's life for a dollar. The mercenary hardly paid any attention to the identification details that flashed on his scanner when he read Catlin's and Pierce's fingerprints, which had been Pierce's intention all along.

"Agent Catlin," the mercenary nodded into the car, "agent Morgan, you're cleared. Welcome to Manhattan."

The masked man stood back from the car and waved his colleagues a signal to let the vehicle pass. Catlin drove the car forward into the darkness of the Holland Tunnel. As they passed the lip of the tunnel, Catlin's cell phone rang, but before she could answer it, the heavy concrete walls cut the signal and the cell went dead.

Dammit, Liz, Belle thought as she dialed the number again, hell of a time to to be screening calls. The phone went straight through to voicemail on the second attempt, and Belle left a message asking Catlin to call her back urgently.

Belle waited a few minutes before trying again, and this time the phone rang twice before Catlin answered.

"Liz, it's Belle, Van Zyl is here. He's going to work out I'm covering for you."

"You're very astute, agent Pearlman."

Van Zyl appeared at Belle's shoulder and snatched the phone from her hand.

Neither Van Zyl nor his goons saw Belle minimize one of the surveillance windows on her computer. As long as Liz and Pierce had the satellite uplink they had a chance of finding whoever was at the end of the communications relay.

"Agent Catlin, do you take me for a complete idiot?" Porter handed Van Zyl his scanner, which displayed Catlin's identification details and the last known location of their use; the Holland Tunnel. "Apparently you've just scanned through the Holland Tunnel. Did you get lost on your way back to Langley, Liz?"

At the other end of the line, Catlin sensed that Van Zyl relished this moment. He now had an excuse to pin any and all failures at her door. Whatever came out of this mess, it would not slow the irrepressible rise of Carl Van Zyl.

"I'm following up a lead," Catlin tried weakly.

"You're harboring a known criminal," Van Zyl cut her off. "Holland checkpoint shows you travelling with an agent Morgan. I knew Pierce wasn't good enough to disappear on his own. I order you to proceed to the nearest police precinct..."

Pierce did not wait for Van Zyl to finish spewing his sanctimonious bullshit over the speakerphone. He grabbed the cell and tossed it out of the window. The phone shattered on the asphalt of Varick Street.

"We'd better deliver," Liz said without taking her eyes off the road, "or I'm going to end up in the cell next to you."

"We need a new car," Pierce observed.

Every society throughout history has held the belief that the end of the world is imminent. Apocalyptic prophecies have dominated global thought since records began. Whether religious, such as the foretelling of the Day of Judgment, or scientific, as with global warming, life has co-existed with the prospect of extinction since humanity developed self awareness. The law of averages, Karo thought as he drove out of the parking lot, dictated that one day the doomsayers would be right. Tonight it would be his privilege to bring the divine eye of judgment upon this deviant nation.

The occupants of the van sat in the same positions they had occupied going into the lot. The only differences were the stack of computer, laser and drilling equipment on the van's flatbed. And the weapons. As well as personal machine pistols for each of the eight men in the van, a small arsenal lay hidden under tarpaulin near the van's rear doors. The muzzle of a heavy machine gun poked out from under the tightly packed green canvas.

As Karo headed down Riverside Drive, he watched the first of the nine vans following him peel away into 135th Street. The second van turned into 133rd Street. Each of the remaining seven vans would turn off Riverside in the minutes that followed. Each van was equipped with exactly the same supply of equipment, and each was headed for a separate destination. It reassured Karo to think that there were now ten autonomous units in play, and that the mission had become unstoppable.

CHAPTER 18

She had not expected grand theft auto to be part of her schedule when the day began. Catlin kept a nervous eye on the street, while Pierce used a scrap of metal to force open the door of an ancient Dodge Challenger. Without proper street lighting, few people went out after dark and Charlton Street was no exception; it was deserted in both directions. Catlin suspected that in addition to the fixed checkpoints, Resolute would sweep the entire island at random, so she stayed alert.

The alarm system managed to emit two high pitched screeches before Pierce disabled it. He started the engine.

As Catlin jumped in the passenger seat, he asked, "Where's the phone?"

Catlin looked at her scanner.

"Financial district."

As Pierce pulled away, Catlin thanked providence for good people. She could only guess that Belle had covered her tracks, because Van Zyl would have cut them off in an instant if he had known that they were still receiving a satellite feed.

The solid steel door that led to the subterranean garage rose slowly but Karo did not allow himself to exhibit any impatience. He replaced the forged security access card in his breast pocket and looked at Rossi, who sat with a stiffness that suggested he was struggling to maintain his composure. This night was the culmination of years of anticipation and although they had incorporated coping mechanisms in their training, talking about how to face a situation and actually facing it were very different. A person could learn to fire a weapon until they could hit a dime blindfold from a hundred paces, but no amount of training could ever prepare that person for the experience of taking a human life. Some events were too profound to prepare for.

Karo focused on the building they were about to enter. The hundred-and-three storey edifice had been completed in 2021 after a prolonged gestation. Initial construction plans had been floated after the financial recovery of 2012, when many companies felt the need to signal a new economic era with expensive headquarters. Then the fuel shocks of 2016 and 2017 had sent the global economy into a downward spiral, and work on the project slowed almost to a halt. By the time the building was completed, the new economic era it had been intended to herald had already passed into history. Instead, the building was a monumental folly to a bygone age of zealous excess.

Once the steel door had retracted into the roof, Karo drove slowly into the underground lot. There was nothing to compare to the waves of anticipation that coursed through his body. No narcotic could ever come close to the raw feeling that overwhelmed him. So many people experienced the highs of life through others, living vicariously through celebrities or fictional characters. For the vast majority, their own interaction with existence was stifled by the steady wage, the monthly loan repayment and health insurance. Karo prided himself that he would give Americans a taste of life in the raw, before they tore themselves apart forever.

The little man always picks up the tab, Rufus thought to himself as he read his copy of Stevenson's Advanced Economic Theory. He was a prime example. A student who was trying to put himself through grad school, he had been forced to take a night job to make the tuition fees. The night job, guarding a New York bank, would previously have been the work of at least ten men, but here he was alone, because the powers that be had found a different way to make the little man pay.

In the golden days of free money and seemingly limitless growth, companies could pass on vast costs to their customers and the economic system would support it because everyone was building in cost inefficiency. When the economic crashes happened and the world stopped growing, companies were at the forefront of cost innovation. The Sentry program had been seen as an excellent way to guarantee corporate, as well as Homeland, security. With mercenaries patrolling the streets of every major city, corporations saw an opportunity to cut back on their own spending. There was a concerted effort from the corporate community to support the Sentry program. When the mercenaries rolled in, the security guards rolled out. Instead of bundling up the costs of security in the price of their products, the corporations had found another way to get in the little man's pocket; taxation.

Rufus looked around the huge lobby and wondered what his life would have been like had he been born fifty years earlier. Everyone said it had been an easier time, where opportunities abounded. There was a sense of sham about things now, Rufus thought, people were going through the motions of a zombie society. There were no opportunities any more, swathes of youth were faced with the prospect of a lifetime of unemployment, so there was no point in going to college. And if there was no point in college, there was no sense in school. The murmurings of social discontent and unrest were turning into calls for action. Rufus knew that the university authorities kept tabs on the handful of radical groups that operated on campus, and he would not have been surprised if the Agency also had a line into things. Positivists like him believed that the system could be fixed and that things could get better, but there was a growing minority who believed the only road to improvement lay through rebellion.

Worry for the future was the last emotion Rufus felt before a bullet cut through his forehead and splintered inside his brain. The force of the silent shot propelled him backwards in his swivel chair, and had it not been for the trail of blood that ran down his face, it would have simply looked like he was asleep on the job.

With smoke still coming from his silenced MP9, Karo crossed the lobby towards the security desk. Behind him, Rossi and the rest of the men started unloading equipment from the elevator. Karo pulled the dead security guard from the chair and dragged his body into a corridor located at the rear of the marbled lobby.

Noah, one of the men from the van, removed his white overalls to reveal a security guard's uniform. As Rossi and the rest of the men transferred equipment into a secure vault elevator located in the east corner of the lobby, Noah took his seat at the security desk and picked up the book that the dead man had dropped. He did a convincing impression of someone who cared about what they were reading.

Karo returned to the lobby and nodded at Rossi, as the vault elevator closed taking the short man and three others into the fortified basement sublevels. Karo entered one of the eight main elevators with the two remaining men, smiling at Noah as he did so. With such simple audacity, they were now in control of Citibank's headquarters.

The bitch was buried, Van Zyl thought as he crossed the pad towards the waiting grav-jet. He was fuming with a fury that was genuine and dangerous. He knew that it could cloud his thought and tried to control it, but he had never experienced such full frontal disrespect and disregard. Catlin had deceived him, put his career at risk and had then compounded it all by hanging up on him.

"Inform NYPD that they have two fugitives in the city. Give them everything they need," Van Zyl ordered Porter, who followed a couple of paces behind him. "And get me John Creed at Resolute. We're going to tie this up fast."

Everything looked calm and peaceful, Catlin thought as she and Pierce walked away from the stolen car and headed towards the imposing building. She double checked her scanner, which showed that the cell phone signal emanated from inside.

They crossed the plaza and approached the glass doors that led to the main lobby. A security guard sat behind a desk and read a large text book.

"Looks fine," Catlin said.

Pierce said nothing, but tapped forcefully on the glass.

The security guard looked up with a start.

"We may have a problem," Noah said as he saw the woman push some official identification up against the glass. The man with her hit the glass insistently.

"Take care of it," Karo's response came via a concealed earpiece.

As Noah stood, he felt inside his jacket and unclipped the restraint strap on the holster of his concealed MP9. He approached the doors and ran a swipe card over a reader.

"Good evening, officers," Noah said. "How can I help you?"

Pierce was in overdrive, his senses sharp looking for telltale signs of anything untoward. The guy felt bad but Pierce could not put his finger on it.

"We're Federal agents," Catlin told the man. "We're in pursuit of a suspect. You been here all night?"

"Sure," the guard said.

When the man's hand made an almost imperceptible move towards his jacket, Pierce noticed the tattoo. It was a small black inscription in Arabic that was permanently imprinted on the underside of his right wrist.

Pierce pulled his pistol from behind his back and shot the man twice in the head.

Catlin was stunned and robbed of speech, as the corpse fell back and hit the hard lobby floor. Pierce stepped forward and pulled the guard's hand out from inside his jacket. The silenced MP9 came with the dead fingers that gripped it. Pierce took the gun, and showed Catlin the tattoo on the underside of the dead man's wrist.

"Sons of September prison tattoo. This guy is Brotherhood. We need back up."

Catlin had not been sure what she expected to find but this was too real. She had not done frontline field work for years and was ashamed to find herself shaking. As she watched Pierce walk towards the security desk, she took out her cell phone and dialed.

The G20 cut through the night sky. Van Zyl watched Porter and his team coordinate with the New York Police Department. In addition to dealing with headquarters, Van Zyl had insisted they call every single precinct commander and put the word out personally. Pierce's photograph was being sent to every precinct house, patrol car and beat cop in the city. Van Zyl wanted Pierce found quickly and was using every ounce of Agency leverage to make this a full court press.

He did not hear his cell phone ring over the rumble of the graviton engines but he felt the vibrate alert in his pocket, and answered.

"Van Zyl."

"Chief, I'm standing in the lobby of the Citibank building with the body of a member of the Sons of September at my feet."

"Liz?"

"He's dressed as a security guard. Pierce was right; something is happening and it is happening now. We believe the Spider may be in the building."

118

"If this is bullshit," Van Zyl began, but Catlin cut him off.

"Just get us help, Carl. If I'm wrong, you can hang me out to dry."

Catlin hung up, and Pierce shook his head slowly.

"Call me paranoid, but I don't trust him."

He picked up the phone on the security desk and dialed nine-one-one. After a brief pause, the call was connected.

"Resolute Corporation. Please state the nature of your emergency."

"I dialed nine-one-one," Pierce said, somewhat bemused.

"All emergency calls are routed here, sir. Please state the nature of your emergency," the disembodied voice responded.

"This is FSA agent Scott Pierce. I've got a possible terrorist attack in progress at the Citibank Building in lower Manhattan. We need back up."

"Yes, sir," the voice reassured him. "I'll notify our command center immediately. What number can you be reached on?"

Pierce gave Catlin's cell number in response to the question, and then hung up.

He turned to Catlin.

"Let's see if we can get eyes on the place."

Inside the Agency grav-jet, Van Zyl was working through the implications of Catlin's revelation, when Porter handed him a phone.

"John Creed for you."

Creed waited patiently for Van Zyl to come on the line. He had been reading the newspaper and eating dinner alone in the Park Avenue apartment Resolute had rented for him, and was glad of the interruption when the telephone rang. One of the benefits of seniority was that he did not have to work nights but after decades devoted to the military, and then the company, Creed had nobody to share them with and experienced the emptiness of time passing alone.

"John, it's Carl," Van Zyl said. "Remember that deep cover agent I mentioned we had inside the Brotherhood?"

"Sure," Creed replied. He had been impressed at the news that the Agency had infiltrated the secretive organization.

"He claims to have uncovered an operation in Manhattan. Citibank headquarters. I'm en route."

"I'll send a team to check it out. See you when you get here."

Creed disconnected and dialed his operations center.

"It's Creed. Put me through to Solomon."

Moments later, Solomon came on the line.

"Sir?"

"We've got a possible situation at the Citibank building. I want you to send a

119

unit to investigate."

"I'll take an assault squad myself," Solomon replied. "We've just had a nine-one-one call from that location."

"Get moving," Creed urged.

"Yes, sir," Solomon said crisply.

Creed put the phone down and headed for the bedroom, where a fresh uniform hung behind the door. He needed to get back to Governor's Island quickly.

The corridor that led from the back of the lobby was empty. Pierce walked ahead of her with the confiscated machine pistol held out in front of him. Catlin had her service pistol out for the first time in over five years and it felt heavy in her hand. Pierce pushed a door marked 'security', which was ajar.

"Jesus," Catlin exclaimed as she walked in and noticed what Pierce was looking at.

Slumped against the wall behind the door was the body of a security guard who had been shot through the head.

Pierce had already turned his attention elsewhere, and Catlin joined him at the huge bank of surveillance monitors that dominated one wall of the security center. One monitor, which was marked 'Vault Level', showed a group of men busying themselves assembling a large robotic drill.

"We can't wait for back up," Pierce said, drawing Catlin's attention to another monitor. This one was marked 'Executive Boardroom', and it showed thirty people huddled together at the far wall. Two men had machine guns trained on this terrified group of night workers. In the center of the room, a man in a janitor's uniform was on his knees, his face contorted in a plea of terror directed at the third terrorist, who held a silenced machine pistol to his head.

"I'm not a patient man," Karo told the pathetic figure who begged for his life. "The encryption key never leaves this building, so I know one of you has it."

Karo looked at the cowards on the other side of the room. Not one of them would risk their life to save the colleague who knelt at his feet. Karo was counting on that cowardice to compel them to reveal the location of the key. They would not trade a life for their integrity of their employer's vault.

"You have one minute to save this man," Karo told them.

Solomon led his squad of heavily armed men into the G20 that hummed on the landing pad. When the last man was aboard, the hatch closed and the grav-jet engines roared, lifting the aircraft into the night sky. The boosters fired, and Solomon consoled himself with the thought that they would be at Citibank in a matter of minutes.

"Thirty seconds," Karo noted, looking at his watch. The man at his feet was

120

sobbing uncontrollably and Karo thought he could smell urine. Sometimes his work was undignified.

The elevator doors opened and Pierce and Catlin stepped onto the executive level on the ninety-eighth floor. Catlin could feel her hands becoming clammy, but she worked hard to control her nerves, and followed Pierce across the large atrium which cut through the top five storeys. The effect of such an airy space so high up was unnerving and only made Catlin feel even more unsteady.

"Ten seconds," Karo said without emotion. A woman on the other side of the room started to cry.

Pierce paused outside the door marked 'Boardroom' and gave Catlin the thumbs up. She nodded automatically, her eyes wide with fear. Pierce could tell she was straining under the pressure of the situation but whatever her emotional state, the truth was the extra gun would be useful.

"He has five more seconds."
Karo looked at the cattle gathered opposite him, and wondered whether it might be easier to kill them all and search their bodies for the key. But if it was secreted in a desk or safe somewhere in the building, they would never find it.
"Kamal Al-Karim!"
Karo turned towards the direction of the shout, and pulled his hostage up from the floor to shield himself.
It was a wise move because his two unshielded comrades were shot dead as they tried to turn their weapons on the man and woman who had infiltrated the room.

Pierce stared at the man in front of him and felt the heat of the emotions surging through his body. This might be the monster that had robbed him of his happiness and forced him into living a dreadful lie for the past five years. The big man had reacted when Pierce had yelled the Spider's real name.
"You are blessed. The Spider has touched many lives," the man said, which confirmed his identity for Pierce. The Spider held a gun to his hostage's head and was well concealed behind the innocent.
Pierce sighted his pistol.
"I've been to hell and back for the chance to stand in the same room as you," Pierce spat out with venom. "You murdered my wife."

Catlin would never have been confident or reckless enough to take the shot. When Pierce squeezed the trigger three times and the hostage and his captor went down, Catlin was convinced that Pierce had killed them both. After a moment, during which her heart leapt into her mouth, Catlin saw the hostage roll onto his side and get to his feet.

The sense of relief in the room was palpable, and the other hostages clustered around the lucky man to express their shared joy at being alive. Catlin thought about the man with the machine gun she had shot dead moments earlier, but as she watched the joy of the innocents, she had no doubt it had been the right thing to do.

Pierce walked up to the dead terrorist, stood over him and stared at his lifeless eyes. Catlin could only imagine what Pierce felt after so many years of struggle. She knew one thing for certain; the dead bastard had not suffered enough.

Catlin was conscious of the men in the basement and wanted to get clear of the building as quickly as possible. She and Pierce had rescued the hostages, they could leave the remaining terrorists to others.

"Scott, we need to get out of here."

Catlin touched him lightly on the arm. He took a moment more to consider the man who lay dead at his feet, then turned and nodded.

"Ladies and gentlemen," Catlin addressed the jubilant hostages. "We need to evacuate the building."

She and Pierce ushered the dazed and ecstatic workers out of the boardroom into the spacious atrium.

The first thing Pierce spotted as he approached the bank of elevators was that one of them was rising.

"We've got company. Everybody back," Pierce said, urging the employees to stay behind him and Catlin.

He dropped to one knee to get a better firing position, and Catlin did the same.

The elevator slowed as it neared the ninety-eighth floor, and Pierce sighted the machine pistol on the line between the two doors.

The moment between the elevator stopping and the doors opening seemed to last an age, and Pierce tightened his grip around the trigger.

When he saw the uniforms, Pierce relaxed. The squad of eight men from the Resolute Corporation spilled out of the elevator into the atrium.

Their commander approached Catlin and offered her his hand.

"Sam Solomon, Resolute Corporation," the man said. "What happened here?"

"Liz Catlin, FSA," Catlin said, as she shook Solomon's hand. "This is Scott Pierce. We bagged three bad guys in there and one in the lobby. There are another four in the basement."

"We're aware of the second team," Solomon said, as he signaled for two of his men to check the scene inside the boardroom.

"We need to get these people out of here," Pierce counseled.

"We've got it covered," Solomon said as he stepped forward to address the employees. "Ladies and gentlemen, can I have your attention? We are working to regain control of the building."

The two men Solomon had sent into the boardroom emerged and shook their heads at him.

Pierce edged up to Catlin.

"Anything strike you as strange about this? How did these guys get all this hardware onto the island? Every vehicle gets scanned, right?"

"Until the building is secure, I'm going to need to take charge of the encryption key," Solomon continued.

Pierce pieced it together the moment the junior executive stepped forward and gave Solomon a computerized chip that hung from the end of a necklace he had concealed under his shirt.

"No!" Pierce yelled, as Solomon turned round to face him, machine gun raised.

"Kill them all!" Solomon ordered, as he opened fire.

The first shots struck a stunned Catlin in the chest. Then the barrage of bullets traced a pepper line up her neck and into her head, as Solomon adjusted his aim.

Pierce looked at Catlin's falling body in dismay and drew his weapon. He returned fire as he dived for the emergency stairwell. Behind him Solomon spewed scorching lead, and the rest of the atrium erupted in violence as the employees lives were ended in screaming slaughter.

CHAPTER 19

When the last of his men had ceased firing, Solomon barked a command.
"Get him!"

He watched them pour into the stairwell and open fire. This Pierce would not last long.

Solomon took a coded radio from his inside pocket and punched in a series of numbers.

In perfect Arabic he said, "Four, this is two. We have a problem, three is dead. Two FSA agents tracked him here."

It took a moment for the man calling himself Rossi to respond from the bowels of the building.

"Is the mission compromised?"

"It is of no consequence," Solomon replied. "We will proceed as planned. I shall leave some men with you to make up the shortfall."

Pierce was running on auto. Catlin's death had not sunk in, and he would not allow it to until he was safe. He leapt the stairs a flight at a time, as bullets whizzed past his head from the floors above. Once again he had underestimated the Brotherhood's reach and he had paid dearly. The Spider was not a bank robber, he was a spy. One of the best Pierce had ever gone up against, and there was no better cover than to infiltrate the organization tasked with protecting New York. There was no way of knowing whether the big man he had shot was the Spider. It could just as easily have been the bastard who had murdered Catlin.

The sound of gunfire in the stairwell was deafening as shots ricocheted all around him. Pierce was running for his life, and had a three floor lead on his pursuers, which was widening with every second. As he hit the eightieth floor landing, Pierce looked up at the stairwell door and saw what he was searching for, a white letter 'E' set against a green plastic advisory sign. He ripped open the door and raced into the open plan office on the other side.

The office stretched out along one side of the building, and Pierce had to reach the other end to reach safety. There was little cover apart from desks and glass partitions that separated clusters of cubicles into work groups. Pierce was almost half way across the open plain, when the first bullets shattered the glass partition next to him. He swerved and dropped behind a desk. He was outnumbered and could not stay put for long.

Pierce rose to his feet and fired a long and wild volley of shots from his machine pistol, which felled one of the seven pursuing mercenaries. The move forced the others to take cover, and momentarily bought Pierce enough time to get moving again. He reached the other end of the open plan office and rounded the corner as another barrage cut into the air where he had been milliseconds earlier.

Up ahead, a green plastic sign hung from the ceiling, the white 'E' indicating that he had reached an evacuation point. Pierce threw himself into the room as the mercenaries rounded the corner and began firing. He slammed the door shut behind him.

The evacuation room doubled as a supply closet, and Pierce pulled a set of shelves down to block the only entrance to the room. He tried to ignore the thunderstorm of bullets that started to tear through the door and shelves, and checked his own weapon. There was one bullet left in the chamber.

Pierce scanned the room. Water cooler bottles stacked on one side, closets lined the wall on the other. A narrow floor-to-ceiling window overlooked the street. Pierce opened one of the closets and started tossing supplies onto the floor. The upended shelves that blocked the door were fast disintegrating.

He had drawn a blank in the first closet, which was full of office supplies, so Pierce moved to the next one along. He tried not to think about the horrendous sound of bullets splintering wood and thudding against masonry. The door would not hold much longer. Pierce saw what he was looking for the moment he opened the closet door, and he reached in to grab a canvas bag from a stack that rested against the back wall. He opened the bag and withdrew a grav-pac, as the door was kicked open.

His old tactical instructor had always said, "Beat the fuckers, and if you can't, act like you can."

Pierce wheeled round and pointed the MP9 directly at the head of the first mercenary through the door.

"Move and he dies," Pierce instructed the man's colleagues. "Drop your weapons."

Pierce knew he would not get all seven men to relinquish arms but the mercenary in his line of fire did so without hesitation. The unarmed man was a shield against most of the other men, only two mercenaries could get their guns into the doorway, and both of them lowered their weapons.

Pierce took aim at the floor-to-ceiling window and fired his last remaining shot. The window shattered, and wind whipped around the room. Pierce took a running jump out of the emergency exit and plummeted towards the sidewalk below.

The grav-pac had been one of the earliest applications of graviton technology. A military replacement for parachutes, it had quickly found a market as a safety product for high-rise buildings and had been declared mandatory for all blocks over fifty storeys.

The proper procedure was to fit the chute and engage the small graviton drive before exiting the building. The user would then float to ground level in a controlled fashion. As he approached freefall velocity, Pierce wondered what kind of stopping power the pac would have at this speed. He fumbled with the four point harness, as the first shots rang out from the window twenty floors above him. He tried not to think about the sidewalk that was only seconds away, and clipped two of the four harness locks together. A bullet clipped his right arm and spun him round, so that he was falling backwards, looking up at the window, where four mercenaries emptied their weapons at him. He ignored the pain of the wound and worked the final two locks. At least he would not know when the sidewalk hit him, Pierce thought as he felt the harness click into place. He hit the button that activated the graviton drive and felt his stomach get sucked towards his shoes.

The grav-pac did not slow him enough for a controlled landing, but it did prevent his death. Pierce hit the sidewalk with a heavy thud and rolled as he had been trained to. Bullets tore chunks out of the concrete around him, and he forced himself to his feet. Pierce raced round the corner and out of sight.

As he rode down in the vault elevator with one of his men, Solomon considered his next move. What the brothers had been unable to do in Cairo, his men would finish here; Scott Pierce would die. His tenacity presented a problem in the form of his Agency colleagues who would no doubt want an explanation for the presence of terrorists on the island. Solomon could offer them the three bodies and claim ignorance of their plan, but that would only lead to an investigative team being dispatched to the building. With Rossi at work in the basement, they could not risk unwanted visitors. No, Solomon would have to take a hard line with any meddlers.

"We lost him," the call came over his secure radio.

"What!" Solomon returned the call.

"He got a grav-pac and jumped."

"Shit!"

Solomon could not take the risk of Pierce getting to a phone. At the very least he had to discredit him. After the way the brothers had blown his cover in Cairo, Solomon believed that Pierce would already be on the edge of suspicion. He knew exactly what to do to push Pierce over the edge. Solomon switched to his official radio and placed a call.

"Command, this is assault team Alpha."

One of the comms officers in the command center acknowledged his call.

"Go ahead, Alpha, this is command."

"We have a terror cell on the island. Scott Pierce, an FSA traitor, is behind it. He just killed another FSA agent, and a group of civilians, and then escaped. Alert all stations and initiate lockdown."

"Sir, the circumstances don't meet the lockdown protocol," came the response.

"Just do it," Solomon yelled, allowing some of his real irritation to burn through. "We've got to stop any hostiles getting off the island."

"Yes, sir."

The great thing about military training, Solomon thought, was that it conditioned people to do whatever was yelled at them.

The elevator doors opened and Solomon stepped into the vault lobby, which was located twelve storeys below ground. Constructed of eight meter thick reinforced concrete, the building specifications estimated it would be able to withstand a nuclear blast less than a block away. Their only way into the vault complex was to obtain the encryption key to the outer doors, which dominated the plain granite lobby. A man Solomon recognized from photographs as Rossi stood in front of the doors with three other men. In front of them was a sophisticated laser drill and some computer equipment.

"I have the key," Solomon said in Arabic.

Rossi took the encryption key from Solomon and inserted it into a reader beside the titanium doors. A screen above the reader displayed the words 'Enter Password', and Rossi used the built-in keyboard to punch in the secret code.

The three feet thick titanium doors slid open majestically to reveal the outer vault, the walls of which were lined with safety deposit boxes. At the far end of the outer vault stood another set of titanium doors, which led to the inner vault and Solomon's prize.

Rossi and Solomon approached the inner doors, and Rossi caressed them delicately.

"One-thousand-and-twenty-eight bit encryption that requires two director level iris scans and voiceprint identification. Its titanium alloy doors are five feet thick and are blast proof," Rossi said in admiration.

"How long will it take you?" Solomon asked.

"Four hours, by the grace of God."

"And the other teams?"

Solomon did not want any further upsets.

"All on schedule."

"Good," Solomon said as he headed for the elevator in the vault lobby. "I must return to my post. These men will stay with you."

Solomon indicated the three mercenaries who had ridden down in the elevator with him.

"Peace be with you," Rossi called out as the elevator doors slid shut.

As the G20 began its descent towards the island, Creed saw one of the massive microwave arrays unfurl from within its concealed bunker at the edge of the base. He hoped to hell that it was just being tested; the alternative was too controversial to even think about.

Inside the command center Phillipe Lopez watched as his colleagues ran through the various stages of the lockdown procedure. The shit was really going to fly for this, Lopez thought, as he worked his own part of the protocol, which was to shut down Manhattan's hard wire telephone network.

"What is going on?" the boss called out as he entered the room.

Lopez felt sorry for Creed; the old hound was always a couple of steps behind the fast dogs.

"We're initiating lockdown," Lopez replied.

"On whose authority?"

Creed strode over to him.

"Commander Solomon's," Lopez said.

He could see that his answer threw Creed into a state of confusion. The man trusted Solomon above anyone else.

"He's en route, sir," Lopez offered. "E.T.A. four minutes."

"He'd better have a damned good reason for this."

Creed backed off and watched the communications and technical teams initiate a procedure that isolated Manhattan from the rest of the world.

Outside, the massive microwave emitter, which was capable of cutting off all cell and radio communications within a three hundred mile radius, continued sucking power from the grid as its systems came online.

Pierce ran until his lungs screamed hot fire. He had ricocheted from one street to another, with no sense of where he was or where he was going. His mind was dominated by the image of Catlin falling back, dead, and it was not until he stopped running that Pierce realized he was on Broadway somewhere between Franklin and Duane. He slumped against a wall and vomited violently. The few pedestrians brave enough to face the streets of New York at night gave him a wide berth; another derelict drunk. Pierce lifted his head to the night sky and yelled with all his remaining breath. It was a guttural cry that stemmed from somewhere primal and as it spewed forth Pierce feared for his sanity. He had been pushed beyond points few men ever go, and he trembled with the effort of holding himself together.

Reality caught up with Pierce and he reached a trembling hand into his trouser pocket and took out the cell phone he had taken from the crashed SUV. He dialed a number and waited to be connected.

Lopez watched the lights blink out on the computerized map of Manhattan. He called out to Creed, who was on the phone.

"Shutting down cell network relay stations. Every mast in Manhattan is coming offline."

One of his colleagues a couple of desks along leaned back and called out, "Cutting cable, hard lines and ISPs."

Lopez wondered how Creed would handle the blowback on this. Even if he countermanded Solomon's order, it would take at least an hour for them to bring all of Manhattan's communication systems back online.

Van Zyl felt sorry for Liz. She had trusted Pierce and paid the highest price. The grav-jet was about fifteen minutes from Governor's Island from where he would be able to coordinate the hunt for Pierce. In the meantime he had John Creed on the line. The commander of the Resolute battalion had explained what his men had found at Citibank, and how Pierce had murdered Catlin to make good his escape. Creed was in the process of telling Van Zyl that the island was being sealed, when Porter approached with another phone.

"This call was patched from Langley. They say it's Pierce," Porter said.

"Hold on, John," Van Zyl said, as he took the second phone.

"Pierce?"

"They killed Liz," Pierce began.

Van Zyl did not wait to hear any more bullshit.

"You're a dead man, Scott. Word's out that you killed Liz."

"What are you talking about?" Pierce said, but every alternate word was lost to a failing cellular signal.

"Don't fuck with me," Van Zyl started until he realized that the line had gone dead.

"Van Zyl?"

Pierce checked the phone and saw that he had no signal. He grabbed a passerby, a young man, who was walking with two friends.

"I need to see your phone," Pierce said in a tone that sounded too close to hysteria.

"Fuck you, crazy man," one of the friends said, pulling the young man away.

Pierce smacked the friend in the mouth. The blow knocked him to the ground.

"I don't have time,"

Pierce rifled through his original victim's pockets and found a cell phone. It had no signal. Across the road, a taxi driver who leant against the hood of his car began cursing his phone for cutting out on him mid-call.

"They're trying to silence me," Pierce observed as he ran into the night.

"What the fuck was that guy on?" the young man said as he helped his friend to feet.

"He's lucky I didn't kill him," the friend replied, as he nursed a bruised lip and tried to conceal his wounded pride.

Creed put down the phone. Van Zyl would arrive soon enough and Creed could really get to work to bring him on side. He suspected he would need all the support he could get to justify the lockdown to Washington, and Van Zyl

130

would not be able to fault Creed for taking drastic action to capture a man that he wanted so badly himself.

One of the technicians, Creed thought his name was Lopez, leant back in his chair to make a status report.

"Cell network is down and we've cut the hard lines. Everything apart from emergency calls, which are routed through us. That takes care of phones, email and Internet."

"Swift work," Creed acknowledged. "Now I just need to know why we've quarantined the most densely populated island on Earth."

"We suspect there is a terror cell operating on the island," Solomon said as he entered. "We need to restrict their ability to operate, and prevent them from being resupplied."

Creed suddenly realized just how much he relied on Solomon. Without him in his customary position in the command center, Creed had been directionless and had watched his men work around him without having a clear view of the strategic objective.

"We're going to get creamed for this," Creed observed.

"If Washington would rather we risked lives," Solomon responded, as he removed his body armor. "I'll happily reopen the island."

Solomon looked at the sad figure he had manipulated for the past few years and saw that the man could not cope without him. It was perhaps right that he did not have long to live, for Creed would not be able to survive the systematic betrayal Solomon had perpetrated. There was time enough to think about killing his patron, but now the prime objective had to be to prevent Pierce from reaching anyone in authority. If word of their mission fell on the right ears, there was still a chance Washington could move to stop it. As long as Pierce was trapped on the island, the destruction of America and everything it stood for was assured. Solomon simply had to feed Creed the right lines to ensure that the lockdown remained in force. He had to keep the weak man strong in the face of inevitable pressure from local officials and bigger fish in Washington. They would all object to the quarantine of one of the United States' foremost cities.

"An Agency task force is en-route. E.T.A. twenty-five minutes. They're going to need full access to the crime scene and a briefing," Creed said from across the room.

Federal agents at the Citibank building was out of the question. Solomon approached Lopez, one of the technicians loyal to him. The man may not be a Brother but his commitment to the cause had been purchased, and Lopez's zealous worship of the almighty dollar rivaled Solomon's passion for the true faith.

Solomon leant over Lopez's shoulder and pretended to check something on the man's computer.

"That task force must never reach Manhattan," he whispered.

CHAPTER 20

There were few genuine beacons left in this dark world. The days of cities blazing with light were long gone, so even a small Internet cafe with a few computers stood out against the darkness. Pierce could see the white screens from almost a block away, and when he pressed his hands against the cafe windows, he knew that Resolute had cut off all communications on the island. The 404 Page Not Found Error messages confounded the customers who sat in front of the machines, and the cafe's frustrated manager could be seen tinkering with the server behind the counter. Isolated in a city of millions, Pierce realized that he needed help.

As he looked out of the command center window, Solomon watched the team of four technicians calibrate the microwave emitter. The giant machine located on the edge of Governor's Island was a marvel of battlefield technology. Originally developed by for the US Army, it was capable of killing the enemy's radio communications without affecting certain frequencies. This meant that the Americans could block all radio traffic but their own. By synchronizing the machine and their radios to randomly alternate frequencies every thirty seconds, the enemy had no chance of cracking the signal embargo.

On the other side of the command center, Resolute's communications officers busied themselves informing the emergency services that they were about to lose radio communication. The city's airports had already been informed to divert the handful of flights that were due in that night, as communications with them would be cut. Solomon marveled that the procedure designed to make the city secure was actually being used to prevent its salvation.

It just wasn't the same, Robert Tunney told himself. Ever since the rent-a-goons had taken over, life as a New York City cop had become strange. With twenty years under his belt, Tunney felt uncomfortable with the thought of what was to come. He and his partner, Jay Roscoe, scanned the almost empty sidewalks of 9th Street, as Tunney drove the patrol car east.

The job of patrolman had evolved and Tunney did not like it; progress was not always a good thing. Twenty years ago as a rookie, Tunney's work had been a mixture of crowd control, crime prevention and working leads for detectives trying to crack big cases. He had felt a moral purpose in his work. Now, his primary function was to keep social order and that troubled him. Resolute handled crime prevention. With every vehicle being searched coming on to the island and then at risk of being searched at random whilst in Manhattan, the average criminal simply could not transport, weapons, drugs or stolen goods. He'd love to know how the terrorists managed it, but that was another story, and one so far removed from his world that Tunney rarely bothered to consider it.

These days, big shot detectives used fancy toys to solve crimes. They seldom sought assistance from the ranks in blue. The DNA database implemented in 2021 meant that at the touch of a button forensics could find out whose hair, skin or fluids had been left at a crime scene. As a result, door-to-door canvasses were rare and Tunney could not remember the last time he took part in a dragnet. People could not move more than a few blocks without running into a Resolute checkpoint. If a fugitive got into a cab he would expose himself the moment the cabbie asked him to use the fingerprint reader to charge his account. Almost every transport and payment system in the world was linked to law enforcement databases and would flag a fugitive in an instant. Tunney almost felt sorry for criminals; the odds were really stacked against them.

Without crime prevention, or solution, the rank and file of the NYPD were left with social order. Their brief was to keep the neighborhoods quiet and keep a lid on any unrest. Tunney had not joined the force to crack innocent heads, and at times he wondered how much longer he could justify this job to himself. During the food riots three winters back, he had seen his colleagues behave in a way that shamed him. Frustrated, angry and hungry citizens had marched on City Hall to protest at ongoing food shortages caused by the perfect storm of fuel scarcity, a poor crop harvest and a terror attack on a major food distribution depot outside of Indianapolis. The marchers had been brutally suppressed by an army of cops, inflaming an already volatile situation.

With social unrest in most of the country, America had watched New York closely. Tunney had heard a rumor that the mayor had gotten a call from the White House threatening to crush his balls if things in New York sparked national anarchy. Whatever the mayor's motivation, police tactical units were given instructions to smash heads and take out the ringleaders by whatever means necessary. The only problem was that this had been a populist movement and that made everyone a ringleader. Everywhere the cops looked they saw an agitator, an enthusiast and a firestarter. So they smashed heads at random, and when the citizens fought back, the cops started to use deadly force against unarmed crowds of men, women and children.

They never talked about it, but Tunney's partner had put three people in hospital. One of them, a middle-aged mother of two from uptown, subsequently died. The M.E. wrote it up as death from unrelated causes, but both Tunney and Roscoe knew the truth, and Roscoe would have to live with that for the rest of his life. And because it was easier to blame the world for a failure than to look inwards for answers, Tunney had seen in Roscoe a microcosm of what had happened to society at large. Roscoe could not accept that he had become a jackbooted murderer, and instead cast blame on the citizens of New York for becoming a bunch of America-hating anarchists. They in turn came to hate the

NYPD for its role in suppressing their anger and killing thirty three citizens in what they saw as legitimate protest. The city had never been the same, and as they patrolled the streets night after night, Tunney knew that it was them and us. He was just not sure which side he was on.

"All units be on the lookout for Scott Pierce."

The call came over the radio and Tunney checked the computer terminal, which displayed a photograph of Pierce to accompany the audio description.

"Category three male, dark hair, six two. Wanted in connection with the murder of Elizabeth Catlin. Suspect is armed and considered highly..."

The radio crackled with static, and Roscoe hit it.

"Fucking piece of crap. How the fuck do they expect us to do our jobs?"

Tunney did not care. He was just glad to have some real police work to think about.

Creed was a pompous asshole, Solomon thought as he watched the older man stride around the command center checking on his staff. Even though he was a religious man, Solomon had great respect for Darwinism, not as an explanation for the natural order of life on Earth, but as a rationale for human society. The idea that man could come from a single cell millions of years ago was preposterous, but the belief that the strong deserve to flourish within society was one that Solomon felt comfortable with. If God had intended the evil of America to prosper, He would have given men like Creed eyes with which to see the conspiracies that beset them. Instead Creed was blind to the fact that he was surrounded by men who would kill him in a heartbeat.

"Microwave emitters operational. All radio traffic, apart from our own, has been killed," Lopez reported.

"What about the exit routes?" Solomon asked.

"Bridges and tunnels are being sealed as we speak."

"By the numbers, people. Let's lock and stock," Creed encouraged.

He was a stupid weak man, Solomon thought, and he deserved to die.

"What the fuck are you doing?" Casper asked as he stepped out of his car.

He was covering the Tokyo desk for the firm and was already late. And in the broking business more than any other, tardiness cost. Ahead of him the Resolute men that guarded the checkpoint on the George Washington Bridge were drawing barricades across the road.

People were going to get pissed, Farley thought, this lockdown shit had better not last long. He tightened his grip on his assault rifle and watched the drivers exit their vehicles. Some of them had waited almost an hour to get to the front of the line, and they were not happy to see the Abrams tank park itself across the mouth of the Midtown Tunnel.

Chadha had not done well at school. He came from a long line of Sikhs who had continued the warrior tradition, although they had all done so in the employ of the US Army. Chadha had been the first to go private, and had joined Resolute three years ago, much to the disapproval of his father and uncles. Over time their views had mellowed, particularly when they had seen Resolute's record of success. As he stood on the hood of the Cougar APV and looked down at the crowd of drivers who were gathered at his feet, Chadha realized that there was no place he would rather be. He was at the center of the action, standing on an armored personal vehicle that blocked the only route across the Queensboro Bridge.

"What the hell is this?" A voice called out from the crowd.

Chadha put the bullhorn to his lips.

"Our orders are to seal the island. There is an imminent terror threat. We ask you all to be patient."

With the click of a remote, Creed turned one of the windows that previously offered a view of Manhattan into a large television screen. The OLED panels switched from transparent window to interactive viewer in an instant and an image of Manhattan from the air filled the screen. The aerial camera was focused on the scene at the Queensboro bridge, where a Resolute platoon commander stood on a Cougar and addressed the crowd. The scroll bar at the bottom of the screen bore the legend, "Manhattan Quarantined", and the anchor provided running commentary of information they were receiving in the studio.

"We're getting reports that Manhattan has been quarantined due to a terror threat," the anchor said, as every phone in the command center started ringing.

Solomon cursed the last vestiges of a free press. Now that the media had hold of the story it would become a sensation and every citizen and official in the city would want to know what the hell was happening.

"This is the first time that any Sentry contractor has invoked the draconian quarantine restrictions of the Sentry Act," the anchor continued. "The White House seems to have been caught off guard, but endorsed the move, saying that Resolute would not have acted without good cause."

"I have Senator Stovall on the line," a telephone operator yelled to Creed.

"Let the shitstorm begin," Creed said as he picked up a nearby telephone. "You'd better be right about this, Sam."

"The White House has just asked news organizations not to broadcast from Manhattan," the anchor said as the image switched back to the studio, "to avoid giving terrorists any publicity for their actions. As a responsible broadcaster, we have taken the decision to support our government in this time of crisis."

Solomon thanked God for the power of fear. The media had silenced itself and he had not had to do a thing.

"What the fuck is happening down there?" Stovall asked as soon as Creed came on the line. He looked at his book lined home office and felt a surge of panic as he wondered about the people he had allowed himself to get into business with.

"We've got a serious situation," Creed offered.

"You only just took over the fucking island, John."

Stovall was not in the mood to be brushed off with platitudes.

"I put my neck on the line with the committee to get you this assignment. Don't fuck it up."

"We'll take care of it," Creed said. "Nobody can criticize us for keeping people safe."

"I told you I didn't want any noise. If people start looking at my political donations..." a panicked Stovall left the remark hanging.

"There is nothing on paper to link us to you, Bob, and nobody is going to start looking at your finances because we close the island."

Creed offered a hollow laugh that told Stovall he was just as uncomfortable with the situation.

"We're just being cautious. It's what the government pays us for."

CHAPTER 21

The solid grey stone of the 10th Precinct exuded a sense of stability, which Pierce craved so badly. His mind was in turmoil and he desperately wanted to curl into a ball to grieve and blame himself for Catlin's death. There were so many things he could have done differently, any one of which might have saved her. Once he had shared his burdensome secret with people in authority, he could indulge this urge to castigate himself, but for now he had to persevere. Just hold it together for a few more minutes, Pierce told himself as he crossed the threshold into the precinct building.

The entrance hall followed the prevailing style of most police buildings. Columns and corners had been torn out and replaced with a stark open plan space that minimized the opportunity for terrorist attack. Two uniformed officers sat by a couple of full body scanners that visitors had to pass through the moment they stepped through the main doors. A solitary bench fixed to one of the walls was the only nod towards human comfort that the room offered. At the far end was a secure two door entry system that led to the motor pool, custody cells and precinct offices. Seated next to the entry system was a corpulent sentinel; a dark haired, overweight desk sergeant who was stationed in a bulletproof booth and monitored access to the building.

Pierce passed through the body scanner without incident, glad that he had lost his weapons during the freefall from Citibank. He approached the desk sergeant and tapped on the glass to get the man's attention.

"I need to see the officer in charge."

The look of recognition that crossed the sergeant's face was unmistakable and Pierce knew he was in trouble. He inched away from the booth.

"What for?" the sergeant asked as he pressed a silent alarm located under his desk.

Pierce had noticed the subtle motion and could tell that the man was trying to buy time. He sensed the two officers leave their posts by the body scanners and knew that other police would be on their way. If he lost control of the situation, he would be locked in a cell and nobody would ever listen to him.

"You know what, I think I'll come back," Pierce said as he walked backwards towards the approaching officers.

"Freeze!" one of the uniformed officers shouted.

Pierce raised his hands and turned around. One of the officers had his pistol trained on him, and the other approached with a set of handcuffs. Pierce waited until the man was close enough, then grabbed the cuffs and used a sweeping kick to knock the officer to the ground. He elbowed the fallen man in the face and seized his holstered gun before his partner had a chance to react.

Crouched down, with the confiscated pistol pressed up against the dazed officer's head, Pierce ordered his partner to, "Back off!"

If pressed, William Moones would have admitted to loving paperwork. There was something satisfyingly certain about filling in forms and filing records. Few things in life had such a distinct sense of closure as signing off a traffic officer's report of a fender bender. The report would get sent to the department's central data server and never be heard of again. It was his skill as an administrator that had ensured Moones's rapid rise to the rank of captain. His men regarded him as a white collar bureaucrat, but it was his ability to keep the appearance of order in an increasingly disordered world that so impressed his superiors.

Moones' office overlooked the open plan room where the homicide, robbery and vice units made their home. A glass partition offered him a clear view of the detectives' desks, most of which were vacant because cost control meant that they only kept a handful of officers on night duty. Opposite Moones' desk was a frosted glass door marked 'Liaison Unit' that led to a room where all the real police work was done. Moones preferred working the night shift, because he had very little to do as the officer in charge. Few men to supervise, very little crime to deal with and ample opportunity to catch up on his administrative duties.

As he absentmindedly chewed on the end of his digital stylus, Moones leant back in his chair and gazed beyond the glass partition into the open plan office. What he saw startled him. A man had a gun to a uniformed officer's head and was leading the human shield towards him. Five uniformed officers and two detectives formed a perverse heptagonal entourage, travelling with the gunman, their own weapons trained on him with every step. Moones recognized the gunman from the earlier flash bulletin that had identified him as wanted killer Scott Pierce.

Moones rushed out of his office, and drew his weapon for the first time in more than a decade.

"Captain, you've got to listen to me," Pierce began, being careful not to give the assembled officers an excuse to shoot him. "My name is Scott Pierce."

"He's wanted for murder," one of the offices noted.

"Put the gun down!" Moones shouted at the suspect.

"You have to listen," Pierce pleaded. "Resolute have framed me because of what I know."

"What do you know?"

The voice came from behind Moones. He turned to see that Tony Jordan, the Resolute liaison officer had joined them in the open plan office. Two of his subordinates had accompanied him and both carried their customary automatic MP9 pistols in hip holsters.

Resolute had followed the Fortress Corporation's practice of keeping three or four liaison personnel in every police precinct in the city. This allowed them unrestricted access to every police commander in the city and gave them early intelligence on any potential threats. It rankled Moones that they had the neighboring office and that there was a connecting door. It was a clear statement of their relative power.

"Whatever it is must be pretty dangerous."

Something passed between Jordan and this man Pierce. Moones could feel something going on beneath the surface that he could not put his finger on. He saw Pierce look from Jordan and his men to the police officers that surrounded him. Perhaps he finally realized that he was truly outnumbered. Whatever the reason, Pierce raised the pistol away from his hostage's head and fixed Jordan with a bitter stare as he did so.

The uniforms and detectives overwhelmed Pierce and knocked him to the floor. He was treated roughly but within the confines of the law as he was disarmed and then handcuffed.

"Captain, call FSA section chief Van Zyl and tell him that I need to talk," Pierce called out to Moones as he was dragged to his feet.

"Shut the fuck up!"

One of the officers smacked Pierce in the mouth, and Moones watched as the men jostled him out of the room towards the elevator that would take him from the second floor down to the basement holding cells.

Jordan approached.

"Captain, I'd like to transfer this man to Resolute headquarters for interrogation."

The request made Moones bristle. It was bad enough that these unelected, unaccountable men were able to keep tabs on his precinct's operations but here was one of their number making a request that was a clear breach of legal procedure.

"I don't think so," Moones responded. "You guys might own the streets, but we're still the law in this town. He'll get arraigned in the morning."

Moones turned away from the mercenaries and headed back into his office. Something about what just happened felt very wrong and he was determined to get to the bottom of it.

That pencil-necked fuck, Jordan thought as he watched Moones shut the door to his office. He needed to be taught a lesson in true power.

"Command, this is tenth precinct liaison," Jordan spoke into his radio.

"Go ahead, Jordan," Sam Solomon responded.

"Pierce just got arrested. The cops refused to hand him over to me," Jordan said.

It had been a smart move on Solomon's part to ensure that every liaison officer in every precinct in the city was loyal to the mission. Jordan's loyalty was being paid for in cold hard cash. If Solomon wanted to exploit their position of trust to rob a bank or two, that was fine with him, provided he got the five million dollars he had been promised.

"Keep me posted," Solomon radioed Jordan.

A look of relief crossed Creed's face, "We can lift the quarantine."

Solomon was not prepared to take the risk that Pierce had got to someone. All it took to blow the mission was one wayward cop to buy Pierce's story and a phone call to be placed to the right extension in Washington.

His life had been defined by instinct. Solomon believed that conscious thought was a barrier to effective action. The mind would always gravitate towards the practical but greatness was never achieved by practicality. Instead, Solomon chose to let God inspire his divine warrior with instinctive answers to the challenges he faced. One such answer presented itself to him now.

"Not yet, sir," Solomon said to Creed. "He may have other operatives on the Island. I'm going to go down there and interrogate him myself."

Creed did not look pleased but Solomon knew the man would not have the strength to disagree with what seemed like a prudent approach.

"Well make it fast, Sam," Creed smiled weakly. "The longer we keep the city in lockdown, the more heat we catch."

Solomon noticed that Lopez was signaling him from the other side of the command center.

"The Agency jet is in range," Lopez whispered as Solomon leant over the back of his chair.

"Destroy it," Solomon replied.

Creed watched his second in command and wondered what was wrong. Something was nagging at him; a feeling of unease that he could neither get rid of, nor bring to the surface. What was clear was that he relied on Solomon too much and it was not healthy for a commander to be so beholden to his deputy. In a few weeks, once a routine had been established in Manhattan, perhaps he would reassign Solomon to command the Washington unit. It would be a big readjustment, Creed thought, but there was something about the way Solomon was behaving tonight that made him feel that it might be the healthy thing to do.

"Sir, I have a Captain Moones on the emergency line," an officer called out to Creed from the bank of communications consoles. "He wants me to connect him to a Chief Van Zyl at the Agency."

"Put him through," Creed said as he picked up the nearest extension.

"This is Resolute Commander John Creed," Creed said when he heard the call connect.

"Commander, this is Bill Moones, tenth precinct," the voice said down the line. "I've got a suspect in my cells and I want to check him out. You think you could patch a call through to the Agency for me?"

"You're talking about Scott Pierce?"

Creed sensed the hesitation at the other end of the line and it made him feel even more uneasy. A New York City police captain should not feel the need to hide things from him. After a moment's pause, Moones's response was non-committal.

"I need to run a background check on the suspect."

This captain may have something to hide, Creed thought, but I don't.

"I'll see what I can do, Captain."

As Creed hung up, he called out to the nearest comms officer.

"Get me Chief Van Zyl."

New York Anti-Aircraft Missile Battery System. The words ran across the top of Lopez's screen, as the targeting system came on line. The Agency G20 was the only bird in the sky around Manhattan so Lopez had no difficulty identifying the target for the drag and drop firing system. He clicked on the tracer signal and a command prompt appeared on screen asking him to confirm the target, which he did. Once the authorization code was entered, the system would automatically fire at the selected target until it was destroyed.

The final command prompt appeared requesting the authorization code. Lopez indicated the screen to Solomon and sat back a little to allow the ruthless man to lean over his keyboard and enter the highly secret firing authorization code.

The words 'System Armed' filled the screen. Lopez wondered whether he would feel guilty about murdering for money. People were frequently killed for things far less noble, he told himself, and the passage of time heals all.

"John Creed," Porter said as he handed Van Zyl the phone.

"Carl, we've got your man. He's at the tenth precinct," Creed started. "The officer in charge wants to talk to you."

The sound of a high pitched alarm is something nobody wants to hear when they're on board an aircraft, and Van Zyl was no exception. He started visibly when the menacing sounded began to emanate from the cockpit.

"What the fuck!" the pilot exclaimed.

"What's the problem?" Van Zyl asked, dreading the answer.

"We've got a missile lock! Manhattan control, this is Federal-Security-Agency-Graviton-Jet-Zulu-Alpha-Charlie-Oner-Sixer-Niner, disengage your missile lock. I repeat, disengage your missile lock."

Van Zyl could hear the pilot trying to maintain his composure.

A much less composed Van Zyl yelled into the phone, "John, we're being targeted by your missile system. What the hell is happening?"

Creed looked around the command center. Everything seemed as it should, but he felt strange, as though he were distant. He looked at the faces of the thirty-or-so men in the room and started to feel very uncomfortable. He tried to tell himself that it was just his imagination that they were looking at him as though he were an outsider.

"Someone give me a status report," Creed called out. "I've got an Agency aircraft that reports a missile lock."

There was no mistaking the silence that greeted his command; the men carried on as though he was not there.

"Creed, you motherfucker," he heard Van Zyl yell down the line. "The pilot says the lock is coming from Governor's Island."

Creed ran to the window. The huge missile battery at the edge of the island was operational and swiveled on its enormous solid steel base as it tracked a target through the sky.

"Disengage missile system," Creed yelled wildly.

Solomon stood on the other side of the command room and stared at him impassively. Frustration, rage and bitter sense of betrayal were just some of the emotions that blazed through Creed. He made a futile dash for the nearest weapons console.

"Take the colonel into custody."

He heard Solomon's words but they had a unreal quality. As two of his own men pushed him to his knees, Creed realized that he was going into shock.

He looked out of the window and saw the incandescent trails of two new stars, as they shot into the sky.

The jet hurtled towards the Earth, and his arms flew up involuntarily. The sudden change of direction and velocity gave Van Zyl a temporary release from gravity, and he reacted badly to it. His final meal spewed out all over the small table in front of his plush chair. Porter glanced in his direction but quickly looked away. Van Zyl shared his subordinate's feeling of shame. Death was defeat. It was the universe's way of declaring him a loser, and the embarrassment he felt at knowing that he was to become yesterday's man far outweighed any sense of dread of the unknown.

The cockpit was alive with activity, as the pilot and co-pilot tried desperately to avoid their fate. Van Zyl heard them shouting about evasive action and countermeasures. The executive officer was frantically alternating radio calls between Resolute command and Washington pleading for assistance. Both failed to respond; the executive officer reported some kind of blanket blockade of radio communications throughout the entire region. Van Zyl felt a series of jolts, which he could only assume were the countermeasures being released.

A massive explosion rocked the aircraft, and Van Zyl was knocked out of his seat to the floor. The pilot reported that one of the missiles had been destroyed by the countermeasures but there was a second headed straight for them. Van

Zyl tried to pull himself up, but the jet was spinning like a pinwheel, and he was flung back to the floor. The last contact he experienced was the soft touch of Porter's hand taking hold of his. He looked up at the man and saw a lake of tears in his eyes. There was no shame in death, Van Zyl thought, it came to us all. A sudden, overwhelming force tore the aircraft apart, and searing light consumed everyone inside.

"What have you done?" Creed asked.

The man was being kept on his knees by two mercenaries loyal to the cause.

"Somebody answer me!"

Solomon had factored this day into their relationship from the outset. He had never allowed himself to get too close to the lazy, malleable man, but he had been happy to allow Creed to come to rely on him entirely. The inequity of their relationship had been obvious to him, but Creed allowed himself to believe that he had found the son he never had. Solomon had initially borne the man no malice; Creed was simply a means to an end. That had changed over the years as Solomon had come to resent the man's stupidity and neediness. It was time to put the distressed creature out of its misery.

"I could not risk letting a team of agents into the city," Solomon offered. "They could have upset my mission."

"What mission?" Creed was genuinely lost. "What are you talking about?"

Solomon neither owed nor felt inclined to give him an answer. He had purchased the loyalty of many of the men in the room and they did not know the full extent of what he had planned. They believed they were part of an elaborate and lucrative heist.

"You may have been the figurehead, John, but this is my company. And I have packed it with men loyal to me."

In his many years of God's work, Solomon had learnt that a man's mind could inflict far more pain than his body. He saw the principle at work that very instant, as Creed came to comprehend the scale and scope of the betrayal. The older man's head sagged, and he lost the feelings of anger that had kept his shock at bay. All that was left was the resignation of the defeated.

Creed lifted his head, his face a window on his inner ruin.

"We built this company together. We're friends, Sam."

Solomon approached Creed and leant down to speak softly in his ear.

"My name is Kamal Al Karim," the man who had been calling himself Sam Solomon whispered. "Your government knows me as the Spider."

The look of realization that crossed Creed's face told Karim that his name had registered. The old man had finally realized the full extent of the betrayal. He had been instrumental in placing the country he loved in the hands of its most feared enemy. Karim drew his pistol and fired three times into Creed's chest.

If any of the men in the command center were shocked by Creed's execution, they knew better than to show it. Karim holstered his weapon and turned to address them.

"We are a breath away from success. You shall all be amply rewarded for your loyalty."

The men returned to their work, as Creed's body was dragged from the room. Karim approached Lopez, who was in the process of placing a call to Agency headquarters in Washington to report the loss of one of their grav-jets.

"I'm taking Alpha Unit to dispose of our problem," Karim told Lopez. "Keep the operation on schedule."

CHAPTER 22

The obsidian black walls of the cell were sheer enough for Pierce's reflection to gaze back at him. He felt ten years older than he looked but he was sure that the stress of the past six years would eventually extract a physical toll. One day he would wake up and see an old man reflected back at him. Until then, his exhaustion and injuries had to be overcome.

Pierce looked at his cellmate, a six-foot-five bare-chested tattooed maniac. The man's barreled torso was a message of hate to the world. A green and blue fire breathing dragon spread its wings across the man's pectoral muscles and underneath was the legend, *"For the weak, death. For the strong, glory."* Scrawled across his abdomen were the words, *"Suicide is a valid option."* His arms were covered in script:

No Mercy.

Fuck The Power.

Choke On My Shit.

A four inch gold chain ran from a piercing in Tattoo's nose to a stud that had been punched into his bottom lip. Pierce had no idea what Tattoo was being held for, but the guy spelled trouble in capital letters.

They shared a ten foot square holding cell constructed from light reactive Geo-Melt, an almost indestructible glass that was used to store nuclear waste. From the inside, the cell walls were midnight black and prevented the inmates from having any view of the world beyond. The police officers on the other side of the cell walls had an unobstructed view of the cell interior. From the outside, the cell walls looked like they were made from clear glass. The Geo-Melt was bulletproof and was virtually impervious to impact. Only military grade lasers could mark its surface. GeoMelt cells were marketed to law enforcement agencies as being escape proof.

Pierce wondered whether surrender had been the right choice. The Resolute officer had made it clear that Pierce would be placing the lives of every police in the room in danger if he shared what he knew. The cops may not have registered the subtext, but the menace in the man's words had been clear. Pierce could only hope that the police captain had the sense to pass his message to Van Zyl. Even if Van Zyl could stop himself from being an asshole for a moment and put some of the pieces together, he might be able to do something.

Tactically, Pierce told himself, the Spider would have to ensure that loyal men were placed in strategic roles and that would have to include the police liaison officers. They were in a position to get early intelligence and to sow misinformation should the scheme be in danger of unraveling. It was unlikely that every man in the battalion was part of the plot, most could be manipulated

147

simply by their drilled-in habit of following orders. Others could be bought without knowing the full extent of the plan. There were probably only a handful of Resolute personnel who knew the truth of the Spider's plans.

Whatever the extent of the conspiracy, Pierce had to do what he could to prevent it. And the Spider now had to answer for the deaths of two people that were close to him. Pierce found himself replaying the moment of Catlin's murder, and immediately stopped it. He would be no good to anyone if he started beating his breast over what he could have done differently. His lamentations would have to wait.

Pierce's thoughts were interrupted by movement. Tattoo got to his feet and lumbered across the cell to tower over him.

"You're in my fucking seat," the painted man said.

Here we go, Pierce thought as he tensed his muscles, but the sound of the cell door opening put an end to any immediate prospect of violence.

The electronic locking system disengaged and the dozen Geo-Melt bolts that locked the door to the cell wall sprang back as one. The door swung open and Captain Moones entered.

He looked at Pierce and said, "We need to talk."

Look at the fucking sheep, Ricky Denilson cursed as he picked his way through the trail of dead metal that snaked back from the Queensboro Bridge. Dozens of unoccupied cars and trucks abandoned by their owners, who clustered around the checkpoint and waited for news of when they would be allowed off the island.

Denilson had sat and stared at the stationary license plate of the car in front for a full five minutes, before he had asked a guy who was coming from the direction of the hold up to tell him what the hell was happening. The guy had explained that Manhattan was in quarantine; some kind of terror threat.

A long criminal record had fostered a healthy disrespect for authority in the thirty-year-old. He saw how society was just a game, where those with power stacked the rules against those without. They made their morality seem absolute, as though it was the holy definition of good and evil, but Denilson knew that it was all bullshit. Some human societies had thought that cannibalism was okay, and had developed a moral code to justify it. The suffering inflicted on the weak and destitute was simply today's version of cannibalism. The murderous ills of poverty, disease and ignorance were cultivated by the rich to maintain the status quo.

Denilson's cynicism had always been useful for justifying his crimes to himself. There was no difference between his robbing a convenience store and a sneaker manufacturer stealing the life and labor of a factory slave in Thailand. During his second four-year stretch for armed robbery, Denilson's views had taken on a political dimension, and he had become involved in Sparta, an underground organization that aimed to implement social change through political revolution.

He had shared a cell with Oscar Abarca, the Californian activist who had been one of the founders of Sparta and Abarca had tutored him in law, philosophy and political theory. The man had changed his life, and Denilson left jail a criminal, but one whose crimes would now have a purpose; to help finance rebellion.

This was not about politics though, this was about pussy, Denilson thought as he approached the mercenary checkpoint. An Indian guy – complete with turban – sat on the roof of an armored truck and cradled a bullhorn. He looked like the unit commander. His men stood around stroking their weapons, while the baa baas muttered discontent but lacked the resolve to act. Denilson strode towards the Sikh.

Chadha observed the motley crowd of New Yorkers from his vantage point on the Cougar's roof, and marveled at the power of conditioning. Our obedience is breed into us from an early age. We are trained to follow the commands of our parents, teachers and bosses. A man with a gun is simply the biggest boss of all. To challenge authority, to break with convention, as he had done when he joined Resolute, was to show true bravery. Here were free Americans who had committed no crime, perfectly happy to see their liberty curtailed in order to defend against a faceless threat. History had taught him that the masses could be controlled by a few determined men, but even he had been surprised how easily Manhattan had been cut off from the world. Chadha wondered whether he would have been so sanguine if he had been on the other end of his men's guns.

The first hint of trouble came when Chadha heard the words, "Hey, motherfucker!"

They had come from the mouth of a wiry guy who had pushed his way through the crowd and now stood in front of the Cougar.

"The last time I checked, this was still America and my rights to life, liberty and the pursuit of happiness were protected by the Constitution."

A little education can be a dangerous thing, Chadha thought as the Central or South American man turned to address the crowd.

"And right now my happiness depends on a hot young thing called Lola who lives on the other side of this bridge."

That got a few laughs from the assembled masses, and Chadha knew he had to take action. Dissent spread like a virulent disease. All it took was one rogue idea to open people's eyes to a different way of thinking.

The agitator sidestepped the Cougar and started climbing over the barricade. Chadha's men looked to him for direction.

"Not even the President of the United States can prevent me from exercising my God-given right to cross this river and nail that sweet ass," the agitator announced as he climbed.

Chadha nodded towards one of his men, who stood on top of one of the concrete blocks that formed part of the barricade. The mercenary brought the butt of his rifle down on the ascending crusader's head, and the man fell off the barricade and landed unconscious on the asphalt.

"You can't do that!"

"Hey!"

"Fucking Nazis!"

These were some of the calls Chadha was able to distinguish from the general discontent of the crowd. As he got to his feet, he drew his pistol and fired it three times into the air.

The shots had the desired effect; silence. Chadha spoke clearly and powerfully.

"We are authorized to use lethal force to quell any dissent. I order you to clear the area."

For a moment Chadha was unsure whether the unconscious sinewy man had done enough to inspire the crowd to challenge his authority. As two of his men dragged the agitator away to be taken to a medical center, Chadha felt the crowd consider the allure of a similar fate. People were happy to lecture on rights, but it took a rare individual to stand up and defend them without thought to personal cost. Chadha had a great deal of respect for the agitator's effort and would see that the man was treated well. He had no respect for the people in the crowd who began to disperse without any resistance, as his men started pushing them back.

"What happened between you and that Resolute prick up there?" Moones asked.

He and Pierce stood near the cell door, and ignored the menacing stare beamed in their direction by Tattoo. Pierce considered his next move carefully. The police captain had inadvertently saved his life by refusing to hand him over to Resolute, but Pierce wondered whether there was anything to be gained by telling him the truth. Right now he was labeled as a cold-blooded killer and could not expect anyone to listen to him. But this officer had come to talk to him for a reason. The man sensed all was not as it seemed, and Pierce came to the conclusion that he had nothing to lose.

"What I'm about to tell you will put your life in danger," Pierce said finally. "You want that kind of weight?"

"I've got to," Moones replied without hesitation. "It's my job."

The police captain listened with increasing dismay, as Pierce told him how his city had fallen into the worst possible hands.

News of Catlin's death had shocked everyone in the room. Their bewilderment was compounded by the official line that Pierce had murdered her. Belle refused to believe that Pierce had anything to do with Catlin's death; she knew how long they had been friends. And there was the rumor that there had been something more intimate while they were both at the Academy.

Belle had tried to reach Van Zyl for orders, but a blackout on everything but Resolute Corporation communication had made contact with the deputy director impossible. Now they were receiving unconfirmed reports that his jet had crashed into the East River, which had filled her with dismay. She could not see the player but the moves were bold enough to suggest a powerful conspiracy.

"Get me any satellite imagery taken over Manhattan in the past hour," Belle commanded one of the analysts. "I'm particularly interested in the site of the grav-jet crash."

Belle turned to the other men and women in the room.

"I don't believe Pierce had anything to do with the embassy bombing or with Liz's murder. He's being played and right now he needs our help. I want us to find a way of cracking Resolute's comms link so that we can hear what's going on. Anyone who wants out can leave now."

Much to Belle's relief, nobody walked out. Instead they busied themselves with the Agency's state-of-the-art technology, in an effort to get to the truth.

Moones leant against the black cell wall, his shoulders slumped. Pierce could see that the man longed for the falsity of what he had just heard. The coherence and conviction of Pierce's story had cut clear fissures in the official Resolute line and Pierce was determined to exploit them.

"Captain, it's really simple," Pierce argued. "Just send a SWAT team down to the Citibank building. Have them go down to the vault. If they find men there, I'm telling the truth. If not, I'll take whatever punishment is coming my way."

Moones weighed up the cost of Pierce's suggestion, and then said, "What the hell."

"Thank you, captain."

Pierce breathed a sigh of relief as he watched Moones use the fingerprint sensor to unlock the cell door.

Moones tried to pick holes in the guy's story as he walked along the block, which was lined with Geo-Melt cells, eight on each side. At the north end of the corridor was a door that led to the booking suite that adjoined the main lobby. The door at the southern end opened onto another corridor that led to the precinct's service areas and the motor pool. Moones stepped through the northern door and nodded to the sergeant who sat behind his desk in the custody suite.

If Pierce was telling the truth, he would not risk his men's lives by sending a SWAT team, he would send every available unit at his disposal and dispatch foot messengers to the three nearest precincts to ask for additional support. This could turn into a shitstorm, Moones cautioned himself, if it pitted the NYPD against the city's private army.

When Moones entered the main lobby the hairs on his neck stood on end. The desk sergeant was hitting his surveillance monitor and swearing at the damned thing to stop acting up. At that moment, eight men in Resolute uniforms stepped into the building. All of them held silenced assault rifles. The silencers, coupled with the look on the face of the man he took to be their leader, told Moones all he needed to know; these men had come to kill Pierce and anyone he might have spoken to.

CHAPTER 23

Karim had taken seven men loyal to him and boarded his G20. All seven men and the flight crew were brothers who had been smuggled into the country by the fat lawyer. They all had false military backgrounds that were almost as impressive as his own. As the grav-jet had flown low and fast over the bay, Karim had marveled at the simple beauty of his enterprise. All it had taken was patience, cunning and determination.

They had been tracking the real Samuel Solomon for years. A non-descript, reclusive Jew who lived at home with his family in Catskill Mountains. After the Rome mission, Karim's American plan had been approved by his superiors. They had seen enough to know that he had both genius and resolve, and as America moved closer to authorizing the Sentry program, Karim's grand scheme could become a reality. The investment was huge, but the payoff would be worth it.

Karim had come to America eight years earlier, two years before the success in London, and disappeared after entering on a false British passport. One of the Brotherhood's donor teams had killed and disposed of the real Sam Solomon, and Karim had assumed his identity. An auto accident was arranged for Solomon's mother, father and brother. Their deaths removed the only people who could blow his cover, and provided a convincing tragedy that explained Solomon's sudden change in lifestyle. He had enlisted in the army and quickly rose through the ranks to join John Creed's unit. Karim had been on the lookout for a suitable front man for their business and he saw in Creed a weak, ambitious and trusting fool.

Karim had introduced Creed to some financiers who were ostensibly distant relatives of Sam Solomon's. In reality, they were paid intermediaries who made a substantial sum for simply laundering Brotherhood money into Creed's hands. That money was used to finance Resolute, America's most successful Sentry company.

Creed had been disinterested in the day-to-day operations of the business, and preferred to seek out patronage and glory. This had left Karim free to structure the company as he had seen fit, and he hired men whose loyalty could be purchased and whose morality was corrupt. As more Brothers entered the country, Karim had been able to build a core of Praetorians around him whose loyalty was beyond question.

The New York contract was the gem in the Sentry program, and Karim had always known Resolute was unlikely to win it in the initial allocation. They were up against established private security companies who had been providing similar services to the American government for many years in occupied territories overseas. Resolute's advantage was that it was effectively run by the Brotherhood's head of military operations. Karim had been able to give Resolute a clean sheet, while feeding his cells restricted Sentry intelligence on his competitors' operations and procedures. With such a contrast between Resolute's success and his competitors' failures, Karim had known it was only a matter of time before they were awarded New York, but he had persuaded Creed to identify a senior politician who could be bought, so that nothing was left to chance. Senator Stovall's support had been instrumental in securing the contract, and Karim was sure once the truth of what he had been involved in became public, Stovall's name would go down in infamy.

The G20 had touched down outside an office block on 23rd Street, and Karim and his men had covered the remaining three blocks on foot. Armed Resolute mercenaries running through the streets did not look out of place, and they had waited until they were outside the precinct building to fit the silencers to their weapons. Karim had commanded his engineering officer to shut down the precinct's eyes and ears. The engineer had activated a miniature communications dish that sent out a signal that would disable all electronic equipment within a one block radius. Once the signal was operational, Karim and his men had entered the solid stone building.

"Shoot them!" Moones yelled as he drew his pistol.

He and his men did not stand a chance, but he was determined to go down fighting. Moones got two loud shots off before a storm of suppressed thunder hit him in the chest and killed him.

"Those were gunshots," Pierce observed. He listened carefully and heard the faint popping of silenced machine-guns, their silencers losing suppressive power with each successive shot.

Pierce did not notice Tattoo sidle up behind him. The huge man whispered in Pierce's ear.

"Sounds like the cops are going to be busy for a while."

The two officers who manned the body scanners were killed with no difficulty. The plain clothed policeman had managed to shoot one of Karim's men in the shoulder, but a volley of bullets had killed him. The desk sergeant had succeeded in activating the alarm, before they had destroyed him and his bulletproof booth with a grenade.

Karim cursed the plain clothed policeman; he had distracted them from their primary objective, which was to kill the sergeant before he could sound the alarm, and now they were paying the price. Police officers stormed into the entrance hall and opened fire. Regular police were quickly joined by SWAT, and the hall became the scene of a pitched battle. Gunfire crackled across the large chamber, and dust and smoke filled the air. The screams of injured cops could be heard between the bullets.

Karim and his men were pinned down behind the scanners by the entrance, while the cops took cover by what remained of the desk sergeant's booth. If they did not take control of the situation soon, Karim knew that they would jeopardize the entire mission. After this attack on one of their precincts, the New York police would believe anything Pierce told them.

Tony Jordan reacted the moment he heard the alarm. He and his men were not cops but they had standing orders to defend the precinct if it was ever the subject of a terror attack. They exited the liaison office to find that the open plan detectives' room was empty. Jordan and his men headed for the elevator, where they found a couple of detectives waiting. They could hear the sound of gunfire echoing up the elevator shaft.

"What's happening?" Jordan asked.

"No idea," one of the detectives replied.

As Jordan and his two men followed the detectives into the elevator, Jordan's earpiece crackled into life.

"Jordan, this is Solomon. SWAT have us pinned down in the lobby. We need your help."

Jordan tapped a button on his radio, which sent a single ping in response to Solomon's message to let the commander know that it had been received.

As the elevator descended, Jordan considered how many lines a man should be prepared to cross in the name of ambition. He was a soldier and had killed scores of men, but what was being asked of him now was the murder of innocents, and the justification was simply his own enrichment.

"Why don't you and I get better acquainted?" Tattoo asked in a tone that made his planned despoliation clear.

Pierce did not pay any attention to the large man, and scanned the cell for a way out. When Tattoo approached and blocked his field of vision, Pierce's eyes fell upon the chain that ran from the man's nose to his lip. It was a stupid thing to wear for anyone intent on physical violence but in Pierce's experience jail cells were not where one found professors.

Pierce reached out and tore the chain from its moorings. The nose ring ripped through Tattoo's nostril and the sudden extraction of the stud left a wet gash in the middle of his lip. The painted man grabbed his nose and hunched over in pain.

Unconcerned, Pierce turned his attention to the cell door. The fingerprint reader would be connected to the locking mechanism, Pierce thought, before he sensed movement behind him.

"Motherfucker!" Tattoo yelled as he lunged forward.

Pierce sidestepped the assault, and punched Tattoo in the neck, as the brute drew alongside him. The sudden, forceful blow knocked the man to his knees, and Pierce used his elbow to finish the job, smashing it into Tattoo's face with enough force to send him into somnolent oblivion.

The sharp end of the nose stud was fine enough to work inside the join where the fingerprint reader attached to the cell door. Pierce leveraged the fingerprint reader free of the door to reveal the wires and circuit boards underneath.

The elevator door opened onto a scene of complete carnage. Bullets whizzed in all directions and there was evidence of grenade damage. The bodies of police officers lay everywhere. Jordan could see the SWAT team ahead of him. They had taken cover behind some rubble and were under fire from Solomon and his men, who were shooting from behind the scanners near the main entrance.

As the two detectives rushed out of the elevator, Jordan came to a decision. He spoke, softly into his neck microphone.

"I can't do it, Sam. These guys are cops."

He looked at the vulnerable police officers who all had their backs to him, and knew that he had made the right decision; there was such a thing as too far.

"Kill him," Solomon said over the radio.

Jordan did not even have time to turn around before his adjutant shot him in the head.

The secret to a successful mission, Karim surmised, was to ensure that paid loyalty was surrounded by true faith. Each police liaison officer in the city had been bought, but at least one of their subordinates was a Brother, sent to keep watch and ensure everyone stayed true to the mission.

From his position behind the scanner, Karim saw his man Darweesh shoot Jordan in the back of the head, before he killed the other Resolute officer who had travelled down in the elevator with him. None of the police officers, including the SWAT team, heard the sound of Darweesh's machine pistol above the tumult of their own gunfire, so they were totally unprepared when the Brother strafed them with burning death.

As the officers who had not been killed immediately turned to engage Darweesh, Karim and his men leapt from their cover and opened fire. When their guns had stopped spitting extinction, Karim estimated that two dozen police officers and a SWAT unit of six men lay dead at their feet.

Darweesh drew Karim's attention to the descending elevator.

"Where is he?" Karim asked of Darweesh in Arabic.

"Cell number three," came the Brother's response.

"Let's move," Karim said to the assembled men.

When he heard the silence, Pierce knew that he did not have long. The final volleys he had heard were the suppressed whelps of silenced armaments; the pattern of shots towards the end of the firefight suggested that the cops had lost. After he had worked the fingerprint reader away from the door, Pierce had quickly found the main circuit board, which linked the reader to the security system.

He believed that he could trip the door by overloading the circuit but he had none of the right tools. Instead, Pierce used Tattoo's chain as a power conduit. He held it to the fingerprint reader's power supply and tried it against various transistors on the main circuit board. There were dozens of transistors, and each was tiny. He had to make contact with them individually to find the correct circuit, and as time passed his nerves got the better of him and his hands started to shake. If whoever was out there killing cops found him here, he would be dead, all prospects of vengeance extinguished with him.

Pierce took a moment to compose himself and watched his fingertips steady. He continued trying transistors, but heard an inner voice telling him that he was wasting his time. The system could not be overloaded by something so brutal and basic, the repressed voice told him. Pierce knew things were bad when his inner gremlin kicked in. It was the same voice that had tried to convince him of the merits of suicide so many times since Eleanor's death. Warriors did not obtain greatness by choosing to die, Pierce told himself, nor did they ever give up hope. He could and would find a way.

A spark from the board told him that he had found the right transistor. Pierce felt the electrical charge run through his fingertips and up his arm, but ignored the jolt and held the chain in position; it would take a moment for the circuit to overload. Every transistor on the board fused, and Pierce heard the satisfying sound of the bolts drawing back into the door.

He stepped into the corridor and turned north, towards the booking hall, but immediately realized his error the moment he saw the first Resolute mercenary step through the door ahead of him. Pierce locked eyes with the man who had killed Catlin for a split second, and both of them knew Pierce was a sitting duck. As the first mercenary raised his weapon to fire, Pierce thought quickly and pulled the cell door wide open, so that it was at a ninety degree angle to the cell wall and blocked half the corridor.

The first bullets embedded themselves in the clear GeoMelt, and Karim watched through the clear bulletproof glass, as Pierce turned on his heels and sprinted towards the door at the southern end of the corridor.

"After him!" Karim yelled.

The stunt with the cell door had bought him precious moments, and Pierce wasted none of them. He burst through the south door, as the Resolute mercenaries reached his cell and kicked the protective door shut. They opened fire, but their bullets hit nothing except masonry and metal; Pierce was already on his way through the service area towards the motor pool.

Tunney had not wanted to come in, but Roscoe had insisted. According to the manual, a defective radio was sufficient reason to return to the precinct, and if an officer were forced to operate a vehicle without a working radio, a formal complaint could be made through the union. Tunney knew what the rules were, but wanted to stay out and finish his shift anyway. When they had passed a Resolute checkpoint, they had been told about the enforced radio silence so everybody was in the same position. But Roscoe had seen the opportunity for some slack time and seized it.

"Rules is rules," he had said.

They pulled into the motor pool and Tunney parked beside a row of patrol cars. The lot was devoid of personnel, which Tunney found strange.

"Where is everyone?" he observed.

He got his answer when he and Roscoe exited the vehicle and heard the distant sound of the precinct alarm. Both men ran towards the service door that led into the building, but were knocked back when the door jerked open and a sprinting man surged into the motor pool. Tunney recognized the guy as the subject of the earlier APB, Scott Pierce. Before either he or Roscoe could react, Pierce had grabbed Roscoe in a headlock and drawn the officer's pistol.

"Shoot the son-of-a-bitch!" Roscoe commanded.

But Pierce had the muzzle of the pistol pressed against his head and Tunney did not feel brave enough to act. His pistol stayed in its holster. Pierce pulled Roscoe towards their patrol car and discarded the human shield as he leapt into the driver's seat.

A group of Resolute mercenaries burst through the service door, as Pierce reversed through the motor pool barrier and out onto the street.

"Motherfucker!" Roscoe yelled. "Come on!"

Tunney joined his partner in the nearest patrol car and the two of them screeched off in pursuit of Pierce.

He was ineffective, but lucky, Karim thought as he saw Pierce disappear into the distance.

"All units," Karim spoke into his official Resolute radio. "Be advised, a terror suspect has escaped from police custody. He is in an NYPD patrol car, number VU one-three-six, that's Victor Uniform one-three-six. Shoot on sight."

"Why divert the manpower," Darweesh asked in Arabic, when Karim had finished his broadcast. "He's alone, cut off from the outside world and up against one of the most highly trained battalions in the world."

"I don't like loose ends," Karim replied.

A group of police officers ran through the service door into the motor pool. They were all in shock after having seen their colleagues lying dead in the main lobby.

"A terror cell attacked the precinct to free Scott Pierce," Karim told them.

"They killed your colleagues, freed Pierce and escaped before we could get here. We didn't see the terrorist's vehicles, but Pierce escaped in a stolen patrol car, number VU 136."

Karim's words had exactly the desired effect; they galvanized the shocked men to action and identified Pierce as an outlet for their rage. Karim watched the six men split into pairs. Each pair took a patrol car and raced out of the garage to wreak terrible vengeance upon the escaped agent.

"Back to the jet," Karim instructed his men.

CHAPTER 24

The ethereal effect of the low level lights made night driving a challenge at the best of times. As the police cruiser raced along Center Street at sixty, Pierce longed for the days of proper illumination. He clipped an old BMW that had stopped at the sound of his siren, and went speeding past in a flashing blur of blue and red. Pierce fought the destabilizing effects of the slight collision, and brought the cruiser under control. He could see the lights of a single cop car behind him. There would be more soon, he thought, as he looked for a way out of this mess.

Pride was a sin, Tunney observed as the ravenous car devoured the road ahead, precisely because it led people to lose control of their reason. He could see that Roscoe was burning with indignation at having been taken hostage, which was why he was driving like a lunatic.

All Roscoe had said on the subject had been: "You should have taken the fucking shot," which was a textbook attempt to pin his burning shame on Tunney. Tunney had said nothing in response, but had made sure his seatbelt was secure when he saw the glare in his partner's eyes.

The stolen patrol car was about half a block ahead of them, and had just sideswiped a BMW. It was a testament to the fugitive's driving skills that he was able to maintain control of the car as it lurched towards a skid. A moment later, Pierce gave them a real demonstration of his prowess as he cut in front of a bus and swung the stolen car into Kenmare Street.

Roscoe mounted the sidewalk on the inside of the bus, and pulled the wheel sharply, sending the car into a punishing turn. Tunney held his breath as they collided with a lamppost, but Roscoe maintained control and gunned the accelerator, which forced the car free and sent it speeding up Kenmare Street in pursuit of Pierce. Tunney was not relieved to see the flashing lights of his colleagues' vehicles as they joined the chase. Now there were just more things on the road for Roscoe to hit.

He had built up a block's lead with the stunt in front of the bus, but Pierce was dismayed to see more flashing lights in the rear-view, as three new vehicles joined the chase. The traffic on the road ahead was light. Cars were mostly used for business and few people had money to burn on using energy for social purposes. The old joke about living to work had come true; most people did very little outside of their jobs and based social activities around their home or immediate neighborhood. Even though traffic was not what it had been in the early part of the century, there were still enough vehicles around to make escape a challenge.

Trucks making deliveries to stores, cabs, a handful of private vehicles and a lot of bicycles. They all came to a halt the moment the heard the siren or saw the flashing lights of Pierce's commandeered police vehicle.

Pierce wove his way through the stationary traffic. He was not worried about hitting any of the vehicles, most of which were equipped with state-of-the-art safety systems. His main concern was the unprotected cyclists who stopped by the sidewalks on either side of the road. As he cut a route along the street, Pierce tried to stay as close to the median as possible. Pierce had no idea where he was heading, but knew that the longer the chase went on, the greater the chances of him being captured. He had to shake these cops.

The hairpin turn seemed to defy the laws of motion. Tunney saw Pierce force the patrol car into an almost ninety degree turn. The car objected and bounced onto two wheels, and for a moment Tunney thought that the vehicle might flip. After a split second's hesitation, the stolen vehicle stopped trying to resist Pierce's mastery, and all four wheels connected with the surface. The pursued car raced up Bowery, as Roscoe slowed to make the turn. Even in his state of temporary insanity he would not be crazy enough to try such a reckless maneuver.

The driver of one of the three cars following them did not have the same good sense, and as Roscoe slowed, he went speeding past and tried to force his vehicle into the turn. The car reacted in the same way as Pierce's had, but this time the driver's judgment crossed the fine line between victory and catastrophe, and the automobile went into a series of savage flips, before it hit a truck and came to a halt.

Pierce caught sight of the flipping car in his mirror, and saw its lights smash as its roof crashed against the road. The drivers of the vehicles coming towards him were shocked to see a police car headed in their direction up a one way street, and stepped on their brakes. Metal crunched against metal, as cars and trucks ran into one another. Pierce avoided the melee and cut across Bowery into Houston Street.

By the time they had turned onto Bowery, the traffic ahead had come to a standstill, and Tunney could see that there had been a number of collisions. He caught a glimpse of the lights of Pierce's vehicle disappearing along Houston. Roscoe slammed the throttle and the car surged forward and cut a diagonal line across Bowery.

Aksel did not intend to be late for his delivery. If he stuck around, he could see himself being forced to give countless interviews to the police about the series of fender-benders around him. His truck had not been hit, so he saw no reason why his business should suffer; he got bonuses for timely delivery. When the second cop car cut in front of his truck, he depressed the accelerator and got moving.

Tunney heard the collisions and turned around to see the remaining two police cruisers collide with a truck that had moved forward and blocked the intersection of Bowery and Kenmare. Both cars were going at such speed and hit the truck with such force that the collisions shunted it ten feet sideways. Without a working radio, there was no way to call for paramedics.

"We should turn back," Tunney said, turning to his partner. "They need help."

"No fucking way," Roscoe gritted his teeth. "This motherfucker is going down."

Ahead of them, Pierce swung his car into Lafayette. Roscoe followed seconds later and the two cars danced around the stationary traffic as they both sped along the road.

The abrupt change from forward to lateral motion pushed the wind from his lungs, and Tunney turned to see that the entire length of his partner's side of the car had buckled from the force of the collision with something huge, something that was grinding them sideways across the street.

Pierce had been calculating his next move, when he had seen the T1 Abrams tank burst from the alleyway to join the pursuit. The huge machine had collided with the pursuing police car and was now shunting it sideways across Lafayette.

The tank executed a sudden turn that worked the mangled car free of its tracks, and it accelerated rapidly in Pierce's direction. As Pierce weaved between the motionless vehicles ahead of him, he saw the staggering sight of the tank ploughing through the line of traffic behind. The nuclear powered behemoth was too large to pick its way through the obstacles ahead of it, and simply drove through or over them. Some drivers fled their vehicles, before they were crushed under the giant's tracks, others tried to pull over to safety. As he checked his rear-view, Pierce saw the storm of metal gaining on him. With a top speed of one hundred and ten miles an hour and no reason to go slow, the tank could move much more rapidly up the street than the weaving police cruiser. It tossed trucks aside as though they were mere toys, and disfigured cars as it drove over them. Chunks of metal and pieces of paneling flew through the air and bounced off the tank in a kaleidoscope of destruction.

Send in your skeletons, Sing as their bones come marching in again
The need you buried deep, The secrets that you keep

Wynn could feel the drum beat vibrate throughout his entire body as he drove north along Lafayette. He had grown up listening to his parent's collection of early twenty-first century music and heard it in an energy that surpassed the dreary trash produced by most contemporary bands. Ryan, who was a hardcore Hoodlum Five fan, had spent most of the night ragging him for his Foo Fighter obsession. All Wynn had been interested in was gathering the courage to finally make his move on Kirstie. He had spent the evening watching her from across the room, listening to his boorish friend extol the merits of bands Wynn hated. His nerve failed him, and after four hours at the party, Wynn put his tail between his legs and drove back towards his parents uptown apartment, with the Foo Fighters' Pretender as his only company.

Next time, Wynn thought – holy shit! The car in front of him swerved off the road onto the sidewalk. All of a sudden cars and trucks ahead of him started to pull to the side of the street.

"Asshole!" Wynn yelled out of the open window.

A cop car raced past and almost took his head off.

"Fucking pig!" Wynn shouted after it.

Thinking that the vehicles had pulled over to allow the cops swift passage, Wynn took advantage of the gap they had created to follow in the police car's wake. He was just admiring his survival-of-the-fittest ingenuity when he glanced in the mirror and saw a huge dark shadow bearing down on him. The tank tracks ripped into the car's trunk. If this didn't kill him, Wynn thought as he unclipped his seatbelt, his father would when he found out about his trashed car. Wynn opened the driver's door and jumped out, just before the tank crushed the car flat.

The guy rolled twenty times before he hit the sidewalk, but he might survive, Pierce thought as he looked in his wing mirror and saw a group of people cluster around the young man who had just leapt from his moving car. These bastards did not give a damn how many people they hurt, and, as if to reinforce the point, one of the buildings ahead of him exploded in a huge fireball. Masonry and glass rained onto the street, as fire licked up the partially demolished walls. Pierce checked his rear-view and saw the tank's main turret lining up for another shot. He swerved just as the shell was fired, and it whizzed through the air beside the cruiser. Pierce did not know how many people were onboard the bus ahead of him, but when that shell hit, and the bus exploded, he was certain they were all dead.

Pierce steered the cruiser onto the sidewalk in order to avoid the flaming bus, which had jack-knifed and now blocked the entire street. Moments after he passed the fireball, the tank tore right through it, chewing flaming metal under its impervious tracks. Pierce recognized that he was putting innocent civilians in harm's way and knew he had to get off the streets. He turned into Fourth Avenue and searched for an escape.

Karim and his men had covered the three blocks back to the grav-jet at a sprint, and were in the air five minutes after Pierce had left the precinct. They had just been getting airborne when a radio report came in telling them that an Abrams had engaged Pierce on Lafayette. The pilot had climbed high, and then had dived into the short, narrow valley that was Fourth Avenue.

The proximity sensors automatically kept the G20 away from the high buildings that loomed on either side. Ahead of them, Karim could see the tank and just beyond it, the flashing lights of Pierce's car.

"Strafe him," Karim ordered the pilot.

Fourth Avenue liquefied as the Vulcan cannons on the G20 pounded the asphalt at a rate of two hundred rounds per second. Cars around him exploded, as bullets cut through their fuel tanks, and Pierce coiled and snaked through the devastation. Behind him the Abrams fired another round, which hit an office block ahead of him. The building exploded, spewing flaming rubble everywhere. The stolen cruiser sped past the building, and raced over a spot that was covered by falling stone a split-second later.

Pierce cut across Fourteenth Street, mounted the sidewalk and smashed through the railings that surrounded Union Square Park. The cruiser juddered violently and threw him around as it travelled across the uneven grassy ground. The treeline provided Pierce with cover from the G20's cannons, which shredded leaf, branch and bark in a blind attempt to hit him. The tank followed, its tracks biting into the rough terrain.

The cruiser careened wildly through the park and burst through the railings on the north western corner. Pierce pointed the car in the direction of the oncoming traffic and headed north up Broadway.

Behind Pierce, the tank fired another shell, which exploded under the car directly ahead of him. The flaming wreckage of the car flipped into the air, and Pierce stepped on the gas, and accelerated through the fireball. He passed directly under the airborne wreck, which crashed to the ground the moment Pierce was clear. A second later, the blazing vehicle was crushed under the relentless tracks of the pursuing tank.

The roadblock Karim had organized had done its job. The traffic on Broadway thinned out and soon Pierce was driving along a deserted street, headed towards an Abrams and two Cougar APVs that formed a barricade further up the street. Karim looked out of the cockpit, as the G20 followed the contours of the road between the narrow buildings. He consoled himself with the thought that Pierce would soon be dead.

The G20 was still firing, and the tank was blasting the road with shells every twenty seconds. The ordnance had the effect of making Pierce feel like he was driving through a volcanic eruption, with fire and brimstone on all sides. When he saw the Abrams and two Cougars ahead of him, Pierce realized why the flow of oncoming traffic had stopped. He was out in the open and his defensive driving could only keep him alive for so long.

Gunner Harvey saw the target approaching. Weapons systems tracked it at eighty miles an hour, and he estimated trajectory based on the vehicle's past erratic swerves. Harvey pressed the trigger, and the high explosive shell erupted from the barrel of the Abrams tank. The shell flew away from the barricade towards the approaching police cruiser and looked to be dead on target, until the driver of the cruiser did something completely unexpected. Travelling at eighty, he veered off the road and crashed down the steps that led to 34th Street Subway Station.

The shell struck the pursuing Abrams tank on its offside track. The force of the explosion combined with the vehicle's high velocity pitched into a sidelong spin. The last thing Gunner Harvey saw as he looked at the targeting display was one-hundred-and-fifty tons of metal flipping directly towards him.

The maneuver impressed Karim. From his vantage point in the cockpit of the G20, he had seen that Pierce had judged his timing perfectly, and had flung the vehicle down the subway steps. Pierce could not have afforded to give any indication of his intention, so no attempt had been made to slow his progress, and the cruiser hit the wall at the bottom of the steps at full speed. Karim tried to see if Pierce emerged from the wreckage, but he was distracted by what happened on the street below, as the Abrams chasing Pierce flipped, spun and finally crashed into the tank in the barricade. The two huge vehicles exploded in a massive, blinding fireball.

"Bring us down," Karim instructed the pilot.

Pierce had cost him a great deal of time and manpower, and had proved himself resourceful enough to remain a threat to the mission. Karim had to know if the cursed man was dead.

CHAPTER 25

The G20 touched down in Herald Square, just behind the burning barricade. Karim led his men out of the aircraft, and ignored the shouts of the Resolute men who were trying to help their colleagues in the burning wreckage. He led Alpha squad around the far end of the barricade, past one of the Cougar armored personnel vehicles, towards the entrance to 34th Street Station.

A cloud of dust was still rising up the steps and Karim could smell burnt rubber, leaking gasoline and scoured metal. He instructed the men to descend with caution, aware that Pierce might be foolhardy enough to think he could overpower one of them. When they reached the bottom of the steps, they found the distorted remains of the police cruiser. The power cells and electric motors had burst through the hood upon impact and lay sprawled over the concertinaed front end. All of the windows had shattered, and Karim could see that all thirty interior airbags had activated.

Karim nudged the driver's door open with the muzzle of his gun, but the car was empty.

"Ya ebn-il-sharmouta," Karim exclaimed.

He checked the metal grating that covered the entrance to the station and found that it gave with a slight pull. Then he saw the tire iron that Pierce must have used to force the padlock. The agent was still alive and on the run.

"Shall we follow him?" Darweesh asked.

Karim hated loose ends but he needed to focus on the mission. Pierce might know pieces of the truth but he had firmly established himself as an enemy of the people and was currently trapped like a rat in the maze of subway tunnels beneath the city. Even if he could evade Resolute checkpoints and the police, and find someone to talk to, it was unlikely they would believe him. And even if they believed him, they would not be able to do anything. The city was isolated from the outside world and in Karim's total control.

"Let's get back to base," Karim said as he started to climb the steps.

When Karim reached the top of the steps he took his encrypted radio out of his breast pocket and typed in a code. He watched the first fire engines race down Broadway towards the burning tanks and waited for Rossi to respond.

The laser drill required three men to operate it. The focal lens directed a powerful beam of blue-tinted light towards the inner vault doors. One man was required to monitor the calibration to ensure that the laser cut a straight and steady path, another ensured the laser's cooling units operated at optimal capacity, and the third operated the gearing mechanism that controlled the laser's forward momentum.

This left Rossi with three men to take care of the safety deposit boxes. Theft was a heinous sin, but rightful plunder in times of war was a duty, and the three men had worked hard to disable the alarm system. Rossi watched as the three faithful brothers used pneumatic jacks to crack open the safety deposit boxes. After each one popped, the men emptied the contents into large sacks, without even looking at what they were taking. The bounty would be valued later, and then sold to support the Brotherhood's ongoing struggle.

Rossi's radio alerted him to an incoming call, and he checked the small LCD display, which identified the caller.

"Two, this is four," Rossi said, "go ahead."

"How much longer?" Two responded.

Rossi checked the gamma image on a scanner that was mounted on a nearby tripod. It showed the laser beam's progress through the inner vault doors.

"Ninety minutes," Rossi replied. "No more."

"The human body can withstand more punishment than most people expect. If you're prepared to learn how to cope with the pain, you can train your body to keep going until you drop."

Pierce smiled as he remembered the words of his combat instructor at the Academy. He had served in the Special Forces first battalion for two years before he had joined the Agency, so he had thought he had known all about pain. But neither the Academy or the army had prepared him for what he felt right now. His bones ached to their very marrow, and he felt that if he did not keep moving, his joints would seize. His heart raced with the simple effort of keeping him upright, and it felt like an overwhelming pressure was crushing his brain. His eyelids were heavy, but he bit his tongue intermittently to ensure they stayed open.

The airbags had exploded the moment the cruiser had made contact with the wall at the foot of the subway steps, but even they could not completely protect Pierce from an eighty-mile per hour impact. He could feel the stabbing sensation of a broken rib. He tried to ignore the stinging sensation coming from his lacerated left arm. And he endured the burning tingles of dozens of wounds on his face, arms and torso, which had been cut by the cruiser's shattered windows. The most recent injuries melded with the ones he had received in the SUV crash and the gunshot wounds to make every step a journey through agony. Pierce knew he was a mess; he only hoped he could keep it together long enough to thwart the Spider.

After the crash, Pierce had used a tire iron to force open the metal gate to the 34th Street station. He had jumped the barriers and descended the stationary escalators to the platforms. Once he had entered the darkness of the northbound tunnel, Pierce felt he was safe - at least temporarily. With all communications cut and the police subverted, Pierce believed his only chance was to get off the island and get to the nearest Agency office in Union City.

All corporations operating under a Sentry contract had to provide details of their communication protocols to Washington. The Department of Homeland Security had initially been reluctant to provide Belle with the algorithm for Resolute's frequency modulator but she had called in a favor from a senior official and had received what she needed within five minutes.

The algorithm generated a random number, which corresponded to a pre-assigned digital frequency. A central processor that was connected to the microwave damper that blocked all other radio signals in New York sent details of the new frequency to every radio on the Resolute network. Every thirty seconds the entire Resolute radio network switched to a new frequency, which made tracking and hacking it almost impossible without the algorithm.

Belle had used the algorithm to listen in on Resolute communications. She had heard the dispatch calls of ambulance and fire service control rooms, which had all been given Resolute radios to communicate with their teams in the field. Belle had grown bored by all the unit chatter that volleyed back and forth, as various Resolute units discussed their deployment. Finally she had heard a call that got her attention; the alert that Scott Pierce had escaped from the 10th Precinct and should be shot on sight.

Belle had put a call in to Resolute headquarters to inform them that the man they were hunting was an Agency operative. She had been told that neither John Creed nor Sam Solomon were available to talk to her, and that it had been Solomon himself who had issued the orders on engagement for Pierce's pursuit. The calls during the ensuing chase had become increasingly frantic, and she had feared for Pierce's life. His evasion and subsequent escape came as something of a relief to the entire team, who had kept up with events when Belle had piped the Resolute signal through the speakers in the operations room.

After the chase, Belle had noticed something strange. A secondary radio signal was piggy-backing on the Resolute frequency. The broadcast duration and pattern had suggested a short conversation, but whatever the signal was, it operated using a one-thousand-and-twenty-eight bit encryption, which was theoretically impossible to crack.

Belle liked a challenge and used a recording of the encrypted broadcast to help her build a key program that would enable her to listen in on this concealed signal. As she sat at her computer terminal writing code, Belle wondered who had hijacked Resolute's signal and what they were saying that was so secret.

"If you had to pick one," Streeter insisted.

"I could give a fuck."

Angel insisted on giving the guys a hard time. As one of the few female platoon commanders within the company, she had a reputation for toughness that needed to be maintained.

"If I may say, ma'am, you're being fucking difficult," Streeter observed.

"Watch your mouth, Streeter."

Angel scanned the immobile vehicles that faced her on the Manhattan side of the Lincoln Tunnel barricade. She and the men had dispersed the drivers just over half-an-hour ago when the order came through from command. Those citizens without anywhere to go were offered refuge in temporary holding pens the company had established on the edge of Central Park. Whatever the heck was happening, the brass was obviously taking it very seriously.

"The Audi," Angel said finally.

"The Z9. Nice pick," Streeter said as he searched for the vehicle's specifications on his Resolute PDA.

The weird thing about service, Angel thought, was the extremes it demanded. One moment she could be called upon to kill or to die herself, the next she would be sitting around on her ass with nothing to do. The contrast between the mundane and the breathtaking was the most difficult part of the job, and many soldiers struggled with it. So they looked for ways to distract themselves, like playing top trumps with the abandoned vehicles that spread out before them.

"You win, ma'am," the voice floated through the still night air. "The Z9 has a top speed of one-eighty-seven."

"When are you men going to realize there's nothing I can't whip you at?"

The second voice belonged to the woman who sat on the hood of one of the Cougar Armored Personnel Vehicles that blocked the mouth of the Lincoln Tunnel.

There were a dozen heavily armed mercenaries stationed at strategic points around her. If she was in charge of the unit, Pierce concluded, she was good. She had set up her lookouts to ensure that there was no way of approaching the tunnel without being spotted. Each man doubled up his line of fire with another, so they had redundancy when it came to their kill zone. Pierce had lost his pistol in the car crash and knew there was no way he could handle these guys unarmed.

He had stumbled through the pitch dark of the subway tunnels, safe in the knowledge that no trains ran at that hour. What had seemed like a good idea could easily have led to his death. The city did not waste energy lighting the subterranean routes under the island, so there had been no way for him to navigate.

"You a friend?" Pierce had heard the voice call out to him from the darkness.

"I need help," he had replied, and in response there came light.

An old flashlight had shone in his face and Pierce had seen two silhouettes behind it, one tall and thin, and the other rotund.

"What's your name?" The tall one had asked.

"Scott Pierce."

"I'm Grundy, and this is Wallace."

Grundy had indicated the fat guy.

"I think we should eat him," Wallace had said.

Pierce had tensed, ready to face whatever came next.

"Relax, he's kidding" Grundy had said. "We're not cannibals, just bums."

In exchange for his watch, Wallace and Grundy, two hobos who had been living under the city for more than ten years, had been willing to supply Pierce with an old flashlight and directions to the Lincoln Tunnel. But now that he had reached his destination, Pierce saw that his efforts had been wasted. The Spider had subverted Resolute as part of his plan and had ensured that there was no way off the island. Pierce was running out of time and options. He needed to find someone who was beyond corruption, but it needed to be a person who had the power to effect change. Someone with the reach to take on the Spider and his cohorts. As Pierce lowered himself back into the storm drain a hundred yards away from the checkpoint, he wondered whether what he was about to do would get him killed.

CHAPTER 26

Pierce remembered the address from the background checks he did on all his business associates. He stood in the archway of an old stone building on West 45th Street and watched the apartment block opposite. It was a sixty storey, expensive piece of post-Obaman real estate, constructed during the final hurrah before things finally turned sour for good. The entire facade was fabricated from glass and steel, a style that offered each apartment floor-to-ceiling windows and the great views that went with them.

A police patrol car turned into the street, and Pierce stepped back into the shadows. The two officers scanned the area, and although they moved slowly, showed no signs of stopping. When they had passed up the street and out of sight, Pierce stepped from his hiding place and crossed the road. He typed an apartment number into an intercom keypad and heard a ringtone. Pierce looked directly at the small fisheye video camera that was part of the intercom security system. After almost a minute, his intrusion was answered.

"What the fuck do you want?"

"I need your help," Pierce said.

"Fuck you!"

"I can make the charges go away."

If this did not work Pierce was out of options; there was no back-up plan. After an interminable pause, the buzzer sounded and Pierce pulled the front door open.

When he walked out of the elevator onto the fortieth floor, Pierce was greeted by a hard punch in the gut. The two apes that had accompanied him down in the elevator in Chicago were waiting for him, and their master, Sullivan stood behind them with a big wide smile on his face.

"You look like shit," Sullivan leered, as the second ape smacked Pierce in the mouth.

The pain was not what pissed him off. Pierce was simply fed up with the disrespect. Ape two came in for another punch, but Pierce ducked inside the sweeping fist as it whistled through the air, and rabbit-punched Two Ape in the Adam's apple. One Ape tried to grab him but Pierce sidestepped and kneed the guy in the groin. There was no point pretending he was in a clean-fighting mood. As both lumbering apes struggled for breath, Pierce approached Sullivan.

"They touch me again and they die," Pierce was very matter-of-fact. "Now do you want to talk business or what?"

"You'd better come in."

Sullivan walked through the double doors that led to his apartment, which was the only one on the floor. Pierce followed, and walked through a small entrance hall that opened onto a two thousand foot open plan living area, which had panoramic views of the city on three sides. For three years Pierce had been the Brotherhood's main importer of heroin into the United States. On paper he had made hundreds of millions of dollars, but in reality the Agency only let him keep what was necessary to maintain appearances. As he walked across Sullivan's living room, Pierce got a taste of the material wealth a real drug dealer could accumulate. Everything was exquisite, from the expensive artwork that dotted the room, to the state-of-the-art speakers that Pierce could see recessed in the walls and ceiling tiles.

Sullivan sat in a cream leather armchair and offered Pierce the matching couch opposite.

"I got to hand it to you," Sullivan began, "you're good. My people are very thorough, and you beat their checks. You a narc?"

"Agency. Six years ago I was Europe section chief working out of London. My wife was killed in the Eurostar bombing."

Pierce paused for a moment. Sullivan was the enemy, a man he had just helped bust, and here he was about to share detailed classified information with him. Until eighteen months ago Sullivan had purchased all his stock from the Fong Fong Boys, a Chinese syndicate that had a line into production in Cambodia. The Agency had shut the Fong Fong operation down, which had created the space for Pierce to step into.

He had followed his standard pattern of undercutting every other supplier and providing the purest quality product. Once the wholesaler felt comfortable, Pierce would up the volumes by offering no money down terms that were too attractive to resist. Every transaction would be monitored by the Agency, which was collecting evidence for future prosecutions. Pierce had been of the belief that they should hold off busting minor players like Sullivan until they had found the Spider, but Washington needed to make its bones. The Agency had to justify the continued investment with a few small successes, so every now and again someone like Sullivan would be reeled in to take a hit. It was risky, but if nobody he did business with ever got busted, that might have looked even more suspicious. They had tried to tread the line carefully, but as Azzam had informed him in Cairo, even the Agency's best efforts had not been good enough.

In normal circumstances Sullivan was the last person Pierce would confide in, not least because the man now had a vested interest in seeing him suffer. But these were not normal circumstances and Pierce recognized that he had run out of options.

"The Agency arranged for me to go deep cover. I was set up as a drug dealer who had been busted on charges of tax evasion. I served two years in Marianna where I saved the life of a man called Idris Rahim, a drug dealer and recruiter for the Sons of September. While I was inside, the Agency hit their drug network hard, which created a need for new blood. My cover made me the perfect candidate and Rahim vouched for me with his masters. When I got out of jail they gave me the central region, but the Agency took out the competition, and soon the Brotherhood gave me control of the entire American operation. All the time I was edging closer and closer to the heart of the organization, hunting the man who was responsible for my wife's death. A man called Kamal Al Karim, otherwise known as the Spider. I believe he's here in New York and that the Brotherhood has taken control of Resolute Corporation in order to launch a major terror attack."

Sullivan considered what he had just heard.

"Why the fuck should I believe you?"

Pierce stared at Sullivan and held his gaze.

"You know how careful you are. You're too smart to get busted by just anyone. I must be Agency, right? And if I'm Agency, what the hell am I doing coming to your apartment asking for help? The only possible reason is that there is a real and imminent danger, and I don't have another soul in this city that I can turn to."

"I help you, and you get the charges dropped?"

Pierce nodded. If they were alive when this was all over, Pierce had no doubt he would be able to convince the Agency to cut Sullivan loose.

If Pierce has any sense, Karim thought, he will stay in the sewers where he belongs. All Resolute personnel and every police officer in the city had been provided with his photograph, so there was little chance of him moving more than a few blocks on the surface without being captured.

Karim and his men had returned to the command center, where Lopez and the rest of the staff coordinated and monitored the quarantine.

"General Caldwell on line one," a communications officer called out.

Karim picked up nearest phone.

"General Caldwell, this is Sam Solomon."

"Where's John?"

Caldwell was Resolute's three star Pentagon liaison and it would be beneath him to talk to a second-in-command.

"He's conducting an inspection of our positions, sir. I can try to raise him for you, but it might take some time."

"Forget it. Listen, Sam, I'm getting it in the neck for this whole lockdown thing. The White House says it's got to be lifted."

"Sir, we've had an attack on one of the city's banks, and a second on a police precinct. The key suspect in these attacks is on the loose somewhere in the city and we have no idea how many cells we're dealing with. If we reopen the city, there's no telling what might happen. Please tell the White House to be patient. We're doing our best."

"Give me something I can go back to them with, Sam."

"Two hours, sir. I can guarantee this will all be over within two hours," Karim said. Then he put down the phone and approached Lopez.

"How are we doing?"

"Latest reports suggest we'll be done within the hour. Apart from number four's team. They're a little behind schedule."

If Karim had not been more experienced in these matters, he might have cursed Pierce and his interference. As it was, he knew that there was always an unexpected element on any mission. The key to success was to be able to neutralize that element as quickly as possible, which is exactly what he had done.

The asshole had some nerve, Sullivan thought, first he gets him involved with fucking terrorists, then he gets him busted and now the guy wants him to help clean up the mess. If things did not work out, at least he would know where to lay hands on Pierce to make sure the man suffered.

It was not politically correct to drive a gas powered SUV, but Sullivan did not give a flying fuck about the environment, and his almost unlimited income meant that gas prices were of no consequence to him. In his line of work it was very useful to have a large high-powered vehicle, and the late model Escalade did just fine.

If the Resolute mercenary disapproved, he did not show it. He simply checked the identities shown on his scanner against the faces of the three men in the car. Sullivan's two bodyguards were in the front seats and he was in the back. One of the mercenary's comrades came round to Sullivan's window and gave his comrade the thumbs up.

"Car's clean," the comrade said, indicating a gamma image of the SUV on his scanner.

"You're free to go," the mercenary said, and he waved Sullivan's vehicle forward.

The SUV passed through the 23rd Street checkpoint and headed into New York's Port Authority Complex.

Desperation makes fools of us all and Scott wondered whether he had placed too much trust in the paroled kingpin. He concentrated on his breathing as a way of stemming any feelings of panic he might experience. They had come to a halt for a second time on the short journey, and Pierce questioned whether he was about to be greeted by the muzzle of a silenced weapon, his body to be disposed of in the murky depths of the Hudson. Instead, when the hatch to the secret compartment was opened, Two Ape offered Pierce a hand out, which he accepted.

The big man pulled Pierce free of the small space that was hidden under the Escalade's rear seats. It must have cost a fortune to have the four-by-two-by-

176

three feet space lined with palladium, but when a person is in the business of smuggling contraband, that investment would have yielded dividends; palladium was the only material that blocked gamma rays and returned a false negative on any vehicle scan. If they got out of this the Agency would be interested to know that at least one dealer had sourced sufficient quantity of the rare metal to construct such a hiding place. And where there was one, there was usually more.

Pierce followed Sullivan into the Port Authority offices of the International Package Corporation. Sullivan was an extremely astute player. He had worked out that a courier company was the perfect front for a heroin distributor. It provided him with a legitimate source of income in which he could bury his illicit one. And it gave him a readymade trafficking network. When Pierce had first made the connect, the Agency had nothing on this four-hundred-million dollar a year operation. Sullivan was simply known as a successful businessman who had purchased a ramshackle courier company at a time when all the sensible money was exiting the transportation business. Over a ten year period he had turned it into one of the fastest growing companies in America. A rare success story in a time of unparalleled economic gloom.

They walked through the deserted reception area, and Sullivan used a pass to open the security door that led to the warehouse area at the back. The dispatch warehouse was dominated by metal framed shelves that were stacked high with parcels. In a small staff area, they found three uniformed employees – their nametags said Chuck, Brad and Winston – playing poker.

Pierce noticed a two foot framed portrait photograph of Sullivan on the warehouse wall above the coffee station, and saw the man in a new light. Like all eminent chief executives, Sullivan understood the power of the cult of personality. As they entered, Pierce saw Brad look from Sullivan to the photograph and back again. He stood up so fast that Pierce thought the guy was going to snap to attention and throw in a salute for good measure.

"Mister Sullivan?"

"Where's your manager?" Sullivan asked.

Chuck and Winston had joined Brad on their feet.

"He got stuck on the other side of the quarantine," Winston offered.

"You think these guys are enough?" Sullivan asked Pierce.

"They're what we've got," Pierce said.

Sullivan took a folded handwritten note out of his inside jacket pocket and walked over to the photocopier, which was next to the coffee station. Pierce caught the man looking at his own portrait, as the machine spewed out dozens of replicas of Sullivan's original missive.

"I want you to deliver these to each and every one of our major Manhattan accounts," Sullivan said, as he handed Brad a stack of copies. Pierce realized the phrase 'major account' was a euphemism for Sullivan's drug buyers.

177

Sullivan looked at Pierce with discomfort.

"We're off the record here, right?"

Pierce nodded, and Sullivan turned back to the three men.

"Tony Vincenzo in Little Italy, Reggie Cannon in Harlem, Alfons Gomez in Nuyorica, Mulligan at the Seventeenth Precinct."

Pierce raised an eyebrow at the last name, but was not surprised to hear that Sullivan had cops selling his product.

"The Suey Sing Boys in Chinatown – get the word out to everyone."

Brad finished reading Sullivan's letter.

"Is this true?"

"Every word," Pierce said. "The city is in grave danger."

Chuck, Brad and Winston split the copies between them, and left the warehouse through the door that led to the loading depot. Pierce joined Sullivan at the window and the two men watched the three couriers jump on their electric motorcycles and speed into the hot summer night.

"What now?" Sullivan asked Pierce.

"I need a gun," Pierce replied.

The New York kingpin smiled.

CHAPTER 27

The encryption had been hard enough to crack but when she discovered that much of the coded radio traffic was in Arabic, Belle had been forced to send for the duty translator. The signals, which were hidden within the Resolute frequency, were fairly infrequent, and originated from a number of locations around Manhattan – Belle had pinpointed seven within New York's financial district.

After a twenty minute delay, Farida, the translator arrived. Belle had planned to play back tapes of earlier communications, but as Farida sat down next to her, a fresh broadcast started between one of the positions Belle had already identified near Wall Street, and a new, unknown location. Belle worked on pinpointing the new coordinates, while Farida translated the Arabic voices she could hear in the decoded communication.

"How much longer, the caller is asking. He identifies himself with the code name number two. The other man says fifteen minutes and identifies himself as number six."

"Is that it?" Belle asked, and Farida nodded.

Fifteen minutes until what, Belle wondered, as the satellite system triangulated the caller's position. The system narrowed its search to the south of Manhattan, then it went further down the map, until it finally pinpointed the radio signal to Governor's Island. Belle checked the system calibration, but knew there was nothing wrong with the machine. Once she had reconciled herself to the fact that the concealed radio signal had originated from Resolute's headquarters on Governor's Island, Belle's imagination started to run wild. If the Brotherhood had managed to infiltrate the Sentry program, anything was possible.

As she stepped away from her desk, Belle hoped that the duty agent-in-charge had the good sense to act fast. She headed for the door.

"If anyone wants me, I'm going upstairs."

Karim admired the New York skyline through the windows of the command center. Even robbed of the sparkling artificial lights that had once made it seem so alive, the city still impressed him. It represented the pinnacle of human ingenuity, one that would probably never be reached again. At least not in his lifetime. What they were about to do would set America back a thousand years, and the rest of the world hundreds. In precarious times it did not take much to send a nation to hell. His plan would have crippled a strong nation but America was already unraveling and would feel its effects a hundredfold. By the time they had dragged themselves back from the abyss, the geo-political map would have changed forever and he and his people would have established an Islamic caliphate that stretched from southern Europe to the tip of Asia.

Six had informed him that his team would be finished in fifteen minutes. The other teams were not far behind. Karim walked over to Darweesh who monitored reports from Resolute units in the city.

"Start preparing the men. It will soon be time for us to leave."

It was approaching midnight and the city was eerily quiet. Angel wondered how much longer they would have to keep the bridges and tunnels sealed. Without the routine of checking vehicles, her men were becoming increasingly distracted. Even Streeter had given up trying to entertain them with his repertoire of games, which was a bad sign. She considered sending some of the platoon on patrol, but her orders had been clear; secure the tunnel at all costs and stay put.

She heard an indistinct distant buzz, which sounded like it was getting closer. The noise echoed around the buildings that towered over the tunnel entrance, and after a moment she remembered where she had heard it before. It was an electric motorcycle, the kind the rich teenagers used to ride in Baghdad. The bike came into view, its lone rider picking his way through the stationary vehicles that blocked the entrance to the tunnel. Angel sensed that this was no ordinary traveler and jumped down from the Cougar's roof to meet him. She approached the barrier that blocked the tunnel entrance and arrived at the same time as the motorcyclist, a confident man in an expensive suit.

"Sir," Angel said, aware that her men had perked up at the arrival of this unexpected traveler, "the tunnel is closed until further notice."

A sound began to echo around the tunnel entrance. Angel could not identify the noise, which reminded her of distant thunder. She looked up at the cloudless sky, and then turned her attention to the motorcyclist.

"My name is Richard Sullivan," the man said, "and I am American citizen. You have no right to restrict my movements."

"I suggest you return home, sir."

The distant thunder grew louder, and Angel started to feel uneasy that she could not identify it. The rumbling was the sort of noise that presaged the arrival of something primal.

Sullivan looked down at his bike, as though he was deep in thought and then said, "You're either part of the problem, or you're part of the solution."

Angel did not like the man's tone, and she found his confidence deeply unsettling. Most people were on edge around armed personnel. This guy acted as though he could not give a damn. And that noise, it was growing louder, which unnerved Angel. She could tell by the way her men were looking around that it also agitated them.

"Sir, I've been very patient with you," Angel said. "Streeter, take this gentleman into custody."

Sullivan took no notice of Streeter's approach.

"Are you going to open this tunnel? Or am I going to have to make you?"

Streeter grabbed Sullivan's arm and asked, "You and whose army?"

Angel saw the look of shock cross Streeter's face and looked down to see Sullivan pressing a machine pistol into the folds between Streeter's body armor.

Sullivan looked directly at Angel and answered Streeter's question.

"New York's."

The thunder became a roar, as hundreds of citizens marched into view, cresting the lip of the tunnel ramp. New Yorkers of all ages, ethnicity and backgrounds advanced on the checkpoint. Policemen, firefighters and paramedics walked alongside gangsters, hoodlums, and thugs. Union workers marched in step with bosses, workers with their employers. Some of them carried weapons, and they all walked towards the Resolute mercenaries in a show of New York's strength and solidarity.

"I suggest you tell your men to throw down their guns," Sullivan said to Angel.

Angel considered the odds and knew it would be pointless to resist. Doing so would lead to the deaths of innocent citizens, and that was not part of her job. If the bosses on Governor's Island wanted the tunnel closed that badly, they could come down here and do the dirty work themselves.

"Drop your weapons," Angel said, as her men were accosted by the army of New Yorkers.

"Wise move," Sullivan said.

He handed his pistol to one of the citizens, a man in a courier's uniform.

"You guys did good," Sullivan told the man, before he kicked the bike into gear.

Two groups of citizens took hold of Angel and Streeter, and other men and women started to move vehicles out of the way to clear the route through the tunnel. Sullivan twisted the throttle and weaved his way through the barricade. Angel watched him disappear into the dark tunnel mouth and wondered where he wanted to go so badly.

The man seated behind the desk looked like a genuine security guard. He was in uniform, he had his feet up and was reading something off a PDA. If Pierce had not recognized him as one of the Resolute mercenaries who had gunned down the Citibank staff earlier in the night, he might have felt uncertain about taking the shot. As it was, he looked down the telescopic sight of the M40 Series 6 that Sullivan had given him and centered the crosshairs on the man's forehead. A solid and steady squeeze of the trigger, and the silent bullet covered the distance between Pierce's place of concealment behind the low plaza wall and the mercenary's head in a split second. It shattered one of the glass panels that encased the Citibank lobby and spread much of the man's brains across the reception wall.

Pierce dropped the sniper's rifle and slung a Heckler & Koch MG7 machine-gun with inbuilt grenade launcher over his shoulder. He ran across Citibank Plaza and stepped through the vacant frame of the shattered window. Pierce pulled a swipe card from the body of the dead mercenary and ran to the emergency stairs that led down to the vault. He checked the door frame for booby traps before he ran the swipe card through the reader, pulled the door open, and stepped slowly and silently down the stairs.

Belle had given Oscar her best interpretation of the intel. If the guy across the desk from her did not have the imagination to put the pieces together, that was his problem, but Belle had already decided that one way or another, Oscar was going to act. Oscar Donnelson was in his mid-fifties and most people viewed him as a stout yeoman. Good at his job, but not stellar. He had taken thirty years to become an agent-in-charge and was unlikely to rise any higher. In the Catlin's absence, he was Belle's reporting superior.

"You think Pierce has been framed?" Oscar checked one more time.

He was clearly nervous about the chain of events that would be sparked by taking Belle's information seriously. Belle nodded.

"The concealed signal originates at Resolute headquarters, which means the Spider has a man on the inside, or is on the inside himself. The whole lockdown could be bullshit designed to help them with whatever the hell they've got planned."

Oscar remained unconvinced.

"If I'm wrong about this, Oscar, they'll write you up in your next performance review," Belle said. "But if I'm right, and you do nothing, I'll make sure they bring you up on charges."

Belle held his gaze to make sure he knew she was serious. Oscar had been in the business long enough to know not to take things personally, and laughed the empty chuckle of a cynic.

"Well that makes my decision a whole lot easier," Oscar said as he picked up the phone.

"We've got a problem," Lopez said as he looked up from his console. "Lincoln Checkpoint is not responding to any calls."

Angel was a reliable soldier, Karim thought as he crossed the command center. She was a good commander and an upright citizen, and Karim cursed every decent fiber of her being. Much as he would have liked to, he had not been able to entirely staff the battalion with insiders – the numbers were just impossible. Of the thousand or so personnel he had under his command in New York, fifty knew the genuine purpose of the mission, and a further three hundred believed they were part of a massive heist – their loyalty purchased with a percentage of the proceeds. That left six hundred and fifty genuine mercenaries who were not

182

in on the plan in any way, and who could only be ordered, manipulated or cajoled into playing their part. Karim regretted his inability to stretch the insiders to cover all of the bridge and tunnel commands. Angel was one of the straightheads and Karim doubted that she, like many of the commanders, would possess the ruthlessness to follow orders and use force to prevent the citizens of New York from breaking the quarantine.

"Dispatch the nearest unit to investigate," Karim ordered Lopez.

Pierce peered through the crack between the open door and the wall. Ahead of him he could see the large doors of the outer vault, which were now fully retracted. Beyond them, inside the outer vault, a large laser drill emitted a brilliant light as it cut through the inner vault door. Three men operated the drill, a fourth supervised, while two other men used some kind of tools to force open two of the many safety deposit boxes that lined the walls of the outer vault.

His breathing steady, Pierce slowly opened the door and stepped through. The MG7 was held high, stock against his shoulder in a reflexive firing position. He crossed the vault's granite floor silently, in an attempt to get a better line of sight on the men who were on the other side of the laser. None of the men had registered his presence, and soon he would be in a position to take them all down unimpeded.

Whether it was the change in air pressure or the almost imperceptible sound of the hinges rotating, Pierce could not say, but something tripped his razor sharp senses to the presence of a sixth man who entered the vault lobby from the men's room behind him. Pierce swiveled on the spot and opened fire at the man who barely had time to register shock at the sight of the unwelcome intruder, before the bullets hit his chest and he dropped to floor, dead.

As the sound of automatic fire echoed around the vault, Pierce turned again and fired a sweeping burst of bullets in the direction of the inner vault. He hit two men, one in the chest, the other in the leg, and the move bought him enough time to dive for cover in the stairwell. The door slammed shut behind him, and gave him a temporary sanctuary in which to think.

Intermingled with the screams of the injured man, Pierce could hear one of the hostiles talking to someone in Arabic.

"Two, this is four. We are under attack!"

"I repeat, we are under attack!"

Karim held his coded radio in disbelief. He could hear the screams of a wounded man in the background.

"I'm on my way," Karim replied. "Hold the position."

If they lost one of the targets, the whole mission would fail, and Karim was not about to let that happen. He addressed Darweesh.

"Assemble Alpha squad on the landing pad immediately. We're leaving."

"We have another problem," Lopez called out from across the room.

Karim patted Darweesh on the shoulder to indicate that he would catch up with his subordinate, and the man hurried from the room.

"What?" Karim said, his patience wearing thin.

"We've lost the Lincoln Tunnel." Lopez wished he had better news for his boss.

Mason sat in the passenger seat of the armored scout vehicle and held the night-vision field glasses to his eyes. A quarter of a mile ahead of him he could see vehicles moving freely through the Lincoln Tunnel. A motley crew of armed civilians had confiscated the Resolute vehicles and stood guard over their conquests; two Cougars, a couple of jeeps, an Abrams and a platoon of Resolute personnel. The thirteen men and one woman were seated near the tunnel mouth, and had their hands and feet bound. Mason's radio crackled into life.

"This is commander Solomon, what's the situation down there?"

Mason thought the boss sounded pissed. With good reason; people seizing control like this was the start of anarchy.

"We've got eyes on the tunnel, sir. Our people have been taken prisoner and their assailants have opened the tunnel in both directions. It looks like word is spreading. Traffic flow has increased in both directions since we got here."

Karim cursed the graves of the people who had dared stand up to him. Pierce had probably already got off the island but it would take him time to get help. Karim intended to make it as difficult as possible for any assistance to get to Manhattan. If the insurrection spread, the citizens would soon grow bold and take control of all the bridges and tunnels. That could not be allowed to happen.

"Instruct 'B' Company to retake the position," Karim ordered Lopez.

"Sir, the mission is almost complete," Lopez objected weakly.

Karim could see the man had no stomach for action, which is why he hid behind a computer.

"You heard me," Karim said.

Lopez turned and relayed the order to captain Mandel, the commander of 'B' Company. The man was another straighthead, but his deputy, who was going under the name Eduardo, was a loyal Brother. Eduardo would ensure that Karim's orders were followed.

"I'm going to deal with the problem at Citibank. Keep things running smoothly, Lopez. All our futures depend on it."

Karim rushed out of the command center, sprinted across the landing pads to join Alpha Squad in the waiting G20. The instant he was aboard, the graviton engines powered up and the jet rose into the sky.

CHAPTER 28

Sullivan rode up to the security checkpoint outside the Federal Building in Union City. An Agency security officer scanned him and the bike, before waving him through towards the concrete monstrosity that sprawled out over a five block area. The low level buildings clustered around a single steel and glass monolith that towered seventy five storeys into the sky. Sullivan roared up to the skyscraper's main entrance, dropped the bike where he stopped, and hurried inside. He passed through a second security check without incident and walked across the large lobby to a desk, where a pretty night receptionist sat reading a book. She looked up at him, as he approached.

"Can I help you, sir?"

"I need to speak to the ranking FSA agent on duty. And I need you to wake the US Attorney attached to this office."

He was outnumbered, but he had the better position, which counted for a hell of a lot. The solid steel stairwell security door was bulletproof and provided impenetrable cover whenever Pierce needed to reload. The hostiles had nothing but the laser drill to shield them, and they were about to find out just how effective that was.

Pierce could hear the jackhammer thuds of bullets striking the steel door. The intimidating noise echoed around the stairwell. He checked the grenade launcher on the MG7 and waited for a lull in fire. If they were professional, the hostiles would use this time to reposition themselves around the vault and make his job more difficult. The jackhammer stopped, and his enemies invited him to poke his head into the vault. Pierce ran the security swipe card through the reader and put his weight against the door, ready to push.

The first thing they did not expect was Pierce's low position. He was on his back, gun held between his knees, and used his feet to kick open the door. The advantage of this firing position was that it gave his enemies a very small target and if they hit anything, it would be feet and butt first. Pierce meanwhile had unrestricted ability to shoot, and he did so, giving the hostiles the second thing they did not expect; a high explosive grenade.

As the enemies' bullets hit high on the door and walls around him, Pierce fired the MG7's grenade launcher directly at the laser drill. The two able and one injured man tried to dive for cover, but there was nowhere for them to go. The high explosive grenade hit the drill and there was a blinding flash and powerful blast, which destroyed the laser and killed all three men. Gunfire from a different direction told Pierce that two of the hostiles had moved and had taken up positions near the vault elevator. Pierce rolled inside the stairwell and allowed

185

the door to slam shut behind him.

They had been minutes away from completing the drilling. Rossi was incandescent with rage. This intruder threatened the entire mission with his pointless violence. He would soon die and they would get another drill from one of the other targets. The destruction of the drill had angered Rossi more than the deaths of his men, who would now be feted as martyrs in paradise.

As he squatted in the elevator archway with his last man, Rossi sighted his weapon low. Let the intruder try and trick them with his strange shooting position. Rossi signaled for his comrade to do the same. They waited quietly, neither wishing to waste any more ammunition on noisy theatrics.

If they were smart, they would have occupied the ground either side of the doorway by now. It was the only guaranteed killzone in the vault. As he sat and listened for clues in the silence, Pierce weighed up whether to gamble on them being smart or stupid. There had been no sounds of movement, and Pierce doubted whether they had been trained for close urban engagement, so he decided to gamble on stupidity.

He slid the swipe card through the reader and kicked the door open. Gunfire erupted the moment the door opened, and the direction of bullet strike told him the men had remained in their positions by the elevator. When they realized he had not come through the door, the firing stopped. As the last of the gunshots echoed around the stairwell, Pierce sprinted through the doorway and dropped to his knees. The momentum he had built up carried him sliding across the hard floor. As he travelled, Pierce opened fire and strafed the elevator. Both targets dropped before they were able to get a shot off.

Pierce got to his feet and checked his surroundings. The hostiles were dead, and whatever they had planned to do was over. Now all Pierce had to do was wait for Sullivan to deliver.

Belle had listened to Oscar put calls into the director of intelligence and the Agency liaisons at the Pentagon and the White House. He had promised to keep her posted, before he had ushered her from the office to give himself a moment's peace to prepare for the storm that would come. Both he and Belle knew how these situations worked; calls would be made and the wheels would start to turn slowly, but they would soon gather speed.

She had returned to the operations room and briefed the team, many of whom now took the opportunity to catch some sleep in their seats. She lay on the couch in Catlin's office and pushed thoughts of Liz from her mind. Belle knew that the moment she relaxed she had a tendency to think dark thoughts. She could not afford to go there now because she might be called upon to support whatever the brass decided to do. Instead, Belle wondered where Pierce was at that very moment, and hoped he was coping with the horrific ordeal he had been put through.

"Come on! When are you guys going to stop sitting on your asses and get after the bad guys?"

Sullivan's irritation was genuine. He had very little respect for the law at the best of times, but tonight's experience added even more color to his views than usual.

After explaining himself to a junior agent, Sullivan had been taken to see Alonso Emerson, the duty agent-in-charge of the Union City office. More time was wasted bringing Emerson up to speed. He had issued orders to his subordinates, offered Sullivan coffee, and then they had waited. One by one the three subordinates came back into Emerson's fiftieth floor office and took up positions around the room. Nothing was said; they just watched Sullivan and waited.

"Are you guys deaf?" Sullivan tried.

"Listen mister Sullivan, we have procedure. We can't just act on the say-so of every nut who walks in here."

Emerson noticed the look on Sullivan's face.

"Not that I'm saying you're a nut job."

Emerson's phone rang, and he answered.

"Emerson. Yes, sir, he's here."

The agent-in-charge switched to speakerphone.

"This is US Attorney Dreyfus," said a voice down the line. "You've got some brass balls waking me up with a crazy story like this."

Sullivan leant in to the speaker.

"Let's cut to the chase, Dreyfus. You know who I am and you know that I'm facing some bullshit trafficking charge. We both know I'll do three years, tops. If this story doesn't check out, I'll tell you where the real bodies are buried."

"What?" Dreyfus asked over the phone.

"Resolute turns out to be clean and I'll turn state's evidence. I tell you everything. All my associates, their business operations, my overseas partners and their financiers: everything. It would be a career-making case. Might even help you with that run for mayor that people keep talking about."

Sullivan knew he had given the man at the other end of the line a great deal to think about. The US Attorney would have a heck of a time holding him to that deal, but Sullivan could sense that he had the man on the hook; the prospect of such a prize was too enticing to resist.

"Emerson," Dreyfus said, "call Washington and check it out."

The debris from the explosion was scattered across the vault. Pieces of the laser drill were imbedded in the walls, and the mangled bodies of the three men who had unwisely chosen to take cover behind it were contorted in strange positions. Pierce searched their pockets for identification and found nothing. No labels in their clothes either. He checked the inner vault door and saw that the laser drill had made a deep incision in the thick titanium. Pierce had a suspicion about what lay inside the inner vault and desperately hoped he was wrong.

His attention was distracted by the sound of a radio broadcast that came from one of the bodies near the vault elevator.

"Four, this is two. Come in," a voice said in Arabic.

Pierce approached and rifled through the dead man's pockets for a coded radio, which was still active. The voice at the other end tried again.

"Four, this is two. What's your status?"

Pierce spoke into the radio, "Four's dead."

"They all are," the voice that was broadcast through the radio's loudspeaker had a certain calm finality to it.

Karim turned off his radio and looked out of the grav-jet window with grim determination. Of all the targets to be attacked it was no coincidence that Citibank had fallen. If that had not been Pierce, it was someone associated with him. The man had moved from being a nuisance to a threat. As the G20 raced through the New York sky towards the financial district, Karim considered how best to neutralize the threat.

Brad had never experienced anything like it. He considered himself a competent drinker and had dabbled with drugs soft and hard, but the high he obtained from liberating the tunnel was in a different league. He had taken a huge personal risk to try and change the world, and it had paid off. The sense of euphoria at their total success had still not worn off. He could see from the beaming smiles on Chuck and Winston's faces that they felt the same way, and became conscious that he had been smiling so much, his jaw was aching.

The traffic flowed in both directions through the tunnel, and each vehicle that passed saluted him and his crew of liberators with a toot of the horn. Brad stood on the hood of an armored personnel carrier, with a confiscated machine gun slung over his shoulder. Underworld bosses he knew only by reputation had responded to Sullivan's letter by sending all the men and women they could muster to support the direct action on the tunnel. It demonstrated to Brad just how much suction Sullivan had in town and engendered a new found respect for his employer. Those mustered men and women now guarded the tunnel entrance and kept watch over the captured Resolute mercenaries. Sullivan had instructed them to hold all prisoners to ensure that Resolute did not launch an attack to retake the position.

Winston's was the first smile to waver, then Chuck's and finally Brad's as they heard the deep rumble that could only be caused by a large military convoy. They all looked at the lip of the tunnel ramp a quarter of a mile away and saw the first vehicle, a jeep, come to a halt. It was quickly joined by four armored personnel carriers and two tanks on either side. Brad watched with growing dismay as the tanks directed the barrels of their huge guns in his direction. The makeshift blockade ran across the entire width of the tunnel ramp and stopped the flow of traffic. Brad's euphoria was replaced with a sense of impotence; without firing a shot, Resolute had effectively reinstated the quarantine.

Captain Lloyd Mandel sat in the rear seat of the jeep and watched the men and women who manned the Lincoln Tunnel checkpoint. A ramshackle group of New Yorkers who had obviously been lucky enough to get the jump on the Resolute platoon they now held captive. Untrained as they were, these people did not realize that taking a position was the easy part; holding it was the real challenge. Mandel's simple maneuver had sealed the breach in the quarantine and traffic was now building up on both sides of the barricade.

"I'll take two platoons to re-capture the position," Eduardo Arroyo, Mandel's second-in-command said.

"There's no need," Mandel countered.

"Our orders were clear."

"The tunnel is sealed. We don't have to put the lives of our own people and those citizens down there at risk."

Mandel felt rising discomfort at Eduardo's demeanor; something had changed. Eduardo was usually a pleasant genial deputy and had never questioned his orders. The feeling of hostility emanating from the man sitting next to him made Mandel wonder if he was the same person he had known for the past two years.

"We must make an example," Eduardo said.

Mandel saw the look that passed between Eduardo and the driver and immediately knew that something was very wrong. He acted quickly, punching Eduardo in the face, as the latter drew his sidearm from its holster. The pistol dropped onto the seat, and Mandel grabbed it. Instinctively he fired at the driver, who had drawn his weapon, and hit the man in the neck. The distraction provided Eduardo with an opportunity, and he launched himself at Mandel. As the two men wrestled for supremacy and control of the weapon, Mandel was shocked by the bitterness with which Eduardo fought; there was real hatred in his eyes.

"What are you doing?" Mandel asked in disbelief, just before the gun discharged into Eduardo's chest. The strange man Mandel thought he knew flew backwards and slumped against the far door of the vehicle, dead.

The door behind Mandel opened, and he swiveled, pistol at the ready. He was greeted by the sight of a squad of his men who had rushed to his aid, alerted by the sound of the first gunshot.

"What the fuck just happened?" a shocked Mandel asked nobody in particular.

189

As his men peered into the vehicle and saw the two dead men, Mandel stepped out of the jeep.

"Get these vehicles moved. Until I find out what the hell is going on, I'm with the people of New York. This tunnel stays open."

There was something familiar about the feeling. A subcutaneous burning that coursed throughout his body. Lopez had experienced it just before the Sharm El Sheikh massacre, when his army unit had been ambushed by a company of mujahedeen. It was the feeling of shame and impotence a person experienced once they realized that things were starting to go very badly wrong. He was feeling it now as he listened to Captain Mandel yelling over the radio.

"I don't give a fuck where he is. I want to talk to Colonel Creed right now!"

"I'm sorry, sir," Lopez replied, "he's been taken sick."

"Patch me through to Solomon."

"He's indisposed, sir. You have your orders, sir."

"Fuck this bullshit," Mandel exploded. "Two of my men just tried to kill me. Until I find out what the hell is going on, me and my boys are parked."

The G20 touched down in Citibank Plaza, and Karim stepped out and walked towards the building. The rest of Alpha Squad headed towards one of the buildings opposite.

"Alpha, this is command," Lopez's voice crackled over the radio.

"Go ahead," Karim responded.

"Mandel refuses to proceed. He killed two of his men when they tried to attack him."

Karim was surprised that Mandel had managed to get the better of Eduardo. The old man could not possibly have matched the Brother's passion and speed. Standing orders for any loyal Brothers were to dispose of their commanders at the first signs of trouble and assume command themselves – much as Karim had done with Creed. In Mandel's case it had not worked, and now he had become an enemy within the organization. There was no immediately obvious solution, so Karim decided to keep the troublemaker sidelined.

"Instruct Captain Mandel to hold his position until I make contact with him," Karim ordered Lopez.

The shattered window and dead security guard told Karim how the intruders had infiltrated the Citibank building. As he stepped over broken glass, Karim wondered what treasures his men would find on their prospecting expedition in the building on the other side of the plaza.

The men's room provided the best angle of fire on both the elevator and the stairwell. The dead body that had blocked the doorway had been dragged into one of the stalls, and Pierce lay on his stomach in a prone firing position, his eyes sweeping from elevator to stairwell and back again. Whichever way they came in, they were dead men.

"Captain Mandel, I have new orders for you, sir," Lopez broadcast.

"This should be good," Mandel responded.

"You're to stay where you are until Commander Solomon contacts you."

"Fine with me. Mandel out."

Lopez sighed, but his troubles were not over.

A comms officer yelled from across the room, "Sir, I have Washington on the line. The Federal Security Agency. They want to talk to Colonel Creed."

The discomfort Lopez felt intensified. Solomon needed to get a handle on the situation soon or Lopez was going to bug out – money or no money.

"Stall them," Lopez called back.

"Colonel Creed is inspecting operations, sir," Lopez heard the communications officer say. "I'll have him call you as soon as possible."

The Montecristo No.2 made any situation more palatable, and as Sullivan sat in Emerson's office holding the beautiful Cuban cigar, the interminable wait did not seem quite so bad.

"Who the hell let him smoke in here?" A voice asked from behind him.

Sullivan turned and saw a fat, middle-aged, balding man who had just entered the room.

"Attorney Dreyfus, sir," Emerson said as he stepped from behind his desk, "this is Richard Sullivan."

Sullivan did not bother to stand, and Dreyfus looked like he had not expected him to do so. The fat man seemed to want to ignore him. No doubt he felt acute embarrassment at having to rely on a common drug dealer for such critical intelligence.

Emerson's phone rang and he answered. After a moment he held it out to Dreyfus.

"They want to talk to you, sir."

"This is Dreyfus."

The call lasted no more than thirty seconds but in that time Dreyfus's face ran a gauntlet of emotions. When he finally put down the receiver, his demeanor had become very somber.

"Washington are taking it seriously. They have intelligence from another source that supports his story."

Sullivan warmed to Dreyfus when the US Attorney had the decency to turn to him and say, "Thank you, mister Sullivan. You've done us a great service."

As the magnitude of the situation sank in around the room, Dreyfus turned to Emerson.

"Wake everybody up," he said. "And I mean everyone."

191

Belle must have drifted off to sleep because she opened her eyes to find Oscar shaking her gently. She was stretched out on the couch in Catlin's office, and sat up with a start.

"It's okay," Oscar offered.

Belle checked her mouth and wiped away the trail of drool that told her she had been deep asleep.

"Well?" Belle asked, her voice undulating and croaky.

"They're taking it seriously. The Agency office in Union City called in a report from a man who claims to have been sent there by Pierce. It looks like you were right: Resolute has been subverted."

Belle took a moment to digest the news.

"What happens now?"

"They're scrambling Special Forces from Bragg. We're going to need the coordinates of all the covert radio signals you found."

Belle's mood brightened. She was back in the game, and would be doing something to catch the bastards that killed her boss.

CHAPTER 29

The alert had called for an airborne briefing, which meant they were being scrambled to an urgent and serious situation. Vincent Neimus watched the men of Echo Company, 3rd Group split into their assigned platoons and board one of eight grav-jets laid out on the landing strip ahead of him. The G30 had been specially constructed for Special Forces by Lockheed Martin. The airframe was ten feet longer than the G20 to allow for a larger equipment store, and the aircraft had heavier armor. In order to power the greater mass at higher speed, the G30 was fitted with more powerful graviton engines that could be supercharged by the onboard miniature nuclear reactor that was an exact replica of the model found in the Abrams T1 tank.

Three minutes had elapsed since the call from the Pentagon had come in and they were now ready to take to the skies. Neimus climbed aboard the lead jet and signaled the pilot to take off. As he strapped himself into his jump seat, Neimus felt the powerful vibration of the graviton engines lift the G30 into the sky. The thrusters kicked in, and as he looked out of the adjacent window Neimus saw Fort Bragg fall away into the darkness.

Pierce heard the sound of the elevator descending. When the doors opened, he realized that in order to get a vantage point on both the stairwell and the elevator, he had sacrificed the ability to look inside the elevator. He was able to see one wall and one corner, which covered about a quarter of the elevator's interior. The doors remained open, but nothing happened. Pierce checked the stairwell, but there was no movement there either.

"She doesn't want to come out," a voice called from inside the elevator. "You won't shoot her will you?"

A thin young woman with tawny skin was pushed out of the elevator. She was weeping and stood forlornly, her shoulders sagging with the weight of her worst fears.

"This is Maria. She cleans the building opposite. You have ten seconds to drop your weapons," the voice instructed. "My men have found a steady supply of innocent citizens, so if you refuse to comply, I will shoot Maria and we shall repeat this process until you surrender."

Maria said nothing, but her eyes pleaded with Pierce, who remained in his prone position, gun targeted on the elevator.

"Five seconds."

As long as he held this position, Pierce was preventing them from completing whatever they had planned, but the price of his resistance would be paid in innocent blood. If he refused to negotiate, they would make him complicit in this woman's murder, and Pierce could not live with that. This was the line he was not prepared to cross – there had to be a better way.

"I'm coming out," Pierce said as he stood.

He flipped the safety on the MG7 and tossed it towards the elevator. Maria wept with relief, as the gun clattered against the granite floor.

Pierce recognized the figure who stepped from the elevator as Sam Solomon, the man who had killed Catlin. He burned with rage, as Solomon trained the barrel of a machine-pistol on him.

"It's clear. Just one man," Solomon said into his coded radio.

"You did this alone?" Solomon asked Pierce, as he backed over to inspect the remains of the laser drill. "You're very resourceful. I had expected to find a SWAT team here at the very least – my men were well trained."

Solomon activated his radio.

"Six, this is two. What's your status?"

"We're through. Laying charges now," the call came back in Arabic.

"Good. I need your drill at target one. Have your men bring it immediately."

Four Resolute mercenaries stepped through the stairwell door and encircled Pierce. Solomon holstered his weapon. He approached and stood eye to eye with Pierce.

"Scott Pierce. The man the Agency sent to find me," Solomon observed. "To kill me? Well here I am."

The pressure of the previous eight years - the grief, the rage, the deceit, the fear, the death – bore down on Pierce as he realized who stood opposite him. At that moment he lost all capacity for rational thought and lunged at the man who had called himself Solomon but was in fact Kamal Al Karim. Pierce jumped on Karim like a wild animal and buried his teeth in the man's neck. It took all four of Karim's men to pull Pierce clear, and when he looked at the Spider, Pierce was disappointed to see that he had only inflicted a flesh wound; the body armor around Karim's neck had prevented Pierce from getting a real purchase.

As Karim staggered to his feet and checked the wound on his neck, Pierce was convinced that he had wasted his only opportunity to kill the man. Shame coursed through his body like an electric current as he waited for the expected bullet to the brain. Instead, Karim let out a long and hysterical laugh that bordered on a scream.

"In another life we would be comrades," Karim said at last. "We are the same. I spent years earning my enemy's trust – just as you did. I even had Creed feeding me information from Van Zyl. Your own section chief did not realize that he had become an unwitting asset to the Brotherhood. It was from him that I found out we had a double-agent in our organization."

Pierce struggled against the four men who held him.

"We are driven by a force of will we cannot explain and every day we strive for greatness. Do you feel the darkness, agent Pierce? I do. It is the sadness we suffer when we think of all our unrealized dreams. You and I have so much to give the world, but in our lifetimes we will only get to share a fraction of that gift. Those people out there would never understand. I'm the only one who understands you, agent Pierce. The only real difference between us is that where you have failed, I shall succeed. Tonight the world shall experience a small taste of my dreams."

The elevator doors opened and four Resolute mercenaries pushed two large canvas covered equipment trolleys into the vault lobby.

"Relax, agent Pierce," Karim said. "I want you to fully appreciate what you are about to see."

Metal clicked against metal as the agents in the room checked their weapons. Sullivan counted thirty men and women, who had been roused from their beds and instructed to return to work as a matter of urgency. Murmurs rippled through the room as the agents wondered aloud what could be so important that it required a complete staff mobilization. Stragglers were arriving every minute, and one of Emerson's subordinates stood at the door and provided them with a Kevlar vest and communicator.

Reluctant as he had been to believe Sullivan's story at the outset, Dreyfus had now become a proselyte and was determined that history should record his part in proceedings. He strode to the front of the briefing room and addressed the assembled agents.

"We have reason to believe that Resolute has been infiltrated by a terror cell, and that an attack on Manhattan is in progress as we speak. The terrorists have sealed the island in an attempt to prevent the world learning the truth. Working with units of the Bronx and Brooklyn NYPD and a Federal taskforce from Queens, our job is to retake Manhattan."

"What about Governor's Island?" Sullivan asked from the back of the room.

If Dreyfus was irritated by Sullivan's intervention, he did not show it.

"That's someone else's problem." He turned his attention to the men and women in the room and said, "The city is counting on us. Let's move."

Sullivan admired the professionalism of the agents who hurried from the room. They had just been presented with an impossible situation, had no time to digest it, and were on their way to confront a faceless enemy, all without question. The trust in their superiors was implicit, and Sullivan envied the certainty that gave them. In his world, life was far more ambiguous.

Belle checked the data one final time. She had registered concealed radio broadcasts from a total of nine locations, including Governor's Island. All of the signals originated from buildings in the financial district, and when Belle had checked the addresses, she had discovered that they were all banks. As Belle transmitted the data to the Special Forces communications officer she had been put in contact with, she wondered whether this was all just an elaborate heist. The Sons of September needed money to finance their operations, and those banks were all bullion depositories, holding billions of dollars worth of gold between them. Much as Belle wanted to convince herself that this was just a sophisticated robbery, she knew that it was not the Brotherhood's style. They would have something far more sinister planned.

"I've just sent the location data," Belle spoke into the radio microphone. "It should be with you now."

"Copy that," came the response. Belle could hear the hum of graviton engines in the background.

Belle sat back in her chair and looked at the expectant faces of the men and women in the operations room.

"There's nothing we can do now but wait," Belle told them, as she offered a silent prayer that their intervention would come in time.

The holographic projector displayed an image of Manhattan in the center of the grav-jet, in between the rows of jump seats that lined either side of the fuselage.

"Uploading location data now," the communications office called from the cockpit.

Flashing beacons appeared on the hologram at locations on the southern tip of Manhattan Island. A separate beacon flashed on Governor's Island.

"The FSA suspects we will find hostiles at these locations," Neimus activated his throat microphone and as he spoke, the radio system carried his voice to the hundred-and-twenty concealed earpieces worn by the men and women of Echo Company. The soldiers in the other seven jets were looking at an exact replica of the hologram that was projected in front of him.

"I want squads three and four to take Governor's Island. Squad two, you're with me on Citibank. We have independent confirmation of hostile activity there. Five and six, and seven and eight, you'll take Bank of America and JP Morgan. Our orders are to secure and hold these locations until a full battalion of the Screaming Eagles can get here from Fort Campbell. This is a no risk operation. The use of lethal force has been authorized, and if in doubt, I suggest you use it."

The Resolute mercenaries had cleared the bodies and debris from the outer vault, and had dragged away the mangled chassis of the original laser drill. Pierce had been handcuffed and was being held at gunpoint with Maria near the vault elevator. Three mercenaries covered them with their automatic weapons. Pierce watched Karim, who seemed unfazed by the alteration to his plans. The mastermind behind Eleanor's death and Catlin's murder was content to watch his men finish the clean-up operation.

The elevator doors opened and four men in black boiler suits pushed a second laser drill into the vault. Pierce tried to remain impassive, but his disappointment must have registered.

"You didn't think that was our only drill?" Karim called out to him. "We have plenty of equipment."

One of the men in black approached Karim, as his associates calibrated the drill to continue working on the inner vault doors.

"Peace be upon you, sir," the man said in Arabic.

"Are the other targets ready?" Karim asked.

"As soon as you give the word."

Karim turned his attention to the laser, which was in the process of powering up.

As the brilliant blue light cut deep into the door, Karim asked one of the operators, "How long?"

The man checked the laser drill's digital display.

"Two minutes," came the response. "Three at most."

Brad watched the heavy military hardware with suspicion. After momentarily blockading the tunnel, the tanks and armored personnel carriers had moved to take up positions by the side of the road. Groups of mercenaries clustered around their vehicles and watched the traffic moving freely through the tunnel. There had been no hostile acts on either side, but Brad found it disconcerting to have such a powerful military force stationed a few hundred yards away. Even though he and his group were clearly breaking the law, these mercenaries did nothing; they just watched and waited.

The first thing Brad felt when he saw the red and blue lights illuminate the tunnel mouth was relief. The Federal Security Agency cars passed through the tunnel and came to a halt near the confiscated Resolute vehicles. Brad jumped down from his vantage point and approached the lead car. A number of men exited the vehicle, and a tall man in a suit approached him.

"Agent Emerson, Federal Security Agency," the man said as he extended a hand.

Brad shook it gratefully.

"You guys did good."

Brad recognized Sullivan's voice and saw his boss step out of one the other electric sedans.

Emerson nodded towards the Resolute convoy parked further up the tunnel ramp.

"Trouble?"

"I thought so at first, but now they're just watching. Like they're waiting for something."

A dozens sets of lights flashed in the tunnel mouth ahead of them. As far as he was concerned, his jeep was now a crime scene and needed police attention before it could be used again, so Captain Mandel stood near one of the Abrams with a squad of his men. Mandel watched as men and women exited the vehicles and approached the people who had taken control of the tunnel checkpoint. The badges on the sides of the cars identified them as Federal Security Agency vehicles, which meant the occupants were most likely FSA agents. Mandel considered what might have brought them to the island in such numbers – he counted over thirty agents – and decided that he had to have guidance. He activated his radio.

"Command, this is Mandel, Bravo Company, come in."

After a moment's pause: "This is command, go ahead."

"I'm looking at a convoy of FSA vehicles that has just crossed the Lincoln Tunnel. I need to know what to do if they try to proceed onto the island."

Another pause, then: "One moment Captain Mandel, I'm patching you through to Commander Solomon."

The radio clicked a couple of times, as the connection was made.

"Mandel, this is Solomon, go ahead."

"I've got thirty FSA agents who've just come through the tunnel. I need orders, sir."

"Captain," Solomon said, "we have reason to believe that those are terrorists posing as FSA agents in order to gain access to the island. Your orders are to engage and detain them. Is that clear?"

"Yes, sir," Mandel acknowledged reluctantly.

"And Captain, when you have done that, I want the tunnel cleared of civilians. I don't care how you do it, but you re-establish control of that damned checkpoint, or it will be your career!"

The men around Mandel had the decency to pretend they had not heard the ass chewing, but Solomon's message was clear; Mandel had a career-defining choice to make. As he watched the people at the tunnel checkpoint, Mandel came to a decision.

"Got trouble with the Agency?" Pierce asked. He had heard Karim's exchange with one of his officers.

"Nothing that a little deception and misinformation can't take care of," Karim smiled back at Pierce. "When the scale of the lie is so huge, people simply cannot comprehend it. They will believe what they want to believe. Whatever makes their lives easier. Captain Mandel will try to arrest your agents, and they shall resist. Two sets of good men and women will die because of their mutual mistrust. But I really must not lecture you. Your agency and its predecessors were experts in sowing deceit. All that is happening now is that we are using your methods."

"All to rob a few banks?" Pierce asked hopefully.

Karim's smile never wavered.

"I am not a thief, agent Pierce."

"We're through," one of the men operating the drill yelled.

Pierce heard the solid sounds of a heavy locking mechanism retracting, and the massive door to the inner vault slid open.

Karim stepped into the cool sanctuary, and the three mercenaries holding Pierce and Maria at gunpoint ushered them in behind him. The entire inner vault was lined with brushed titanium and cold air blasted in from vents concealed in the ceiling. At the far end of the inner vault was another titanium door. This one was smaller and less imposing than the one Karim's men had just opened. The walls of the inner vault were lined with eight huge mainframe computer servers. Massively powerful machines with large disk arrays that whirred quietly. Karim stepped up to the first server and gently caressed it.

"The financial backbone of America is run through ten banks," Karim said, confirming Pierce's worst fears. "Eighty percent of all transactions, deposits, stock and financial deals rely on their systems. In 1993 my predecessors bombed the World Trade Center. In 2001 they succeeded in destroying it. All that effort was expended in the belief that if the building came down, it would cripple your economic system. They were naive. They did not understand the fail-safes built into your system. Tonight we shall finish what they set out to achieve. With no financial system, America will tear itself apart."

Karim turned to his men.

"Set the charges."

One of the Resolute mercenaries removed the canvas sheets that covered the equipment trolleys they had brought down earlier, and revealed two four-feet-by-four-feet stacks of high explosive devices.

Pierce noticed that two other mercenaries had approached the small titanium door at the far end of the inner vault. One of them carried a laptop, which he placed on a counter next to the keypad that operated the locking mechanism on the small door.

As his men took the explosive charges off the trolley and attached them to the servers, Karim continued.

"To destroy an empire, one must impoverish it. Egypt, Greece, Rome, Great Britain – all pushed over the edge by their empty treasuries. America is already on the edge. You cannot provide your citizens with energy, and they are unwilling to provide you with warriors. Just like ancient Rome, you rely on paid mercenaries to keep you safe. It is a sign of your weakness, a testament to your failure. All we shall do is give the country a push over the edge, towards anarchy. With no way to prove what's yours and what's your neighbor's, and no money to buy anything, just how long do you think the country will last?"

CHAPTER 30

The mercenaries seemed to be mobilizing for action. At the crest of the ramp, an older man, whom Sullivan assumed must be the commander, was issuing orders to his troops. They could all hear the sound of the tanks and armored personnel vehicles rumbling to life. The smart thing to do right now would be to jump in one of the cars and make a run for Union City. Instead Sullivan found himself walking up the tunnel ramp alongside Emerson.

"Stay back," Emerson instructed him.

"I'm not one of your cops," Sullivan replied. "I'm a New Yorker, and I can go where the hell I like."

Emerson was wise enough not to press the issue. The way Sullivan saw it, if things kicked off, he was just as dead down by the tunnel as he was next to Emerson. Sullivan's only fear was that this unit was staffed with terrorists, but, he told himself, if that were the case, they would already be dead.

As they approached the commanding officer, all the mercenaries around him raised their weapons and aimed them at Emerson and Sullivan.

"Hands up!" a voice yelled.

Both men complied, but kept walking. They stopped when they were about ten yards from the mercenaries. The old commander sized them up, and then approached with two of his men.

"My commanding officer tells me that I should open fire on you guys. That you're insurgents posing as Feds."

Sullivan shook his head, and the mercenary commander looked him and Emerson up and down very carefully. He addressed his next remark to Emerson.

"You look like you were born in that suit."

Emerson smiled.

"Alonso Emerson, Federal Security Agency."

"Lloyd Mandel, and I don't have the first fucking idea who I'm working for."

The three men smiled, as Mandel extended his hand in friendship.

All eight computer servers had been wired with explosives. There were forty charges in all, five for each machine, and sixteen detonators. Without close examination, Pierce could not be sure of the design, but at a guess it seemed like the detonators were paired for each server; one primary, one failsafe. They were timed devices, and from the spirit levels on them Scott surmised that they were rigged to blow at the first hint of motion or tampering. One of the mercenaries was calibrating the final pair of detonators.

The two men at the far end of the vault had succeeded in using a cracking program to break the keypad code and had managed to get the small titanium doors open. Beyond them lay the bank's bullion vault; a long, narrow, low ceilinged tunnel that was lined with pallet after pallet of gold bars. Pierce had watched Karim's men move the gold from the bullion vault onto the equipment trolleys and then on to some unknown destination outside the bank.

"I thought you weren't a thief," Pierce observed.

"I'm not," Karim countered. "I'm an opportunist. Call it a tax to finance the costs of war."

The man who had been calibrating the detonators approached Karim.

"We're ready."

Karim activated his Resolute radio.

"Command, this is Solomon. Take out the back-up centers."

Lopez had been inside the back-up networks for twenty minutes. Accessing the networks had been the greatest achievement of his life. In computer hacking terms, it was his Everest. Lopez's computer screen displayed a map of the United States that showed the location of sixteen data centers that provided secure data back-up to all ten banks. Each bank had at least two back-up providers, and eight shared services at the same locations, which had made his job slightly easier. The servers in the banks' headquarters were solid state systems with a random intermittent network link, which made them impossible to hack. The back-up data centers were networked, which meant they could be hacked – in theory.

The initial probes on their systems had been carried out six months ago, since when Lopez had tried various ways to crack the firewalls that protected the data centers. Some of them were so advanced, Lopez had initially been unable to locate the data center on a network. Over time however, and with the advanced computer equipment they were authorized to requisition from the military under the Sentry program, Lopez had been able to build a complete picture of the data centers, all their security systems and their fail-safes. He had spent two months coding a virus that, once inserted into a data center's systems, would destroy every byte of data it held.

"I'm on it, sir," Lopez radioed back to Solomon.

He typed a command on his keyboard and earned his five million dollars. His computer screen displayed the words, 'Sending Corrupt Data Kernel.'

"It's done," Lopez's voice was broadcast through Karim's radio.

"These men believe we're destroying the back-up centers to keep the authorities busy while we make our escape," Karim said to Pierce. "Only a handful of my true Brothers know about the explosive charges we have placed in each bank. Without the back-up centers, all that stands between America and anarchy are ten computer systems, which will be destroyed in a matter of minutes."

Vimal had the best job in the world. He sat in the five desk office and played Rise of The Titans on his Apple G-Player. Through the glass panels that separated the office from the super-cooled bunker, Vimal could see hundreds of hardened servers. Every night he and his partner in crime, David Lee, would drive out to Melvindale, go through the security checks and take the elevator a thousand feet down to the bunker that was built into an abandoned salt mine. All they had to do was watch the machines and make sure nothing ever happened to them. In the five years that he had been working at Tellerdyne Systems, Vimal had never had to lift a finger. So he and Lee did whatever they wanted. Lee had been at Tellerdyne for eight years and had completed a distance learning computer sciences Phd through the University of Detroit. He now spent his time developing specialist Internet security software, which he sold through a data broker. Vimal tested video games for a software house that was based in California.

They had been so idle for so long that neither man was sure what to do when the first alarm went off. Lights started flashing all over the server control panels that dominated the north wall of the office. As they approached the sophisticated machine Vimal and Lee exchanged looks.

"What the hell is it?" Vimal asked.

Lee typed a command on the central keyboard and hit enter.

The main screen flashed up the words, 'Total System Failure", and then went blank. Behind them, in the cold chamber beyond the glass panels, hundreds of computer servers went dead simultaneously.

Total System Failure.

Lopez watched the words blinking on his computer screen. The machine reported that every single server at the sixteen target locations had been destroyed. This was going to affect more than just the banks. Internet service providers, payroll companies and government would have all had data stored at those locations. Lopez had just created a heck of a lot of work for the country's data programmers.

"Sir, we're picking up something on radar," one of the technicians reported.

Lopez walked across the command center and looked at the man's screen. It showed eight intermittent radar signatures approaching Manhattan.

"Alpha Squad, this is command," Lopez spoke into his radio.

"Go ahead, command," Karim said.

"The back-up centers have been destroyed."

"Excellent work."

"There's something else, sir," Lopez continued. "Our sensors are picking up eight aircraft approaching New York. It looks like they're trying to fly below radar. The signatures are bigger than standard G20s. At a guess, I'd peg them as Special Forces."

Pierce did not bother to hide his pleasure at hearing those words.

"They're too late. Evacuate those loyal to us. Leave the rest of the battalion to take the heat," Karim ordered.

"Copy that," Lopez said. "See you at the rendezvous point, sir. Command out."

Karim watched as his men pulled the last of the gold out of the inner vault.

"We're finished here," he said, and nodded at the three men who guarded Pierce and Maria.

The mercenaries backed through the outer vault, keeping their weapons trained on Pierce as they did so. Karim followed them out. Pierce placed a hand on Maria's arm as a signal for her to keep still; they did not need to do anything to antagonize these killers.

"She's served her purposed," Pierce called out to Karim. "Let her go."

"I thought you might like the company," Karim replied. "Enjoy the show, agent Pierce."

Karim pulled the encryption card from the reader by the outer vault doors, and they began to swing shut. The three mercenaries kept their weapons trained on Pierce until the outer vault doors sealed. Pierce heard the rubber pressure seal activate with a hiss. Four feet of solid titanium now separated them from the outside world. Pierce scanned his surroundings, desperately searching for a way out.

The man was tenacious, but sooner or later the abyss waited for us all. As he made his way up the stairwell, Karim could not help but admire Pierce. The man had continued to fight even when it made no rational sense to do so. It was the kind of devotion and belief that made great Brothers.

Special Forces might be on their way but that was of no consequence. The detonators would be primed once he and his men were clear of the building, and two minutes later America's reign of terror would be over. As a bonus, they had looted the gold reserves of all ten banks, which would net almost three hundred billion dollars. Enough money to finance the caliphate he and his Brothers had long dreamed of.

Karim had started to allow himself to think about how he and the Sons of September were going to realize that dream when he heard the start of the broadcast.

"This is Captain Lloyd Mandel, 'B' Company, broadcasting on Resolute open frequency nine."

Mandel stood on the turret of an Abrams tank and addressed the assembled ranks of the hundred-and-eighty men and women under his command. His words were carried to the entire battalion by an open radio microphone his communications officer had rigged for him. He had taken the news well, given that he had just discovered his role in placing the city in grave danger. Once he had heard the story from Emerson and the man called Sullivan, Mandel had determined to do whatever it took to thwart the sons-of-bitches that had made a fool of him. Sullivan and Emerson stood with the rest of the FSA agents on the fringe of the crowd.

"The Federal government has reason to believe that Resolute Corporation has been infiltrated by subversive elements," Mandel continued. "They believe that there are terrorists within our ranks."

"That spineless motherfucker!" Karim yelled. He had known there was little chance of Mandel opening fire on the FSA agents, despite his orders, but he had not expected the weak man to cave in quite so quickly.

As he crossed the lobby and followed his men towards the three Grav-jets stationed in Citibank Plaza, Karim activated his radio.

"Lopez, shut that lying asshole down. Block his signal!"

"The 101st Airborne are en route and have orders to seize control of the city."

Mandel's voice was broadcast with crystal clarity by the command center's speaker system. Lopez had shuddered when he had heard the word terrorist. They were supposed to be robbing banks. The thing with the back-up centers was smoke and mirrors to keep the Feds busy. There was no plan to...

All the pieces clicked into place and Lopez realized that he had been played for a fool. He looked around the room and wondered which of the men were puppets like him, and which were genuine believers. From the expressions on the faces of the men around him, most were having exactly the same thoughts.

"Lopez!" Solomon's voice crackled through the airwaves.

There was nothing to be gained by playing any further part in proceedings. Lopez backed discretely towards the door. All he had to do was get a grav-jet off the island and he could disappear into the ether forever.

"Lopez, you asshole!" Solomon tried desperately.

Lopez was almost at the door when the first bullet tore through his liver. A volley of shots followed it, and shredded his chest. As he lay dying, Lopez watched a dozen loyal Brothers order the technicians and communications officers back to their stations at gunpoint.

"Because the government cannot know which of us to trust, I'm ordering all patriotic and loyal personnel to absent themselves from the field," Mandel said as he surveyed the eyes of his troops. Emotions were mixed, but Mandel picked up a prevailing sense of shame.

"You are to join me and 'B' Company in Central Park, by the Wolman Rink. Any Resolute employees found outside Central Park will be considered hostile and shall be treated accordingly."

"We have restored order, sir."
Karim recognized Sohal's voice over the radio.
"God be praised," Karim replied in Arabic.
"Lopez is dead."
Karim barely registered the news as he stood in Citibank Plaza and watched his men transfer the Citibank gold from the equipment trolleys into the three waiting Grav-jets. They were about half way through the process of strategically distributing hundreds of ingots around the airframes.
"We need to slow the Green Berets down," Karim said. "Have one of the technicians give them a warm welcome before you evacuate."

Sohal stood over a technician and nudged the man with the muzzle of his machine-gun. He usually found that words were unnecessary in such situations and if there was any talking to be done he let his weapon make matters clear for him. In this instance, the technician was an alert young man and had listened carefully to Karim's broadcast. He typed some commands on his computer terminal, and the screen was filled by the words, 'Automated Air Defense Batteries Activated.'
Sohal stepped over to the command center window and watched the large missile batteries swivel into action, as their sophisticated computer brains tracked the approaching targets. Satisfied that the machines were working as they should, Sohal turned to the men in the command center.
"Everybody out," he ordered.

They were six minutes out and Neimus was making his final equipment checks, when the pilot alerted them to the hazard.
"Buckle up rodeo riders, we just got a hostile missile lock."
Neimus punched a command into the computer panel on his jump seat and a hologram of Manhattan was projected into the center of the aircraft. The computer fed threat data from the pilot's systems into the hologram and highlighted a dozen missile batteries on the perimeter of the island and a further four on Governor's Island.
"Let me make a call," Neimus radioed the pilot, and then switched frequencies.
"Guardian Angel," Neimus began, "this is Freebird. We have multiple hostile locks and need assistance."

To the casual observer the holographic displays would have looked like an indecipherable jumble, but to the six combat technicians that operated the system, the holograms told them all they needed to know about any battlefield and the airspace around it. Major Lewis Saxton had commanded the combat team on board the Battle-Jet for the six months since its launch, and had seen action all over the world. He had never expected the huge, three hundred foot long, six storey jet to be positioned in low orbit above Manhattan.

The two recently commissioned airforce Battle-Jets were America's newest and most secret battlefield weapons and were used to support Special Forces deployments. Bristling with surveillance equipment and weapons, the massive aircraft had been in development for over a decade as the military sought to harness graviton technology on an industrial scale. Dozens of supercharged graviton drives kept the huge jet two-hundred-thousand feet above the Earth's surface, well out of the reach of any land based weapons.

One of the holographic displays showed the view Neimus had of Manhattan, with the sixteen missile batteries highlighted by flashing cursors.

"Take them out," Saxton instructed Cabe, one of the combat technicians. Cabe used his motion sensitive gloves to highlight all sixteen flashing cursors, selected a weapon from a drop down menu and hit the fire button.

As eight of the Battle-Jet's twenty-two missile batteries each fired a warhead, Saxton sent a radio broadcast back to the Special Forces grav-jet.

"Freebird, this is Guardian Angel. Thunder and lightning is on its way."

When the eight large warheads were clear of the Battle-Jet, their nose cones split and their outer casings fell away to reveal a dozen missiles inside each one. After a second's freefall, the missiles' thrusters kicked in, and sent the swarm speeding towards the Earth.

The military convoy travelled along 8th Avenue, swelled with each passing minute by more and more Resolute vehicles that had surrendered their positions. As agreed, Emerson's fleet of FSA cars escorted the convoy, but they kept a discreet distance so as not to add to the indignity felt by the Resolute personnel. In a short space of time they had gone from being defenders of the city to suspected enemies of the state.

As he sat in the lead Cougar, Mandel consoled himself with the thought that whatever evil was planned, the men and women who had chosen to join him would play no further part in it.

The incandescent auroras of sixteen shooting stars caught Sohal's attention as he crossed the landing pad towards one of the waiting grav-jets. He was not possessed of a great deal of knowledge beyond the Holy Book, having been deprived of a proper education as a child. Whatever the gaps in his learning, Sohal did not need to be a master of physics to know that the stars were coming straight towards Governor's Island. Others had seen the approaching objects and some of them had already started to run. Sohal simply stood on the landing and turned to face his destiny. He had been a good soldier and his place in paradise was guaranteed.

The network might have agreed to a broadcast embargo but that did not mean they stopped covering the unfolding situation. Pound for pound, aviation fuel was more expensive than gold, but a story this big merited a blank check. Ray kept the chopper steady, facing the bird south into a northerly wind. Behind him the camera operator captured footage of the large convoy of Resolute vehicles that they had followed through the streets of the city. The convoy had come to a halt in Central Park, and more vehicles continued to arrive by the minute. Faith, the network's onboard correspondent, had expressed her frustration at their inability to listen into what the mercenaries were saying, but hers was an impossible ambition. Thanks to Resolute's microwave damper, which Ray could see on Governor's Island, he was unable to even communicate with air traffic controllers at the Jersey heliport.

Ray was looking south towards the Statue of Liberty when a number of objects passed through his field of vision at supersonic speed. Sixteen missiles struck the automated batteries and the microwave emitter on Governor's Island. The explosions were tremendously powerful. They destroyed or badly damaged almost every structure on the island and illuminated the night sky for miles around. Ray spun the helicopter around so that the camera operator could get a shot of the aftermath.

"Why aren't we live?" Faith exclaimed in frustration. "This is Pulitzer material!"

Just as they were coming to terms with the drama of the situation, a further series of explosions erupted at multiple locations on Manhattan Island, as missiles struck the automated batteries around the island's perimeter.

Ray looked at the developing warzone that was the city he liked to call home and asked his passengers, "What the fuck is going on?"

The explosions provided the city with more artificial light than it had experienced for many years. Karim could see the glow from three of the blasts over the tall buildings that surrounded Citibank Plaza. From their positions, he knew that the Americans had somehow managed to destroy the missile batteries.

"Command, this is Alpha, come in," Karim said into his radio.

A faint buzz was the only response.

"Command?"

Karim's radio crackled into life, but it was a voice he neither expected nor welcomed.

"Resolute battalion, this is United States Special Forces. Throw down your weapons and proceed to Central Park. Any resistance will be suppressed. Any aircraft that take to the skies will be shot down."

Karim looked at the three G20s that were almost fully loaded with gold. Sacrifices would have to be made.

"We leave by truck," Karim instructed Darweesh.

"What about the gold?"

"Leave it," Karim replied as he took a remote detonator from his side pocket. He punched in a code and flipped the trigger switch. Let these soldiers come, Karim thought, the beast they protected was already dead.

Pierce could not see a way to open the outer vault doors and the inner door had been damaged beyond repair. He paced between the inner and outer vaults and wracked his brain for a solution. Maria watched him silently. Pierce suspected she might be in shock, which was probably an advantage in their present circumstances. His only consolation was that the detonators had not been activated. Perhaps the Spider had encountered resistance outside the bank. It was possible that Sullivan had convinced the Feds to make a direct assault, or maybe Special Forces had intervened.

All such hopes were immediately extinguished the moment the red LEDs on the detonators flashed into life and the countdown began. Sixteen timers displayed '2.00' in illuminated red digits. They simultaneously flipped to '1.59' and Pierce knew that if he did not think of something quickly, he and the girl would be consumed in a gruesome fiery death.

CHAPTER 31

There was no experience like it. The pressure of trying to keep one's cool in the face of impossible odds tested the caliber of a person's character. Pierce could only think of one slim possibility for survival. He picked up a scrap of metal from the destroyed laser drill and used it to force open the outer casing on the first computer server. Inside he found a large RAID disk array.

"How much do you know about computers," Pierce asked Maria, as the countdown passed through '1.43'.

"Nothing."

"Watch what I do," Pierce said hurriedly.

He flipped the shut down switch for the RAID array, and the system cycled through the power down sequence. While the machine closed down its processing units, Pierce moved to the next server, forced the casing open and flipped the shutdown switch.

"Only a handful of people outside the government know that these banks run a final failsafe. There is an encrypted hard-line between the ten banks that maintains a mirror of all ten banks' records on all of their machines."

'1.27'

Pierce went back to the first machine and flipped four catches that held the disk array in place. With one fluid movement he extracted the large super-cooled disk system, which looked like a medium sized, black safety deposit box.

"I'm going to shut down the machines, but I need you to pull the disk arrays out. You have to wait until the servers have powered down or there is a risk you'll corrupt the data. Do you understand me?"

Maria nodded uncertainly. Pierce could see that she was questioning his use of their final few moments, but she was too battered by the whole experience to raise any objections.

'1.18'

Pierce forced open the third machine and switched it off and then moved on to the fourth.

"The Spider must know about the final failsafe, which is why he has gone to such lengths to destroy these computers. A nuclear attack or wholesale bombing of the city would not do it. There would be too much chance of one bank's systems surviving."

Machines five, six and seven were cracked and shut down, as Maria pulled the second disk array free.

'1.03'

"If we can save these disks, we can save the entire system," Pierce said as he shut down the final server.

"How?" Maria asked as she pulled the disk from the third machine.

'0.55'

"I'm working on it," Pierce said as he ran over to the laptop that had been left connected to the keypad at the far end of the inner vault. He studied the hacking program that had been used to force open the doors to the bullion vault.

'0.41'

Maria grabbed the fourth disk pack and pulled it clear, as Pierce worked on the computer. If he could find a way to re-task the hacking program, they might just have a chance.

'0.36'

Pierce saw Maria's hands start to tremble as she tried to pull the fifth disk free. She tried not to look at the numbers as they sequenced down towards zero, but the detonators stared her in the face.

"You can do this, Maria," Pierce called over to her as calmly as he could.

'0.28'

Pierce finished typing and the computer displayed the prompt, 'Hit Enter to Initiate.' There was no time to test the system, so Pierce could only hope that his work would be adequate. He ran over to the eighth machine and pulled the disk array clear, as Maria pulled out number five.

'0.21'

Maria was shaking uncontrollably as she tried to remove the sixth disk. Pierce pulled out number seven and rushed to help her with the final machine.

'0.15'

He grabbed the final array and tossed it into the bullion vault. The array's shockproof casing would protect the disks inside from any damage. Pierce grabbed Maria and pushed her towards the bullion vault.

"Inside!"

'0.08'

As Maria ran inside, Pierce gathered up the disk arrays.

'0.06'

He tossed them into the vault.

'0.05'

And ran towards it.

'0.04'

As he passed the laptop, he hit the enter key.

'0.03'

The titanium doors started to close, as Pierce dived into the bullion vault.

'0.02'

Pierce pulled Maria deep into the bullion vault, as far away from the doors as possible.

'0.01'

The titanium doors slid shut and sealed, and Pierce hoped that their blast-proof design was robust enough to contain what would hit them from the other side.

'*0.00*'

The detonators triggered a colossal explosion on the other side of the bullion vault doors, and everything went black.

CHAPTER 32

When the Apocalypse began, it would look something like this, Ray thought as ten monster explosions detonated across Manhattan. From his vantage point in the cockpit, Ray saw the initial blasts tear through the buildings on the southern tip of the island, then, one by one, the buildings started to collapse. Massive monuments to an age of prosperity reduced to flaming rubble in moments. There was so much happening that the camera operator did not know where to focus his lens. After the missile strike on Governor's Island, the radio had crackled back to life. Faith was using it now to get the latest updates from her sources in Washington and to instruct the network of the urgency for a live feed.

The silhouetted figures of squads three and four fell through the sky, grav-pacs slowing their descent as they neared the surface of Governor's Island. The first skirmishes broke out before they had even touched down. Through the G30's observation window, Neimus saw muzzle flashes, as his soldiers opened fire on a handful of mercenary stragglers who had not been killed by the missile strike.

"Thirty seconds to target," the pilot advised his passengers, as the speeding grav-jet left the firefight on Governor's Island in the distance.

Thank God for television, Joe Conroy thought. If every night was like this one he would have killed himself years ago. The cable had gone out when the Stormtroopers had shut down Manhattan. Even his neighbors in the building who had digital satellite had lost their signal. Resolute had not instituted a curfew, but Joe knew better than to be out on the streets on a night like this. His brother had given up trying to get home to his wife and kids in Jersey and sat next to Joe drinking beer in the 141st Street apartment. They had tried to find out what the heck was happening, but like in so much of life these days, the truth was hidden. With no television, no Internet and nothing but his neighbors' intermittent rumors and speculation, Joe became increasingly bored.

When the first earthquake came, Joe had rushed to the only south facing window in the apartment, which was in his kitchen. The pots hanging from the rack had rattled against one another with the aftershocks, but when Joe looked south he saw that it was no earthquake. The bright lights of multiple explosions had illuminated the dark sky.

"TV is back," Joe's brother had called to him from the sitting room.

They had immediately flipped through the news stations but none of them were carrying anything about the situation in Manhattan. It was like they were living in a different world.

When the second earthquake hit, Joe had rushed to his kitchen window again, and had seen so many of the skyscrapers that loomed over the island crumple towards the earth like old men dying. It was only after the second set of explosions that the outside world finally connected with Joe's surreal night.

"We interrupt this broadcast to bring you an update on the situation on Manhattan."

Joe heard the announcer's voice from the kitchen and ran back into the sitting room.

The television broadcast aerial footage of a city in flames. Multiple fires raged in the rubble of the destroyed buildings in the financial district. Smaller fires could be seen at locations around the perimeter, and the flashes of scattered machine-gun peppered the length and breadth of the island.

"This is Faith Kitsantonis," the reporter voiced over the images. "Earlier tonight Resolute Corporation instituted a quarantine of Manhattan Island in order to deal with an ostensible terror threat. The Federal Security Agency now has reason to believe that Resolute itself has been infiltrated by insurgent elements and has been subverted in order to launch a massive attack on the island. As authorities struggle to discern friend from foe, my sources in Washington tell me that Resolute forces have been ordered to withdraw to Central Park and that units from the FSA, NYPD and Special Forces are engaging any mercenaries who refuse to comply. We have been informed that the only active infantry battalion in the United States, the 101st Airborne, is en route to restore order. As you can see from these images, Manhattan is in chaos, with firefights between mercenaries and law enforcement personal across the island. There have been multiple explosions, with wholesale demolition of buildings within the financial district. At this stage there is no way of knowing how many lives have been lost. We'll try to make more sense of the chaos as events unfold."

Stovall suffered from insomnia at the best of times. It seemed as though lack of sleep was part and parcel of a senator's life. Tonight had been different. Rather than the usual accelerated thinking he experienced when he shut his eyes and struggled to disconnect from the day's events, now he felt the ulcerated burning of worry in his solar plexus. Something had felt wrong with what was happening in Manhattan and the illicit donations Resolute had made to his campaign meant that he was exposed. Unable to drift off, Stovall had switched the television on to an old comedy movie.

When the news bulletin interrupted the film, Stovall knew his career was over. He had been manipulated by the very forces he had devoted his life to destroying. They had targeted him where he was weakest; his pocketbook and he would now pay the price. Stovall did not need to see any more of the catastrophe unfolding in New York. He turned off the television, and lay his head against the pillow. A strange calm swept over him, and as he drifted to sleep he knew that the only role he had left in life was to wait for men with handcuffs to knock on his door and take him away to answer for his greed.

This had not been a controlled demolition; the explosion had been designed to cause as much damage as possible. The massive Citibank tower had toppled into the adjacent building and taken that down with it. The G30s of One and Two squad landed in Citibank Plaza, which was now covered with burning rubble. As Neimus exited the jet, he ordered his men to investigate the three Resolute G20s that were stationed at the edge of the Plaza. Neimus surveyed the scene of devastation and wondered whether anyone could have survived.

The mercenaries that congregated in Central Park had the dejected look of a defeated army. Sullivan counted twenty two Abrams tanks, four dozen Cougar armored personnel carriers and many more jeeps and trucks, all parked idle on the grass. Several hundred men and women had surrendered their small arms, which were stacked in neat piles and guarded by Emerson and his agents. As soon as the news broke, New Yorkers started to drift by in their dozens and then hundreds to see the mercenaries surrender. The crowd of several hundred citizens was kept at bay by members of the New York Police Department. Sullivan thought about Pierce, the man at the center of the storm, and wondered whether he had made it.

Two of his men had died before his unit had split into opposing groups. The moment Mandel's broadcast had changed their perspectives on good and evil, one of Chadha's men, Nick Stelios, had opened fire indiscriminately and killed Teddy and Lomax. As the men split for cover, uncertain of who to trust, Chadha had exchanged gunfire with Stelios. The enemy had quickly revealed themselves, as Chadha had quickly come under fire from three other men in his unit.

Six apparent loyalists, led by Chadha, traded shots with four hostiles, led by Stelios – both sets of men using the Resolute vehicles at the Queensboro Bridge checkpoint for cover. Chadha had longed to distinguish himself in action with Resolute, but he had never expected his opportunity to come like this.

"Drop your weapons!" a voice said through a bullhorn.

Chadha turned to see that a fleet of police vehicles had pulled up at the checkpoint. Regular units and a SWAT team had their weapons trained on both sets of Resolute men.

"Do as they say," Chadha commanded.

While he and the five men loyal to him threw down their guns and placed their hands on their heads, the hostiles were foolhardy enough to turn their weapons on the police. A storm of gunfire from dozens of police officers brought their resistance to an end and the Queensboro Bridge checkpoint fell quiet.

Once the nature of the situation had become clear, Brad and his people had felt no qualms at handing over control of the tunnel to the Federal Security Agency. The FSA, supported by a team of hastily assembled cops, now searched every vehicle that tried to leave the island. The hunt was on for the terrorists, as the city strived to reassert control of its destiny. The New Yorkers that had seized the tunnel kept a watchful eye on proceedings as they struggled to adjust to becoming simple civilians once more.

Karim looked at the line of traffic ahead of them. He and a dozen of his men sat in the back of one of the vans Rossi and Karo had used to transport the bank infiltration team to the city. Another two vans were behind them, further down the line. The remaining five vans had been instructed to use alternative routes off the island.

Karim's van was stacked in a queue of vehicles waiting to get through the Lincoln Tunnel. A crowd of citizens by the tunnel mouth watched police and plain-clothed agents search every vehicle that tried to leave the island.

"We could fight our way through," Darweesh said to Karim in Arabic.

Karim calculated their chances of success. Even if they could get through the tunnel, the firefight would draw the attention of every law enforcement agency on the other side. There was a better way.

"Instruct all loyal units to return to Citibank," Karim told Darweesh. "If we are to be martyrs, we shall take many more American souls with us."

CHAPTER 33

Closing the door had been simple. The real challenge had been to program a time delay into the bullion vault's locking mechanism. Pierce had estimated twenty five minutes would give the fires caused by the explosion sufficient time to burn out. So after the initial blast, which the titanium door had successfully protected them from, he and Maria had sat in the pitch darkness of the bullion vault. Pierce had asked her about her life, and had taken great pleasure in hearing about her husband and two children. Her voice drifted out of the darkness and for a time Pierce was able to share in her peaceful, productive existence. Her concerns at whether her children's talents were being recognized and developed by their teachers put his own challenges in perspective. These were the people he had sacrificed a large part of his life to save, their existences, the very essence of what America stood for.

As he sat in the darkness listening to this small, beautiful life tell its story, Pierce experienced a moment of clarity. Since Ellie's death, his life had been defined by that single, terrible moment. Everything he did was tied to that monstrous event and his life-force had been spent in search of revenge. Maria was proof that there were billions of better reasons to fight – reasons that did not stoke the feelings of anger, impotence and frustration that he had not been able to save his wife. The voice in the darkness was a life he had saved and as a result the three souls closest to her would be spared the savagery of grief he knew so well. For the past six years, rage had consumed him and he had lost his way. The voice in the darkness helped guide him back. As the bitterness left him, Pierce knew he would never forget Eleanor but from this moment on he would chose to remember how she had lived, not how she had died.

The locking mechanism clicked and the heavy bullion vault door slid open. Beyond it Pierce could see the red glow of emergency lighting, the source of which was obscured by clouds of gas from the fire extinguisher system.

"Hold your breath," Pierce instructed Maria, as he grabbed her arm and ushered her into the inner vault, which was filled with Argonite gas.

Red hot twisted metal was strewn all over the place, and Pierce picked their way through the debris with care. The force of the explosion and subsequent fireball had melted the safety deposit boxes in the outer vault, with the result that the chamber now looked like a vision of hell. Red hot clumps of semi molten steel dripped from the walls and the granite floor was cracked and disfigured, with lava like clumps of red hot concrete poking through.

Pierce was relieved to see that the force of the explosion had blown the slightly weaker outer vault doors off their runners, and sent them crashing into the far wall of the vault lobby, where the elevator had once been.

The vault was designed to withstand a nuclear blast two blocks away but the building above it had not been constructed to withstand an explosion of the size it had just experienced. As Pierce tentatively pulled open the stairwell door, he saw that the building had collapsed. Dust and smoke filled the air and, three flights up, the stairwell was blocked by rubble and debris that was still on fire. With access to the elevator destroyed by the outer vault doors, this was their only way out.

"You can breathe again," Pierce told Maria as he shut the stairwell door. Dust and smoke was not great, but unlike the Argonite gas, it was not immediately dangerous.

Pierce took Maria's hand and led her up the steps.

The fire crews worked hard to extinguish the flames. Governor's Island had been secured and the squads at the other locations had reported similar destruction to that which lay before Neimus at Citibank. The search of the three Resolute Grav-jets had revealed billions of dollars of gold bullion and Neimus could only assume that the arrival of Special Forces and threat of force had caused the insurgents to alter their plans.

Advance units of 101st Airborne were thirty minutes away, and Neimus was waiting for orders for his squads. There were plenty of bad guys in the city and law enforcement radio traffic spoke of sporadic firefights all over the island.

"I've got something," one of the firefighters shouted from the south east corner of what had once been the Citibank building.

The firefighter held a gamma scanner and was one of a number of men searching the rubble for survivors. The building had fallen towards the north west, so there was very little rubble and debris over the south east corner. Neimus approached and saw an image on the scanner that looked like two people struggling to climb through a mass of rubble.

"Get that robot over here!" the firefighter called out to his colleagues.

A huge remote control Excavator robot stood idle near the specially designed firetruck that had transported it to the scene. At the firefighter's call, the operator used the remote control panel to bring the huge machine to life. It lumbered over to the scene on six heavy metal legs. Its mantis like chassis linked the legs to four arms that ended in massive claws, which immediately got to work shifting large chunks of rubble from wherever the firefighter directed.

They had squeezed through two flights of fallen masonry and rubble when Pierce heard the sound of machinery. Dust and small pieces of debris fell from the stairwell above, as large chunks of the building were pulled from their path. After a few minutes, Pierce could see the first beams of artificial lights from the torches carried by their rescuers.

220

The Excavator had cleared four storeys of rubble when a dust-covered hand poked through a small crack; there were survivors. The final few chunks of rubble were removed slowly and carefully, and the Excavator's claws transformed into a platform upon which the survivors – two of them – could be lifted to safety.

The woman was immediately covered with a blanket and taken to a waiting ambulance. The man, who looked far more battered and bruised than the woman, resisted the firefighters' attempts to give him assistance and scanned the uniforms of the Green Berets on the scene. He approached Neimus.

"Scott Pierce, FSA."

"Vincent Neimus."

As the two men shook hands, Neimus could see that Pierce was breathing the balmy night air with the quiet satisfaction of a man who had never expected to breathe again. After a respectful pause, Neimus asked, "You look like you've been through hell. What happened here?"

"They tried to destroy the banking system. Your men need to get down to the bullion vault. They will find eight disk arrays, which need to go to the computer crimes division in Washington. They'll know what to do."

The first bullet killed a firefighter standing ten feet away. The second struck one of the Green Berets in the head. The automatic gunfire spread from the southern end of the plaza like a deadly swarm.

Karim was glad that he had radioed all units to return to Citibank. The Brothers had accomplished their mission but it looked as though the Almighty had decreed that it would be their last. They could not escape the island without a fight, and any American units they encountered would engage them with ferocity and enthusiasm, little knowing that the system they sought to defend had already been destroyed. Better he and his men should martyr themselves in a way that matched their tremendous achievement. In order to achieve the spectacular death Karim desired, he needed a grav-jet but he had suspected that the three jets abandoned at Citibank would have already been impounded and had rightly guessed that he would need all the support he could get to seize one of them.

When the eight vans full of men and two Resolute Cougars had converged on Citibank Plaza, Karim thanked Allah for his foresight. Two Special Forces G30s lay next to his own jets – they were a gift from above. The graviton drive of a standard G20 could be used to destroy a couple of blocks, but the graviton drives combined with the nuclear reactor onboard the G30 could wipe out at least half of the city. Karim knew he must have one of the Special Forces grav-jets. All that stood between him and glory were two squads of Green Berets and some firefighters.

Karim had instructed his men via their coded radios. The Cougars were to use their mini-guns to strafe the plaza while his men engaged the Green Berets and kept them busy long enough for him to get to one of the flying atom bombs.

His own machine pistol had signaled the start of the assault and he watched with satisfaction as a fireman and then a Green Beret had fallen. The Cougars had then filled the plaza with bullets, supported by the ninety men under his command – a mixture of Rossi's and Karo's Brothers and his own Resolute personnel - who fought with savage enthusiasm.

They were seriously outnumbered and outgunned. Eight Green Berets caught in the open died almost instantly. The remainder sought cover in the rubble of the destroyed building. These bastards knew no rules of war and killed firefighters indiscriminately. As he and Neimus took cover behind a huge cornerstone, Pierce saw Karim at the southern end of the plaza.

"Echo company, this is squad one, we have engaged the enemy and need support. All squads rally to my location!" Neimus yelled into his radio.

Pierce crawled into the open to grab a machine gun from the body of a fallen Green Beret. He scrambled back behind the stone and joined Neimus in the firefight. The first grenades from the Cougar's launchers hit three Green Berets who had dug in behind a concrete support forty feet away. The explosion set Pierce's ears ringing.

As the mayhem of battle raged around him, Pierce wondered why Karim had returned. He could understand that the insurgents would not be able to get off the island but they could have tried to find somewhere to hide – Manhattan was a big place. To return to the scene of the crime was suicide...and the moment he thought of the word, Pierce had his answer. He raised his head over the cornerstone, firing his machine gun as he did so, and looked for Karim. Across the Plaza he saw two men, Karim and one other, climb aboard one of the Special Forces G30s.

"Cover me," Pierce instructed Neimus as he started to run.

Neimus watched the crazy man run into the open and instinctively started to target anyone who posed a threat to him. Two hostiles went down under a volley of shots from Neimus's weapon, and Pierce took out another as he shot his machine gun on the move. The sudden dash made no sense, Neimus thought; they had a strong, defendable position here. Then he saw the G30 rise into the sky and understood why the terrorists had returned. Neimus emptied his weapon with renewed passion – Pierce was about thirty feet from the second G30 and even if it meant that nobody else survived, that man had to make it to that aircraft.

With twenty feet to go, one of the Cougars targeted him. As the heavy caliber bullets spat into concrete inches away from him, Pierce dived for cover behind the body of a dead Green Beret. He hauled the corpse into position in front of him and held it in place, as the dead man danced under the barrage of shots.

Pierce dared not raise his head, but he was a sitting duck and knew it would only be a matter of time before the hostiles flanked his position. The would be coming up alongside him at any moment and there was not a damned thing he could do about it.

The force of the explosion knocked Pierce back five feet. He looked up to see what was left of the Cougar in flames. The second Cougar was hit by a missile strike from the sky and Pierce raised his head to see two G30s hovering above the plaza. A cloud of Green Berets fired at Karim's men, as their grav-pacs brought them rapidly to Earth.

Pierce covered the final twenty feet, sprinted into the cockpit of the G30 and launched the jet into the sky.

"Guardian Angel, this is Freebird," Neimus said into his radio as he watched Pierce pilot the second G30 into the sky. "We've got a hostile jet in the air. Echo Company, squad two, identifier Charlie, Kilo, Foxtrot, Niner, Lima. Request immediate strike."

Neimus fired over the top of the cornerstone as he waited for a response. The reinforcements from three and four squads were tipping the balance against the hostiles.

"Freebird, this is Guardian Angel," the radio crackled. "Showing a negative on that transponder identifier. That aircraft does not register on our system."

Without a transponder lock, there was no way to track the grav-jet unless it popped up on radar. As long as the pilot kept it close to the city's buildings, the aircraft would remain invisible.

"Find that jet," Neimus yelled into his radio. "Find it and destroy it."

"Keep it steady," Karim instructed Darweesh as he worked on the G30's graviton drive control system. "They will not be able to locate us."

Darweesh sat in the co-pilot's seat, while Karim worked on the ship's computer at the flight engineer's station. He had disabled the aircraft's transponder signal as they had climbed away from the firefight in the plaza. Without it the Americans would not be able to find the G30 before it was too late.

The jet was now hovering twenty feet above the roof of a skyscraper on Fifth Avenue, concealed from radar by its proximity to the building.

"I'm sending the Graviton drive and nuclear reactor into simultaneous meltdown. In three minutes this aircraft will explode with the force of a thousand suns."

CHAPTER 34

As he piloted the G30 into the sky, Pierce heard Neimus's communication with his tech support over the aircraft's radio. If they did not find Karim's jet soon, the city would pay dearly. Pierce crested the skyline and dialed a number on the grav-jet's communication system.

She had sent the rest of the team home with instructions to get some sleep. The next few days would be extremely busy, of that Belle was certain. The administration would want to know exactly how something like this could have happened. Belle had not followed her own advice and had remained in the operations room watching events unfold on CNN. The balance of power appeared to be shifting, with the network now reporting that law enforcement agencies controlled over ninety percent of the island. The final few pockets of resistance were in the process of being put down.

Belle wondered about the Brotherhood's destruction of buildings in the financial district. If their intention had been to take lives, there were far more populous neighborhoods on the island.

The phone shook her from her thoughts.

"Pearlman," Belle said as she answered.

"Belle, it's Scott."

Pierce's voice was accompanied by the low rumble of a graviton drive.

"I don't have time to explain. I need you to find a G30. It will be hiding somewhere in Manhattan. Transponder has been deactivated."

Belle activated the holographic interface of her computer and brought up the Agency's satellite systems.

"Tell me it's not what I think it is," Belle said as she worked. Access to military grade G30s was severely restricted. The combination of nuclear reactor and graviton drive had the potential to be fiercely destructive.

"Find it, Belle."

Pierce's response told her all she needed to know.

The satellite system scanned the island for graviton emissions. Belle cross referenced what the computer found with aircrafts that showed active transponder locations. There was one graviton drive registering in Mid-town that had no transponder. Belle brought up a visual satellite image and saw the dark outline of a jet hovering over the roof of a building.

"Got it. Fifth Avenue. I'm sending you the coordinates now."

"How much longer?" Darweesh asked Karim.

The ship's computer was flashing a constant warning message, and alarms had started to sound in the cockpit, but Karim ignored them and worked to override the aircraft's automatic safety systems.

"Two minutes," Karim replied, as the ship started to shudder with the build up of power in the graviton drive.

The first volley of cannon fire buffeted the G30 over the edge of the roof. The G30's sensors showed minor structural damage and the radar displayed a contact three hundred yards to their rear.

Karim punched in the last set of safety overrides and rushed to the pilot's seat. He assumed the controls and pushed the aircraft into an almost vertical nosedive.

Missiles had been out of the question with the G30 so close to the residential building, so Pierce had used the jet's guns instead in an effort to force Karim's aircraft clear of any human shields. When the G30 went into a whining nosedive, Pierce followed, piloting his jet down into the narrow canyons of Manhattan.

The two jets flew fast and low along Fifth Avenue and blew out the windows of every building and vehicle that they passed. Cannon fire from Pierce's jet buffeted Karim's ship and sent it bouncing into the buildings either side of the street. The collisions tore off huge chunks of building facades.

Even with the automatic proximity system, Karim struggled to bring the ship under control. The barrage of cannon fire was simply too destabilizing. He could not risk a full collision with the buildings around him – not when he was so close to success.

Aware that he did not have the luxury of time on his side, Pierce locked onto his target and fired a graviton-seeking missile.

More alarms sounded in the cockpit as the G30's computer told Karim that a missile was headed directly for them. Karim deployed countermeasures and put the aircraft into a steep climb.

The countermeasures burst from the tail section of Karim's jet and detonated moments later to create a cloud of flak. The missile exploded on contact with the cloud, and Pierce flew through the ensuing fireball to match Karim's steep climb, firing his cannon as they ascended vertically parallel to a skyscraper.

Darweesh looked at the building directly beside them, as his body strained to cope with the pressure of the vertical climb.

"I am prepared for paradise," Darweesh said to Karim in Arabic. "Crash the jet into the building."

The brother of all Brothers did not look at him as he maintained mastery over

226

the aircraft. He simply said, "If we crash before the graviton drive reaches critical mass, our deaths will be for nothing."

Over Karim's shoulder Darweesh could see the ship's computer indicate that they had ninety seconds until critical mass. A short time to wait for perfection.

Pierce saw the G30 top out and spin on its axis in a sudden change of trajectory, and once again he matched the move. They were now travelling high above the city, dodging in and out of the tips of the giant buildings. Let's see how the guy copes with raw emotion, Pierce thought as he activated the radio.

"Kamal Al Karim," the voice said over the radio. "This is Scott Pierce."

The name was like a knife in Karim's back. If the man survived, there was a chance that the disks had too. If the disks had survived, he had one chance to ensure their destruction. The epicenter of the graviton explosion had to be at Citibank. Karim reversed the thrusters and the aircraft came to a virtually immediate standstill.

It was not the reaction Pierce had expected, but it was a reaction. He sped past Karim's jet, and rather than slow down, put his own into a banking turn. As he swooped fast and wide, Pierce saw the other aircraft turn and head south. He opened fire with his cannon and sent four missiles towards Karim.

This man was a menace, Karim thought, as the jet was buffeted by cannon fire. Almost every alarm in the cockpit was going off, as the aircraft's graviton drive started to go into meltdown, and the ship's computer tried to warn him of the approaching missiles. Karim could not take the risk of the ship being destroyed before the drive reached critical mass. Pierce would have to be dealt with.

Another burst of countermeasures detonated, but this time two missiles exploded on contact and the other two flew through the cloud of flak unscathed. When Pierce passed through the fireball, he realized he had lost visual on Karim's jet. He checked his radar display and saw the signature of Karim's jet a hundred yards above and behind him. The Spider had used the countermeasures as cover for a sudden change in position. The move had also confused the remaining two missiles, and Pierce's computer now told him that they were locked onto his graviton drive. As cannon fire from Karim's guns hit his jet, Pierce deployed his countermeasures and pulled into a steep climb.

One of the missiles struck the countermeasures, but the other got through and hit the rear section of Pierce's aircraft. The explosion took out one of the aircraft's graviton engines and buffeted the aircraft badly, shaking Pierce to the bone.

Karim had a direct line on Pierce's lame and damaged jet and fired four missiles towards it. Behind him the computer countdown informed them that they had twenty seconds until critical mass. The rear section of the jet now shuddered violently as the graviton drive approached meltdown.

As the computer reported the damage suffered by the ship, Pierce realized there was no way he could beat Karim in a dogfight. It also reported a massive leak of gravitons in the vicinity, which meant Karim's ship was now approaching critical mass. With four missiles speeding towards him and no way to evade, Pierce had one last hope. The radar display showed that Karim was directly to the rear of his jet, matching speed and trajectory as they headed towards the southern tip of Manhattan.

Pierce lined his G30 up as best he could, deployed his countermeasures, and hit reverse thrusters, just before hit pulled the lever on his ejector seat.

Karim saw the jet spray countermeasures across the sky, which detonated in a cloud of flak. They were now only ten seconds away from critical mass, but Karim took satisfaction in the knowledge that Pierce would die before them as three of the missiles avoided destruction. The fourth missile hit the countermeasures and exploded. What Karim saw next robbed him of all hope of glory. If Karim had been looking at the radar display instead of out of the cockpit he might have noticed Pierce's jet travelling in reverse. Instead, when it burst through the flaming cloud of countermeasures, Karim had no time to react. The two jets collided. Karim and Darweesh were killed instantly and the debris from the two jets, including the shielded graviton drive and nuclear reactor fell harmlessly towards the waters of the New York Bay.

The first rays of sunshine were lighting up the world, as Pierce's grav-pac slowed his descent towards the ground. He made contact with the hard soil of Liberty Island, rolled and got to his feet to watch the flaming pieces of the G30s splash into the water half a mile way. High in the sky above him dozens of G30s streamed over Manhattan and disgorged hundreds of soldiers from the 101st Airborne.

Pierce unclipped his grav-pac, turned and walked towards the visitors' center and the Statue that stood high above it.

The crowd was getting restless, so Lyle had Buddy on his shoulders to avoid the boy getting jostled and crushed. About a thousand people stood in the parking lot outside the Ralph's supermarket. Lyle and the boy had been there since seven a.m. and were near the front. Ahead of them a line of cops tried to hold back the crowd that was straining to get into the store when it opened. Since the thing in Manhattan four days ago, shops had operated restricted hours because nobody could access their bank accounts to pay for things. Those lucky enough to hold cash struggled to find places to spend it because the dollar had gone into freefall globally. The television had said there were small towns in the Mid-West that had gone back to barter. But that kind of civilized behavior just would not work in the metropolitan cities where a warped form of the pioneer spirit was very much in evidence. It was every man for himself.

"Return to your homes!" a voice yelled through a bullhorn.

Lyle could not see the speaker, but guessed it was one of the cops further down the line.

"You have acted on false information. This store is out of stock and will remain closed for the foreseeable future."

"Fuck you!" a voice yelled.

"You're lying!" came another.

Lyle could sense that the mood of the crowd had changed and just as he started to push his way towards its edge, a trash can went sailing through the air in front of him and smashed through one of the store's windows.

Seeing the opening, desperate people ignored the police cordon and surged through the broken window. One of the police officers fired warning shots into the air, but he was quickly disarmed and trampled under the crowd.

Tempted as Lyle was by the thought of the supplies within, he continued to fight against the flow of the crowd, aware that Buddy was gripping his head with every terrified ounce of his strength. They made it clear of the surge, and Lyle congratulated himself on the wisdom of his decision when he heard the sound of gunshots coming from inside the supermarket.

Her coverage of the battle for Manhattan had brought her international recognition and the network wanted to capitalize on it, so she was now their point reporter on all the big stories. Faith looked down from her vantage point in the chopper at the riot in central Chicago, and struggled to know where to begin. They were due to go live in ten, and somehow Faith had to convey to viewers that they were witnessing the beginning of the end of civilization. What had started as a peaceful protest against the banks and conglomerates attended by over one hundred thousand people had degenerated into a full scale riot, with protesters engaged in running battles with police. Since the kneejerk suspension of the Sentry program, out of shape, out of practice police-forces across the country had suddenly been expected to resume full responsibility for maintaining law and order. The transition could not have come at a worse possible time. The anger that people felt at the loss of their money, their inability to pay for goods and the consequent food shortages all over the country, was now boiling over into large-scale civil unrest. What scared Faith was that from where she was sitting, it seemed that the forces of law and order were losing. The system might be broken, but it was the only one they had ever known. She did not dare imagine the chaos that would follow if the government could not re-establish some kind of order and the country was allowed to descend into mob rule.

Denilson looked across the doorway at the man opposite him, who held a Sig Sauer K17 automatic pistol. Denilson's own fingers were wrapped around an old 45 Magnum, which felt reassuringly heavy. He knocked on the door of the large house in East Hampton and waited. There was no response, but his brother Spartans had been watching the place for two days and knew there were hoarders living inside. Denilson nodded at the two men, who stood behind him and held a battering ram. They drew the ram back and smashed the door open in one fluid, forceful motion.

The householders were not aware of the new order of things. The Imperative of Community as Abarca described it. The Spartans were robbing any businesses or individuals that hoarded and were distributing the stolen produce to the poor and needy. The Imperative of Community valued the alleviation of common suffering more highly than the pleasure of the individual – it was the new order.

The two shotgun blasts that came through the doorway and hit one of the Spartans in the chest showed that the occupants of this house were set in their old capitalist ways. They were beyond saving, Denilson thought as he stepped through the doorway and opened fire.

Of all the possible outcomes, Sullivan had not expected this one. He watched the President, who sat nine seats away from him on the front row of the podium at the New York Stock Exchange. Men in suits came and went with frightening frequency, each whispering something in the President's ear and receiving a whispered reaction or instruction in return. Two seats closer to the President than him was Emerson and next to him was US Attorney Dreyfus. Both of them were basking in the recognition they had received for their roles in the liberation of Manhattan.

Sullivan looked out at the assembled press corps and wondered what the heck the President could say to make the shitstorm better. The country was on its knees and soon the anarchists would kick it face first into the gutter. Sullivan was considering a move to Europe. He had spread his wealth wisely and had a nice villa in the hills above Nice. The loss of part of his fortune in the destroyed banking system pained him, but at least he was not like the vast majority of Americans who had lost everything.

The smoke from his Monte Cristo swirled around his mouth – nobody had the guts to tell a hero of the Battle of Manhattan that he could not smoke in the Stock Exchange – and Sullivan thought about Scott Pierce. He had simply disappeared and nobody seemed to know whether he was even alive. Sullivan put money – Euros or Yen – on his survival. From what he had heard from Emerson, Pierce had given the bad guys a real run for their money.

The afternoon sun glared down on the Alabaster Mosque. Azzam stood in the courtyard of the mosque of Mohamed Ali and marveled at the magnificence of the Spider's scheme. It had been an unqualified success, and from what he had seen on the news, America was now near the end. The loss of Karim and his men had been a setback, but to expend their greatest tactical mind in the achievement of such a monumental goal was a fair price to pay. They would have their reward in Paradise.

As the pink, sweaty lawyer walked across the courtyard, Azzam wondered what message Karim wanted him to hear. The fat man had been adamant that Karim had left a recording for Azzam to receive upon his death and had insisted on delivering it to him in person.

"I was ordered to give you these," David Helmer said as he handed Azzam a scanner and a cellphone.

"By whom?" Azzam asked, suddenly realizing that in his euphoria he had stumbled into a trap. He looked around him uncertainly.

Helmer backed away without responding, and the cellphone started to ring. Azzam answered.

"One move and you're dead," Pierce said.

The fat Egyptian's apartment that had been scouted out by Saul and Wycliff was the perfect vantage point. As he looked down the sight of the sniper's rifle, Pierce could see Azzam alone in the otherwise deserted Citadel courtyard. He fixed the crosshairs on the target's head.

"Agent Pierce," Azzam's voice came through the earpiece Pierce wore, "so you survived? Go ahead and kill me. My work is done."

"Turn on the screen," Pierce replied.

He nodded at Belle who sat in front of a flight case full of computer and communication equipment.

"The audience is watching," Belle said into her radio.

There was a certainty in Pierce's voice that worried Azzam. He complied with

231

the instruction out of morbid curiosity and switched on the scanner, which was set to receive CNN. As he looked at the anchor, Azzam felt a sinking feeling in his stomach.

"We're now going live to the President who is at the New York Stock Exchange," the anchor said.

The image cut to another of the President approaching a dais. He was surrounded by dozens of officials and police officers on a podium in the New York Stock Exchange.

"My fellow Americans," the President began, "in recent years our nation has endured a prolonged campaign of violence perpetrated by evil men intent on destroying our way of life. This week saw the culmination of their efforts; an assault on our financial system. An assault they had planned for years. But even with their best preparation, they were unable to harm us. We have kept our banks and businesses closed so as not to alert them to the failure of their plan, but we have been able to restore all our financial systems and data. Whilst painful, this brief period of deprivation and uncertainty has enabled our intelligence agencies to track down the perpetrators and smash their operations."

When the President paused and a small screen within a screen appeared on the scanner, Azzam knew that this message might be being broadcast to billions of people, but it was meant for him personally. As the President stood silently, Azzam looked at the image within the smaller screen and saw a boy he knew as Imran being arrested in his pigeon-hole lined apartment by agents of the brutal Pakistani Inter-Services Intelligence.

The small screen went black for a split second then cut to an image of Senator Stovall being led away from his house by a team of FSA agents.

The next image disturbed Azzam greatly. It showed David Helmer, Yaseen and his men in the Citadel parking lot. They lay spread-eagled on the ground and were being frisked by members of Mabahith Amn al-Dawla al-'Ulya, the Egyptian secret service.

"I would like to send a personal message to our enemies," the President continued. "I know you are out there watching this. The lesson you are about to learn is that you mess with America at your peril."

Azzam saw the President's demeanor change as he returned to the business at hand. The American leader was proud to be able to say the words that came next.

"It is with great pleasure," the President said, "that I declare this market and with it the United States of America open for business."

The President rang the opening bell and the screen on Azzam's scanner went dark.

"Impossible," Azzam said into the cellphone.

"I wanted you to know that you had failed," Pierce said, as he squeezed the trigger. He saw the bullet tear into Azzam's skull and watched the great Engineer's corpse slump to the ground.

Pierce put the sniper's rifle to one side, and he and Belle walked out of the apartment in silence. Once they were gone, a cleanup crew would remove every trace of evidence that they had ever been there.

They walked down the stairs and exited the building into the baking sun. Pierce looked at the crystal clear blue sky as they crossed the dusty sidewalk towards the waiting car, and wondered what the future held for him. There would be a future, of that he was sure. Eleanor's memory was sacred to him and he had been through too much to throw his life away in a statement of grief. The men responsible for her murder were now dead, and Pierce felt that was sufficient sacrifice.

Whatever the shape of his future, it would begin with a difficult farewell. Catlin's funeral was in two days. His old friend, the woman who had watched over him for five years, one of the few people in the Agency, in the whole world, he could genuinely trust was gone. The grief he felt for Catlin merged with his general physical and emotional exhaustion to make Pierce feel punch drunk.

As Belle climbed into the front seat of the car, Pierce slid into the back. He was relieved to finally be able to rest.

The guy was an Agency legend, Belle thought as she watched the lone figure of Scott Pierce sprawl across the back seat and shut his eyes. The tragedy was that he would never receive any recognition; what he had gone through for his country could only ever be whispered about in soundproofed corridors by a privileged few.

Belle tapped Saul's leg, and the young man put the car into gear, pulled into the flow of traffic and headed towards the airport.

Lightning Source UK Ltd.
Milton Keynes UK
UKOW040418291112

202910UK00001B/78/P

Pathology for the Primary FRCS

Pathology for the Primary FRCS

D. L. Gardner MD, FRCPath

Professor of Histopathology,
University Hospital of South Manchester;
Examiner in Pathology to the Royal College
of Surgeons of Edinburgh

D. E. F. Tweedle ChM, FRCSEd

Consultant Surgeon
University Hospital of South Manchester;
Examiner in Pathology to the Royal College
of Surgeons of Edinburgh

With a Foreword by
Sir James Fraser, Bt, BA, ChM, FRCS, FRCP

Edward Arnold

First published in Great Britain 1986 by
Edward Arnold (Publishers) Ltd, 41 Bedford Square, London WC1B 3DQ

Edward Arnold (Australia) Pty Ltd, 80 Waverley Road, Caulfield East,
Victoria 3145, Australia

Edward Arnold, 3 East ·Read Street, Baltimore, Maryland 21202, U.S.A.

British Library Cataloguing in Publication Data

Gardner, D.L.
Pathology for the Primary FRCS
1. Pathology — Problems, exercises, etc.
I. Title   II. Tweedle, D.E.F.
616.07'076   RB119

ISBN 0-7131-4497-1

Text set in 10/11pt Times Roman Compugraphic
by Colset Private Limited, Singapore
Printed and bound in Great Britain by Richard Clay (The Chaucer Press) Ltd,
Bungay, Suffolk

Foreword

There have been many publications within the field of pathology that are entirely specific in both title and objective and this is unquestionably true of this volume. Professor Dugald Gardner and Mr David Tweedle have chosen the simple and obvious title *Pathology for the Primary FRCS* for their book. It is, therefore, specifically relevant to that examination but there are, I believe, two principle reasons why it should be welcomed and will prove to be a significant contribution to the medical literature.

The first is of course because it is directed to young surgeons who are preparing for the Primary Fellowship, and this volume presents a comprehensive collection of responses to the whole range of questions that they are likely to meet during the examination. Each of the answers is succinct and yet full in its content and each, if relayed to the examiner, will in all probability ensure success. There is no other single book that can provide this cover.

The second reason why it should be welcomed is less obvious and in many ways reflects the spirit of the Primary Fellowship. There have been many and sometimes justifiable criticisms of the examination but no one can doubt that it has firmly held to its original objectives which are that every surgeon who holds a Fellowship has, or more correctly, at some time has had a sound knowledge and understanding of the Basic Sciences as they relate to clinical practice. It is accepted that a great deal of the detailed information that is necessary in order to pass the examination may not be entirely relevant for the average surgeon but the discipline involved in obtaining that information cannot be lost. This is all the more significant when applied later in his career both to the every day problems of patient care and even more so when he decides to concentrate on a single specialty and has to relearn the essential basic sciences. *Pathology for the Primary FRCS* by its very nature serves a similar purpose. Although its reader may have a single immediate goal to pass the examination, it would not be possible to complete its study without retaining a mass of information, and because of its particular construction, without obtaining and retaining an understanding of pathology in its widest context that will not easily be forgotten.

There is another reason why this book should be welcomed. Its unique format is such that it can also be regarded as a concise encyclopaedia or even an ABC of surgical pathology. When compared with the usual major textbooks it offers to all surgeons a much more useful, comprehensive and practical handbook. The information on any single topic may not be in great depth and there are no references, but there must be many who will welcome the opportunity to consult the volume, to refresh their memory in some areas and to learn for the first time in others. It does not purport to be a book to be read straight through from cover to cover but whether as an aid to success in the examination, a mental discipline or a reference volume there can be no doubt that it is a most interesting educational development and that it will occupy a useful place on any surgeon's bookshelf.

J.D.F.

Preface

This short book provides candidates with answers to those questions most likely to be asked during the oral (**viva voce**) examination in Pathology for the first part (**Primary**) of the **FRCS** diploma. The subjects described have each been raised as topics in these examinations in recent years. There is no published syllabus for the primary pathology FRCS examinations but the contents of this volume, carefully indexed, come close to providing one. The primary examinations for Fellowship of the four Royal Surgical Colleges are individual in style and content; there is a heavy component of Immunology, Microbiology and Serology, with frequent digressions into Haematology and Clinical Chemistry. The book closely reflects this bias. The subject matter is arranged alphabetically according to the subjects of the major questions that have been asked.

Particular thanks are due to Mr Iain D. Gardner FRCS, Dr Alastair M. Lessells MRCPath, Mr Philip Schofield FRCS, Mr Leslie Turner FRCS, and Dr Katie Whale MRCPath, who have given much advice and constructive criticism, and to our publishers, Edward Arnold Ltd, for tolerance and understanding during the book's gestation.

1986   **D.L.G.**
                                                                                            D.E.F.T.

Abbreviations

CT   Computerized axial tomography
EM   Electron microscopy
UVL   Ultraviolet light

Abrasion

An abrasion is an epidermal injury caused by friction. It is the mechanical rubbing or scraping away of part or the whole of the epidermis. During a fall from a motor cycle, for example, the skin is abraded from exposed parts of the limbs. Healing is rapid and complete.

Abscess

An abscess is a localized collection of **pus** (p. 163). Diseases in which abscess formation predominates are said to be **suppurative**.

Abscesses form at sites of tissue injury, irritation or infection when persistent inflammation (p. 116) accompanies cell death. Neutrophil polymorphs aggregate and an inflammatory exudate develops. Extension of the injury and irritation or persistence of infection results in the injury and death of increasing numbers of cells. Cell proteins are denatured. A collection of cell and tissue debris forms. Small molecules are liberated, attracting water by osmosis. The contents of the abscess may be fluid, semifluid, caseous or granular. Osmotic changes determine that abscesses tend to swell.

Unless the abscess is drained or excized, granulation tissue begins to form and fibrosis results in **encapsulation**. The loss of overlying tissue may allow an abscess to point at and rupture through an epithelial surface. A chronic abscess may display **dystrophic calcification** (p. 39).

In abscesses caused by infection, living or dead bacteria are often present. Many bacteria thrive at abscess margins but anaerobes such as the Actinomyces (p. 3) grow centrally. Micro-organisms may survive mainly inside or outside phagocytes.

Acidaemia/Acidosis

Acidaemia is a decrease in the pH of the blood below 7.36, i.e. an increase in the hydrogen ion concentration above the normal value.

Acidosis is an accumulation of hydrogen ions (H^+) or a loss of base that will produce acidaemia in the absence of compensatory mechanisms. Examples are renal and pulmonary failure, diabetic ketoacidosis and duodenal fistula. Acidaemia produced by metabolic acidosis may be prevented by a compensatory respiratory alkalaemia.

Alkalaemia/Alkalosis

Alkalaemia is an increase in the pH of the blood above 7.44.

Alkalosis is a loss of H^+ ions or an accumulation of base that will produce alkalaemia in the absence of compensatory mechanisms. Examples are hyperventilation due to thyrotoxicosis or anxiety, overventilation with a mechanical ventilator, and loss of gastric acid by vomiting or aspiration.

Acquired immunodeficiency syndrome (AIDS)

AIDS is a newly-recognized, epidemic form of immunodeficiency caused by a human lymphocytotrophic virus, HTLV-III. There is a high mortality rate. The clinical syndrome is dominated by opportunistic infection (p. 101) and by the onset of neoplastic diseases such as Kaposi's sarcoma (p. 167), a malignant neoplasm that is rare under the age of 60 years except in Central Africa.

The virus is introduced directly into the blood of five susceptible groups of people: homosexuals; heroin addicts; Haitian (and other Caribbean and Central African) populations; and those receiving repeated blood transfusions with haem derivatives. AIDS can be transmitted by blood products as well as by blood, and haemophiliacs are therefore very vulnerable. Heterosexual transmission is much more frequent in Africa than in Europe and the U.S.A.

The AIDS virus is a human T-cell retrovirus that transforms lymphocytes and destroys the cell-mediated immune response. Sufferers are then vulnerable to infection with other viruses such as cytomegalovirus and herpes simplex; with atypical mycobacteria; and with protozoa and fungi such as *Pneumocystis carinii, Toxoplasma gondii,* Candida species and *Cryptococcus neoformans.* The pattern of spread bears a close resemblance to that of hepatitis B, and virus is present in blood and other body fluids.

Steps taken to control AIDS are (1) the elimination from blood donation of those who are carriers of the virus: one in 20 000 blood donors have anti-HTLV-III antibody in their serum, and (2) the heating of blood products such as the Factor VIII given to haemophiliacs. The virus of AIDS is heat sensitive and it was hoped that virus would be inactivated by exposure to a temperature of 56 °C for 30 minutes. However, a temperature of 80 °C for three days is now judged necessary to treat Factor VIII preparations.

Attempts are being made to manufacture vaccines using recombinant gene technology. It is possible that such active protective agents may become available within five years.

Acromegaly, gigantism

Acromegaly, from 'akron' (extremity) and 'megas' (great) describes the excessive size of the hands, feet, jaw and face which results when a primary functioning neoplasm of the anterior pituitary, usually an adenoma, secretes excess growth hormone (GH). The viscera are also enlarged. When such a neoplasm liberates excess GH before the growth of the long bones has ceased, the condition of **gigantism** follows.

Older classifications describe the endocrine cells of the anterior pituitary as eosinophils (acidophils), basophils and chromophobes. The techniques of antibody-labelling now demonstrate that eosinophils secrete either GH or prolactin. The former, GH-secreting cells are called somatotrophs; the latter prolactin-secreting cells are called lactotrophs. The neoplasms that result in acromegaly and gigantism are somatotroph cell adenomas.

The term **local gigantism** has been used to described the excessive growth of an appendage, for example a finger or a limb. However, this local phenomenon, which may be congenital, is not due to the action of excess GH but is usually attributable to neurofibromatosis (von Recklinghausen's* disease).

Actinomycosis

Actinomycosis is an infection with anaerobic or microaerophilic filamentous, branching bacteria of the genus Actinomyces.

The actinomyces grow best in situations remote from blood vessels. Another genus of the same family of organisms, the Nocardia, are strict aerobes and may extend widely within tissues that retain a blood supply. *Actinomyces israelii*, a normal buccal commensal, may cause chronic purulent infection in man. *A. bovis* can be transmitted from cattle to human tissue.

The lesions of actinomycosis are deep-seated, indolent, persistent, and destructive. Tissue injury leads to abscess and then to sinus formation. Colonies of the organism grow in the centre of the abscess, far from the nearest source of oxygen. The colonies seen in the pus released from such sites are recognized as pin-head sized **sulphur granules**. Affected tissues include the jaws and tongue, and the vermiform appendix. Rarely infection occurs in association with an intrauterine contraceptive device that has been present for a long time.

Acute tubular necrosis

Acute tubular necrosis is the death of renal tubular cells that may follow hypotension or reduced cardiac output from any cause. It may also follow damage by endogenous agents such as haemoglobin and myoglobin, by unidentified substances in patients with obstructive jaundice, and by exogenous poisons such as heavy metals and carbon tetrachloride.

In an established case, the kidneys are enlarged, the cortex swollen and pale. There is tubular degeneration and necrosis. The terminal portion of the proximal convoluted tubules and the distal convoluted tubules are most vulnerable. The tubules are distended with casts and there is interstitial oedema. Acute renal failure is likely. In some cases the diagnosis of tubular necrosis is clinical rather than pathological: the cell injury may be very mild. Moreover, renal tubular cells have excellent powers of recovery by regeneration. At first, the regenerating cells lack a brush border and are unable to conserve sodium so that there is a persistent diuresis. Ultimately, they differentiate and sodium conservation resumes. In survivors, there is no residual microscopic evidence of damage to the tubules.

---

*Friedrich Daniel von Recklinghausen (1833–1910), Professor of Pathology at Königsberg, Würtzburg and Strasbourg, described neurofibromatosis in 1882 and, confusingly for modern students, osteitis fibrosa cystica (hyperparathyroidism) (p. 154) in 1890.

Adenoma

An adenoma is a benign neoplasm of glandular epithelium.

Adenocarcinoma

An adenocarcinoma is a malignant neoplasm of glandular epithelium.

Aflatoxins

Aflatoxins are toxins from the fungal genera Aspergillus and Penicillium which occasionally grow on foods such as stored, wet groundnuts. An aflatoxin causes acute enteritis and hepatitis that may progress to liver failure. Repeated ingestion leads to liver-cell carcinoma in experimental animals and aflatoxins may contribute to the great frequency of primary hepatocellular carcinoma in parts of Africa.

Ageing

Ageing, growing old, consists in the degenerative changes in tissues and organs that ultimately determine the life span. In the sense that it is inevitable, ageing may be regarded as physiological.

Modern surgery in Western countries is dominated by problems created by the ageing of tissues and their altered responses to disease. All cells have a built-in, genetic programme that ensures that they survive for only a limited, finite time. When a cell reaches this time limit, it may be said to be **senescent**: it becomes abnormally susceptible to the expression of disease processes such as cancer and atheroma. The tissues may no longer be capable of mounting normal defence reactions against, for example, infection.

Premature ageing or **progeria** and extreme longevity suggest the limits of human survival; they reflect the operation of endocrine factors or responses to chemical or environmental agents that accelerate or protect against senescence.

Among the changes of ageing in man are greying and loss of hair; loss of teeth; osteoporosis; wrinkling of the skin with elastosis of the dermis; decreased stature; muscle atrophy and physical weakness. Senile dementia is frequent and one common cause is Alzheimer's disease.

Agglutination reaction

Agglutination reactions are antigen-antibody reactions in which particulate antigens such as red blood cells or bacteria are linked by the **antigen binding fragments** (Fab) of an immunoglobulin molecule. Because IgM antibodies (p. 112) are polymers with five peptide subunits they are very efficient agglutinating and cytolytic agents; they bind five times as many antigenic sites as IgG and, under some circumstances, ten times as many.

Agglutination reactions are common, important serological tests. The **Widal reaction** is employed to search for antibody against the O and H antigens of *Salmonella typhi, S. paratyphi* A and B, and non-specific Salmonellae. Agglutination studies for Brucella are often carried out at the same time. When enteric fever (p. 76) is suspected, a rising titre of anti-*S.typhi* or *S. paratyphi* antibody, assessed on the basis of two specimens of serum obtained at 4–7 days interval, can confirm the formation of new antibody. This conclusion is permissible provided that natural antibody and antibody formed after inoculation with typhoid–paratyphoid (TAB) vaccine can be excluded and that there has not been a previous episode of clinical or of latent infection.

Albinism

Albinism is the complete absence of melanin pigment from the skin, hair, retina and other parts. The heritable occurrence of albinism is the result of the lack of tyrosinase or of another enzyme from melanin-producing cells (p. 140). **Albinoidism** is incomplete albinism, i.e. the hair and skin are darker than in albinism and the eyes appear normal.

Albumin

The plasma contains two major proteins, albumin, 42–54 g/l, and the globulins (p. 88). Fourteen to 15 g of albumin are made each day, but when there is serious loss the rate of synthesis can be doubled. Albumin is mainly extracellular: 40 per cent is intravascular. The plasma half-life is 18–20 days and the molecule is very stable. The functions of albumin include:

1. the provision of one of many sources of amino acids;

2. the control of the distribution of body water by oncotic pressure;

3. the transport of elements such as Ca, Mg, Cu, Zn; of hormones such as T3 and T4; of bilirubin; of free fatty acids; of amino acids; and of many drugs.

Aldosterone

Aldosterone is a steroid secreted by the cells of the zona glomerulosa of the adrenal cortex; it increases renal tubular Na^+ reabsorption and K^+ and H^+ excretion. In the ileum and colon there are comparable effects. The loss of Na^+ in sweat and saliva is diminished.

Hyperaldosteronism

Excess aldosterone causes sodium retention and hypertension but usually no oedema. Much potassium is lost. The muscles are weak and there may be flaccid paralysis. Hyperaldosteronism may be primary or secondary.

Primary hyperaldsteronism (Conn's syndrome)   This is usually caused by an adenoma of the adrenal cortex but may be due to bilateral adrenal cortical hyperplasia or, rarely, to carcinoma. The condition was first recognized and described in detail by M.D. Milne in Manchester.

Secondary hyperaldosteronism   A condition which may be a consequence of increased secretion of renin due to renal artery stenosis or from a renin-secreting renal tumour. Inappropriate secretion of excess aldosterone may occur in cardiac failure and in cirrhosis. The secretion of aldosterone is increased following injury or operation. The magnitude and duration of this increase is proportional to the severity of injury or operation. The increase is prolonged if there are postoperative complications, in particular local or systemic infection (sepsis).

Amoebiasis

Amoebiasis is infection by the intestinal protozoon, *Entamoeba histolytica* or by the free-living *Naegleria fowleri*.

Intestinal amoebiasis can be contracted in any part of the world. Amoebic cysts are ingested with food or water under conditions of poor sanitation. Flies may convey cysts to foodstuffs. After ingestion, the amoebae that evolve may live for long periods in the gut without causing dysentery, that is, without invading gut tissue. However, when invasion and tissue necrosis result, the amoebae can pass from the gut to the liver. A hepatic abscess containing typical 'anchovy-sauce' pus may be formed. The organism may also be transported to the lung and to the brain. In diagnosis, free *E. histolytica* are sought in specimens of fresh, warm stool but are often not detected. Pus, secretions or biopsy specimens must be stained by the periodic acid-Schiff method. Serological confirmation of diagnosis should be sought by applying an immunofluorescence test to the material.

The saprophytic amoebae have been found in fresh-water baths and tanks and can harbour *Legionella pneumophila* (p. 128).

Amyloid

The amyloids are a family of insoluble fibrillar glycoproteins, chemically distinct but with identical physical properties.

The chemical composition of the amyloids is well understood. Each molecule consists of an individual protein molecule and a smaller antigenic P substance common to all the amyloids. The amyloids are divided into five categories according to the chemical structure of the protein (Table 1).

Table 1   Classification of amyloid

Type	Clinical syndromes	Fibril	Plasma precursor
AA	Secondary to rheumatoid arthritis bronchiectasis, tuberculosis	AA protein	SAA
AL	Myeloma or lymphoma	AL often made of λ light chains	Ig light chains
AE	Localized masses and organ deposits	AE polypeptides	Neurosecretory polypeptides e.g. calcitonin
AS	Senile: brain, heart	AS protein	Not known
AH	Heritable	Prealbumin in some forms	Not known

All amyloids show a molecular arrangement described as a β-pleated sheet. This means that the dyes used in staining for amyloid are incorporated in a similar laminar fashion between the sheets of the protein, giving a doubly refractile appearance when viewed with plane-polarized light. **Congo red** is one of the stains most commonly employed. This red stain seen in polarized light appears apple green, not red. Very small amounts of amyloid can be detected and the staining technique is highly sensitive.

The five types of amyloid of known nature and cause are (1) AA, deposited in blood vessel walls in chronic inflammatory disease; (2) AL, laid down during the development of some immunocytic diseases and in the growth of plasma-cell myeloma; (3) AE, accumulated locally at sites of apudomas (p. 15); (4) AS, amassed in the old (senile); and (5) AH, aggregated as one result of a group of rare, heritable diseases. When a cause can be demonstrated, amyloid is said to be **secondary**. When no demonstrable cause for amyloidosis can be found, the term idiopathic or **primary amyloidosis** is used. Formerly, it was believed that the sites of primary amyloid, such as the tongue and heart, were characteristic. At present, in Western countries, the commonest cause of amyloidosis is rheumatoid arthritis but the disorder is also encountered in other chronic inflammatory conditions particularly tuberculosis, bronchiectasis and chronic osteomyelitis.

The spleen, kidneys, liver and other viscera, become enlarged and develop a waxy appearance because of the deposits. A simple autopsy test with iodine gives the affected tissue a mahogany brown colour that resists decolorization with sulphuric acid. In biopsy practice amyloid is sought by needle. The most rewarding biopsy sites are the rectal mucosa and the kidney.

Anaemia

Anaemia is a reduction in the concentration of haemoglobin in the circulating blood below the normal range (Table 20, p. 204).

Anaemia is the result of a diminution either in the number of circulating red blood cells or in the concentration of haemoglobin in each cell. Normally the haemoglobin concentration in the circulating blood of adults is 12–18 g/dl. The range for healthy men is 13.5–18.0 g/dl and for adult women 11.5–16.4 g/dl. In women, the concentration before the menopause is usually about 1 g/dl lower than after menopause.

The causes of anaemia may be:

1. a defect in the formation of haemoglobin, due for example to iron deficiency, or in the numbers or maturation of red blood cells, due for example to a deficiency of cyanocobalamin (vitamin B_{12}) (p. 201). Anaemias in which there is defective haemoglobin and/or red cell formation are **dyshaemopoietic**;

2. excessive red blood cell destruction, as in the hereditary or acquired haemolytic anaemias: hereditary spherocytosis (p. 91) is an example of the former, malaria of the latter. This class of anaemia is said to be **haemolytic**;

3. blood loss attributable to acute or chronic bleeding (p. 34). This category of anaemia is **haemorrhagic**.

Anaphylaxis

Anaphylaxis, an exaggerated reaction, is the opposite of prophylaxis which is a term for guarding or prevention. The word anaphylaxis describes a severe type I hypersensitivity reaction (p. 102) to a second exposure to a foreign antigen against which the individual has already formed antibody. The responsible antigen is usually protein. The initial, sensitizing injection is symptomless. The second, challenging injection, causes the most severe response when given not less then 10–14 days later. This challenge provokes a profound systemic reaction with shock, oedema and cardiorespiratory failure that is often quickly fatal.

Anaphylaxis is now rarely encountered in the course of human immunization. Active immunization has largely superseded passive, and foreign proteins for parenteral injection, such as insulin or antihaemophiliac globulin, are purified and given in very small amounts.

See Mast cells (p. 139)

Anaplasia

Anaplasia is the reversion of a cell line to a less differentiated and more primitive type which may resemble that of the embryo. When anaplasia is extreme, the identity of the tissue from which the anaplastic cells originate may no longer be apparent. Loss of differentiation (dedifferentiation) is one important sign of dysplasia, precancer or cancer.

Aneurysm

True aneurysm   This is an abnormal, localized dilatation of a blood vessel.

Aneurysms may be classified

morphologically, as saccular, fusiform, berry, dissecting, arteriovenous, communicating, and cirsoid; or

functionally, (causally) as congenital, mycotic (infective), syphilitic, traumatic, and atherosclerotic.

The principal complications of arterial aneurysms are thrombosis, rupture, and a mechanical disturbance of surrounding tissues. A classical but now rare example of the latter complication is the erosion of the vertebral bodies but not of the intervertebral discs by the posterior extension of an enlarging saccular, syphilitic aortic aneurysm.

False aneurysms   These are blood-filled spaces in continuity with the circulation. Part or all of the wall of the aneurysm is formed of non-vascular tissue.

Angiogenic factors

Angiogenic factors   These are chemical substances that lead to the growth of blood vessels into (1) tissues that are normally avascular, like hyaline articular cartilage, or (2) tissues that require a vascular supply to grow beyond a small, critical size, like islands of cancer cells. Similar factors assist the growth of blood vessels into healing infarcts.

1. In rheumatoid arthritis, inflammation leads to the replacement of marginal cartilage by a soft rim (pannus) of vascular granulation tissue, catalysing the onset of fibrous ankylosis. An angiogenic factor may take part in this process. A factor that protects cartilage against vascularization may simultaneously be depleted.

2. Explants of neoplastic tissue can survive if the mass is no more than 1 mm in diameter. Beyond this size, the establishment of a vascular network is critical to neoplastic growth. Equally, a reduction in blood supply to a neoplasm that has already exceeded the critical size of 1 mm^3 may result in necrosis.

Anoxia

Anoxia is the absence of oxygen from the whole environment or from parts of organs or tissues.

Tissues such as the central nervous system that normally receive a very large proportion of the highly oxygenated arterial blood and that use only aerobic respiration to provide cell energy tolerate anoxia for only 2–4 minutes before permanent cell injury is caused.

Tissues such as articular cartilage that respire at low rates, and if necessary by anaerobic glycolysis, can withstand long periods of anoxia. Pieces of cartilage removed from the body may have cells still able to metabolize 3–4 weeks after excision.

Other tissues and organs range in order of sensitivity to anoxia, from highly sensitive (cardiac muscle, renal tubules) to relatively insensitive (skin, fascia, tendons, ligaments, aponeuroses). The degree of injury and the extent to which tissues and organs are likely to be injured by anoxia is suggested in Table 2, in which the relative oxygen consumption of some important tissues is shown.

See Ischaemia (p. 125).

Table 2 Relative oxygen consumption at 37 °C of some representative body tissues.

Organ	Oxygen consumption (ml/min/kg)
Heart	94
Kidney	61
Liver	33
Brain	33
Skeletal muscle	2–3
Articular cartilage	very small

Antibacterial agents

Bacteria can be killed within the tissues by cellular and humoral mechanisms and by some antibiotics; they can also be killed outside the body by antiseptics and disinfectants but these agents may also kill normal cells if they come in contact with them. The immunological mechanisms that kill bacteria within tissues are described on p. 108.

Oxygen-independent mechanisms   These are mainly lysosomal.

Oxygen-dependent mechanisms   Phagocytosis is followed by bacterial destruction; there is a sudden burst of oxygen consumption.

Defects of phagocytosis arise when cytotoxic drugs or ionizing radiations deplete the bone narrow of leucocyte precursors. Rarely, defective phagocytosis is encountered in inherited oxidase deficiencies, for example, in chronic granulomatous disease.

Antibiotics

An antibiotic is a substance produced in vitro by bacteria or fungi, and capable of killing (bactericidal) or inhibiting (bacteriostatic) the growth of other micro-organisms in vivo and in vitro. Many antibiotics can now be made synthetically.

The main groups of antibiotics active against bacteria are:

1. those that impair the synthesis of the structural mucopeptides of the bacterial wall, especially of Gram-positive bacteria, e.g. **penicillin**.

2. those which affect the function of bacterial membranes, including pseudomonas species, e.g. **polymyxin**.

3. those which interfere with nucleic acid synthesis, e.g. **rifampicin, nalidixic acid** and **metronidazole**.

4. those which interfere with protein synthesis, e.g. the aminoglycosides such as **streptomycin** and **gentamicin**.

Other antibiotics are active against protozoa, worms and fungi.

Antiviral agents are few. They may act on the free virus, e.g. isoquinoline; at the stage of virus absorption or penetration, e.g. idoxuridine; or at the stage of viral assembly or release, e.g. methisazone. The **interferons** (p. 119) are being tested for clinical use in the early treatment of common viral diseases such as influenza. They have attracted more interest as anti-cancer agents.

Antibiotic resistance

Many strains of common hospital pathogenic bacteria such as *Staphylococcus aureus* are resistant to antibiotics. The frequency of resistance is proportional to the extent to which an antibiotic is used in the hospital. An increasing proportion of bacteria is now resistant to more than one antibiotic.

The resistance of a bacterial strain to an antibiotic may be acquired by two alternative mechanisms.

First, the elimination of sensitive strains. Some resistant bacteria are always present. In the case of resistance to penicillin this may be due to the possession of an enzyme, penicillinase, which has the capacity to destroy the antibiotic. With the administration of the antibiotic clinically, there is selective pressure so that the proportion of sensitive organisms declines. The proportion of resistant organisms increases until they predominate.

Second, previously sensitive strains may acquire resistance by mutation which may be (a) by transduction, the mechanism by which bacteriophage (p. 26) injects new genetic material into bacteria; (b) by the acquisition of a plasmid containing a new genetic programme; or (c) by chromosomal change. Examples of these forms of mutation are (a) the development of penicillin resistance by *Staphylococcus aureus*; (b) gentamicin resistance; and (c) streptomycin resistance.

The advice of a bacteriologist, based on the results of cultures, is desirable before deciding, in a particular case, the antibiotic of choice. Fortunately, strains of organisms such as staphylococci that are resistant to penicillin may retain sensitivity to other agents such as cloxacillin, to the cephalosporins and to alternative compounds such as gentamicin.

The proportion of antibiotic–resistant strains in a particular hospital tends to rise if the use of a single antibiotic is continued. However, it is often possible, in prophylaxis, to restrict the use of an antibiotic to a period of 24–48 hours.

Antibody

Antibodies are immunoglobulins (p. 111); they are formed when antigen (See this page) in suitable form gains access to the lymphoid tissues, transforming B lymphocytes to plasma cells. Particular regions of each antigen molecule, with a characteristic shape, are antigenic determinants; they ensure the uniqueness of the response. When these sites are identified as foreign, plasma cells are stimulated to form greatly increased amounts of immunoglobulins that bind specifically with the foreign antigen. Each clone of plasma cells forms only one class of antibody immunoglobulin. The formation of antibody in response to antigen does not occur when antigens are exchanged between identical twins and antibody is not formed in animals in which the immune mechanism has been ablated at an early age, for example by thymectomy in newborn mice. The capacity to form antibody may be deficient (p. 110) or suppressed (p. 115)

Antigen

An antigen is a large, natural or synthetic, organic molecule, usually protein but sometimes polysaccharide, nucleic acid or lipid, which can provoke an immune response when it has access to the immune surveillance system of a mature, non-identical individual.

Although an antigen is generally a single substance, the large molecule is complex. One part determines the degree of the immune response, another the specificity. Those parts of the antigen that react with cells or antibodies in the immune response are **antigenic determinants**; the rest of the antigen is the carrier. **Haptens** are small molecules, not themselves antigenic; they can elicit antibody formation when attached to a large carrier molecule. Penicillin is an example of a hapten.

The route by which an antigen reaches foreign, immunoreactive tissues influences the cellular events leading to immunization. Whether the antigen enters by intradermal, intravenous, respiratory or other pathway modifies the recipient's response just as do the amount and concentration of antigen. Administered orally, many antigens are destroyed or changed by digestion so that antigenic reactivity is lost or specificity altered. Nevertheless, some protein antigens can be absorbed unchanged from the intestine. One consequence may be the development of food or milk allergy in atopic persons (p. 103)

Antigens are more likely to provoke an immune response if they are retained locally in tissues. Substances such as oil or killed mycobacteria-in-oil which encourage this persistence are called **adjuvants**.

The likelihood of an immune reaction being of a humoral, antibody-mediated (p. 108) or of a cellular form (p. 109) is influenced by the mode of presentation of antigen to the immunoreactive tissues. Antigens such as the vaccine of yellow fever virus given for prophylactic immunization are administered intramuscularly or subcutaneously. There is quick absorption and a brisk formation of antibody. When a cellular response is desired, antigen absorption is slowed by the addition of adjuvant; intradermal injection is chosen or the antigen is given as a preformed antigen-antibody complex.

Antigen, antibody measurement

Many techniques of measurement use radioactive isotopes as labels that can be measured with precision: these methods are the basis of **radio-immunoassay**.

Antigen
Antigen can be measured by techniques in which unlabelled antibody is added to the material to be tested. Anti-immunoglobulin labelled with a radioactive isotope is then used to measure the quantity of antigen–antibody binding. The technique is very sensitive and small amounts of polypeptide hormones, tumour markers, hepatitis B_S antigen and other proteins, as well as smaller molecules including digoxin, morphine-like compounds, steroids and the prostaglandins, can be assayed.

Antibody
Antigen can be stuck on beads of polymer or in plastic wells and incubated with the solution to be tested. An anti-immunoglobulin is added that has been labelled with a radioactive isotope such as ^{125}I, ^{3}H or ^{14}C. The amount of antibody bound to the known quantity of antigen is then determined by counts of emitted x-rays or β-particles.

Antineoplastic drugs

Antineoplastic drugs are classified according to their chemical structure.

Antimetabolites
These drugs are structural analogues of essential components of DNA such as purines and pyrimidines; or of precursors or cofactors essential for the synthesis of the nucleic acids. Methotrexate is a structural analogue of folic acid, for example, and competes with this molecule, preventing nuclear maturation.

Alkylating agents
In these compounds alkyl groups are substituted for some of the hydrogen atoms, preventing DNA replication and RNA transcription. Irradiation with x- or γ-rays has similar effects and these agents are said to be radiomimetic. Melphalan and cyclophosphamide are examples of alkylating agents.

Antibiotics
Many potent antibiotics such as daunorubicin and its analogue doxorubicin (Adriamycin) inhibit the synthesis of DNA and/or of RNA.

Vinca alkaloids
These substances dissolve the protein of the spindle apparatus essential for the mitotic division of cells (p. 51). Vincristine is such an agent.

Some antineoplastic drugs such as methotrexate and vincristine are effective in only one of the four phases of mitotic division (p. 50). They are said to be **phase specific**. These drugs are inactive against cells that do not divide frequently; they must be given repeatedly to be effective. Some drugs are active against cells in all phases of the mitotic cycle and are said to be **phase non-specific**. These compounds are active against slowly growing tumours.

Antisepsis: asepsis

Antisepsis is the prevention of the growth and multiplication of the micro-organisms that cause sepsis (p. 168). Asepsis is the exclusion of these organisms from the tissues. The terms antisepsis and asepsis are often used synonymously but should be clearly distinguished.

Antiseptics are mild disinfectants (p. 72) devoid of significant irritative and sensitizing properties, and suitable therefore for application to the skin. **Asepsis** is achieved by excluding micro-organisms from the operating theatre and by sterilizing all instruments, dressings and appliances used in surgery.

In surgical practice, the principles of antisepsis and asepsis are used together. Before Lister* the majority of surgical wounds became infected, although Semmelweiss** had greatly reduced the frequency of postpartum sepsis by introducing the practice of the washing of hands and the cleaning of instruments before examining an obstetric patient. Since Lister's time, it has become obligatory to sterilize instruments before use, generally by heating in an autoclave. The patient's skin at and near an operating site is usually prepared by shaving or depilation. Soaps have an important antiseptic activity that is greatly enhanced by the mechanical removal of skin bacteria during preoperative washing. Agents such as ethanol, detergents and chlorhexidine are then applied. For abraded skin or healing wounds, less irritating solutions such as the iodophor povidone-iodine (Betadine) are used.

Antiseptic care includes regular cleaning of the walls and floors of the hospital wards and operating theatres, the use of dressing rooms on wards and the sterilization of endoscopic instruments. Isolation units segregate patients infected with highly pathogenic organisms such as *Pseudomonas aeruginosa* and individuals at particular risk. Among these are patients requiring immunosuppressive therapy for organ transplantation, who exemplify the need to prevent contact with pathogenic organisms.

The techniques of antisepsis and asepsis are effective against most vegetative forms of bacteria, but spores and some viruses are frequently unaffected. Even when operations are performed in specially designed theatres in which the site of operation is exposed only to filtered air, there remains a small incidence of wound infection caused by organisms that escape these exacting preventative measures.

Aplasia

Aplasia is a total deficiency of growth of an organ or tissue due to a failure of

---

*Joseph Lister (1827–1912), the 'father' of antiseptic surgery, described his pioneer investigations on the value of carbolic acid dressings and the carbolic acid spray in 1867. His studies showed how the very high rate of postoperative sepsis in the Glasgow Royal Infirmary, often as much as 30 per cent, could be greatly reduced by preventing the access of bacteria to wounds.
**Ignaz Philipp Semmelweiss (1818–1865), Hungarian by birth, showed these dramatic results in Vienna 20 years before Lister's observations.

cell division. The defect may be congenital, e.g.
at any time of life, e.g. when bone-marrow cel.
radiation.

See Hypoplasia (p. 106).

APUD cells

The term APUD, an acronym, is applied to a family of endo
distributed throughout the gastrointestinal tract and presen
epithelial structures such as the prostate and bronchus. The c   the
capacity for **a**mine **p**recursor **u**ptake and **d**ecarboxylation before   .reting a
variety of active substances. The word APUD was coined to describe the cell
type.

APUD cells arise from the embryonic ectoderm: they share common properties with cells derived from the neural crest. The endocrine properties of
these argentaffin cells include the ability to synthesize and secrete amines
such as 5-hydroxytrytamine and polypeptides such as insulin, glucagon and
gastrin (pancreatic islets); gastrin and enteroglucagon (stomach); secretin
and gastric inhibitory polypeptide (duodenum), enteroglucagon (intestine);
and calcitonin (thyroid C cells). The bronchial argentaffin endocrine
cell is the Feyrter cell. Some APUD cells can synthesize more than one
hormone.

Monoclonal antibodies against APUD-cell secretions are now widely used
in diagnostic histopathology. These methods allow the exact identification
of the hormone and thus of the cell type; by means of the immunoperoxidase
technique, they can be applied to formalin-fixed, paraffin-embedded
sections.

APUDomas

APUDomas are neoplasms of APUD cells.

The neoplastic cells secrete the endocrine product(s) characteristic of the
parent cell; the neoplasms are therefore functional and each may cause a
clinical syndrome that reflects the synthesis of the hormone. Pancreatic
islet-cell neoplasms, for example, result in clinical syndromes characteristic
of the effects of excess insulin (**insulinoma** of β-cells) or glucagon
(**glucagonoma** of α-cells).

Other neoplasms synthesize ectopic, inappropriate hormones including
corticotrophin (ACTH), antidiuretic hormone (ADH) or vasointestinal
polypeptide (VIP). Occasionally, APUDomas of two or more cell types arise
synchronously and lead, for example, to the effects of excess anterior
pituitary, parathyroid, adrenal cortical and pancreatic endocrine secretion
simultaneously with the onset of peptic ulcer. These syndromes are termed
Multiple Endocrine Neoplasia (MEN) syndromes (p. 101).

Arterial injury

Arteries are resistant to minor trauma. The walls of arteries are very resilient.

Physical injury by high-velocity projectiles such as rifle bullets, is immediately destructive. Mechanical penetration by needle puncture is quickly

by healing, but larger stab wounds such as those incurred during
al catheterization or caused by knives, may result in the delayed development of false aneurysms. Arteries are not immediately damaged by ionizing
radiation, but 'endarteritis' (endarterial fibromuscular hyperplasia) usually
develops and interferes with tissue healing after any subsequent surgery.

The arterial wall also resists most chemical injuries; however, strong acids
applied externally or local injections of steroidal anaesthetic agents can
cause sufficient injury to lead to thrombosis.

Hypersensitivity vasculitis is a form of immunological injury: soluble
immune complexes lodged in the vessel wall incite inflammation, with focal,
segmental vascular destruction.

Arteries resist external neoplastic cell infiltration as long as blood flow is
active.

Arterialization

The word arterialization is used in two ways.

In the first sense, a vein is said to be arterialized when it is placed in
functional continuity with an artery, for example, when part of a saphenous
vein is used to construct a coronary artery bypass. The vein forms new
smooth muscle, becomes thicker and stronger but is susceptible to arterial
disease, in particular atheroma.

In a second sense, venous blood is said to be arterialized when it is exposed
to oxygen in the lungs.

Arteriosclerosis

Arteriosclerosis means a 'hardening of the arteries'. The word is used more
liberally to indicate all forms of degenerative arterial disease and it therefore
embraces atheroma (p. 17), atherosclerosis and Mönckeberg's medial
sclerosis.

Arteriolosclerosis is an analogous term for diseases, such as hypertensive
hyalinization, of arterioles.

Asbestos/asbestosis

Asbestos Asbestos is an inorganic fibrous silicate which had great practical value because it could be spun into yarns and fabrics for heat-resisting
material, and was used to lag boilers and pipes and to make brake linings.

More than 90 per cent of the asbestos used in the recent past in the UK was
chrysolite, i.e. white asbestos. During the manufacture of asbestos-
containing materials, a fine dust was created of which the smaller particles
may be inhaled into the bronchioles and alveoli. The dust is fibrogenic. The
diffuse pneumoconiosis which may eventually result from the inhalation of
asbestos is termed **asbestosis**. This disorder is scheduled for compensation
as an industrial disease; it is often complicated by the development of
tuberculosis.

Asbestos dust is carcinogenic. There is an increased probability of developing bronchial carcinoma. Particular importance is attached to the

induction of the rare tumour, **mesothelioma** of the pleura which is recognized up to 40 years after limited exposure to asbestos dust and which is believed to occur in populations living near industrial asbestos plants as well as among workers or former workers in these plants.

Astrocytes

Astrocytes are the predominant glial cell. The other neuroglia are the oligodendrocytes and the ependymal cells. Although astrocytes are of neuroectodermal rather than of mesodermal origin, it is convenient to draw an analogy between astrocytes and fibroblasts: the cells share common supportive and reparative properties. Microglia are mononuclear phagocytes (p. 155).

Astrocytes grow well in culture when there is a reduction in oxygen tension. When neurones are lost in the human brain or spinal cord, astrocytes multiply **(astrocytosis)**. The division of astrocytes is a response to hypoxia or hypoglycaemia; the presence of paired or clustered astrocytes is evidence of neuronal loss. Multinucleate, giant forms may be present, or the cell body may swell. These fattened cells are called gemistocytic astrocytes or **gemistocytes** (German: gemästete, i.e. fattened, a term also encountered in the so-called mast cell, p. 139). Astrocytes are found near inflammatory, ischaemic or neoplastic lesions and in oedematous white matter. They also appear in excess in special circumstances such as chronic liver failure.

Gliosis   This is the proliferation of the fibrillary processes of the astrocyctes. Glial fibres are therefore cytoplasmic. Although gliosis is occasionally physiological, it generally represents a reparative mechanism following, for example, ischaemic injury.

Atheroma

Atheroma, commonplace in Western societies, is the progressive accumulation of lipid-rich plaques in the intima of medium-size and large musculoelastic systemic arteries. Occasionally there are deposits in the pulmonary-artery intima and beneath the endocardium.

Morphology
The plaques of atheroma acquire a characteristic yellow colour and a grumous consistency: the name atheroma describes this porridge-like material. Small islands of atheroma may be found in infancy and childhood; they are frequent in early adult life. These limited, simple intimal atheromatous plaques become hard and thickened by the formation of new collagen. The term **atherosclerosis** is then used to describe the ageing lesion in which deposits of calcium often occur.

Causes
Atherogenesis, the development of atheroma, has been studied in man and experimentally.

Endothelial injury   Clues to its origin come from the frequent presence of atheroma at sites of turbulent blood flow, such as the most proximal parts of the coronary arteries, and in regions of high blood pressure and rapid flow. Hydrodynamic factors and mechanical injury to the endothelium are therefore invoked. An early view was that local endothelial injury provoked thrombus formation and that this lesion, in turn, covered by endothelium, became an atheromatous plaque. The concept has been retained but much modified. However, the passage of a balloon catheter into the arterial tree of an animal, stripping islands of endothelial cells, is indeed followed by atheroma at the injured sites.

Platelets   Atheroma does not develop if blood platelets are absent; platelets play a critical part in atherogenesis. Platelets adhere to the connective-tissue collagen exposed by endothelial cell loss and are activated; they liberate a growth factor that acts upon medial smooth-muscle cells. Muscle cells migrate into the intima and multiply. The smooth-muscle cells synthesize new collagen and proteoglycan. The intima increases in thickness and extent.

Lipid   The accumulation of lipid in the intima is a central abnormality in atherogenesis. Populations with high living standards, high intakes of fat containing saturated fatty acids and high plasma levels of low density lipoproteins (LDL) (p. 52) have an incidence of atheroma much greater than identical ethnic groups living in conditions of malnutrition. Plasma LDL levels are particularly high in diabetes mellitus and in familial hyperlipoproteinaemia. In both disorders, atheroma is common and severe. It is suspected that lipid accumulates in the arterial intima at sites of smooth muscle multiplication, but these cells themselves may synthesize lipid or avidly phagocytose lipid micelles.

Predisposing factors

Factors **predisposing** to atherogenesis include age, sex, diet, sedentary occupations, endocrine disorders such as diabetes mellitus and myxoedema, hypertension and cigarette smoking.

Atheroma is a disease of young and middle-aged men in well-nourished societies. The frequency of severe disease is much higher in men than women until the age of 45–50 when, after the menopause, the frequency of complicated atheromatous lesions in women is as great as in men. Atheroma is less severe among athletes than among those who do not practice regular, vigorous exercise.

Surgical consequences of atheroma

Because of the high frequency of atheroma in Western society, the disorder has come to be of great surgical importance and many cases present as surgical disorders.

The **anatomical lesions** of atheroma and atherosclerosis are located mainly at the sites of origin of the cerebral, coronary, intestinal, renal and limb arteries. Partial occlusion by the plaque itself, superadded thrombosis, regional ischaemia and infarction or gangrene are the most common pathological results; aneurysms develop that may be saccular, fusiform or dissecting. The common consequences are stroke, myocardial infarction, intestinal infarction, renal ischaemia, secondary hypertension and lower-limb gangrene. The more slowly developing results of atheroma such as angina pectoris and aneurysm can be treated by surgical techniques such as angioplasty, vascular grafting or the implantation of substitute plastic vessels.

Atrophy

Atrophy is a decrease in the size of one or more cells of a tissue or of a part or organ.

The umbilical tissues, for example, atrophy following birth. Muscle and bone atrophy accompany disuse; pressure, ischaemia, nerve injury or mechanical obstruction may each contribute to atrophy under particular circumstances. Rudimentary embryonic tissues such as those of the branchial clefts wholly or partly atrophy before or shortly after birth. In vascular organs such as the kidney, the anatomical distinction between atrophy, due for example to arterial occlusion, and aplasia (p. 14), may be difficult. The persistence of a related but independent organ of normal size such as the ureter may allow renal atrophy to be confirmed. The atrophy of nerves is a special case: following proximal injury, Wallerian degeneration (p. 149) interrupts the structure of axons peripheral to the site of injury. The atrophy of heart muscle cells in old age is often termed brown atrophy, since a lipofuscin pigment accumulates inside the cells. A diminishing quantity of contractile protein leads to the reduced size of the cell.

See Hypertrophy (p. 106).

Sudeck's atrophy   An acute atrophy of bone, usually of the hand or foot, at the site of injury. There is osteoporosis due to vasospasm.

Autoclave

An autoclave is a strong metal container in which surgical instruments and, if necessary, dressings and clothes, are sterilized by steam under high, measured pressure. Steam is more effective than dry heat in sterilization procedures; it has greater powers of penetration and effectively denatures the proteins of most micro-organisms.

The autoclave is first sealed. The air in the autoclave is then entirely replaced by steam. The temperature is raised, causing the atmosphere to be saturated with water vapour at high pressure and temperature. Autoclaves are single- or double-jacketed. The single-jacketed autoclave closely resembles a kitchen pressure cooker. The outer jacket of the double-jacketed autoclave is heated by an external source of steam which also supplies the inner chamber.

Using this system, it has been found that steam is effective in killing bacteria, bacterial spores and the majority of viruses provided that sufficient time at the chosen temperature, the **holding time**, is allowed. The holding times required are:

(at 132 °C)	27 lb/in²*	for 2 min
(at 121 °C)	15 lb/in²	for 12 min
(at 115 °C)	10 lb/in²	for 30 min

See Sterilization (p. 176)

Autoimmunity

Autoimmunity is a description for an immunological or hypersensitivity reaction directed against antigens of the 'self'. It is misleading in the sense that, by definition, immune responses cannot be generated against normal autoantigens. Autoimmune reactions occur because part of the 'self' is changed: antigenic determinants become chemically altered and 'foreign', and self-tolerance (p. 113) is lost. Either humoral or cell-mediated reactions occur against them and the tissue injury caused in this way may be sufficiently severe to lead to an **autoimmune disease**. Among the antigens of the 'self' that can be involved in autoimmune disease are:

Antigen	*Disease*
Soluble, circulating immunoglobulin	Rheumatoid arthritis
Soluble, non-circulating intrinsic factor	Pernicious anaemia
Cell surface receptors (insulin receptor)	Diabetes mellitus
Cell surfaces (heart muscle)	Rheumatic fever
Extracellular antigens, renal, pulmonary basement membranes	Goodpasture's syndrome
Mitochondria	Primary biliary cirrhosis
DNA	Systemic lupus erythematosus
Smooth muscle	Chronic active hepatitis

Autolysis

Autolysis is self-digestion. It is caused by any circumstance such as hypoxia or poisoning that impairs cell metabolism, disturbing the active processes by which the cell walls and those of intracellular organelles retain their structural integrity and specialized functions. Among the organelles affected by hypoxia are the **lysosomes** (p. 135): their hydrolytic enzymes are activated by the acid environment that results from a failure of dying cells to lose H^+ ions by aerobic respiration. These enzymes begin to digest the injured cells themselves and the molecules of the surrounding matrix. The process is accelerated by high body and ambient temperatures and slowed by a reduction in temperature.

The term **cloudy swelling** was used to mean the appearance of cells which became pale and swollen when temporary hypoxia or metabolic failure led to

---

*1 lb/in² = 6.894 × 10³ N/m² (≈ 6.9 kPa)

defective osmotic regulation. The appearances were therefore indistinguishable from the early effects of autolysis.

Autopsy

Autopsy is the procedure of determining, by personal inspection of the body after death, the site and nature of disease. It is a **postmortem examination**.
Necropsy is an alternative name for autopsy.

Bacille Calmette et Guérin (BCG)

BCG is an attenuated strain of *Mycobacterium tuberculosis bovis* that has been grown for long periods on artifical media in a laboratory. The organism loses its virulence but retains its antigenic structure so that it can induce hypersensitivity when injected into a non-immune individual.

BCG vaccination protects efficiently against the hazards of primary tuberculous infection: it is therefore given to all children in the UK who have been shown, by the demonstration of a negative Mantoux test (p. 139), not to have had contact with *Myco. tuberculosis* by the age of 13.

Rarely the small subcutaneous granuloma caused by BCG, microscopically identical with the lesion of active tuberculosis, fails to heal and requires excision for cosmetic reasons.

Bacteria

Bacteria are a small and relatively unorganized, free-living form of uni-cellular life. Bacteria are a species distinct from the plants and animals: they are classified with the algae, fungi and protozoa. There are no specific intra-cellular organelles such as mitochondria and no membrane around the double-stranded DNA.

Organisms in which the nuclear DNA is not arranged in an orderly, definitive form are said to be **prokaryotes**. Bacteria are in this category. Less primitive organisms in which the DNA is in organized nuclei are **eukaryotes**; they include unicellular forms such as the protozoa and multicellular forms such as man.

Cocci are spherical cells: the most important are streptococci (p. 179) which are bacterial cells arranged in chains, and staphylococci (p. 175) which are bacterial cells arranged in groups and clusters. Neisseriae and pneumococci form pairs. **Bacilli** are rod-shaped cells.

The main groups of bacteria are (1) the Gram-positive (p. 25), spore-bearing organisms such as the Clostridia; (2) the Gram-positive, non-sporing bacteria such as the Corynebacteria; (3) the Gram-negative bacilli such as Brucella, the pseudomonads and the Enterobacteria; (4) the acid-fast bacilli such as the Mycobacteria. **Vibrios** are short, curved rods. *V. cholerae* is an example.

The living material of a bacterium is circumscribed by a thin cytoplasmic membrane. The membrane is covered by a rigid supporting cell wall. Occasionally there is an additional protective polypeptide or polysaccharide capsule. In Gram-positive bacteria, the cell-wall is of small amount and simple structure. In Gram-negative bacteria, the cell wall is of very large amount and complex structure: there is lipid, polysaccharide, protein and the lipo-polysaccharide of endotoxin (p. 185). The composition of the bacterial cell wall is important in determining antibiotic sensitivity. When the cell wall is removed or damaged, a living form remains that is an **L-phase** organism.

Some bacteria are motile and have spiral filamentous flagellae. Other bacteria such as the gonococci have fimbriae that enable the organism to attach to the surface of an epithelial cell of the host.

Certain bacterial species such as *Bacillus* and *Clostridium* develop highly resistant **spores** that are a resting phase. Spores can survive long periods of adverse environmental conditions. Spores are more resistant than vegetative bacteria to heat, drying, ultraviolet light, ionizing radiation and dis-infectants. Germination takes place when the environment becomes less hostile. The spore contains antigens not present in the vegetative cell. *Clostridium tetani* forms a drumstick-shaped structure: there is a round, project-ing terminal spore. Neither *Bacillus anthracis* which forms an oval, central spore, nor *Clostridium welchii* which forms an oval, near-terminal spore, do so in living tissues.

Bacterial culture

Bacterial identification requires that the micro-organisms be recovered from patients, wounds, staff, or fomites thought to be infected, and introduced into a culture medium in which they will grow quickly. The general and specific nutritional requirements of the bacteria must be met so that sources of energy, salts, amino acids and cofactors should be present, as well as substances preferred by individual organisms. General growth media are prepared so that they support the multiplication of as wide a range of bacte-ria as possible. Such media are easily and cheaply produced from hydrolysed horse serum protein to which are added meat extract, yeast and sodium chloride. Sometimes the whole medium is made synthetically.

Media are frequently enriched by the addition of horse blood, e.g. **blood agar**, and adjusted to suit the cultural requirements of fastidious micro-organisms by the introduction of agents such as bile salts, and indicators to demonstrate significant changes in pH, e.g. **MacConkey's bile-salt agar.**

Among the physical conditions to be considered when the growth of bacte-ria is attempted are:

oxygen requirements;
occasionally, as with *Brucella abortus*, carbon dioxide;
temperature, the optimum being 37 °C for most human pathogens;·
water – drying impairs growth;
pH – many organisms grow best at a neutral or slightly alkaline pH;
light – ultraviolet light is inhibitory.

Growth media are poured into plastic Petri dishes or tubes. Bacteria grow on the surface of agar or blood agar as pinhead-size colonies. Organisms such as β-haemolytic streptococci (p. 179) produce a haemolysin that breaks down the red blood cells of the medium around their colonies, creating a wide zone of haemolysis. Other bacteria such as the Salmonellae grow best on agar reinforced with bile salts. Intestinal pathogens do not ferment lactose and this can be shown by incorporating an indicator, neutral red, in a lactose-containing medium together with bile salts. *Escherichia coli* of enteropathogenic strains are an exception; they are an important cause of infantile gastroenteritis but ferment lactose.

With colonies formed after as little as 24 hours growth under optimum conditions, simple tests of bacterial identity can quickly be performed. Parts of the golden yellow colonies of *Staphylococcus aureus* (p. 175), for example, can be picked off the surface of the medium, added to a drop of citrated plasma on a glass slide and allowed to mix for a few seconds while the slide is closely observed for the formation of a coagulum that indicates the production by the organism of the enzyme coagulase. This is the **coagulase test** (p. 176). The identification of this enzyme establishes that the staphylococcus is of a pathogenic strain, although coagulase-negative staphylococci are increasingly implicated in infections associated with foreign bodies such as heart-valve prostheses.

Some slowly growing organisms such as *Mycobacterium tuberculosis* grow best on complex media such as coagulated egg containing glycerol. The **Lowenstein-Jensen medium** is often used.

Anaerobic organisms such as *Clostridium welchii (Cl. perfringens)* and *Cl. difficile* only grow in atmospheres from which oxygen has been excluded. The common anaerobic streptococci and organisms such as *Bacteroides* are cultured similarly. One device used to culture anaerobes is the **Gaspak system**, which consists of a pack of powdered sodium borohydride to which water is added, generating hydrogen and carbon dioxide. The pack is placed inside a strong polypropylene jar in the lid of which is a platinum catalyst. The lid of the jar is screwed down firmly and the atmosphere of the jar replaced by the hydrogen generated by the addition of water to the Gaspak.

In general, a qualitive assessment of bacterial growth is made, but when a quantitative assessment is necessary (e.g. for the determination of significant bacteriuria) a measured volume of the specimen is cultured and the number of colonies counted after a specified period of incubation. The count may be expedited by the use of an image analyser: a touch-sensitive probe is employed to record the presence of each colony.

Bacterial growth

Bacteria divide by simple binary fission: a cross-wall extends inwards and divides the cell into two equal parts. Before division occurs, the cells increase in size. Division of *Escherischia coli* can occur every 15–20 minutes under optimal conditions and continues exponentially until energy sources are curtailed. There are large differences in the frequency of bacterial division. The rate of bacterial cell division depends on the genus as well as on the conditions of growth so that *E. coli* divides every 15–20 minutes whereas *Myco. tuberculosis* divides only every 12 hours.

In practice, an initial **lag phase** is succeeded by a phase of **logarithmic growth**. The rate of multiplication then remains stationary before declining and ultimately ceasing. These phases are shown in Figure 1, which also demonstrates the changes seen, in culture, in the total number of bacteria and in the number of living cells. By 5–6 hours, sufficient growth has occurred to permit preliminary identification by modern chemical techniques. By 18–20 hours, enough bacteria have formed to cause a tube of broth in an incubator at 37 °C to become turbid. This is a rough guide to the time taken for significant wound infection to be established clinically.

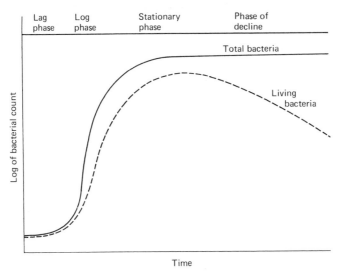

Fig. 1　Typical bacterial growth curve comparing total number of bacteria with those that are viable and capable of dividing to form colonies.

Bacteraemia

Bacteraemia is the presence of bacteria in the blood stream. Small numbers of bacteria are often present in the blood stream of normal persons. Transient bacteraemia may occur after brushing the teeth. The organisms are quickly destroyed in normal subjects but may produce infection of abnormal cardiac valves or of prostheses or cannulae. Patients with known cardiac valvular disease must be given antibiotics during the period of any surgical operation. Dental extractions, dental manipulations and orthodontic procedures are among other common procedures for which antibiotic cover is required. See Viraemia (p. 196). See Septicaemia (p. 168).

Bacterial identification

Bacteria in sufficient numbers are recognized in films made on glass slides and stained. Exudates, pus, cerebrospinal fluid, synovial fluid and cell smears can be shown to contain organisms the appearances of which may allow provisional identification. For example, the presence of many Gram-positive staphylococci (p. 175) in fulminating enterocolitis; of chains of Gram-positive streptococci in wound infections; or of the colonies (sulphur granules) of *Actinomyces israelii* in suspected actinomycosis, provide evidence to enable treatment with antibiotics to be started.

Tests for lactose fermentation (intestinal pathogens are non-fermenters); motility (*Proteus* species); anaerobiasis; (*Clostridia*); enzymes (pathogenic staphylococci); and agglutination by group-specific antisera (β-haemolytic streptococci) are among the methods that can be employed to carry identification further. To determine the source of an organism in an outbreak of infection requires other special techniques. One example is the use of (bacterio)phage typing (p. 26) in tracing the source of a wound infection.

Gas chromatography permits bacterial identification by biochemical criteria; and identification techniques can be assembled 'on-line' in automated apparatus so that many specimens can be handled simultaneously.

Bacterial stains

Although suspensions of bacteria can be seen with dark ground illumination, the light microscopy of smears and sections for surgical diagnosis requires the use of selective stains. Gram's stain is the most useful.

Gram's stain allows bacteria to be divided into broad classes that differ in properties such as growth characteristics, preferred environments, toxin production and antibiotic sensitivity. The categories are (1) Gram-positive, (2) Gram-negative, and (3) bacteria which do not stain with Gram's stain but may, like the mycobacteria, be acid-fast.

The Gram stain, simple and easy to perform, is of great practical importance: it can be applied not only to tissue sections but to smears or sediments of pus, cerebrospinal fluid, pleural and other exudates, and to faecal material. Methyl or crystal violet is poured onto a bacterial smear fixed by gentle heat. The dye is mordanted (secured) by a solution of iodine in potassium iodide, Gram's iodine. When the violet-stained smear is washed with alcohol or acetone one class of bacteria, the **Gram-negative**, are decolorized; they are rendered visible by applying a counterstain which colours them red. The **Gram-positive** bacteria retain the original violet stain.

The mechanism of the Gram stain relates to bacterial structure (p. 21). The cytoplasmic membrane, the cell wall and the outer membrane together form a cell envelope. Bacterial cell walls are strong, rigid, resistant structures surrounding the cytoplasmic membranes of the cells. The cell wall of Gram-positive bacteria is relatively thin. Gram-negative bacteria have a further complex lipid outer membrane, outside the wall. Gram-positive bacteria do not have this structure. Among the consequences of this difference are the greater susceptibility of Gram-positive than Gram-negative bacteria to the antibacterial actions of agents such as penicillin, lysozyme, acids, some dyes and iodine, but a lesser susceptibility to antibody and complement, proteolytic enzymes and alkalis.

The cell walls of the third category of organism, notably *Mycobacterium tuberculosis*, *Myco. leprae*, and of some nocardia, e.g. *Nocardia asteroides*, contain a wax that stains poorly with Gram's method. When heated with carbolfuchsine in the **Ziehl-Neelsen** method, the wax retains this red dye which then resists decolorization by strong acids and by ethanol. The organisms are said to be **acid and alcohol fast**: they are seen against a background provided by a counterstain which may be blue (methylene blue) or green (malachite green). **Auramine** is a fluorescent yellow dye or stain that is now preferred for the demonstration of *Mycobacterium tuberculosis*. The dye cannot be employed as a food colorant or skin antiseptic: it is a carcinogen. Whereas to search a smear for mycobacteria with the Ziehl-Neelsen method requires 20 minutes with a x100 oil-immersion microscope objective lens, auramine can be used readily with a x25 objective lens and a search completed in 2–3 minutes.

The word 'fast', of Anglo-Saxon origin, indicates the strength with which the carbolfuchsine is retained. Mycobacteria that show this important property include those causing human and animal tuberculosis and leprosy; animal pathogens such as the vole bacillus and the avian bacillus (*Myco. avium*); saprophytes such as the smegma bacillus (*Myco. smegmatis*); and numerous 'atypical' mycobacteria such as *Myco. kansasii, Myco. marinum, Myco. intracellulare* and *Myco. fortuitum*. These organisms are normally not pathogenic but are able to cause disease under special circumstances such as those of immunosupression (p. 115) or local injury (p. 194).

Bacteriophage

Bacteriophages (phages) are viruses that multiply in bacteria; virulent phages cause the host bacterium to lyse. Large bacteriophages resemble syringes in shape and in function; the head contains double-stranded DNA. There is a hollow tail with a base plate where the virus attaches to the bacterial cell wall. Phage DNA is transferred to the bacterium through the tail in the process of **transduction** and integrated into the genome of the bacterial cell which then manufactures new phage protein and nucleic acid. Eventually, the parasitized bacterial cell is disrupted by lysis.

Phages can be used to type bacteria: thus, different strains of an organism such as *Staphylococcus aureus* display different susceptibility to different phages. Twenty-four staphylococcal phage types can be recognized. The identification of a single phage type of staphylococcus in an outbreak of wound infection can assist in tracing the source of the infection. The organisms are isolated from the wound and, subsequently, from a carrier, who may be a surgeon, a member of the nursing staff or the patient himself. Confirmation of the source of the infection is achieved when the bacteria from both subjects are shown to belong to a single phage type.

Bacteroides

Bacteroides are an important Gram-negative, non-sporing anaerobic family of bacilli that are prolific commensals of the lower intestinal tract of man. They are frequently present in the mouth and oropharynx. Bacteroides may exist in the lower genitourinary tract in the female and can cause infection after abortion or childbirth. Normally, Bacteroides are not highly invasive but they are potentially pathogenic. When there is local tissue injury, as in surgical procedures on the large intestine, or when metabolic disorders such as diabetes mellitus or immunosuppression impair host resistance, Bacteroides may cause local infection. Less often they gain access to the blood stream. Metastatic infection, for example of the brain, may ensue. Postoperative bacteraemic shock may result. Bacteroides are relatively resistant to the penicillins but respond to metronidazole and to the lincomycins.

Basal-cell carcinoma

Basal-cell carcinoma (BCC) is a common neoplasm of the skin of older people, particularly of whites such as the sheep farmers of Queensland, long exposed to the intense UVL of sunny, subtropical climates. The neoplasm, which may be multifocal, arises from the basal cells of the epidermis of the face, eyelids, forehead and other frequently exposed parts; it is locally invasive. Untreated BCC may progress to gross tissue destruction, causing the loss of an ear or the nose or penetration of a cranial bone with exposure of the meninges. BCC does not metastasize. Although ulceration is common, so that the older term **rodent ulcer** is still used, solid and micro-cystic forms are frequent. Biopsy of all suspect skin lesions is mandatory. The specimen must include a margin of normal tissue. Excision is curative and the neoplasm responds to radiotherapy.

Bile

Bile, the exocrine secretion of the liver, comprises cholesterol, phospholipids, bile acids, bile pigments, inorganic ions and water. Abnormalities in the proportions of these constituents often contribute to the development of biliary calculi (p. 42). Bile is also a vehicle for the excretion of toxic substances of high molecular weight.

Bile acids

Cholic acid and chenodeoxycholic acid are conjugated with taurine (from meat) and glycine (from vegetables) to form water-soluble detergents, the bile acids. These acids are essential for the emulsification of triglycerides in the small gut and assist their enzymatic hydrolysis. The sum of the bile acids in the liver, biliary apparatus, gut and body fluids constitutes a metabolic pool.

Obstruction to the outflow of bile by calculi, tumours or fibrosis of the biliary tract or pancreas, leads to steatorrhoea and the excretion of bile acids in the urine. The synthesis of bile acids is reduced by hepatocellular disease which may also lead to steatorrhoea. A reduction in the bile-acid pool may follow disease or resection of the distal ileum, the main site for the reabsorption of bile acids in the enterohepatic circulation. The incidence of biliary calculi in these patients is much increased (p. 42).

A proportion of the bile acids is deconjugated in the bowel by bacterial action. In patients with abnormally large bacterial populations e.g. with incomplete intestinal obstruction or with blind loops, the level of free bile acids and their metabolites may be very high. There is evidence that this may contribute to the development of large-bowel neoplasms. Reflux of bile acids into the stomach and oesophagus is a cause of gastritis and oesophagitis and this sequence may be important in the development of gastric carcinomas.

Bile pigments

Bile pigments are derivatives of the porphyrin **haem**, the oxygen-carrying part of the haemoglobin molecule. Ageing red blood cells are broken down each day in very large numbers. Red blood cell destruction takes place in the mononuclear macrophages of the reticuloendothelial system, in particular in the sinusoidal cells of the red pulp of the spleen (p. 173). Within these cells, haem is freed and converted to **bilirubin**, a water-insoluble, iron-free molecule that leaves the macrophages attached loosely to plasma albumin. The bilirubin–albumin complex is conveyed in the blood to the liver, entering the hepatocytes. Within these cells, bilirubin is conjugated with glucuronic acid to form a water-soluble glucuronide that is excreted in the bile. The normal plasma concentration of total bilirubin, largely unconjugated, is less than 15 μmol/l. In the small gut, bilirubin glucuronide is converted by bacterial action to a mixture of colourless compounds called **faecal urobilinogen** ('stercobilinogen'). However, oxidation easily converts these colourless substances to orange-red **faecal urobilin**. The major portion of the faecal urobilinogen is absorbed from the gut and recirculated like the bile acids. A small fraction is excreted in the stool, producing its characteristic colour, and an even smaller fraction of the reabsorbed urobilinogen in the blood stream is excreted as **urinary urobilinogen**.

The presence of excessive quantities of bilirubin in the blood and body fluids constitutes **jaundice** (p. 125). In the presence of hepatocellular disease, reabsorbed faecal urobilinogen is incompletely excreted; excess urobilinogen is then detected in the urine. A comparable excess of urinary urobilinogen is also a consequence of a high rate of red cell lysis, for example in familial spherocytosis (p. 91). Since there is no impediment in this condition to the escape of conjugated bilirubin bile salts from the liver into the gut, they do not appear in the urine. The accompanying jaundice is said to be 'acholuric'. By contrast, with an obstruction to biliary excretion and consequential jaundice, conjugated bilirubin fails to reach the gut, jaundice is manifest, bilirubin and bile salts appear in the urine, but urobilinogen disappears.

Biopsy

The word **bios** in ancient Greek meant life. Biopsy is the examination of living tissue or cells. In practice, biopsy is usually undertaken to establish diagnosis but may be required to stage a lymphoma before chemotherapy or radiotherapy; to assess endocrine status; or to judge the progress of a disease in response to treatment.

Small biopsies

Small specimens sufficient for diagnosis can be obtained by scraping or shaving a skin surface or by passing a spatula or swab across a mucosal surface, techniques used in the diagnosis of skin diseases such as leucoplakia with pruritus and oral and pharyngeal disease. Scraping may not yield enough tissue for adequate assessment of the depth and extent of a neoplasm. Small, solid samples are obtained by needle biopsy or fibreoptic endoscopy.

Needle biopsy   If the tissue is sufficiently soft, adequate biopsy specimens can be obtained with hollow needles. Needle biopsy is employed on a very large scale for the study of tissues ranging from breast and thyroid to synovia. Comparable specimens can readily be obtained from bone by rotary cutting trephines with serrated ends, operated manually or by motor. Tissue is now often derived from structures within the thoracic or abdominal cavities by percutaneous puncture using needles guided by ultrasonography or computerized axial tomography (CAT).

Fibreoptic endoscopy and biopsy   Endoscopy is the examination of the interior of the body by means of an instrument which incorporates an optical system and a source of light.

Instruments for endoscopy may be rigid or flexible. Using the principles of fibreoptics, flexible endoscopes are now made from parallel bundles of very fine plastic fibres along which light can pass without distortion. It is therefore posssible to examine the coelomic cavities, the genitourinary tract, the respiratory tract and the gastrointestinal tract from either end. The endo- and myocardium are accessible to cutting devices introduced via a brachial artery. Most endoscopes contain channels through which small pieces of tissue or fluid may be collected under direct vision for biochemical, cytological or histological examination; still and television cameras can be fitted to record the investigation.

Larger biopsies
Larger biopsies are conveniently obtained by knife. Depending upon the size of the lesion and the relative size of the specimen, the biopsy may be **excisional** or **incisional**. Excision is often preferred, in the case of suspected neoplasms, to minimize the risks of disseminating cancer cells and of implanting them into healthy tissue. In the case of foci of infection, excision diminishes the hazards of disseminating the organism. An important advantage of excision is that it guarantees the provision of microscopic sections representative of the material under investigation.

Processing   The precise manner in which biopsy specimens are handled after they are obtained is crucial to microscopical interpretation. Cell preparations and smears, spread on slides, can at once be fixed by an alcohol spray. Small fragments of skin are placed in Bouin's fluid. Samples obtained at endoscopy and larger pieces of tissue are fixed in 10 per cent neutral formalin. In all cases, the volume of fluid used should be at least 10 times that of the specimen.

For electron microscopy, the help of skilled technical staff is advised; minute tissue samples, very carefully selected and manipulated without pressure or distortion are rapidly introduced into cold buffered 2 per cent glutaraldehyde.

For frozen section, small, thin blocks, stuck to metal stubs, are quenched in alcohol or acetone chilled to -70 °C with isopropane or in liquid nitrogen at -196 °C, and transferred to a cryostat (p. 67) or to the stage of a freezing microtome.

See Histology (p. 99). See Histological stains (p. 100).

Birth

Birth is the process by which the fetus attains independent existence.

There are many coincidental changes: the whole right ventricular output of blood is passed through the pulmonary artery and the ductus arteriosus closes. The pulmonary air spaces are inflated. Red-cell formation in organs other than bone marrow is curtailed and soon ceases. Maternal plasma IgG passed across the placenta is catabolized to be replaced by infantile IgM and, later, IgG. The thymus involutes and the large fetal adrenal cortex becomes smaller.

The hazards of birth range from mechanical, hypoxic and vascular injuries to the central nervous system, to umbilical sepsis; the acquisition of parasitic disease such as toxoplasmosis; and persistent hyperbilirubinaemia, i.e. jaundice, attributable to impaired bilirubin conjugation.

Bleeding

Bleeding may follow injury to arteries, capillaries or veins. Bleeding stops due to a combination of vascular contraction, plugging of the puncture by platelets, and the formation of a clot (p. 56).

The **bleeding time** is the time taken for a small skin wound made with a needle or stylet to stop bleeding; it varies from one to nine minutes. An excessive bleeding time is usually due to a combination of failure of vascular contraction and either thrombocytopenia or thrombocytopathia. Abnormalities of platelet function and of coagulation are described on pp. 60 and 59. Small haemorrhages into the skin, epithelium or peritoneum are **petechiae**. Larger areas of flat haemorrhages are **ecchymoses. Purpura** (Latin: purple) describes either petechiae or ecchymoses. Purpura may be due to disease of small vessels or platelet abnormalities.

If bleeding produces a swelling, the lesion is a **haematoma** (p. 91).

Non-thrombocytopenic purpura   This describes bleeding due to damage to small vessels. **Scurvy** (p. 168) was one of the first diseases to be identified in this group. The causes of petechial haemorrhages in scurvy are thought to include the inadequate intercellular support for the blood vessels due to abnormal connective tissue. **Henoch–Schönlein purpura** is a disease of young people that follows infection, usually streptococcal. In addition to skin lesions, there is bleeding into the gut wall, producing abdominal colic and even intussusception. Acute glomerulonephritis occurs and death may follow. Henoch–Schönlein purpura is an immune-complex disease and complexes can be demonstrated in the affected tissues. Purpura is also observed in patients with severe **infections** such as meningococcal septicaemia, diphtheria, typhus and some virus diseases including those of childhood. Capillaries are damaged by toxins released by the infective agents although thrombocytopenia and disseminated intravascular coagulation (p. 73) may contribute to the injury.

Telangiectasia   Telangiectasia is a persistent condition of multiple dilated blood vessels. Telangiectases can be distinguished from purpura since they disappear under pressure applied with a glass slide. Previously unexplained bleeding into the gastointestinal tract has recently been shown often to be due to telangiectasia. **Hereditary haemorrhagic telangiectasia** is inherited as an autosomal dominant trait. There are microvascular dilatations in the skin, mucosa and gastrointestinal tract.

Blood-borne infection

The majority of infecting viruses and rickettsia, but few bacteria and fungi, enter the blood. Whereas viraemia is clinically silent, bacteria and fungi multiply extracellularly and may release toxins, causing severe disease.

In systemic virus disease, the organism quickly reaches the blood after passing through an epithelial surface. **Primary viraemia** results. Thus, in measles, virus multiplies briefly at an infected site such as the bronchiole, and passes through lymphoid tissue to the blood. Distant organs such as the brain are then invaded. The blood is then re-seeded, and a massive **secondary viraemia** develops with the infection of a further series of tissues. In measles, these include the skin where a rash (exanthem) occurs. The frequency of viraemia explains why blood, plasma and blood products are important sources of common viruses such as those of hepatitis (p. 96), and why blood transfusion can be hazardous.

In systemic bacterial disease, bacteria commonly enter the blood by chance (bacteraemia) (p. 24). Foci of metastatic infection arise when there is a localizing factor, such as a congenitally bicuspid aortic valve or a mitral valve disorganized by rheumatic fever, or when resistance is impaired. Thus, bacterial endocarditis may follow bacteraemia by organisms of the *Streptococcus viridans* group after dental manoeuvres, and osteomyelitis follows local trauma in growing bones when there is transient *Staphylococcus aureus* bacteraemia. In a few instances, widespread foci of infection are regular features of a bacterial disease: typhoid (*Salmonella typhi*) and anthrax (*Bacillus anthracis*) are examples.

Micro-organisms may also be carried free in the plasma, in the erythrocytes, leucocytes or platelets, or in a combination of these compartments (Table 3).

Table 3 Blood-borne infection: examples of micro-organisms carried in blood in human disease

	Free in plasma	Within mononuclear phagocytes	Within polymorphs	Within erythrocytes
VIRUS	Poliovirus	EB virus		Colorado tick fever virus
	Yellow fever virus	Measles virus		
BACTERIA	*Streptococcus pneumoniae* *Bacillus anthracis*		pyogenic bacteria	*Bartonella bacilliformis*
PROTOZOA	*Trypanosoma cruzi*	*Leishmania donovani* *Toxoplasma gondii*		*Plasmodium falciparum*

According to the site of infection, the spread of micro-organisms within the body may be initially within the systemic, pulmonary, or portal circulations. Retrograde emboli and paradoxical routes are possible.

Blood culture

Blood culture is used to detect and identify bacteria present in (bacteraemia) or multiplying in (septicaemia) the circulation. The number of organisms is often small and relatively large volumes of blood are used to inoculate a variety of culture media. The natural bactericidal or bacteriostatic actions of the blood are minimized by using large bottles of culture medium, diluting the blood, or by adding substances to inhibit antibacterial action. Initial tests for bacteraemia are now often made by an automated radiometric culture technique: multiple samples can be grown overnight to give early evidence of infection.

Ten millilitres of blood is taken by venepuncture after treating the skin with an antiseptic such as chlorhexidine. The blood, withdrawn by presterilized plastic syringe, is introduced into culture bottles the tops of which are sterile (Viskaps) or are treated with antiseptic. Dilution of the blood by the culture medium is enough to liberate bacteria from fibrin clots. Anticoagulants such as liquoid (sodium polyethanol sulphonate) can also be used for this surpose: liquoid has the advantage that its inhibitory effect on bacterial growth is slight and it exerts a neutralizing effect on the natural bactericidal action of the blood.

The media now in use will support the growth of most pathogens. However, the addition of a bile salt, sodium taurocholate, can be used to assist the recovery of *Salmonella typhi* and *S. paratyphi*. Anaerobic organisms such as *Bacteroides* and the obligate anaerobic streptococci found in the female genital tract are of particular importance in surgical bacteriology and additional cultures are set up in selected media to support their growth (p. 23).

Repeated attempts to recover bacteria from a case of suspected infection should be made before the method is abandoned. Six separate attempts are advised. When a patient has already been treated with antibiotics, the inhibitory effects of these compounds may be blocked by adding to the culture media agents such as para-aminobenzoic acid (PABA) which competes with the tetracyclines, or penicillinase which destroys penicillin.

Blood groups

Human red blood cells are divided into a series of groups on the basis of the presence or absence of surface antigens. Thirteen groups are of major significance. They are ABO, rhesus, MNSs, P, Lutheran, Kell, Lewis, Duffy, Kidd, Diego, Yt, I and Xg. An individual is said to be of a particular blood group when his/her red cells bear the appropriate antigen.

The surfaces of human and of many other mammalian red blood cells have polypeptide or carbohydrate **blood group antigens**. When blood is transfused into a recipient whose red-cell antigens are of a different structure, antibody formation is provoked. Serious reactions are likely when a second transfusion is necessary. In the case of the ABO antigens, the situation is made more complex by the fact that each individual's plasma contains natural, complementary antibodies. Adverse reactions (p. 36) are therefore probable on the first occasion of an incorrectly matched blood transfusion.

ABO blood groups   These are the most important. All human red blood cells inherit either A or B antigenic substances or neither. Therefore four ABO blood groups are designated (Table 4) depending on whether antigens A and B exist together (group AB), separately (groups A or B) or not at all (group O). Because the ABO antigens and antibodies are shared within a single species, they can be described as isoantigens and as isoantibodies respectively (iso = equal). The serum of persons who are of group A contains antibodies called (haem)agglutinins against the red cell antigens of group B and vice versa. When the red cells bear both A and B antigens, and the group is AB, no serum agglutinin is present; when the group is O, haemagglutinins against both A and B agglutinogens are identified. The haemagglutinins are IgM antibodies. After birth they form naturally in response to normal exposure to the bacterial polysaccharide antigens of the gut. These polysaccharides resemble the A and B antigens. The individual responds, however, only to polysaccharides absent from his/her own red blood cells so that a person who has inherited group A red cell antigen forms only anti-B haemagglutinins and vice versa. The autoantigenic substances are tolerated.

It is highly unlikely that an individual can possess red blood cells with antigens of more than a single ABO group. When however, in special circumstances, two or more embryos share a single placenta, a phenomenon much more common in cattle than in man, a mixture of blood-forming cells takes place; the individual then shares red blood cells and red blood cell antigens of more than one blood group and is said to be a **chimaera**. The word chimaera derives from the name of the mythical Greek creature that enjoyed the head of a bull and the hind limbs of a horse. Chimaeras are frequent in cattle with multiseptate placentas.

Table 4   The ABO blood groups

Group	Genotype	Red-cell agglutinogens	Serum agglutinins	Frequency (%)
AB	AB	A + B	none	3
A	AA or AO	A	anti-B	42
B	BB or BO	B	anti-A	9
O	OO	none	anti-A and anti-B	46

Rh blood group (rhesus, from the monkey, *Macaca rhesus*).   Rhesus antigen is present on the surfaces of the red blood cells of 85 per cent of individuals in the UK, who are therefore said to be Rh-positive. The Rh antigen is coded by three pairs (alleles) of closely related genes Cc, Dd and Ee so that each individual locus is CDe, cDe, CDE and so on. D is the most frequent of the dominant genes; most Rh-positive individuals in the UK are D rather than C or E. There are large racial differences in the frequency with which the Rh antigen is present; in China, only 55 per cent of the population is Rh-positive.

Individuals who lack the Rh antigen and who are therefore said to be Rh-negative, do not possess natural anti-Rh antibodies in their plasma. If a Rh-negative patient is transfused with Rh-positive blood, anti-Rh antibodies may be formed. Repeated transfusion provokes increasingly high antibody titres and may result in transfusion reactions with haemolysis and the other undesirable effects characteristic of incompatible blood transfusion (p. 37).

An analogous situation arises when a Rh-negative mother bears a Rh-positive child. Small numbers of the fetal red blood cells escape across the thin placental barrier in which the maternal and fetal endothelial cells are separated only by a narrow lamina of extracellular matrix and basement membranes. The fetal red cells stimulate antibody formation by the maternal immune system. Anti-Rh, IgG (but not IgM) antibodies then pass back across the placental barrier into the fetal circulation. Binding to fetal red blood cells, this IgG antibody fixes complement and causes haemolysis. The resulting **haemolytic disease of the newborn** may be mild and associated only with transient postnatal jaundice. However, high serum concentrations of bile pigment tend to accumulate in the basal ganglia and can culminate in the severe neurological syndrome of kernicterus.

It is most important to identify susceptible, Rh-negative mothers and to search for anti-Rh antibody early in pregnancy. It has been found that the intra-amniotic injection of anti-Rh antibody can prevent haemolytic disease by preventing access of fetal Rh-positive cells to the maternal circulation. Anti-D antibody is the most valuable for this purpose. Alternatively, exchange transfusion of the newborn infant can be employed to remove all fetal red blood cells prejudiced by bound maternal anti-Rh antibody.

Blood group incompatibility

Blood for transfusion is said to be incompatible with that of a recipient when it includes red cell antigens that can react with natural (e.g. ABO) or acquired (e.g. Rh) antibodies present in the recipient's plasma, or when it contains antibodies able to combine with recipient's red blood cell antigens. Normally, blood of the same ABO group as that of the recipient should be chosen for transfusion. Transfusion is only permissible when the ABO and Rh groups of both donor and recipient have been established and after a compatibility test has been performed in the laboratory. This test is necessary since very occasionally transfusion reactions may result from severe incompatibility of one of the rarer blood group systems such as Kell, Duffy or Kidd, the identification of which is not part of routine blood grouping. Blood of group O, so-called universal donor blood, should be transfused in emergency only if it has been shown to contain low titres of anti-A and anti-B isoagglutinins, because rare transfusion reactions are attributable to a response between the donor plasma antibodies and recipient red blood cells.

Blood loss

Blood loss may be slow and clinically imperceptible; at an obvious rate; or disastrously rapid.

The continual slow loss of blood, often from capillaries or small veins, results in hypochromic, microcytic (iron deficiency) anaemia (p. 8). Very rapid blood loss, from arteries, large veins or ruptured viscera, results in haemorrhagic shock or death. If massive haemorrhage is not fatal, vasoconstriction of peripheral and of visceral arterioles diminishes perfused territories. The circulating blood volume is reduced with no immediate alteration in the packed cell volume. In the absence of intravenous or intra-arterial transfusion, the circulating blood volume is gradually restored by the passage of interstitial tissue water into the blood stream. The diffusion of water in this way is a result both of osmotic change and of lowered arteriolar filtration pressure. There is a consequential fall in the red cell and haemoglobin concentrations and in the packed cell volume. Ultimately, accelerated haemopoiesis, recognized by the presence of reticulocytes in the circulation, restores red blood cell mass and haemoglobin concentration to normal.

Small wounds of very vascular tissues such as the scalp may be responsible for disproportionately severe bleeding and a substantial blood loss. Injury of some tissues that are very vascular, such as the liver, leads to a disproportionately heavy blood loss. Surgeons often underestimate the volume of blood lost during operation. The volume of blood collected in aspiration ('suction') apparatus should be measured and swabs weighed. An allowance is necessary for drying of blood by evaporation.

In severe injuries, it is convenient to estimate a loss of 500 ml of blood from each superficial wound as large as an open human hand, or each deep wound the size of a closed human fist. Particular dangers are offered by the concealed haemorrhage of closed fractures, especially those of long bones. Bone is very vascular and much blood may be lost both from the fracture and from the surrounding lacerated muscle and soft tissues. Thus volumes of blood lost from common fractures may be:

Site of fracture	Litres of blood lost
humerus	0.5 – 1.0
radius + ulna	0.5
femur	0.5 – 1.5
tibia + fibula	0.5 – 1.0
pelvis	1.0 – 3.0

Other causes of concealed haemorrhage include injuries to abdominal viscera with the intra- or retroperitoneal accumulation of blood, and concealed accidental haemorrhage in pregnancy. Intra- and postpartum haemorrhage are usually manifest. The rapid loss of blood into the gastrointestinal tract is generally revealed as haematemesis or melaena. In haemoptysis, blood loss is rarely massive.

Blood storage

The storage of whole blood is possible at low temperature. Without special cryoprotectants, whole blood cannot be frozen without damaging the red blood cells. The optimum temperature for preservation is 4–6 °C; at this temperature, bacterial proliferation is greatly slowed, but not prevented.

After 21 days, stored blood must be discarded: ageing red blood cells lyse and the oxygen-carrying capacity of the blood diminishes.

Whole blood is best stored in refrigerators under the immediate supervision of a haematologist or pathologist; the refrigerator should be used for this purpose only. An anticoagulant is added to the whole blood at the time of collection. Sodium citrate (p. 55) is preferred. When removed from the refrigerator for use, blood should be allowed to warm before infusion. In temperate countries, blood should not be returned to storage if it has been outside the refrigerator for more than 30 minutes. Whole blood can also be stored for periods of up to three months if it is mixed with glycerol as a cryoprotectant, rapidly frozen, and held at -90 °C, a technique that requires very costly equipment.

Plasma, fibrinogen and other blood proteins can be preserved by freeze-drying.

Blood transfusion complications

Blood transfusion may be complicated by hydrodynamic, thrombotic, haemorrhagic, infective or immunological phenomena.

Hydrodynamic phenomena
Air may be introduced inadvertently into the venous or arterial circulation during transfusion: air embolism (p. 75) results. Formerly the most common cause of air embolism was the injection of air into bottles of blood to increase the rate of flow in emergency. There are now more effective methods using peristaltic pumps or the manual compression of envelope containers.

Microaggregates of red and white blood cells and platelets may form in stored blood; they are removed by filters of small pore size inserted in the transfusion set.

Intravenous infusion of any fluid may precipitate heart failure and oedema. This is particularly likely to occur following infusion of blood and other oncotic fluids which do not quickly leave the circulation.

Thrombotic and haemorrhagic phenomena
Mechanical inflammation of the vessel wall can be caused by a needle or catheter. Thrombosis commonly follows and embolism is a possible sequel.

The amount of citrate (p. 55) used as anticoagulant in stored blood is insufficient to produce hypocalcaemia and coagulopathy even after large transfusions. If there is bleeding following transfusion, a haemolytic reaction to the transfusion of incompatible blood should be suspected (see below). Lysis of incompatible cells releases thromboplastic substances; disseminated intravascular coagulation (DIC) (p. 73) may develop.

Infective phenomena

Bacterial   The administration of blood containing significant numbers of viable bacteria is rare. Septicaemia after transfusion is therefore very infrequent. Nevertheless, stored blood is an excellent culture medium and blood should not be given if it has been out of cold storage for longer than 30 minutes.

Viral   Prospective donors are tested for anti-AIDS virus antibody and blood for donation is examined for the presence of hepatitis B surface antigen and antibody (p. 12). In spite of this screening, there is a small but definite risk of developing hepatitis B after blood transfusion. This risk is greatly increased following the infusion of pooled plasma. In communities where donors are paid, the likelihood of non-A, non-B hepatitis is high.

Immunological phenomena

Allergic   Allergic reactions such as urticaria and fever occur after 1 per cent of blood transfusions. The reactions are due to antigens in the donor blood to which the recipient is hypersensitive or to antibodies from donors who are hypersensitive to antigens in the recipient's blood. Anaphylaxis is rare.

Haemolytic   Haemolytic reactions are due to transfusion of incompatible blood (p. 32). They are likely to be due to a clerical error in the laboratory but may result from a mistake made at the bedside. The incidence of incompatible transfusion is reduced when homologous blood, i.e. of the same ABO and Rh groups (p. 32) as those of the recipient, is transfused. The isoantibodies in the blood of some donors of group O may be of such a titre that they will lyse the red cells of recipients with blood of groups AB, A or B. More rarely, a haemolytic reaction is due to incompatibility within one of the many other subgroups. If a haemolytic reaction is recognized early and the transfusion stopped, the only consequence may be the development of haemolytic jaundice. If the reaction is severe, haemoglobinaemia, haemoglobinuria and renal tubular necrosis are likely.

Bone marrow after blood loss

Normal red bone marrow derives its colour from the developing red and white blood cells. Yellow marrow retains the ability to produce red blood cells but is predominantly fat, as the colour suggests. At birth, all the bones contain some red marrow and islands of haemopoietic cells may still be present in the liver. By the age of 20 years, red marrow is found only in the skull, scapulae, clavicles, sternum, ribs, vertebrae, pelvis and in the proximal ends of the long bones.

In patients with anaemia due to chronic blood loss the yellow marrow turns red as it once again begins to produce red blood cells. After a single large haemorrhage there is no immediate increase in the apparent quantity of red marrow but examination of its content reveals a qualitative change: there is an increase in the relative number of the red blood cell series compared to the leucocyte series. An increase in the relative quantity of red-cell precursors such as basophilic erythroblasts indicates the onset of rapid production of red blood cells.

Botulism

Botulism is a rare form of food poisoning in which a neurotoxin formed by the anaerobe *Clostridium botulinum* (the 'sausage' bacillus) (p. 56) causes a paralysis that may be fatal.

The organism is a widely distributed saprophyte, present in soil and vegetable matter. Spores are formed that can resist the sterilizing action of moist heat at 100 °C for several hours; they germinate in foods such as meat and sausage that have been improperly canned or bottled. After germination, the organism forms one of the most potent of known toxins. Taken by mouth, the toxin is absorbed from the gut and acts on the cholinergic motor endplates of the nervous system, causing paralysis of muscles including those of the diaphragm and eye.

In infancy, *Cl. botulinum* is believed to be an occasional cause of neonatal gastroenteritis.

Burns and scalds

Burns are injuries caused by excessive dry heat, scalds by excessive moist heat. Burns are usually of external body surfaces, although hot gases may burn the trachea and bronchi. There is a direct relationship between the extent of injury and both the temperature to which the skin is exposed and the time of the exposure. A flash burn at 10 000 °C for 1/1000 second can cause injuries comparable with a hot water bottle at 45–55 °C left in contact with a limb overnight.

Severity   Burns may be superficial, with destruction of part of the thickness of the skin, or deep, with whole-thickness skin loss. In cutaneous burns, if the applied heat is sufficient, a central zone of coagulation or carbonization is surrounded by zones of partial injury in which cell function is disturbed without being lost, allowing signs of injury such as inflammation to develop. Red blood cells lyse within small blood vessels. At the margin of the burn, thrombosis occurs.

Effects   The most important immediate effect of a severe burn is shock and fluid loss. The severity of these disturbances is in proportion to the area of the body that has been injured. A 'rule-of-thumb', the so-called 'rule-of-9s', allows a rapid clinical assessment of the severity of the injury and a calculation of the initial requirements for intravenous fluid replacement. The anterior and posterior surfaces of the trunk and the lower limbs each represent 18 per cent of the body surface; each upper limb and the head represent 9 per cent and the perineum 1 per cent.

Caisson disease

Caisson disease is a syndrome of multiple infarcts caused by the gaseous emboli that may occur in divers and those working under high atmospheric pressures.

In the building of the underwater foundations of bridges and in deep-sea diving, men work in air under high pressure. The gases of the air pass into solution in the body fluids. When decompression occurs quickly, nitrogen, which comprises nearly 80 per cent of the dissolved air, comes out of solution and forms small bubbles which act as gaseous emboli. The bubbles lodge in capillaries or terminal arterioles in territories such as those of the brain and spinal cord where there are 'end-arteries'. Ischaemia results and foci of necrosis cause permanent injury. In bone, aseptic necrosis may predispose to osteoarthrosis, particularly of the femoral head.

Calcification

Calcification is the deposition of insoluble inorganic calcium salts (mineral) in living tissues.

Calcification is an essential, normal part of bone formation; it is closely dependent on normal concentrations of vitamin D, parathormone and calcitonin. Bone mineral is calcium phosphate and calcium carbonate together with small amounts of sodium, magnesium, fluoride and other ions. The calcium salts are present as a mixture of crystalline calcium hydroxyapatite and amorphous calcium phosphate. The hydroxyapatite crystals, delicate, needle-shaped and 100 nm long, accumulate in clusters in relation to bone collagen; they are laid down under the influence of osteoblastic alkaline phosphatase.

As bone forms in zones of endochondral ossification, the matrix near cartilage cells that are undergoing degeneration becomes provisionally mineralized by the deposition of crystalline calcium hydroxyapatite: this deposition is an essential preliminary to the ingrowth into the avascular growth cartilage of sinusoidal capillaries. Provisional calcification is only possible when vitamin D is available. Where mineralization is proceeding during appositional bone growth at mineralization fronts, the mineral deposited is insoluble amorphous calcium phosphate; the formation of insoluble calcium hydroxyapatite crystals follows.

Pathological calcification

Pathological calcification is a common consequence of local or systemic disease. The mineral is calcium hydroxyapatite but other insoluble calcium salts, particularly calcium pyrophosphate, are often deposited.

Heterotopic   Calcification outside sites where mineral is normally deposited is said to be heterotopic.

Metastatic   When abnormal calcification is a sequel to excessively high levels of plasma calcium, due, for example, to hyperparathyroidism or resulting from excess vitamin D, the mineralization is said to be metastatic. The tissues in which the calcium salts come out of solution are themselves structurally and functionally normal. The mineral is precipitated in parts such as arterial walls, gastric mucosa, lungs and the renal interstitium. Metastatic calcification is also encountered in multiple myeloma, sarcoidosis and carcinoma of the breast, and may be caused by administering excess vitamin D or excess calcium.

Dystrophic   Frequently, abnormal calcification occurs in diseased tissues; the circulating and extracellular fluid levels of calcium, phosphate, parathormone, vitamin D and calcitonin are normal. Under these circumstances, calcification is said to be dystrophic. Dystrophic calcification is a feature of senescence and is commonly recognized in the media of musculoelastic arteries such as the radial and popliteal, when the phenomenon is still referred to as Mönckeberg's medial sclerosis. Dystrophic calcification follows acute pancreatitis and occurs in sites of inflammation such as the walls of abscesses, chronic foci of fibrocaseous tuberculosis, sites of parasitic infestation or cysts and densely fibrotic scar tissue; it is also commonplace in complicated atherosclerosis, the walls of aneurysms and cardiac valves, particularly the aortic. Some common malignant neoplasms undergo dystrophic calcification; sand-like, psammoma bodies may be formed. Radiographic and microscopic recognition of calcification in the form of calcium hydroxyapatite is a valuable diagnostic sign of carcinoma of the breast.

Calcinosis
A form of dystrophic calcification. Calcifying tendinitis is calcinosis confined to a tendon. Calcinosis is also a feature of tissues affected by systemic sclerosis, a systemic connective tissue disease. The term 'CREST syndrome' describes systemic sclerosis with calcinosis, Raynaud's phenomenon, oesophageal hypomotility, sclerodactyly and telangiectasia. Tumoral calcinosis is a rare example, displaying a familial trait, occurring in young individuals, often negroid, and affecting soft tissues anterior to the shoulder joint.

Calcium

Calcium (Ca), an element essential for normal life, is required for the formation, growth and maintenance of bone. Extracellular concentrations of Ca^{2+} ions regulate transmembrane potentials and the contractility of muscle cells: low concentrations initiate myofibrillar relaxation. Calcium ions are necessary for the coagulation of blood (p. 57).

Serum concentrations are normally 2.30–2.65 mmol/l; approximately 40–50 per cent is physiologically active, free, ionized Ca: 40–50 per cent is non-ionized and bound to plasma protein, principally to albumin, the distribution being dependent upon plasma pH. The remaining 5–10 per cent of Ca is in the form of complexes with organic acids. Hypoalbuminaemia leads to a fall in total serum Ca without altering muscle contractility, nerve conduction or coagulation. Because total serum Ca is measured when a routine test is requested, the concentration of plasma proteins should be considered when assessing the significance of the results.

Calcium balance is regulated by intestinal absorption, by renal excretion and by the avidity of storage in bone. These processes are controlled by the activities of parathormone, the vitamins D, and calcitonin; and by the permissive effects of growth hormone, cortisol, the sex hormones and triiodothyronine. Consequently, abnormal serum concentrations may result from a very wide variety of disorders.

Hypercalcaemia

Very high levels of plasma calcium are recognized in primary hyper-parathyroidism (p. 154). Causes of less severe hypercalcaemia include metastatic carcinoma of the bronchus, breast and kidney; multiple myeloma; inappropriate secretion of parathormone-like polypeptides by bronchial carcinoma; sarcoidosis; Paget's disease of bone; prolonged immo-bilization; the treatment of osteomalacia with excess vitamin D; hypervita-minosis D of infancy; hyperthyroidism; and hypoadrenocorticalism.

The **milk-alkali syndrome** (p. 1) is not common in this era of H2 recep-tor antagonists but occurred in patients with peptic ulceration who con-sumed huge quantities of milk and alkalis. The large amounts of Ca absorbed from the bowel in this syndrome led to nephrocalcinosis which was made worse by the alkalosis. Severe renal failure followed.

Hypercalcaemia releases excess gastrin; peptic ulceration is more common in the presence of hypercalcaemia, particularly in patients with hyperpara-thyroidism. Pancreatitis is also frequent in patients with hypercalcaemia. The cause is unknown but it has been suggested that Ca may induce the con-version of trypsinogen to trypsin in the pancreatic ducts.

In all forms of hypercalcaemia, metastatic calcification is likely to affect the kidneys and renal failure with nephrocalcinosis may occur. Calcification of the coronary arteries is one consequence.

Hypocalcaemia

The many causes of osteomalacia and rickets contribute to hypocalcaemia, of which tetany (p. 182) is one sign. Renal disease and hypoparathyroidism resulting from surgical or radiation injury to the parathyroids may exert the same effect. Low serum concentrations of Ca can also accompany acute pancreatitis. Rare causes include renal tubular disease, the effects of diuretics such as frusemide, malignant hyperpyrexia and leukaemia.

Calculus

A calculus (stone) is a concretion formed in an excretory duct or fluid-containing viscus. Biliary and urinary calculi are commonplace but salivary, prostatic and pancreatic calculi are found less frequently. **Lithiasis** is the formation of calculi.

Primary calculi

Primary (metabolic) calculi form in the absence of local disease. In the past, nidi such as bacteria and debris produced by inflammation were considered to be responsible for the origin of all calculi.* Now, however, the majority of calculi are thought to derive from the secretions of the ducts and organs in which they are found. Substances of low molecular weight such as calcium, that occur naturally within the secretions, are held in solution by adsorption onto large molecules such as glycoproteins or mucins. Calculi may be formed

---

*Berkeley George Andrew Moynihan (1865–1936), First Baron Moynihan of Leeds, suggested that 'a gallstone is a tombstone to the memory of the germ which lies within it'.

by an increase in the concentration of the crystalloids or a decrease in the concentration of the carrier molecules.

The composition of primary calculi is naturally that of a crystalloid (p. 69) such as cholesterol or cystine. Primary calculi of pure cholesterol, bile pigment, cystine and xanthine may be radiolucent but frequently contain small quantities of calcium or magnesium that render them opaque.

Secondary calculi

Calculi that form around a foreign body such as a suture, desquamated cells or organisms, are said to be secondary. Secondary calculi consist predominantly of radio-opaque salts of calcium and magnesium.

Effects of calculi

Calculi, particularly biliary, may be clinically silent and discovered accidentally at radiological or postmortem examination. However, even those that are clinically silent are likely to cause disease. Until the calculus is passed spontaneously or removed surgically, there may be complete or partial obstruction to the outflow of secretion. If the obstruction is partial or intermittent, there may be proximal dilatation such as hydroureter or hydronephrosis. If the obstruction is complete, all secretion may be stopped. In one kidney, if the other is functioning, disuse atrophy accompanies compensatory hypertrophy of the other. A calculus impacted in the common bile duct produces obstructive jaundice. A calculus impacted in Hartmann's pouch produces a mucocele of the gall bladder (p. 143); if infection supervenes, it gives rise to empyema of the gall bladder. Rarely, a calculus may ulcerate through the wall of the gall bladder into the duodenum to produce gallstone ileus.

Obstruction of the salivary ducts is usually partial, producing a painful distension of the salivary gland from which the duct originates. When there is obstruction and subsequent stasis, infection occurs within the duct, predisposing to the development of secondary calculi. A vicious circle is established. The origin of the infecting organisms is sometimes obscure: although those found in patients with cholangitis are usually enteric, there is little to confirm that the infection is ascending in nature. An empyema of the gall bladder may develop from a mucocele and a hydronephrosis may be converted to a pyonephrosis. Acute sialadenitis with suppuration may occur. Urinary calculi may damage the urothelium, producing haematuria. It is not certain that carcinoma of the gall bladder is more frequent in patients with biliary calculi than in the general population, but chronic inflammation predisposes to the development of cancer (pp. 44, 146).

Biliary calculi

Primary

(a) Pure cholesterol calculi are pale yellow, ovoid and smooth-surfaced. They are single ('solitaire'). Cholesterol in bile is kept in solution in a micelle of cholesterol, bile salts and, to a lesser extent, by phospholipid. Some calculi are formed in patients who excrete excess biliary cholesterol but the majority are due to a decrease in the bile salt pool. Cholesterol calculi are particularly likely to form in patients with hepatocellular disease, or after disease or resection of the terminal ileum (p. 27), in those taking a contraceptive pill and during the last trimester of pregnancy due to hormonally induced stasis in the biliary tree. Cholesterol calculi are uncommon in patients with cholesterolosis of the gall bladder (so-called 'strawberry gall bladder').

(b) Pigment stones, of calcium bilirubinate, are usually multiple, black, friable and irregular in shape. They are formed by the excretion of excess bile pigment and are frequent in patients with congenital haemolytic anaemia (p. 8). By contrast with cholesterol stones, they are more common amongst Africans and Asians than among Europeans.

Secondary
The majority of biliary calculi in the Western world are 'mixed'; they are of mixed shape and size and mixed constitution; they contain predominantly cholesterol but also pigment and calcium salts. Cholecystitis frequently develops in a gall bladder that contains calculi: the centre of the stone is likely to be composed of cholesterol or pigment with successive layers of other substances deposited around it. Calculi frequently develop as 'families'; due to their large number and rapid and concurrent growth, they press upon one another, forming multifaceted surfaces.

Urinary calculi
The majority are formed in the kidney. Some vesical calculi are formed in bladder diverticula or when there is outflow obstruction, particularly if there is coexistent infection. Urinary calculi may also form around foreign bodies such as hairgrips, pieces of catheter or sutures introduced from outside.

Primary
(a) *Cystine.* Cystine is poorly soluble. In patients suffering from cystinuria, pale yellow or white calculi may form.

(b) *Xanthine.* Xanthine is also poorly soluble. In xanthinuria, reddish brown calculi may form.

(c) *Oxalate.* The aetiology of oxalate calculi is unclear. They may occur in patients suffering from the metabolic disorder oxalosis but in the majority of patients who have oxalate calculi, no metabolic disorder can be identified. The calculi are hard, dark brown in colour and have an irregular surface which is particularly likely to produce mucosal damage.

(d) *Urate.* These calculi are common in patients with gout. They are hard and brown in colour but have a smooth surface.

(e) *Calcium.* Calcium is an inevitable component of secondary calculi (see below) but in many patients the cause of calculi containing large quantities of calcium is excessive urinary excretion of this element. Hypercalciuria is found following prolonged immobilization, hyperparathyroidism, renal tubular acidosis, sarcoidosis, chronic pyelonephritis and increased absorption of calcium from the bowel due to hypervitaminosis D.

Secondary

Secondary calculi may form after the introduction of a foreign body into the bladder, around a primary calculus, or following severe urinary-tract infection. They are friable, white and smooth-surfaced mixtures of calcium and magnesium ammonium phosphates and calcium carbonate. **Randall's plaques** are areas of dystrophic calcification in renal papillae: they arise because of the high calcium content in that part of the kidney; it has been postulated that they lacerate through the pelvic mucosa and act as nidi for calculus formation but they are frequently identified in patients without urinary calculi.

Cystine, oxalate, and urate calculi form in an acid urine but the phosphates of secondary calculi are deposited in an alkaline urine particularly in infection due to Proteus, bacteria which split urea and liberate ammonia. Infection is likely when there is stasis due to obstruction.

Salivary calculi

Salivary calculi contain calcium phosphate and carbonate: they form around a central nidus of desquamated epithelial cells and bacteria following infection and are most frequent in the submandibular duct.

Prostatic calculi

Prostatic calculi, of calcium phosphate and carbonate, form in the ducts of elderly patients with benign nodular prostatic hyperplasia; they are multiple. Prostatic secretions become inspissated to form corpora amylacea which act as nidi.

Pancreatic calculi

These calculi are found occasionally in the major ducts in chronic pancreatitis. They comprise calcium phosphate and carbonate.

Cancer

Cancer is the common name for all malignant neoplasms (p. 146).

Neoplasms are encountered in all forms of multicellular life, animal and plant, and cancer may therefore be one inevitable consequence of such life.

Carbuncle

A carbuncle is a large zone of infection of skin and subcutaneous tissue caused by pathogenic staphylococci, particularly by *Staphylococcus aureus*.

Carbuncles are prone to occur in individuals, and especially in diabetics, in whom resistance to infection by pyogenic organisms is low. The affected site is covered by hair-bearing skin and a hair follicle may be the portal of entry of bacteria. Characteristically, the site is one where the skin is relatively thick and firmly attached to the subcutaneous tissue: the back and the back of the neck are particularly susceptible.

There is widespread, diffuse subcutaneous tissue necrosis, contrasting with the localized focus of necrotic subcutaneous tissue in a boil (furuncle) (p. 85). There are multiple openings (sinuses) on the surface and through these thick pus is discharged.

Carcinogen, carcinogenesis

A carcinogen is an agent that causes the development of a neoplasm. Strictly, carcinogenesis, the production of a neoplasm by such an agent, describes the origin only of malignant epithelial neoplasms (carcinoma, p. 49). **Oncogenesis** includes the origin of all benign and malignant growths; in practice the word carcinogenesis is used instead.

Carcinogens are physical, chemical or viral agents; they are environmental hazards. There may be both a racial and a genetic predisposition to their effects. The likelihood of development and growth of a neoplasm is increased by occupational, dietary and social exposure to the influence of carcinogens.

Mechanisms of carcinogenesis

Carcinogens act by causing changes in the genetic code (p. 87). Normal genes may or may not be expressed, a concept of altered differentiation. Mutations may occur. Alternatively, new information may be introduced into the cell genome, e.g. by virus infection. As a result of such changes, the mechanisms that control cell growth are lost or altered. DNA is directly or indirectly changed. Neoplastic cells divide frequently: contact inhibition of cell division is no longer effective. The cell surfaces are altered and negative charges increase. Lectins, proteins that bind to surface glycoproteins, agglutinate some neoplastic cells. Chalones lose their regulatory function.

All carcinogenic influences produce irreversible effects. The actions, for example, of small doses of ionizing radiation or of minute amounts of a chemical carcinogen, are additive, even over long time intervals.

There are thought to be two stages in carcinogenesis. For example, a single small amount of benzpyrene applied to the skin is without visible effect. The subsequent repeated application to the same site of an irritant but non-carcinogenic substance such as croton oil, leads to neoplastic growth. The benzpyrene is said to **initiate** carcinogenesis; the croton oil **promotes** carcinogenesis. Initiation is irreversible, promotion reversible. The croton oil acts as a **co-carcinogen**, but many agents are effective by themselves and are **complete carcinogens**.

Field change

In carcinogenesis, agents initiating or promoting the growth of neoplasms act upon wide fields of organs or tissues. Neoplasms may grow at any focus within those fields which are unusually susceptible to neoplasia. In hereditary multiple polyposis of the colon, for example, several neoplasms may arise simultaneously in various parts of a single organ. Such neoplasms are said to be multifocal. Other regions of the affected tissue may show precancerous changes such as dysplasia (p. 74) or carcinoma-in-situ (p. 49).

Chemical carcinogens

The first evidence of the part that chemicals could play in carcinogenesis was the description by Pott* of scrotal cancer in those who had been chimney sweeps as boys. Soot contains coal tar which is carcinogenic due to the presence of hydrocarbons such as 3, 4-benzpyrene. These hydrocarbons are found in the air of industrial towns, in the exhaust gases of internal combustion engines and in cigarette smoke. At least 11 classes of inorganic and organic chemicals are now known to be carcinogenic; many thousands of compounds have been incriminated.

Carcinogenic polycyclic hydrocarbons bear a generic resemblance to cholesterol (p. 52) and to the steroid hormones. Structurally, these carcinogens are very similar to inert molecules. Whether an individual compound is an active carcinogen or an inactive compound is determined by small but critical changes in structure; 1:2,5:6-benzanthracene is a potent carcinogen; 1:2,3:4-dibenzanthracene is inactive. Carcinogenic activity is related to water solubility and an ability to react with DNA.

Carcinogenic aromatic amines attracted attention after the rise of the synthetic aniline dye industry. Aniline is not carcinogenic but derivatives of the associated compounds β-naphthylamine and benzidine are. β-Naphthylamine induces bladder cancer in species with glucuronidase. β-Naphthylamine is converted to the carcinogen 1-hydroxy-2-aminonaphthalene in the liver where it is safely conjugated with glucuronic acid. The deconjugation of this soluble product in the bladder permits local carcinogenesis which is therefore remote, tissue selective and species specific.

Other important chemical carcinogens include:

azo dyes
  e.g. the artifical colouring agent dimethylamino-azobenzene ('butter yellow');

aminofluorenes
  e.g. the insecticide 2-acetylaminofluorene;

nitrosamines
  e.g. the solvent dimethylnitrosamine;

alkylating agents, linking directly to DNA
  e.g. methylmethanesulphonate; mustard gas;

microbial toxins
  e.g. aflatoxin (p. 4);

inorganic compounds
  e.g. asbestos (p. 16); salts of nickel, chromium, cadmium.

Physical carcinogens

Squamous carcinoma of the hands of radiologists was recognized within a few years of the introduction of x-rays for diagnostic radiology. Ionizing radiations, particularly x- and γ-rays (p. 122) are potent cytotoxic agents; they are also effective carcinogens. Particulate radiation in the form of neutrons and α-particles exerts similar effects. β-Particles (electrons) are carcinogenic provided they gain access to cells after injection, inhalation or ingestion.

---

*Percival Pott (1714–1788) described occupational cancer in 1775 in 'Chirurgical observations relative to the cataract, the polypus of the nose, the cancer of the scrotum etc'.

Solar ultraviolet light (UVL) is less effective as a carcinogen. It is non-ionizing: its influence is limited to exposed skin surfaces. Malignant melanoma (p. 138) and basal-cell carcinoma (p. 27) are produced in white people working in hot, sunny climates such as that of Queensland, Australia.

Ionizing radiations remove electrons from intracellular molecules, creating free radicals that can react with DNA. The mitotic phase of cell division is most susceptible. Consequently, cell populations in tissues such as the testis, bone marrow, small intestinal epithelium and lymph nodes, where divisions are numerous, are particularly vulnerable. Tissue such as brain, hyaline cartilage and cornea are tolerant of high doses of ionizing radiation. Radiation injury to the cornea is a result of altered collagen cross-linking.

Other important physical carcinogens include:

1. atomic bomb explosions; reactor accidents — leukaemia; carcinomas of breast, lung and thyroid

2. occupational inhalation or ingestion of uranium (mines) or radon (watch-dial painters) — bronchial carcinoma osteogenic sarcoma

3. angiography with thorotrast (thorium dioxide) — haemangiosarcoma; cholangiocarcinoma.

Virus carcinogens

Both DNA and RNA viruses (p. 196) can cause neoplasms. Oncogenic DNA viruses permanently change the genetic structure of host cells, but do not kill them; the cells are non-permissive of viral multiplication. The altered morphology and intercellular junctions of the infected cells, their changed chromosomes, the expression of fetal antigens and a tendency towards anaerobic glycolysis, are among aspects of cell life that are transformed. DNA virus genome is integrated directly into the chromosomes of the host cells. To be oncogenic, an RNA virus must first be transcribed by a unique enzyme system. The enzyme is **reverse transcriptase**: its presence in a cell is highly indicative of the influence of an oncogenic RNA virus.

Oncogenic viruses are transmitted horizontally, e.g. by contact, from individual to individual; or vertically, across the placenta.

RNA viruses that are oncogenic often multiply within transformed cells. Of the RNA tumour viruses, the Rous sarcoma virus has one gene (src) necessary for cell transformation but not for viral replication. The src gene codes for a single protein that may be responsible for the complex changes of cancer-cell transformation: the src gene is an example of an **oncogene**. Normal cells have similar genes which have oncogenic potential; these are cellular oncogenes.

Examples of viruses causing neoplasms

Epstein–Barr (EB) virus Epstein–Barr virus is ubiquitous. It causes glandular fever (infectious mononucleosis) in young adults from upper social groups. The virus is closely associated with **Burkitt's* B-cell lymphoma** in malaria-ridden parts of Africa, and with nasopharyngeal carcinoma in South China.

EB virus infection results in humoral antibody formation but chronic, latent virus infection persists. Lymphocytes are infected and more virus is formed in immunosuppressed than in normal persons. Burkitt's lymphoma is found most commonly in children in malarial districts. This curious geographic distribution is not because EB virus and the malarial parasite are both carried by mosquitoes but because malaria probably disturbs the surveillance mechanism of the immune system. Transformed, malignant B (plasma) cells grow unhindered because T helper cells are compromised.

Lymphomas that develop when cytotoxic drugs are used to produce immunosuppression before organ transplantation are frequently caused by EB virus and are of Burkitt (transformed B-cell) type. In infectious mononucleosis, by contrast, the transformed cells are killed. In SE Asia where **nasopharyngeal carcinoma** is exceedingly common, there is an inherited defect in the capacity to respond to cells transformed by EB virus. The deficiency is indicated by the inheritance of particular HLA types.

See Hepatocarcinoma (p. 99)

Kaposi's sarcoma (p. 167).

Rous't sarcoma virus   Rous' sarcoma virus is the cause of chicken sarcomas. It was the first oncogenic virus discovered. The virus is seen by EM as C-type particles, the genome lying centrally within the particle.

Mammary neoplastic (tumour) viruses   Mammary neoplastic viruses cause breast carcinomas in mice. In 1936 Bittner identified female mice with a high or a low incidence of mammary neoplasia. Mothers of a high-incidence strain conveyed cancer to offspring of a low-incidence strain who were not at risk when suckled by mothers of a low-incidence strain. The so-called Bittner RNA virus was transmitted in the milk.

Tumour (neoplastic) necrosis factor (TNF)

The serum from animals injected with agents such as BCG or with bacterial endotoxin contains a polypeptide that kills neoplastic cells. TNF also originates from macrophages. Human TNF can be manufactured by recombinant gene technology.

Carcinoid

Carcinoids are APUDomas (p. 15).

These functioning neoplasms arise from the enterochromaffin cells of the appendix, small intestine, rectum, colon, oesophagus and stomach in this order of frequency, but identical neoplasms occur in the breast, thymus,

---

*Denis Burkitt (b. 1911). His African B-cell lymphoma is believed to have been described in detail by the missionary Sir Albert Cook in an unpublished report.

†Francis Peyton Rous (1879–1970) described the chicken sarcoma virus in 1910 and was awarded the Nobel prize for this work in 1966.

liver, gall bladder, lung and ovary. They are small, yellow and grow slowly, invading the intestinal wall which they may penetrate. The microscopic structure is of nests of cells of a uniform structure, closely related to a meshwork of small, thin-walled blood vessels. Appendiceal carcinoids rarely metastasize: they are encountered by chance when appendicectomy is undertaken in young adults. Small intestinal carcinoids grow to a larger size, may be multiple and metastasize to the liver, lymph nodes, lungs and bone; they may therefore lead to the carcinoid syndrome.

Carcinoid syndrome

The carcinoid syndrome comprises vasomotor disturbance (facial flushing, cyanosis), intestinal hypermotility, episodes of bronchoconstriction, and right-sided cardiac disease in individuals in whom a carcinoid neoplasm, usually of the small intestine, has formed large hepatic metastases.

The cells of carcinoids secrete 5-hydroxytryptamine (5-HT), histamine, kallikrein and prostaglandins. They may also form ACTH, insulin, gastrin, calcitonin and other hormones. The major cause of the symptoms and signs of the carcinoid syndrome is 5-HT. Normally degraded by a healthy liver, in the presence of large hepatic metastases (which also secrete it), 5-HT enters the vena cava and promotes pulmonary valvular stenosis and endocardial fibrosis; it is then degraded to 5-hydroxyindolacetic acid (5-HIAA) in the pulmonary circulation and excreted in the urine. The other symptoms and signs of the carcinoid syndrome are attributable to bradykinin and the prostaglandins, which are not metabolized in the lung and enter the systemic circulation.

Carcinoma

A carcinoma is a malignant neoplasm arising from epithelial cells.

Carcinoma-in-situ

Carcinoma-in situ describes the appearance of a malignant neoplasm (p. 146) in which an island of epithelial cells has assumed the cytological features of carcinoma but in which the basement membrane has not been breached and invasion has not begun.

A distinction is drawn between atypical hyperplasia, dysplasia, and carcinoma-in-situ, but the differentiation demands skill, experience and judgement in microscopy. Applied to the skin, the uterine cervix, the bronchus and the stomach, the diagnosis of carcinoma-in-situ indicates an excellent prognosis by contrast with invasive carcinoma. The individual, desquamated cells of carcinoma-in-situ can be recognized in smears (p. 69) as cancer cells.

Cell

Cells are the structural and functional units of all living creatures.

The human body comprises 10^{13} cells: each is bounded by a **plasma membrane** of lipid in which proteins are embedded. The cell usually contains a conspicuous **nucleus** in which is concentrated all the chromosomal DNA (p. 70). The nucleus, separated from the non-nuclear content of the cell, the **cytoplasm** (cytosol) by a double membrane, includes a smaller **nucleolus** in which the ribosomes are assembled. Continuous with the outer membrane of the nuclear envelope is the **endoplasmic reticulum** (ER). Rough ER bears the ribosomes engaged in protein synthesis; smooth ER lacks ribosomes and is closely concerned with lipid metabolism. The sacs of the **Golgi apparatus** process and package large molecules before they are delivered to other organelles or secreted.

The cytoplasm contains a skeleton of protein filaments including the centrioles and microtubules, actin filaments which determine cell contractility and movement, and intermediate filaments (p. 120). Intermediate filaments include the polypeptides keratin, the neurofilaments and vimentin. **Mitochondria** are the power-houses of the cells, using oxygen to make high-energy ATP. Within the cytoplasm are scattered **lysosomes** (p. 135) and **peroxisomes** that generate and destroy hydrogen peroxide.

Cell growth and division

The multiplication of very large numbers of cells each day is necessary to replace those lost by senescence and injury. There is a cycle (Figure 2) of cell division in most human body cells, although some, such as the neurones, skeletal muscle cells and red blood cells (which possess no nucleus) do not divide after maturation. Neurones regenerate by molecular replacement. In tissues such as those of the lining epithelia, cells divide rapidly and continuously throughout life; the cycle of cell division and growth may be as brief as 8 hours. In many other tissues, the capacity for division is rare. Occasionally the cycle of division is as long as 100 days.

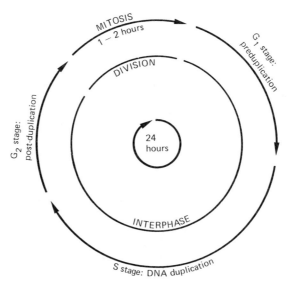

Fig. 2   The stages of mitotic cell division.

The period between cell divisions is the **interphase**. In a 24-hour cell cycle of growth and division, 90 per cent of the time is occupied by interphase, so that the process of division itself, **mitosis** lasts for only 1–2 hours. During interphase, cells synthesize structural and enzymic proteins and other components. The mass of the cell doubles and mitosis commences.

Interphase begins with a G_1 phase (Figure 2) of high synthetic activity. Nuclear DNA is replicated during a small part of interphase, in a period termed the S (synthesis) phase. This is the time when each chromosome (p. 52) divides to form a pair of identical 'sister chromatids'. A further G_2 growth phase follows. The period of division is the M (mitotic) phase, in which there is first nuclear division, mitosis, and then cytoplasmic division, cytokinesis. Early in M phase the divided chromosomes condense and can easily be seen by light microscopy. The phases of cell division influence treatment by antimitotic drugs (p. 13).

Mitosis
Mitosis is the process by which the genetic material of the cell divides in half during somatic cell division; one member of each chromosomal pair passes to each daughter cell.

Meiosis
Meiosis is reduction division, the process by which the germ cells divide to form gametes, the spermatozoa and ova, each of which has only 23 chromosomes.

Cell movement
Many cells are freely mobile. All cells display movements of components such as cilia, microvilli and mitochondria. Movement is readily demonstrated when phagocytes are encouraged to attack pathogenic micro-organisms; within 30 minutes, a polymorph will adhere to vascular endothelium and begin to emigrate from the blood stream towards a bacterium. In cell culture, fibroblasts travel across a glass surface by extending a leading edge which attaches to the surface before pulling the rest of the cell forwards. Changes in cell shape, the movement during cell division, the extension of epidermal squamous cells across a healing excised wound (p. 93), and the movement of young fibroblasts during the growth of granulation tissue are probably all the result of molecular changes in cytoplasmic microtubules, actin filaments and intermediate filaments. How these processes are regulated is not understood.

Cellulitis

Cellulitis is the rapid, diffuse spread of non-suppurative inflammation along connective-tissue planes.

The cause of cellulitis is bacterial. The most frequently recognized micro-organisms are group A β-haemolytic streptococci, but other aerobic and anaerobic organisms may be responsible, and of the latter the Clostridia are the most important.

Streptococci produce a considerable variety of exotoxins including fibrinolysin, haemolysin and the enzyme, hyaluronidase. Hyaluronidase depolymerizes the glycosaminoglycan chains of connective-tissue matrix proteoglycans. It is this action above all which accounts for the nature of cellulitis. Formerly, hyaluronidase was 'spreading factor' and the use of this old name serves to recall its essential action. The characteristic toxins and enzymes of the causative bacteria combined with the connective-tissue planes create a rapidly extending, diffuse swelling with ill-defined, slightly raised margins. Lymphangitis and lymphadenitis (p. 132) may be evident for the same reasons. Tissue necrosis, the proliferation of other organisms and suppuration may occur but, generally, the infection responds early to antibiotic therapy.

Chemotaxis

Chemotaxis is the unidirectional movement of leucocytes towards chemical agents at sites of injury or inflammation.

Among the agents responsible for chemotaxis are the components of complement (p. 62); products of bacteria and of polymorphs; lymphokines (p. 105) and substances formed in injured tissues. The components of complement that are chemotactic include C5 fragments, the C567 complex, and a C3 fragment. They can be generated both by antigen/antibody interaction and directly, by bacterial, plasma and tissue proteases. Movement takes place along a gradient of chemical concentration. Polymorphs move rapidly and can accumulate at injured sites within 30 minutes. Monocytes move much more slowly.

Cholesterol

Cholesterol is a lipid. It is an organic hydrocarbon, widespread in nature; it is found in all normal diets and can be synthesized in all body tissues. Ninety five per cent is within cells, 5 per cent in the blood. The ring structure of cholesterol (cyclopentenoperhydrophenanthrene) is common to many classes of biological compounds including steroid hormones, bile acids and vitamins as well as drugs such as digoxin.

Cholesterol and cholesterol esters, all insoluble in water, are carried in the circulation as low-density lipoproteins (LDL), particles formed of cholesterol, other lipids and proteins; the plasma concentration of cholesterol is 3.6–7.8 mmol/l. Cell-surface receptors allow LDL into cells. Plasma concentrations of cholesterol are high in rare hereditary conditions such as the hyperlipoproteinaemias and in diabetes mellitus. In familial hypercholesterolaemia, for example, there are no cell-surface receptors but very high levels of LDL. Raised concentrations of LDL may be associated with a predisposition to atheroma (p. 17) and its complications. Low concentrations of LDL, with an increase in the high-density lipoprotein (HDL) fraction, are protective against these disorders.

Chromosomes

Chromosomes are the forms or packets in which the genetic material (chromatin) of the cell, deoxyribonucleic acid (DNA), is organized.

Chromosomes can only be identified as discrete structures during cell division. Between divisions, the nuclear chromatin is coiled into a tangle of delicate blue-staining strands which appear as punctate bodies inside the nuclear membrane.

When cell division is arrested at metaphase in cell cultures by the spindle poison colchicine, 23 pairs of chromosomes can be identified within each human somatic cell. They can be categorized, grouped and numbered in the **karyotype**. The groups represent chromosomes that share similar sizes and shapes. Forty-six chromosomes are seen in each dividing human somatic cell. The **autosomes** are the 44 non-sex chromosomes; the other two are the **sex chromosomes**. In the nucleus of the female somatic cell, there are two X chromosomes; in the male somatic cell, one X and one Y. According to Mary Lyon's hypothesis, in the female cell one of the X chromosomes exerts a predominant, controlling influence. The other can sometimes be seen at the internal nuclear margin as the so-called Barr body.

Ploidy   This comes from the ancient Greek for 'form', and describes the number of sets of chromosomes in the cell nucleus. A normal number of sets of chromosomes is said to be **euploid**. Each normal human somatic cell, with its complement of 23 chromosome pairs is **diploid**; those cells that have undergone reduction division in meiosis have 23 single chromosomes and are **haploid**.

Chromosome abnormalities

Many abnormalities are large and can be seen with the light microscope when the karyotype is studied.

The majority of abnormalities are acquired either (1) during the formation of the gamete, (2) in fertilization, or (3) during early mitotic cell division in the embryo. Although some acquired abnormalities can be shown to be the result of exposure to ionizing radiation or to the action of chemicals, viruses or hormones, many have no demonstrable cause. Occasionally chromosomal abnormalities are inherited.

Heteroploidy is an abnormal appearance of the karyotype: the alteration may be in (1) the number of chromosomes, or (2) their shape or form. Heteroploidy is a frequent cause of spontaneous abortion, particularly in older mothers.

Alteration in numbers of chromosomes

Aneuploidy is an alteration in the total number of chromosomes in the somatic cell from the normal, euploid 46, other than a multiple of this number. When there is an increase in the number of chromosomes that is a multiple of the normal diploid number, the cell is said to be **polyploid.** **Triploidy** (69 chromosomes) or **tetraploidy** (92 chromosomes) are usually lethal conditions in man: they are found in 15 per cent of spontaneous abortions. There are exceptions: Purkinje cells are normally and safely tetraploid and megakaryocytes are **octaploid** (184 chromosomes).

Alteration in shape or form of chromosomes

Deletion is the loss of part of a chromosome. **Translocation** is the movement of part of one chromosome to another. Both deletion and translocation are encountered in the abnormal karyotypes seen in most malignant neoplasms.

Varieties of chromosomal abnormality

Some chromosomal abnormalities are particulary frequent.

(a) Congenital autosomal anomalies

Autosomal abnormalities are usually incompatible with life. An exception is **Down's syndrome**. A small additional chromosome is present at number 21 in group G: the diploid number of chromosomes is increased to 47 and the designation **trisomy 21** is an alternative name for the disorder.

A few children with Down's syndrome do not have trisomy 21; instead, the long arms of chromosome 21 are translocated to another chromosome.

Down's syndrome is increasingly common among children of older parents, and 60 times as common in children born to mothers over 45 years as it is to those of mothers less than 30 years. There is defective cerebral development and mental retardation. Cardiac malformation, flat occiput, slanting mongoloid eyes and increased susceptibility to infection with diminished life span are some of the clinical features.

(b) Congenital sex chromosome anomalies

In live children, abnormalies of sex chromosomes are more common than autosomal anomalies. The relatively trivial effects of aneuploidy of the sex chromosomes are due firstly to the small size of the Y chromosome, which carries little genetic information except the determination of sex, and secondly to the partial suppression in most normal cells of one X chromosome.

Klinefelter's syndrome   With a karyotype of 47 XXY, this is present as an anomaly in 1 in 600 'males'. The presence of the Y chromosome determines that part of the male phenotype is expressed but there is testicular and seminiferous tubule atrophy, and no germ cells. Subjects are usually detected during investigations for infertility.

In the **XYY syndrome**, occurring in about 1 in 2000 male births, there is an association with aggressive behaviour in about 3 per cent of cases. Those with this syndrome constitute a significantly large proportion of violent criminals in maximum-security prison hospitals.

Turner's syndrome   This karyotype, 45 XO, is expressed as small stature in infertile women with hypoplastic, fibrous ovaries and failure to menstruate. It occurs in 1 in 2000 newborn females but many die before birth.

(c) Chromosomal anomalies and malignant neoplasms

Abnormal numbers of mitotic figures are found in the majority of malignant neoplasms and are a distinguishing feature of precancerous states such as intraepithelial neoplasia of the uterine cervix. The number of chromosomes is often in the ranges 40–50 or 60–90. Chromosomal numbers of 37–38 are frequent in carcinoma of the breast.

There are simultaneous abnormalities of shape and size, and bizarre forms, some very large and long, are found. These abnormal forms are **markers** (p. 192) for malignancy. In chronic myeloid leukaemia, for example, one of the small chromosomes of pair 22 is replaced by the minute Philadelphia chromosome, Ph[1]: part of autosome 22 is translocated to autosome 9. Later, a second Ph[1] may appear.

Cicatrization

Cicatrization is the formation of a scar.

Cirrhosis

Cirrhosis literally means 'yellow-coloured' or 'tawny' (a brown colour with much yellow or orange). In practice, the term cirrhosis is applied to a progressive, chronic, fibrotic disease of the liver. Bands of new fibrous tissue extend haphazardly across and within anatomical lobules. They constrict the portal venous circulation and portal hypertension results. The residual liver cells respond by regeneration so that islands of new, young hepatocytes form. The liver becomes hard and nodular as well as small and yellow-brown.

Causes
The most common and most important cause of hepatic cirrhosis in the West is alcoholism. Importance causes of cirrhosis in Eastern countries are protein malnutrition, hepatitis B (p. 96) and metazoal (worm) diseases. Hepatic cirrhosis may result from chronic, heritable metabolic disorders such as haemochromatosis (storage of excess iron) and Wilson's disease (storage of excess copper), or from an inherited deficiency of α_1-antitrypsin. Other forms of cirrhosis follow chronic obstructive biliary disease or jejuno-ileal bypass. Cirrhosis is also associated with chronic active hepatitis and primary biliary cirrhosis, probably on an autoimmune basis.

Surgical significance
In surgical practice it is important to note that hepatitis B virus (p. 96) can be found in cirrhotic livers and in ascitic fluid and other material many years after acute hepatitis B has resolved. Tests for HBsAg (p. 98) help to identify carriers; those with HbeAg are highly infective. Patients with cirrhosis have diminished humoral and cellular immunocompetence and the morbidity and mortality of all operations are increased.

Citrate intoxication

Citrate intoxication may result when patients with severe hepatic failure are rapidly transfused with large quantities of citrated blood or plasma.

The rapid transfusion of citrated blood or plasma may produce a dangerous rise in plasma citrate concentration with subsequent hypocalcaemia. Cardiac arrythmias and arrest have been observed. In the past it was believed that this hazard was common: calcium gluconate was given intravenously as a preventative measure. The quantity of citrate now used for blood storage makes this an unnecessary precaution for most transfusions, but when two or more litres of blood are given in 20 minutes or less the danger of citrate intoxication remains.

Clostridia

Clostridia are common anaerobic bacteria that can cause dangerous human diseases including tetanus and gas gangrene. They are large, Gram-positive, metabolically active, spore-bearing, saprophytic organisms. The spores germinate in warm, moist conditions when there is very little oxygen. The majority of Clostridia grow in soil, water or decomposing plant and animal material. Some, notably *Cl. welchii* (*Cl. perfringens*) and *Cl. sporogenes*, inhabit the human intestinal tract, invading the tissues and blood at death to cause putrefaction. A few, behaving as opportunistic pathogens, produce disease when vegetative forms develop and attack injured or devitalized tissue. These pathogens all liberate powerful exotoxins. *Cl. welchii* and *Cl. septicum* are causes of gas gangrene; *Cl. tetani* causes tetanus; and *Cl. botulinum* botulism. Their spores resist the actions of many commonly used antiseptics and disinfectants.

Cl. welchii forms four main exotoxins, α, β, ϵ, and ι. Alpha toxin is the major agent in all strains and is capable of causing death in laboratory animals. Alpha toxin is the principal cause of the toxaemia of gas gangrene; it is heat-stable and produces necrosis and haemolysis. Some strains of *Cl. welchii* also form an enterotoxin that can lead to food-poisoning.

Cl.tetani produces an extremely potent neurotoxin, tetanospasmin, that travels along motor nerves after adsorption by motor end-plates at sites of infection. *Cl. tetani* also forms a haemolysin. The lethal dose of the neurotoxin for a mouse is approximately 1×10^{-7} mg. The initial response is local tetanus affecting the muscle supplied by the motor nerves first affected. However, toxin passes to ascending levels of the spinal cord (ascending tetanus) and may also reach the brain stem via the blood, travelling downwards to motor nerves such as those supplying the muscles of the mouth and jaw. The toxin impairs normal inhibition of impulses that reach the motor neurones from the brain, and tetanus (p. 182) results.

Cl. botulinum produces a toxin that is one of the most powerful known; it is a neurotoxin, acting on the parasympathetic nervous system. It paralyses the muscles of the eye, pharynx and larynx, and results in botulism (p. 38).

Cl. difficile is an important cause of antibiotic-associated colitis (p. 162). In adults *Cl. difficile* can survive antimicrobial treatment, multiply and produce a potent toxin that may lead to severe and potentially fatal pseudomembranous colitis (p. 162).

Coagulation

Coagulation (clotting) of the blood is the conversion of the soluble plasma fibrinogen into the insoluble substance fibrin to form a **clot** or coagulum.

When coagulation occurs in the living circulation, the resultant mass is a **thrombus** (p. 183).

Under normal circumstances coagulation prevents dangerous haemorrhage; the processes of coagulation work in conjunction with the antagonistic mechanism of fibrinolysis. This homeostatic action may be unbalanced in inappropriate circumstances, causing tissue injury. At the site of injury to a blood vessel there is a haemostatic plug composed largely of platelets. Subsequently successive layers of fibrin are deposited.

The coagulation mechanism is complex, involving many substances in a **cascade**. International agreement now designates a roman numeral for each substance (fibrinogen is factor I) and proceeds in a retrograde fashion through the sequence of reactions. The existence of a Factor VI is now doubted. Other platelet and lipid factors have been identified and designated by arabic numerals. Factor 3 is the only one of importance.

Factor I, **fibrinogen**, is a plasma protein produced by the liver. When plasma clots, the fluid that remains lacks fibrinogen and is called **serum**. The conversion of fibrinogen to fibrin is brought about by the proteolytic enzyme **thrombin**.

Factor II, **prothrombin** is an inactive glycoprotein normally found in the blood and produced by the liver. In coagulation, it is converted into an active form, thrombin, by activated thromboplastin in the presence of calcium ions.

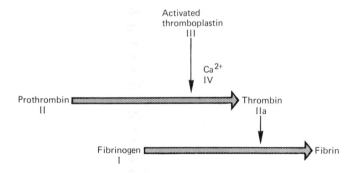

Fig. 3a   Blood coagulation. The final common pathway.

Factor III, **thromboplastin,** has not been characterized. The term 'thromboplastic activity' is often used. Thromboplastic activity can be produced intrinsically (from the blood) or extrinsically (from the tissues).

Factor IV, **calcium ions,** help to accelerate the conversion of fibrinogen to fibrin; they are essential for the other reactions in coagulation. In practice, hypocalcaemia is never sufficiently severe to interfere with clotting.

The extrinsic system

Tissue thromboplastin (extrinsic prothrombin activator) is rapidly formed following local trauma in the presence of factors IV, V, VII and X.

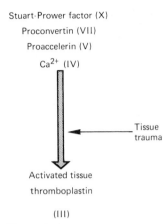

Fig. 3b   Blood coagulation. The extrinsic system.

Factor V, **proaccelerin**, is a labile factor destroyed by heat; it is a plasma protein.

Factor VII, **proconvertin** is a heat-stable factor present in serum.

Factor X, **Stuart–Prower factor**, is a thermolabile protein present in serum, and named after two patients in whom its deficiency was first identified.

The intrinsic system

Blood thromboplastin (intrinsic prothrombin activator) is formed by factors IV, V, VIII, IX, XI, XII and platelet factor 3.

First there is activation of factor XII as a result of contact of blood with a foreign surface. The early stages of the sequence are slow. Once thrombin has been formed, the process is greatly accelerated and the term 'cascade sequence' has been used to describe it.

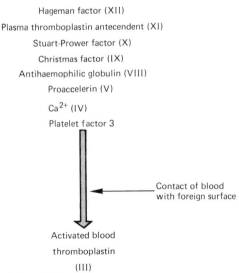

Fig. 3c   Blood coagulation. The intrinsic system.

Factor XIII **(fibrin stabilizing factor)**. The ultimate stage in clot formation is the production of a network of fibrin resistant to digestion by plasmin (p. 78). Peptide bonds form between fibrin polymers under the enzymic control of factor XIII.

Coagulopathies

The term coagulopathy is given to a defect in the coagulation mechanism (p. 56).

In modern laboratories it is possible to measure the concentration of many of the individual coagulation factors. If this facility is not available, it may be possible to deduce from simple tests which factor is deficient in the patient's plasma or serum: some factors are sensitive or resistant to heat or freezing; others can be adsorbed onto aluminium hydroxide. Tests used to assess the common pathway, the extrinsic system, the intrinsic system, or a combination of these include:

(a) **Bleeding time** (p. 30).
(b) **Capillary fragility (Hess' test)** – a positive test is the occurrence of purpura of the skin below a tourniquet applied to the arm for five minutes at a pressure between diastolic and systolic blood pressure. The test is positive in thrombocytopenia, but there is a poor correlation with the platelet count and positive tests have been obtained in normal people. It is also positive in scurvy.
(c) **Platelet count** – the normal range is $150–400 \times 10^9/l$. Thrombocytopenia exists with counts below $100 \times 10^9/l$ and thrombocytosis above $500 \times 10^9/l$. The accuracy of counting can be low even with automated equipment such as the Coulter 20 counter and figures outside the normal range may not be significant in diagnosing these conditions.
(d) **Platelet adhesion** – platelet counts are performed before and after exposure to foreign surfaces such as Cellophane and glass.
(e) **Platelet aggregation** – the amount of light transmitted through a suspension increases as the platelets aggregate.
(f) **Clot retraction** – the clot from healthy blood begins to retract 30–60 minutes after the sample is taken. In patients with thrombocytopenia, the clot is like a jelly and does not retract.
(g) **Fibrinogen concentration** – normally, 2–4 g/l plasma.
(h) **Fibrinogen titre** – thrombin is added to dilutions of plasma. Clot formation is observed in vitro with dilutions up to 1:32 to 1:64.
(i) **Whole blood clotting time** – in glass tubes the clotting time is 5–15 minutes and in silicon-coated tubes, 20–60 minutes. The normal clotting time requires an adequate intrinsic system, an adequate final common pathway, and normal platelet function.
(j) **Plasma thrombin time** – thrombin and calcium are added to the patient's plasma and compared with a known normal control. The thrombin time is increased if there is an inadequate concentration of fibrinogen; it is prolonged by heparin and other anticoagulants.
(k) **Prothrombin time** – the patient's plasma is incubated with calcium and a brain extract (which provides extrinsic thromboplastic activity). The

time taken for a clot to form is compared with a control plasma and expressed as a ratio. The test assesses the extrinsic system and the final common pathway.

(l) **Kaolin–cephalin clotting time** (formerly the partial thromboplastin time). Patient's plasma is added to calcium and cephalin, a phospholipid, in a glass tube. The presence of the phospholipid makes the test independent of the platelet count; the glass provides a foreign surface for activation of factor XII. The time taken for a clot to form is compared with a normal control.

The kaolin-cephalin clotting time is a more sensitive method of assessing the intrinsic coagulation system and the final common pathway than the whole blood clotting time.

(m) **Thromboplastin generation test** – this assesses the factors involved in the intrinsic system. If plasma adsorbed onto aluminium hydroxide is incubated with serum, platelets and calcium, clotting occurs in 8–10 seconds. If clotting is delayed, the deficient factor can be ascertained by replacing either the patient's plasma, serum or platelets with normal plasma, serum or platelets.

Summary: assessment of bleeding disease before surgery

Bleeding diseases encountered in surgery can be adequately assessed by four tests: the platelet count, the bleeding time, the prothrombin time (PT), and the kaolin–cephalin clotting time (KCCT). From this combination, the following conclusions can be reached:

KCCT and PT normal – **platelet or vessel defect;**
KCCT and PT abnormal – **defect in common pathway;**
KCCT abnormal and PT normal – **defect in intrinsic system;**
KCCT normal and PT abnormal – **factor VII deficiency.**

Platelet abnormalities

Insufficient platelets may be formed; they may mature abnormally; or they may be destroyed in excess. Alternatively, there may be increased platelet formation and abnormal platelet function. Platelets are destroyed in autoimmune diseases and their function disturbed in a wide variety of conditions ranging from haemophilia (p. 92) and Christmas disease to other, rarer disorders.

Thrombocytopenia   This is a decrease in the number of circulating platelets. It may be caused by **deficiency** of bone-marrow megakaryocytes. This defect, which leads to an increased bleeding tendency, may be due to replacement of the bone marrow by metastases or leukaemia, or to the effect of a variety of chemicals and toxins such as cytotoxic drugs, gold, poisons, uraemia and septicaemia. The **maturation** of megakaryocytes may be abnormal in patients with megaloblastic anaemias. There may be excessive **destruction** of circulating platelets in disseminated intravascular coagulation (DIC) (p. 73), immune thrombocytopenic purpura (see below) and hypersplenism.

Thrombocythaemia Thrombocythaemia is an increase in the number of circulating platelets. Haemorrhagic thrombocythaemia is the platelet component of polycythaemia rubra vera. Although the platelet concentration is grossly elevated, there may be defective platelet function in clot formation. Similar abnormalities may occur with other myeloproliferative disorders such as chronic myeloid leukaemia.

Platelet function may be affected by anti-inflammatory drugs such as aspirin, vitamin K antagonists, and cytotoxic drugs. Platelet function is also defective in von Willebrand's disease (see below).

Immune thrombocytopenic purpura (p. 163) This is an autoimmune disease in which antiplatelet antibodies can be demonstrated in half the patients. There is excessive destruction of platelets in the spleen. The adult form is chronic but in infants the disease may be acute and does not recur after treatment by steroids and/or splenectomy.

Clotting abnormalities

Haemophilia (p. 92) Although the bleeding may be severe enough to induce haemorrhagic shock, the major mortality and morbidity are due to cerebral haemorrhage and haemarthrosis respectively.

Christmas disease This was named after the first patient in whom it was identified. There is an inherited deficiency of factor IX, transmitted in the same manner as haemophilia.

von Willebrand's disease (p. 92) This is due to a deficiency of a factor essential for the formation of factor VIII; it is transmitted as an autosomal dominant trait with partial expression. Thus, the disease occurs in its fully expressed form in homozygotes. Unlike haemophilia, heterozygotes are affected to a lesser extent. Platelet function is also defective in both heterozygotes and homozygotes and there is a prolonged bleeding time. This associated defect may also explain why, in patients with von Willebrand's disease, there is bleeding into the skin and mucous membranes rather than into the joints.

Other very rare deficiencies of factors II, V, VII, X, XI, and XIII have been described. They cause haemophilia-like diseases.

Anticoagulant therapy and prophylaxis
When thrombosis is evident or anticipated, anticoagulant therapy may be required.

Heparin Parenteral heparin inhibits coagulation at several stages in the coagulation sequence; it appears to be particularly effective in preventing the activation of factors II, IX, X and XI and probably VII. Therapy may be monitored using the kaolin–cephalin clotting time or the prothrombin time.

Vitamin K antagonists Vitamin K is required for the synthesis of factors II, VII, IX and X in the liver. Warfarin is the most commonly used antagonist. Therapy can be monitored by the prothrombin time.

Collagen disease

This term has been used in two entirely distinct ways.

In the first, obsolete usage, collagen disease was a term introduced in 1941 to describe disorders such as systemic sclerosis, systemic lupus erythematosus and rheumatoid arthritis, with diffuse abnormalities of collagenous structures. There is no evidence that any primary disturbance of collagen is responsible for these conditions although collagen may be disorganized secondarily or laid down in excess.

In the second, modern usage, collagen disease (or, better, **disease of the collagen molecule**), refers to the numerous genetic disorders in which there is an inherited fault in the synthesis, secretion, maturation or cross-linking of collagen. The majority of the diseases of the collagen molecule are rare; they include osteogenesis imperfecta and the Ehlers–Danlos syndromes.

Colloid, colloidal solution (sol)

A colloidal solution (a sol) is one in which there are dispersed particles between 1 and 100 nm in diameter. The colloid is the **disperse** or discontinuous phase, the medium in which the particles are dispersed is the **dispersion medium** or continuous phase. Because of their mass and large surface areas, the particles display properties like Brownian movement; they scatter light and can be measured by nephelometry. They can be brought out of the disperse phase by techniques such as high-speed centrifugation.

In an old, obsolete sense, the word colloid, from the ancient Greek for glue, meant a jelly-like material. Colloid is still employed in this way to describe thyroid acinar colloid, colloid goitre and colloid carcinoma.

Commensal organisms

Commensal (symbiotic) organisms depend upon the life of other animals or plants, living as their tenants but not at their expense. The advantages of symbiosis are often mutual and may be crucial to the survival of either organism. For example, bacteria thrive in the distal part of the small intestine and synthesize essential nutritional substances such as vitamin K.

Complement

Complement (C) is a complex of 21 proteins present in the plasma that act together, in a cascade of events, to cause cell and bacterial lysis, cell death and some of the phenomena of inflammation.

The breakdown of bacteria by lysis is made possible by plasma or serum containing specific antibacterial antibody. This process does not occur if the serum has previously been heated to 56 °C for 30 minutes. This simple test was used by Bordet* in 1895 to show that there was a factor in normal and immune serum that **complemented** the specific antibacterial activity of

---

*Jules Jean Baptiste Vincent Bordet (1870–1961) was awarded the Nobel prize in 1919 for his studies of immunity.

antibodies. The breakdown of red blood cells by anti-red cell antibodies was also shown to rely on the presence of this complementary activity (C). The release of haemoglobin from red cells became a simple test for the presence and activity of C.

Classical pathway of complement activation

The actions of the numbered components of C are aided by cofactors and amplified or inhibited by subtle mechanisms. The proteins function in groups. The usual sequence by which C is activated begins when antibody binds to antigen. Unfortunately for readers, the sequence does not exactly correspond to the numerical order of the C components. One IgM or two adjacent IgG molecules interact with the antigen. Three functional C units form: the first (C1) recognizes the antigen-antibody complex; the third (C3) then attacks the bacterial wall or cell membrane. Together, this sequence is said to be the classical pathway of cell lysis.

Alternative pathway of complement activation

This alternative mechanism does not depend upon the initial binding of antibody to antigen. The alternative pathway was discovered in laboratory studies which showed that the protein, properdin, acts in this way: it can activate C3 in the absence of antibody or of C1, C4 or C2. In surgery, the alternative pathway is important because some Gram-negative bacteria and viruses can be neutralized by this mechanism.

Complement fixation   This is the basis of sensitive and specific serological **complement fixation tests** that search for the presence of antibody against bacteria such as those causing syphilis (Wasserman reaction (p. 174)) and viruses such as rubella. The test can also be used to detect humoral responses to other foreign proteins and cells such as those of malignant tumours and tissue transplants.

The C fixation test is best viewed in two stages.

1. When antibody present in a patient's plasma is encouraged to react in a tube with a known antigen, in the presence of a limited amount of C, the latter is bound (fixed), activated and consumed.
2. An indicator system is then used to detect any remaining C. The indicator comprises sheep red blood cells coated with enough anti-sheep RBC antibody to lyse the red blood cells if C is present but not enough to agglutinate these cells or lyse them in the absence of C.

If the C fixation test is positive, that is, if the patient's plasma contains antibody, C will have been used up (fixed) in the first stage of the reaction. No lysis of red blood cells will occur in the second stage.

Congenital disease

A disease or abnormality is said to be congenital when it is present at birth. Congenital diseases may be inherited or acquired.

Many congenital defects such as syndactyly, oesophagotracheal fistula, cardiac malformation and spina bifida are apparent at or shortly after birth. Others, such as branchial cyst, bicuspid aortic valve or accessory rib, may not be identified until much later, perhaps in adult life.

The causes of **inherited congenital disease** are considered on p. 118.

The causes of **acquired congenital disease** can be classified as:

1. Agents such as ionizing radiation, viruses and mutagens **acting on the gamete** provoking genetic mutation.

2. Substances **acting on the zygote**, embryo or fetus that alter organogenesis. Thus thalidomide, a tranquillizer taken by many pregnant women, led to defective limb development. Cigarette smoking is associated with an increased probability of the risk of the stillbirth of a malformed fetus and the smoke may contain chemicals with a thalidomide-like action.

3. Viruses, such as that of rubella, acquired by the mother during early pregnancy and **acting directly on viscera** such as the heart and eye to impair development.

4. Hormones such as hydrocortisone or oestrogens **taken by the mother** during early pregnancy.

5. Physical agents such as ionizing x- or γ-radiation or α- or β-particle-emitting isotopes, to which the growing zygote, fetus or embryo can be exposed during the intrauterine development.

Connective tissues

The connective tissues, of mesodermal origin, provide support for the viscera, the structural and mechanical basis of the musculoskeletal system, the non-mineral elements of bone and an integral part of many abnormal tissues especially those of scirrhous neoplasms, and granulation and scar tissue.

Connective tissue may be **compact** (dense) or **loose**. There are three components in addition to water: cells, structural fibrous proteins (collagen and elastin) and giant, carbohydrate-rich, protein-containing molecules, the proteoglycans. The extracellular materials constitute an intercellular matrix. The structural proteins and the proteoglycans are manufactured by the connective-tissue cells.

Water   The water content of connective tissue is 70–74 per cent.

Cells   Connective tissue cells are typified by the fibroblast.

Fibrous proteins   The fibrous, structural proteins provide strength by resisting tensile stress. They are particularly important in tendons. The main fibrous, structural protein is **collagen** which comprises 15 per cent of the dry weight of the whole body but 50 per cent of the dry weight of tissue such as hyaline articular cartilage. At least 11 genetically distinct types of collagen are now known: each has a different primary amino-acid composition. Type I collagen is bone collagen, type II the main collagen of cartilage, type III of vascular and developing tissue and type IV of basement membranes.

Elastic material has two components: the protein **elastin** and a micro-fibrillar glycoprotein. **Glycoproteins** are proteins with a small quantity of associated carbohydrate (less than 5 per cent of the molecular weight).

Proteoglycan   Proteoglycans comprise a protein core to which numerous polysaccharide chains are attached to give a molecule shaped like a bottle brush. The protein component represents less than 5 per cent of the molecular weight. The proteoglycan molecules unfold to an extent determined by the nearby fibrous proteins; they retain much water. Lying within the expanded proteoglycans, water provides resistance to compressive stress, the most important characteristic of hyaline articular cartilage.

The normal formation of connective tissue, for example in scars, depends upon the availability of substances such as ascorbic acid (p. 201) which is essential for the maturation and stability of collagen, and pyridoxine and copper that are necessary for the synthesis and maturation of elastic tissue.

Connective-tissue disease

Connective-tissue diseases are **primary**, local or systemic disorders of the connective tissue system (p. 64). Many diseases affect or involve the connective tissues **secondarily**: they are excluded from the present concept.

Primary connective-tissue diseases are occasionally inherited, but are more often, acquired. In the latter, the role of an inherited predisposition is often suspected. In rheumatoid arthritis (RA), for example, the histo-compatibility antigen HLA DR4 occurs with greater frequency than in the normal population. In ankylosing spondylitis (AS), an association with HLA B27 (p. 189) is very strong.

Interest has centred on those connective-tissue diseases in which a disturbance of the immunological mechanism is suspected. In systemic lupus erythematosus (SLE), for example, antibodies are formed against many constituents of the patient's own tissues and blood: they are autoantibodies (p. 20). One of the most important is anti-ds (double stranded) DNA.

A role for virus infection is proposed in RA, SLE and polyarteritis nodosa. Patients with RA often have raised titres of antibody against Epstein–Barr virus and it is suspected that the virus alters the regulatory functions of T suppressor lymphocytes (p. 133). NZB/NZW disease of mice and Aleutian disease of blue mink provide interesting animal models in which virus infection disorganizes immunoregulatory mechanisms (p. 108).

Contracture

A contracture is a prolonged, irreversible replacement of part of subcutaneous tissue, skeletal muscle or tendon by fibrous connective (scar) tissue rich in collagen and of low vascularity. The fibrous tissue shrinks as the collagen matures; deformity results.

Dupuytren's contracture   This affects the fascia of the palm; it is often bilateral. There is a familial tendency. Alcoholic cirrhosis is a predisposing factor and the disorder is much commoner in males than in females.

Contusion

A contusion or bruise is a lesion caused by a crushing injury which does not break the epithelium. Capillaries and small vessels within and deep to the epithelium are damaged, with extravasation of small quantities of blood.

Corticosteroids

The corticosteroids are a group of compounds synthesized from cholesterol by the cells of the adrenal cortex; they are essential for life. Some corticosteroids are secreted from the adrenal cortex directly into the blood stream, acting as hormones. Adrenal corticosteroids have profound effects on physiological processes, particularly the control of the intermediary metabolism of carbohydrates, fats and proteins; the regulation of water and electrolyte exchange; the mediation of local and systemic responses to injury and stress; and the modulation of both humoral and cell-mediated immunity. The most important corticosteroids in man are cortisol (hydrocortisone) and aldosterone (p. 5). Chronic hypoadrenocorticalism is Addison's disease. Hyperadrenocorticalism is one cause of Cushing's syndrome.

Cortisol

Cortisol stimulates gluconeogenesis from glycogen and protein and the blood glucose concentration is raised. It promotes renal retention of sodium and loss of potassium but is far less effective, in this regard, than aldosterone. It corrects the extracellular dehydration and intracellular overhydration of adrenocortical insufficiency. It is said to have a 'permissive' role in facilitating the vasoconstrictive effect of catecholamines upon arterioles, thereby increasing mean arterial pressure. Erythropoiesis is stimulated, and leucocytosis is caused, with eosinophilia. Lymphoid tissue atrophies. Antibody production falls, with a reduction in the severity of inflammation and allergy and decreased speed and adequacy of wound healing. In experimental shock, cortisol can stabilize lysosomal membranes if administered before the stimulus.

Crohn's disease (regional enteritis)

Crohn* and his colleagues first described a chronic inflammation of the terminal ileum in 1932. The cause of the disease is still unknown. Subsequently it has become apparent that any portion of the bowel from the lips to the anus may be involved, but the terminal ileum is the commonest site. Other viscera may be affected.

---

*Burrill Bernard Crohn (1884–1984) with L. Ginzburg and G.D. Oppenheimer, described 'regional ileitis' in 1932. Crohn was a minor contributor to the research and unhappy that his name was associated with the disorder.

Macroscopic changes

Mucosal ulcers develop into fissures which penetrate the wall of the gut, separating islets of less diseased mucosa which protrude due to oedema. The bowel is thickened and serosal involvement is obvious. Usually, the disease process is discontinuous: normal bowel intervenes between diseased segments forming so called 'skip' lesions. Ulceration in the skin, indistinguishable histologically from that seen in the bowel, has also been described.

Histological changes

Microscopically, there is early involvement of all layers of the bowel. In the large bowel, this helps to distinguish the condition from ulcerative colitis, in which the disease is initially confined to the mucosa. The finding of granulomata containing Langhans' giant cells and epitheloid cells in the bowel or local lymph nodes is almost pathognomonic of Crohn's disease. Giant cells and epitheloid cells may also be found in the fissures. Endarteritis with perivascular infiltration by lymphocytes is a common feature, particularly in elderly patients.

Complications

Fibrosis and stricture are common. They are often multiple, particularly in the terminal ileum. Intestinal obstruction may occur. When the small bowel is involved, malnutrition is likely and megaloblastic anaemia (p. 201) develops due to either a deficiency of vitamin B_{12} or of folic acid. Chronic or acute loss of blood may occur. Crohn's disease is one of the commonest causes of fistula formation. Fistulae form between the loops of the diseased bowel, between the bowel and the abdominal wall or between the bowel and other viscera. Malabsorption and malnutrition are particularly severe in these patients. Acute ('toxic') dilatation of the colon may occur and perforation may follow with generalized or localized peritonitis and abscess formation. Perforation of the colon may occur in the absence of dilatation. Perforation of the small bowel is uncommon: the diseased segment usually adheres to another structure and fistulae arise.

Systemic disorders are commonly associated with Crohn's disease. Cutaneous lesions and ophthalmitis may occur. The incidence of cirrhosis, sclerosing cholangitis, ankylosing spondylitis and arthritis is higher than in the general population, and amyloidosis may develop.

Cryostat

A cryostat is a form of refrigerator.

In surgical pathology the term cryostat is used to describe an insulated cabinet containing a microtome; low temperatures are maintained by refrigeration. Small pieces of fresh tissue can quickly be cut in the cryostat, before staining and microscopic examination. Sections examined in this manner are often of poorer quality than those obtained by fixation and embedding in paraffin-wax, but they are usually sufficient to allow the general pathologist to inform a surgeon whether the tissue is neoplastic or from an inflammatory lesion. Exceptionally, an entire diagnostic tissue pathology service can be maintained by cryostat techniques used by special staff.

Crystal deposition

Crystals of normal components such as cholesterol often form within the body. Other crystals, such as those of urates, grow when a normal constituent is present in excess. Crystals of abnormal constituents such as corticosteriods are sometimes introduced therapeutically. Insoluble crystals can excite inflammation and lead to **crystal deposition diseases**. The best known of these disorders is gout.

Gout

Gout is a clinical syndrome in which inflammation of joints and connective tissue arises in some individuals who have a persistently high serum concentration of urate. Insoluble, needle-shaped crystals of monosodium urate form in the extracellular connective tissues. Crystal growth is likely in and around synovial joints and in the connective tissues of the lobe of the ear, the arteries and the kidney. Some crystals are phagocytosed by neutrophil polymorphs, but tend to disrupt the membranes of phagolysosomes so that lysosomal enzymes are released into the tissues. Crystals also bind protein, activate complement and cause inflammation which can become chronic if effective prophylaxis with uricosuric drugs such as allopurinol is not arranged. Chronic inflammation excites a foreign body, macrophage reaction and fibrous tissue forms, leading to a crystal granuloma to which the name **tophus** is given. Cartilage and bone can be destroyed.

Gout is usually **primary**. When there is excess formation of urate derived from nucleoprotein breakdown in chronic leukaemia or myeloproliferative disease, the occurrence of gout is **secondary**. Secondary, **saturnine** gout can arise from lead poisoning.

Chondrocalcinosis (calcium pyrophosphate deposition disease)

Chondrocalcinosis is a clinical syndrome resembling gout. It was formerly called pseudogout. Chondrocalcinosis is due to the formation of insoluble crystals of calcium pyrophosphate dihydrate. The distinction between these two causes of acute arthritis is essential because of the availability of effective specific treatment for gout. The differentation is made quickly and easily from synovial fluid by the use of a microscope fitted with polarizing filters. Urate crystals are negatively birefringent, pyrophosphate crystals positively birefringent. It may be possible to make this distinction with tissue sections.

Calcium hydroxyapatite deposition disease

Calcium hydroxyapatite (bone) crystals are individually too small to be seen by light microscopes in body tissues and fluids; they can, however, be identified by electron microscopy. They may cause synovial inflammation.

Other crystal deposits

Cholesterol crystals, derived from red-cell membrane lipoprotein, are common at sites of old haemorrhage. They may also develop from bile deposited in the wall of a chronically inflamed gall bladder. Xanthine, hypoxanthine and cystine crystals deposits are rare.

Crystalloid

A crystalloid is a soluble substance or solute the particles of which, in solution, are less than 1 nm in diameter.

In an older sense, the term defined a crystal-like material, distinct from the less readily soluble, glue-like colloids (p. 62).

Cystinuria

In this disease, which is transmitted as an autosomal recessive trait, there is defective tubular reabsorption of cystine, lysine, arginine and ornithine. Although the urine of heterozygotes contains more cystine than that of normal subjects, the concentration does not usually exceed the limit of solubility. In homozygotes, the urine becomes saturated with cystine and calculi (p. 41) are formed. Cystine is more soluble in an alkaline urine.

Cytodiagnosis

Cytology is, literally, knowledge or understanding of cells.

Cytodiagnosis is a diagnosis made by the microscopic examination of cells obtained by smears, scrapings, brushings, aspirations or lavage. **Exfoliative cytology** is the study of cells obtained by these methods. Cells in suspension can be spread evenly on a glass slide by a Cytospin centrifuge. After spreading, the smears must be immediately fixed: an aerosol of alcohol is convenient.

The final interpretation of cell smears and sediments is a matter for expert pathological opinion: the identification of cells from a malignant neoplasm, for example, is determined on the basis of nuclear and cytoplasmic abnormalities (p. 147). However, valuable **screening** programmes can be maintained by skilled technical personnel; the early recognition of potentially malignant disease of the uterine cervix is the aim of the most widely practiced programme.

Death

Death is the cessation of vital function in an organism, tissue or cell.

The clinical and pathological definitions of death have excited controversy.

Clinically, there may be irreversible cessation of cerebral function, indicated by electroencephalographic (EEG) changes, while cardiac, renal and respiratory function may be retained. Although the body therefore appears alive, the state of the central nervous system determines that independent life is no longer possible and that the individual is therefore dead.

Pathologically, the death of tissue is recognized when cell nuclei are irreversibly injured or lost, when membrane stability can no longer be maintained or when the activity of essential enzymes ceases. To identify cell death in sections, the pathologist relies on secondary criteria such as the loss of stainable glycogen or of cardiac muscle cell striations. The histological features of cell death are detectable in inverse relationship to the metabolic activity of the parent tissue. Cerebral neurones reveal ultramicroscopic signs of permanent injury within two minutes, heart-muscle cells within 15 minutes, renal tubular cells within 60 minutes but articular chondrocytes only after many days.

Deoxyribonucleic acid (DNA)

DNA, deoxyribonucleic acid, is the chemical basis of genes (p. 87); it codes all genetic information. Each generation of cells inherits a programme of instructions to reproduce the form and behaviour of the parent cells.

DNA is arranged spatially as a double helix, that is, as two very long molecular threads. Each thread is a helix, not intertwining with the other but wound around an imaginary centre. Viewed from the end, the assembly resembles a cylinder with a central space.

Each of the two threads of the double helix of DNA is an enormously long chain of the sugar deoxyribose and of phosphate. The arrangement of the phosphate radicals, substituted through hydroxyl groups, is directional. Any process or change passing along the thread is 'forwards' or 'backwards' so that 'forwards' in one strand equates with 'backwards' in the other. Consequently, the arrangement is that of an 'anti-parallel' double helix.

Each deoxyribose in a DNA strand is substituted with one of two purine or two pyrimidine bases. The purine bases are **adenine** and **guanine**; the pyrimidine bases are **thymine** and **cytosine**. Their spatial arrangement is such that the thymine of one helical strand is always opposed to the adenine of the other, the guanine to the cytosine.

When the proportions and arrangements of the bases are considered along the helical DNA strand, the numbers of individual bases are found to vary widely. The arrangement of the adjacent bases in one strand is however very exact: three adjacent bases, a triplet, in one helical strand code for each amino acid. These base triplets determine the sequence of each polypeptide chain that forms along the axis of ribonucleic acid (RNA). Because four distinct purine and pyrimidine bases occur in DNA, there are 64 different possible coding triplets or **codons**. Theoretically, therefore, 64 different amino acids can be made. However, only 21 different amino acids exist in normal body tissues.

See Ribonucleic acid (RNA) (p. 166)

Desmoplastic response

The desmoplastic response is the formation, by an epithelial neoplasm, of a stroma of collagen-rich, connective tissue.

Desmoplasia is most conspicuous in scirrhous (hard) breast cancers but is often encountered in malignant neoplasms of the stomach, colon, bile duct and other sites. Initially, collagen is formed by the malignant epithelial cells themselves. Subsequently, fibroblasts extend from the host tissue with new, young, host blood vessels so that the neoplasm is provided with mechanical support and a vascular supply.

Diabetes mellitus

Diabetes (flowing through) mellitus (sweet, sugar-like) is a state of hyperglycaemia and glycosuria due to a relative lack of circulating insulin.

There are two categories of diabetes mellitus: type 1 (childhood and adolescent onset) and type 2 (adult, late onset). Type 1 diabetics are prone to severe disease and often survive only by the repeated injection of insulin ('insulin-dependent' diabetes).

There is deficient production of insulin by the pancreatic islets* in one per cent of the population: a hereditary disposition suggests transmission by an autosomal recessive gene with incomplete penetration. The condition can also follow destruction of the pancreas by neoplasms, inflammation and pancreatectomy. The abnormal metabolism can also be produced by excessive quantities of hormones with antagonistic effects to insulin such as catecholamines, glucocorticoid hormones, glucagon and somatotrophin. Thus, diabetes mellitus is a feature of Cushing's syndrome and acromegaly.

The clinical scene in untreated, severe diabetes mellitus is dominated by thirst, hunger and weight loss. The osmotic effects of excess renal tubular glucose cause polyuria and there is a constant hazard of disordered fluid balance.

In addition to inadequate quantities of glycogen in muscles and liver, patients with diabetes suffer from muscle wasting due to increased gluconeogenesis from protein. There is an increased oxidation of fat resulting in ketosis (p. 127). The stress of surgery and anaesthesia accentuates these phenomena. In diabetic patients undergoing operation, the safest procedure is to stop the usual insulin or oral hypoglycaemic preparation on the day of operation, to infuse isotonic solutions of glucose until a satisfactory oral intake can be re-established and to inject amounts of insulin indicated by measurements of the blood glucose concentration.

Complications
1. Coma – hyperglycaemia and hypoglycaemia are causes of unexplained loss of consciousness.
2. Arteriopathy – diabetics develop several forms of vascular disease. Atheroma is more common in diabetics that in the general population and the basement membranes of capillaries such as those of the glomeruli are thickened. In addition, there is hyaline sclerosis of arterioles. These smaller, peripheral vessels are affected predominantly in the retina (where microaneurysms are common), heart, kidney, large bowel and limbs. Amputation for gangrene can therefore sometimes be confined to an affected toe in a diabetic when a much more extensive procedure would be required in a non-diabetic with gangrene due to atheroma of proximal, larger arteries.
3. Infection – diabetics are prone to many types of bacterial infection including wound infections. They are particularly likely to develop cellulitis

---

*Paul Langerhans (1847–1888) described the pancreatic islets in 1869 in an inaugural dissertation published in Berlin when he was 22. He became Professor of Pathological Anatomy at Freiburg-im-Breisgau.

or a carbuncle. This susceptibility to infection is believed to be due to impaired immune responsiveness rather than to the relatively high glucose content of the tissues. In addition phagocytosis is defective.
4. Neuropathy – diabetics frequently suffer from peripheral neuropathy. Together with arterial disease, this makes them susceptible to the development of painless 'trophic' ulcers.

Disinfection

Disinfectants are chemical substances that kill bacteria and, with less certainty, their spores. Disinfectants reduce a bacterial population but cannot bring about sterility. The distinction between a disinfectant and an antiseptic is quantitative: the former can be regarded as a powerful form of antiseptic, suitable for application to inanimate objects.

In wards and clinics, disinfectants are used to treat containers, dishes and instruments that require to be made safe quickly and easily, regardless of their subsequent sterilization and laundering. In laboratories and mortuaries, disinfectants are used to make dishes, plates, tubes and jars safe to wash and transport.

Examples of disinfectants include

1. **Phenols** such as lysol and cresol which are effective in the presence of organic matter.
2. **Hypochlorite**, less toxic than the phenols and easily removed by washing but ineffective in the presence of much organic matter. It may be combined with a detergent. Eusol (Edinburgh University Solution of Lime) is a mixture of calcium chloride and boric acid which yields hypochlorite.
3. **Formaldehyde**, which kills bacterial spores as well as vegetative bacteria. It is used as a liquid or gas. Ten per cent aqueous formaldehyde quickly disinfects contaminated surfaces. Formaldehyde is also used to kill the bacteria used in some vaccines.
4. **Metal salts**, such as mercuric chloride and organic metal compounds, such as merthiolate.
5. **Ethylene oxide gas**, particularly valuable in disinfecting plastics and polymers found in apparatus such as renal dialysis and extracorporeal circulatory machines. There are hazards because ethylene oxide in air is explosive, but a non-explosive mixture can be made in carbon dioxide.
6. **Chlorhexidine** ('Hibitane') 0.5 per cent in 70 per cent ethanol or in water. This halogenated compound is as effective as 1 per cent iodine in ethanol and is devoid of the risk of irritation of the skin and sensitization.
7. **Chloroxylenols** ('Dettol') and **chlorophenols** are weak disinfectants. They cause little irritation and are of low toxicity.
8. **Hexachlorophane**, often with a detergent or soap, is a very mild disinfectant, able to kill pyogenic cocci but not *Pseudomonas aeruginosa*. Toxic effects can result if hexachlorophane is absorbed systemically from very large surfaces such as those of burns.
9. **Quaternary ammonium compounds** such as cetrimide ('Cetavlon') are weak disinfectants with no action against *Pseudomonas aeruginosa*.

Pasteurization
Biological materials that are easily damaged and foodstuffs such as milk, can be disinfected (but not sterilized) by moist heat at temperatures below 100 °C. The process is called **pasteurization***. In one common variety of pasteurization, milk is held at 63–66 °C for 30 minutes. All non-spore-forming pathogenic bacteria including *Myco. tuberculosis, Brucella abortus*, salmonellae and streptococci are killed, but hepatitis B virus, *Coxsiella burnetii* (the cause of 'Q' fever), bacterial spores and protozoa are not destroyed.

In a comparable procedure, prolonged washing in very hot water at 70–80 °C can be used to disinfect some hospital and kitchen equipment.

See Antiseptics (p. 14)
Sterilization (p. 176)

Disseminated intravascular coagulation (DIC)

In disseminated intravascular coagulation (DIC) abnormal quantities of fibrin may be formed in the circulation. DIC is common after severe injury, during cardiothoracic surgery, in patients with acute pancreatitis, in endotoxic shock and following incompatible blood transfusion. This intra-vascular coagulation consumes large quantities of the coagulation factors and afibrinogenaemia and thrombocytopenia result. Consequently, the alternative term, **consumptive coagulopathy** has been used. The excess fibrin may obstruct small vessels, causing infarction. Fibrinolysis is stimulated. Although fibrinolysis removes some of the fibrin, the breakdown products have an additional anticoagulant action and severe microscopic bleeding occurs.

Diverticulum

A diverticulum is a pouch or cul-de-sac of an organ. Some diverticula, such as those of the oesophagus and intestine, are congenital: **Meckel's diverticulum** is part of the residue of the vitellointestinal duct. Many diverticula are formed by mechanical or hydrodynamic forces that push part of the wall of a hollow organ outwards: these are **pulsion diverticula**. Other **traction diverticula** are created when contracting scar tissue pulls the wall of the viscus outwards.

False diverticula form by the protrusion of a mucosa through a defect in the muscle coat of a hollow organ.

---

*Louis Pasteur (1822–1895) established the nature of fermentation and disproved the concept of the spontaneous generation of micro-organisms. He successfully protected sheep against virulent anthrax and devised a vaccine for the treatment of patients bitten by dogs or wolves with rabies.

Duct obstruction

Ducts such as those of the salivary glands and pancreas, the bile duct, ureters and eustachian tubes are often obstructed. Lesions causing obstruction may lie (1) outside the duct, (2) within the duct wall, or (3) in the lumen.

The effects, which are specific to each organ or gland, lead to malfunction and loss of tissue. Hydronephrosis and mucocele of the gall bladder exemplify this sequence: renal cortical atrophy and fibrosis, and fibrosis of the gall bladder are likely consequences respectively. The most important and most common result of duct obstruction is infection. Bacteria may ascend in a retrograde direction within the lumen of the duct or within adjacent lymphatics. Alternatively, blood-borne organisms can lodge in tissue proximal to an obstructed duct. Cholangitis and some cases of pyelonephritis are examples.

Dysplasia

Dysplasia (dys = altered; plasia = growth) is a loss of or reduction in the degree of differentiation of cell types. In stratified squamous epithelium, for example, there is a loss of the capacity of the cells to form keratin and the emergence of cells resembling those of the young stratum germinativum.

Many believe that dysplasia is an early stage of carcinogenesis and the word dysplasia in a biopsy report is liable to be misinterpreted by the surgeon if it is applied to non-neoplastic disorders.

In dysplasia, cell nuclei lose their mature polarity. The size of the nuclei increases so that the nuclear: cytoplasmic ratio rises, approaching those of embryonic or 'blast' cells. The chromosome number increases, deviating from the diploid number. The abnormally large number of chromosomes is reflected in the high nuclear chromatin content. Among these large, deeply-staining nuclei, mitotic figures become numerous and the appearances of the tissue merge with those of carcinoma-in-situ.

The term dysplasia is also used to describe an abnormality of organ growth. Renal dysplasia is one example: a small, poorly-formed kidney contains cartilage and is accompanied by other abnormalities of the genitourinary tract.

Elastosis

Elastosis is any degeneration of elastic tissue. In old age, **senile elastosis**, with a proliferation of dermal elastic material of fragmented character and poor mechanical quality, is commonly observed. **Solar elastosis** is a basophilic change in dermal collagen and a degeneration of dermal elastic material that develops after prolonged exposure to sunlight. Irradiation of the skin by x- or γ-sources leads to similar changes.

Embolism

Embolism is the process by which a solid, liquid or gas enters and lodges within blood or lymphatic vessels during life. Emboli are often formed of an individual's tissues or cells but may be composed of foreign substances.

Solid emboli   These are very common. The most frequent form is a portion of thrombus detached from a leg or pelvic vein entering the right side of the heart and lodging in the pulmonary arteries. Embolic thrombi are often carried in the left systemic arterial circulation from the internal surface of a cardiac infarct or an atherosclerotic plaque, to lodge in an artery such as the renal, carotid or popliteal. Other solid emboli include parts of plastic cannulae, fragments of foreign bodies such as talc and metal objects including bullets and shrapnel.

Fluid emboli   Fluid emboli are formed of material such as fat (p. 77) that is fluid at body temperature but differs from plasma in viscosity, density and solubility. Amniotic fluid is a source of microscopic pulmonary embolism in difficult labour.

Gaseous arterial emboli   Gaseous emboli may be of nitrogen released into the plasma during decompression after working for long periods in air held at high atmospheric pressure. Caisson disease (p. 38) results. The other non-physiological gases such as helium do not dissolve sufficiently to cause symptoms.

A comparable form of venous gaseous embolism can be caused by the accidental introduction of air. This is a hazard encountered during the measurement of central venous pressure, during the mechanical procedure of abortion and during operations on the neck. Continuous ultrasonic monitoring of the neck veins minimizes the risk during this latter form of surgery, allowing small air emboli to be quickly identified.

Venous air embolism of as little as 50 ml may be rapidly fatal. When the right atrium is occupied by air, venous return is impeded and cardiac output ceases.

Empyema

Empyema is the collection of pus in a cavity bounded by mesothelium or epithelium.

Empyema thoracis
The collection of pus in the pleural cavity is the most frequent form of empyema. Infection may extend to the pleura from an infected lung, as in lobar pneumonia due to *Streptococcus pneumoniae* or in bronchopneumonia; from the exterior, as in perforating injury; or from the subdiaphragmatic tissues, especially the liver. Where the lung infection reflects progressive bronchial disease, a bronchopleural fistula can result: air may then gain access to the pleural cavity, with resultant pyopneumothorax and mediastinal shift. Rarely, as in amoebiasis, a liver abscess can extend via the pleura and lung to a bronchus.

Empyema of the gall bladder
This complication occurs in 3–5 per cent of elderly patients with acute cholecystitis.

Endotoxic shock

Endotoxic shock results from the entry into the blood of large numbers of dead Gram-negative bacteria, particularly *Escherichia coli, Proteus vulgaris, Pseudomonas aeruginosa* and *Klebsiella aerogenes*. The syndrome is caused by the lipopolysaccharides that are part of the membrane that lies on the outside of the bacterial cell wall (p. 21) and that constitute endotoxin. By contrast with exotoxins (p. 185), endotoxins are therefore structural components of bacteria.

Endotoxic shock is particularly likely after gastrointestinal surgery or when intestinal perforation has occurred. It is also a complication of urological and pelvic surgery and of infected burns. Endotoxic shock is increasingly probable when immunosuppression has predisposed to Gram-negative bacterial infection.

There is diminished peripheral arteriolar resistance, the effect of the released histamine and kinins; activation of complement by the alternative pathway; hypotension; and disseminated intravascular coagulation (p. 73).

See Renal cortical necrosis (p. 165)

See Shwartzman reaction (p. 171).

Enteric fever

The term **enteric fever** includes typhoid and paratyphoid fevers, caused respectively by *Salmonella typhi*, and *Salm. paratyphi A and B*.

These are diseases of populations where poor hygiene and sanitation prevail. Typhoid and paratyphoid fevers are clinically and pathologically similar: only bacteriological studies can distinguish them with certainty. Paratyphoid B is the most frequent form of enteric fever in the UK. Infection is conveyed by contaminated food or water. The organisms in typhoid often survive in symptomless carriers. Faecal carriage may be due to the persistence of *Salm. typhi* in the gall bladder, a state which can cause epidemics if the individual is a food-handler. Not all faecal carriers are cured by cholecystectomy and in these patients, some other gastrointestinal reservoir must be responsible. Urinary carriers are both less common and much more dangerous than faecal carriers because of the ease with which urine can spread infection.

In a preliminary incubation phase, *Salm. typhi* multiplies in the lymphoid tissues of the gut, enters the blood stream and begins to cause febrile illness. The phase of incubation coincides with anti-*Salm. typhi* antibody formation; during the phase of bacteraemia, blood culture may be positive. The organisms are disseminated widely but small intestinal infection dominates the disease so that intestinal haemorrhage and perforation are important causes of death. The ileal ulcers that form from Peyer's patches are longitudinal; unlike tuberculosis, healing is not complicated by fibrosis and obstruction.

Vi antigen

Vi antigen is a heat-sensitive antigen present on the surface of salmonellae. As its name indicates, it is a measure of **vi**rulence. Fully formed, Vi antigen prevents agglutination by anti-O-(somatic) antibody: Vi may therefore protect the pathogenic organisms against phagocytosis and against the bactericidal actions of serum.

Erysipelas

Erysipelas ('red skin') is a form of cellulitis caused by β-haemolytic *Streptococcus pyogenes*. **Surgical erysipelas** develops at the site of wounds, for example, after inguinal herniorrhaphy.

The infection spreads quickly; the involved skin is warm, slightly firmer than normal and reddened. There is often no obvious point at which the organisms can be seen to have gained access to the subcutaneous connective tissues and the infection is self-limiting. The red coloration of the skin is the result of intense vascular congestion. The clinical significance is not the local disease but the profound systemic effects of the streptococcal toxins on the patient.

Exudate

An exudate is the outpouring of fluid rich in protein and derived from the plasma during acute inflammation. The selective filtration mechanism of the normal post-capillary venule is impaired and the escaping water is accompanied by large amounts of proteins including fibrinogen and the immunoglobulins. Leucocytes and some red blood cells are usually present.

By contrast with exudation, the protein content of a **transudate** is small. Transudates form, for example, in cardiac failure and as a result of mechanical obstruction to venous return.

Fat embolism

Fat embolism is the obstruction of pulmonary and systemic capillaries by droplets of fat that enter or form within venules or sinusoids after two per cent of cases of severe injury (p. 74).

Fat embolism characteristically follows severe injury, in particular fracture. The syndrome may occasionally be detected after less severe soft tissue trauma, particularly of adipose tissue. The time interval between injury and fat embolism is, on average, two days.

Lodging haphazardly within the vessels of the lungs, brain, kidneys and skin, where they are seen after the staining of frozen sections by dyes such as Sudan III, scattered fat droplets cause foci of tissue ischaemia and hypoxia. The tissue injuries of fat embolism may be anoxic. Alternatively, they have been attributed to the actions of lipoprotein lipase. Fatty acids freed within injured tissues are themselves irritant.

A clinical syndrome may result, with respiratory distress and defective arterial oxygenation, disturbed cerebral function, petechial skin haemorrhages and the presence of fat in the urine and in the sputum. The cerebral hypoxia is due to a defect in oxygen exchange in the lungs. Death is likely. However, microscopic fat embolism without previous evidence of clinical disease is commonly recognized post mortem.

The cause of fat embolism is disputed. Fat may be liberated directly from the marrow of fractured bone into the circulation. It is easy to envisage embolism after fracture of large bones, particularly when metal rods or prostheses have been inserted into marrow cavities. It is less easy to explain fat embolism in the absence of bony injury or orthopaedic manipulation. An acute disorder of the mechanisms regulating fat solubilization has therefore been considered and it has been suggested that plasma lipids coalesce in the plasma because of a defect in the mechanism that keeps lipids in solution: micelles of phospholipid may join to form droplets.

Fatty change

Fatty change is the abnormal accumulation of liquid, stainable (sudanophilic) fat by cells that, in health, contain little or none.

Ultramicroscopic fat droplets are seen in normal cells as varied as the chondrocyte and macrophage. In the latter cell, so-called lipid myelinoid bodies, the remnants of lipoproteins, lie within single, membrane-bounded vacuoles.

Fatty change is a valuable, common indication of cell injury; the disorder is frequently caused by starvation, hypoxia, ischaemia or by cell poisons. Fatty change is recognized, for example, in heart-muscle cells in severe anaemia, in hepatocytes in cardiac failure and ethanol poisoning, and in skeletal muscle cells as a result of the action of the α-toxin of *Clostridium welchii*.

Fibrinolysis

Fibrinolysis is the dissolution of a fibrin clot or coagulum.

The formation of fibrin is an important homeostatic mechanism (see Coagulation, p. 56). Although the prevention of bleeding by the formation of thrombi may be life saving, it may subsequently be desirable to dissolve thrombi in vessels such as end-arteries to restore flow to the tissues beyond the obstruction. Tissue fibrin is removed when organization follows inflammation (p. 116). There is normally a balance between coagulation and fibrinolysis within the blood. Any imbalance may produce inappropriate coagulation or hypofibrinogenaemia (see Disseminated intravascular coagulation, p. 73).

The fibrinolytic system is activated following injury, haemorrhage, anaphylaxis and other forms of shock, and after exercise.

Both clot dissolution (fibrinolysis) and coagulation are achieved by activation of inert precursors. The sequence is shown in Figure. 4. In fibrinolysis, kinases are liberated from precursors in the blood or tissues or from bacteria (streptokinase and staphylokinase) and these in turn convert inert blood proactivator into an activator. In a similar manner to coagulation, an activator can be produced directly by tissue damage. Inactive **plasminogen**, a plasma protein synthesized in the liver, is converted to the active fibrinolytic enzyme **plasmin** by such intrinsic and extrinsic activators.

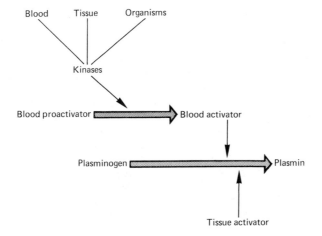

Fig. 4   The fibrinolytic system.

Therapeutic fibrinolysis can be used to treat local coagulation. The use of purified extracts of snake venom in this way has been frustrated by the adverse systemic effects of the preparations. Similarly disappointing results have been obtained in the therapeutic use of the fibrinolysis inhibitor ε-aminocaproic acid in the treatment of local haemorrhage.

See Coagulation (p. 56).

Fibrosis

Fibrosis is the process by which vascular tissues and organs effect **repair** when reconstitution of the part, by cell division within the uninjured remnant, is not possible.

Repair by regeneration is rapid in the skin, the liver, the renal tubules, the bone and the adrenal cortex. By contrast, cardiac-muscle cells and the smooth-muscle cells of arteries divide infrequently and repair is likely to be fibrous. Fibrosis is a response of fibroblasts: the cells are activated and form new type III collagen. The collagen matures and the fibrous tissue becomes denser, stronger and less vascular. X- and γ-radiation are particularly likely to promote fibrosis in tissues exposed to their effects.

In avascular tissues such as hyaline articular cartilage, repair by fibrosis is not possible. In the central nervous system, repair is by the analogous process of gliosis (p. 17). Occasionally, as in hypertrophic scar or keloid formation (p. 126), excess fibrous tissue is formed. A similar process is caused by drugs such as methysergide and propranolol, which may lead to retroperitoneal fibrosis. Ethanol is associated with hepatic cirrhosis (p. 55).

Heredity may determine the development of **fibromatosis** although in the most frequent form, Dupuytren's contracture, alcoholic cirrhosis, injury and diabetes mellitus may contribute to the onset (p. 66).

Fistula

A fistula is an abnormal communication between two epithelial surfaces. It may be congenital or acquired.

Developmental defects can persist as fistulae: failure of the urachus or of the vitellointestinal duct to atrophy, are examples.

Fistulae can form, for example, between the stomach and transverse colon because of chronic peptic ulceration, between the gall bladder and the duodenum as a result of the presence of biliary calculi, between different parts of the small and large intestine because of a combination of infection and local ischaemia or because of therapeutic irradiation, and between the trachea and oesophagus or colon and urinary bladder on account of tissue destruction by a malignant neoplasm. Fistulae are said to form between blood vessels but these are more accurately described as arteriovenous aneurysms (p. 9).

Fixation of tissues and cells

In pathological practice, tissues and cells are 'fixed' in fluids or gases that prevent autolysis and putrefaction and that harden the material before dehydration, embedding and sectioning. Without adequate fixation, the interpretation of a biopsy section may be difficult or impossible.

The most commonly used fixative **for light microscopy** is ten per cent formaldehyde (formalin); formalin is often made up in isotonic (0.9 per cent) saline. Since formaldehyde oxidizes in air to become formic acid, it is customary to add to the solution a salt such as magnesium hydroxide that combines with the unwanted acid, or to buffer the formalin as it is prepared. **For EM,** 1 per cent glutaraldehyde at 4 °C is used. Fresh glutaraldehyde is kept in refrigerators near operating theatres where renal, neoplastic and other EM biopsies are collected.

Surgical specimens must not be allowed to dry; they should be placed expeditiously in large containers in which the volume of fixative should be not less than ten times the volume of the specimen. Tissues should not be allowed to stick to the bottom of the container. Specimens should be delivered promptly to the laboratory on the day of operation, properly identified.

Foreign bodies

Foreign bodies comprise material that is physically, chemically or immunologically distinct from the native tissues of the host.

Materials of an immense variety are introduced accidentally or deliberately into the tissues or tissue spaces. The response which follows the introduction of a sterile foreign body varies in intensity according to the degree of physical and chemical irritation provoked. There is often an initial acute inflammatory reaction, overtaken by the arrival of mononuclear phagocytes derived from the blood. Endeavouring to phagocytose the foreign material, these macrophages tend to fuse to form multinucleated (foreign body) giant cells (p. 88). Unless the foreign material is disgested or destroyed, the inflammatory and cellular reaction persists, causing granuloma formation and sometimes a sinus or fistula.

Foreign bodies such as particles of silicate, fragments of cobalt-chrome steel or pieces of suture material have individual chemical or physical properties. The foreign-body reaction to them is characteristic and is influenced by their form, e.g. whether they are smooth or rough, finely or coarsely particulate. The identity of the foreign body can be suggested microcopically and proven by electron probe x-ray microanalysis, or by histochemical or immunocytochemical tests.

When host tissue such as kidney, bone, or myocardium undergoes infarction, the residual dead, sterile tissue becomes antigenically distinct from those of the host. Active inflammation is characteristic of the margins of infarcts and the response is comparable to the reaction to a foreign body.

Fracture

Fracture is the breaking of a hard material or tissue. The term is applied to bone and cartilage. Fracture may be a natural response by normal tissue to excessive direct or indirect force. Abnormal tissue is often unable to withstand physiological stresses: fracture of this diseased tissue is said to be pathological (p. 83).

Healing

Haematoma   Immediately after fracture, blood escapes in large amounts from injured periosteal, endosteal and marrow blood vessels and nearby soft tissue (p. 91). Blood coagulates in extravascular planes, forming a haematoma between and around the fractured bone ends. The extent of the haematoma is affected by the degree to which the bone ends are displaced. Fragments of ischaemic bone are scattered at the fracture site. Inflammation is excited by the local tissue injury. Polymorphs and then macrophages accumulate at the site and engulf and destroy cell debris.

Granulation tissue   Within a few hours, repair begins. Capillary endothelial buds and dividing fibroblasts extend from nearby viable tissue into the haematoma. The increased vascularity results in local osteoporosis of nearby bone. Type I bone collagen is laid down together with a non-collagenous matrix rich in proteoglycan. The response is the formation of granulation tissue: it fills the space between the bone ends within two to seven days.

Provisional callus   Within one to two days of injury, osteoblasts of the surviving periosteal and endosteal surfaces are activated. Together with the fibroblasts of the granulation tissue, these osteoprogenitor cells synthesize a microskeleton of osteocollagen which, with the associated proteoglycan, is called **osteoid**. Alkaline phosphatase formed by these cells catalyses the deposition of bone mineral in this extracellular matrix. The mineralized osteoid is described as woven bone. The irregular pattern of its microskeleton of collagen can be detected with polarized light. The new vascular, woven bone gradually fills the zone between the fractured bones and forms a spindle-shaped mass external to the bone contours. The mass is now said to be a **provisional callus**. It has a splint-like, supportive function and is well formed during the 5–15 days after injury. Particularly beneath the periosteum, islands of cartilaginous matrix also form: they characterize sites where there is relative ischaemia and are more extensive when immobilization is defective and healing delayed.

Callus   Within 14–21 days, osteoclasts begin to remove the woven bone of the provisional callus by phagocytosis and degradation of this mineralized tissue. These cells do not digest cartilage. Resorption is accompanied by a vigorous process of further orderly, lamellar bone formation. Arrays of activated osteoblasts synthesize osteocollagen and proteoglycan and catalyse mineralization by alkaline phosphatase activity. This lamellar bone is the **definitive callus**.

Remodelling   Infuenced by the stresses of weight-bearing and movement and by electrical forces, the excess external (subperiosteal) and internal (medullary) callus is now insidiously remodelled, restoring the shape and architecture of the bone to meet the stresses of normal movement and load-bearing. Restoration is never perfect. The site of even the oldest fracture can be identified as a zone of subperiosteal irregularity. Fractures of normal bones in childhood heal most completely although the growth of an affected long bone can be excessive.

Delayed union (healing)   Healing of uncomplicated fractures may be delayed by:

1. *Movement*. Shearing movements disturb granulation tissue and exacerbate inflammation. Distraction may also delay union, whereas compression can lead to rapid healing.
2. *Infection*. Bacterial infection prolongs and exaggerates inflammation. Pus may accumulate; abscesses form and osteomyelitis leads to ischaemic necrosis.
3. *Ischaemia*. Fracture can irretrievably injure the arterial blood supply to bone and joint tissue. Bone necrosis is an early consequence. More often ischaemia is partial, and the growth of granulation tissue and the formation of osteoid impaired. Delayed healing is more likely where arterial supplies are precarious, as in fracture of the neck of the femur, or where blood vessels are abnormal, as in the aged.
4. *Systemic disease*. Renal failure with uraemia, diabetes mellitus and malnutrition are examples of disorders in which fracture healing is often impaired.

Delayed healing is a characteristic of compound fractures.

Non-union (absence of healing)
Soft tissue may lie between the opposed parts of a fractured bone. Union is then impossible. An example is the interposition of the tendon of the tibialis posterior in fracture of the medial malleolus. Any factor predisposing to

delayed healing may result in a failure of the union of a fracture if the factor is sufficiently severe or prolonged. More frequently, osseous union is substituted by fibrous union.

Fibrous union

Fibrous union is, in effect, repair as it is seen in soft, non-mineralized connective tissue. Fibrous union therefore represents defective mineralization: it may result from local or systemic causes.

Pseudoarthrosis
(see p. 162)

Fracture, pathological

Pathological fractures are produced by the application of normal forces to diseased bones.

Any localized or generalized bone disease may lead to a reduction in bone strength, and the causes include both heritable and acquired bone disorders. A very common cause of pathological fracture is metastatic carcinoma. Comparable fractures may be due to simple cysts or giant-cell tumours. Pathological fractures may be a feature of generalized disease including osteoporosis (p. 152), osteomalacia (p. 151), osteitis fibrosa cystica (p. 154), osteogenesis imperfecta (p. 119) (in which there is reduced bone density), Paget's disease of bone (p. 153) and osteosclerosis (in which there is increased bone density). Pathological fractures can heal readily provided the cause is effectively treated.

Fracture, spontaneous

Spontaneous fractures are caused in normal bone by the sudden application of unexpected forces. In one example a normal lower limb bone can break readily when a single step downwards is taken in darkness: there is no protective contraction of the skeletal muscles acting about the nearby joints.

Stress or fatigue fractures are caused by the repetitive application to normal bone of small forces, each episode alone being insufficient to produce a fracture. Fatigue fractures of the tarsal and metatarsal bones are common among joggers and soldiers ('march fracture'), and among ballet dancers. Avulsion of the spinous process of the seventh cervical vertebra (so called 'clay-shovellers disease') is another example.

Frozen section

Frozen sections are cut to enable the rapid biopsy or necropsy diagnosis of a disease.

Tissues such as breast cannot easily be cut into sections sufficiently thin to be examined microscopically until they have been infiltrated and supported by a wax or resin. Freezing offers an alternative to this time-consuming procedure.

Freezing is quickly accomplished by a spray of ether, by a jet of compressed CO_2, by immersion in alcohol cooled by solid CO_2 ('dry ice') and isopentane at -70 °C, or in liquid nitrogen at -196 °C. Immediately after freezing, sections can be cut on a simple microtome fitted with a razor, or as is now often the case, in a cryostat (p. 67).

The cut, frozen section is lifted from the microtome into a bath of a dye such as toluidine blue or into two stains in sequence: haematoxylin (blue) and eosin (red) stain nuclei and cytoplasm respectively. The stained section is placed on a glass slide, wiped dry, covered with a drop of gelatin and a cover slip and at once examined microscopically.

The entire procedure occupies on average 8–10 minutes. The facility of frozen section is enhanced if the pathologist can be given prior warning that the procedure is required, and if a laboratory with freezing microtome or cryostat can be sited beside the operating theatre. It is essential to appreciate that there are some conditions, such as malignant melanoma and papillary carcinoma of the thyroid, that cannot reliably be diagnosed by frozen section in a non-specialized laboratory. There are other disorders such as cystic mastopathy that can be subject to frozen section but offer such difficulties of interpretation that the pathologist may be right to refuse comment except on a subsequent paraffin section.

Functioning neoplasms

Functioning neoplasms secrete hormones, enzymes and/or pharmacologically active substances. There are two categories:

1. In the first, an islet-cell neoplasm of the pancreas, for example, may secrete excess insulin or glucagon. Other examples include the multiple endocrine adenomas (p. 101). The secretions are those of the normal endocrine cells but are produced in excess.

2. In the second, hormones or other substances are secreted by cells that do not normally form these substances. The formation is ectopic or **inappropriate** and may be excessive. Thus, lung cancers often secrete ACTH. In ten per cent this produces Cushing's syndrome. Many more neoplasms, particularly oat-cell carcinoma, produce ACTH detectable only microscopically as granules within the cytoplasm of the cancer cells. The cells of oat-cell carcinoma may also secrete other humoral substances such as excess vasopressin and oxytocin. Renal-cell carcinomas can secrete parathyroid hormone, and hepatocarcinoma can form gonadotrophin.

The mechanism and reasons by which the cells of a non-endocrine neoplasm synthesize and secrete excessive amounts of a hormone are not known. It is assumed that all such cells are genetically programmed to make the majority of human proteins. If the latent ability to express endocrine polypeptide products is derepressed, for example by the action on the cell of an exgenous carcinogenic agent such as virus, then the neoplastic cells may become autonomous.

Fungi

Fungi are members of a group of non-vascular plants that have no chlorophyll. They are excluded from the algae and higher plant orders because of their reproductive and vegetative structures. Some are sources of antibiotics. Others are saprophytes. A few cause human disease.

Mycoses
Mycoses are specific superficial or invasive fungal infections.

Superficial mycoses such as candidiasis (*Candida albicans*) are opportunistic; the organism thrives when mucosal pH is changed or mucus secretion impaired. The fungus also multiplies when antibiotics have changed regional bacterial flora or when immunosuppressive or cytotoxic therapy has impaired host defence mechanisms.

Invasive mycoses are much more frequent in subtropical or tropical countries. Some are systemic and airborne. They may be endemic (histoplasmosis: *Histoplasma capsulatum*) or epidemic (coccidioidomycosis: *Coccidioides immitis*). Others, of particular dermatological and surgical importance, are locally invasive: they include South American blastomycosis (*Blastomyces dermatiditis*), maduramycosis (*Madurella mycetomi*; Allescheria). Invasive fungi such as *Aspergillus fumigatus* or Mucor widely infiltrate tissues that have been prejudiced by ischaemia or neoplastic growth, in immunosuppression and in those given cytotoxic agents.

Mycetism
Mycetism is an illness due to the ingestion of fungi such as mushrooms.

Mycotoxicosis
Mycotoxicosis is the poisoning produced by the injection of food contaminated by poisonous fungi. Ergot and aflatoxin (p. 4) poisoning are examples.

Furuncle

A furuncle or boil is a localized infection of the skin that results in the formation of a small abscess. The causative organism is usually *Staph. aureus*. The infection originates in an obstructed hair follicle.

Gangrene

Gangrene is an ancient term, used inconsistently, describing necrosis (death) of part of the body. It is synonymous with putrefaction.

The initial change is a loss of blood supply to a part such as a limb or a segment of gut. Vegetative saprophytic bacteria already present on or in the tissues then multiply, breaking down the tissues by enzymatic degradation. The responsible organisms tend to be micro-aerophilic or anaerobic. The result is a mass of discoloured, softened, foul-smelling tissue, the high water content of which accounts for the description '**wet (or moist) gangrene**'.

Extensive tissue death is not always followed by gangrene. Saprophytic organisms may not be present: their growth may be prevented by antibiotics. The dead tissue then dries slowly by **mummification**, retaining its form. The effects are identical with those seen when the dead body lies in a dry, sterile environment as did Egyptian mummies. The description '**dry gangrene**' sometimes given to this process of mummification is misleading. Mummification is encountered relatively frequently in patients with slowly advancing occlusion of limb arteries.

Gas gangrene   This dangerous form of spreading tissue necrosis is liable to occur when the spores of Clostridia gain access to a wound in which there is extensive soft-tissue or muscle injury. Dirty wounds contaminated by soil are particularly at risk. Within the injured tissue where O_2 tension is low, *Clostridium welchii* multiply as vegetative bacteria. They form potent exotoxins which themselves break down tissue. The important α-toxin of *Cl. welchii*, for example, a haemolysin, kills muscle cells and destroys fat. Further tissue injury is caused by *Cl. oedematiens* and *Cl. septicum*. A vicious circle is established and proteolysis and saccharolysis, with gas production, are caused by enzymes that are among the toxins liberated in the injured tissues by *Cl. histolyticum* and *Cl. sporogenes*.

Synergistic gangrene   This may arise at sites of ulceration due to trauma or virus infection. Two bacterial species, *Borrelia vincentii* and fusiform bacteria of the bacterioides group, *Fusobacterium fusiforme*, live in symbiosis in sites such as the normal gum. When the resistance of such tissues to invasion is lessened, e.g. as a result of immunosuppression, granulocytopenia or nutritional deficiency, vastly increased numbers of these micro-organisms form and cause progressive local tissue destruction. Synergistic gangrene is particularly likely when wound hygiene is poor. Orofacial gangrene (cancrum oris) is one instance.

Fournier's gangrene   Fournier's gangrene arises without an immediately recognizable injury, destroying the tissues of the scrotum or vulva.

Meleney's gangrene   This is progressive gangrene at the site of an accidental abrasion of the skin. Like idiopathic scrotal and vulvar gangrene, the lesion has been attributed to the action of anaerobic streptococci, but an amoeba may be implicated.

Gardner's syndrome

The American geneticist E.J. Gardner first described a hereditary disease in which the occurrence of multiple polyps in the colon is associated with benign osteomas of the skull and benign neoplasms of soft tissues, including desmoid neoplasms, cutaneous fibromas, and neoplasms of sebaceous glands. The disease is transmitted as an autosomal dominant trait with a high degree of penetrance. As in patients with polyposis coli (p. 158), there is a greatly increased risk of development of carcinoma of the colon.

Subsequently it has become apparent that patients with Gardner's syndrome are also likely to develop polypoidal neoplasms of the stomach, duodenum, particularly of the papilla of Vater, the biliary tract, and the small bowel.

Genes

A gene is the part of a molecule of DNA (p. 70) that determines the inheritance of a characteristic.

The DNA of each cell nucleus is visible at the beginning of cell division as the **chromosomes** (p. 52). Each gene encodes the information for the construction of a single molecule of protein. The bases (nucleotides) of the DNA strand are arranged in a precise order: three nucleotides ('words') form a **codon**. Each amino acid of a protein molecule is specified by the structure of an individual codon so that guanine-uridine-guanine (GUG) is translated into valine; guanine-adenine-guanine (GAG) into glutamic acid, and so on.

In the case of proteins such as enzymes, two or more independent genes may code for different parts of the enzyme protein. Usually, these different regions lie close together but occasionally, as in the case of the regions coding for the α- and β-chains of haemoglobin, the genes are on different chromosomes.

Genes determine the transfer of genetic information (p. 118). Mendel's laws (p.88) established the independent segregation of genes and their assortment. Modern evidence shows, however, that genes on the same chromosome may be linked; that separated genes may recombine; that genes vary in the degree to which they express their influence, so that there is complete or incomplete penetrance; and that genes exert their effects at different phases of development. A single gene may influence many characteristics (**pleiotropy**) or many genes may regulate one characteristic (**polygenic inheritance**).

Mutation

Mutation is a change in a gene usually comprising the replacement of one base (nucleotide) in the DNA of the gene by another base. The change is heritable. There is a corresponding alteration in cell structure or behaviour. The focal nature of the chemical change has led to the term 'point mutation'. A classical example is the emergence of the sickle-cell trait (p. 171). The original gene and the new, mutant form are **alleles**: they are alternative genes at a single locus. The mutation of sex cells results in the production of mutant individuals in the progeny.

Genetics

Genetics is the study of inheritance.

Individuals vary in shape, height, colour, intelligence, behaviour and in every other bodily characteristic. The genetic constitution determining these characteristics is the **genotype**. The physical and mental features themselves constitute the **phenotype**. Some conditions such as chondrodystrophy and alkaptonuria are wholly genetic; others such as burns, fractures and carbuncles may be wholly environmental. In conditions such as peptic ulcer, cholelithiasis, pigmented skin neoplasms and Crohn's disease, both genetic and environmental factors may play important roles.

In **Mendelian inheritance**, the appearance of characters in the offspring or progeny follows the laws first established by Mendel.* In the case of each nuclear gene, two of the four cells that are formed by meiosis (p. 51) inherit the gene from one parental cell; the other two cells inherit the gene from the second parental cell.

Giant cells

Giant cells are simply very large cells. They may have single nuclei but are frequently **multinucleated** or multilobed.

The presence of many nuclei in a large cell is an indication of abnormal nuclear division during mitosis, or a sign of cell fusion. Thus, the multinucleated giant cells encountered in viral infections such as measles demonstrate that the virus has impaired nuclear division; the multinucleated (Langhans) giant cells of tuberculosis (p. 190) are indications that macrophages have fused in their efforts to engulf and destroy mycobacteria.

The largest **normal** cells in the human body are those of skeletal muscle (Muscle 'fibres'). The longest cells are the neurones transmitting impulses between the foot and the spinal cord. Normal giant cells, including the osteoclast, the skeletal muscle and cardiac muscle cells and those of the cytotrophoblast are often multinucleate. The nucleus of the megakaryocyte is multilobed; there are 184 chromosomes but the cell is not multinucleate.

Abnormal giant cells are typified by the multinucleated foreign-body giant cell that phagocytoses particulate debris in injured tissues, the multinucleated Langhans giant cell (p. 190), the multinucleated 'mulberry' giant cells of virus infections such as measles, and the mirror-image, twin nucleus Reed–Sternberg cell of Hodgkin's lymphoma. The measles multinucleated giant cell is named the Warthin–Finkeldy cell, the giant cell of the xanthomas, the Touton cell.

Globulins

Globulins are proteins synthesized in the liver.

The normal plasma concentration of globulins is 22–31 g/1. Their molecular weight varies from 50 000 up to many millions. They can be separated into different components, the α_1-, α_2-, β- and γ-globulins, by electrophoresis and ultracentrifugation. Individual globulins can be identified by immunoelectrophoresis. The **cryoglobulins** precipitate out of solution in the cold. The most important globulins are the **immunoglobulins** (p. 111).

Gloves

The wearing of sterile gloves is a highly desirable feature of the surgeon's fight to avoid sepsis. Gloves were adopted for surgical operations by Halsted;† they reduce but do not eliminate the possibility of transferring

---

*Gregor Johann Mendel (1822–1884). Mendel was a monk who lived in Brno and made studies of peas in investigations that were rediscovered in 1900, 16 years after his death. Mendel's work founded modern genetics.

†William Stewart Halsted (1852–1922), the first Professor of Surgery at the Johns Hopkins Medical School, had rubber gloves made (1889) to protect the hands of an operating theatre nurse whose skin was sensitive to mercuric chloride.

pathogenic bacteria such as *Staphylococcus aureus* from a surgeon's hands to a sterile surgical wound.

Surgical gloves must be sufficiently thin to be flexible and to allow tactile sensation but sufficiently thick and strong to prevent organisms passing to the surgical field. During operations, rubber and latex gloves often perforate. The likelihood of perforation increases with the duration and scale of surgery. Modern gloves are made of latex. Lubrication is necessary before they can be donned: the lubricant is usually a starch powder (p. 181). Sterile gloves should be worn on wards for all procedures, such as lumbar puncture, in which asepsis is necessary. The likelihood of cross-infection in a ward is reduced if nursing staff are encouraged to use disposable, clean but not necessarily sterile gloves for each dressing.

See Granuloma, starch (p. 181).

Grading of neoplasms

The grading of neoplasms is a microscopic procedure of value to the clinician that allows attempts to predict responses to treatment.

In Broder's classification, malignant epithelial neoplasms can be divided into four grades: in grade I, more than 75 per cent of the cells are well differentiated; in grade II, 50–75 per cent; in grade III, 25–50 per cent; in grade IV, less than 25 per cent of the cells are well differentiated.

Such a precise numerical system is rarely used; it is time-consuming and histopathologists usually simply report a neoplasm as being well-differentiated, poorly-differentiated or undifferentiated. In terms of prognosis there may be more important features to consider such as the clinical staging (p. 174). Microscopic grading is often of value to the radiotherapist; the well-differentiated neoplasms are less radiosensitive than the poorly differentiated.

In assessing the degree of differentiation the histopathologist takes account of the size and shape of the cells; the ratio between cell and nuclear size; the number of mitotic figures and, in neoplasms of glandular epithelium, the extent to which the neoplasm has reproduced a glandular structure. In squamous carcinoma of the skin, the amount of cornification is considered. Attempts are made to grade sarcomas, in a similar manner, but this is difficult and the degree of correlation between prognosis and grading is less than with carcinomas.

Granulation tissue

Granulation tissue is the young, vascular connective tissue that forms when healing occurs by repair rather than by regeneration.

Leucocytes, in particular macrophages, digest cell debris. Vascular, endothelial buds extend into the injured part: the vessels soon become arterioles, capillaries or venules. Fibroblasts divide and a matrix of proteoglycan and young collagen is deposited between the blood vessels. With time, vascularity diminishes and the residual collagen constitutes a scar (p. 168).

Granulation tissue is characteristic of healing by second intention. The healing surface is punctuated by small, pink dots or granules the appearance of which is due to the presence of arcades of young blood vessels seen at the surface before it is covered by regenerating epithelium.

Granuloma

A granuloma is initially an aggregate of macrophages. With time, organization occurs and the granuloma comes to be an island of fibrous connective tissue with many small, thin-walled blood vessels. There is a close resemblance to granulation tissue. Granulomas, in spite of their name, are not neoplasms: the suffix '-oma' is misleading.

The macrophages of granulomas resemble the cells of some epithelia, and were misleadingly called 'epithelioid' cells. In many types of granuloma, macrophages are accompanied by activated mononuclear phagocytes and by lymphocytes. In some instances, small numbers of neutrophil and eosinophil polymorphs are seen. The varied nature and maturity of the cells present helps to differentiate granulomas from neoplasms.

Many granulomas are evidence of chronic bacterial (staphylococcal, tuberculous, leprous), protozoal (leishmanial), fungal (coccidioidal), or parasitic (filarial) infection. Others result from immunological reactions or autoimmune disease (p. 20) (spermatic, pulmonary, rheumatoid). Physical agents such as retained oil, suture material and foreign bodies elicit granulomas, as do chemical agents like beryllium. Some granulomas, such as those of Crohn's disease and sarcoidosis, do not yet have a defined cause.

Growth

Growth is the progressive development and increase in size of part or the whole of an organism. Growth of the whole body takes place during the period from fertilization to maturity but individual normal tissues grow in response to functional demand or to compensate for structural loss.

The ancient word growth, an Anglo-Saxon term, is also used in common speech as a synonym for neoplasia.

The rate of fetal growth, indicated by body length (stature), is highest midway through pregnancy. The rate slows late in pregnancy, accelerating briefly after birth. The rate of growth in childhood declines until puberty when it accelerates again. The long bones effectively cease growing at 16 years in girls, 18 years in boys. Height declines in old age.

Factors affecting growth of stature are both genetic and environmental. Growth is closely controlled by the growth hormone of the anterior pituitary and influenced by thyroid hormone and by adrenal and testicular androgens. Malnutrition slows growth, as does any severe systemic disease. The body tissues and organs have growth patterns that are regulated differentially. The growth processess and the factors that control them also influence tissue and organ maintenance, regeneration (p. 164) and repair.

Gunshot and missile wounds

Gunshot and missile wounds are produced by the sudden dissipation of energy in the tissues.

Three main factors determine the severity of a wound: the velocity of the missile; its mass; and its composition. The kinetic energy of a missile is proportional to the square of the velocity when compared to the mass. Wounds produced by high-velocity rifles are much more severe than those produced from small-calibre hand guns. It is safer to be struck by a slowly moving, 12 pound cannonball than it is to be hit by a bullet from a modern military rifle. High-velocity missiles produce widespread tissue cavitation due to the creation of pressure waves transmitted radial to the trajectory. Although the size of a wound is proportional to the calibre of a bullet, small, soft bullets often fragment upon impact and produce a correspondingly larger wound.

Particular forms of injury are caused by special varieties of missile or explosion. Bomb explosions in enclosed spaces produce lung injury, underwater explosions injure the unprotected abdominal viscera, and blunt injuries by rubber bullets or cricket balls cause indirect effects including cardiac arrest and, in survivors pericarditis.

H2 Receptor antagonists

By convention, it is agreed that H1 receptors regulate mucosal blood flow and H2 receptors regulate acid secretion. Consequently, drugs acting upon H2 receptors are known as H2 receptor antagonists. This group of drugs, which includes cimetidine and ranitidine, prevents the stimulation of gastric secretion of acid by histamine without altering the large increase in gastric mucosal blood flow that histamine causes. In addition to their effect upon histamine-stimulated secretion of acid, H2 receptor antagonists also inhibit all other stimulators of acid secretion such as gastrin, insulin and food.

Haematoma

A haematoma is a swelling composed of blood, resulting either from injury, from vascular disease, or from a disorder of coagulation.

Haemolysis

Haemolysis is the breaking down of red blood cells with the release of haemoglobin. It is the normal fate of ageing red blood cells (p. 92) within the reticuloendothelial cells of the spleen (p. 173). Large-scale rapid haemolysis may lead to haemoglobinaemia and haemoglobinuria.

Red blood cell survival can be measured in vivo by labelling a sample of cells with radioactive chromium (^{51}Cr) and reintroducing them into the circulation. A tendency for abnormal haemolysis can be recognized in vitro by suspending red blood cells in serial dilutions of saline. Healthy red cells begin to break down in 0.5 per cent saline; abnormal cells show a much greater osmotic fragility and begin to break down at concentrations of saline nearer to the normal plasma figure of 0.9 per cent.

Excessive haemolysis is a characteristic of mismatched blood transfusion (p. 36), of the heritable haemolytic anaemias such as spherocytosis (p. 8) and of the haemoglobinopathies such as sickle-cell disease (p. 171). Excessive haemolysis alsos accompanies the numerous acquired haemolytic anaemias. Haemolysis may be a feature of any form of splenomegaly and is characteristic of protozoal diseases such as malaria.

Haemolysis is used as an end-point in the complement fixation reaction (p. 63). It is an undesirable change in blood collected carelessly for haematogical or serological tests and may occur if the collected blood is left standing for a few hours at room temperature before it is centrifuged.

Haemophilia

Haemophilia A is a rare and potentially fatal inherited disorder of the clotting mechanism of males transmitted as a X-linked recessive characteristic by mothers who, because of the dominant influence of their second X chromosome (p. 53), show no clinical abnormality.

The affected male has a relative deficiency of factor VIII. A deficiency of factor IX gives rise to the closely similar **haemophilia B** (Christmas disease), named after the first individual to be identified. The abnormality in haemophilia is a defect in the intrinsic clotting mechanism. The bleeding time is normal but there is a tendency for severe or fatal bleeding to occur after minor injuries or incisions such as dental extractions. Bleeding into joints occurs after minor trauma. Severe crippling arthropathy results, with ankylosis and deformity.

In **von Willebrand's disease**, there is a deficiency of the von Willebrand factor, necessary for the formation of factor VIII. The abnormality is an autosomal dominant characteristic. Both bleeding and clotting times are prolonged.

Haemopoiesis

Haemopoiesis is the production of blood cells.

In the fetus, red and white blood cells and platelets are formed in the bone marrow, spleen and liver. The marrow site is said to be medullary; the spleen and liver are extramedullary. After birth, haemopoiesis is soon confined to the axial skeleton and long bones; in the adult, zones of red, haemopoietic marrow remain only in the axial skeleton, ribs and skull, and in the proximal one third of the humerus and femur.

The red blood cell precursors are large **erythroblasts**: as they mature, they become smaller and acquire cytoplasmic haemoglobin before losing their nuclei. As mature cells, they survive 80–120 days in the circulation before undergoing destruction in the spleen.

White-cell precursors, **myeloblasts,** are at first undifferentiated; they acquire characteristic granules and are called myelocytes before they mature to become neutrophil, eosinophil and basophil granulocytes.

Platelets (p. 157) are derived from **megakaryocytes**. Each cell breaks up to form up to 3000 small, freely movable particles with no nuclei.

See Bone Marrow after blood loss (p. 37).

Hamartoma

A hamartoma is a non-neoplastic, congenital malformation that constitutes a neoplasm-like mass or nodule.

Unlike a neoplasm, a hamartoma grows at the same rate and proportion as the tissue in which it arises. There is no capsule. The tissues of which a hamartoma is formed are often vascular, but, as in the case of the pulmonary hamartoma which is composed of hyaline cartilage, other mesenchymal or epithelial tissues may be present. Many hamartomas are formed of an admixture of tissues but one tissue predominates. Although arising in utero and present at birth, hamartomas may only be recognized in later life: they shrink with advancing age.

Healing

In a general sense, to heal is to cure a disease, to restore to health. In a specific, surgical sense the term is applied to the restoration of the tissues of a wound to normal.

Healing of tissues that retain a capacity for cell division is by **regeneration**. Thus, the epidermal cells of the skin and those of the liver, renal tubules, bone and adrenal cortex regenerate by mitotic division. By contrast, the central nervous system, hyaline cartilage and heart muscle heal by **repair** (p. 79). This is the substitution of fibrous or glial tissue for a defect.

Wound healing

When the edges of a clean, sterile surgical wound are directly apposed, the rapid division of epidermal cells and the localized formation of a young, subepidermal fibrovascular scar (p. 168) lead to healing **by first intention**. This process is encouraged by careful wound closure but is impeded around the tracks of sutures.

In pre-Listerian days, surgical wounds were allowed to remain open, the edges separate. New, young vascular granulation formed the base of the healing wound and healing was then said to be **by second intention**. This precaution was taken to overcome infection and is still practised today with heavily contaminated wounds. Another approach to such wounds is to excise the damaged edges with primary closure of healthy tissue to promote healing by primary intention. If such a wound becomes infected but the infection resolves, healing can be said to be **by third intention**.

Three features characterize wound healing, whether or not it is by first or second intention:

Epithelial overgrowth   Within a few hours there is increased basal-cell division at the edges of the wound; undifferentiated epithelial cells migrate down the edges. In healing by second intention, it takes much longer for the epithelial cells to completely cover the wound. Stratification then begins. The cells differentiate and mature.

Connective-tissue repair   Following early inflammation there is an ingrowth of highly vascular granulation tissue into the base of the wound. In wounds healing by first intention the connective tissue is rapidly covered by epithelial cells; in wound healing by second intention, much granulation tissue is formed to fill the defect before there is complete epithelial over-growth. Between the 5th and 15th day of wound healing there is a rapid increase in collagen content and a great increase in the strength of the wound. The granulation tissue becomes less vascular and less cellular. There is re-modelling of collagen with increased cross-linkage between collagen fibrils.

The relatively avascular tissue, composed predominantly of collagen, is a **scar** (p. 168). Replacement of collagen is a continual, slow process in old wounds: they may break down if the patient develops scurvy (p. 168).

Wound contraction   In a large wound, contraction causes centripetal movement of the skin edges and reduces the necessity for epithelial replace-ment. There is a lag period of three to four days before contraction begins: it is usually complete by the 14th day. Contraction is an important component of wound healing, particularly by second intention, and a wound may be reduced by as much as 80 per cent in size. The connective-tissue cells that predominate in early healing, (myo)fibroblasts, contain many contractile intermediate filaments (p. 120). Contraction of these filaments produces active cell movement which is the most important factor in wound con-traction. Later, as collagen matures, interfibrillar cross-linking contributes strongly to the contraction that is characteristic of scar tissue. Contracture (excessive contraction) (p. 65) or cicatrization (p. 55) occur after wound healing is complete and may, for example, produce immobilization of joints in patients who have sustained severe burns.

Heart failure

Heart failure exists when the heart is unable to maintain a circulation suffi-cient for the need of the body in spite of an adequate venous filling pressure.

Mechanisms   The heart fails either because of an overwhelming load of work or because cardiac muscle is abnormal. These factors may coexist.

Increased load may be imposed by a demand to expel a higher volume of blood per unit time than normal, **volume load**, or because of increased resistance to the expulsion of blood from the heart, **pressure load**. Examples of failure due to volume load include anaemia and thyrotoxicosis, in which a high cardiac output is required to become increasingly higher; and mitral and aortic valve incompetence, in which the heart attempts to expel both the normal ventricular volume of blood and that which regurgitates through the abnormal valve. Examples of failure due to pressure loads are systemic hypertension and aortic stenosis.

Impaired cardiac-muscle function is usually the result of coronary artery insufficiency but cardiomyopathy and amyloidosis are other causes.

Effects   As the heart responds to an increased work load, the ventricle dilates and cardiac muscle hypertrophies. Cardiac output then becomes inadequate and there is a progressive retention of Na^+, and thus of water, due in part to impaired glomerular filtration but largely to increased renal tubular Na$^+$ reabsorption. Hyperaldosteronism (p. 5) is characteristic only of advanced cardiac failure. These changes together culminate in rising venous pressure and in capillary and venous stagnation ('congestion') in the viscera.

In **left heart failure** due to defective function of the left ventricle or atrium, there is engorgement of the pulmonary veins and capillaries and ultimately pulmonary oedema. Causes include systemic hypertension, aortic and mitral valvular disease, myocardial infarction, and cardiomyopathy.

In **right heart failure** due to defective function of the right ventricle or atrium, there is engorgement of the liver, kidneys, other organs and systemic veins, and oedema. The causes include many forms of pulmonary disease such as chronic bronchitis and emphysema, but right heart failure is a common result of left heart failure.

Surgical significance   Heart failure poses many problems for surgeons and anaesthetists. There may be

defective metabolism of anaesthetic agents and drugs;
defective tissue perfusion with impaired regulation of
    water balance, gaseous exchange, pH and electrolytes;
inadequate cardiovascular response to haemorrhage;
increased susceptibility to venous thrombosis and its
    complications.

Acute heart failure occurs in shock (p. 169) of which many instances are cardiogenic.

Heat excess, effects of

Local
The local effects of heat on a tissue depend upon the temperature attained. Tissue is irreversibly injured by temperatures exceeding 45 °C. Up to a temperature of 50 °C there is profuse vasodilatation with an increase in vascular permeability and the formation of a protein-rich exudate. Above 50 °C there is denaturation of protein and inactivation of intracellular enzymes. Sludging of blood and intravascular haemolysis are recognized.

Systemic
The systemic effects of heat may be due either to fever or to the exposure of the unacclimatized body to excessive temperature and high humidity. The major cause of 'heat stroke' is inadequate loss of heat by cutaneous evaporation.

Diathermy
The heat used to coagulate tissue by diathermy is generated by high-frequency electric currents. Temperatures in excess of 1000 °C can be produced. By altering the frequency and current it is possible to use the same apparatus either to cut or to coagulate tissue.
See Burns and Scalds (p. 38).

Hepatitis

Hepatitis is inflammation of the liver. The inflammation may be focal or diffuse, acute or chronic.

Acute hepatitis of surgical significance is usually viral although inflammation of the liver can be bacterial (e.g. portal pyaemia), protozoal (e.g. amoebiasis), or metazoal (e.g. hydatid disease; schistosomiasis).

Acute viral hepatitis is a result of liver-cell injury caused by the hepatitis viruses (Table 5), by the Coxsackie B and herpes simplex viruses in neonates, by the virus of yellow fever, by cytomegalovirus, by rubella virus in the embryo or adult, by the Epstein–Barr virus in glandular fever, and by the herpes simplex and varicella zoster viruses in immunosuppressed subjects.

Chronic hepatitis is said to be persistent or active. The former is a self-limiting process and is innocuous; the latter, in which a disturbance of the immune mechanism has been provoked, is progressively damaging and is likely to lead to cirrhosis (p. 55) and its consequences.

Hepatitis B

Hepatitis B (HB) is caused by a DNA virus, a member of the Hepadna group. A small number of animals are susceptible to hepatitis due to a virus of identical morphology, but the animal virus is antigenically distinct from the human agent.

Virus structure   The virion or Dane particle, is a 42 nm diameter icosahedron. There is an inner 27 nm diameter core containing DNA, and an outer envelope. The DNA is circular and in part double-stranded: the amount is very small.

Three viral antigens can be detected:

1. Hepatitis B surface antigen (HBsAg) (formerly Australia antigen). This antigen exists on the outer surface of the Dane particle, and in the serum as numerous small, non-infective particles. They are aggregates of excess envelope protein and lipid.

2. Core antigen (HBcAg) which encloses the viral DNA core.

3. HBeAg, formed as a result of the breakdown of core antigen released from infected liver cells. The appearance of e antigen in the serum is closely correlated with viral replication in these cells.

Following infection, antibodies are formed against all three of these antigens but the significance of their identification differs in an important sense. Infected persons and carriers have HBsAg and anti-HBcAg but lack anti-HBsAg in their blood. On recovery from infection, HBsAg disappears from the blood and anti-HBsAg is later demonstrable, together with anti-HBcAg.

Patients with acute hepatitis and carriers of virus bearing the e antigen are particular hazards for the transmission of infection by inoculation injury, by perinatal infection in pregnant women and by sexual contact.

Table 5   The hepatitis viruses and their properties

	HA	HB	H non-A, non-B
Nature of virus(es)	RNA ss; 27 nm icosahedral non-enveloped; enterovirus-like	DNA part ds, part ss; 42 nm icosahedral, enveloped; unique structure	At least 3 viruses. One is a 27 nm diameter non-enveloped icosahedron, distinct from hepatitis A and B viruses. The second is a poorly understood, enveloped RNA virus. The third is not characterized
Transmission route	faecal-oral	by blood, blood products, other body fluids; sexual contact	Like HA or like HB
Incubation period	15–40 days	50–180 days	
Mechanism of tissue injury	liver cells injured directly by virus	liver cell injury is associated with immunological response	
Diagnosis			
virus in faeces	from 2 weeks before onset to 1 week after recovery	absent	by exclusion of HA, HB, CMV and EB
virus in blood and body fluids	from 2 weeks before onset to 2 weeks after recovery	from incubation to months or many years after recovery; in blood 6–8 weeks before onset. Persistence in carriers may be indefinite	
anti-HBs	no	yes	no
Chronicity			
persistence of virus	no	yes	yes
chronic hepatitis	no	yes	yes
cirrhosis	no	yes	yes
predisposition to hepatocarcinoma	no	strong virus may be oncogenic	not demonstrated

Clinical manifestations   HB has a mean incubation period of about 100 days. Raised serum levels of enzymes such as AST (p. 205) precede the insidious onset of jaundice which may persist for four to twelve weeks. Fifty per cent of infections are subclinical. Those who have had the infection, clinically or subclinically, may persist as symptomless carriers. A carrier is a person who has been found to have HBsAg for not less than 6 months.

HB infection is important in surgery because the virus persists for months or years after the acute infection has subsided, in blood and body fluids. Seven to ten per cent of surivors in Western Europe become carriers. Virus is transmitted by direct contact with blood or blood products or by other body fluids. Most carriers have apparently had an anicteric infection. Patients who have become jaundiced almost invariably recover. Carriers are very frequent among drug addicts (50 per cent), among those who have been tattooed, and among male homosexuals. There is also a high incidence of HB among the populations of SE Asia and in other places where the liver is prone to injury because of malnutrition or other coincidental disease. A large proportion of the infections in SE Asia is among neonates. The carrier rate in these populations can vary from 10 to 30 per cent. Predisposition to infection may be racial, as it is among the Chinese. Many patients contract infection and become carriers as a result of perinatal infection transmitted by carrier mothers at the time of birth. Others who have a high chance of becoming symptomless carriers if exposed to HB infection are individuals with chronic uraemia, those treated with immunosuppressive drugs and those with defects such as Down's syndrome (p. 54).

Patients requiring very large quantities of blood or blood products such as Factor VIII prepared from large pools of plasma have an increased likelihood of contracting HB but no increased tendency to become carriers: their immune mechanisms are normal. There is a potentially increased risk of infection among staff working in units where blood and blood products are frequently used in treatment and in laboratories dealing with blood, blood products or unfixed tissues, but precautions now effectively prevent this hazard.

Recognition of carriers   Screening tests for HBsAg on serum are the basis for the identification of acute HB and carriers.

Pathogenesis   Identification of HBeAg confirms that the HB virus is actively replicating and causing liver damage. As replication proceeds, anti-HBcAg antibody is formed; its early presence does not provide a measure of protection. Indeed, liver injury in hepatitis B is mainly due to cell-mediated hypersensitivity associated with anti-HBc. By contrast, humoral antibody is associated with anti-HBs. It has been shown that complexes of HBe and anti-HBe can cause arteritis, glomerulonephritis and synovitis.

Vaccination   Active protection against HB is possible by administering a killed vaccine of HBsAg obtained from the plasma of HB carriers. Partial protection after inoculation injury or sexual contact can be attained by the administration of hyperimmune globulin prepared from donors who are anti-HBsAg-positive. Combined active and passive immunization has also been shown to be highly effective.

Carcinogenesis   HB is closely associated with the high incidence of hepatocarcinoma in SE Asia. The carrier state, chronic hepatitis and cirrhosis precede neoplasia. HB virus can be identified in the cancer cells.

Hepatitis Non-A, Non-B
At least three other agents, for which no laboratory tests are available, are known to cause viral hepatitis. One type has clinical features and an epidemiological behaviour similar to HA. The other two viruses together account for more than 50 per cent of cases of hepatitis following blood transfusion, in haemophilia and in drug addiction. They behave and spread like HB. In transfusion hepatitis, there is an incubation period of 2–16 weeks and a 20 per cent chance of developing chronic hepatitis.

Hepatitis A
Hepatitis A is mainly of medical significance.

Hepatorenal syndrome

The term has been applied to patients dying from liver failure in whom there is also evidence of renal failure. The justification for the term hepatorenal syndrome is now questioned. In many patients there is histological evidence of renal damage with tubular necrosis. The association is commonly observed following operations for long-standing obstructive jaundice and it has been suggested that renal damage is produced by bacterial endotoxins liberated from Gram-negative micro-organisms in the bile.

Histology

Histology is the microscopic study of tissues. Histological preparations are often of crucial importance in surgical diagnosis and treatment.

To prepare tissue for microscopic study, it is necessary to harden the material by fixation (p. 80) or freezing; to cut sections sufficiently thin for light to be transmitted easily through them; and to provide optical contrast by colouring the thin sections with dyes (stains). Fixation has the added importance of preserving tissue by preventing autolysis and putrefaction. Stains allow the selective distinction between a very wide variety of cell and tissue components.

Blocks of tissue, often about 1.5 × 1.5 × 0.4 cm in size, are cut carefully from the specimen; compression by forceps and scissors distorts the tissue and must be avoided. The blocks are placed in the rectangular plastic capsules of a processing system such as the Tissue Tek. The capsules are carefully labelled in pencil and transferred to an automatic processing machine, e.g. the Histokine, which passes the blocks through a sequence of ethanol of increasing concentrations, to remove water. After dehydration, ethanol is replaced with xylol. The next move is into molten paraffin wax. The paraffin wax should have a melting point high enough to remain solid on the warmest days. The plastic capsule with its block is brought out of the Histokine paraffin bath onto a warm plate. The tissue is carefully repositioned, the capsule filled with paraffin, cooled and opened. The rectangular block of paraffin wax with its contained tissue is now prepared for sectioning.

Sections, usually 5–7 μm thick, are cut with microtomes. **Microtomes** are very strong, heavy metal machines in which an embedded tissue is moved across the blade of a steel alloy or glass knife: the predominant movement may be rotary or rocking but, for special purposes such as the cutting of very hard tissues, horizontal sledge microtomes with tungsten steel knives are used.

Each section is fixed to a glass slide and the paraffin wax removed with xylol. However, the cells and nuclei of the wet section can only be visualized by special techniques such as phase-contrast microscopy. It is therefore essential to expose the section to one or more stains.

In modern diagnosis, increasing use is being made of 0.5–1.0 μm thin sections made from tissue embedded in high-density polymers. Fine cellular detail can be resolved and the precision of diagnosis enhanced. The hardened materials are cut by costly, specialized microtomes.

Histological stains

Stains are dyes and chemicals used to colour cells, tissues and micro-organisms to make them visible. Stains create optical contrast. In routine surgical diagnosis, it is convenient to apply one dye, haematoxylin, to colour the nucleus and a second, eosin, to colour the cytoplasm. Primary stains can be combined with counterstains or, as in the trichrome methods, a series of dyes can be employed allowing a considerable number of different tissue structures to be identified with reasonable confidence.

Stains are often used to give information about individual tissue components. In scars, scirrhous carcinoma, and tuberculosis for example, the presence of collagen is demonstrable by the van Gieson or picro-Sirius red stains. Elastic material, in breast carcinoma or aneurysm, is shown by methods such as Weigert's resorcinol–fuchsine. Basement membranes are displayed by silver stains, amyloid by examining Congo red-stained sections with polarized light, and mucins and glycogen by mucicarmine or the periodic acid-Schiff (PAS) methods. Fat is sought in tissues where fat embolism or fatty change are suspected and is demonstrated when fresh or formalin-fixed tissue is cut in the frozen state and stained with Sudan III without dehydration in fat solvents.

Histochemical techniques   These permit elements such as iron and copper to be identified. In enzyme histochemistry, the fresh tissue is exposed to a substrate which yields a characteristic colour at the sites of activity of enzymes such as prostatic acid phosphatase.

Immunocytochemical methods   These techniques are widely employed and allow the immunoglobulins, complement, fibrin, and innumerable other antigens, including tumour markers and hormones, to be demonstrated at their sites of formation or binding. The immunoperoxidase technique for demonstrating cell antigens is now preferred because stored formalin-fixed, paraffin-embedded tissues can be used effectively: in the alternative immunofluorescent dye techniques, fresh frozen tissue is usually required and the sections are cut in a cryostat. It is impracticable to re-examine blocks from the file. A further method of rapidly growing importance is the use of antibodies labelled with minute particles of gold, the immunogold technique: the method is applicable to light-microscopy or to EM.

Hormones

A hormone is a substance formed by an endocrine cell or gland in one part of the body and transmitted by a portal or systemic circulation, to which the secreting cells are intimately related, to another site where it exerts a characteristic effect. Many hormones, such as prolactin and TSH are glycoproteins; some, such as corticotrophin and parathormone, are polypeptides; others, such as the adrenal corticosteroids and the sex hormones, are steroids; while a few, such as the adrenal medullary catecholamines, are phenols.

Hormones may be synthesized and secreted by ectopic endocrine tissue and by neoplasms of endocrine organs. Occasionally, in the **Multiple Endocrine Neoplasia (MEN) I and II syndromes,** several adenomas secrete an excess of a number of different hormones simultaneously. In MEN I, there are neoplasms and/or hyperplasia of the parathyroid, pituitary, adrenal cortex and pancreas. Gastric hypersecretion and peptic ulceration are found. In MEN II, adrenal medullary phaeochromocytomas occur, with medullary carcinoma of the thyroid, and parathyroid adenoma or hyperplasia, but there is neither pancreatic islet-cell neoplasia nor peptic ulcer.

Hormones are occasionally secreted **inappropriately** (p. 84) and paradoxically by cells of neoplasms arising from non-endocrine tissues. The cells of an oat-cell carcinoma of the bronchus, for example, often secrete corticotrophin and may cause Cushing's syndrome.

Hospital infection

The frequency and mortality of bacterial infections contracted in hospital is much greater than in the general population. Hospitalized patients are often seriously ill, their defence mechanisms prejudiced. Infections are a major cause of morbidity in patients undergoing operation; they may occur in the wound, in the abdominal and thoracic cavities and their organs, in bones and in the brain. The bacteria that cause these infections are often of low virulence in the general population in whom they may be carried unnoticed. Due to the depressed immunity of the aged and ill in hospital, these organisms become highly pathogenic. One example is *Strep. millerei*; another is *Pseudomonas aeruginosa*. When bacteria behave in this way, the consequence is an **opportunistic infection.**

The source of infection may be the patient himself as in gas gangrene of an above-knee amputation stump; it is then termed **self (auto)-infection.**

Cross-infection describes infection from a source other than the patient. The origin may be another patient, contaminated equipment or instruments or a member of staff who may be an asymptomatic carrier. Organisms carried in this way often develop resistance to the commonly used

antibiotics. *Pseudomonas aeruginosa* and *Staphylococcus aureus* are common examples.
    See Bacteriophage (p. 26)
        Wound Infection (p. 203)

Hydronephrosis

Hydronephrosis is dilatation of the renal pelvis and calyces; it is produced by obstruction to the flow of urine and, according to the site of obstruction, there may also be hydroureter.

Congenital obstruction is usually due to valve-like folds of mucosa at the pelviureteric or the vesicourethral junctions, in the ureter or in the urethra. Acquired obstruction may be due to urethral strictures, to prostatic hypertrophy, or to the presence of calculi in the bladder, ureters or pelvis, or to surgical injury. If the obstruction is in the bladder, prostate or urethra, hydronephrosis is likely to be bilateral. In unilateral disease, the contralateral kidney undergoes compensatory hyperplasia.

Obstruction to the outflow of urine may be partial or complete. The degree of dilatation after partial obstruction is greater than when obstruction is complete. In both instances, the affected kidney atrophies. Renal tubules are first affected but, ultimately, glomeruli become collagenous. Infection is common.

Hyperplasia

Hyperplasia is an increase in the number of cells in an organ or tissue.
    See Aplasia (p. 14)
        Hypoplasia (p. 106).

Hypersensitivity

Hypersensitivity is a condition in which undesirable tissue damage follows the development of a state of humoral or cell-mediated immunity. Hypersensitivity is particularly likely when large amounts of foreign antigen persist as antibody formation is occurring. Individuals sensitized by first exposure to foreign antigen develop a beneficial primary immune state. Later exposure to the same antigen boosts this immunity. Hypersensitivity represents an exaggeration or perversion of this secondary reaction.

There are four types of hypersensitivity. Types I, II and III hypersensitivity are 'immediate' and are mediated by reactions between antigen and humoral antibody. Type IV hypersensitivity is 'delayed' and is mediated by T-lymphocyte surface receptors.

Type I hypersensitivity

Anaphylaxis (p. 8)   This is the opposite to prophylaxis (p. 109) which is a protective, beneficial state. The responses of type I hypersensitivity may be generalized or localized depending on how antigen reaches the sensitized tissues.

Some individuals exposed to certain foreign antigens are prone to form class IgE antibodies. The Fc, non-antigen-binding parts of IgE molecules have an affinity for the surface of mast cells (p. 139) and basophil leucocytes: these antibodies have been called **reagins**. When there is further contact with the original sensitizing antigen, antigen molecules link the free, Fab parts of the IgE molecules, causing the mast cells or the basophil leucocytes to release the contents of their granules into the nearby tissues or circulation, respectively. The mechanism of degranulation is the production of cyclic adenosine monophosphate (cAMP) and cyclic guanidine monophosphate (cGMP). These agents alter the organelle membranes and lead to the escape of the contents of the granules. Histamine, heparin, the leukotrienes, a platelet activating factor and an eosinophil chemotactic factor are among the substances released.

Generalized anaphylaxis in man is rare: the injection of antitetanus serum (ATS), insect or arthropod stings, or the systemic administration of penicillin may produce this life-threatening result.

Local anaphylactic reactions in man are commonplace: they include hay fever, extrinsic asthma and urticarial responses to foods. The old term atopic* allergy† is still used.

Type II hypersensitivity – cytotoxic/cytolytic

Cytotoxic and cytolytic hypersensitivity is directed against cells by antibody molecules bound to cell surfaces. One result is to facilitate phagocytosis. Contact with macrophages is promoted. This action is brought about (a) by opsonic adherence by Fc receptors, or (b) by immune adherence caused by the binding of the C3 component of complement. The complement system can directly injure the plasma membrane of the cell. A red blood cell can be lysed by a single site binding C3, but to cause lysis, the involvement of several C3 binding sites is usually needed. IgM is particularly effective because of its 5 pairs of binding sites.

Cytotoxic hypersensitivity is exemplified by the haemolytic reactions accompanying the transfusion of incompatible blood (p. 37), by many autoimmune reactions (p. 20) and by some drug reactions.

Cells coated with small numbers of IgG molecules can also be killed by non-sensitized phagocytic or even non-phagocytic cells bound to their target cell by the Fc receptor part of the IgG. Polymorphs, blood moncytes and the small K (killer) cells can act in this way. The process is called **antibody-dependent, cell-mediated cytotoxicity** and may be important in killing virus-infected cells. Eosinophils act correspondingly to destroy the larvae of the helminth Schistosoma (p. 202).

Type III hypersensitivity – immune-complex-mediated

Free, soluble antigen and antibody, present in the circulation in appropriate (optimal) proportions, can combine to form **immune complexes** the presence of which can be shown by laboratory tests. Immune complexes can be found

---

*Atopy** means that **familial**, genetic development of hypersensitivity to the antigens causing allergy.

†**Allergy** originally meant 'altered' reactivity; it is now synonymous with hypersensitivity.

locally in tissue sections by the application of suitably-labelled anti-immunoglobulin and anti-complement antibodies. Complexes are detected in the circulation by precipitating them with polyethylene glycol or by identifying the extent to which they bind to the walls of complement-coated plastic tubes.

When there is excess antibody, the complexes are large, insoluble and tend to be phagocytosed by cells of the reticuloendothelial system. When there is excess antigen, the complexes are smaller and soluble. Soluble immune complexes lodge in or pass through blood vessel walls, fix complement, and initiate inflammatory, tissue-damaging reactions. Polymorphs are attracted by chemotaxis. In turn, these cells release enzymes such as elastase and neutral collagenase. Platelets aggregate and thrombus formation is encouraged.

Systemic immune complex disease   This was first recognized when **serum sickness** followed early attempts at prophylactic, passive immunization against tetanus and diphtheria. Antitoxins were prepared in horses. Since the immunoglobulins could not be concentrated, it was necessary to administer as much as 150 ml of horse serum to provide prophylaxis. The huge quantities of foreign horse proteins elicited antibody formation in the patient. Within 10–14 days, the large amount of persisting, soluble horse protein antigen formed soluble circulating complexes with the modest but increasing numbers of anti-horse antibody protein molecules. Lodging in the small terminal blood vessels of the joints, kidney, heart and skin, these complexes caused a potentially fatal syndrome (serum sickness) comprising arthritis, glomerulonephritis, oedema, cutaneous vasculitis and carditis.

Local immune complex disease   This, the **Arthus reaction**, is an inflammatory response produced by injecting antigen locally into the dermis of individuals with high levels of circulating antibody. Antigen forms a local, insoluble precipitate with antibody within venules; complement is bound, and C3a and C5a together release histamine and provoke the chemotaxis of polymorphs. Comparable responses occur in the lungs of sensitized persons on exposure to actinomycetes (in hay mould), and in patients in whom antibiotics or chemotherapeutic agents kill micro-organisms, thereby releasing antigens (as in lepromatous leprosy and syphilis). Reactions of this kind typify autoimmune disease (p. 20) such as systemic lupus erythematosus. In rheumatoid arthritis, an analogous reaction occurs when immune complexes form in synovial tissues. Immune complex vascular disease with hepatitis B as antigen can be found in 50 per cent of cases of polyarteritis nodosa.

Many immune complex diseases are acute. However, if antigen persists, for example, because of indolent infection or autoimmune response, immune complex deposition may be recurrent and the resulting disease long-lasting.

Type IV hypersensitivity – cell mediated
Type IV hypersensitivity is exemplified by the Mantoux reaction (p. 139).

The state of cell-mediated hypersensitivity can be transferred from one animal to another by T lymphocytes or by a lymphocyte transfer factor extracted from them, but not by the tranfer of antibody. The macrophage reactions of cell-mediated hypersensitivity are brought about by the **lymphokines**, polypeptides produced by sensitized T cells. One lymphokine impedes the movement of macrophages and is called 'migration inhibition factor' (MIF); another is a chemotactic factor and a third is a macrophage activating factor. The macrophages in cell-mediated hypersensitivity are activated therefore by the specific behaviour of the antigen that has sensitized the T lymphocytes; the properties of the resultant 'activated macrophages' are exerted non-specifically. Advantage has been taken of this behaviour in the attempted treatment of some cancers by BCG vaccination (p. 21).

Cell-mediated, delayed hypersensitivity is of crucial importance in determining the cell injuries and tissue lesions of infection by some bacteria e.g. *Mycobacterium tuberculosis* (p. 190), by fungi, and by viruses, e.g. measles virus. Type IV hypersensitivity is responsible for many examples of transplant rejection (p. 188) and for skin reactions to important, small molecules such as neomycin, paraphenylenediamine (in hair dyes), and nickel and chromates which bind to protein and act like haptens.

Hypersplenism

The term hypersplenism implies over-activity of the spleen with trapping and destruction of all blood cells, producing pancytopenia. There is usually splenomegaly but the degree of hypersplenism is not related to the size of the spleen.

Splenomegaly may occur during acute or chronic infections or may be due to replacement of splenic tissue by neoplastic or storage diseases (e.g. Gaucher's disease). The spleen is also enlarged in patients with haemolytic anaemia in which it is an organ of destruction of the red blood cells, and in other anaemias when it reverts to its fetal role as an organ of red cell production. In **Banti's syndrome**, splenomegaly and hypersplenism are secondary to portal hypertension due to cirrhosis or portal vein thrombosis. In **Felty's syndrome**, there is hepatomegaly, splenomegaly and hypersplenism, producing anaemia and leucopenia in patients suffering from rheumatoid arthritis.

Hypertension

Hypertension is the persistence of raised blood pressure within the systemic, pulmonary or portal circulations. Pressures may be recorded directly in the arterial, capillary or venous parts of a circulation; indirect measurements, by manual or electronic devices, may be of the systolic, diastolic, or mean blood pressures.

In the case of systemic arterial hypertension, a patients' blood pressure is best measured under basal, resting conditions. The recognition of systemic hypertension is only certain by comparing a series of these basal measurements with those from a control population of the same race, sex and age. An individual can be said to be hypertensive when blood pressure exceeds two standard deviations above this norm.

Hypertrophy

Hypertrophy is an increase in the size of the individual cells of an organ or tissue, often resulting from increased work demand, or from an endocrine stimulus, and leading to an overall increase in size of the part relative to that of other normal organs and tissue.

See Atrophy (p. 19)

Hypervolaemia

Hypervolaemia is a significantly increased circulating blood volume.

An abnormally high total blood volume may be due to an increase in the red blood cell volume (polycythaemia: p. 157) or to an increase in the plasma volume. Polycythaemia may be a primary disorder (polycythaemia vera) but myeloproliferation is often induced by chronic hypoxia in cardiac or respiratory disease, by the haemoglobinopathies, and by renal disease in which there is increased production of erythropoietin.

An increase in plasma volume may be produced by an excess of sodium in the plasma as a consequence of increased secretion of aldosterone (hyperaldosteronism: p. 5). This increased secretion may be primary (Conn's syndrome), due to adrenal cortical hyperplasia or neoplasia. More commonly hyperaldosteronism is secondary to congestive cardiac failure or cirrhosis; it appears to be an inappropriate physiological response. The cause is unknown. Hyperaldosteronism is a component of Cushing's syndrome (p. 66).

Hypovolaemia

Hypovolaemia is an abnormal reduction in blood volume.

A low total blood volume can follow haemorrhage or the loss of plasma or total body water. The kidneys, and to a lesser extent the brain and heart, are the organs at risk. Initially the body responds by secreting additional catecholamines. Peripheral vasoconstriction results. A reduction in circulating blood volume then maintains blood pressure. Antidiuretic hormone and aldosterone are secreted to conserve water and sodium. Total blood volume is restored after an initial period of haemodilution.

Ultimately, any residual reduction in red blood cell volume is corrected by haemopoiesis.

Hypoplasia

Hypoplasia is the defective formation or underdevelopment of a tissue, organ or part.

See Aplasia (p. 14).

Hypothermia

Man is warm-blooded and constantly loses heat to the environment.

Hypothermia, a reduction in temperature, is usually harmful but can be used with benefit to protect against cell injury.

Systemic (generalized) hypothermia

Generalized hypothermia is said to exist when the internal body (core) temperature falls below 35 °C: it may be due to excessive heat loss (e.g. exposure) or to decreased heat production (e.g. hypothyroidism). By contrast with normal individuals in whom muscular activity can generate heat, the surgical patient is often immobile and may be unconscious.

The systemic response to cold is influenced by the degree of hypothermia. As the temperature falls to 35 °C, the body attempts to conserve heat by peripheral vascoconstriction and to maintain vital centres at normal temperature by increased cardiac output. Below 32 °C, metabolic activity is depressed and cardiac output is reduced. Below 24 °C all thermoregulation is lost and the body loses heat uncontrollably to the environment. Patients with hypothermia are often old, malnourished, and have core temperatures below 32 °C. Newborn infants are also particularly at risk. Death is due to ventricular fibrillation which may occur at 30 °C.

Generalized hypothermia was used in patients undergoing cardiac surgery to reduce tissue metabolism and the requirement for oxygen. With more efficient extracorporeal systems, this use of hypothermia is less common.

Local hypothermia

The adverse local effects of cold vary in severity in proportion to the rate and degree of heat loss and according to the nature and mass of the exposed tissue. The skin and subcutaneous tissues of the periphery of the limbs are the most vulnerable but the ears and nose are also susceptible to cold injury. Raynaud's phenomenon (p. 164) is one consequence. Very rapid and extreme chilling causes slowing and cessation of cell metabolism; ultimately, there is intracellular ice crystal formation. The clinical effects of cold are, however, dominated by vascular changes.

Brief cooling to a low temperature, or prolonged mild cooling, injure the endothelium of capillaries and result in oedema and superficial vesication. The mildest injury is a **chilblain**, a tender, erythematous swelling with inflammatory changes in subcutaneous fat.

When chilling is both rapid and severe, there is vascular occlusion by plugged masses of red blood cells. There may be no overt evidence of ischaemia until the temperature rises and the circulation is re-established. More serious injuries of this kind occur in mountaineers when vascular occlusion leads to tissue infarction with the subsequent loss of digits. **Frostbite** is the formation of ice in tissues. Subsequent thawing destroys cells by the breakdown of osmoregulation. In **trench (immersion) foot**, prolonged exposure to cold water causes extensive injury. **Gangrene** (p. 85) may complicate cold injury. Occasionally **mummification** (dry gangrene) (p. 85) results.

Local hypothermia may be induced for therapeutic reasons: thus, local anaesthesia can be produced by spraying the skin with ethyl chloride.

Cryosurgery

Cryosurgery is a destructive procedure that can be performed using very cold probes. The probes may be cooled by liquid nitrogen at –196 °C or, more commonly, by decompressing pressurized gaseous nitrous oxide. Using the latter, rapid freezing of tissue to temperatures lower than –20 °C is obtained and this is sufficient to produce intracellular ice crystals. The probes also possess a mechanism for rewarming, the process that destroys the cells. Freezing should be repeated for maximum effect. Capillaries and small vessels in the 'ice ball' are also destroyed. Blood in large arteries may freeze but does not coagulate; upon thawing, a normal circulation is restored as the artery wall is not damaged. Since nerve endings are destroyed, the procedures of cryosurgery are usually painless.

Immobilization

Immobilization is a hazard for all patients. The **systemic effects** include disturbances of fluid balance, nutrition and intestinal function so that dehydration, weight loss and constipation follow. Prolonged immobilization may lead to osteoporosis, and loss of skeletal calcium can result in the formation of renal calculi. There is tendency to deep venous thrombosis, and pulmonary embolism is a common result. Bronchopneumonia may develop. Gravitational (pressure) ulcers are probable.

The **local effects** include local osteoporosis, formation of fibrous adhesions, ankylosis of limb joints, localized oedema, epidermal atrophy, and muscle wasting.

Immune response

The immune response gives rapid, specific and beneficial protection against pathogenic micro-organisms and other antigens by the formation of antibody, **humoral immunity**, and by the provision of sensitized lymphocytes, **cellular immunity**. However, immune responses can be damaging to the tissues of sensitized individuals who are then said to display **hypersensitivity** (p. 102). Occasionally, tolerance fails or the immune mechanism ceases to distinguish between the constituents of the individual (the 'self') and those of foreign antigens: the essentially protective reactions are perverted to create a paradoxical **autoimmunity** and even autoimmune disease (p. 20).

Humoral immunity
Humoral immunity follows the synthesis and secretion of antibodies by plasma cells. These immunoglobulins (p. 111) circulate in the blood stream, reaching the extracellular tissue spaces but not the cerebrospinal fluid.

Antibacterial immunity   Humoral immunity protects against many bacteria including *Str. pneumoniae* and *Neisseria meningitidis*, and against bacterial exotoxins such as those of the clostridia (p. 56). However, humoral immunity is relatively ineffective in responding to organisms such as the mycobacteria which live within macrophages (p. 137).

Protection is provided by three main mechanisms:

1. By the action of C8 and C9 on the bacterial cell wall. This sequence is important for the destruction of Gram-negative bacteria. Antibody binds to

the bacterial wall; complement is fixed; and the consequent damage allows lysozyme to destroy the wall and thus the micro-organism.

2. By opsonization (p. 151). Gram-positive bacteria are not susceptible to complement. Antibody binds to antigenic sites on Gram-negative bacterial cell walls, allowing complement to be fixed. Polymorphs and macrophages have receptors that bind to these sites by opsonic adherence, facilitating phagocytosis of the bacteria and consequent bacterial destruction.

3. By the neutralization of bacterial exotoxin. This effect can be secured actively by toxoid (p. 185) given in advance of exposure to infection.

Antiviral immunity   Humoral immunity is ineffective against viruses, all of which are obligate intracellular parasites inaccessible to antibody. Antibody therefore plays little part in recovery from viral infection. However, small amounts of circulating antiviral antibody are able to neutralize virus at sites of entry or bind to virus in the stage of primary viraemia. The active stimulation of antiviral antibody formation to provide protection against viruses such as poliovirus, using orally administered attenuated strains, or the passive administration of preformed anti-measles virus gamma globulin, are examples of effective antivirus prophylaxis attributable to humoral antibody. The presence of antiviral antibody in rising titres can be a useful diagnostic aid in suspected viral disease.

Antibody can also prepare the way for the destruction of injured cells such as those infected with virus, by taking advantage of the properties of K (killer) lymphocytes. These K cells have receptors that bind to the constant (Fc) region of antibody immunoglobulin molecules; they are entirely distinct from sensitized cytotoxic T cells (p. 133). In this way, a target cell bearing specific antibody can be non-specifically destroyed.

Cell-mediated immunity
Cell-mediated immunity is a necessary defence mechanism in dealing with intracellular micro-organisms, particularly viruses, the mycobacteria and some protozoa that are little affected by antibodies. It is a property of T lympocytes (p. 133). The features of cell-mediated immunity are also characteristic of reactions with certain chemical haptens, of transplant (graft) rejection (p. 188) and of the delayed type IV hypersensitivity reaction (p. 104).

The pathological characteristics of T-cell-mediated responses are typified by the response of the sensitized or immunized individual to *Mycobacterium tuberculosis* (p. 190) as seen in the Mantoux (tuberculin) reaction (p. 139).

Immunity

Immunity is the specific state of resistance to the harmful effects of foreign antigens, particularly those causing microbial disease. The resistance may be **general**, including all those heritable, nutritional and metabolic factors that raise the state of resistance, or **local**. Immunity may be **natural**, or it may be **acquired**, actively or passively. It is used in prophylaxis.

Active immunity   Active immunity is conferred, for example, by recovery from infection with micro-organisms such as *Bordetella pertussis* or measles virus.

Passive immunity   This may be conferred on the newborn by the transplacental transfer of maternal IgG but not by the much larger IgM antibody molecules. In later life, passive immunity is given by the parenteral injection of sera containing preformed antibodies such as those in convalescent serum, or of antibody preparations such as purified anti-measles immunoglobulin. In modern surgery, passive immunity is largely confined to prophylactic treatment against serum hepatitis and gas gangrene. Where possible, it is preferred to boost active immunity by the further injection of the appropriate antigen, for example, hepatitis B virus vaccine or tetanus toxoid. A hazard for the passive administration of crude animal serum containing antibody is the development of serum sickness (p. 104) in response to the presence of the foreign animal serum proteins.

Immunodeficiency

Immunodeficiency may be a **primary** congenital or heritable defect, or a **secondary** result of disease, of drugs, infections, irradiation and other causes.

Primary immunodeficiency
Primary immunodeficiency can be classified (1) according to whether B cells, T cells or both are defective or absent, and (2) according to the phase of B- or T-cell development and function that is affected. The classification is explained by Figure 5.

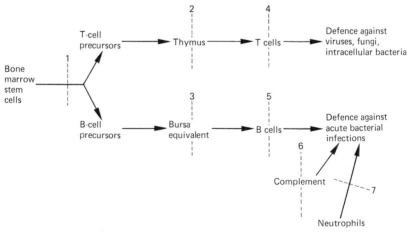

Fig. 5   Causes of immunodeficiency. 1.Combined immunodeficiency; 2.Thymic aplasia (di George); 3.Agammaglobulinaemia (Bruton); 4.Secondary T-cell deficiency (e.g. in Hodgkin's disease); 5.Secondary B-cell deficiency (e.g. in multiple myeloma); 6.Complement deficiency (primary or secondary); 7.Chronic granulomatous disease. (Modified from Taussig, 1984. *Processes in Pathology and Microbiology*. Oxford: Blackwell Scientific Publications.)

There are many categories of more or less severe primary immuno-deficiency disease: they are rare conditions. Examples are:

1. A complete lack of B cells, and thus of antibody synthesis, as encountered in **Bruton-type agammaglobulinaemia**. The affected infants are highly susceptible to bacterial infection but have a normal degree of immunity to viral, mycotic and mycobacterial disease.

2. A complete lack of T cells, and thus of cell-mediated immune responses, as seen in the **Di George syndrome**, in which the thymus does not form. Individuals with this rare syndrome have normal humoral immune responses to pyogenic bacterial infections but display little resistance to viral infections such as measles and chickenpox, and to mycobacterial infection. The local injection of attenuated *Mycobacterium tuberculosis* in BCG vaccination is followed by progressive local and even systemic infection. Smallpox vaccination leads to extensive local skin disease and the possibility of systemic vaccinia.

3. In severe forms of **combined immunodeficiency** both B-cell and T-cell formation is defective and there is a lack both of humoral and of cell-mediated immune responses. Consequently, an extreme defect of resistance to all forms of infection prevails.

Secondary immunodeficiency

Disease of the lymphoreticular tissues may lead to secondary immunodeficiency. Although the cells of myeloma usually secrete large quantities of monoclonal immunoglobulin, there is an overall B-cell deficiency resulting in a defect of humoral immunity. Hodgkin's lymphoma, with a neoplastic proliferation of mononuclear macrophage-type cells, is associated with a deficiency of T cells and lowered resistance to viral, mycobacterial and fungal infections.

Immune suppression (p. 115) and immunodeficiency are associated with an increased frequency of cancers such as leukaemia, lymphoma and malignant melanoma. Sometimes these cancers are caused by oncogenic agents such as EB virus, latent within the B cells of normal adults. Cytotoxic T cells normally regulate the tranformation of EBV-infected cells, and suppression or lack of T-cell activity allows infected B cells to express themselves as neoplasms.

Immunoglobulins

Antibodies are large proteins of the γ-globulin group. They are termed immunoglobulins. There are five classes; all share some features. The molecular characteristics that the immunoglobulins have in common are indicated in Figure 6, which illustrates diagramatically an immunoglobulin monomer.

Immunoglobulin molecules have two functional ends. The first is formed of a pair of antigen-combining sites which can be separated by enzyme digestion into two identical Fab fragments. The second has a less variable

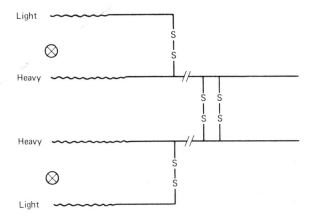

Fig. 6   Antibody (immunoglobulin) molecule.
〜〜 = variable regions
—— = constant regions
// = sites where papain divides Fab and Fc fragments
⊗ = antigen-combining sites
S – S = disulphide bonds.

structure and, because it can easily be crystallized, is termed Fc. The immunoglobulin molecule is based on two longer amino-acid chains each with a molecular weight of about 60 000 and said therefore to be 'heavy'; and two shorter 'light' chains each with a molecular weight of about 22 000. The four chains are arranged in a Eiffel-tower-like structure, the central part or hinge region of which offers considerable flexibility.

In the course of a lifetime, however, an individual's immune system may be expected to interact with a huge number and variety of foreign antigens. The immune system is normally able to distinguish all these antigens from those of the 'self'. It is clear that, within the five classes of immunoglobulin, an enormous number of detailed variations in molecular structure are possible; these variations are confined to the variable (Fab) end of the Ig molecule. The five classes of Ig also have other characteristic and constant structural and biological properties. These are a function of the easily crystallizable, constant (Fc) part of the molecule.

The five classes of Ig in quantitative order are IgG, IgA, IgM, IgD and IgE. The 'heavy' chains are of five different types corresponding to the five classes of Ig: the heavy chains are designated γ, α, μ, δ, and ϵ. In a typical molecule, the 'light' chains are either one of two different types: they may be κ (kappa) or λ (lambda). An entire IgG molecule could therefore be $\gamma_2\kappa_2$, an entire IgA monomer $\alpha_2\kappa_2$. The classes and main biological properties of the immunoglobulins are shown in Tables 6 and 7.

Table 6 Immunoglobulin classes

Immunoglobulin class	IgG	IgA	IgM	IgD	IgE
Molecular weight	150 000	160 000 (or, as dimer, 320 000)	900 000	185 000	200 000
Serum concentration (g/l)	6–16 g/l	0.5–4 g/l	0.4–1.2 g/l	20–50 μg/l	0.1–0.4 μg/l
% total serum Ig	80	13	6	0–1	0.002
Number of basic 4-peptide units	1	1 or 2	5	1	1

Immunological tolerance

The immune mechanism distinguishes the antigens of the 'self' from those which are foreign. The failure to react to 'self' antigens constitutes natural tolerance; but tolerance can be acquired or transmitted. Tolerance can also be lost or 'broken', a change that provides a key to autoimmunity (p. 20).

Some tissues such as the lipoproteins of the central nervous system, the cornea, the lens, and the colloid of thyroid follicles are effective antigens but do not establish contact with the immune mechanism because there is a blood/brain barrier or lack of vascular supply.

Newborn mice can be induced to tolerate skin grafts from foreign donors. The state of tolerance is specific, that is, confined to the antigen used; it persists to adult life. Very young, immunologically immature animals are readily tolerized. After tolerization, they become susceptible to infective agents such as rubella virus that cause malformations, and to tumour viruses.

Adult animals can be tolerized by suppressing or depleting the lymphocyte population when antigen is given or by giving antigen that cannot effectively be processed by macrophages. Protein antigens can tolerize in low or in high doses. Between these low and high zones, intermediate amounts of antigen cause antibody formation.

The clonal selection theory This theory postulates that all lymphocytes able to react with antigens of the 'self' are eliminated early in life after contact with these antigens. The lymphocytes that remain are only capable of reacting with foreign antigens. This explanation offers a basis for transplantation reactions (p. 187), known to be largely mediated by T cells. However, T and B cells respond differently. T cells are more easily tolerized. Thus, in low-zone tolerance only T cells are unresponsive, whereas in high-zone tolerance both T and B cells are affected. It is possible to break the state of low-zone tolerance by activating B cells. Slight changes to antigen may be sufficient to accomplish this effect. Suppressor T cells are bypassed; helper T cells remain to aid the production of antibody production by B cells. The results may include autoimmune thyroiditis and can offer a partial explanation of the cross-reaction of anti-streptococcal antibody with cardiac and synovial cells in rheumatic fever.

Table 7 Biological properties of the immunoglobulins (Igs)

Main Properties	IgG Most abundant of the Igs; combats micro-organisms and toxins extracellularly	IgA Major Ig in seromucous secretions	IgM Good agglutination: secreted early in immune response	IgD On lymphocyte surface	IgE Protects external surfaces. Symptoms of atopic allergy
Complement fixation by:					
(i) Classical pathway	++	−	+++	−	−
(ii) Alternative pathway	−	±	−	−	−
Crosses placenta	+	−	−	−	−
Fixes to homologous mast cells	−	−	−	−	+
Binds to macrophages, polymorphs	+	±	−	−	−

Tolerance can also be the result of a suppression of the immune response. The suppressor T cells that effect this change can be transferred passively to other hosts. T-cell suppressor activity diminishes with age. The increased tendency of autoimmune diseases in the old may be a result of this change.

Immunosuppression

Suppression of the T-cell immune reaction against a graft is required to permit prolonged survival of the transplanted organ or tissue. Among the effective immunosuppressive drugs are:

Corticosteroids.
Analogues of DNA bases which compete in DNA synthesis; 6–mercaptopurine and azathioprine are important examples.
Alkylating agents such as cyclophosphamide.
Antibiotics such as actinomycin which block protein synthesis, and cyclosporin A, a valuable suppressor of T but not B cells. Cyclosporin A may permit virtually permanent tolerance of a graft.
Antilymphocytic serum, purified as antilymphocytic IgG.
It is of interest that several important immunosuppressive drugs were first employed as cytotoxic drugs (p. 13) in the therapy of cancer. A number of other immunosuppressive compounds are carcinogens. The common bond between these drugs is a similarity to bases of the DNA molecule.
A hazard of prolonged immunosuppression is the emergence of an unexpectedly high incidence of neoplasms, particular lymphomas. The mechanism of neoplasia may be a failure of T cells to suppress the multiplication of B cells bearing tumour-promoting agents such as the Epstein–Barr virus.

Implantation

Implantation is the act of setting a piece of tissue from one part of the body into another site. The term is also applied to the insertion of foreign bodies, such as radioactive needles, in the treatment of cancer, and in the implantation of avalon sponges in the treatment of rectal prolapse.
To flourish, tissue implants require particular environments and stimuli (see Transplantation p. 187). Implantation dermoid cysts are usually found on the fingers but may occur at any site at which squamous epithelium is driven beneath the skin by a penetrating wound. Other epithelia undergo similar displacement. Thus, implantation cysts may form in the lower rectum following haemorrhoidectomy or polypectomy, and neoplastic cells may be implanted in wounds or suture lines. Theoretically, the implantation of neoplastic cells might be expected at needle biopsy but in practice this is very rare.

Incision

An incision is an interruption to a body tissue produced by cutting.

Infarct

An infarct is the dead tissue remaining when the oxygen, nutrition or blood supply to a tissue or organ is quickly reduced below a critical level. Infarction is therefore ischaemic necrosis of tissue.

The sensitivity of tissues to ischaemia varies widely (p. 9). A two-minute deprivation of blood flow to the brain is sufficient to cause tissue death, whereas gastrointestinal organs can withstand at least an hour of ischaemia. Isolated articular cartilage may survive days or even weeks.

Infarcts are described as red or white (pale). When afferent vessels are end arteries, as in the case of the spleen or kidney, the infarcted tissue remains pale. In the lung, blood continues to flow through the bronchial arteries and the ischaemic tissue becomes 'stuffed' (infarcted) red or purple.

Ischaemia (p. 125).

Infection

Infection is the invasion of the body by pathogenic or potentially pathogenic micro-organisms, and their subsequent multiplication in the body.

Infections may be **direct** for example, after contact, or **indirect** when they are transmitted by an intermediate agent such as food, fomites or by insect or arthropod vectors.

Inflammation

Inflammation is the response of living, vascularized tissues to injury caused by chemical, physical, immunological or infective agents. Inflammation is usually beneficial and protective. The process of inflammation may, nevertheless, exert damaging effects upon the tissues in which it develops. Inflammation may be acute or chronic (pp. 101, 203).

Acute inflammation

There are five main clinical (cardinal) signs: redness, swelling, pain, heat and loss of function. These signs reflect a complex series of molecular and microscopic changes centred upon the arterioles, capillaries and venules. The changes of inflammation cannot develop in ischaemic tissue; the inflammatory responses at sites of infarction, for example, are confined to the surrounding zones where vascular perfusion continues. The phenomena of acute inflammation depend upon the formation or activation of a series of chemical mediators. There are important secondary alterations in the behaviour of the circulating leucocytes, in tissue mononuclear phagocytes and in mast cells.

Vascular changes   Three of the five clinical signs of inflammation can be reproduced by drawing a pin-head firmly across the surface of the skin. The flexor surface of the forearm is a convenient site to observe. A **triple response** results. This reaction, described by Lewis* (1922), comprises an immediate

---

*Thomas Lewis (1881–1945) first suggested that a histamine-like substance ('H-substance') was responsible for the skin changes in anaphylaxis.

dull red **flush** in and around the site of injury; a wider zone of reddening, the **flare**; and a more slowly developing **weal** along the track of the pin-head. The flush is due to the dilatation of venules; it results from the rapid activation locally of chemical mediators, particularly histamine. The flare is caused by arteriolar dilatation which results from an axon reflex and which leads to a rise in local temperature. The weal is oedema.

Chemical mediators   There are three groups of mediators corresponding to three phases of acute inflammation: early (histamine); intermediate (kinins); and prolonged (prostaglandins and leukotrienes). **Histamine**, Lewis's 'H' substance, is responsible for the immediate, transient changes in vessel permeability. It is manufactured in and released from mast cells near blood vessels. The **kinins**, polypeptides made by the action of enzymes (kallikreins) on plasma precursors (kininogens), also increase vascular permeability and aid leucocyte margination and migration. Kallikreins are activated by Hageman factor (factor XII, p. 58). In the delayed, later phase of acute inflammation **prostaglandins** are quickly manufactured from arachidonic acid as they are needed: the phospholipase of neutrophil polymorph lysosomes is one source. However, arachidonic acid is also the precursor of the **leukotrienes**, formed by neutrophil polymorphs and by mast cells. Leukotrienes are potent chemotactic agents for neutrophil polymorphs; they increase endothelial 'stickiness'.

Oedema   One effect of histamine is to cause the endothelial cells of the venules to separate. Fluid rich in protein escapes from the plasma through these gaps. Among the proteins are fibrinogen and the immunoglobulins. Fibrinogen polymerizes to form fibrin, the accumulation of which is commonplace at inflammatory foci. Fluid containing only smaller molecules crosses the endothelial cells by pinocytosis. The volume of fluid leaving the venules in inflammation exceeds that returning by osmosis. Oedema (p. 149) results: the fluid is an exudate (p. 150).

The flow of lymph from the inflamed part increases as extravascular tissue fluid accumulates. The inflammatory agents and the products of tissue injury are conveyed to local and thence to regional lymph nodes. Lymphadenopathy develops.

Leucocyte behaviour   At inflammatory foci, axial blood flow in post-capillary venules slows. The central column of red cells and leucocytes is dispersed. Within a few minutes, the most numerous white cells, the polymorphs, adhere to the 'sticky' endothelium. Inserting cytoplasmic processes between the endothelial cells, the polymorphs move actively to the extravascular tissue spaces; they are followed slowly by mononuclear macrophages, passively by red blood cells. Chemotactic influences draw the leucocytes towards the inflammatory focus. Reactions between the defensive white cells and the damaging agent initiate processes such as antibody production and phagocytosis.

Chronic inflammation
Among the numerous causes of chronic inflammation are (1) persistent

infection by organisms resistant or inaccessible to antibiotics, (2) the formation of granulation and fibrous tissue in the wall of an abscess, (3) the presence of foreign bodies ranging from non-absorbable suture material to particles of dirt and bullet fragments, (4) the local extension of malignant neoplasms, and (5) recurrent mechanical abrasion or ulceration. Chronic inflammation is characteristic of the granulomatous infections, tuberculosis, syphilis and leprosy. The mycobacteria survive within macrophages. Foci of ischaemic necrosis defeat attempts at resolution and repair; caseous, necrotic tissue debris persists for long periods. Where particles of metal, dirt or crystals are present, macrophages unite in a common purpose, fusing to form **foreign-body giant cells** (p. 88).

Fibrosis is the ultimate fate of chronic inflammatory foci. However, pus, foreign bodies, persistent infection or irritation also prevent healing. One result is the escape of pus to epithelial surfaces through sinuses or fistulae. The persistence of chronic infection in, for example, osteomyelitis or tuberculosis is the basis for **amyloidosis** (p. 6).

Inhalation

The inhalation of nasopharyngeal secretions or vomit is likely in heavily sedated patients, after operation and in those who remain supine and unconscious. According to the nature of the inhaled material, there may occur bronchial irritation, excess mucus secretion and subsequently delayed bronchopneumonia; the collapse of one or more pulmonary lobes; or sudden, early death due to anoxia or vagal cardiac stimulation.

In fires and explosions, noxious and hot gases are often inhaled, damaging the trachea and bronchi directly. The onset of pulmonary oedema may then lead to death from respiratory failure.

Inheritance

Inheritance is the derivation of characters from parents and ancestors and their expression in the progeny. It is a function of the genetic information exchanged when two gametes unite at fertilization. The zygote obtains half its genetic information from each parent; the information is coded by the base triplets (codons) of DNA (p. 70).

Abnormal inheritance
Abnormal inheritance is a result of alterations in the genetic code or in chromosome structure, caused, for example, by ionizing radiation, virus infection, chemical agents or hormones acting on the gonads or on germ cells prior to fertilization. There may be alterations (1) in sex-linked; (2) in autosomal inheritance; or (3) in characteristics transmitted by polygenic multifactorial inheritance. Single-gene defects are inherited according to Mendelian principles (p. 87).

Abnormal sex-linked inheritance   The pattern of abnormal inheritance is determined by whether the single mutant gene is located upon the X or Y

chromosome and whether the trait is recessive or dominant. The only known abnormal Y-linked fault is 'hairy ear' trait, which is transmitted from male to male. In abnormal X-linked recessive inheritance, e.g. haemophilia or colour blindness, transmission from male to male cannot occur. Females suffer very rarely. The mutant gene is carried by females; half of the sons suffer from the disease and half the daughters are carriers.

Abnormal sex-linked inheritance may be dominant or recessive. In abnormal X-linked dominant inheritance, e.g. vitamin D resistant rickets, all the daughters of affected men have the disease but none of the sons. All children of affected homozygous females and 50 per cent of the children of heterozygous affected females suffer from the disease.

Abnormal autosomal inheritance   There is a similar frequency of disease phenotype in males and females.

In abnormal autosomal dominant inheritance, e.g. in hereditary spherocytosis (p. 91) or in familial polyposis (p. 158), 50 per cent of the children of an affected individual suffer from the disease but its severity varies due to differing degrees of penetration. Thus, in some the disease cannot be detected clinically and the gene is said to be non-penetrant. However, the genetic defect is still present and may be transmitted to the next generation in whom a severe form of the disease may occur.

In abnormal autosomal recessive inheritance, e.g. cystic fibrosis or in phenylketonuria, the parents are often consanguineous. The condition occurs in 25 per cent of the offspring.

Abnormal polygenic inheritance   In many disorders there is no evidence of Mendelian inheritance, yet a familial predisposition or a relatively high frequency among identical twins suggests that genetic factors are operative. Under these circumstances it appears that the disorder is inherited on a polygenic basis, the actions of several genes combining. Carcinoma of the breast and rheumatoid arthritis are examples. Alternatively, there may be non-penetrance, or the condition may arise as a consequence of an environmental influence acting upon a genetically determined abnormality.

Interferons

Nature and origins

The interferons (IFN) are a family of small proteins formed by cells infected with virus. Interferons non-specifically interfere with and inhibit virus multiplication in other cells. Interferons are also made by activated T lymphocytes. The different sources and varied structure of the interferons has led to their classification as groups IFN-α, IFN-β and IFN-γ.

Once virus has entered a cell, double-stranded RNA activates an interferon gene and synthesis follows. Interferon is best formed in cells infected by viruses that do not quickly cause cell death. IFN-γ is produced like a lymphokine after sensitized T cells have bound specific antigen.

Actions

Interferons (Table 8) are potent therapeutic agents: a dozen molecules only can give a cell resistance to virus infection. They are under trial for early, active protection against diseases such as influenza, the common cold, herpes-virus infections and hepatitis B, and offer hope as cytotoxic agents in the therapy of malignant disease of breast, bone marrow and skin. However, these properties are complicated by the hazards of bone-marrow cell depression.

Table 8   Properties of the interferons

Antiviral agents
Inhibit cell division
Increase antigen expression
Boost action of 'natural killer' (NK) cells
Regulate immune functions of cells
Amplify ability of some neoplastic cells to activate complement via alternative pathway.

Intracranial space-occupying lesions

The brain is surrounded by incompressible cerebrospinal fluid and contained within the rigid cranium. In addition to local injury, any lesion occupying space within the cranium may exert widespread mechanical effects irrespective of the nature of the lesion or of the anatomical site. Infratentorial lesions produce raised intracranial pressure more rapidly than do supratentorial lesions.

The **anatomical changes** attributable to raised intracranial pressure include flattening of the gyri, subfalcine herniation of the cingulate gyrus, uncal herniation and coning of the medulla. The transmission of pressure to the pons may produce bilateral pontine haemorrhage. There may be coincident internal non-communicating hydrocephalus, and if the rise in intracranial pressure is sustained and the patient survives, the inner table of the skull may display atrophy due to pressure from cerebral gyri.

The **clinical features** of generalized raised intracranial pressure include vomiting, headache and epileptiform convulsions. Compression of medullary centres may prejudice respiration, cardiac output, blood pressure and thermoregulation. Coma follows. Medullary coning may follow injudicious lumbar puncture.

The space-occupying lesions may be benign or malignant neoplasms, subdural venous and extradural arterial haemorrhage, intracerebral haemorrhage, abscess and arterial aneurysm.

Intracytoplasmic filaments

All cells contain fine, delicate cytoplasmic filaments which can be viewed by EM and identified by monoclonal antibodies. Occasionally, as in muscle, the number of filaments is very large. The filaments in muscle are thick (myosin) and thin (actin and tropomyosin B). Other filaments, intermediate in diameter between actin and myosin are (1) prekeratin tonofilaments, (2) vimentin, (3) desmin, (4) neurofilaments and (5) glial fibrillary protein.

Intracytoplasmic filaments help to identify cancer cells, degenerative diseases and metabolic disorders. Actin and myosin filaments are found in striated muscle neoplasms, tonofilaments in squamous carcinoma. Increased numbers of neurofilaments are present in ageing neurones and in nerve cells in Alzheimer's and other neurological diseases, glial fibrillary protein in glial scars and some astrocytomas. Desmin filaments are prominent in heart muscle in some cardiomyopathies and after treatment with anabolic steroids. Vimentin filaments predominate in ageing and degenerate chondrocytes, in synovial cells in rheumatoid arthritis, and in synovial sarcoma.

Invasion

Invasion is the aggressive intrusion of living cells or micro-organisms into tissue. The word is used in several ways. Degradative enzyme activity is always the responsible mechanism.

Pathogenic bacteria such as *Streptococcus pyogenes* penetrate tissue planes quickly, causing disorders such as cellulitis. Hyaluronidase is the agent that facilitates this invasion. Malignant neoplasms invade directly, by lymphatic or blood vascular permeation, or by metastasis. Collagenase, hyaluronidase and lysosomal proteases degrade connective-tissue molecules and assist the invasive process. In inflammatory connective-tissue disease such as rheumatoid arthritis, activated macrophages release neutral collagenase, elastase and cathepsins. Cartilage matrix is degraded. Macrophages, lymphocytes, capillary endothelial cells and young fibroblasts extend into the cartilage, replacing it by granulation tissue.

Irradiation

Tissues may be exposed accidentally or deliberately to electromagnetic or particulate (Table 9) radiation. Exposure to non-ionizing, ultraviolet irradiation in the form of sunlight is a universal experience. Exposure to ionizing x- and γ-radiations is an occupational hazard among radiographers, workers in nuclear reactors and space travellers.

Electromagnetic radiation

X-rays (röntgen* rays) are produced deliberately from cathode ray tubes. They are also emitted incidentally from high-energy sources such as electron microscopes and, in nature, from stellar sources.

The wavelength of x-rays varies considerably. The short wave ('harder') x-rays used in radiotherapy penetrate tissues to a much greater extent than do the longer wave ('softer') x-rays used in radiodiagnosis. The damaging effects of diagnostic x-rays are diminished by combining low doses with image amplification. In the laboratory, x-rays can be used to identify exactly very small amounts of elements such as iron, calcium or lead in tissue sections.

---

*Wilhelm Konrad von Röntgen (1845–1923) discovered x-rays by chance in 1895. They were later re-named Röntgen rays.

Table 9   Radiation characteristics

ACOUSTIC RADIATION
  Wavelength in soft tissue = approximately 1 mm

ELECTROMAGNETIC RADIATION
  energy increases as wavelength decreases

Form	Mean wavelength
Radio	1500– 10 m
Infra red	700–600 nm
Visible	600–400 nm
Ultraviolet	400–250 nm
X-ray	1.0 nm
γ-ray	0.1 nm
Cosmic	very short

PARTICULATE RADIATION

Particle	Penetration	Mass	Charge
Electron (β-particle)	0.5 cm/MEV	1/100 (H nucleus)	–
Positron		1/100 (H nucleus)	+
Proton	Short	1	+
Neutron		1	nil
α-particle	Short	4 (Helium nucleus)	+ +
Heavy nuclei			–

Gamma-rays are of very short wavelength and high energy. They are emitted spontaneously by many natural and by some artificial radioactive isotopes. Radium, the first known source, was described by the Curies in 1898. Stellar γ-rays reach the earth as cosmic rays and therefore comprise part of the background radiation to which all living creatures are continuously exposed.

Ultrasonic and laser radiations are described on p. 195 and p. 128 respectively. Other uses for electromagnetic radiation include microwave ovens, TV sets and radar.

Particulate irradiation

Tissues may be exposed to α-particles (nuclei of helium atoms), β-particles (electrons), deuterons, protons and other particles, depending on the source. Many radioactive isotopes used safely in diagnosis are rapidly decaying β-emitters with short half-lives. Phosphorus (^{32}P), yttrium (^{90}Y), and tritium (^{3}H) are examples. Alpha-particle emitters such as thorium (^{232}Th), previously employed in the form of colloidal thorium dioxide (thorotrast) as a contrast medium for angiography, are potent carcinogens.

Isotopes

An isotope is a nuclide (Table 10) of a particular chemical element which has the same atomic number (of protons) but a different mass number (protons + neutrons) from other nuclides of the same element. Thus, an isotope is an element that has the same atomic number but a different atomic weight as another element. Some elements consist of several isotopes and the atomic weight is the mean of their weight.

Table 10   Some definitions of terms used in nuclear physics

A *nuclide* is a species of atomic nucleus as characterized by charge, mass number and quantum state, capable of existing for a measureable lifetime. A *daughter nuclide* originates from a nuclide by radioactive decay.
Nuclear isomers are separate nuclides. However, transient excited nuclear states and unstable intermediates in nuclear reactions are not described in this way.
The *half-life* of a radioactive material is the time during which half the original nuclei disintegrate.
The *specific activity* of a compound is proportional to the number of radioactive atoms present.

When the nuclear composition of an element is unstable, the nuclei may undergo spontaneous disintegration with the emission of α- or β-particles or γ-radiation, and the isotope is said to be radioactive. Some **radioactive isotopes** exist naturally but many others now used in diagnosis are prepared artificially by bombarding a stable element in a reactor or cyclotron.

Biological effects of radiation
The biological effects of any form of radiation (Tables 11 and 12) depend on the frequency of exposure, the intensity (energy) of the radiation, the duration of exposure and the nature of the tissue (Table 13). The tissue effects are cumulative and damaging. They are due to the absorption, by cells and cell nuclei, of energy.

Table 11   Old (CGS) units of ionizing radiation

röntgen **(R)**:   a measure of the radiation source, equivalent to the ionization produced in air by x- or γ-radiation. The name of the unit was adopted in 1928 in honour of W.K. Röntgen. 1 R is the quantity of radiation such that the associated corpuscular emission in 1 cc of air produces 1 electrostatic unit of charge.

rad: a measure of absorption.
1 rad is the deposition of 100 ergs/g material, at the point of interest, by ionizing radiation.

curie **(Ci)**:   a measure of radioactivity, originally related to the activity of radium (^{226} Ra).
1 Ci is 3.7×10^{10} disintegrations/second.

rem is a unit of radiation dose which expresses, on a common scale for all ionizing radiations, the presumed biological damage incurred by exposed persons. It is obtained by applying a correction factor to the absorbed dose in rads.

Table 12   New (SI) units of ionizing radiation

1. gray (Gy):   a gray is the measure of absorbed radiation dose. It is equivalent to 100 rad.

2. becquerel (Bq):   a becquerel is a measure of radioactivity and is equivalent to 2.703×10^{-11} Ci.

3. sievert (SV):   a sievert is a measure of dose equivalence. One Sievert corresponds to 100 rem.

Table 13   Relative radiosensitivity of different cells

High (radiosensitive)	lymphocytes immature blood-cell precursors intestinal epithelium thymocytes spermatogonia oögonia
Intermediate	endothelium basal epithelium hair follicles fibroblasts lens growing cartilage parenchyma of liver, pancreas, kidney, endocrine glands, glandular epithelium, breast, skin
Low (radioresistant)	blood muscle mature connective tissue bone, mature cartilage nerve tissue

The biological effects of both electromagnetic and particulate radiation are in proportion to their energy and their capacity to penetrate tissues. Electromagnetic radiations such as short-wavelength x- and γ-rays have the highest energy, penetrate furthest and produce severe tissue disturbance by the transfer of energy. Large particles such as helium nuclei (α-particles) possess similar properties. Cells are injured and killed. The primary site for lethal cell injury is the nucleus. Mutations are caused in surviving cells. The mutations are usually recessive. Occasionally, there is major chromosomal injury. There is ionization of cell water. Protein is denatured and cell membranes, organelles and enzyme systems are disorganized.

The **short-term effects** of ionizing irradiation are recognized in tissues in which there is rapid cell turnover (Table 13). The nucleus is particularly vulnerable during division. The cells of the gastrointestinal tract, those of the lymphoid tissues and bone marrow, the spermatogonia and ögonia are most readily injured. Externally, the skin may be desquamated.

The **long-term effects** of ionizing radiation include local neoplasia, particularly of the skin (squamous carcinoma) and bone marrow (leukaemia). The frequency of congenital defects in the progeny is increased. Many long-term effects result from occlusion of small blood-vessels.

According to the mass of tissue irradiated and the nature of the exposed tissue, a series of post-irradiation syndromes can be defined (Table 14).

Table 14   Clinical syndromes following whole-body irradiation

Syndrome	Dose needed to cause onset	Signs	Death
bone marrow	275–500 R	marrow aplasia	30 days
intestinal	700–1000 R	anorexia and diarrhoea	7–15 days
central nervous	10 000 R	convulsions	a few hours to days

Ischaemia

Ischaemia is the partial or complete reduction in blood flow to a tissue or organ. Ischaemia is frequently caused by vascular diseases such as atheroma or thrombosis, by arterial obstruction in trauma or surgery, by irradiation – a potent cause of arterial intimal proliferation and thus of radiation nephritis – and by the action of vasoactive drugs such as the catecholamines. All are potent causes of reduced arterial blood flow. Incomplete or slowly developing ischaemia often causes tissue atrophy. Sudden complete ischaemia usually results in infarction (p. 116) or gangrene (p. 85).

The different organs and tissues display wide differences in susceptibility to the injurious effects of ischaemia (Table 15). It is convenient to consider the organs and tissues in three groups, of high, medium, and low susceptibility. The sensitivity of a part to ischaemia is in proportion to the rate of aerobic respiration of the cells of the part. One index of this respiratory activity is the size and number of the mitochondria. Another indication of sensitivity to ischaemia is the number of capillaries per unit mass of tissue: cardiac muscle and brain cells are highly sensitive, skeletal muscle is of modest sensitivity, and hyaline cartilage and cornea, which are avascular, are tolerant of ischaemia.

Table 15 Sensitivity of tissues to ischaemia (See Table 2)

High sensitivity	
Brain	Renal cortex
Spinal cord	Liver
Heart muscle	Adrenal cortex
Pituitary	
Moderate sensitivity	
Bone	Renal glomeruli
Skeletal muscle	Small intestine
Tendon	Stomach
Skin	
Low sensitivity	
Hyaline cartilage	
Cornea	
Intervertebral disc	

The effects of ischaemia on a tissue or part are modified by the existence of an alternative, collateral circulation and by temperature. Thus, the sudden lodging of an embolus in the femoral artery is much less likely to cause infarction than an embolus entering the arcuate artery of a kidney. Equally, tissues cooled during the interruption of arterial blood flow during open heart surgery are much less likely to sustain ischaemic injury than are tissues maintained at normal body temperature.

See Anoxia (p. 9).

Jaundice

Jaundice is a yellow discoloration of the tissues due to an excessive quantity of bilirubin in the body tissues. It is hyperbilirubinaemia.

Jaundice is first apparent when the concentration of bilirubin reaches 100–150 μmol/l. Biochemical jaundice is said to occur when the concentration exceeds the upper normal limit of 20 μmol/l in the blood, but discoloration of the tissues is not apparent. According to the cause the bilirubin may be water-soluble, conjugated bilirubin; insoluble, unconjugated bilirubin (p. 28); or a mixture of both.

Jaundice is subdivided into prehepatic, hepatic and posthepatic categories. Frequently there is overlap, particularly when the jaundice has been present for some time. Thus, in hepatic jaundice due to viral hepatitis, the jaundice is initially due to cellular dysfunction, but eventually tissue swelling produces obstruction to the excretion of bile in the canaliculi. An obstructive factor is added.

Prehepatic jaundice (haemolytic)

There is increased production of bilirubin due to increased destruction of red blood cells. Although there is an excessive quantity of bilirubin in the blood stream, it is unconjugated and cannot pass through the glomerular capillary basement membrane into the urine. An old name for this condition is acholuric jaundice. There is an increased quantity of stercobilinogen in the faeces and of urobilinogen in the urine.

Hepatic jaundice (hepatocellular)

There is liver-cell damage by micro-organisms, chemicals or toxins. Acute viral hepatitis is one cause. The liver cells of all individuals may be damaged directly by chemicals such as ethanol, carbon tetrachloride, methotrexate and many other chemotherapeutic agents (p. 13). Damage may also be induced in some persons who are hypersensitive to substances such as halothane and para-amino salicylic acid (PAS).

Defective conjugation of bilirubin occurs in the Crigler–Najjar syndrome. Gilbert's disease is a familial condition in which there is inadequate concentration of the conjugating enzyme to cope with normal rates of haemolysis.

Posthepatic jaundice (obstructive)

There is obstruction to the excretion of conjugated bilirubin. In the Dubin–Johnson syndrome, there is a hereditary failure of transport of conjugated bilirubin from the microsomes to the biliary canaliculi. Obstruction in the biliary tract may be **intrahepatic**, due for example to neoplasms or in the later stages of hepatitis, or **extrahepatic**, due for example to obstruction of any part of the extrahepatic biliary system by neoplasms, stones or abscesses. The conjugated bilirubin is highly soluble and passes through the glomerular basement membrane. The urine is dark. The bilirubin does not reach the lumen of the intestine. The stools become pale, due to an increase in the quantity of fat; they lack stercobilinogen.

Keloid

A keloid is a hard, smooth, raised erythematous scar. During the first two or three months of healing any scar may hypertrophy, but the majority regress so that within a year the scar is pale and not raised. In some patients the growth of scar tissue is progressive and massive. Ugly hypertrophic lesions result. The deposition and maturation of collagen is essential for the healing of wounds (p. 93). In keloids, excess collagen is apparent microscopically and the fibre bundles become hyalinized. After each excision, keloid is liable to recur. Treatment by ionizing radiation is often attempted.

The cause(s) of keloids are uncertain. Their formation is more common in coloured races, in whom they may be encouraged for cosmetic reasons in females and in the young. They are particularly likely to occur after burns, following wounds about the ear and neck and after tattooing. It has been suggested that they are due to the implantation of keratin and hair into the dermis; they can be produced experimentally by this means.

Ketosis

Oxidation of fatty acids in the body results in an increase in the plasma concentrations and urinary excretion of acetoacetate and β-hydroxybutyrate. Traditionally, the term 'ketone bodies' is used to describe these products; when they are found in abnormal concentration, the term 'ketosis' is used. However, neither substance is a ketone and β-hydroxybutyrate is not a ketoacid. The term ketosis probably arose because of the observation that acetone, a ketone, could be detected in the breath and urine of diabetics and fasting or fat-fed subjects. Neither acetoacetate nor β-hydroxybutyrate is harmful. Utilization of these substrates is an important homeostatic response to starvation, reducing the requirements for gluconeogenesis from protein.

Ketosis is an important sign that a patient may be suffering inappropriate starvation.

See Acidosis (p. 1).

Koch's postulates

In the early years of bacteriology, Koch* established strict criteria by which the causal relationship between a bacterial species and a disease could be irrefutably confirmed. The criteria, Koch's postulates, were (1) that a bacterium be detected in the body in all cases of the disease; (2) that the bacterium isolated from a case should be grown in pure culture; and (3) that the isolated bacterium should then be shown to be capable of causing the original disease when inoculated in pure culture into a susceptible animal.

Koch's postulates are not applicable to all micro-organisms. For example, the causal association between *Mycobacterium leprae* and leprosy was not seriously questioned during the first 100 years after its discovery although it was only in 1974 that the bacillus was successfully grown, first in the

---

*Robert Koch (1843–1910) was at first a general practitioner in Niemegk and Rakwitz, later an army surgeon, and finally Director of the Institute for Infectious Diseases in Berlin. Having shown that a single disease, anthrax, was caused by a single bacterial genus, he resolved the problem of how to grow bacteria in culture. He discovered *Myco. tuberculosis* in 1882, *Vibrio cholerae* in 1883 and tuberculin in 1890. He became Nobel laureate in 1905.

foot-pad of the mouse and then, very recently, in the armadillo. The requirement that a virus be isolated from a disease, grown in pure culture and then used successfully to reproduce the disease experimentally has not been met in the case of many common human disorders.

Laceration

A laceration is an interruption in the continuity of an epithelium, produced by a tearing injury.

Laser

LASER is an acronym for Light Amplified by Stimulated Emission of Radiation.

A laser is a device containing an element which, when stimulated by light energy of sufficient intensity, emits a beam of light that is coherent, monochromatic, highly directional and of great intensity.

Lasers are used in ophthalmology to treat retinal and choroidal disease and in plastic and dental surgery and cancer therapy. However, lasers are potent sources of eye injury since the eye lens can focus an intense beam of laser light onto an area of the retina as small as 10 μm². Retinal injury is thermal. Laser light can be delivered through fibres inserted in endoscopes.

Three media are in common use in surgical lasers. They are CO_2 gas; argon gas; and neodymium: yttrium-aluminium-garnet (Nd:YAG) (Table 16). The wavelength of a laser determines the depth of penetration and the absorption of the beam. The absorption of argon light by blood is a hindrance in bloody fields of surgery. The maximum energy (wattage) released by a laser also varies and restricts the practical use of CO_2 and of argon lasers. It is likely that many other crystals capable of laser emission will be developed so that, in the future, it will be possible to select more exactly than at present the best medium for a particular clinical requirement.

Table 16 Wavelength and depth of penetration of lasers

Medium	CO_2 gas	Ar gas	Nd: YAG crystal
Wavelength (μm)	10.6	0.5	1.1
Penetration (mm)	1	2–3	5–7

Legionnaires' disease (Legionellosis)

Legionnaires' disease is a form of pneumonia caused by the small Gram-negative bacillus, *Legionella pneumophila*. The organism is very difficult to demonstrate in tissues; it produces an exotoxin. Outbreaks have occurred in hospitals. The source of infection is drinking water and moist air from air-conditioning plants. Those contracting legionellosis in hospitals include staff and healthy visitors. However, immunosuppressed patients are particularly vulnerable and surgery in immunoincompetent individuals may be a risk factor for *Legionella pneumophila* infection.

Leproma

A leproma is the granuloma of lepromatous leprosy, that is, leprosy in which the locally destructive effects of *Mycobacterium leprae* are shown. The granuloma may appear as a nodule or macule. Microscopically, there are many foamy macrophages within which the organism survives for very long periods.

Leucocytes

Leucocytes are the 'white' cells of the blood and tissues, although a single cell is transparent rather than white. Small numbers can be seen easily only if special devices such as phase-contrast microscopy are used or if the cell is stained. However, great numbers of leucocytes in blood allowed to stand uncoagulated in a tube occupy so much of the sedimented mass that they appear as a white layer, an observation that led to the origin of the term 'buffy coat' and to the recognition of leukaemia (p. 130).

There are three main categories of leucocyte: granulocytes (50–90 per cent), lymphocytes (5–45 per cent) (p. 132) and monocytes (5 per cent) (p. 136). Platelets (p. 157) are, by convention, described separately not because of their small size but because each is only part of a parent cell. Mature granulocytes are polymorphonuclear (polymorphs): the single nucleus is divided into lobes or segments the number of which increases with the age of the cell. The granular series is predominantly (80 per cent) neutrophil.

The cytoplasm of **neutrophil polymorphs** contains two types of granules, the lysosomes (p. 135) and the specific, azurophilic granules. Neutrophil polymorphs move very quickly to sites of inflammation, attracted by chemotaxis. They pass through blood-vessel walls within 20–30 minutes and surround and phagocytose foreign material and bacteria. Neutrophil polymorphs live only 3–4 days. In an abscess, the activated proteolytic enzymes from dead cells are released, digesting surrounding tissue components, fibrin and cell debris. The residual products constitute pus (p. 163).

Eosinophil granulocytes (2 per cent) contain large granules of rhomboidal shape. Eosinophil polymorphs are found in inflammatory reactions of a hypersensitivity form, for example, in response to parasitic and protozoal antigens and in anaphylaxis. They predominate in the rare **eosinophilic granuloma**.

The granules of **basophil** granulocytes (0.4 per cent) are distinct from those of mast cells (p. 139) but it is assumed that the cells have comparable functions. They contain histamine, leukotrienes and other mediators of acute inflammation and anaphylaxis and are presumed to play a role in these reactions. They also release a platelet-activating factor.

Leucocytosis

Leucocytosis is an increase in the total number of leucocytes in the circulating blood above the normal number of $6-10 \times 10^9/l$. An increase in the total number of neutrophil granulocytes is **neutrophil granulocytosis**, in the number of lymphocytes, **lymphocytosis**, and so on. When a change occurs in the total white cell count, it is important to distinguish whether there is a relative alteration in the proportions of the individual leucocyte populations. Thus, in sepsis, a relative and absolute increase in the neutrophil granulocytes is usual; in many virus infections, a relative and absolute lymphocytosis is common but there may be lymphopenia.

Leucopenia

Leucopenia is a diminution in the total number of leucocytes normally present in the blood below the normal total count of $6-10 \times 10^9/l$. Correspondingly there may be **lymphopenia**, a feature of many virus infections, or **granulocytopenia**, a consequence of the action of drugs such as cytotoxic agents (p. 13) and some antibiotics.

The total loss of granulocytes is **agranulocytosis**.

Leucoplakia

Leucoplakia is a local lesion of the mouth, vulva, penis or bladder in which smooth, dry, white, thickened patches result from chronic irritation. They are precancerous.

(Leukos: white; plasis: plate)

Erythroplasia

Erythroplasia, a term analogous to leucoplakia, describes red, papular eruptions of the penis (Queyrat's erythroplasia) or mouth. Erythroplasia is synonymous with **erythroplakia**.

(Erythros: red; plasis: plate)

Leukaemia

Leukaemia, literally 'white blood'*, is a potentially fatal neoplastic disease of the leucocytic precursor cells of the bone marrow. There is characteristically a release of a great excess of one or other of the immature granulocytic, lymphocytic or mononuclear cells, into the circulating blood. The leukaemias are said to be acute or chronic. In chronic lymphocytic or chronic granulocytic leukaemia, the enormous excess of leucocytes can be seen in the buffy coat (p. 129).

Consequent upon the successful use of cytotoxic drugs, the prognosis in many forms of leukaemia, such as the acute forms of childhood, is much improved.

There are other, poorly understood leukaemia-like disorders. Hairy-cell leukaemia, for example, a lymphocytic and monocytic neoplasm, is an insidious cause of splenomegaly and pancytopenia. The peripheral blood mononuclear cells have hairy, cytoplasmic projections and contain rod-shaped inclusions.

---

*Described by John Hughes Bennett (1812-1875) in 1845, the essential neoplastic nature of the disease was recognised by R. Virchow (p. 183) six weeks later.

Liver failure

In liver failure there is defective synthesis of protein and other macro-molecules, impaired conjugation, defective intermediary metabolism, and often hyperbilirubinaemia.

Causes.   Liver failure occurs because of destruction of the parenchyma (hepatocytes) or replacement by fibrous tissue (cirrhosis: p. 55). The hepatocytes may be damaged by chemical reagents (e.g. halothane), drugs (e.g. paracetamol) and organisms, particularly viruses (e.g. hepatitis B and the non A, non-B viruses) (p. 96). Cirrhosis may supersede progressive hepatitis but may be due to severe right heart failure (cardiac fibrosis) or persistent, intermittent biliary obstruction (secondary biliary cirrhosis). The Budd-Chiari syndrome is a rare condition in which the radicles of the hepatic vein undergo progressive intimal fibrosis. The cause is unknown.

Effects.   The effects of liver failure are widespread. Approxmately half the glycogen reserve of the body is stored in the liver, which is also the site of gluconeogenesis from other carbohydrates and amino acids. In the experi-mental animal, total hepatectomy results in death from hypoglycaemia. A plethora of protein deficiences occurs. There is a fall in the concentration of serum albumin; the subsequent decrease in oncotic pressure is one factor in the production of ascites. Most of the proteins required for blood coagula-tion (p. 56) are synthesized in the liver, and defective coagulation is an early feature of hepatic failure. Much of the insulin released into the portal circu-lation from the pancreas is normally used by liver cells. In parenchymal liver disease, increased quantities of insulin reach the systemic circulation where they induce an increased uptake by skeletal muscle of the branched-chain amino acids leucine, isoleucine and lysine. At the same time, the aromatic amino acids methionine, phenylalanine and tyrosine, normally metabolized in the liver, reach the circulation in excess. It is believed that the change in the normal plasma ratio between aromatic and branched-chain amino acids induces alterations in the concentrations of neurotransmitters in the central nervous system. These defects may produce a coarse tremor of the skeletal muscles, disorientation, coma and death.

Many drugs are detoxified by the liver and excreted in the bile after conjugation with amino, organic, or mineral acids (e.g. glutamic, glucuronic and sulphuric acids respectively). Consequently patients with hepatic failure may be abnormally sensitive to drugs such as opiates.

Lymph nodes

Lymph nodes are encapsulated masses of lymphoid tissue into which lymphatic vessels drain. They are often oval or bean-shaped; the size is highly variable, ranging from 2–5 mm in diameter to 2 cm or more. There is an outer cortex and an inner medulla. Afferent lymphatic channels enter the periphery of the node where the channels offer access, for example, to groups of metastatic carcinoma cells. Efferent vessels emerge from the hilus, the part where blood vessels enter and leave.

B-cell areas   The cortical lymphoid follicles are formed of large numbers of smaller mature lymphocytes. Within these islands, there are often germinal centres containing larger proliferating cells, reticular macrophages and dendritic macrophages. These centres are sites of B-cell memory: they respond to antigenic stimuli. The cells around the follicle become plasma cells and synthesize antibody.

T-cell areas   A second population of lymphocytes, controlled by the thymus, comprises the paracortex, that is, the cortical region remote from the follicles. In this region, cell proliferation is seen during T-cell-mediated reactions (p. 133). Among these reactions are skin-graft rejection; hypersensitivity to tuberculoprotein; and contact dermatitis, the result of sensitivity to small molecules such as metals, dyes and plastics.

The respiratory tract, gut and urinary tract are protected by non-encapsulated lymphoid tissues, of which the pharyngeal tonsils provide one example. There is a particular association with IgA and IgE synthesis and the term mucosal-associated lymphoid tissue (MALT) has been used.

Lymphadenitis; lymphangitis

Lymphadenitis is inflammation of lymph nodes; it is commonly due to infection but may be caused by physical and chemical agents such as x-rays and silicates. Lymphadenitis may be diffuse in systemic infection, or localized to specific anatomical regions.

Acute lymphadenitis   This often follows infection within an epithelium. If the lymphadenitis is due to streptococci, suppuration may occur within the node. Most forms of acute lymphadenitis resolve completely.

Chronic lymphadenitis   Chronic inflammation of lymph nodes was commonly due to tuberculosis. Sarcoidosis, brucellosis and lymphogranuloma venereum, more common in negro races, are other causes. Within the affected nodes, there is hyperplasia of the reticuloendothelial cells with many altered macrophages. The phagocytes are frequently clustered and the term granulomatous lymphadenitis is often used. In chronic inflammatory lymphadenitis, the lymph nodes are frequently matted together by perilymphadenitis. An abscess may develop and discharge spontaneously to the nearest epithelial surface, forming a sinus.

Lymphangitis   This is inflammation of lymphatic channels. In the skin, lymphangitis shows as red lines defining the course of the affected lymphatics.

Lymphocytes

Lymphocytes are the class of white blood cells responsible for immune reactions.

Lymphocytes originate from stem cells in the bone marrow and circulate in large numbers in the blood stream to the spleen, lymph nodes, gut, tonsils and thymus. They leave the blood stream through the walls of specialized 'high endothelial' venules and subsequently return to the blood stream via the thoracic duct. The peripheral blood normally contains 2–3 × 10^6 lymphocytes/l so that these cells comprise 20–45 per cent of the leucocyte population of the blood. Morphologically, lymphocytes are small, round cells with relatively large, round nuclei, little cytoplasm and few organelles. Lymphoblasts and young lymphocytes are larger than mature cells. Functionally, the main property of lymphocytes is to act as units of immunological memory. Each lymphocyte inherits the capacity to recognize a single foreign antigen (p. 12).

Lymphocytes differentiate into two classes of cell, B (bursa-dependent) and T (thymus-dependent): these classes cannot be distinguished morphologically.

After antigenic recognition, **B lymphocytes** are transformed. Some B lymphocytes become plasma cells and undertake the slow and limited manufacture of antibody (p. 12) in a **primary response**. Others multiply by mitotic division and provide a population of cells that can yield a rapid, amplified **secondary response** on subsequent exposure to the same antigen. These characteristic B-lymphocyte reactions are the essential basis for humoral immunity (p. 108) and for many hypersensitivity responses (p. 102).

Eighty per cent of blood lymphocytes are **T lymphocytes**. They circulate continually from the blood to the lymph, returning from lymphoid tissue to the blood directly or via the thoracic duct. T lymphocytes appear identical to B lymphocytes but behave quite differently. The circulating T cells monitor the body for foreign antigen but do not respond to 'self' antigens to which they display tolerance (p. 113). Passing to the thymus, the T lymphocytes acquire the property of recognizing molecules such as mycobacterial cell-wall peptide (p. 25). Recognizing antigen by inherited information, the T cells develop cell-surface receptors that specifically bind this antigen and are triggered by it. In this way, a signal is generated that profoundly modifies (transforms) T-lymphocyte behaviour. The transformed cell enlarges and becomes a lymphoblast. Of these activated cells, one population releases lymphokines, one becomes cytotoxic, the **killer** T cell, and another preserves permanently a **memory** of the antigen. In addition, some T lymphocytes co-operate with B lymphocytes and stimulate their reactions to foreign antigen: these are the so-called **'helper'** cells. Other T lymphocytes **suppress** T-cell function.

The T-lymphocyte reactions form the essential basis for cell-mediated immunity and for type IV (delayed) hypersensitivity (p. 104). They depend on the presence and normal function of the thymus.

Lymphoedema and lymphangiectasia

Lymphoedema is an accumulation of tissue fluid due to defective lymphatic drainage. The fluid has a high content of protein but not as high as that of an exudate (p. 77).

Secondary lymphoedema Lymphoedema is usually secondary due to damage to lymphatic channels by surgery, radiotherapy or trauma. The channels may also be obliterated by infection. The 'peau d'orange' appearance of the breast, from obstruction of the lymphatic channels by carcinoma, is one example. The arm on the affected side may become oedematous due to involvement of the axillary lymph nodes by dissemination, surgical transection or radiotherapy.

Primary lymphoedema This is much less common; it may be due to aplasia, hypoplasia or ectasia of the lymphatics. The condition may become apparent in adolescent or adult life. Milroy's disease is a variety of congenital lymphoedema inherited as an autosomal dominant with incomplete penetration. All forms of primary lymphoedema affect the lower limbs more than the upper.

Elephantiasis Persisting lymphoedema provokes an overgrowth of the epidermis and fibrous tissue; the oedema does not 'pit'. In patients with filariasis, the lymphatics of the groin are blocked by the worms, which also provoke inflammation. Gross elephantiasis of the legs and genitalia may be produced.

Lymphatic cysts Congenital cysts of the lymphatics are found within the abdominal and thoracic cavities. Cystic hygromas occur in the region of the embryonic jugular lymph sac.

Lymphomas

Lymphomas are neoplasms arising in the lymphoid tissue of lymph nodes and, less often, in the spleen, bone marrow, liver and gut. They are closely allied to the leukaemias, from which they are distinguished by the absence of excess neoplastic cells from the blood circulation.

There are two categories of lymphoma: the more frequent Hodgkin's lymphoma and the less frequent non-Hodgkin lymphoma.

Hodgkin's lymphoma
Hodgkin's lymphoma occurs in two distinct age groups: young adults, and middle-aged and older persons. The disease is confirmed at biopsy when the characteristic large Reed-Sternberg cell with its paired, 'mirror image,' ovoid or bean-shaped nuclei is found.

Four microscopic **grades** (p. 89) are recognized, in increasing order of malignancy: lymphocyte-predominant (15 per cent), nodular sclerosing (40 per cent), mixed cellularity (30 per cent), and lymphocyte-depleted (15 per cent).

There are four clinical **stages** (p. 174). In increasing order of malignancy they are recognized when

1. a single lymph node or group of nodes is affected;
2. two or more groups of nodes are involved but the disease is confined to parts above *or* below the diaphragm;
3. the disease is confined to lymph nodes but groups of nodes both above *and* below the diaphragm are affected;

4. tissues such as the spleen, bone marrow and liver, beyond lymph nodes, are involved.

The behaviour and prognosis of Hodgkin's lymphoma are related to microscopic grade and to clinical stage.

Although the cause(s) of Hodgkin's disease are not known, there are similarities to granulomatous infection. A geographic clustering of cases supports this view. Cell-mediated immunity is depressed.

Non-Hodgkin lymphoma

Most of these neoplasms are derived from B lymphocytes. Multiple myeloma (p. 143) is a malignant lymphoma of plasma cells. A few non-Hodgkin lymphomas such as the Sézary syndrome come from T cells and, occasionally, non-Hodgkin lymphoma arises from histiocytes.

Non-Hodgkin lymphomas are follicular (nodular) or diffuse. Follicular lymphomas have a better prognosis. Diffuse lymphomas are themselves divisible into those of low and those of high malignancy. Some follicular lymphomas change terminally and become diffuse.

The non-Hodgkin lymphomas that arise from B lymphocytes come from the cells in and around the cortical follicles of lymph nodes. These lymphoid cells are small or large and are called centrocytes or centroblasts respectively. On this basis, the B-cell non-Hodgkin lymphomas have been classified as:

1. small lymphocyte type;
2. plasmacytoid lymphocyte type;
3. follicle-centre cell type, follicular or diffuse, centrocytic or centroblastic;
4. immunoblastic, a category found in old persons in whom polyclonal hyperglobulinaemia is accompanied by haemolytic anaemia.

Burkitt's lymphoma (p. 48) is a particular diffuse, neoplasm of poorly differentiated B-lymphocytic origin.

Lysis

Lysis is the recovery from an infectious disease. There is a gradual fall in temperature accompanying a disappearance of symptoms.

Lysis or, more accurately, **cytolysis** also means the dissolution or distintegration and, consequently the death of cells by immunological, chemical or physical agents or by virus or enzyme action. In **immune cytolysis**, cell-membrane injury begins when part of the C5b-9 unit of complement (p. 62) is inserted into the lipid bilayer: a channel is created which pierces the cell membrane, allowing water to enter by osmosis and the contents of the disrupted cell to escape.

Lysosomes

Lysosomes are very small, intracellular cytoplasmic organelles. They are characteristic components of phagocytes (p. 155) and are therefore important functional units of macrophages (p. 136) and of neutrophil polymorphs

(p. 129). In the polymorph, lysosomes are seen as the blue-staining (azurophilic) granules.

Lysosomes are storehouses of inactive, degradative enzymes that become activated when exposed to an appropriate substrate at acid pH. The enzymes include a nuclease, cathepsin B, glucuronidase, a collagenase, and plasminogen.

Lysosomal enzymes are activated during the process of phagocytosis (p. 155). Endocytosis of a foreign solid such as a staphylococcus results in the formation of a **phagosome**, with which the lysosomal membrane fuses to form a **phagolysosome**. The lysosomal enzymes are activated within the phagolysosome because of a change in pH, and digestion of the foreign solid takes place. Subsequently, the residue of the digested material is expelled from the cell by **exocytosis**, although undigested material such as haemosiderin may remain inside a **telolysosome** for very long periods.

Lysosomal enzymes are also activated indiscriminately if the normal processes of cell respiration and metabolism break down. Thus, in hypoxia or shock, when there is impaired tissue oxygenation or vascular perfusion, at sites of ischaemia and under the influence of cell poisons or toxins, cell membranes lose their semipermeability, and alterations in cell pH occur. In this way, lysosomal enzymes are enabled to degrade the constituents of the cell itself and, in turn, those of surrounding tissue. This is the mechanism by which **autolysis** (p. 20) takes place. When lysosomes were first discovered, their role in autolysis was quickly discerned and they were called 'bags of death' by their discoverer, Christian de Duve, in 1955.

Lysozyme

Lysozyme* is an enzyme with antibacterial properties, present in tears, nasal and bronchial secretions and in other unlikely sites such as uncooked egg white. Lysozyme can be said to be an antibiotic. Both lysozyme and penicillin act by disrupting the same chemical component of bacterial cell walls.

Macrophages

Macrophages are large phagocytic cells. A **mononuclear macrophage system** is recognized. It includes blood monocytes derived from bone-marrow precursors; the mononuclear phagocytes of the lung, serous surfaces, central nervous system (microglial cells), synovia and skin (Langerhans cells); and the less mobile histocytes of the loose connective tissue.

The cells of the system possess the property of processing antigens in an early phase of the immune response (p. 108) and this characteristic distinguishes mononuclear phagocytes from the endothelial cells of the reticuloendothelial system (p. 166) with which, however, they share the property of avid phagocytosis.

---

*Alexander Fleming (1881–1955) identified lysozyme in nasal secretions in 1922. Seven years later, he published his classical paper describing the inhibitory action of a mould, *Penicillium notatum*, on the growth of staphylococcus colonies.

Structure

Macrophages are recognized by their large size, filopodia, indented uniform nucleus, lysosomes, and phagocytic vacuoles. Their cell-surface antigens can be used as markers for their presence and are identifiable by monoclonal antisera. Their phagocytic potential can be tested in vivo by the injection of dyes or particulate material into the circulation, in vitro by adding similar substances to cell suspensions or monolayer cultures. The cell surfaces of macrophages bear receptors for the Fc end of immunoglobulin molecules, enabling the phagocytes to kill non-specifically or by activating complement.

Function

1. Macrophages phagocytose foreign or necrotic material including bacteria and carbon particles, the residue of infarcted heart, lung and bone, and plastic and metallic implants, including sutures. Antigens processed in this way may be passed to lymphocytes, leading to immune reactions (p. 108). Complement bound to the macrophages assists the phagocytosis of those bacteria that have been opsonized.

2. Macrophages play a special part in granuloma (p. 90) formation. In tuberculosis for example, *Mycobacterium tuberculosis* remains alive within some macrophages. Many others, not phagocytic, aggregate together and effect the destruction of the organism. Because of the resemblance of these macrophages to some forms of epithelium, they are still sometimes called **epithelioid cells.**

3. They are activated by lymphokines (p. 105). Activated macrophages are effective in destroying ingested bacteria such as brucella, mycobacteria and salmonella.

4. Macrophages kill neoplastic cells by a non-specific cytotoxic mechanism activated by lymphokines. This action is by contact, not by phagocytosis. Neoplastic cells may also be killed by a specific antibody-associated mechanism involving macrophage Fc receptors.

5. They take part in amyloid formation.

Malignant cachexia

Malignant cachexia is a state of extreme ill-health accompanying the growth of a malignant neoplasm. There is anaemia, malnutrition, hypoalbuminaemia, loss of weight, circulatory impairment and muscle weakness. The changes of malignant cachexia may appear when only a localized, small neoplasm is present, of insufficient size to induce these changes physically. The possibility of the selective uptake of vitamins or essential amino acids by the neoplasm is one explanation for the syndrome; another is the secretion of humoral agents which inhibit intermediary metabolism.

Malignant; malignancy

These terms refer to invasive neoplasms and distinguish them from benign. Malignancy denotes spread by metastasis. Occasionally, the word malignant is used to other senses such as 'malignant' hypertension but it is better to use an alternative term such as 'accelerated' hypertension.

Malignant melanoma

Melanoma is a neoplasm derived from melanin-forming cells. The word melanoma should not be used without a qualifying adjective. In North America, in particular, melanoma implies a malignant neoplasm.

Malignant melanoma arises from melanocytes in the skin, the eye, or the mucous membrane of the oropharynx, nasopharynx, oesophagus and vagina, sometimes from a pre-existing junctional naevus. Malignant change in a pre-existing naevus may be suggested by an increase in size and a change in colour together with exudation, ulceration or bleeding. Malignant change is more common in naevi of the palms, soles and genitalia. Subungual naevi are particularly prone to malignant change. Malignant melanoma is more common in white races and individuals exposed to ultraviolet light than in dark races.

Microscopically there are numerous mitotic figures, with hyper-chromatism. The cytoplasm contains granules of melanin. These cells show widespread invasion of the dermis and, frequently, the entire thickness of the epidermis. In some cases the differentiation between a large compound naevus and a malignant melanoma may be difficult.

The prognosis of melanoma varies considerably; many surgeons are unjustifiably gloomy. For unknown reasons the prognosis is much better in women than in men. The prognosis with peripheral lesions is better because treatment is more effective. The prognosis is worse with lesions showing nodularity.

See Naevus (p. 144).

Malnutrition

The word malnutrition describes clinical conditions arising out of imperfect nourishment. The deficiency in the diet may be highly specific, e.g. vitamin C, or there may be a general deficiency of all the ingredients required in a normal diet. Such cases of starvation are usually described as protein-energy malnutrition but this term has no exact definition. Malnutrition is most frequent in impoverished, underdeveloped countries, particularly among children. In the West, malnutrition is most frequently seen in patients with serious disease of the gastrointestinal tract.

Beri-beri
A disease due to lack of thiamine and characterized by neuropathy, mental deterioration, oedema and heart failure (p. 94).

Kwashiorkor
A disease of growing infants characterized by a low concentration of plasma albumin, together with oedema, normocytic anaemia, and an enlarged fatty liver. Ultimately, cirrhosis develops. Kwashiorkor is common in Africa, Asia and parts of South America and is due to a dietary deficiency of protein.

See Anaemia (p. 7) Scurvy (p. 168)
Osteomalacia (p. 151) Osteoporosis (p. 152)
Trace elements (p. 186) Vitamins (p. 199).

Mantoux test

The Mantoux test is the intradermal injection of 1–3 units of an antigen, the **purified protein derivative (PPD)** of *Myco. tuberculosis* with Tween 80 added as a stabilizer.

PPD is the concentrate of a culture of *Myco tuberculosis* on synthetic medium, purified by ultrafiltration and by the precipitation of the protein with trichloroacetic acid. **Old tuberculin** is the original preparation of tuberculin, a fraction or extract of the *Myco. tuberculosis*, filtered and concentrated from glycerin-broth cultures of the organism.

In a sensitized person, the injection of PPD is followed after 5–8 hours by a slowly developing focus of inflammation. A zone of oedema is surrounded by a wider area of erythema. Inflammation becomes maximal after 24–48 hours. The indurated zone is measured after three days. If a biopsy is made, the microscopical reaction is found to be dominated by mononuclear phagocytes ('epithelioid' cells: p. 137). A granuloma (p. 90) forms.

A positive reaction in the Mantoux test indicates individuals who have, at some time, been infected with *Myco. tuberculosis* or inoculated with BCG (p. 21). Non-reactors are still at risk of developing tuberculosis.

A difficulty in interpreting the Mantoux test is the possibility that in the face of massive active tuberculous infection, a positive test may become spuriously negative, as it may in the severely malnourished. In some countries, infections with 'atypical' mycobacteria (p. 143) are relatively frequent: the Mantoux test is usually negative but may be weakly positive.

Mast cells

Mast cells are large and mononucleate. They were given their name because they are stuffed (gemästete) with basophilic granules which are easily broken down and lost. Mast cells are widely dispersed near blood vessels, in loose connective tissue and in the lung. The basophilic granules stain with metachromatic dyes because of their content of heparin; in man, the granules also contain and release histamine, platelet-activating factor, leukotrienes and a substance chemotactic for eosinophilic polymorphs.

One mechanism for the release of chemical mediators from mast cells is the binding of IgE antibody to the cell surfaces in individuals sensitized to antigens such as the house mite and pollen. Degranulation results and the chemical mediators liberated from granules cause symptoms such as those of hay fever and allergic asthma (p. 103). Another response is attributable to the liberation of the small C3a and C5a fragments of complement during complement activation: these fragments are anaphylatoxins. In turn, they release histamine and other substances, explaining some of the symptoms of anaphylaxis (p. 102).

Melanin

Melanin is a brown-black pigment formed in the skin and to a lesser extent in other tissues, in amounts determined by racial and genetic factors. It is produced from tyrosine by **melanocytes**. There is disagreement as to whether the precursor cells, **melanoblasts**, are ectodermal in origin or migrate to the epidermis from the neuroectoderm. Many consider them to be part of the APUD system (p. 15). The production of melanin is controlled in some species by a melanin-stimulating hormone (MSH) released from the pars intermedia of the pituitary gland. Melanin escapes from local sites of formation; **melanophores** are phagocytes that take up the pigment.

Large amounts of melanin may be formed by the cells of malignant melanomas (p. 138). An excess of melanin is synthesized in the skin in Addison's disease (p. 66) and in haemochromatosis (bronzed diabetes) and melanosis is a normal consequence of sunburn and ionizing radiation.

Melanosis

Melanosis is the excessive pigmentation of body surfaces by melanin. Melanosis of the skin is commonly a sequel to exposure to the ultraviolet light of the sun; however, other sources of UVL such as lamps can produce the same effect. Melanosis often follows therapeutic x- or γ-irradiation and, in disorders such as Addison's disease, is one result of the actions of excess adrenocorticotrophic and related hormones.

Conjunctival melanosis   This is produced by the proliferation of atypical melanocytes in the conjunctiva. Ultimately, malignant change ensues.

Melanosis coli   Melanosis coli is the presence of macrophages laden with melanin-like pigment in the lamina propria of the large intestine. The origin of the pigment is uncertain. Many believe that the pigment comes from purgatives containing anthracene but some have suggested that the pigment is derived, in constipated individuals, from the degradation of phenylalanine or tyrosine in the diet.

Metabolic response to trauma

After injury (trauma) or operation, a sequence of changes affects many aspects of intermediary metabolism. The sequence is known as the metabolic response to injury. Changes in metabolism after injury or operation are governed by alterations in the secretions of the catabolic hormones adrenaline, noradrenaline, cortisol and glucagon, and by the anabolic hormones insulin and somatotrophin.

Catabolic phase

Following surgery, metabolic expenditure exceeds that observed before injury. Surgeons often refer to this phase as the 'catabolic response to surgery'. The systemic result is weight loss and a reduction in body protein, fat and carbohydrate. The net catabolic effect is a consequence both of decreased molecular synthesis and of increased molecular breakdown. Protein may be mobilized for repair and for gluconeogenesis. All body proteins, whether skeletal, visceral or circulating, are functional or structural: they are not stored, and any reduction implies disordered function or abnormal structure.

The length of the catabolic phase varies according to the severity of injury; after elective operations it is usually not more than five days. After severe injury, particularly after burns or sepsis, catabolism prevails over anabolism for weeks and the patient may die.

Anabolic phase

The recovering patient enters an anabolic phase. The tissue lost during the catabolic phase is replaced. Most of this loss is made good within one month following an elective operation. However, a year may elapse before the body is entirely restored to its normal state.

Consequences

The pattern of response to injury is inherited and may have survival value. Injured animals mobilize fat and carbohydrate for energy, protein for repair: they cannot hunt for food. Such a response may be inappropriate in a patient in hospital. If the stimulus of injury is sufficiently severe or prolonged a patient may die as a consequence of continuing excess catabolism. Unlike starvation, the provision of nutrients does not influence the catabolic phase significantly.

Metaplasia

Metaplasia is the change of one type of differentiated tissue to another differentiated type. An example is the change of the normal pseudostratified columnar ciliated epithelium of the bronchus to stratified squamous epithelium, under the influence of chronic irritants or carcinogens such as those of cigarette smoke.

Metastasis

Metastasis is the distant extension of the cells of malignant neoplasms. Metastasis may be direct, by natural channels or ducts, or by the blood, lymph or other body fluids. In the circulation, blood-born metastases may be arterial or venous, within the systemic, pulmonary or portal distributions. Metastasis may be **retrograde** when, because of altered hydrodynamics, the normal direction of flow is reversed. **Paradoxical** metastatic spread is possible when there is an abnormal communication, such as a patent interatrial septum, between the arterial and venous circulations.

Some locally invasive neoplasms such as basal-cell carcinoma do not metastasize. More often, metastasis, as in breast carcinoma, is widespread long before the primary neoplasm is apparent clinically.

Lymphatic permeation

Lymphatic permeation is the direct extension of the cells of malignant neoplasms as continuous columns into and along lymphatic channels.

Permeation is a characteristic of carcinoma. One common example is gastric carcinoma of the diffusely infiltrating type.

Metazoa

The *Metazoa* are a subkingdom of the *Animalia* which contains all the multicellular forms except the *Parazoa* (sponges) and the *Mesozoa*. The *Metazoa* therefore include the multicellular parasites such as worms and flukes (p. 202).

Monoclonal antibodies

A **clone** is a group of identical cells, all derived from a single ancestor.

The term monoclonal antibody is used to describe antibody molecules that have identical antigen specificity: they are produced by a single clone of B cells. They are made in cell cultures. These cultures are now manufactured in bulk commercially. Antibody-producing cells from the lymphoid tissues of an animal sensitized to a particular antigen are fused with myeloma cells to make 'hybrid myeloma' cells. These cells are grown in culture as a so-called **hybridoma**. The hybridoma cells combine the permanent growth potential and high rate of immunoglobulin protein synthesis of the myeloma with the specificity of the original animal antibody. The immunoglobulins made in bulk from such propagated cells are then available for diagnostic use.

The ready availability of monoclonal antibodies against an almost limitless range of antigens has begun to revolutionize laboratory diagnosis in those countries where the high cost of these reagents can be met. Among the antigens that can be detected specifically and with great sensitivity are hormones such as ACTH and parathormone; markers for individuals cancer cells and macrophages; transplantation antigens (p. 189); bacterial serotypes; cell proteins such as actin and myosin; and drugs such as digoxin.

Monoclonal antibodies are proving particularly valuable in radioimmune assays (p. 13) and in establishing the histological identity of neoplasms such as lymphomas, APUDomas and angiosarcomas.

It is also possible to employ monoclonal antibodies to target cancer cells in vivo. If the antibodies are 'labelled' with an appropriate radioactive isotope such as ^{14}C, ^{3}H or ^{32}P, the β particles emitted by the isotope can be expected to irradiate and destroy selectively the cancer cells.

Mucus

Mucus is the viscid, watery secretion of epithelial cells and some glands. The major component of mucus is mucin, a glycoprotein. The cells that secrete mucus vary in form; the majority are distended in the shape of a goblet. The protein component of mucus is synthesized in the endoplasmic reticulum. The carbohydrate component is added within the Golgi apparatus.

If there is inflammation of the epithelia lining the respiratory, gastrointestinal or genitourinary tracts, mucus secretion is increased and microscopic examination shows an increase in the number of goblet cells which are greatly distended with mucus. In **cystic fibrosis** (mucoviscidosis), the mucus-secreting cells of the sweat glands, bronchi, intestines and bile ducts, as well as the pancreas secrete an abnormally viscous mucin which ultimately obstructs the ducts of the glands; they subsequently atrophy. If the duct or orifice of any organ containing mucus-secreting cells is obstructed, a **mucocele** (p. 42) may be produced, e.g. in the lip, appendix or gall bladder. Some neoplasms of the breast, stomach and large intestine are composed predominantly of cells secreting mucin. Pseudomucinous cystadenomas of the ovary may rupture, releasing mucin intraperitoneally.

Mycobacteria

Mycobacteria are rod-shaped bacilli closely related to the actinomycetes and nocardia. All have a wax-like material in their cell walls which determines that they are acid and alcohol-fast (p. 25). Mycobacteria divide infrequently and grow very slowly (p. 23) even on special culture media such as Lowenstein–Jensen. The organisms are identified by these selective media. The distinction between strains is made by assessing antibiotic sensitivity, by growth characteristics, and biochemically. The inoculation of guinea-pigs is no longer used for this purpose.

Mycobacterium tuberculosis hominis causes human tuberculosis and *Myco. tuberculosis bovis* may infect man and other animals as well as cattle. Other mycobacteria cause skin ulceration. Atypical (opportunistic) mycobacteria such as *Myco. kansasii* and *Myco. intracellulare* are only occasionally pathogenic but the former can cause arthritis and the latter lymphnode disease, pulmonary disease or disseminated infection in immunocompromised patients. Leprosy is the result of infection with *Myco. leprae.*

Myeloma

A myeloma is a unique malignant neoplasm derived from a single clone of plasma cells. The neoplasm is **monoclonal** (p. 142). Although uncommon, myeloma is the most frequent primary neoplasm of bone and bone marrow in elderly persons. The multiplication of myeloma cells begins simultaneously in many sites and the name **multiple myeloma** is used. The proliferating cells destroy the bone and cause hypercalcaemia. The skull, ribs and vertebrae are most susceptible but pathological fracture of a limb bone may be the first sign of disease.

All the cells of one myeloma synthesize and secrete a single, identical immunoglobulin, usually IgG or IgA or a single, identical light chain which may be κ or λ (light-chain myeloma). The immunoglobulins and light chains are differentiated by immunoelectrophoresis. The light chains from myeloma proteins are secreted in large amounts in the urine as so-called Bence Jones protein, a material which comes out of solution on gentle heating, redissolving with further heat. In ten per cent of cases, amyloidosis (p. 6) develops. The amyloid protein in myeloma, AL protein, is more frequently derived from κ than from λ light chains. Myeloma protein accumulates in the renal tubules and death occurs from renal failure.

Heavy-chain diseases These are lymphocytic and plasmacytic lymphomas associated with the excess production of the Fc fragments of γ, α or μ heavy chains.

Myositis ossificans

Myositis ossificans is metaplasia of mesenchymal tissue with bone formation. The process is analogous to the cell changes that occur at sites of fracture healing. In the callus formed around a fracture, fibroblasts and osteoblasts are indistinguishable and are differentiated by the nature of the nearby extracellular matrix that they secrete. The fibroblasts and osteoblasts have separate identities but come from the same stem cell: their mutability explains the response seen in myositis ossificans.

Traumatic myositis ossificans
Localized myositis ossificans, **myositis ossificans circumscripta**, may follow repeated trauma to a muscle (e.g. rider's bone in the tendinous origin of the adductor longus muscle). It also occurs after a single episode of trauma (e.g. in the tendinous insertion of the brachialis anterior muscle after supracondylar fracture of the humerus). The ossification is within an organized haematoma. There is argument as to whether the osteoblasts arise from the periosteum or from totipotent mesenchymal cells in the haematoma.

Progressive myositis ossificans
Myositis ossificans progressiva is a rare hereditary disease in which ossification occurs in fascia, aponeuroses, tendons and muscles. The disease begins in childhood with painful swellings in these tissues; they subsequently ossify. There is an intermittent course. Ultimately the body becomes rigid and death is due to pneumonia. Other congenital skeletal abnormalities such as microdactyly and absence of digits are often associated with this disease.

Naevus

A naevus or 'mole' is any congenital spot or blemish of the skin. In practice, the term naevus is, however, restricted to mean a neoplasm of those skin cells which can form melanin and which are often but not always pigmented. Benign (pigmented) naevi may be junctional, intradermal, compound, juvenile, or blue. The malignant counterpart of a junctional naevus is malignant melanoma (p. 138).

Junctional naevus
The fetal migration of melanocytes from the neural crest to the epidermis is nearly complete at birth. Aggregated at the epidermodermal junction, these cells may grow to form a junctional naevus. In 98 per cent of intradermal naevi (see below) examined before puberty, junctional change is present and it is reasonable to ascribe the origin of intradermal naevi to these cells.

Intradermal naevus
Present at birth or manifest later, the intradermal naevus (common mole) becomes more prominent at puberty. Melanin pigment is often not present. Unless there is an overlying junctional naevus, malignancy rarely supervenes.

Compound naevus
Junctional change and intradermal naevus together constitute compound naevus. The junctional activity cannot be detected clinically.

Juvenile spindle-cell naevus
This compound naevus includes single and multinucleated giant cells. There is no malignant predisposition and fibrous replacement and involution often occur.

Blue naevus
The blue naevus comprises deeply pigmented, dopa*-positive cells deep within the dermis. Histologically, the lesion is identical with the mongolian spot found in the mid-sacral skin, and the naevus of Ota found in the eye and skin of the face.

Fewer than 10 per cent of malignant melanomas arise from pre-existing naevi. Those that precede malignant melanoma are usually flat, hairless and light to dark brown. Raised, hairy, papillary naevi uncommonly become malignant.

Necrosis

Necrosis is the death of part or the whole of a tissue; the physical form of the dead tissue varies both according to the cause, and to the composition of the tissue. Among the varieties of necrosis are:

Aseptic necrosis, a term applied to necrosis of part of a bone resulting from ischaemia. A common example is aseptic necrosis of the head of the femur after fracture or in caisson disease, or in the course of renal dialysis.

Caseous necrosis (p. 190), the breakdown of tissue under the influence of *Mycobacterium tuberculosis*, with conversion to a cheese-like material which may form a 'cold' abscess, i.e. an abscess with little surrounding inflammation.

Coagulative necrosis, the conversion of dead tissue to a firm mass, as in ischaemic infarction of a kidney or of the myocardium. Structural proteins are retained but DNA and RNA are lost.

Colliquative necrosis, the conversion, by autolysis, of necrotic tissue to a fluid, as in a cerebral infarct.

Fat necrosis, the breakdown of fatty tissue with subsequent acute inflammation and sometimes haemorrhage. Trauma to breast or synovial tissue, the release of activated pancreatic enzymes and bacterial infection are known causes.

---

*Dopa, dihydroxyphenylalanine, is a precursor of tyrosine and of melanin (p. 140).

Fibrinoid necrosis, a descriptive term for the necrotic zones seen for example in the intima and media of arteries which come to have staining properties identical with those of fibrin. In the necrotic zones other plasma proteins are also found.

Hyaline necrosis (Zenker's degeneration), a term applied to the segmental skeletal muscle necrosis caused by *Salmonella typhi*.

Ischaemic necrosis, death of tissue due to the cutting off of the blood supply. Aseptic necrosis is one variety.

Mummification, the process sometimes called dry gangrene (p. 85).

Pressure necrosis, tissue death due to local vascular stasis or ischaemia e.g. bedsore.

Radiation necrosis, tissue death caused by the local action of ionizing radiation.

See Gangrene (p. 85)
   Infarct (p. 116).

Neoplasms

A neoplasm is an abnormal mass (tumour) of tissue the growth of which exceeds and is unco-ordinated with that of the normal body tissues, persisting in the same excessive manner after cessation of the stimuli which evoked the change.

There is an irreversible alteration in the genetic material of somatic or germ cells leading to uncontrolled, purposeless multiplication. The neoplasm often appears in the host tissue as a swelling but diffuse growth or ulceration may occur. Neoplasms are not properly regulated by the growth-control mechanisms of the host; nevertheless, their increase beyond a diameter of about 1–2 mm depends upon the provision by the host of a vascular supply. Nor are they usually responsive to the host's immune mechanism or endocrine system. In some ways therefore a neoplasm behaves like a parasite, in others like the embryo, extending at the expense of the host (mother). The tendency is, however, towards host destruction and two broad categories of neoplasm are recognized according to the behaviour of the neoplasm, its structure and the degree of destruction produced.

Benign neoplasms
Benign neoplasms are well-differentiated (p. 74): their cell structure and arrangement closely resemble those of the parent tissue. They are classified by histogenesis, that is, by the tissue of origin (Table 17). There is often a true collagenous capsule. Growth is slow and may even cease. The cells seldom display mitotic activity. Metastasis does not occur, but local recurrence after excision or treatment is not exceptional. Mechanical effects may develop and in the case of neoplasms of the brain, encased within the rigid skull, these effects (p. 120) may be fatal. Occasionally, benign neoplasms may be the source of haemorrhage.

Table 17 Classification of neoplasms according to histogenesis and behaviour

Epithelial

benign
papilloma
adenoma

malignant
carcinoma: a prefix such as 'adeno-' is added to indicate a glandular origin

Mesenchymal

benign
fibroma
lipoma
chondroma

malignant
fibrosarcoma
liposarcoma
chondrosarcoma

Haemopoietic
Hodgkin's lymphoma
non-Hodgkin lymphoma
myeloma
leukaemia
primary polycythaemia

Neural
glioma
neurilemmoma
neuroblastoma and ganglioneuroma
chromaffinoma

Miscellaneous
chordoma
malignant melanoma
embryonic neoplasms, e.g.
nephroblastoma
teratoma
choriocarcinoma

Some benign neoplasms secrete hormones and other humoral substances such as catecholamines and 5-hydroxytryptamine; the endocrine or chemical secretion may lead to a characteristic clinical syndrome. Thus, eosinophilic adenoma of the anterior pituitary may cause gigantism or acromegaly; a β-cell adenoma (insulinoma) of the pancreas may provoke hyperinsulinism; and adenoma of a parathyroid gland may culminate in osteitis fibrosa cystica (p. 154).

Malignant neoplasms

The critical characteristic of a malignant neoplasm is uncontrolled, distant spread. Malignant neoplasms invade and destroy host tissue locally, and extend directly and by metastasis to a wide variety of remote anatomical sites.

Malignant neoplasms are composed of cells that have lost some or most of their resemblance to the structure and function of the parent tissue. The growth of malignant neoplasms is usually rapid. Mitotic figures are seen frequently: many are abnormal. There is aneuploidy (p. 53). In the absence of effective treatment, the outcome of the growth of a malignant neoplasm is death, the result of injury to essential structures such as brain, liver or lung or of secondary haemorrhage, ulceration or infection.

Malignant neoplasms often but not always retain structural, antigenic or functional characteristics that allow them to be classified according to the tissue or organ of origin (Table 17). Malignant neoplasms of epithelia are **carcinomas**. They are much more common than malignant neoplasms of mesenchymal connective tissues, the **sarcomas**, and of those of the haemopoietic and lymphoreticular tissues, the **leukaemias** (p. 130) and **lymphomas** (p. 134). Nevertheless, many malignant neoplasms display so few of the features of any normal tissue that they can only be described as **undifferentiated** and anaplastic. Under these circumstances, the pathologist can offer only limited guidance to the surgeon. The advent of EM in diagnosis and the use of labelled antibodies to identify neoplastic antigens and markers means that the proportion of neoplasms categorized as 'undifferentiated' is diminishing.

The abnormalities of cell behaviour which determine the pattern of growth of a malignant neoplasm include (1) loss of normal contact inhibition of cell growth; (2) loss of the regulation of cell growth and synthesis by feedback inhibition and (3) loss of the regulation of cell motility.

Embryonic neoplasms
Embryonic neoplasms arise during embryonic, fetal or postnatal development; they derive from organ rudiments while these are still immature. They should be distinguished from teratomas.

Examples of embryonic tumours include:

Neuroblastoma of the adrenal medulla
Medulloblastoma of the cerebellum
Retinoblastoma of the retina
Nephroblastoma of the kidney (Wilms' tumour: p. 201).

Mixed neoplasms
A mixed neoplasm is composed of cells of two or more kinds of neoplastic tissue. In a fibroadenoma of breast, for example, there is abnormal growth both of epithelial and of connective tissue. Even more complex arrangements are found in the rare mixed neoplasms of adult uterus and thyroid, so that in the malignant mixed mesodermal neoplasm of the uterus, striated muscle, cartilage and epithelial components are present: the metastases may be carcinomatous or sarcomatous.

Some embryonic neoplasms also display divergent differentiation, forming tissues not normally present in the part or organ. Rhabdomyoblasts comprise an important element of the embryonic neoplasm of the kidney, Wilms' tumour (p. 201). By contrast, the neoplasm that was formerly called mixed tumour (neoplasm) of the salivary glands is now believed to be wholly epithelial and is therefore named pleomorphic salivary-gland adenoma.

Teratomas
Teratomas are neoplasms formed of two or more tissues foreign to those in which the neoplasm arises. Teratomas are distinct from but may superficially resemble non-neoplastic aberrations of development such as heterotopic tissues and conjoined ('Siamese') twins. The diversity of the

tissues of a teratoma demonstrate that the neoplasm is not the result of metaplasia from organs and tissues such as the ovary, testis, mediastinum, retroperitoneal, presacral and coccygeal tissues that are the sites in which teratomas most frequently arise.

Nerve damage

The nature of the damage to a nerve depends upon the type of injury which there may have been: contusion, compression, stretching or laceration. Each injury may occur with or without complete disruption: the simplest is **neuropraxia** with no anatomical disruption. After injury, there is a period in which axons are unable to re-establish normal membrane potentials. Complete recovery of function can be expected within 50–100 days.

Degeneration
Following disruption of an axon (axonolysis), the axis cylinder swells. The myelin fragments and is ingested by phagocytes. In the segment distal to the injury these changes are known as **Wallerian degeneration**. In myelinated fibres, degeneration extends proximally to the first node of Ranvier. At the same time, the nerve cell undergoes chromatolysis: the Nissl granules disappear, a change shown by EM to be a loss of endoplasmic reticulum. Lysis of the whole cell is **neurolysis**.

Regeneration
Regeneration occurs as neurofibrils emerge from the proximal end of the injured axon and grow into the regenerated distal sheath. The rate of growth is about 1 mm/day. Many or all of the fibrils fail to reach their appropriate end organ. If the severed ends of the injured nerve are widely separated, regeneration is slow or impossible. Fibrous tissue proliferates and forms a **traumatic neuroma**. Recovery is better in purely motor or purely sensory nerves: it is more likely that each proliferating fibril will reach an appropriate end organ. Recovery in a mixed nerve is often poor since motor nerve neurofibrils may grow down sensory sheaths and vice versa.

In surgical treatment, careful apposition of the nerve endings using an operating microscope gives the best results. Autografts offer an alternative. Grafting may be as beneficial as resuture if only small segments are replaced in either purely motor or purely sensory nerves.

Oedema

Oedema is the presence of excessive fluid in the intercellular, extracellular and interstitial tissue spaces, due to the increased escape of fluid from capillaries and venules. Oedema may be localized or generalized. Excess fluid leaves the blood vessels when the factors described by Starling's hypothesis are disturbed.

Ascites Ascites is the accumulation of excess fluid within the peritoneal cavity as the result of exudation or transudation. The corresponding terms for the pericardial and pleural cavities are **hydropericardium** or pericardial effusion, and **hydrothorax** or pleural effusion, respectively.

There are two categories of oedema.

In the first, a **transudate**, the permeability of the vessel walls is unchanged. The increased escape of fluid is due to an increase in the pressure difference between blood pressure and plasma osmotic pressure at the arterial end of the capillary, or to a decrease in the difference at the venous end of the capillary. Examples include cardiac failure and nutritional oedema. The accumulated fluid has a low protein content.

In the second, an **exudate** (p. 117), the permeability of the small blood vessels to protein, particularly to albumin, is increased because of inflammation, injury or metabolic disorder. The ratio between arterial and venous blood pressure and plasma osmotic pressure remain unchanged.

There are occasions, as in the tissue hypoxia of congestive cardiac failure, when both categories of oedema coexist. Other changes such as secondary hyperaldosteronism (p. 5) also play a simultaneous part in the redistribution of fluid.

Causes   The common causes of oedema include (a) increased capillary permeability to protein, as in acute inflammation, (b) increased venous (and thus capillary) hydrostatic pressure, as in cardiac failure (when the oedema is generalized) or in venous thrombosis of a limb, (when it is localized), (c) lymphatic obstruction, such as occurs after radical mastectomy or in the worm infestation of filariasis, (d) nutritional oedema and the oedema of the nephrotic syndrome, when plasma albumin concentrations fall, and (e) pulmonary oedema, in which increased pulmonary venous pressure due, for example, to left ventricular heart failure, vasoconstricting agents and neurogenic factors are all active.

Operating theatres

Modern operating theatres are designed so that microbiological contamination of sterile areas is reduced to a minimum. Entering a theatre suite, all staff change into clean clothes and wear clean caps to cover their hair. Patients are transferred across a physical barrier from the trolley used to transport them from the ward, to another, clean trolley that never leaves the theatre suite. Dirty instruments, gowns, drapes and pathological specimens are taken from the theatre complex by a different route from that used for patients and surgical staff.

The most important feature of operating theatre design is the ventilation system. Air from outside the hospital is pumped into the operating theatre after passing through filters that remove bacteria. There should be a smooth, orderly (laminar) flow of air with complete replacement of the whole air volume, i.e. displacement of contaminated air, at 5–10 minute intervals. Downward displacement of air is more effective than lateral displacement in minimizing the dispersion of bacteria and dust. The air should be heated or cooled, saturated with water vapour or dehumidified to maintain an environment of ~20 °C and 40–60 per cent humidity; this is appropriate for patients, but sometimes uncomfortable for staff. Thermoregulation in anaesthetized patients is paralysed: the patient loses heat and fluid to the environment.

When operating on patients in whom wound infection is likely to prove particularly devastating e.g. in hip replacements, specially designed ultra-clean air enclosures or transparent plastic envelopes are used to isolate the wound from all personnel except the surgeons.

Opsonins

Opsonins are IgG antibodies against the antigens of bacterial capsules or cell walls.

Opsonins prepare bacteria for phagocytosis. They are particularly effective against extracellular pyogenic micro-organisms, especially those, such as *Streptococcus pneumoniae*, that are encapsulated. Neutrophil granulocytes and macrophages identify the free Fc part of the opsonizing antibodies (p. 109) that are attached to the bacterium, because of Fc receptors on their surfaces. Some bacteria possess mechanisms to counter opsonization. Thus the opsonization of *Staphylococcus aureus* can be prevented by a wall component, **protein A**, that blocks the free Fc end of the antibody molecule.

Organization

Organization is the conversion to and replacement of an inflammatory exudate or of thrombus, by granulation tissue (p. 89). Organization, with the subsequent formation of scar tissue, bands and adhesions, is a feature of healing by fibrous repair.

Osteomalacia/rickets

Osteomalacia is inadequate mineralization of bone matrix (osteoid) formed normally and in normal amounts. Before the growth of bone ceases and while endochondral ossification continues, the effects of inadequate mineralization are complex and the disease is called **rickets**. The causes of osteomalacia/rickets are (1) inadequate dietary vitamin D and calcium, (2) defective absorption of vitamin D, or (3) defective utilization of vitamin D. Osteomalacia affects four per cent of the old people of Western Europe. In the old, and in infancy, dietary deficiencies can be easily corrected. However, osteomalacia/rickets can be an intractable problem in countries where social and religious practices prevent exposure to sunlight, a source for the synthesis of a vitamin D in the skin (p. 200).

Osteomalacia is sensitively diagnosed by biopsy of the iliac crest. The seams of non-mineralized bone can be measured and the response to treatment followed closely. Osteoid can be labelled and bone growth measured by a preliminary dose of the fluorescent antibiotic tetracycline, which binds to osteoid (and dentine). The serum concentrations of calcium and phosphate are low but serum alkaline phosphatase activity is elevated. A particular form of osteomalacia has complicated renal dialysis with soft water containing aluminium, and osteomalacia is one of several forms of renal bone disease.

Osteomalacic bone is weak. Pathological fracture occurs. Zones of incomplete pseudofracture, Looser's zones, detectable in the bone cortex by x-ray, are characteristic.

Osteomyelitis

Osteomyelitis is infection of the medullary cavity of bone. The term is taken to mean any form of bone infection.

The causative organism in idiopathic disease is usually *Staphylococcus aureus*. Characteristically, *Staph. aureus* gains access to the blood stream of a child or adolescent from a small lesion such as a boil. The skin lesion may not be detected. Bacteria lodge in the end-arteries of metaphyses such as those of the femur or tibia. An abscess forms. Infection with *Pseudomonas aeruginosa* may follow compound fracture in road-traffic accidents. Many other bacteria have been implicated, and *Haemophilus* is a recognized agent in children. *Mycobacterium tuberculosis* evokes a particular form of osteomyelitis of the vertebral bodies, and of bone near infected joints. Tuberculosis (p. 190) of bone is frequently termed osteitis rather than osteomyelitis and is sometimes given special designations such as **Pott's* disease**, tuberculous vertebral osteitis. Among the other bacteria associated with osteomyelitis are *Brucella abortus* and Salmonella species including *Salm. typhi*. Infection is occasionally caused by fungi, viruses and other parasites.

In the absence of antibiotic treatment, bone necrosis culminates in the formation of a **sequestrum**. Extension of infection to the periosteal surface provokes periosteal new bone formation and the development of an enveloping **involucrum**. Infection rarely spreads through the epiphysis to the nearby joint. Among the complications of persistent and inadequately treated disease is amyloidosis.

Osteoporosis

Ostepoporosis is a reduction in the density of bone: unlike osteomalacia (p. 151) the bone formed is fully mineralized.

Throughout life, bone is continually lost and replaced. The balance of this daily turnover becomes negative in the most common forms of osteoporosis: imperceptibly, loss exceeds formation. Since there is neither fault in calcium metabolism nor abnormally raised bone destruction, serum concentrations of calcium, phosphate and alkaline phosphatase are normal and there is no demonstrable increase in the excretion of calcium.

The most common categories of osteoporosis are those accompanying old

---

*Percival Pott (see also p. 46n), the greatest surgeon of his time, gave a classical description (1779) of spinal curvature due to tuberculous osteitis, but did not himself recognise its tuberculous nature.

age in both sexes (senile osteoporosis), those occurring in women after the menopause (postmenopausal osteoporosis) and those attributable to the influence of drugs such as corticosteroids and to diseases such as rheumatoid arthritis. However, osteoporosis is also a result of endocrine diseases such as hyperthyroidism and Cushing's syndrome; the disorder develops in the course of protein deficiency and in heritable diseases of bone such as osteogenesis imperfecta.

The loss of strength of osteoporotic bone means that pathological fracture is commonplace: the femoral neck and the vertebrae are vulnerable. Radiological diagnosis is insensitive: a loss of about 25 per cent of bone mass is the smallest recognizable change. Iliac-crest biopsy or assessment by nuclear magnetic resonance are more sensitive. The histological changes are pathognomonic.

The term osteoporosis is also used when neoplasms such as metastatic carcinoma, leukaemia, or myeloma, destroy bone directly. In contrast to idiopathic and senile osteoporosis there is hypercalcaemia and an increased urinary loss of calcium and hydroxyproline.

Paget's disease of bone'

Paget's* disease of bone, osteitis deformans, is a frequent **local** disorder, affecting single or multiple islands of cranial, pelvic, tibial or femoral bone in old persons. Rarely, the disorder is **generalized**. Excess local bone formation, indicated by high vascularity and the presence of many osteoblasts, is accompanied by vigorous reabsorption by the numerous osteoclasts. The result is the formation of zones of heavy, dense bone with a mosaic pattern and low mechanical strength.

Paget's disease is the most common known cause of osteogenic sarcoma. Where limb blood flow is very large, high-output cardiac failure may develop.

The cause of Paget's disease remains obscure; paramyxovirus infection, autoimmunity and disordered endocrine regulation of bone growth have been considered. There is a beneficial response to therapeutic calcitonin.

Paget's disease of breast

Paget's† disease of the female breast is a chronic eczema-like lesion of the nipple and areola associated with the presence of an intraduct carcinoma. Paget's disease of the breast accounts for less than five per cent of all mammary carcinomas and occurs in relatively elderly subjects. The tissue change that causes the eczematous reaction is the presence in the epidermis of large, pale vacuolated malignant (Paget) cells with hyperchromatic nuclei. The Paget cells are frequently seen to be undergoing mitotic division. It is

---

*Sir James Paget, *Bart.*, (p. 1814–1899) described osteitis deformans, Paget's disease of bone, in 1877. Paget was a keen observer and a fine surgical pathologist. He identified the worm *Trichinella spiralis* in muscle that he was dissecting as a first-year student.
†Sir James Paget, also described the skin changes of intraduct carcinoma of the breast, Paget's disease of the nipple, in 1874.

believed that they are intra-epidermal metastases from the underlying carcinoma. Histologically, Paget's disease of the breast must be differentiated from carcinoma-in-situ and from intra-epithelial malignant melanoma.

Papilloma

A papilloma is a nipple-shaped or stalked benign neoplasm of epithelium. Papillomas may be villous (seaweed-like) as in the urinary bladder, or less prominent (sessile), as on the weight-bearing skin.

The term 'papillary' is applied to other structures, including carcinomas, to describe their macroscopic shape and histological pattern; examples include papillary cystadenocarcinoma of the ovary and papillary carcinoma of the thyroid.

See Adenoma (p. 4)
   Papillary adenoma (p. 158)
   Polyp (p. 158).

Parasites

Parasites are animals or plants which live in or upon another organism, the host, and draw their nutritional requirements directly from it without bestowing benefit.

Parathyroid disease

Hyperparathyroidism
The parathyroid glands are sites for hyperplasia, adenoma or primary carcinoma.

Hyperplasia is the most common cause of **primary hyperparathyroidism**. The aetiology is unknown. Hyperparathyroidism also results from the growth of a single, functioning adenoma or, rarely, from a functioning carcinoma. Primary hyperparathyroidism may also be caused by the inappropriate secretion of excess parathormone from functioning, nonparathyroid tumours (p. 101). The effect is upon the skeleton. If diagnosis is delayed, osteoporosis and osteitis fibrosa cystica may develop with ectopic calcification: it is common in renal tubules and constitutes a form of nephrocalcinosis. Renal calculi, peptic ulceration and pancreatitis are frequent.

Secondary hyperparathyroidism arises as a result of hypocalcaemia produced by another disease such as chronic renal disease with hyperphosphataemia. There is depression of the concentration of serum Ca^{2+} and hyperplasia of the parathyroid glands. Occasionally, they become autonomous. Adenomata may develop within the enlarged glands, so that these patients are said to suffer from **tertiary hyperparathyroidism**. The skeletal changes of the primary, secondary and tertiary forms are identical.

Hypoparathyroidism
The parathyroid glands may be excised by accident, at thyroidectomy. Tetany (p. 182) due to hypocalcaemia, is one result. Atrophy or hypoplasia are rare.

Phagocytosis

Phagocytosis is the ingestion, by any living cell, of foreign or of altered, autologous solids; it is a common characteristic of macrophages (p. 136) and neutrophil polymorphs (p. 129). Cells in which phagocytosis is a predominant characteristic are **phagocytes**.

The most common materials ingested by phagocytosis are old red blood cells (in the spleen), injured or anoxic body cells, bacteria, immune complexes, and foreign bodies ranging from insoluble fibres, polymers and metals to crystals (p. 68).

The double-layered cell wall of a phagocyte throws out a pseudopod-like process which closes around an object such as a bacterium to form a vacuole, the **phagosome** (p. 136). This process of ingestion is **endocytosis**. Digestion of the engulfed solid takes place within the phagosome. The products of digestion are later excreted from the cell by **exocytosis**, a process of 'reversed phagocytosis'. If digestion is incomplete, residual dead or living objects may remain within the phagocyte indefinitely. The carbon that accumulates in lung lymphoid tissue originates in this way, rendering the pulmonary and lymphoid tissues of city dwellers permanently grey-black.

Pigmentation

Pigmentation is the coloration or discoloration of tissues by the formation or deposition of a coloured substance. Pigmentation may be generalized or localized. The physiological pigments are organic compounds: they often contain metals such as iron or copper.

Generalized, physiological yellow, brown or black skin pigmentation is usually racial; there is much melanin in the basal layer of the epidermis. Generalized pigmentation is exaggerated in causcasian races by UVL and is common in pregnancy (**chloasma**). The prolonged, excessive ingestion of dietary articles such as carrots can result in a temporary, yellow skin coloration due to carotene.

Localized melanin pigmentation is recognized in the axillary and perineal skin and in the facial skin of white persons exposed to sunlight.

Depigmentation
Generalized lack of pigment is characteristic of albinism (p. 5): there is a genetic deficiency of tyrosinase.

Localized depigmentation, **vitiligo**, is the focal absence of melanocytes.

Pigmentation diseases

Abnormal pigmentation may be genetic or environmental in origin, and generalized or localized in distribution. There may be:

1. Excess production of melanin due to:
(a) Solar or artificial UV radiation. The skin darkens and freckles appear. The effects are precancerous.

(b) X- and γ-rays. After a long latent period, excess melanin forms.

(c) Heat (infra-red radiation). Local pigmentation of the face develops in furnacemen. A similar change occurs in the shins of elderly women.
(d) Hypoadrenocorticalism (p. 66) or hyperadrenocorticalism (p. 66).
(e) Naevi (p. 144) and malignant melanomas (p. 138).
(f) Neurofibromatosis.
(g) The Peutz–Jegher syndrome (p. 159).

2. Excess production or accumulation of derivatives of haemoglobin due to:

(a) Haemosiderosis. Excess iron is stored as the brown pigment haemosiderin. Generalized haemosiderosis can follow parenteral iron therapy, multiple transfusions of blood and haemolysis (p. 91). In haemochromatosis some of the pigment is haemosiderin, some lipofuscin and some melanin. Localized aggregates occur in contusions (p. 66).
(b) Jaundice (p. 125).
(c) Porphyria. Porphyrins are tetrapyrroles, natural components of haemoglobin. Small quantities of iron-free porphyrins are normally present in the plasma and the urine. In porphyria, abnormal quantities are formed due to an inborn error of metabolism, and the skin becomes photosensitive. If the urine is left standing it turns a very deep red colour. Porphyria may be acquired as a consequence of ingestion of some metals, organic agents and drugs.
(d) Carboxyhaemoglobin and methaemoglobin change the colour of the blood to a persistent bright pink and to dull blue respectively. The tissues are correspondingly discoloured.

3. Ingestion, inhalation, or injection of foreign organic or inorganic compounds

Organic   For example the prolonged exposure of the skin to trinitrotoluene (TNT) during the manufacture of this explosive.

Inorganic   For example the following:
Carbon:	anthracosis of the lungs of city dwellers and coal workers following inhalation.
Iron:	siderosis of the lungs of iron-ore miners following inhalation.
Bismuth:	discoloration of the small intestine following the ingestion of bismuth-containing medicines.
Mercury and Arsenic:	discoloration of the skin due to prolonged therapeutic administration.
Lead:	plumbism due to the swallowing or inhalation of dry lead paint. A blue line forms at the junction of teeth and gums.
Silver:	argyria, due, e.g. to the prolonged medicinal painting of the mucosae with silver nitrate.
Gold:	chrysiasis caused by numerous injections for rheumatoid arthritis.

Tattooing   This is a Tahitian word, and means the production of indelible markings in the skin, usually as a decorative pattern, by puncturing the skin and inserting pigments such as carbon (black) and mercuric sulphide (red). Tattooing also occurs around entry wounds caused by gunshots at close range.

Plasma cells

Plasma cells are mature antibody-secreting cells. They are derived from activated B lymphocytes (p. 133). The less mature, antibody-forming cells are plasmablasts.

Morphologically, plasma cells are 15–20 μm in diameter, round or ovoid. They have eccentric nuclei which, in paraffin sections, display peripheral clumps of nuclear chromatin, giving a cartwheel appearance. There is a basophilic cytoplasm containing many ribosomes and much rough endoplasmic reticulum. A large Golgi vacuole is prominent.

Functionally, the formation of large numbers of plasma cells, plasmacytosis, is characteristic of the tissue reactions in chronic inflammatory diseases such as rheumatoid synovitis and syphilis, in both of which high titres of antibody are encountered. However, plasmacytosis is also found at sites of local injury to adipose tissue.

See Lymphocytes (p. 133)
Myeloma (p. 143).

Platelets

Platelets are convex, anucleate cells, 2–5 μm in diameter. They are formed by the disintegration of megakaryocytes. Each megakaryocyte may give rise to more than 3000 platelets. Normally there are 150–400 × 10^9 platelets/l in blood; they are phagocytic and have granules that are lysosomes, and dense bodies containing calcium, ADP and 5–HT. The platelet membrane has an associated phospholipid, platelet factor 3, part of the blood clotting mechanism. Platelets are vigorously contractile, 15–20 per cent of their protein being actomyosin.

Platelets have two distinct haemostatic functions: the prevention of leakage of red cells from sites of minor endothelial damage and the formation of thrombus (p. 183). Platelets can be given in concentrated suspension, by transfusion. Platelet concentrates are prepared fresh, since stored platelets live less than 24 hours.

See Thrombocytopenia (p. 60)
Thrombocythaemia (p. 61).

Polycythaemia

Polycythaemia is an abnormal increase in the number of circulating red blood cells in excess of 7 × 10^9/l; there is a rise both in total blood volume and in the packed cell volume (PCV) which may be as high as 60 per cent. There is consequently an increase in haemoglobin concentration to a level of more than 18 g/dl. Because of the increased proportion of red blood cells, blood viscosity is high; sludging occurs and there is an abnormal tendency to thrombosis.

Polycythaemia may arise without demonstrable cause: it is then described as **primary** or true polycythaemia (**polycythaemia vera**). **Secondary** polycythaemia occurs when there is a persistent stimulus to new red blood-cell formation caused by life at high altitude, by chronic heart failure, by chronic respiratory disease, by the persistent binding of carbon monoxide to haemoglobin in heavy smokers, or by excess secretion of erythropoietin by a renal neoplasm.

The imprecise term 'relative polycythaemia' is occasionally used to describe the increased proportion of red blood cells, the PCV, that is a transient result of fluid loss due to burns or fulminating gastroenteritis. There is no increase and there may, indeed, be a decrease in total blood volume and the disorder is better described as **haemoconcentration**.

Polyp

A polyp is a pedunculated cell mass arising from an epithelial surface as a result of neoplasia, metaplasia or inflammation; some polyps are hamartomas. Most polyps are gastrointestinal and neoplastic. When the surface of a polyp forms finger-like processes, the polyp is said to be **villous**.

The majority of polyps are benign; a few are malignant. It is important that surgeon and pathologist should agree the criteria used to define malignant change. There is an initial zone of cellular atypia. Later, epithelial cells are judged to be neoplastic because they have extended through the muscularis mucosae and invaded the connective tissue stalk of the polyp. Carcinoma of the colon is much more common in those who have large benign intestinal polyps than in those who have not. There is evidence that many if not all carcinomas of the large intestine arise in benign polyps.

Pseudopolyp

Pseudopolyps are polyp-like masses of vascular granulation tissue and glandular crypts, partly or wholly covered by hyperplastic colonic epithelium. The pseudopolyps, long and pendulous or shorter and broad, are conspicuous, very numerous and characteristic in ulcerative colitis. Unlike the true adenomatous polyp, there is no distinction between the structure of the body of the pseudopolyp and the stalk. Both lesions may occur together.

Polyposis

Polyposis is the simultaneous occurrence of many polyps. In the gastrointestinal tract several hundred may coexist.

Familial (adenomatous) polyposis coli   This is inherited as a Mendelian dominant characteristic with incomplete penetrance. It is transmitted by either sex. In this condition there may be as many as several thousand or as few as 200 polyps throughout the large intestine; most are in the rectum. In familial polyposis, the lesions are rarely detected before the age of 10 years. Their presence is precancerous and 80 per cent of subjects with familial polyposis develop malignant neoplasms. Carcinoma is diagnosed on average

at the age of 40 years in subjects with familial polyposis coli compared with a mean age of 60 years in the general population.

Gardner's syndrome (p. 86)   This is an unusual variant of familial adenomatous polyposis.

Peutz–Jegher syndrome   This syndrome arises in young, female brunettes. There is melanin pigmentation of the mucosae, for example of the mouth, and numerous polyps throughout the length of the gastrointestinal tract. The polyps are hamartomas: they are recognized in adolescence or early adult life and cause recurrent intussusception.

Potassium depletion

Potassium (K) depletion is characteristic of vomiting, aspiration and severe diarrhoea, and develops after surgical operations or other injury, and in starvation. Much potassium may be lost from a villous papilloma of the large intestine (p. 154).

The body of a healthy 70 kg male contains approximately 3000 mmol of potassium (K) within the cells but only 60 mmol outside the cells: the extracellular concentration of K does not indicate total body K content. Potassium has profound effects upon neuromuscular conductivity. Muscular weakness develops when the serum K concentration falls to about 2.5 mmol/l. Because of its low concentration in the extracellular fluid, the rapid loss of moderate amounts of potassium soon causes symptoms of K depletion. Patients suffering from villous papilloma of the large bowel may lose up to three litres of mucus per day, containing 120 mmol/l of K. Following operation or injury (p. 140) the urinary excretion increases from about 50 mmol/day to 100 mmol or more. The potassium/nitrogen ratio in muscle is 3 mmol K/gN; after surgical operation, the urinary excretion is 5–15 mmol K/gN. During starvation, the urinary K/N ratio is similar to that in muscle.

See Metabolic response to trauma (p. 140)

Precancer

A precancerous state is one in which the invasive and metastatic changes of cancer have not occurred; these changes may be manifest if appropriate circumstances arise. The precancerous condition may be inherited, e.g. multiple polyposis of the colon (p. 158). Alternatively, precancer may be due to environmental agents. Thus, permanent changes in genetic structure may be caused by subcarcinogenic doses of ionizing radiation (p. 121) or by a chemical that is an initiator (p. 45), not a promoter of cancer.

Precancerous states are distinguished from carcinoma-in-situ (p. 49) in which a cancer has formed but has not yet begun to invade.

see Carcinogenesis (p. 45).

Precipitation – precipitin test

Precipitation is an immunological phenomenon observed when a solution of antigen reacts with a solution of antibody in a tube. The molecules combine to form deposits of protein complexes. By varying the amount of antigen added, the proportion of antigen to antibody that yields the largest precipitate is found; this is the **optimal proportion**. The amount of protein deposited can be measured. The precipitin test is used by forensic scientists to search for antigens in stains.

Agar precipitation   A similar test can be carried out in agar gel. Opaque precipitin lines form in the gel and indicate where serum antibody is reacting in optimal proportions with known antigen, or where unknown antigen is reacting with known antibody. Such an immunodiffusion test, using small wells cut in an agar layer on a microscopic slide, is used to identify HbsAg in human serum. As a tube test, immunodiffusion provides a relatively insensitive means of recognizing types and strains of bacteria, fungi and viruses such as meningococci and histoplasma.

Immunoelectrophoresis   This is a further modification in which serum proteins are separated on a glass slide by an electric current and identified by the addition of antiserum to produce precipitation. The precipitated complexes are stained and their pattern identified. Diagnostic patterns are given by myeloma proteins and in disorders such as aspergillosis.

Prostheses

Prostheses are artificial parts. They are made from a wide variety of materials including metals, plastics, ceramics and glass. No foreign substance introduced into the body is entirely inert: all foreign bodies provoke inflammation of varying severity. Typically, there is a chronic response with macrophages and giant cells predominating. The severity of the response is determined by the physical state of the substance as well as its chemical nature. Highly polished surfaces produce less reaction than rough surfaces. Brisk inflammatory responses are provoked by powders. Adjacent metal components must be of the same composition; an electrochemical potential may be established between metals of differing composition with subsequent damage both to the components and to the nearby tissue.

Metals
Stainless steel, vitallium (an alloy of cobalt, chromium and molybdenum) and tantalum are commonly used: they are almost inert, and are employed in orthopaedics for plates, pins and the components of arthroplasties. Formerly these metals were used as mesh for the repair of hernias: the wire often fractured after some months but by then its tensile strength was no longer required. Other more expensive alloys are being used more frequently for arthroplasty: all give rise to microscopic particles that initiate a characteristic macrophage response.

Plastics
Polytetrafluoroethylene (PTFE, Teflon) is an inert, rigid and unwettable plastic often used to make intravenous cannulae. Polyethylene and polypropylene are similar plastics. Dacron resembles Teflon but its wettable surface makes it more suitable for arterial prostheses. Ivalon sponge produces a severe reaction and the resulting fibrosis can be used to treat rectal prolapse.

Siliconized rubbers (Silastic)
Although more expensive than the plastics, siliconized rubber materials are inert and soft. Tube drains, urinary and intravenous catheters, and mammary implants containing liquid silicon are used with increasing frequency.

Ceramics
Ceramics are finding an increasing place in arthroplasty but glass is no longer used for this purpose and foreign-body reactions to glass or glass fibre are now usually accidental or occupational.

Carbon fibre
Carbon fibre has been used successfully to repair tendons and ligaments. It is a strong and relatively inert material.

Protozoa

The protozoa are unicellular animals with a range of functions comparable to those of the metazoa. Individual parts of the cell of a protozoon serve special purposes; although therefore it is convenient to group the protozoa as flagellates, amoebae, sporozoa and ciliates, their taxonomic classification is complex. In man, protozoa are responsible for worldwide endemic diseases of which many have surgical significance. Examples are as follows.

Malaria
Plasmodium falciparum malaria may simulate many other febrile diseases. Several cases of cerebral malaria occur in the UK each year in travellers returning from abroad. Blackwater fever, with renal tubular obstruction, results from sudden massive haemolysis.

Trypanosomiasis
Trypanosoma cruzi causes Chagas' disease in Central and South America. Mega-oesophagus and megacolon are common complications. *Trypanosoma brucei* causes sleeping sickness in sub-Saharan Africa.

Leishmaniasis
Leishmania donovani causes visceral disease of the lymphoid tissues and spleen, and cutaneous and mucosal ulceration in Asia and Africa, in the Mediterranean and in tropical South America.

Amoebiasis

The intestinal pathogen *Entamoeba histolytica* causes amoebic dysentery and liver abscess. A free-living protozoon, *Naegleria fowleri*, has been identified in meningo-encephalitis.

Toxoplasmosis

Toxoplasma gondii infection is widespread but often silent. The central nervous system is vulnerable to intrauterine, transplacental infection. Chorioretinitis is a serious complication. Stillbirth may result. Postnatal infections are mild. Infants can contract the infection from kittens.

Giardiasis

Infection with *Giardia lamblia* is a common hazard of travel in Eastern Europe and South America. The organism is transmitted as cysts. Infection is usually silent but may become chronic and cause intestinal malabsorption and steatorrhoea. The protozoon thrives on the mucosal surface of the duodenum and proximal jejunum where it can be recognized by endoscopic biopsy.

Trichomoniasis

Trichomonas vaginalis is a common cause of silent venereal infection in the female, but acute vaginitis may occur. In the male, infection is symptomless or associated with urethritis.

Pneumocystis infection

Pneumocystis carinii causes a plasma cell pneumonitis in premature infants and in immunosuppressed adults. The infection is encountered in the acquired immunodeficiency syndrome (AIDS) (p. 2).

Pseudarthrosis

A pseudarthrosis is a false joint formed in living bone and connective tissue because of heritable or of acquired disease.

Inherited pseudarthrosis   This is a rare connective-tissue disease.

Acquired pseudarthroses   These may form at sites where the healing of fracture of a long bone is delayed or prevented. The predisposing factors include inadequate immobilization after fracture, impaired local blood supply and the presence of necrotic or foreign tissue.

Pseudomembranous colitis

Treatment with broad-spectrum antibotics may be quickly followed by the explosive onset of a potentially fatal pseudomembranous colitis (PMC). There are focal adherent yellow mucosal plaques, with an exudate of fibrin and inflammatory debris. Untreated, the acute disorder may progress to complete mucosal necrosis.

At first it was believed that the antibiotic destroyed the normal gut bacterial flora, allowing an enormous proliferation of *Staphylococcus aureus*, which in turn could be eradicated by an appropriate antibiotic such as erythromycin.

Now it is clear that the stools of more than 90 per cent of patients with PMC contain *Clostridium difficile* or its exotoxin. PMC usually follows the use of lincomycin and clindamycin but has been observed following the use of the majority of potent systemic antibiotics. *Cl. difficile* is sensitive to vancomycin and this provides effective treatment. However, the way in which *Cl. difficile* exerts its toxic action is not wholly understood. It is important to note that before the antibiotic era major surgical procedures alone could provoke PMC. Surgery can alter the susceptibility of the gut to colonization.

In diagnosis, it is simpler to test the stool for the cytopathic exotoxin of *Cl. difficile* than to culture the organism.

Pseudomyxoma peritonei

In pseudomyxoma peritonei, mucinous material fills the peritoneal cavity. The usual sources are the cells of a mucinous cystadenoma or mucinous cystadenocarcinoma of the ovary; it may also come from rupture of a mucocele of the vermiform appendix. In this condition, non-neoplastic mucin-secreting cells spread throughout the peritoneal cavity where they multiply; they do not invade deeper tissues. The prognosis is poor.

Purpura

Purpura is bleeding into the skin or mucosae. It is caused by deficient numbers of platelets or defective function. The haemorrhages of purpura are petechiae or ecchymoses.

Pus

Pus is the detritus of broken-down tissue together with the pyknotic fragments of nuclear debris. Many dead and some living neutrophil polymorphs are usually present. Occasionally, macrophages are frequent. The causative micro-organisms, parasites, or foreign bodies can often be recognized within the pus.

The appearance of pus is strongly influenced by the nature of the tissue injury. Tuberculous pus, for example, appears like pale cream cheese and is **caseous**. Amoebic pus resembles orange-brown anchovy sauce. Staphylococcal pus is yellow, thick and viscous. Haemolytic streptococcal pus is thin, watery and blood-stained, and the pus in *Pseudomonas aeruginosa* infections is green. Anaerobic organisms often impart a foul smell to pus.

See Abscess (page 1)

Putrefaction

Putrefaction is the decomposition of dead animal and vegetable matter by saprophytic bacteria and other organisms. Enzymatic degradation of protein produces cadaverine, putrescine, trimethyl amine, ammonia, hydrogen sulphide and mercaptans. There are consequently nauseating odours; absorbed, these products are toxic.

See Gangrene (p. 85).

Pyaemia

Pyaemia is the presence and multiplication of pyogenic bacteria in the blood and their carriage by microemboli to other organs. The possibility that pus may actually be present in the blood was disproved by Virchow (p. 183). He showed that what was thought to be pus was in fact numerous leucocytes. The effect of pyaemia is to produce microabscesses distal to the source of the emboli. Thus, **systemic pyaemia** results in abscesses in viscera such as the kidney, whereas **portal pyaemia** leads to abscesses in the liver.

Pyrogens

Pyrogens are substances that produce fever. Some are formed by bacteria. Among the most important are pyrogens produced by water-borne bacteria: they are filtrable and thermo-stable. Others include foreign proteins and an **endogenous pyrogen** produced by polymorphs; it is a lipoprotein and causes the fever that develops during severe, acute inflammation. Endogenous lipoprotein, like other pyrogens, acts on the temperature-regulating centres of the brain.

Raynaud's phenomenon

Raynaud's phenomenon is digital ischaemia due to vascular spasm. When severe and prolonged, infarction of the tips of the digits may occur. Raynaud's phenomenon is often initiated by minor degrees of environmental cold but excess vasoconstriction sufficient to cause Raynaud's phenomenon can occur at a relatively high ambient temperature.

Systemic connective tissue disease, macroglobulinaemia and prolonged occupational exposure to vibration are underlying causes. A comparable form of vascular occlusion may also occur if **cryoglobulins** are formed in excess by multiple myeloma. An occasional response, similar to Raynaud's phenomenon, is the activation of haemagglutinins and haemolysins that are normally inactive at 37 °C. The red blood cells agglutinate in small, peripheral vessels. Haemolysis may then lead to so-called **'cold' haemoglobinuria**.

Regeneration

Regeneration is the repair of an injured part, tissue or cell by the formation of virtually identical structures.

Regeneration is most complete and the capacity for reformation greatest in simple creatures such as the newt, where a whole amputated limb can be manufactured. In man regeneration is vigorous in highly vascular tissue such as facial skin, liver, renal tubules, bone, gut and stomach and in haemopoietic bone marrow. It is limited in skeletal muscle, arterial media and pretibial skin, and does not occur in the neurones of the central nervous system, the cornea and hyaline cartilage. Where regeneration is not possible in a living part, **repair** takes place by the formation of a substitute vascular connective tissue, which ultimately becomes collagenous fibrous tissue (p. 79).

In some cases (for example, the adrenal cortex and the renal proximal convoluted tubules) destruction or removal of one of two paired organs very quickly provokes a peak of mitotic activity in the cells of the remaining organ. The total mass of the combined, paired organs, is restored within four weeks, provided anterior pituitary function is maintained.

Renal cortical necrosis

In a small group of patients who die in shock, the kidneys show a dramatic change in colour: each cortex is intensely pale and has undergone massive, bilateral infarction. The medullae are spared and appear normal. The appearances are absolutely distinct from the ill-defined pallor of acute renal tubular necrosis (p. 3), a much more frequent but less severe and reversible complication of shock.

In classical form, bilateral renal cortical necrosis is seen in uncontrolled eclampsia. The small renal veins are blocked by fibrin plugs. The cause of this change is unknown but there is an association with Gram-negative bacterial infection. The changes of renal cortical necrosis are very similar to those of the experimental generalized Shwartzman phenomenon (p. 171)

Resistance to infection

Resistance to bacterial and viral infections may be natural or acquired. Some races appear to be susceptible to agents such as *Mycobacterium tuberculosis*, but poverty, overcrowding, malnutrition and lack of health care and vaccination are among factors that influence this assessment. Geographical isolation can prevent exposure to common infective agents such as measles virus so that, when the susceptible population is exposed to the micro-organism, a devastating epidemic may result.

Non-specific resistance   Virulent, pathogenic micro-organisms encounter cell surfaces and cells. Inflammation normally results and the inflammatory response (p. 116) can therefore be said to provide a first line of host defence: the responses are sometimes characteristic of particular bacteria or viruses, and the local reactions to *Streptococcus pyogenes* and *Herpes simplex* provide examples. In systemic infection, pyrexia can impede bacterial multiplication. Among the non-specific agents providing resistance to viral infection are the interferons (p. 119).

Specific resistance   Specific resistance is given by the immune mechanism (p. 108). Immunity may be active or passive. The mechanisms of active immunity appear less effective in the premature or small infant and in the aged than in normal adults.

Resistance to infection is impaired when two or more infections coincide; when the immune mechanism is imperfect or is compromised; and when dehydration, shock, tissue injury and mechanical factors contribute to abnormal organ function.

Reticuloendothelial system

The reticuloendothelial system (RES) is a family of cells, widely distributed throughout the body, and sharing the properties of phagocytosis and intravital staining. RES cells derive from primitive reticulum cells which differentiate in the bone marrow to become the precursors of the red and white blood cells and platelet series. RES cells are grouped in organs such as the spleen but they are also dispersed in vascular and stromal tissues. The cells of the RES can therefore be said to be intravascular or extravascular. The **intravascular** cells include the blood monocytes and the endothelial cells of the liver capillaries (Kupffer cells), lymph node sinuses, splenic sinuses, and the adrenal and hypophyseal capillaries. The **extravascular** cells are the macrophages of the connective tissues; these cells may be 'fixed' in location or may 'wander' freely as they enter the tissues from the blood.

Functions of the RES

1. Phagocytosis   The destruction of aged normal red blood cells is a function of splenic RES cells; abnormal red cells such as those of congenital spherocytosis (p. 91), sickle-cell anaemia and malaria are similarly treated. The fixed and wandering tissue macrophages engulf and destroy micro-organisms and foreign bodies as part of a defence against infection and injury; they also phagocytose particulate contrast media and dyes.

2. Immune response   Foreign antigens are phagocytosed by macrophages, catabolized and presented to lymphocytes with which they co-operate to promote cell-mediated or humoral immunity. This property of antigen localization is not shared by the vascular endothelial cells of the RES. The term **mononuclear phagocyte system** (p. 136) has therefore been proposed to described that part of the RES concerned with the immune response.

3. Proliferation   Exposed to micro-organisms, foreign material and carcinogens, the RES is prone to proliferate reactively or by neoplasia. The response may be generalized, as in sarcoidosis, lymphoblastic lymphoma or the storage diseases; or localized, as in granulomatous infection, fibrous histiocytoma or xanthoma.

Ribonucleic acid (RNA)

RNA is a very long, thin, chain-like molecule; it closely resembles DNA (p. 70) but is usually present as a single helical chain. RNA is formed of four nucleotides in which the constituent bases are linked to the sugar ribose. Like DNA, three of these bases are adenine, guanine and cytosine. Whereas DNA contains thymine, in RNA the fourth base is uracil.

The nucleotide sequences of DNA and RNA are complementary. Cells contain several kinds of RNA, each with a different function.

RNA is present both in nuclei, where it constitutes much of the **nucleolus**, and in the cytoplasm as the **ribosomes**. Inherited information, incorporated in the genetic code of nuclear DNA, is conveyed from the nucleus to the cytoplasm by **messenger RNA** (mRNA). **Transfer RNA** (tRNA) then brings individual amino acids to the correct assembly points on the membranes of the endoplasmic reticulum where peptide and protein synthesis take place.

Both mRNA and tRNA are crucial to the exact synthesis of all macro-molecular structures, including enzymic and structural proteins.

Saprophyte

A saprophyte is a vegetative organism such as a bacterium that survives on dead or decaying matter.

Sarcoid

Sarcoid* is a descriptive term for a granuloma, composed of epithelioid-like mononuclear cells arranged in follicles but without the caseous necrotic centre characteristic of tuberculosis. The granuloma often contains Schaumann bodies, and multinucleate giant cells that may be very large. There is no doubly-refractile foreign material and the lesion is sterile. **Sarcoidosis** is a local or widespread, multisystem disease. The lymph nodes are firm, grey-pink and rubbery in consistency. The cause(s) are not known. Hypersensitivity to mycobacteria, mineral dusts and pine pollen are among the agents proposed. The intradermal Kveim test is often positive, and there may be hypercalcaemia because sarcoidosis stimulates vitamin D activity.

Sarcoma

A sarcoma* is a malignant neoplasm of mesenchymal tissue. Suffixes such as fibro-, chondro-, angio-, and myxo- are added to indicate the differentiation shown by the neoplastic cells and demonstrated by the extracellular matrix that is formed. When more than one extracellular matrix material is present, the neoplasm is designated by the most mature material seen. Thus, even minute islands of osteoid are sufficient to categorize a mainly collagenous neoplasm as an osteogenic sarcoma.

Sarcomas have a solid, flesh-like structure with many small, thin-walled blood vessels. The neoplastic cells lie close to the basement membrane of these vessels and gain ready access to the circulation. Consequently, blood-borne metastasis to the lungs is common.

Rarely, the microscopic features of carcinoma and sarcoma coexist. The term **carcinosarcoma** can then be applied.

Kaposi's sarcoma   This is a vascular, spindle-cell sarcoma resembling an

---

*The prefix sarc-, from the Greek sarcos (flesh-like), is used to describe the naked-eye appearances of both sarcoid and sarcoma.

angiosarcoma. The component cells are endothelial. Starting as blue-red, lower limb skin nodules, the neoplasm spreads proximally and may involve viscera. Inflammation is excited and there is a similarity to granulation tissue.

Kaposi's sarcoma is endemic and relatively frequent in parts of Central Africa; until recently it was rare elsewhere. Now the neoplasm has excited interest because it is unusually frequent among sufferers from the acquired immunodeficiency syndrome (AIDS) (p. 2). In these individuals, the immune response to the neoplasm may be defective; the neoplasm behaves aggressively and two out of five sufferers die within one year.

Scar

A scar is a focus or island of fibrous connective tissue which forms when healing occurs by repair. Scar tissue is prolific when healing is delayed and complicated by infection or by the presence of foreign bodies. Scar tissue, initially pale pink, abundant and soft, becomes dense, hard, pale and contracted with time. These changes are accompanied by an increase in strength and are closely related to the formation and maturation of the type III collagen. The formation of a scar is dependent on the availability of essential nutritional factors such as ascorbic acid. However, scar formation is not impaired in old age. Abnormal scars form in rare inherited diseases of collagen such as the Ehlers–Danlos syndromes (p. 62)

Scurvy

Scurvy is a disease of connective tissue, due to deficiency of vitamin C (ascorbic acid). Man does not possess the enzymes necessary to synthesize ascorbic acid. As this simple compound is essential for the formation of normal collagen, for the maintenance of normal connective-tissue matrix and for the healing of wounds, the consequences of long-standing deficiency are disastrous. Petechial and gingival haemorrhages occur, wounds heal poorly and display low tensile strength. There is osteoporosis and teeth may loosen. The effects of restoring vitamin C to the diet are dramatic and within 12 hours new collagen synthesis is detectable.

Sepsis

Sepsis describes infection with pyogenic, i.e. pus-forming, bacteria. The word originates from the Greek for putrefaction but it is no longer used in this sense.

Septicaemia

Septicaemia is the multiplication of bacteria in the blood, associated with a failure of bactericidal mechanisms to overcome the number of organisms being released into the circulation.

Shock

Shock is the aggregate of disturbed body functions accompanying and immediately following severe injury or infection. Shock may be produced by any interference with cell metabolism but the majority of cases are due to inadequate tissue perfusion:

Neurogenic (vasovagal) shock   A subject may faint because of emotion or pain. Loss of consciousness is due to vagal stimulation and hypotension induced by medullary stimuli; there is concurrent bradycardia, distinguishing the condition from hypovolaemic shock. The same vagal response may occur under dental anaesthesia in the upright, seated position. Unless blood flow is quickly restored, cerebral infarction may occur.

Hypovolaemic (oligaemic) shock   Fluid may be lost as blood, plasma or water. Ultimately there is a reduction in circulating blood volume, and tachycardia.

a. **Haemorrhagic.** The most common cause is blood loss from the gastro-intestinal tract. Peptic ulcer is a common agent. Other sources of haemorrhage include ruptured abdominal aortic aneurysm, placenta praevia and ruptured ectopic pregnancy. Early vasoconstriction and reduced blood volume are followed by the diffusion of interstitial fluid into the intravascular compartment, with haemodilution and a restoration of blood volume. With natural recovery increased haemopoiesis is evident from the reticulocytosis that continues until the red blood cell mass has been restored to normal.

b. **Plasma loss.** The rapid loss of plasma is most commonly due to burns or scalds. Plasma collects in blisters under the epithelium and exudes from the exposed subepithelial tissues, but the greatest loss is into the interstitial tissue spaces. Other causes are severe crushing injuries to the limbs, carcinomatosis peritonei, and peritonitis such as that associated with acute pancreatitis.

c. **Water and electrolyte loss.** Shock may follow the inadequate intake or excessive loss of water and electrolytes. The most common reason is severe diarrhoea due to dysenteric organisms; the most severe cause is cholera due to the toxins of *Vibrio cholerae*.

Cardiogenic shock   Cardiac output is severely reduced following myocardial infarction, myocarditis, cardiac tamponade, dissecting aortic aneurysm or the onset of arrhythmia. There is metabolic acidosis due to underperfusion of the tissues.

Pulmonary shock   Patients with severe pulmonary lesions such as embolism, atelectasis, pneumothorax and haemothorax exhibit the classical features of shock.

Septic shock   Many organisms can liberate exotoxins (e.g. clostridia, staphylococci) or endotoxins (coliforms) which are potent causes of normovolaemic shock. Endotoxic shock (p. 76) results from the liberation of the lipopolysaccharide of the cell wall from dead Gram-negative bacteria. To promote shock, it is not necessary for the bacteria to reach the bloodstream: shock results from the actions of the toxins alone, so that the term 'bacteraemic' shock is often inappropriate. All tissues may be damaged by bacterial endotoxins but the lungs are particularly susceptible.

Anaphylactic shock   Antigen–antibody interactions in the body liberate vasoactive substances such as histamine. Such hypersensitivity is more common in atopic individuals. The blood pools in the capillaries and there may be laryngeal oedema.

Irreversible shock   When the shocked state is established, the tissue injuries caused by the initial shock perpetuate the disorder. Metabolic acidosis due to underperfusion of tissue in cardiogenic shock has a deleterious effect upon cardiac output: the shock progresses rapidly. Lysosomal proteases are activated extracellularly and degrade susceptible tissues such as the liver and the renal tubules, causing cell injury and death. There is a high mortality rate.

Shock lung

Some severely injured patients with shock respond initially to haemodynamic resuscitation but die ultimately from pulmonary failure, a syndrome termed shock lung (post-traumatic pulmonary insufficiency or the **adult respiratory distress syndrome** (ARDS)). The most common cause is sepsis, particularly when combined with inadequate perfusion. Other factors of possible importance are massive blood transfusion, particularly if the blood is not filtered to remove microaggregates (p. 36), the excessive infusion of saline, prolonged ventilation (particularly with high oxygen partial pressures), and direct or indirect pulmonary damage by inhalation, shock waves or blows to the chest. Circulating endotoxin is important and the syndrome is analogous to the generalized Shwartzman reaction (p. 171). All these factors may act through a final common pathway affecting the surfactant lining the pulmonary aveoli. A reduction in the quantity or a change in the nature of pulmonary surfactant (a lipoprotein) may be the common denominator in the aetiology of ARDS.

There are petechial haemorrhages and engorgement of the capillaries and small veins in the lung. Alveolar congestion and patchy atelectasis is more evident in the lower and middle lobes. The surface tension of the alveolar surfactant increases. Within 24 hours there may be intra-alveolar haemorrhage and a hyaline membrane lines the alveolar walls. Thromboemboli are observed in small vessels. Interstitial and alveolar oedema increases. There is haemorrhagic consolidation of the lungs. By the fifth day infection is the predominant feature with confluent bronchopneumonia. There is a very high mortality. In survivors, pulmonary fibrosis is a sequel.

Shwartzman phenomenon

Gregory Shwartzman, a New York bacteriologist, described* an unusual dermatological response to the injection of a filtrate from a broth culture of *Salmonella typhi.*

Local Shwartzman reaction   In the local form of response to Gram-negative bacterial endotoxin, he first inoculated rabbits intradermally with endotoxin. Twenty four hours later, he injected the same material intravenously. Although, clearly, the animals had not formed antibody to the material first injected, haemorrhagic necrosis of skin developed at the original injection site after a few hours. The response was accompanied by the formation of platelet thrombi in venules, and closely resembled the vascular reactions in disseminated intravascular coagulation (DIC) (p. 173).

Generalized Shwartzman reaction   An analogous response of generalized character is observed when both injections of Gram-negative bacterial endotoxin are intravenous. The animal dies of endotoxic shock (p.76) 24 hours after the second injection. There is intravascular coagulation and renal cortical necrosis.

Sickle-cell phenomenon

Sickle cells are red blood cells the shape of which is altered because of the presence of an abnormal **sickle cell haemoglobin**, HbS. Normal adult haemoglobin (HbA) and HbS possess the same solubility when oxygenated. On deoxygenation, HbS becomes poorly soluble and forms a semi-fluid gel. The affected cells are curved. Flow through capillaries is obstructed and blood viscosity is increased. The sickled cells are avidly phagocytosed by the reticuloendothelial cells of the spleen and their decreased life-span is the reason for the development of **sickle-cell anaemia.**

Inheritance
The presence of HbS is the result of an inherited defect in the genetic coding for glutamic acid. This amino acid normally occupies position 6 in the β-polypeptide chain of the haemoglobin molecule. Inheritance of the sickle-cell trait determines that glutamic acid is replaced by valine. When an individual is **heterozygous** for this defect, both HbA and HbS are formed. The individual is then said to have the **sickle-cell trait**. The red blood cells do not deform in vivo, but sickling can be induced by exposing them in the laboratory to an atmosphere containing less oxygen than normal. When the sufferer is **homozygous**, normal HbA is not formed. The red blood cells readily deform in vivo and sickle-cell anaemia develops. Other phenomena frequent in this disorder are hyperostosis of the skull, with frontal 'bossing' and fibrosis and calcification of the spleen.

---

*Gregory Shwartzman (1896–1965). Studies on Bacillus typhosus toxic substances. 1. Phenomenon of local skin reactivity to *B. typhosus* culture filtrate.

The high frequency with which HbS is inherited in some Negro populations in whom malaria is infrequent, suggests that the possession of HbS confers a genetic advantage in heterozygous persons.

Clinical effects

Because of shifts in populations the sickle-cell trait and disease are being recognized with increased frequency in Europe. Sickle-cell disease may create difficulties for the surgeon. The anaemic patient responds poorly to infection and trivial bacterial infection can precipitate widespread sickling with tissue infarction. Septicaemia may develop. Patients may display acute abdominal and lower thoracic symptoms and signs that can mimic other intra-abdominal catastrophes.

Sinus

In anatomy, a sinus is a wide venous channel, a pouch or recess, or an air-containing cavity lined by mucosa.

In pathology, a sinus is a narrow, infected tract leading from an abscess to the skin or a body cavity. It is lined with granulation tissue and is a consequence of incomplete resolution of an inflammatory process. This may be due to a retained foreign body such as a non-absorbable suture or dead bone, or to constant reinfection, or to the presence of indolent, chronic infections such as tuberculosis or actinomycosis. Eventually, sinuses are lined with epithelium and become chronic.

Sludging of blood

Blood is said to sludge when red blood cells stick together and form columns (rouleaux) in the circulation.

Any form of shock may result in a redistribution of blood within the macro- and micro-circulations. In the micro-circulation, there is a pooling of blood in the capillaries and rouleaux are formed. This process is distinct from true aggregation in which there is chemical bonding. In some circumstances the rouleaux may disintegrate.

Sludging is common after major burns. It is a common feature of extracorporeal circulations and a component of the generalized Shwartzman phenomenon (p. 171). There is tissue anoxia and micro-infarcts may be caused.

Dextrans of low molecular weight in electrolyte solutions reduce the tendency for rouleau formation: the polymer induces electrostatic charges on the surface of the red blood cells which then repel each other.

Space travel

The experience of space travel has thrown light on many pathological processes. For example, inactivity and weightlessness promote a negative nitrogen balance, skeletal muscle atrophy, loss of bone mineral and electrolyte disturbances. Many of these changes can be corrected or avoided by exercises performed in space craft.

Laboratory studies in space have been very detailed. Calcium disorders promote red blood-cell aggregation, whereas zero gravity by itself simply diminishes red-cell sedimentation. So far, however, no surgical operation has been performed in the weightless state. Nor is there evidence of the hazards of prolonged exposure to ionizing radiation that accompanies extra-terrestrial travel.

Spleen, functions of

The sinusoids of the **red pulp**, lined by vigorously phagocytic cells, engulf and destroy aged and abnormal red blood cells. In splenomegaly from a wide variety of causes this function is exaggerated (**hypersplenism**), Red blood cells are susceptible in the haemoglobinopathies and in hereditary sphero-cytosis. The phagocytes, part of the reticuloendothelial system (p. 166), avidly phagocytose cells coated with abnormal antibodies in disorders such as the acquired haemolytic anaemias. In this process of erythrophagocytosis, injured and effete red blood cells are broken down and the products meta-bolized. The protein moiety of haemoglobin is degraded, the iron, detached from haem, is incorporated in the body's iron stores, while the porphyrin is changed to bilirubin and metabolized by the liver.

In the fetus, the spleen is a site of haemopoiesis: this function may be retained after birth or resumed if much bone marrow is replaced or destroyed.

The **white pulp**, comprising 25 per cent of the body's lymphoid tissues, has immunological functions important for defence against micro-organisms. The white pulp harbours macrophages, and in this part of the spleen bacteria coated with opsonic antibody are phagocytosed and destroyed.

Splenectomy, effects of

Loss of splenic tissue leads to a reduction in the capacity of the spleen to remove immature or abnormal red cells from the circulation and these cells are therefore found in increased numbers in the blood following splenectomy. Target cells, reticulocytes and siderocytes appear within a few days, and granulocytosis persists for two weeks but declines quickly to be replaced by lymphocytosis and monocytosis. Occasionally, thrombocyto-sis is marked and thrombosis and embolism occur.

Following splenectomy, all patients are more prone than normal to infection, particularly by encapsulated bacteria such as *Streptococcus pneu-moniae*. Death from septicaemia may follow. Such infections are more com-mon after elective splenectomy than following splenectomy for trauma. It is known that after splenectomy, splenic cells or small islands of splenic tissue may survive. The continuous function of these splenunculi or *accessory spleens*, confirmed by radioactive isotope tests, can permit the resumption of some normal splenic function or the re-emergence of a disease, such as haemolytic anaemia, for which spelenctomy had been performed.

Squamous carcinoma

Squamous carcinomas are common epithelial neoplasms in which the cells show light microscopic or EM evidence of differentiation towards stratified squamous epithelium, with or without keratinization. The light microscopic features include intercellular ('prickle') process formation and neoplastic cells are arranged as 'nests,' often with central keratin. The EM features include the presence of cytoplasmic filaments, keratohyaline granules and intercellular junctions. There are no intracellular lumina but long slender microvilli may exist within intercellular spaces.

Squamous carcinomas of the skin of the hand were the first neoplasms attributable to ionizing radiation. Later, experimental squamous carcinomas were produced by painting the skin of mice with coal tar and, subsequently, with carcinogens such as dibenzanthracene. Squamous carcinomas often arise from metaplastic epithelium such as that lining the bronchi in cigarette smokers; they may also derive from ectopic islands of squamous epithelium or from teratomas.

Staging of malignant neoplasms

The **stage** of an invasive neoplasm is the extent to which it has spread from its site of origin and is one guide to prognosis. Staging is of surgical importance and enables the merits of different forms of treatment to be compared.

Dukes' method   A method of staging was devised by Dukes for carcinoma of the rectum: the stage was assessed according to whether there was extension outside the wall and whether lymph nodes were affected.

The TNM system   Subsequent studies of rectal carcinoma and of neoplasms of other organs suggested that even more detailed staging may have clinical relevance. A system has now been devised applicable to malignant neoplasms at any site. A classification devised by De Noix, the TNM system, has been modified and applied to many tumours by the Union Internationale Contre le Cancer. Within this system, a tumour is staged according to three criteria:

T – the extent of the primary Tumour
N – the involvement of regional and more distant lymph Nodes
M – the existence of distant Metastases.

There can be subdivisions within each category. A carcinoma of the colon with a colovesical fistula and spread to the para-aortic lymph nodes but no distant metastases is designated T3a/N4/M0. With the help of sophisticated radiology such as CT scanning, this method of staging may be attempted preoperatively. During an operation, staging can be undertaken by frozen section and confirmed postoperatively by paraffin section. Staging of some neoplasms before operation correlates poorly with staging after operation. Neoplasms that show little spread may have been identified early or may be growing slowly: a good prognosis may be a consequences of either.

Standard tests for syphilis (STS)

Although *Treponema pallidum*, the cause of syphilis, can occasionally be identified in primary lesions by dark-ground microscopy, the bacterium cannot be grown in culture. The diagnosis of syphilis therefore rests on methods for the demonstration of antitreponemal antibodies in serum. This problem does not arise in the diagnosis of gonorrhoea, since *Neisseria gonorrhoeae* can easily be cultivated. A complement-fixation test for anti-gonococcal antibodies is only used to screen asymptomatic female patients.

Early workers used an extract of syphilitic tissue as antigen to detect antitreponemal antibodies. It was soon found that normal tissue extracts could be substituted for syphilitic. An alcoholic preparation of heart muscle was very effective. The specific reagent in heart is a substance called cardiolipin; it is now employed, together with lecithin and cholesterol, as a substitute for the ideal antigen, *T. pallidum*, that is not available. However, positive STSs obtained with cardiolipin are not wholly specific for syphilis. Two strains of treponeme, the first *T. pallidum, strain Nichols*, the second *T. phagedenis, biotype Reiter*, are employed in additional confirmatory procedures. The three antigens, cardiolipin, *T. pallidum, strain Nichols* and *T. phagedenis, biotype Reiter* each detect different treponema-related antibody.

Thus, there are two groups of commonly used STSs: (a) antilipoidal, and (b) antitreponemal. The antilipoidal tests are flocculation reactions such as the Venereal Disease Research Laboratory Test (VDRL) and complement-fixation reactions such as the Cardiolipin Wasserman Reaction (CWR). The antitreponemal tests are the *T. pallidum* Haemagglutination Test (TPHA) and the Fluorescent Treponemal Antibody-Absorption Test (FTA). In practice, the VDRL, CWR and TPHA tests are used for screening sera, and the FTA test to increase sensitivity and specificity.

The classical **Wasserman reaction** (WR) has been employed for many years as a test for specific anti- *T. pallidum* antibody. Its use is decreasing. The Wasserman reaction is a **complement-fixation test**. A measured amount of complement (p. 62) is added to patients' serum together with cardiolipin antigen. If antilipoidal antibodies are present, they unite with the antigen and bind complement. An indicator system is then added to determine whether complement remains. The indicator system comprises (1) sheep red blood cells, and (2) rabbit anti-sheep red blood cell antibody. If haemolysis does not occur, the WR is positive. If no antibody is present in the patient's serum, complement is not consumed and the sheep red blood cells lyse; the test is then negative.

Biological false positive STSs may arise in recent respiratory-tract infections or in pregnancy. False positive STS may persist in systemic lupus erythematosus and other autoimmune diseases (p. 20).

Staphylococcus

Staphylococci are Gram-positive cocci that form grape-like clusters. *Staphylococcus aureus* exists in the nose and on the moist skin of many healthy persons and leads to opportunistic infection when skin or mucosae are damaged. Common suppurative infections caused by *Staph. aureus* include boils and carbuncles, wound infection and bronchopneumonia. Pyaemia, osteomyelitis and bacterial endocarditis are occasional results. *Staph. aureus* often causes hospital infections, particularly of the newborn, the old, and the surgical patient, and is responsible for some outbreaks of food-poisoning.

Pathogenic *Staph. aureus* invade and destroy tissue locally, causing suppuration. The virulence of *Staph. aureus* is due to a combination of numerous surface components, toxins and enzymes that enable the bacteria to resist phagocytosis, kill leucocytes, and avoid opsonization. Among these virulence factors are

1. A cell-wall structural protein, **protein A**, which binds to the Fc region of IgG, inhibiting opsonization (p. 109).
2. **Coagulase**, an enzyme that activates prothrombin, leading to the local formation of a fibrin barrier that impairs the movement of leucocytes towards the micro-organisms. The production of coagulase is a good index of pathogenicity. This enzyme is sought in colonies under investigation by means of a simple slide test.
3. **Leucocidin**, a toxin that kills leucocytes.
4. **α-Haemolysin** (α-toxin) a toxin which kills leucocytes, causes vascular smooth-muscle contraction, lyses red blood cells and contributes to death if pyaemia or septicaemia develop.
5. **Enterotoxins**, of which six types are known. Food poisoning results when enterotoxin, formed by bacterial multiplication in contaminated food, is ingested. These toxins resist heat.

The source and spread of staphylococcal infection in a surgical ward is investigated by phage typing (p. 26). Some phage types are more virulent than others and are especially likely to be responsible for surgical infections. Most strains of *Staph. aureus* remain sensitive to cloxacillin, the cephalosporins and gentamicin, but 50 per cent of strains encountered in the community and 85 per cent in hospital are resistant to benzyl penicillin. Strains resistant to cloxacillin are a growing problem in hospital.

Sterilization

Sterilization is the entire destruction of micro-organism including their spores and cysts. **Disinfection** (p. 72) is the destruction of living infective cells, usually by chemical means. Although some spores may be killed by disinfectants, the majority are resistant. Weak disinfectants are called **antiseptics** (p. 14).

Physical

(i) Heat   Moist heat is more effective than dry. Moist heat penetrates better than dry heat and denatures the proteins of the microbial cell wall. Boiling at 100 °C, at normal atmospheric pressure, is effective only if continued for many hours. Bacterial spores and hepatitis B virus withstand short periods of boiling. Bacteria, fungi and their spores are destroyed in 10 minutes by steam at 126 °C, in 15 minutes by steam at 121 °C but only after one hour by dry heat at 160 °C.

In the **autoclave** (p. 19), steam is heated to a temperature of 121 °C by increasing the pressure. The steam condenses upon the cool instruments and packages within the autoclave, giving up the large amount of latent heat of vaporization required for its production. It is essential that the steam is able to penetrate all containers. The sterilizing cycle must be sufficiently long to ensure that this happens. Sterilization by steam under raised pressure is the most commonly used method in hospitals and in industry.

Many articles will not withstand the high temperatures required for sterilization by dry heat. However, if they tolerate these temperatures, it is possible to sterilize such articles in sealed containers which may then be opened for a scrub nurse to remove the sterile contents in the operating theatre. Dry heat may be produced by infra-red irradiation as well as in ovens, and microwave ovens have been used in laboratories.

(ii a) Irradiation, non-ionizing   Micro-organisms can be killed by sunlight and by artifical UVL of wavelength less than 330 nm. UVL of relatively low energy does not penetrate far.

(ii b) Irradiation, ionizing   Gamma rays penetrate the plastic containers used in surgery and are employed commercially to sterilize heat-labile articles, plastic syringes and dressings.

(iii) Filtration   Bacteria and spores can be removed from heat-labile solutions (such as mixtures of amino acids and glucose) and from gases by filtration through earthenware, sintered glass or seitz (asbestos) filters. Cellulose acetate (millipore) membrane filters can be chosen with a pore size sufficiently small to remove mycoplasmas and viruses. The efficiency of sterilization is determined by this pore size.

The air entering operating suites is filtered to remove dust particles that carry bacteria, but the glass-fibre filters do not remove particles as small as individual bacteria or spores.

Chemical
Few chemical disinfectants (p. 72) are reliable in effecting sterilization. Those that can kill bacterial spores must be used in proper conditions of temperature and moisture and in sufficient concentrations; organic matter such as blood, pus and dirt decreases their effectiveness.

(i) Formaldehyde   Many heat-labile instruments such as cystoscopes can be sterilized by exposure to formaldehyde vapour at 80 °C for two hours. The vapour is produced by the addition of formaldehyde to steam.

(ii) Ethylene oxide   At room temperature, ethylene oxide is a highly explosive gas. It is mixed with carbon dioxide for safety and used to sterilize heat-labile instruments. The gas penetrates rubber or plastic; it is toxic but is only released from these materials over a period of days.

(iii) Glutaraldehyde   Solutions of glutaraldehyde sterilize endoscopes and other instruments containing plastic or rubber. Unfortunately, glutaraldehyde may cause contact dermatitis in nurses subjected to frequent exposure while preparing endoscopes.

Indicators of sterilization

When heat is used, a continuous recording of temperature from the coolest lower part of the autoclave should be made during the period of sterilization. Browne's tubes placed amongst the instruments enable confirmation that articles have been exposed to sufficient heating. These glass tubes contain a fluid that changes from red to green upon exposure to a temperature of 115 °C for 25 minutes (type 1) or 15 minutes (type 2). Sterile packs can be identified by the colour of the heat-sensitive inks used in the Bowie-Dick test. A colour change develops after sufficient heating.

Confirmation of sterilization by methods other than heat can only be determined by including samples of living but non-pathogenic bacteria and spores with the materials to demonstrate the destruction of these micro-organisms by the sterilization process.

Sterilization of ventilators

There are two types of ventilator. The first type is used for comparatively short periods in anaesthetized patients undergoing operations; the second is used for prolonged ventilation of severely ill patients, usually in Intensive Care Units (ICU).

Anaesthetic ventilators

In this type of ventilator, the expiratory circuit from the patient is the key component. Ideally, this circuit would be changed for each patient. In practice, this procedure is not followed: the components made of rubber, plastic and metal offer poor media for growth and do not become infected. Cleaning with disinfectants at regular intervals is a sufficient precaution. However, the expiratory circuit should be changed and disinfected when it has been used in a patient with pulmonary tuberculosis or obvious pulmonary sepsis. In view of the known virulence of the organism, the same practice should be observed after anaesthetizing a patient with hepatitis B. Similarly, the complete ventilator should be disinfected along with all the other contents of the theatre after an operation has been performed for gas gangrene.

Methods of sterilization vary according to the type of ventilator: the manufacturer's instructions should be followed. Modern ventilators are designed so that they can be dismantled to allow easy access to the contaminated units. The most effective method of avoiding infection is to use disposable components but these are expensive. Some components can be sterilized by autoclaving but this reduces the life of the part. Other components (particularly transducers and electronic devices) are damaged by heat. Pasteurization and the use of various disinfectants is possible but less effective than expensive techniques employing ethylene oxide and gamma irradiation.

ICU ventilators

Patients requiring prolonged ventilation are usually infected with virulent bacteria that are resistant to antibiotics. Sterilization of the inspiratory and expiratory circuits is essential before the ventilator is used for another patient. Most intensive care units are now equipped with ventilators that incorporate disposable circuits.

Storage diseases

In a storage disease, there is an inherited biochemical deficiency of an enzyme, so that intermediary metabolities or products accumulate in excess, often in the viscera.

The majority of storage diseases are inherited as autosomal recessive characteristics (p. 119). In the eight known types of **glycogen storage disease**, there is an enzyme deficiency affecting carbohydrate metabolism. Excess glycogen accumulates mainly in either liver or heart. In the **mucopolysaccharidoses**, lack of a single lysosomal enzyme results in the accumulation of glycosaminoglycans in brain, skeleton and skin. In the **mucolipidoses**, there is a comparable lysosomal deficiency affecting multiple enzymes, so that both glycosaminoglycans and lipids accumulate.

Streptococcus

Streptococci are Gram-positive, spherical bacteria, multiplying to form chains of organisms. They are facultative anaerobes: they grow better anaerobically than aerobically. Some are micro-aerophilic. An important category, often associated with pelvic infection, is anaerobic. Those bacteria which produce clear zones of haemolysis around their colonies on blood agar plates, are said to be β-haemolytic (*Streptococcus pyogenes*); the streptococci that cause green coloration around their colonies are α-haemolytic. Streptococci that do not cause haemolysis are said to be γ-haemolytic.

(a) The β-haemolytic streptococci (*Strept. pyogenes*) are classified into 17 Lancefield groups, labelled A–S. Classification by agglutination reactions using specific antibacterial antisera stuck onto latex particles helps to identify human pathogens quickly. The majority of β-haemolytic streptococci causing human infections are of group A. Group B attacks the neonate. Groups C and G are increasingly recognized as important pathogens. Group D are the faecal streptococci (enterococci); they are frequent causes of urinary-tract infection and, after the coliforms, are the most common cause of biliary infection.

Strept. pyogenes can be further divided into more than 50 Griffith serotypes using a classification based on an M surface bacterial antigen.

Among the important biological activities of *Strept. pyogenes* are the production of haemolytic exotoxins that can damage polymorphs and other cells; of erythrogenic (scarlet fever) exotoxin; of a fibrinolysin called streptokinase; of hyaluronidase, so-called 'spreading factor' (p. 152); of DNAase, an enzyme able to degrade nuclear material in pus; and of NADase and DPNase, enzymes that kill leucocytes.

The spread of infection can be traced by searching for antistreptolysin D, anti-DNAase B and anti-hyaluronidase.

(b) The α and non-haemolytic streptococci are found in the mouth and pharynx. The viridans group, *Strept. viridans*, is associated with dental sepsis and is still a relatively common cause of bacterial endocarditis.

Stress

Stress may be psychological or physical. Prolonged mental distress can reduce resistance to disease and increase the probability of a fatal outcome to infection and injury. There is an effect upon the immune mechanism, related to the regulatory mechanisms of the hypothalamo–pituitary–adrenal cortical axis. Physical stress increases the rate of the adrenal secretion of cortisol; there are changes in the appearance and behaviour of the cells of the zona fasiculata, which becomes lipid-depleted. Under these conditions, relatively minor surgical and anaesthetic procedures, such as those used in dentistry, may cause serious effects including neurogenic shock and cerebral infarction.

Superinfection

This term is used to describe two situations:

1. Infection with an organism that supersedes infection by a different agent ('secondary infection'). In one example, superinfection with *Pseudomonas aeruginosa* is common in infected burns and in the lungs of patients requiring prolonged ventilation; in another, superinfection with *Candida albicans* is increasingly common in patients surviving septicaemia.
Overwhelming infections of this kind may result from impaired immunity following initial infection by other organisms; the infection can then be considered to be 'opportunistic' (p. 101).

2. Infection with an organism that is a normal commensal but which expresses its latent pathogenicity due to a change in its environment. Thus, staphylococcal enteritis may occur when the other organisms which predominate in the gastrointestinal tract are eradicated by the use of oral antibiotics (p. 162).

Suture materials

Clean surgical wounds of epithelial and vascular tissue usually heal quickly but the restoration of even 50 per cent of normal mechanical strength to tissues with much collagen such as the linea alba, requires three or more months. Suture materials play an important part in achieving complete healing.

An ideal suture material can be sterilized without damage, is chemically and biologically inert, and retains sufficient tensile strength to ensure wound integrity until healing is complete. The ideal material does not delay healing; if bacteria enter the wound it does not increase their pathogenicity. When healing is complete, the suture is absorbed.

These ideal properties cannot be found in a single material.

Absorbable sutures

Absorbable sutures are degraded by enzymatic dissolution. Implanted **catgut**, a material obtained from the submucosa of the small intestine of the sheep, produces a profuse tissue reaction within 24 hours, with oedema and polymorph infiltration. Catgut delays healing but it is usually rapidly dissolved, with reduction in tensile strength. After catgut has been tanned with chromic acid, its absorption is delayed and its capacity to cause inflammation reduced. **Collagen** sutures are obtained from the Achilles tendon of cattle and provoke less tissue reaction. Synthetic polymers of glycolic acid (dexon and vicryl) are less irritant than catgut or collagen but enzymatic dissolution is equally rapid.

Non-absorbable sutures

Non-absorbable sutures resist enzymatic dissolution; they fragment and lose tensile strength over a period of months. Non-absorbable sutures are made as a single strand (monofilament) or as a number of strands twisted or braided together (multifilament). There is a greater tissue reaction to multifilament than to monofilament sutures, and bacteria may lodge in the interstices of multifilament sutures in infected wounds. Sutures made of the natural fibres, silk, cotton and linen are made in a multifilament pattern and induce a tissue reaction almost as severe as that caused by catgut. These sutures are being replaced by inert synthetic plastics such as polyamide (nylon) and polypropylene (prolene). Metal sutures made of stainless steel or tantalum are almost inert, as is carbon fibre.

Talc granuloma

The latex gloves (p. 88) used by surgeons require a lubricant and a finely divided powder has proved to be ideal. Unfortunately, in the past, the powder used was often talc (magnesium silicate); talc was insoluble and free powder was liable to produce a granulomatous inflammation within wounds and body cavities. A chronic inflammatory response developed around the particles. Foreign-body giant cells were evident. Peritoneal adhesions induced intestinal obstruction, and sometimes sterility due to involvement of the Fallopian tubes. Talc was replaced by powders made of starch or from the spores of the moss *Lycopodium clavatum*. Although these powders are more soluble and less irritant than talc, they are still capable of inducing inflammation. Gloves are now lubricated with powder made from potassium bitartrate, which is completely soluble and does not cause inflammation. Recently, a leading manufacturer has produced gloves that do not require lubricating powder.

Teratoma

Teratomas are neoplasms formed of two or more tissues foreign to those in which the neoplasm arises. Teratomas are distinct from, but may superficially resemble, non-neoplastic aberrations of development such as heterotopic tissues and conjoined ('Siamese') twins. The diversity of the tissues of a teratoma demonstrates that the neoplasm is not the result of metaplasia from organs and tissues such as the ovary, testis, mediastinum, retroperitoneal, presacral and coccygeal tissues that are the sites from which teratomas most frequently arise.

Tetanus

Tetanus is the disease caused by **tetanospasmin**, the neurotoxin of *Clostridium tetani* (p. 56). It is a major cause of death in poor, agricultural populations living in warm climates among whom neonatal tetanus is common. The spores of *Cl. tetani* are present in soil, dust or dirty clothing, and have been found in surgical catgut. The spores readily gain access to the umbilicus and to wounds of all sizes. Stab and puncture wounds, even though very small, may be potent causes of tetanus. Ischaemia, contamination by foreign bodies, and the existence of other forms of bacterial infection, particularly those caused by pyogenic cocci and by *Cl. welchii*, predispose to the growth of *Cl. tetani*.

Tetanus is a disease of poverty, accident and war, but fatal cases in Western populations have resulted from a single prick by a rose thorn or splinter. The spores of *Cl. tetani* have occasionally been identified in air entering operating theatres.

Germination of the spores of *Cl. tetani* and the growth of vegetative bacteria are essential for neurotoxin formation. This growth is possible only in conditions of very low oxygen tension.

The most effective defence against tetanus is the proper surgical treatment of wounds, and immunization. Active immunization offers protection if immunity is maintained by booster injections of toxoid at five- to ten-year intervals. Antibiotics help to prevent the growth of *Cl. tetani*.

Tetany

Tetany is the painful tonic spasm of muscle induced by changes in the concentrations of extracellular ions.

Neuromuscular irritability can be increased by a reduction in the concentrations of Ca^{2+}, Mg^{2+} and H^+ ions, or by an increase in the concentrations of Na^+, K^+ and OH^- ions. The commonest cause of tetany is hypocalcaemia, but changes in the concentration of more than one ion frequently coincide. Spontaneous 'main d'accoucheur' exemplifies classical tetany and there may also be paraesthesiae and spasms of laryngeal and abdominal muscles. **Latent tetany** can be diagnosed by inducing the main d'accoucheur (Trousseau's sign) using a tourniquet applied to the upper arm. Latent tetany can also be caused by tapping a branch of the facial nerve: twitching of the facial muscles develops (Chvostek's sign).

Tetany is a rare complication of partial thyroidectomy as it is unusual for all the parathyroid glands (p. 154) to be removed or their blood supply to be damaged. More commonly, tetany is seen after total thyroidectomy. It does not occur in every patient because glandular tissue is sometimes located in the mediastinum or elsewhere. Tetany is also unusual following operations on the parathyroid glands unless pre-operative hyperparathyroidism (p. 154) has been severe.

Tetany may be induced by severe metabolic acidosis (p. 1). A more frequent cause is respiratory alkalosis (p. 1).

Thrombus

A thrombus is a solid mass formed in the living circulation from the constituents of the blood. It is distinguished from a **clot** or coagulum, which is a solid mass formed when coagulation of the blood occurs outside the circulation in vivo or in vitro. Emboli commonly form from thrombi (p. 74).

Young thrombi are firm, grey-purple and retain the shape of the vessel from which they can be lifted. Where platelets and fibrin predominate, a thrombus appears pale; where many red cells remain within the mass, the thrombus is dark red. The gradual extension of thrombosis beyond the site at which the process began leads to a propagated or **consecutive thrombus**. As organization begins, thrombi adhere to the vessel wall (**mural thrombus**). The alternating, laminated surface structure of an old thrombus, caused within an aneurysm, for example, by the differential contraction of platelets and fibrin, gives rise to the **lines of Zahn**.

A **postmortem clot** appears softer and gelatinous; it is purple-black, retains no constant shape and resembles blackcurrant jelly. If coagulation occurs in these circumstances after the red blood cells have sedimented, the plasma clot resembles **chicken fat**.

The causes of thrombosis constitute Virchow's* triad:

1. Changes in the coagulation mechanism of the **blood**. Examples include the increased number of platelets that follows surgery or injury, the increased adhesiveness of the young platelets formed at this time, the haemoconcentration of fluid loss and polycythaemia, and disorders such as cold antibody formation, in which there is an intrinsic cause for thrombosis.

2. Changes in the **endothelium**. The lining endothelium and endocardium lose their normal smooth surface when atherosclerotic plaques are present, when congenital anomalies exist, or when extraneous catheters, implants, artificial valves or synthetic materials are introduced. Local injury, by exposing the collagen of the basement membrane, activates platelets and promotes thrombosis. Injured tissue liberates thromboplastin. Prostacyclin synthesis is inhibited. Although veins have an intrinsic endothelial fibrinolytic system (p. 78), it is readily disturbed.

3. Haemodynamic alterations in **blood flow** are caused by the presence of aneurysms, valve deformities, shunts, bypasses and other artificial or abnormal communications. Turbulent flow results; normal, orderly laminar flow is lost. Platelet deposition and thromboplastin activation are

---

*Rudolf Ludwig Karl Virchow (1821–1902), author of *Cellular Pathology* (1858), was Professor of Pathology in Würtzburg and Berlin. He defined amyloid, thrombus and leukaemia, and showed that the cell is the unit of disease. His publications numbered 2000, and he edited 179 volumes of his own Archives. He was a pathologist, an anthropologist, a social reformer, and a politician.

encouraged. In the venous system, blood flow is readily obstructed, for example, by forces such as the pressure of a limb on an uneven surface, of heavy bedclothes on vessels in the leg and, in pregnancy, of the uterus upon pelvic veins. Venous stasis is also associated with the diminished movement that accompanies bed rest.

Tissue culture

Cells can **grow** in vitro. Small pieces of tissue can be **maintained** without cell growth.

Cell culture
Cells from many tissues and organs can be grown outside the body, without a supporting stroma or blood circulation. To encourage cell multiplication, they are separated from the parent tissue, cut into pieces, mixed with an enzyme to assist disaggregation, and suspended in a fluid medium in a flask or hollow slide where the growth of a **monolayer** of cells can be watched. Alternatively, a **suspension** of cells can be made and free cell growth encouraged.

The media in which cells are grown are either entirely **synthetic**, i.e. composed of amino acids, carbohydrates, salts and cofactors mixed in proportions calculated to resemble closely those of physiological extracellular fluids, or they may be wholly or partly **natural**, in the sense that they include serum. 'Conditioned' medium from other successful cultures contains factors that catalyse further new cell growth. Special forms of culture are adopted to enhance the study of particular cell lines, e.g. haemopoietic cells can be induced to form colonies in agar gel and neoplastic cells can be explanted to sites such as the anterior chamber of the eye.

The practical applications of cell culture include the use of monkey kidney cells to allow viral growth and identification, the growth of cells in searches for carcinogens, the growth of macrophages in tests of immunity mediated by lymphocytes or lymphokines, and the culture of connective tissue cells to test and identify pharmacological agents.

Organ culture
Organ culture implies the maintenance of very thin slices or minute solid parts of tissue in special dishes or chambers without cell multiplication. In the Trowell chamber, tissue samples are explanted under sterile conditions onto the surface of a fine metal mesh which is perfused with a fluid medium. The explants are placed in a sterile chamber containing an appropriate oxygen/carbon monoxide gas mixture and incubated at 37 °C.

Organ cultures are valuable ways of examining drug action and can be used as bioassay systems for hormones such as ACTH. Parts of neoplasms can be maintained in organ culture to study their characteristics.

Toxins

Many animals and plants form complex chemicals toxic to man. Among those that have achieved notoriety is ricin (castor seeds: *Ricinus communis*).

In surgery, bacterial toxins are of special significance: they are liberated from the bacterial cell (exotoxins) or are an integral part of its structure (endotoxins).

Exotoxins

Exotoxins are synthesized by actively growing bacteria; they exert their pathogenic effects remotely from the organism that produces them. Most bacteria producing exotoxins are Gram-positive; a few, including *Vibrio cholerae* and *Shigella shigae*, are Gram-negative. The lesions produced by exotoxins are widespread; the site of bacterial infection, however, remains localized. Exotoxins are proteins of high molecular weight and are therefore sensitive to heat. When partly changed by chemicals such as formaldehyde, which destroy pathogenicity, exotoxins retain their antigenicity and can therefore be used safely for active immunization. The altered, non-pathogenic toxin is called a **toxoid**.

Exotoxins exert specific effects on selected tissues where they are enzyme inhibitors. For example, the exotoxin of *Corynebacterium diphtheriae*, formed by bacteria localized to the throat and nasopharynx, inhibits cell protein synthesis and acts on the myocardium, nerves and adrenals. The α-toxin of *Cl. welchii* (p. 56) is a phospholipase and acts on the phospholipids of the cell membranes of red blood cells. The exotoxin of *Cl. tetani* (p. 56) potentiates neurotransmission at the synapse of the upper motor neurone with the anterior horn cells of the spinal cord, whereas the neurotoxin of *Cl. botulinum* (p. 56), the most potent of all bacterial exotoxins, blocks transmission at cranial motor-nerve endings. The actions of the haemolytic, cytolytic and leucocidal toxins of the pathogenic staphylococci (p. 175) and streptococci (p. 179) are equally specific.

Endotoxins

Endotoxins are phospholipid–polysaccharide–proteins of the outer layer of the cell wall of Gram-negative bacteria. When endotoxin is incorporated in the plasma membranes of host leucocytes, macrophages, endothelial cells and platelets, it seriously disturbs cell function. The lipid mainly determines toxicity, the carbohydrate antigenic specificity. Endotoxins resist heat, but are of low potency and specificity; they cannot be changed to toxoids. Combination with antibody does not destroy their toxicity and they cannot be used in immunization.

The effects of endotoxin are simulated by the generalized Shwartzman reaction (p. 171). Endotoxin is an exogenous pyrogen (p. 164), provoking leucocytes and macrophages to release endogenous pyrogen that acts on the temperature-regulating centre of the hypothalamus. Repeated exposure to endotoxin results in some tolerance, and the activity of mononuclear phagocytes may be enhanced. Pyrogenic endotoxin may come from saprophytic Gram-negative bacteria that have grown in fluids used for intravenous administration: the endotoxin is not destroyed by autoclaving. Similar organisms may multiply in fluids that have been autoclaved but are contaminated during storage.

See Endotoxic shock (p. 76).

Trace elements

Minute (trace) quantities of certain dietary elements are required for normal growth and function. Lack of trace elements are rare causes of well-recognized deficiency syndromes.

Most trace elements are cofactors for enzymes. Iron, zinc, copper, cobalt, manganese, iodine and fluorine are known to be required by man. Chromium, selenium, molybdenum, nickel, silicon, tin and vanadium are needed by other animals and may be essential for man.

Iron
Iron is a crucial part of haemoglobin and myoglobin and an ingredient of the peroxidases and the cytochromes.

Zinc
Zinc is a component of enzymes such as carbonic anhydrase, lactate dehydrogenase and the carboxypeptidases. Zinc is necessary for the healing of wounds; in depleted patients, the local application or systemic administration of zinc accelerates wound healing. There is no effect upon wound healing in normal individuals.

Copper
Copper is a component of cytochrome oxidase, monoamine oxidase, and tyrosinase. Copper deficiency impairs the maturation of red and white blood cells and the mineralization of bone. In the absence of copper, hair is depigmented and cerebral function deteriorates.

Cobalt
Cobalt, part of vitamin B_{12} (p. 201), is required for the normal function of the nervous system and for the development of red and white blood cells.

Manganese
Manganese is necessary for the activity of enzymes such as pyruvic carboxylase that catalyse oxidative phosphorylation. Manganese deficiency is extremely rare.

Iodine
Iodine is required for the iodination of tyrosine in the formation of tri-iodothyronine (T3) and thyroxine (T4).

Fluorine
Fluorine assists the development of healthy teeth and the formation of normal bone. Added to drinking water, calcium fluoride prevents dental caries. However, fluoride in great excess causes skeletal abnormalties.

Transcoelomic spread

Transcoelomic spread is the extension of the cells of a primary or metastatic malignant neoplasm across a body cavity.

Upon reaching the serosal layer of a viscus, a neoplasm often provokes an effusion through which malignant cells may pass to other organs. The commonest instances of transcoelomic spread is within the abdomen, particularly from neoplasms of the stomach, pancreas, colon and ovaries, but spread can occur throughout the pleural cavity from neoplasms of the breast or lung.

Krukenberg (neoplasm) tumour

The name Krukenberg* tumour is still given to bilateral ovarian metastasis from a mucin-secreting carcinoma of the stomach or colon. The neoplasm may reach the ovaries by transcoelomic spread. However, the surface of the ovaries is often free of deposits, and similar neoplasms have been found **within** the ovaries in patients with mucin-secreting carcinoma of the breast. Consequently, retrograde lymphatic or haematogenous spread is an acceptable alternative explanation for this mode of extension.

Pseudomyxoma peritonei (p. 63).

Meigs' syndrome

In Meigs' syndrome, pleural and peritoneal effusions accompany benign ovarian fibroma. The cause of the effusions is not understood; they may occur in the absence of a peritoneal neoplasm.

Transplantation (grafting)

A graft or transplant is an organ or piece of tissue deliberately implanted:(1) in a different site in the same individual, or (2) in the same or different site in another individual. Occasionally in trauma a portion of one tissue is accidentally implanted in an abnormal site. Tissue is transplanted from a **donor** to a recipient or **host**.

Tissue for transplantation may be living and survive in its original form: it is then said to be **vital**. By contrast, grafted tissue such as bone may be dead; it is then said to be a **static** graft, performing a passive, mechanical function and acting as a nidus for the new growth of cells derived not from itself but from those of the recipient.

A transplant from one site to another in the same individual is an **autograft** (Table 18). A transplant from one individual to another of the same species was said to be a **homograft** but the lack of genetic identity is indicated better by the term **allograft**. Transplants between different species, xenografts, display species differences in tissue antigenic structure: the genetic relationship is **xenogeneic**. When transplanted human tissue has a genetic structure identical with that of the receipient, e.g. if donor and recipient are identical twins, they are said to be **syngeneic**. When the donor and recipient are dissimilar twins or are unrelated, the genetic relationship is **allogeneic**.

---

*Friedrich Ernst Krukenberg (1870–1946) described intra-abdominal secondary tumours of the ovaries in a thesis published when he was only 25. He later became Professor of Ophthalmology at Halle.

Table 18   Terms used in tissue transplantation

Relationship between donor and host	Genetic term	Transplant
Same individual		Autograft
Identical twin	Syngeneic	Isograft
Different individual	Allogeneic	Allograft*
Different species	Xenogeneic	Xenograft†

* old term: homograft †old term: heterograft

Other terms denote the anatomical site of grafts. When a graft is sited in the tissue from which it came, as in the case of corneal grafts, it is said to be **isotopic**. If a graft is placed within the same type of tissue as its origin but in a different anatomical position, as for example in the case of skin from the thigh grafted to the arm, it is **orthotopic**. When a graft is inserted in a different type of tissue, it is **heterotopic**.

Distinct surgical procedures characterize different kinds of graft. Autografts, such as those used in head and neck surgery, can be established by means of a temporary pedicle. Many of these are now sustained by free vascular anastomosis using an operating microscope. Allografts, such as those of whole kidney, liver and heart, are also established by vascular anastomosis: they are wholly disconnected from the donor site of origin before implantation and are also therefore said to be '**free**' grafts. There are exceptions: if a grafted tissue has no blood supply of its own, as in the case of the epidermis, articular cartilage and cornea, it can survive without a vascular pedicle.

Graft rejection

Autograft rejection   The reasons for autograft rejection are vascular, mechanical, endocrine and microbial.

An autograft that has an adequate blood supply and receives appropriate mechanical, nervous or hormonal stimuli, is not rejected provided that the transplanted tissue is healthy and sterile. If rejection occurs, it is most likely to be due to inadequate vascularization or to infection.

Allograft rejection   The main reasons for allograft rejection are immunological.

When a visible, carefully sited graft from one individual to another unrelated person is rejected, the process is usually immunological. The recipient's circulating lymphocytes recognize antigens in the graft that are foreign and not present on the surfaces of the recipients own body cells. The cell surface antigens recognized at graft rejection are **histocompatibility antigens** (p. 189). Occasionally, a graft is rejected very rapidly indeed because of the presence of preformed antibodies. After months or years of normal function, a graft may be rejected because of slowly progressive arterial obliteration. Graft rejection patterns are conveniently classified according to this time scale.

Hyperacute rejection   Within a few minutes of transplantation blood flow through the graft is seen to decrease rapidly; the vessels are obstructed by polymorphs and fibrin and the graft becomes ischaemic and necrotic.

Hyperacute graft rejection is brought about by antibodies already present in the recipient's circulation; the antibodies include those formed against red and white blood cells during pregnancy and after previous blood transfusion.

Acute rejection   In man, allografts become vascularized and may function well for the first week. However two to three weeks after transplantation, a graft may be rejected. Two mechanisms are active: one of the two is predominant:

In **parenchymal** rejection, the homograft is infiltrated with host T lymphocytes and rejection is cell-mediated. Vascular changes in the graft are minimal.

In **vascular** rejection, the small vessels of the graft become blocked by platelet aggregates and fibrin. Fibrinoid change is recognized in the walls of the small arteries and immunoglobulins are demonstrable. There is little lymphocytic infiltration: rejection is mediated by circulating antibodies.

Chronic rejection   Rejection due to narrowing of the vessels may occur months or years after transplantation. The intima becomes thickened; the deposition of fibrin and platelets is followed by collagen and proteoglycan formation.

Second set phenomena   After graft rejection, a second graft (second set) may be implanted from the same donor; it is rejected at an increased rate. The mechanism is immunological and is a consequence of sensitization of the recipient to histocompatibility antigens of the donor cells. Sensitized lymphocytes bring about this accelerated rejection.

Histocompatibility antigens

These antigens can be recognized on the surfaces of lymphocytes taking part in the transplantation rejection reaction. The antigens are inherited and are coded by genes on somatic chromosome 6 in a region called the major histocompatibility complex (MHC). In man, this region is termed Human Leucocyte Antigen system A (HLA). Maps have been made of the MHC and they show three main sites where genes code for HLA antigens: (i) A,B and C; (ii) D; and (iii) others. The antigens coded by HLA-A,B and C are 44 000 MW glycoproteins. Together with a smaller 12 000 MW α_2-microglobulin chain, they are **class I MHC** molecules. The molecules coded by the HLA-D region are pairs of polypeptides called **class II MHC** molecules. The MHC includes genes coding for some components of complement.

The outcome of allografting is best when the HLA antigens of donor and host are matched before transplantation; the result is also improved if blood group and other, minor histocompatibility antigens are matched. There is international collaboration to ensure that the optimum use is made of donor organs.

The tests for HLA-A,B and C antigens are serological: the lymphocytes or other cells from a prospective donor are tested against anti-HLA sera. The sera come from multiparous women who have reacted to form antibodies against paternal antigens on fetal cells, from recipients of multiple blood transfusions, or from individuals subject to planned immunization schedules. Monoclonal antibodies to individual HLA antigens are available for testing.

The tests for HLA-D antigens may still be cytological, using time-consuming procedures such as the mixed lymphocyte reaction. Even these tests are not yet available in all centres. Fortunately, anti-HLA-D antisera and monclonal antibodies are now on sale so that the important procedure of matching prospective donor material for the antigenic products of all the HLA loci (A,B,C and D) is practicable in district laboratories in the UK.

Graft-versus-host reaction

When foreign cells were injected into young (particularly embryonic) animals, some died from a wasting disease that became known as **runt disease**. The disease is an example of a graft-versus-host reaction. The reaction takes place when a host contains tissue antigens not present in grafted material, when the grafted cells are immunologically competent and when the host is tolerant of the graft. Lymphocytes, included with the graft, attack the tissues of the host.

This reaction may be seen following allogeneic transplantation of bone marrow to patients whose marrow has been destroyed during the treatment of leukaemia. In these patients the disease is usually limited to exfoliative dermatitis, anorexia, diarrhoea and opportunistic infection.

Tuberculosis

Tuberculosis is an infectious disease caused by *Myco. tuberculosis* (p. 25). The usual agent is *Myco. tuberculosis hominis*. Man is also susceptible to *Myco. tuberculosis bovis*, which infects cattle and other animals, but rarely to *Myco. avium*, the avian pathogen; however, avian tuberculosis is usually fatal. Other mycobacteria, some opportunistic in behaviour, can also cause human disease.

At sites of infection, mycobacteria are phagocytosed by macrophages and may remain alive within these cells for long periods. Many macrophages and tissue cells die and a focus of ischaemic, caseous necrosis results. The focus is surrounded by residual, living macrophages (epithelioid cells) and by lymphocytes responding to mycobacterial antigen by cell-mediated immunity (p. 109). Some macrophages fuse to form 'Langhans'* giant cells (p. 88). The focal lesion originating in this way is a granuloma: it is called a **tubercle**. The skin reactions in a positive Mantoux test (p. 139) and the response at sites of BCG vaccination (p. 21) are microscopically identical.

Mycobacterium tuberculosis reaches the tissues by the inhalation of droplets expectorated or expelled when patients with open disease cough, speak or sing. Large droplets are particularly hazardous, and bacteria can survive in dust. Infection can also be spread directly, to the small intestine, for example, when milk contaminated with *Myco. bovis* is drunk. The

---

*Theodor Langhans (1839–1915) described the mutlinucleated giant cells of tuberculosis in 1867. He also drew attention to the giant cells in Hodgkin's lymphoma and gave his name to the cells of the cytotrophoblast.

inoculation of virulent mycobacteria instead of an attenuated vaccine caused a disaster in Lübeck in 1933. Small numbers of organisms are sufficient to cause disease in susceptible individuals.

Primary disease   Infection of an individual who has not previously been in contact with pathogenic myobacteria leads to a **primary** disease: there is neither acquired immunity nor hypersensitivity. The lung is a common site and a peripheral Ghon focus with lymphatic spread and regional lymph-node disease constitutes a **primary complex**. The organisms may gain entry to the blood stream from necrotic lymph nodes adjoining the pulmonary vein and blood-borne **miliary** spread is then a complication. In cases where the intestine is infected, the bacteria multiply in and cause circumferential ulcers of the lymphoid tissues and of the adjacent mucosa. Ileocaecal tuberculosis may provoke intestinal obstruction. When mesenteric lymph nodes are in turn infected, the description '**tabes mesenterica**' can be used.

Post-primary disease   If there has been previous, healed or localized infection or vaccination with BCG, the **post-primary** response to infection is much modified by cell-mediated, delayed hypersensitivity (p. 104). There is little humoral immunity. The organisms elicit a vigorous inflammatory reaction, **Koch's phenomenon**, generally in the apex of a lung lobe, and infection, localized to this site, becomes chronic with slowly progressive caseous tissue destruction and fibrosis. Healing and fibrosis are greatly accelerated by the use of antibiotics such as rifampicin, streptomycin, isoniazid, pyrazinamide and ethambutol. Surgical removal of lung segments or lobules is now rarely necessary to control advanced disease.

Tumour

A tumour is a swelling. The word tumour is very commonly used instead of neoplasm (p. 146). However, many swellings are not neoplasms and the majority of cancers never appear as external swellings.

Tumour (neoplastic) antigens

Many, but not all, neoplastic cells bear antigens distinct from those of the host. Neoplastic cells transplanted to sensitized, genetically identical (syngeneic) animal hosts, are rejected. The antigens responsible for rejection are neoplasm (tumour) specific transplantation antigens (TSTA): they are entirely distinct from the histocompatibility (HLA) antigens identified in the rejection of transplants between unrelated individuals. TSTA can only cause the rejection of small numbers of cancer cells: larger masses are unaffected.

The foreign antigens of neoplasms which encourage destruction by host lymphocytes are located at the cell surface. In experimental cancers caused by chemicals, the TSTA are unique to the individual neoplasm. In experimental cancers caused by oncogenic viruses, surface antigens may be shared whether the morphology of the transformed cells is the same or not. These virus coded antigens may be part of the virus itself, but other neoplastic antigens of virus-transformed cells are not part of the virus. Some virus-coded antigens may be intracellular and do not influence immunological rejection. Addition antigens normally found only in embryonic cells are formed ('expressed') by many neoplasms. These oncofetal antigens have value in diagnosis (p. 193).

Tumour (neoplastic) growth

The growth of the most malignant neoplasms is rapid, but no more rapid than that of normal embryonic or of regenerating adult tissue. Explants of neoplasms to animals form masses each about 1 mm in diameter: thereafter, continued growth and viability depends upon the provision of a blood supply. New vessels grow in from the host and a fibrovascular stroma forms. The provision of this blood supply is stimulated by **angiogenic factors** (p. 9). Substances like protamine, which block angiogenesis, can cause experimental neoplasms to regress.

The overt metastasis of human neoplasms may not be apparent until long after a primary malignant neoplasm is recognized clinically, although neoplastic cells have been disseminated at an early period. This behaviour is characteristic of malignant melanoma and of carcinomas of the breast and kidney. The neoplastic cells are said to be dormant; reactivation is likely to result from a change in the host's immunological status, or from local endocrine, chemical, physical or mechanical factors.

Tumour (neoplastic) markers

As neoplastic cells grow, they may produce proteins, polypeptides and other compounds not normally synthesized by the tissue in which neoplastic development is occurring. Some of these products are intracellular enzymes; others are hormones or embryonic, oncofetal proteins (p. 193). The identification of these altered enzymes, or of increased levels of plasma hormones and oncofetal antigens, is of diagnostic importance and may assist prognosis.

Some examples of neoplastic markers are:

Enzymes
The granulocytes of chronic granulocytic leukaemia display a deficiency of lysosomal alkaline phosphatase and the cells of acute lymphocytic leukaemia lack an enzyme necessary for the synthesis of asparagine. The cells of prostatic carcinoma form an acid phosphatase which escapes into the blood. Twelve per cent of cancers liberate the alkaline phosphatase (AP) that is formed normally by the placenta (carcinoplacental AP: Regan isoenzyme).

Hormones
Functioning neoplasms of endocrine tissues secrete hormones appropriate to the parent tissue. For example, adrenal cortical adenomas may secrete aldosterone or cortisol.

Many other non-endocrine neoplasms including common carcinomas such as those of the lung, kidney and liver secrete **inappropriate**, ectopic hormones (p. 84); cytoplasmic, secretory granules can be identified by electron microscopy. Thus, the cells of oat-cell bronchial carcinoma often release ACTH, gonadotrophin or ADH.

Embryonic (fetal) proteins (oncofetal antigens)

Many malignant neoplasms form and secrete proteins into the blood which are normally synthesized only by embryonic or fetal tissue. These oncofetal antigens can be recognized by radioimmune assay (p. 13).

Carcinoembryonic antigen (CEA) can be detected in the blood of many patients with a variety of malignant neoplasms including carcinoma of the colon and hepatocarcinoma but also in many individuals without neoplasms but with disorders such as chronic inflammatory bowel disease. The antigen, a glycoprotein, normally part of the plasma membrane of embryonic intestinal cells, is in no sense specific for a particular neoplasm: the titre of CEA may be an aid to monitoring the response of a neoplasm to treatment. Regression of the cancer leads to a fall in plasma levels of CEA and a rise in titre is often apparent before recurrence of the neoplasm is evident clinically.

Alphafetoprotein (AFP) is present in the serum of patients with hepatocarcinoma and testicular teratomas, and in those with viral hepatitis.

Oncofetal antigens behave as neoplasm (tumour) specific antigens (TSA) (p. 148): they are distinct from the neoplasm (tumour) specific transplantation antigens (TSTA) (p. 191). TSA elicit an immune response.

Ulcer

Ulcers are interruptions in the continuity of an epithelial or endothelial surface.

An ulcer may penetrate through the skin or gastrointestinal mucosa into other nearby tissues. A slough of dead tissue and acute inflammatory exudate forms in the floor of the ulcer. Ulcers may be produced by any of the mechanisms that initiate acute inflammation. Healing takes place by repair or regeneration (p. 164). If the ulcer has become chronic, repair by scar tissue formation is almost inevitable. Sometimes the contraction induced by this fibrous repair may produce stenosis. Pyloric stenosis resulting from duodenal ulceration is one example. If an ulcer extends deeply, it may penetrate arteries or veins. Two examples are haemorrhage from the retroduodenal artery produced by a posterior duodenal ulcer, and bleeding from the long saphenous vein produced by a varicose ulcer. In the gut, penetration by an ulcer may lead to perforation with the release of intestinal contents into the peritoneal cavity or the development of an internal fistula.

Peptic ulcers

Peptic ulcers occur in the gastrointestinal tract due to autodigestion of the epithelium by pepsin; they are one possible result of the use of non-steroidal, anti-inflammatory drugs. The Gram-negative bacterium, *Campylobacter pyloridis*, has also been found to be a common associate of chronic gastritis and of peptic ulceration. Pepsin is active at an acid pH, so that peptic ulcers are found in the lower oesophagus (due to the reflux of gastric contents), in the stomach, in the duodenum, and in sites such as Meckel's diverticulum, where ectopic gastric mucosa may persist. Although there is usually evidence of increased secretion of hydrochloric acid, 'peptic' ulceration can be observed in patients in whom secretion of acid is reduced. In these patients, other enzymes and agents such as bile may produce ulceration.

Healthy mucosae are protected from normal enzymatic activity by the glycoproteins of the surface mucus. The ability to resist acid digestion, a function of the tight junctions of normal gastric cells, is reduced at sites of anastomosis, particularly when the jejunum is involved. Consequently, **stomal or anastomotic ulceration** is likely to occur at the site of gastrojejunal anastomosis unless acid secretion has been reduced by either vagotomy or antrectomy.

Chronic ulcers

There are many other causes of chronic, persistent ulceration. **Varicose ulcers** are very frequent. The oxygen transport to the tissues is normal but the transport of oxygen across the cells in the base of the ulcer is impeded by fibrin. Among the most frequent tropical ulcers are schistosomal ulceration of the bladder (*Schistosoma haematobium*) and of the large intestine (*S. mansoni*). In **Buruli ulcer**, *Myco. ulcerans*, acquired from reeds at river margins in Australia, Africa and other countries, causes a chronic, sclerotic lesion.

Malignant ulcers

Some ulcers are cancerous *de novo*; in others, malignant change supervenes in chronic ulceration. An ulcerated basal-cell carcinoma of the skin is a '**rodent' ulcer**. Carcinoma arising in chronic varicose ulcer of the leg is **Marjolin's ulcer**. Similar changes may occur in tropical and in syphilitic ulcers.

Ulcerative colitis

Ulcerative colitis is an inflammatory bowel disease (p. 66) usually confined to the mucous membrane of the large intestine. The small intestine is not involved.

Onset

Inflammation with ulceration usually begins in the rectum and spreads proximally. In patients with total colitis the severity of the inflammation is greater distally than proximally. Exudative inflammation extends into the submucosa only in severe cases. Unlike Crohn's disease (p. 66), granulation tissue and giant cells are not seen; fibrosis with shortening of the large bowel occurs only in chronic cases. Small 'crypt' abscesses are present: they are due to blockage of the crypts of Lieberkühn. Polymorphs abound in the mucosa. In the submucosa, lymphoctyes, plasma cells and eosinophils are seen. In severe, acute cases and in longstanding disease, both the mucosa and submucosa may be destroyed. Crypt abscesses coalesce, producing longitudinal ulcers between which the surviving mucous membrane is thrown up into inflammatory pseudopolyps (p. 158). The aetiology of ulcerative colitis is unknown.

Complications

Patients may lose around 100 g of protein in the stool daily. Malnutrition is inevitable in longstanding cases. In the young, this leads to stunted growth and delayed puberty. Anaemia from chronic blood loss is frequent; acute haemorrhage may occur. In acute fulminating colitis, **toxic dilatation of the colon** and subsequent perforation may develop. Although fibrosis is uncommon, strictures may be produced in a few patients in whom there is remission after longstanding disease. Patients who have had total colitis and who have suffered symptoms for more than ten years have a greatly increased risk of developing carcinoma of the colon when compared with the general population.

Systemic disease

Other disorders are common. There is frequently sclerosing cholangitis and hepatocellular fatty change; in a few patients liver disease progresses to biliary cirrhosis. Iridocyclitis, arthritis and a variety of dermatitides are found, and amyloidosis may occur.

Ultrasound

Ultrasonic vibrations are sound waves of high frequency inaudible to man. The lower limit of ultrasonic vibration is 20 kHz. The (much higher) frequency range used in medicine is 1–15 MHz. Ultrasonic vibrations may be either pulsed or continuous. The intensity with which ultrasound is delivered can be varied; it is measured in watts per square centimetre (W/cm^2).*

Diagnostic ultrasound Low-intensity waves have no effect upon the material through which they pass and can be used for the non-invasive imaging of tissues. This is particularly useful in differentiating between solid and cystic masses. The technique is used to identify gallstones, intra-abdominal abscesses, and ovarian and thyroid masses, and to demonstrate the tissues of the growing fetus. With a special probe it is possible to obtain fluid for cytological examination and biopsy material for histological examination. Using the Doppler technique of change in frequency induced by motion, ultrasonic vibrations can be used to measure blood flow: the apparent frequency of the sound varies with the relative movement of the source, the observer, and the medium through which the sound is propagated.

Therapeutic ultrasound High-intensity vibrations affect the tissue through which the waves pass. Energy is given up in the form of heat and this can be utilized by physiotherapists to promote resolution of soft-tissue injuries. At higher levels of intensity, cavitation of tissue may be produced. This destructive capability is used to destroy the vestibular labyrinth in patients with Menière's disease. Calculi may be shattered by ultrasonic vibrations; unfortunately, the ureter or bile duct may also be damaged.

   Degradation of DNA can be produced by high-intensity vibrations but there is no evidence that this change can occur in the diagnostic range of ultrasonic vibration.

---

*A watt is a unit of power which, in one second, produces 1 joule of energy.

Varix, varicosity

A varix is an enlarged, dilated and tortuous venous channel. In the systemic circulation, varicosities are commonplace in the large veins of the leg. In the portal circulation, varicosities develop in portal hypertension at sites such as the lower end of the oesophagus, where the portal and systemic circulations are in continuity.

Viraemia

Viraemia (p. 31) is the presence of virus in the blood. When virus gains access to a tissue and multiplies, the affected cells are injured or killed. Virus particles pass from the extracellular tissue fluid, enter lymphatics and are taken up by macrophages. Relatively small numbers reach the blood stream via the thoracic duct in a phase of **primary viraemia**. Settling in individual organs after clearance from the blood, virus multiplies in large numbers. The **secondary viraemia** that follows marks the acute onset of the clinical disease.

Virchow's* node

This name is given to a left supraclavicular lymph node enlarged because of its involvement by metastatic gastric or other intra-abdominal carcinoma, and referred to as a 'signal node'. Recognition of the enlarged node is Troisier's sign.

Virus

Viruses are very small infective agents, incapable of independent life and multiplication outside living cells.

Structure
An infective virus particle is called a **virion**. The particle comprises nucleic acid and a surrounding protein coat. The nucleic acid is DNA or RNA. The protein coat is the **capsid**. It is made up of units called capsomeres the arrangement of which gives virus particles their characteristic shape: they are either compact, 20-sided **icosahedrons** or elongated cylinders in which the protein is arranged around the nucleic acid as a **helix**.

Properties
Viruses are distinguished from other forms of life by:

- their very small size: the largest, pox viruses, are scarcely as large as a staphylococcus. Because of their small size, they can pass through filters that retain bacteria: hence the old term, 'filtrable' viruses;
- their simple chemical structure, of one nucleic acid and a few protein molecules;

---

*See page 183(n).

- their orderly construction with an icosahedral or helical shape;
- their response to the interferons (p. 119);
- their resistance to most antibiotics;
- the possibility that they can be crystallized;
- their lack of a cell wall, of mitochondria and of ribosomes;
- their inability to replicate outside host cells and their dependence on host cell synthesis for replication;
- their lack of binary fission as a mechanism of division.

Classification

Viruses are classified by the nature of their nucleic acid (Table 19) and by size; the classes are divided into families and genera.

1. By nucleic acid. The nucleic acid is DNA or RNA; it is arranged as single strands (ss) or as double strands (ds).

2. By size. The largest, vaccinia, is half the size of a small bacterium; it can therefore be seen with a good light microscope. The smallest, including the polioviruses, can only be viewed by EM. Size can be determined by passing viruses through filters of known pore size and by high-speed centrifugation. EM is a convenient method of study and can sometimes be accomplished very quickly. Formerly, in a suspected case of smallpox, variola virus could be distinguished from varicella (chickenpox) virus in 10–15 minutes.

Sterilization

Most viruses survive and are conveniently stored at temperatures as low as -70 °C or in a dry state after freeze-drying. The majority, including HTLV-III (p. 2) are killed by moderate heat. There are important exceptions. The viruses of serum hepatitis and poliomyelitis resist much higher temperatures. Viruses are not destroyed by pH changes from 5 to 9; those with a lipid-containing envelope are sensitive to ether. Hydrogen peroxide and other oxidizing agents such as hypochlorite are good virus disinfectants. Phenols are seldom effective, although this depends on the concentration. Viruses with envelopes are sensitive to bile. Many viruses are inactivated by ultraviolet light, and dyes such as acridine orange, which penetrate the nucleic acid, increase this susceptibility.

A small number of effective antiviral agents (p. 11) such as idoxuridine and acyclovir have been discovered. Viruses resist antibacterial, antibiotic and chemotherapeutic agents, which can be used to rid diagnostic material of bacteria when viruses are being sought in the laboratory.

Routes of infection

Many viruses are swallowed with food or water (poliovirus; hepatitis A). Some are inhaled (measles, influenza, smallpox). Other viruses can be

Table 19   Classification/nomenclature of viruses

Family	Genus	Structure	Species	Disease
CLASS I ds DNA e.g. Herpetoviridae	Herpes virus	enveloped icosahedron 180–200 nm	HSV type 2	genital herpes cervical carcinoma
			EB virus	Burkitt's lymphoma Nasopharyngeal carcinoma
	Hepadna	non-enveloped icosahedron Dane particle = 42 nm	Hepatitis B	serum hepatitis
CLASS II ss DNA e.g. Parvoviridae	Parvovirus	non-enveloped icosahedron 18–26 nm	Norwalk virus and similar agents	gastroenteritis
CLASS III ds RNA e.g. Reoviridae	Rotavirus	non-enveloped, double-walled icosahedron 60–80 nm	Rotavirus (3 types)	gastroenteritis
CLASS IV ss RNA e.g. Picornaviridae	Enterovirus	non-enveloped icosahedron 20–30 nm	Polio 3 types	poliomyelitis
	Rhinovirus		Rhinovirus 113 types	common cold
CLASS V ss RNA e.g. Paramyxoviridae	Paramyxovirus	Enveloped, helical 150 nm	Para-influenza	acute respiratory infections
e.g. Orthomyxoviridae	Influenza virus	Enveloped, helical 100 nm	Influenzavirus (types A0,A1,A2,A3)	influenza
Unclassified		Non-enveloped icosahedron 27 nm	Hepatitis A	infectious hepatitis

inoculated directly in blood and blood products or by contaminated instruments and needles (HTLV-III, hepatitis B). A further category is conveyed to the human host by intermediary vectors including the mosquito (yellow fever), the sandfly (dengue) and the tick (arboviruses).

Effects on the host

Infection begins when virus attaches to cell surfaces by adsorption. Virus nucleocapsid is covered by plasma membrane lipoprotein as virus penetrates the cell wall. Entering the cell, virus loses this protein and becomes uncoated. The synthesis of viral protein and the replication of virus nucleic acid then begin. However, in this phase of multiplication the formation of new infective particles is latent; there are no clinical signs of disease. Eventually, viral multiplication leads to viraemia (p. 196) and virus localizes in individual organs and tissues.

Virus may kill cells by lysis; infection may be manifest or abortive. Alternatively, infective virus may persist within the cell, in a steady state, without killing the cell. Virus can be integrated into cell nucleic acid, remaining latent, or can transform cells, causing them to behave as neoplasms (p. 146).

Slow viruses

Virus diseases with very long incubation period, of two, three or many more years, are caused by 'slow' viruses.

Slow viruses include agents such as the measles virus, which can cause the changes of subacute sclerosing panencephalitis. There is a further group which include the particles causing Jakob-Creutzfeld disease, kuru and (in sheep) scrapie. These strange disorders share the features of unusually long incubation periods, destructive lesions of the central nervous system, and mental disorder with death. When clinical manifestations begin, progress may be rapid. Death is invariable in kuru, for example, and occurs within 12 months. These 'unconventional' slow virus agents are extremely resistant to normal methods of sterilization; the agents are very small and contain little or no nucleic acid, so that the possibilities for genetic coding are limited. The term **prion** (proteinaceous infective agent) has been introduced to describe these virus particles. It is possible that some forms of amyloid fibrils (p. 6) are prions. It is remotely possible that similar viruses cause progressive diseases such as multiple sclerosis.

Vitamins

Vitamins are substances which cannot be synthesized in the body and which are required in very small quantities for specific purposes, for example, to act as coenzymes. The first compounds of this kind to be identified were amines: they were termed vitamines (vital amine). Vitamins A, D, E and K are soluble in fat, vitamins B and C in water. It is now recognized that there are 8 components in the vitamin B complex. A number of substances have chemical compositions closely similar to the other vitamins: these analogues have comparable biological activities.

Vitamin A (retinol)   This vitamin is required for the normal growth of epithelia of the gastrointestinal, genitourinary and respiratory systems and of the retina. Retinol also affects the integrity of cartilage. Vitamin A deficiency causes keratinization and metaplasia of these epithelia; vitamin A excess may impair development of the central nervous system.

Vitamin D   Vitamin D is a steroid which is modified metabolically before it can exert its biological activities. Most vitamin D comes from the conversion of 7-dehydrocholesterol, a component originating in dairy foods and fish liver oil, to cholecalciferol (vitamin D_3). The conversion takes place in the skin and is caused by solar UVL. An alternative source of vitamin D is ergocalciferol (vitamin D_2) which can be synthesized commercially but which can also be obtained by irradiating the ergosterol of fungi and yeasts with UVL. The amount of vitamin D_2 in the diet is small but the biological activity of vitamin D_2 is greater than that of vitamin D_3.

Vitamin D is changed to a steroid hormone, $1,25\text{-}(OH)_2D_3$, in the kidney: this active metabolite increases the absorption of calcium and phosphorus from the intestine and the deposition of these substances in bone.

Lack of vitamin D results in rickets or osteomalacia (p. 151); excess dietary vitamin D can promote formation of renal calculi.

Vitamin E (α tocopherol)   This is a powerful anti-oxidant. There are several tocopherols with biological activity. Deficiency of vitamin E is related to sterility in rats but vitamin E lack has not been shown unequivocally to cause human disease.

Vitamin K   Vitamin K is required for the formation of a number of blood coagulation factors (see p. 56). Vitamin K_1 (phylloquinone) is present in green vegetables; vitamins K_2 (menquinone) and K_3 (naphthoquinone) are synthesized by intestinal bacterial which can be destroyed by oral antibiotics. Vitamin K deficiency can develop rapidly in patients with disturbed fat digestion and absorption.

Vitamin B   The B vitamins are a complex of chemically dissimilar substances all of which are water-soluble and all of which come from similar dietary sources. Consequently, a deficiency of one member of the complex is commonly associated with a deficiency of the others.

Thiamine, vitamin B_1, is a coenzyme required for the oxidation of carbohydrates. Deficiency causes beri-beri.

Riboflavine, vitamin B_2, is a component of flavoproteins which are required for a number of oxidation reactions. Deficiency of this vitamin produces abnormalities in epithelia, particularly angular stomatitis.

Nicotinic acid (niacin or nicotinamide) is a component of coenzymes NAD and NADP. Prolonged deficiency produces widespread metabolic disturbances; the subsequent disease, pellagra, is characterized by delirium, dermatitis and gastroenteritis (diarrhoea).

Pyridoxine, vitamin B_6, is a coenzyme required for transamination, deamination and decarboxylation. The metabolism of the amino acid tryptophane is particularly affected. Pyridoxine deficiency results in dermatitis and abnormal function of the central nervous system.

Folic acid is a coenzyme required for the synthesis of purines and pyrimidines; it is consequently vital for the synthesis of DNA, and for cell division and maturation. Deficiency of the coenzyme produces abnormalities which are particularly severe in cell populations with a high turnover rate such as those of the bone marrow.

S^1-**deoxyadenosylcobalamin**, vitamin B_{12} is a coenzyme located in mitochondria whose precise function is uncertain. Like folic acid deficiency, lack of cyanocobalamin results in abnormal haemopoiesis and anaemia (p. 7). In addition, there are degenerative changes of some cells of the central nervous system. The vitamin is synthesized from an **extrinsic factor** which can only be absorbed in the distal ileum with the aid of a glycoprotein, **intrinsic factor**, secreted by gastric parietal cells. Together, these compounds form a haemopoietic principle stored in the liver.

Deficiency of vitamin B_{12} may occur in spite of a normal dietary intake of extrinisic factor, due to:

1. lack of intrinsic factor (e.g. pernicious anaemia, partial gastrectomy);

2. malabsorption (e.g. Crohn's disease, ileal resection);

3. bacterial overgrowth in the ileum (e.g. blind-loop syndrome).

Biotin is a coenzyme required for carboxylation and decarboxylation. Deficiency may result in seborrhoeic dermatitis, paraesthesiae and lethargy, depending upon the severity.

Pantothenic acid is a component of coenzyme A required for the oxidation of carbohydrate and fatty acids and for the synthesis of cholesterol, steroid hormones and triglycerides. Deficiency is rare but paraesthesiae and fatigue may result.

Vitamin C (ascorbic acid)   Vitamic C is a strong reducing agent whose precise function is unknown. However, in the absence of ascorbic acid, proline is not hydroxylated: hydroxyproline is an essential part of the collagen molecule. Prolonged deficiency results in **scurvy** (p. 168). Ascorbic acid is also required for the hydroxylation of dopamine to noradrenaline and in the synthesis of other steroid hormones.

Wilms' (neoplasm) tumour

Wilms' tumour, **nephroblastoma**, is the result of a defect of the embryonic development of the kidney occurring in the fetus or infant. It is an embryonic neoplasm: the cells that give rise to the neoplasm have the ability to differentiate into tissue derived from more than one germ layer. Among the tissues present are renal tubular epithelium, rudimentary glomeruli, connective tissue and smooth muscle.

Worms (helminths)

Helminths are elongate, legless animals. Those that parasitize man belong to the phyla *Nematoda* (roundworms) and *Platyhelminthes* (flatworms). The flatworms are subdivided into two classes, *Trematoda* (flukes) and *Cestoda* (tapeworms).

Man is infected (1) by eating undercooked meat (trichinosis); (2) by eating undercooked fish (*Diphyllobothrium latum*: anaemia; *Clonorchis sinensis*: liver disease); (3) by drinking contaminated water (*Dracunculus medinensis* – guinea worm); (4) by low standards of hygiene (hydatidosis); (5) by penetration of the skin in infected water (schistosomiasis); (6) by arthropod bites (elephantiasis, onchocercosis); or (7) coincidentally, as aberrant infestations, by worms that normally parasitise other hosts (toxocariasis).

Helminths cause human disease most commonly in tropical or subtropical countries where the opportunties for infestation are frequent. However, some helminthic diseases such as ascariasis, toxocariasis, trichinosis, taeniasis and echinococcosis are encountered in all countries.

Schistosomiasis   This is widespread in South America and the Caribbean, in Africa and Arabia (*Schistosoma mansoni*), in the Middle East (*Schistosoma haematobium*) and in Southeast Asia (*Schistosoma japonica*). The worms cause intestinal ulceration and fistulae with papillomata, precancerous bladder irritation, and intestinal fibrosis and cirrhosis, respectively.

Ascariasis (*Ascaris lumbricoides*)   Ascariasis is contracted by eating food contaminated with human faeces. Ileal obstruction, biliary obstruction, acute suppurative cholangitis and acute pancreatitis are among the mechanical effects that may complicate the presence of these numerous, large helminths.

Toxocariasis   This is contracted by young children from soil contaminated by puppies (*Toxocara canis*) and kittens. Retinal invasion can cause choroidoretinitis or a localized mass resembling neuroblastoma.

Trichinosis   This is conveyed by eating·undercooked pork containing the larvae of *Trichinella spiralis*. The larvae encyst in skeletal muscle: myalgia and eosinophilia are two of the effects.

Taeniasis   Taeniasis, with the intestinal development of the pig tapeworm *Taenia solium* or the beef tapeworm *T. saginata*, causes no symptoms. However, **cysticercosis**, the consequence of swallowing the eggs of *T. solium*, may cause focal lesions in skeletal and cardiac muscle, subcutaneous tissue and brain. After a long latent period, epilepsy may develop. Multiple sclerosis may be simulated and hydrocephalus can result.

Ecchinococcosis (hydatidosis)   This arises from ingestion of the dog tapeworm *Echinococcus granulosus*. Eggs are ingested and hatch in the duodenum. Embryos are carried in the blood to the liver, lungs, spleen, bones and brain. The resultant hydatid cysts may be single or multiple.

Wound

A wound is an interruption or break in the continuity of the external surface of the body or of the surface of an internal organ, caused by surgical or other forms of injury or trauma. The word 'wound' means a disruption of the continuity of the tissue but it is taken to include contusions and fractures as well as external injuries.

Wound infection

Small numbers of bacteria usually gain access even to clean surgical wounds; larger numbers of bacteria invariably contaminate open wounds incurred by accident.

Wounds may be infected by bacteria present within the patient (**endogenous** infection) or by bacteria introduced from the environment (**exogenous** infection). In **cross-infection** there is bacterial spread from person to person either from another patient, from a nurse or from the surgeon. Wound infection is frequent when there has been extensive injury with the presence of foreign bodies, as in road-traffic accidents. Before the introduction of antiseptic surgery (p. 14) the majority of incisions became infected and septicaemia was a common cause of death.

The organisms that survive on the skin of the patient are likely to be staphylococci (p. 175). The bacteria that gain access to wounds from endogenous faecal sources include those of the *Bacteroides* group (p. 26), *Bacillus* species, enterobacteria, *Streptococcus* species, enterococci, and clostridia.

Whether overt clinical infection is likely to develop or not can be estimated by the degree of bacterial contamination. Four categories can be listed:

Clean wounds   These are incisions in patients in whom aseptic techniques have been observed, in whom a hollow, muscular organ has not been opened and in whom no infection has been found.

Potentially contaminated wounds   These are incisions for operations in which organs have been opened but in which contamination due to a failure of aseptic technique has not occurred.

Contaminated wounds   In this category are traumatic wounds of less than four hours duration, surgical wounds following operations for acute inflammatory conditions without the formation of pus, and wounds in patients in whom there was a failure of aseptic technique, e.g. inadvertent contamination during colectomy.

Dirty wounds   These wounds include those that have been untreated for longer than four hours, and incisions in patients in whom a perforated viscus or pus is found at operation.

The anticipated approximate proportion of clinical infections is 2 per cent for clean wounds, 10 per cent for potentially contaminated wounds, 20 per cent for contaminated wounds and, 40 per cent for dirty wounds.

The frequency of wound infection increases exponentially with the length of operation, probably because of increases in the extent of tissue trauma and in the extent of contamination (p. 203). A haematoma is a good site for bacterial multiplication. The frequency of infection also rises with the duration of the preoperative hospital stay: there is a growing opportunity for the skin to be colonized by pathogens. Many of these pathogens may have acquired resistance to the antibiotics in common use in an individual hospital.

Systemic factors that predispose to wound infection include extreme youth or age, diabetes mellitus, impairment of the mechanisms of defence against bacteria (p. 21) and immunosuppression. Wound infection is unexpectedly frequent in the presence of jaundice.

Table 20   Normal values in venous whole blood (B) serum or plasma (S) or in arterial whole blood (A)
The values given, particularly those for haemoglobin and red blood cell concentrations, vary according to age and sex and according to the method of measurement used by individual laboratories.

Sodium	S	132–145 mmol/l
Potassium	S	3.4–5.0 mmol/l
Calcium	S	2.1–2.7 mmol/l
Magnesium	S	0.7–1.0 mmol/l
Chloride	S	95–105 mmol/l
Phosphate (inorganic)	S	0.8–1.4 mmol/l
Zinc	S	10–222 μmol/l
Copper	S	13–24 μmol/l
Iron	S	10–34 μmol/l
Total iron binding capacity	S	45–72 μmol/l
Glucose	B	3–5 mmol/l
Ketones	B	80–140 mmol/l
Lactate	B	0.4–1.4 mmol/l
Pyruvate	B	45–80 μmol/l
Total protein	S	62–82 g/l
Urea	B	2.5–7.5 mmol/l
Creatinine	S	60–120 μmol/l
Albumin	S	42–54 g/l
Globulin (total)	S	22–31 g/l
α_1	S	2–4 g/l
α_2	S	5–9 g/l
β	S	6–11 g/l
γ	S	7–17 g/l
IgG	S	6–16 g/l
IgA	S	0.5–4.0 g/l
IgM	S	0.4–1.2 g/l
IgD	S	20–50 μg/l
IgE	S	0.1–0.4 μg/l

Table 20 – *Continued*

Triglycerides	S	0.3–1.7 mmol/l
Fatty acids (total)	S	3.6–18 mmol/l
Fatty acids (free)	S	0.35–1.25 mmol/l
Cholesterol (total)	S	3.6–7.8 mmol/l
Cholesterol (free)	S	1.1–2.6 mmol/l
Phospholipid	S	1.6–3.2 mmol/l
Bilirubin	S	1–20 μmol/l
Alkaline phosphatase	S	25–110 IU/l
AST	S	5–45 IU/l
Lactate dehydrogenase	S	200–450 IU/l
ALT	S	5–40 IU/l
γ-glutamyl transpeptidase	S	5–65 IU/l
Amylase	S	70–300 IU/l
Fibrinogen	B	2–4 g/l
Fibrinogen degradation products	B	6 mg/l
Prothrombin time	B	11–13 sec
Platelet count	B	$150–400 \times 10^9$/l
Haemoglobin	B	11.5–18.0 g/dl
Red blood cells	B	$3.9–6.5 \times 10^{12}$/l
White blood cells (total)	B	$4–11 \times 10^9$/l
Neutrophils	B	40–75%
Lymphocytes	B	20–45%
Monocytes	B	2–10%
Eosinophils	B	1–6%
Basophils	B	1%
Oxygen	A	9.5–14.5 kPa
Carbon dioxide	A	4.5–6.0 kPa
Bicarbonate	A	24–28 mmol/l
pH	A	7.36–7.44

Index